THE
BORGIAS

THE
BORGIAS

TWO NOVELS IN ONE VOLUME

JEAN PLAIDY

BROADWAY PAPERBACKS
NEW YORK

B
BROADWAY

This is a work of fiction. Names, characters, places, and incidents either are the product
of the author's imagination or are used fictitiously. Any resemblance to
actual persons, living or dead, events, or locales is entirely coincidental.

Madonna of the Seven Hills copyright © 1958, 1974 by Jean Plaidy,
copyright renewed 1986 by Jean Plaidy

Light on Lucrezia copyright © 1958, 1976 by Jean Plaidy,
copyright renewed 1986 by Jean Plaidy

All rights reserved.
Published in the United States by Broadway Paperbacks, an imprint of the
Crown Publishing Group, a division of Random House, Inc., New York.
www.crownpublishing.com

Broadway Paperbacks and its logo, a letter B bisected on the diagonal,
are trademarks of Random House, Inc.

The two novels contained in this volume were originally published separately in
hardcover and in slightly different form as *Madonna of the Seven Hills* and *Light on Lucrezia*
by Robert Hale, Ltd., London, in 1958 and G.P. Putnam's Sons, New York,
in 1974 and 1976 respectively.

Library of Congress Cataloging-in-Publication Data is available on request.

ISBN 978-0-307-95686-6

Printed in the United States of America

Book design by Maria Elias
Cover design by Jim Massey/Laura Klynstra
Cover photographs: (Lucrezia): Michael Nelson, (Pope): Eric Thayer/
Getty Images, (ring): Bruno Morandi/The Image Bank/Getty Images,
(cross): Godong/Robert Harding World Imagery/Getty Images,
(church): Sites and Photos/Samuel Magal/Mix: Subjects/Getty Images

10 9 8 7 6 5 4 3 2 1

First Edition

Contents

MADONNA OF
THE SEVEN HILLS

A NOVEL OF THE BORGIAS

AUTHOR'S NOTE

I hope that my readers will bear in mind the proverb Altri tempi, altri costumi, and adjust their mental vision to the fifteenth century when Popes took their vows of celibacy merely as a form, and when murder was so commonplace that an old Tiber boatman on seeing the body of the Pope's son thrown into the river did not think it necessary to report it because he saw bodies thrown in every night.

Only by judging the Borgias against their own times can they arouse our sympathy, and only if they arouse our sympathy can they be understood. Below are some of the books which have been of great help to me:

Lucrezia Borgia: A Chapter from the Morals of the Italian Renaissance. Ferdinand Gregorovius.

The Life and Times of Lucrezia Borgia. Maria Bellonci. Translated by Bernard Wall.

Lucrezia Borgia. Joan Haslip.

The Life of Cesare Borgia. Raphael Sabatini.

Lucretia Borgia, The Chronicle of Tebaldeo Tebaldei, Renaissance Period, Commentary and Notes by Randolph Hughes. Algernon Charles Swinburne.

Life and Times of Roderigo Borgia, Pope Alexander VI. The Most Rev.
Arnold H. Mathew, D.D.

Chronicles of the House of Borgia. Frederick Baron Corvo.

Hadrian the Seventh. Frederick Rolfe (Frederick Baron Corvo).

Alma Roma. Albert G. MacKennon, M.A.

Cesare Borgia. Charles Yriarte. Translated by William Stirling.

Cesare Borgia. William Harrison Woodward.

An Outline of Italian Civilization. Decio Pettoello.

History of the Italian Republics in the Middle Ages. J. C. L. Sismondi.
(Recast and Supplemented in the light of historical
research by William Boulting.)

*Memoirs of the Dukes of Urbino: Illustrating the Arms, Arts and Litera-
ture of Italy from 1440 to 1630.* (3 Vols.) James Dennistoun
of Dennistoun.

J.P.

THE BIRTH

OF LUCREZIA

I t was cold in the castle, and the woman who stood
at the window looking from the snowy caps of the mountains to the
monastery below thought longingly of the comfort of her house on the
Piazza Pizzo di Merlo sixty miles away in Rome.

Yet she was content to be here for it was Roderigo's wish that their
child should be born in his mountain castle; and she could feel nothing but
delight that he should care so much.

She turned her back on the majestic view and looked round the room.
The bed was inviting, for her pains were becoming more frequent. She
hoped the child would be a boy, since Roderigo could do so much more
for a boy than for a girl.

Already she had given him three handsome sons, and he doted on
them, particularly, she believed, on Cesare and Giovanni; but that was
because Pedro Luis the eldest had been sent away. It was sad to lose him
but it was a wonderful future which would be his: education at the Spanish
Court, where he was to receive the dukedom of Gandia. And there would

be equally grand opportunities for the others—for Cesare, for Giovanni, and the unborn child.

Her women were hovering. Madonna should lie down now, they advised, for the child would surely soon be born.

She smiled, wiping the sweat from her forehead, and allowed them to help her to the bed. One touched her forehead with a sweet-smelling unguent which was cool and refreshing; another put a goblet of wine to her lips. They were eager, these women, to serve Vannozza Catanei, because she was beloved by Roderigo Borgia, one of the greatest Cardinals in Rome.

She was a lucky woman to have become so dear to him, for he was a man who needed many mistresses; but she was the chief one, which in itself was something of a miracle since she was no longer young. When a woman was thirty-eight she must indeed be attractive to hold the attention of such a one as Cardinal Roderigo Borgia. Yet she had done it; and if there were times when she wondered whether he came to see their children rather than for the purpose of making love to her, what of that? Sons such as Pedro Luis, Cesare and Giovanni could make a stronger bond than passion; and if, in the future, there were younger and more beautiful women to charm him, she would still be the one who had given him his favorite children.

So she would be contented—when the pains were over and the child born; she was sure the baby would be healthy and handsome; all her children were. They had all inherited her golden beauty and she hoped the new child would, for it delighted their father. So she must be pleased that he had insisted on bringing her here to his castle at Subiaco, even though the journey had been long and tedious and the wind was fierce in the Apennines. He wished her to have their child in his palace, and he wished to be near her when it was born. That would have been less simple to achieve in Rome, for Roderigo was after all a man of the Church sworn to celibacy, and here in the mountain fastness of the Subiaco castle he could give way to his joy with an easier mind. So she would soothe herself while she waited by thinking of her beautiful house on the Piazza Pizzo di Merlo in which, due to the bounty of Roderigo, she lived so graciously. She delighted in the Ponte quarter in which there was always so much going on. It was one of the most populous districts of the city, and merchants and bankers abounded there. It was favored by the most notorious and prosperous of the courtesans, and dominated by the noble family of Orsini who had their palace on Monte Giordano, and whose castle, the Torre di None, was part of the city's wall.

Not that Vannozza considered herself a courtesan. She was faithful to Roderigo and regarded him as her husband, although of course she knew that Roderigo, being a Cardinal, could not marry, and that if he had been able to he would have been obliged to look for a wife in a different stratum of society.

But if Roderigo could not marry her he had been as considerate as any husband. Roderigo, thought Vannozza, was surely the most charming man in Rome. She did not believe she was the only one who thought this, although a man such as Roderigo would certainly have his enemies. He was made for distinction; his eyes were on a certain goal, the Papacy, and those who knew Roderigo well would surely feel that he had an excellent chance of achieving his ambition. No one should be deceived by those gracious manners, that enchantingly musical voice, that attractive courtesy; they were so much a part of Roderigo, it was true, but beneath the charm was a burning ambition which would certainly carry him as far as he intended it should.

Roderigo was a man whom Vannozza could adore, for he had all the qualities which she admired most. Therefore she prayed now to the saints and the Virgin that the child which she was about to bear should have charm and beauty (for Roderigo, possessing the former to such a degree, was very susceptible to the latter) and that should she, herself a matron of thirty-eight, fail to arouse his sexual desire she could continue to bask in his gratitude for the children she had borne him.

How long would the children be kept under her roof? Not long, she imagined. They would depart as Pedro Luis had departed. Roderigo had fine plans for the boys; and Vannozza, beloved of the Cardinal though she might be, had little social standing in Rome.

But he would remember that part of her lived in those children, and she would continue in her charming house, the house which he had given her. It was the sort of house which was possessed by the nobles of Rome, and she delighted in it. She had enjoyed sitting in the main room of the house, the whitewashed walls of which she had decorated with tapestries and a few pictures; for she had wanted to make her house as luxurious as that of the great families—the Orsinis and the Colonnas. Her lover was generous and had given her many presents; in addition to her tapestries and paintings she had her jewelry, her fine furniture, her ornaments of porphyry and marble, and—most treasured of all—her *credenza*, that great chest in which she stored her majolica, and her gold and silver goblets and drinking vessels. The *credenza* was a sign of social standing, and Vannozza's eyes shone every time she looked at hers. She would walk about her beautiful house, touching her beautiful possessions and telling herself in the quiet coolness she enjoyed behind its thick walls that she had indeed been a fortunate woman when Roderigo Borgia had come into her life and found her desirable.

Vannozza was no fool, and she knew that the treasures which Roderigo had given her were, in his mind, as nothing compared to those she had given him.

Now the pain was gripping her again, more insistently, almost continuously. The child was eager to be born.

In another wing of his castle of Subiaco the great Cardinal also waited. His apartments were far from those of his mistress for he did not wish to be distressed by the sound of her cries; he did not wish to think of Vannozza's suffering; he wished to think of her as she had always taken pains to be in his presence—beautiful, light-hearted and full of vitality, even as he was himself. In childbirth Vannozza might fail to be so and he preferred to remember her thus, as he was a man who hated to be uncomfortable; and Vannozza in pain would render him so.

Therefore it was better to shut himself away from her, to wait in patience until the message came to him that the child was born.

He had turned from the shrine before which he had been kneeling. The lamp which burned constantly before the figures and pictures of the saints had shone on the serene face of the Madonna, and he had fancied he had seen reproach there. Should he, one of the mightiest of Cardinals, be praying for the safe delivery of a child he had no right to have begotten?

Could he expect the Madonna to grant him a son—a beautiful healthy boy—when, as a son of the Church himself, he was sworn to celibacy?

It was an uncomfortable thought and as Roderigo always turned hastily from such, he allowed himself to forget the shrine and looked instead at the emblem of the grazing bull which adorned the walls, and which never failed to inspire him. It was the emblem of the Borgias and one day it would be, so determined Roderigo, the most feared and respected symbol in Italy.

Ah yes, it was comforting to contemplate the bull—that creature of strength, peacefully grazing yet indicative of so much that was fierce and strong. One day, pondered the Cardinal, the Borgia arms should be displayed all over Italy, for it was the dream of Roderigo that the whole of Italy would one day be united, and united under a Borgia. Another Borgia Pope! Why not? The Vatican was the center of the Catholic world; certainly the Vatican should unite a divided country, for in unity there was strength, and who more fitted to rule a united Italy than the Pope? But he was not yet Pope, and he had his enemies who would do all in their power to prevent his reaching that high eminence. No matter. He would achieve his ambition as his uncle Alfonso had achieved his when he had become Pope Calixtus III.

Calixtus had been wise; he had known that the strength of a family was in its young members. That was why Calixtus had adopted him, Roderigo, and his brother Pedro Luis (after him he had named Vannozza's eldest boy), that was why he had enriched them and made them powerful men in the land.

Roderigo smiled complacently; he had no need to adopt children; he had his own sons and daughters. The daughters were useful when it came to making marriages which would unite eminent families with the Borgias; but sons were what an ambitious man needed and, praise be to the saints, these were what he had, and he would forever be grateful to the woman, who was now in childbed in this very castle, for providing them. Pedro Luis in Spain would ensure that country's benevolence toward his father; dashing young Giovanni—for him Roderigo had the most ambitious plans, for that best loved of his sons should command the armies of the Borgias; and Cesare, that bold young scamp (Roderigo smiled with pleasure at the memory of his arrogant little son), he must perforce go into the Church, for, if the Borgias were to achieve all that Roderigo planned for them, one of them must hold sway in the Vatican. So little Cesare was destined to follow his father to the Papal Chair.

Roderigo shrugged his shoulders, and smiled gently at himself. He had yet to achieve that position; but he would; he was determined that he would. The gentle smile had faded and for a few moments it was possible to see the man of iron behind the pleasant exterior.

He had come far and he would never go back; he would prefer death rather. He was as certain as he was that a child was being born in his castle of Subiaco that one day he would ascend the Papal throne.

Nothing . . . nothing should stand in his way, for only as Pope could he invest his sons with those honors which would enable them to work toward that great destiny which was to be the Borgias'.

And the new child? "A boy," he prayed, "Holy Mother, let it be a boy. I have three fine sons, healthy boys, yet could I use another."

He was all gentleness again, thinking of the nursery in the house on the Piazza Pizzo di Merlo. How those two little ones delighted in the visits of Uncle Roderigo! It was necessary at present that they should think of him as "uncle"; it would be quite inconceivable that he—a Holy Cardinal—should be addressed as Papa. "Uncle" was good enough for the present; one day those little boys should know who they really were. He looked forward to his pleasure in telling them. (Roderigo enjoyed bringing pleasure to those whom he loved but if there was any unpleasant task to perform he preferred others to do it.) What glorious fate awaited them because he, the illustrious Cardinal, was not merely their uncle, but their father! How Cesare's eyes would flash—the arrogant and delightful little creature! How Giovanni would strut—dear, best-beloved Giovanni! And the new child . . . he too would come in for his share of honors.

What were they doing now? Disagreeing with their nurse-maid, very likely. He could imagine the threats of Cesare, the sullen anger of Giovanni. They were brimming with vitality—inherited from Vannozza as well as from their father, and each knew how to achieve his desires. They would get the better of twenty nursemaids—which was what he must expect. They were the sons of Roderigo Borgia, and when had he failed to get his way with women?

Now he was thinking of the past, of the hundreds of women who had pleased him. When he had first gone into the Church he had been dismayed because celibacy was expected of him. He could laugh at his naïvety now. It had not taken him long to discover that Cardinals, and even Popes, had their mistresses. They were not expected to lead celibate lives, only to appear to do so, which was quite a different matter. Not continence but discretion was all that was asked.

It was a solemn moment when a new life was about to begin; it was even more solemn to contemplate that, but for an act of his, this child would not have been preparing to come into the world.

He sat down and, keeping his eyes on the grazing bull, recalled those incidents in his life which had been of greatest importance to him. Perhaps one of the earliest and therefore the most important, for if it had not happened, all that had followed would not have been possible, was when his uncle Calixtus III had adopted him and his brother Pedro Luis and promised that he would treat them as his own sons if they would discard their father's name of Lanzol and called themselves Borgia.

Their parents had been anxious that the adoption should take place. They had daughters—but Pope Calixtus was not interested in them, and they knew that no better fate could befall their sons than to come under the immediate patronage of the Pope. Their mother—the Pope's own sister—was a Borgia, so it merely meant that the boys should take their mother's name instead of their father's.

That was the beginning of good fortune.

Uncle Alfonso Borgia (Pope Calixtus III to the world) was Spanish and had been born near Valencia. He had come to Italy with King Alfonso of Aragon when that monarch had ascended the throne of Naples. Spain—that most ambitious Power which was fast dominating the world—was eager to see Spanish influence throughout Italy, and how could this be better achieved than by the election of a Spanish Pope?

Uncle Alfonso had the support of Spain when he aspired to the Papacy, and he was victorious in the year 1455. All Borgias were conscious of family feeling. They were Spanish, and Spaniards were not welcome in Italy; therefore it was necessary for all Spaniards to stand together while they did their best to acquire the most important posts.

Calixtus had plans for his two nephews. He promptly made Pedro Luis Generalissimo of the Church and Prefect of the City. Not content with this he created him Duke of Spoleto and, in order that his income should be further increased, he made him vicar of Terracina and Benevento. Pedro Luis was very comfortably established in life; he was not only one of the most influential men in Rome—which he would necessarily be, owing to his relationship with the Pope—he was one of the most wealthy.

The honors which fell to Roderigo were almost as great. He, a year younger than Pedro Luis, was made a Cardinal, although he was only twenty-six; later there was added to this the office of Vice-Chancellor of the Church of Rome. Indeed, the Lanzols had no need to regret the adoption of their sons by the Pope.

It had been clear from the beginning that Calixtus meant Roderigo to follow him to the Papacy; and Roderigo had made up his mind, from the moment of his adoption, that one day he would do so.

Alas, that was long ago, and the Papacy was as far away as ever. Calixtus had been an old man when he was elected, and three years later he had died. Now the wisdom of his prompt action in bestowing great offices on his nephews was seen, for even while Calixtus was on his death-bed, there was an outcry against the Spaniards who had been given the best posts; and the Colonnas and the Orsinis, those powerful families which had felt themselves to be slighted, rose in fury against the foreigners; Pedro Luis had to abandon his fine estates with all his wealth and fly for his life. He died shortly afterward.

Roderigo remained calm and dignified, and did not leave Rome. Instead, while the City was seething against him and his kin, he went solemnly to St. Peter's in order that he might pray for his dying uncle.

Roderigo was possessed of great charm. It was not that he was very handsome; his features were too heavy for good looks, but his dignity and his presence were impressive; so was his courtly grace which rarely failed to arouse the devotion of almost all who came into contact with him.

Oddly enough those people who were raging against him parted to let him pass on his way to St. Peter's while benignly he smiled at them and gently murmured: "Bless you, my children." And they knelt and kissed his hand or the hem of his robes.

Was that one of the most triumphant hours of his life? There had been triumphs since; but perhaps on that occasion he first became aware of this great power within him to charm and subdue by his charm all who would oppose him.

So he had prayed for his uncle and had stayed with him at his bedside while all others had fled; and although his magnificent palace had been sacked and looted, he remained aloof and calm, ready to cast his deciding vote at the Conclave which would follow and which assured Aeneas Sylvius Piccolomini of becoming, as Pius II, the successor of Calixtus.

Pius must be grateful to Roderigo, and indeed he was.

Thus Roderigo came successfully through the first storm of his life and had assured himself that he was able to stand on his own feet, as poor Pedro Luis had not been able to do.

Roderigo collected his brother's wealth, mourned him bitterly—but briefly, for it was not in Roderigo's nature to mourn for long—and found himself as powerful as he had ever been, and as hopeful of aspiring to the Papal throne.

Roderigo now wiped his brow with a perfumed kerchief. Those had been times of great danger, and he hoped never again to see the like; yet whenever he looked back on them he was aware of the satisfaction of a man who has discovered that the dangerous moment had not found him lacking in shrewd resourcefulness.

Pius had indeed been his good friend, but there had been times when Pius had found it necessary to reprove him. He could recall now the words of a letter which Pius had sent to him, complaining of Roderigo's conduct in a certain house where courtesans had been gathered to administer to the pleasures of the guests. And he, young handsome Cardinal Roderigo, had been among those guests.

"We have been informed," wrote Pius, "that there was unseemly dancing, that no amorous allurements of love were lacking, and that you conducted yourself in a wholly worldly manner."

Roderigo threw back his head and smiled, remembering the scented garden of Giovanni de Bichis, the dancing, the warm perfumed bodies of women and their seductive glances. He had found them irresistible, as they had him.

And the reproof of Pius had not been serious. Pius understood that a man such as Roderigo must have his mistresses. Pius merely meant: Yes,

yes, but no dancing in public with courtesans, Cardinal. The people complain, and it brings the Church into disrepute.

How careless he had been in those days, so certain was he of his ability to win through to his goal. He had determined to have the best of both ways of life. The Church was his career, by means of which he was going to climb to the Papal throne; but he was a sensualist, a man of irrepressible carnal desires. There would always be women in his life. It was not an uncommon foible; there was hardly a priest who seriously took his vows regarding celibacy, and it had been said by one of the wits of Rome that if every child came into the world with its father's clothes on, they would all be dressed as priests or Cardinals.

Everyone understood; but Roderigo was perhaps more openly promiscuous than most.

Then he had met Vannozza, and he had set her up in a fine house, where now they had their children. Not that he had been faithful to Vannozza; no one would have expected that; but she had remained reigning favorite for many years and he adored their children. And now there was to be another.

It was irksome to wait. He, who was fifty, felt like a young husband of twenty, and if it were not for the fear of hearing Vannozza's crying in her pain he would have gone to her apartment. But there was no need. Someone was coming to him.

She stood before him, flushed and pretty, Vannozza's little maid. Even on such an occasion Roderigo was aware of her charms. He would remember her.

She curtseyed. "Your Eminence . . . the child is born."

With the grace and agility of a much younger man he had moved to her side and laid beautiful white hands on her shoulders.

"My child, you are breathless. How your heart beats!"

"Yes, my lord. But . . . the baby is born."

"Come," he said, "we will go to your mistress."

He led the way. The little maid, following, realized suddenly that she had forgotten to tell him the sex of the child, and that he had forgotten to ask.

THE BABY WAS brought to the Cardinal who touched its brow and blessed it.

The women fell back; they looked shame-faced as though they were to be blamed for the sex of the child.

It was a beautiful baby; there was a soft down of fair hair on the little head, and Roderigo believed that Vannozza had given him another golden beauty.

"A little girl," said Vannozza, watching him from the bed.

He strode to her, took her hand and kissed it.

"A beautiful little girl," he said.

"My lord is disappointed," said Vannozza wearily. "He hoped for a boy."

Roderigo laughed, that deep-throated musical laugh which made most people who heard it love him.

"Disappointed!" he said. "I?" Then he looked round at the women who had come closer, his eyes resting on them each in turn, caressingly, speculatively. "Disappointed because she is of the feminine sex? But you know . . . every one of you . . . that I love the soft sex with all my heart, and I can find a tenderness for it which I would deny to my own."

The women laughed and Vannozza laughed with them; but her sharp eyes had noticed the little maid who wore an expectant expression as Roderigo's glance lingered upon her.

She decided that, as soon as they returned to Rome, that child should be dismissed and, if Roderigo should look for her, he would look in vain.

"So my lord is pleased with our daughter?" murmured Vannozza, and signed to the women to leave her with the Cardinal.

"I verily believe," said Roderigo, "that I shall find a softer spot in my heart for this sweet girl even than for those merry young rogues who now inhabit your nurseries. We will christen her Lucrezia; and when you are recovered, Madonna, we will return to Rome."

AND SO ON that April day in the Borgia castle at Subiaco was born the child whose name was to be notorious throughout the world: Lucrezia Borgia.

THE PIAZZA
PIZZO DI MERLO

How delighted Vannozza was to be back in Rome! It seemed to her during those months which followed the birth of Lucrezia that she was the happiest of women. Roderigo visited her nurseries more frequently than ever; there was an additional attraction in the golden-haired little girl.

She was a charming baby—very sweet-tempered—and would lie contentedly in her crib giving her beautiful smile to any who asked for it.

The little boys were interested in her. They would stand one on either side of the crib and try to make her laugh. They quarrelled about her. Cesare and Giovanni would always seize on any difference between them and make a quarrel about it.

Vannozza laughed with her women, listening to their bickering: "She's *my* sister." "No, she's *my* sister." It had been explained to them that she was the sister of both of them.

Cesare had answered, his eyes flashing: "But she is more mine than Giovanni's. She loves me—Cesare—better than Giovanni."

That, the nursemaid told him, will be for Lucrezia herself to decide.

Giovanni watched his brother with smoldering eyes; he knew why Cesare wanted Lucrezia to love him best. Cesare was aware that when Uncle Roderigo called it was always Giovanni who had the bigger share of sweetmeats; it was always Giovanni who was lifted up in those strong arms and kissed and caressed before the magnificent Uncle Roderigo turned to Cesare.

Therefore Cesare was determined that everyone else should love him best. His mother did. The nurserymaids said they did; but that might have been because, if they did not, he would have his revenge in some way, and they knew that it was more unwise to offend Cesare than Giovanni.

Lucrezia, as soon as she was able to show a preference, should show it for him. He was determined on that. That was why he hung about her crib even more than Giovanni did, putting out his hand to let those little fingers curl about his thumb.

"Lucrezia," he would whisper. "This is Cesare, your brother. You love him best . . . best of all." She would look at him with those wide blue eyes, and he would command: "Laugh, Lucrezia. Laugh like this."

The women would crowd round the crib to watch, for strangely enough Lucrezia invariably obeyed Cesare; and when Giovanni tried to make her laugh for him, Cesare would be behind his brother pulling such demoniacal faces that Lucrezia cried instead.

"It's that demon, Cesare," said the women to one another, for although he was but five years old they dared not say it to Cesare.

One day, six months after Lucrezia's birth, Vannozza was tending her vines and flowers in her garden. She had her gardeners but this was a labor of love. Her plants were beautiful and it delighted her to look after them herself for her garden and her house were almost as dear to her as her family. Who would not be proud of such a house with its façade, facing the piazza, and the light room with the big window, so different from most of the gloomy rooms in other Roman houses. She had a water cistern too, which was a rare thing.

Her maid—not the one whom Roderigo had admired; she had long since left Vannozza's service—came to tell her that the Cardinal had called, and with him was another gentleman; but even as the girl spoke Roderigo stepped into the garden, and he was alone.

"My lord," cried Vannozza, "that you should find me thus. . . ."

Roderigo's smile was disarming. "But you look charming among your plants," he told her.

"Will you not come into the house? I hear you have brought a guest. The women should have attended to you better."

"But it was my wish to speak to you alone ... out here while you worked among your flowers."

She was startled. She knew that he had something important to say, and she wondered whether he preferred to say it out of doors because even in well-ordered houses such as hers servants had a habit of listening to what they should not.

A cold fear numbed her mind as she wondered if he had come to tell her that this was the end of their liaison. She was acutely conscious of her thirty-eight years. She guarded her beauty well, but even so, a woman of thirty-eight who had borne several children could not compete with young girls; and there could scarcely be a young girl who, if she could resist the charm of the Cardinal, would be able to turn away from all that such an influential man could bring a mistress.

"My lord," she said faintly, "you have news."

The Cardinal lifted his serene face to the sky and smiled his most beautiful smile.

"My dear Vannozza," he said, "as you know, I hold you in the deepest regard." Vannozza caught her breath in horror. It sounded like the beginning of dismissal. "You live here in this house with our three children. It is a happy little home, but there is something missing; these children have no father."

Vannozza wanted to cast herself at his feet, to implore him not to remove his benevolent presence from their lives. They might as well be dead if he did. As well try to live without the sun. But she knew how he disliked unpleasant scenes; and she said calmly: "My children have the best father in the world. I would rather they had never been born than that they should have had another."

"You say delightful things ... delightfully," said Roderigo. "These are my children and dearly I love them. Never shall I forget the great service you have done me in giving them to me, my dearest love."

"My lord. . . ." The tears had come to her eyes and she dashed them away, but Roderigo was looking at the sky, so determined was he not to see them.

"But it is not good that you should live in this house—a beautiful and still young woman, with your children about you, and only the uncle of those children to visit you."

"My lord, if I have offended you in some way I pray you tell me quickly where I have been at fault."

"You have committed no fault, my dear Vannozza. It is but to make life easier for you that I have made these plans. I want none to point at you and whisper: 'Ah, there goes Vannozza Catanei, the woman who has children and no husband.' That is why I have found a husband for you."

"A husband! But, my lord . . ."

Roderigo silenced her with an authoritative smile. "You have a young baby in this house, Vannozza; she is six months old. Therefore you must have a husband."

This was the end. She knew it. He would not have provided her with a husband if he had not tired of her.

He read her thoughts. But it was not entirely true that he was weary of her; he would always have some affection for her and would continue to visit her house, but that would be mainly to see his children; there were younger women with whom he wished to spend his leisure. There was some truth in what he was telling her; he did think it wise that she should be known as a married woman, for he could not have it said that his little ones were the children of a courtesan.

He said quickly: "Your husband's duties will be to live in this house, to appear with you in public. They will end there, Vannozza."

"Your lordship means?"

"Do you think that I could mean anything else? I am a jealous lover, Vannozza. Have you not yet learned that?"

"I know you to be jealous when you are a lover, my lord."

He laid his hand on her shoulder. "Have no fear, Vannozza. You and I have been together too long to part now. It is solely for the sake of our children that I take this step. And I have chosen a quiet man to be your husband. He is a good man, a man of great respectability, and he is prepared to be the only sort of husband I could content myself with giving you."

She took his hand and kissed it.

"And your Eminence will come and visit us now and then?"

"As ever, my dear. As ever. Now come and meet Giorgio di Croce. You will see that he is a mild-tempered man; you will have no difficulty with such a one, I do assure you."

She followed him into the house, wondering what inducement had been offered to this man that he had agreed to marry her. It was not difficult to guess. There would be scarcely a man in Rome who would refuse to marry a woman whom the influential Cardinal had selected for him.

Vannozza was uneasy. She did not care to be bartered thus, as though she were a slave. She would certainly keep Giorgio di Croce in his place.

In her room which overlooked the piazza he was waiting. He rose as they entered and the Cardinal made the introductions.

The mild-tempered man took her hands and kissed them; she studied him and saw that his pale eyes gleamed as he took in her voluptuous charm.

Did the Cardinal notice? If so, he gave no sign.

From the loggia of her mother's house Lucrezia looked out on the piazza and watched with quiet pleasure the people who passed. The city of the seven hills outside her mother's house fascinated her, and it was her favorite pleasure to slip out to the loggia and watch people passing over the St. Angelo Bridge. There were Cardinals on white mules whose silver bridles gleamed in the sunshine; there were masked ladies and gentlemen; there were litters, curtained so that it was impossible to see the occupants.

Lucrezia's wide wondering eyes would peer through gaps in the masonry as her fat little fingers curled about the pillars.

She was two years old but life with her brothers had made her appear to be more. The women of the nursery loved her dearly for, although she was like her brothers in appearance, she was quite unlike them in character. Lucrezia's was a sunny nature; when she was scolded for a fault, she would listen gravely and bear no malice against the scolder. It was small wonder that in that nursery, made turbulent by the two boys, Lucrezia was regarded as a blessing.

She was very pretty, and the women never tired of combing or adorning that long hair of the yellow-gold color which was so rarely seen in Rome. Lucrezia was already, at two—like her brothers she was precocious—aware of her charm, but she accepted this in quiet contentment as she accepted most things.

Today there was a hush over the house, because something important was happening, and Lucrezia was aware of the whispers of serving men and maids, and of the presence of strange women in the house. It concerned her mother, she knew, because she had not been allowed to see her for a whole day. Lucrezia smiled placidly as she looked on the piazza. She would know in time, so she would wait until then.

Her brother Giovanni came and stood beside her. He was six years old, a beautiful boy with auburn hair like his mother's.

Lucrezia smiled at him and held out her hand; her brothers were always affectionate toward her and she was already aware that each of them was doing his best to be her favorite. She was coquette enough already to enjoy the rivalry for her affections.

"For what do you watch, Lucrezia?" asked Giovanni.

"For the people," she answered. "See the fat lady with the mask!"

They laughed together because the fat lady waddled, said Giovanni, like a duck.

"Our uncle will soon be here," said Giovanni. "You are watching for him, Lucrezia."

Lucrezia nodded, smiling. It was true that she always watched for Uncle Roderigo. His visits were the highlights of her life. To be swung in those strong arms, to be held above that laughing face, to smell the faint perfume which clung to his clothes and watch the twinkling jewels on his white hands and to know that he loved her—that was wonderful. Even more wonderful than being loved so much by her two brothers.

"He will come today, Lucrezia," said Giovanni. "He surely will. He is waiting for a message from our mother."

Lucrezia listened, alert; she could not always understand her brothers; they seemed to forget that she was only two years old, and that Giovanni who was six and Cesare who was seven seemed like adults, grand, large and important.

"Do you know why, Lucrezia?" said Giovanni.

When she shook her head, Giovanni laughed, hugging the secret, longing to tell yet reluctant to do so because the anticipation of telling so pleased him. He stopped smiling at her suddenly and Lucrezia knew why. Cesare was standing behind them.

Lucrezia turned to smile at him, but Cesare was glaring at Giovanni.

"It is not for you to tell," said Cesare.

"It is as much for me as for you," retorted Giovanni.

"I am the elder. I shall tell," declared Cesare. "Lucrezia, you are not to listen to him."

Lucrezia shook her head and smiled. No, she would not listen to Giovanni.

"I shall tell if I want to," shouted Giovanni. "I have as much right to tell as you. More . . . because I thought to tell first."

Cesare had his brother by the hair and was shaking him. Giovanni kicked out at Cesare. Cesare kicked back, Giovanni yelled and the two boys were rolling on the floor.

Lucrezia remained placid, for such fights were commonplace enough in the nursery, and she watched them, content that they should be fighting over her; she was nearly always the cause of these fights.

Giovanni was yelping with pain, while Cesare shrieked with rage. The maid-servants would not come near them while they fought thus. They were afraid of those two boys.

Giovanni who was being held down to the floor by Cesare, shouted: "Lucrezia . . . our mother is . . ."

But he could say no more because Cesare had his hand over his brother's mouth. His eyes looked black with rage and his face was scarlet. "I shall tell. It is my place to tell. Our mother is having a baby, Lucrezia."

Lucrezia stared, her eyes wide, her soft babyish mouth open in astonishment. Cesare, watching her amazement, was placated. She was looking at him as though he were responsible for this strange thing. She made him feel powerful, as she had ever since she had been a baby and he had hung over her crib and watched her little fingers curl about his thumb.

He released Giovanni and both boys got to their feet. The fight was over; it was one of many which took place every day in the nursery. Now they were ready to talk to their little sister about the new baby, to strut before her and boast of all that they knew concerning the great events which went on outside their nursery.

Vannozza lay waiting for the Cardinal to visit her. A boy this time, but she was uneasy.

She had good reason to be.

The Cardinal had continued his visits during the two years of her marriage, but they had been less frequent and she had heard a great deal of gossip about the charming young women in whom he was interested.

Giorgio was a good man, a meek man, as the Cardinal had declared him to be; but even the meekest men are yet men, and Vannozza was possessed of voluptuous and irresistible charm. There had been long summer evenings—the cool of the evening was the best part of the day—when they supped in her lovely vineyard in the Suburra, when they had talked and grown drowsy and afterward gone into the house, each feeling stimulated by the presence of the other.

After all, they were married, and Roderigo's visits were so infrequent.

It was to be expected, of course, even though the rule had been laid down that Giorgio was merely to share the public rooms of her house.

Could Roderigo blame her? She did not think he would. But if there was a question of the child being his, he might feel less inclined to do for it what he planned to do for the others.

When a woman held a child in her arms, a child of a few hours, how could she help it if for a short while that child seemed more precious to her than anything else on Earth? Cesare would always hold first place in her affections; but at this time as she lay exhausted in her bed the little newcomer—her Goffredo—being the most helpless of her brood, must, she decided, have the same opportunities as his brothers.

He looked exactly as the others had; indeed it might be little Lucrezia who lay in her arms now, a baby a few hours old; and there was no doubt who her father was. Goffredo might be Roderigo's son. With such a lover and a husband living under her own roof, even Vannozza could not be sure. But she must do all in her power to make the Cardinal sure he was the child's father.

He was coming to her bedside now. Her women stepped back in awed reverence as he approached.

"Vannozza, my dear!" His voice sounded as tender as ever, but he rarely showed anger, and she could not tell what his feelings were toward the child.

"A boy this time, my lord. He is very like Lucrezia . . . and I fancy I see Your Eminence in that child every day."

A plump white hand, sparkling with gems, touched the baby's cheek. It was a tender, paternal gesture, and Vannozza's spirits rose.

She picked up the child and held him out to the Cardinal who took him from her; she saw his face soften in a look of pride and joy. It was small wonder, she thought then, that many loved Roderigo; his love of women and children made them eager to please and serve him.

He walked up and down with the child, and in his eyes was a faraway look as though he were seeing into the future. Surely that meant that he was making plans for the new-born boy. He did not suspect. He must have compared himself with Giorgio and asked himself how any woman could consider the little apostolic clerk, when she must compare him with the charming and mighty Cardinal.

He put the baby back into her arms and stood for a while smiling benignly down at her.

Then he said slyly, "Giorgio? He is pleased?"

THere was a period in Lucrezia's life which she would remember until the day of her death. She was only four years old, yet so vivid was the memory that it was imprinted forever on her mind. For one thing it was the beginning of change.

Before that time she had lived the nursery life, secure in the love of her mother, looking forward to the visits of Uncle Roderigo, delighting in the battle of her brothers for her affection. It had been a pleasant little world in which Lucrezia lived. Each day she would take her stand on the loggia and watch the colorful world go by, but all that happened beyond her mother's house seemed to her nothing more than pictures for her idle pleasure; there was an unreality about all that happened on the other side of the loggia and Lucrezia was safe in her cozy world of love and admiration.

She knew that she was pretty and that no one could fail to notice this because of her yellow hair and her eyes which were light blue-gray in color; her eyelashes and brows were dark and inherited from her Spanish ancestors, it was said; and it was this combination which, partly because it was so unusual, was so attractive. She had the arresting looks of one who was only part Italian, being also part Spanish. Her brothers also possessed this charm.

The serving-maids could not help embracing her, patting her cheeks or stroking her lovely hair. "Dearest little Madonna," they would murmur, and they would whisper together about those enchanting *occhi bianchi* which were going to make a seductress of their little Madonna.

She was happy in their affection; she would snuggle up to them, giving love for love; and she looked forward to a career as a seductress with the utmost pleasure.

Little Lucrezia up to that time believed that the world had been made for her pleasure—her brothers had the same feeling in regard to themselves—but because Lucrezia was by nature serene, ready to be contented, and could only be pleased herself when she pleased others, her character was quite different from those of her brothers. Cesare's and Giovanni's young lives were darkened by their jealousy of each other; Lucrezia knew no such jealousy. She was the Queen of the nursery, certain of the love of all.

And so, up to her fourth birthday the little girl remained shut in her world of contentment which wrapped itself about her like a cozy cocoon.

But with the fourth birthday came the first indication that life was less simple than she had believed it to be, and that it did not go on forever in the same pleasant pattern.

At first she noticed the excitement in the streets. There was much coming and going across the bridge. Each day great Cardinals, their retinues with them, came riding into Rome on their mules. People stood about in little groups; some talked quietly, some gesticulated angrily.

All day she had waited for a visit from Uncle Roderigo, but he did not come.

When Cesare came into the nursery she ran to him and took his hands, but even Cesare had changed; he did not seem as interested in her as before. He went to the loggia and patiently she stood beside him, like a little page, humble, waiting on his pleasure as he liked her to; yet he said nothing, but stood still, watching the crowds in the streets.

"Uncle Roderigo has not come to us," she said wistfully.

Cesare shook his head. "He will not come, little sister. Not today."

"Is he sick?"

Cesare smiled slowly. His hands were clenched, she saw, and his face grew taut as it did so often when he was angry or determined about something.

She stood on the step which enabled her to be as high as his shoulder, and put her face close to his that she might study his expression.

"Cesare," she said, "you are angry with Uncle Roderigo?"

Cesare caught her neck in his strong hands; it hurt a little, this trick of his, but she liked it because she knew that it meant: See how strong I am. See how I could hurt you, little Lucrezia, if I wished to; but I do not wish to, because you are my little sister and I love you because you love me . . . better than anyone in the world . . . better than our mother, better than Uncle Roderigo, better, certainly better, than Giovanni.

And when she squealed and showed by her face that he was hurting— only a little—that meant: Yes, Cesare, my brother. You I love better than any in the world. And he understood and his fingers became gentle.

"One is not angry with Uncle Roderigo," Cesare told her. "That would be foolish, and I am no fool."

"No, Cesare, you are no fool. But are you angry with someone?"

He shook his head. "No. I rejoice, little sister."

"Tell me why."

"You are but a baby. What could you know of what goes on in Rome?"

"Does Giovanni know?" Lucrezia, at four, was capable of sly diplomacy. The lovely light eyes were downcast; she did not want to see Cesare's anger; like Roderigo she turned from what was unpleasant.

The trick was successful. "I will tell you," said Cesare. Of course he would tell. He would not allow Giovanni to give her something which *he* had denied her. "The Pope, who you know is Sixtus IV, is dying. That is why they are excited down there; that is why Uncle Roderigo does not come to see us. He has much to do. When the Pope dies there will be a Conclave and then, little sister, the Cardinals will choose a new Pope."

"Uncle Roderigo is choosing; that is why he cannot come to see us," she said.

Cesare stood smiling at her. He felt important, all-wise; no one made him feel so wise or important as his little sister; that was why he loved her so dearly.

"I wish he could choose quickly and come to see us," added Lucrezia. "I will ask the saints to make a new Pope quickly ... so that he can come to us."

"No, little Lucrezia. Do not ask such a thing. Ask this instead. Ask that the new Pope shall be our Uncle Roderigo."

Cesare laughed, and she laughed with him. There was so much she did not understand; but in spite of the threatening strangeness, in spite of the gathering crowd below and the absence of Uncle Roderigo, it was good to stand on the loggia, clinging to Cesare's doublet, watching the excitement in the square.

※※※

Roderigo was not elected.

The excitement, watched by the children, persisted throughout the city. The scene had changed. Lucrezia heard the sounds of battle in the streets below, and Vannozza, in terror, had barricades put about the house. Even Cesare did not know exactly what it was all about, although he and Giovanni, strutting around the nursery, would not admit this. Uncle Roderigo only visited the house briefly to assure himself that the children were as safe as he could make them. His visits now were merely to see the children; since the birth of little Goffredo he had ceased to regard Vannozza as his mistress, and now there was another baby, Ottaviano, whom Vannozza made no pretence of passing off as his. As for little Goffredo, Roderigo was enchanted by the child, who was turning out to be in every way as beautiful as his elder brothers and sister. Roderigo, having need of sons and being susceptible to beautiful children, was more often than not inclined to give Goffredo the benefit of the doubt, and the attention he bestowed on the others was then shared by the little boy. Poor little Ottaviano was an outsider, ignored by Roderigo, though dearly loved by Vannozza and Giorgio.

But during those weeks there was little time even to regret Roderigo's absence; the children could only look out on the piazza with amazement at the changing scene.

Innocent VIII had become Pope and he had allowed Cardinal della Rovere, who was the nephew of the deceased Sixtus, to persuade him to make war against Naples. The powerful Orsinis who, with the Colonnas, dominated Rome, were friends and allies of the Neopolitans, and this gave them an excuse for rising against the city. They put Rome almost into a state of siege and their old enemies, the Colonnas, lost no time in going into battle against them. Therefore, the streets of Rome, during that period which followed the death of Sixtus and the election of Innocent were the scenes of many a fierce battle.

The children—Cesare, Giovanni and Lucrezia—watching behind the barricades saw strange sights in the city of Rome. They saw the fierce Orsinis coming out in force from Monte Giordano to attack the equally fierce and bloodthirsty Colonnas. They watched men cut each other to pieces in the piazza immediately before their eyes; they saw the way of lewd soldiery with the girls and women; they smelled the hideous smells of war, of burning buildings, of blood and sweat; they heard the cries of victims and the triumphant shouts of raiders.

Death was commonplace; torture equally so.

Little Lucrezia, four years old, looked on at these sights at first with wonder and then almost with indifference. Cesare and Giovanni watched with her and she took her cue from them.

Torture, rape, murder—they were all part of the world outside their nursery. At four years of age children accept without surprise that which is daily paraded before their eyes and Lucrezia was to remember this time of her life not as one of horror, but of change.

THE FIGHTING DIED down; life returned to normal; and two years passed before there was another and this time a more important change for Lucrezia, a change which marked the beginning of the end of childhood. She was nearly six, a precocious six. Cesare was eleven and Giovanni ten; she had been so much their companion that she had learned more than most children know at six years of age. She was as serene as ever, perhaps a little more eager now to provoke that rivalry between her brothers than she had been, understanding more than ever what power it gave her, and that while each sought to be her favorite, she could be the most powerful person in the nursery.

Certainly she was serene, for she was wise; she had come to her power through her brothers' rivalry and all she had to do was award the prize— her affection.

She remained the darling of the nursery. The maids could be sure that there would be no tantrums from Lucrezia; she was kind to little Goffredo whom his brothers scarcely deigned to notice on account of his youth; and she was equally kind to little Ottaviano whom her brothers would not notice at all. They knew something about Ottaviano which made them despise him, but Lucrezia was sorry for him, so she was particularly kind.

Lucrezia enjoyed her life; it was amusing to play one brother off against the other, to worm their secrets from them, to use this rivalry. She liked to walk in the gardens, her arms about Giovanni, being particularly loving when she knew Cesare could see her from the house. It made her feel warm and cozy to be loved so much by two such wonderful brothers.

When Uncle Roderigo came she liked to climb over him looking close into his face, perhaps putting out a delicate finger to touch the nose which seemed gigantic, to caress the heavy jowls, to bury her face in his scented garments and to tell him that the smell of him reminded her of her mother's flower gardens.

Uncle Roderigo loved them all dearly, and came often with presents; he would have them stand round him while he sat on the ornamental chair which their mother kept for him, and he would look at them all in turn— his beloved children whom, he told them, he loved beyond all things on Earth; his eyes rested most fondly of all on Giovanni. Lucrezia was aware of this; and sometimes when she saw the dark look it brought to Cesare's face she would run to Uncle Roderigo and throw herself at him in order to turn his attention from Giovanni to herself.

She was often successful, for when Uncle Roderigo's long fingers caressed her yellow hair, when his lips touched her soft cheek, there would be a special tenderness which he could only give to her. He would hold her more tightly to him and kiss her more often.

"My enchanting little one," he would murmur. "My little love."

Then he ceased to watch Giovanni so devotedly and that pleased Cesare who did not mind Uncle Roderigo's loving Lucrezia. It was only Giovanni who aroused his jealousy.

Then Vannozza might appear at the door holding little Goffredo by the hand, pushing him forward; and Goffredo would break from his mother and run shrieking with joy, shouting: "Uncle Roderigo, Goffredo is here." He would be dressed in his blue tunic, which made him look as beautiful as a painted angel in one of the pictures which their mother cherished; and Uncle Roderigo would hesitate—or pretend to hesitate—for one second before he picked up the beautiful little boy. But only when Vannozza had gone would he smother him with kisses and take him on his knee and let him pull gifts from the pockets of his robes, while he called him "My little Goffredo."

Ottaviano never came. Poor Ottaviano, the outsider; he was pale and delicate and he coughed a great deal. He was very like Giorgio, who was kind but who must be, so Cesare commanded, ignored by them all, since he had nothing to do with them.

But it was through Ottaviano and Giorgio, those two who were regarded as insignificant by the three children in the nursery, that change came into their lives.

They grew listless, both of them. The weather was sultry and it was said that there was pestilence in the air. Giorgio grew paler and thinner each day until he took to his bed and there was quiet throughout the house.

Vannozza wept bitterly, for she had come to love her meek husband, and when he died she was very sad. It was not long afterward that little Ottaviano, suffering in the same way as his father had, took to his bed and died. Thus in a few months the household had lost two of its members.

Lucrezia wept to see her mother unhappy. She missed little Ottaviano too; he had been one of her most faithful admirers.

Cesare found her crying and wanted to know why.

"But you know," she said, her light eyes wide and wondering. "Our father is dead and our little brother with him. Our mother is sad and so am I."

Cesare snapped his fingers angrily. "You should not weep for them," he said. "They are nothing to us."

Lucrezia shook her head and for once she would not agree with him. She had loved them both; she found it easy to love people. Giorgio had been so kind to her, Ottaviano had been her dear little brother, so she would insist on weeping even though Cesare forbade her.

But Cesare must not be crossed. She saw the dark angry look come into his eyes.

"Lucrezia, you shall not cry for them," he insisted. "You shall not, I say. Dry your eyes. Look here is a kerchief. Dry them and smile. Smile!"

But it was not possible to smile with all her grief upon her. Lucrezia tried, but she remembered the kindness of Giorgio and how he had carried her on his shoulder and looked so pleased when people had admired her yellow hair; she remembered how little Ottaviano had a habit of creeping close to her and slipping his little hand in hers; she remembered how he used to lisp her name. She could not smile, because she could not forget that she would never see Giorgio and Ottaviano again.

Cesare seemed as though he were finding it difficult to breathe, which meant he was very angry. He took her by the neck, and this time there was more anger than tenderness in the gesture.

"It is time you knew the truth," he said. "Have you not guessed who our father is?"

She had not thought of possessing a father until Giorgio came into the house, and then, as Vannozza called him husband, she had thought of him as father, but she knew better than to say that Giorgio was their father; so she was silent, hoping Cesare would relax his hold on her neck and let the tenderness return to his fingers.

Cesare had put his face close to hers; he whispered: "Roderigo, Cardinal Borgia, is not our uncle, foolish child; he is our father."

"Uncle Roderigo?" she said slowly.

"Of a certainty, foolish one." Now his grip was tender. He laid his lips on her cool cheek and gave her one of those long kisses which disturbed her. "Why should he come here so often, do you think? Why should he love us so? Because he is our father. It is time you knew. Now you will see that it is unworthy to cry for such as Giorgio and Ottaviano. Do you see that now, Lucrezia?"

His eyes were dark again—not with rage perhaps, but with pride because Uncle Roderigo was their father and he was a great Cardinal who, they must pray each day, each night, might one day be Pope and the most powerful man in Rome.

"Yes, Cesare," she said, for she was afraid of Cesare when he looked like that.

But when she was alone she went into a corner and continued to weep for Giorgio and Ottaviano.

But even Cesare was to discover that the death of those whom he had considered insignificant could make a great difference to his life.

Roderigo, still solicitous for the welfare of his ex-mistress, decided that, since she had lost her husband, she must be provided with another; therefore he arranged a marriage for her with a certain Carlo Canale. This was a good match for Vannozza since Carlo was the chamberlain of Cardinal Francesco Gonzaga, and a man of some culture; he had encouraged the poet, Angelo Poliziano, in the writing of *Orfeo*, and had worked with distinction among the humanists of Mantua. Here was a man who could be useful to Roderigo; and Canale was wise enough to know that through Roderigo he might acquire the riches he had so far failed to accumulate.

Roderigo's notary drew up the marriage contracts and Vannozza prepared to settle down with her new husband.

But as she had gained a husband she was to lose her three eldest children. She accepted this state of affairs philosophically for she knew that Roderigo could not allow their children to remain in her house beyond their childhood; the comparatively humble home of a Roman matron was not the right setting for those who had a brilliant destiny before them.

Thus came the greatest change of all into Lucrezia's life.

Giovanni was to go to Spain, where he would join his eldest brother, Pedro Luis, and where his father would arrange for honors to fall to him; and those honors should be as great as those which he had given to Pedro Luis. Cesare was to stay in Rome. Later he was to train for a Spanish Bishopric, and to do this he must study canon law at the universities of Perugia and Pisa. For the time being he was with Lucrezia but they were soon to leave their mother's house for that of a kinswoman of their father's; therein they would be brought up as fitted their father's children.

It was a staggering blow to Lucrezia. All that had been home to her for six years would be home no longer. The blow was swift and sudden. The only one who rejoiced in that household on the Piazza Pizzo di Merlo was Giovanni, who strutted about the nursery, wielding an imaginary sword, bowing in mock reverence before Cesare whom he called my lord Bishop. Giovanni, intoxicated with excitement, talked continually of Spain.

Lucrezia watched Cesare, his arms folded across his breast, his face white with suppressed anger. Cesare did not rage, did not cry out that he would kill Giovanni; for once Cesare was beaten.

The first important change of their lives had been reached and they all had to accept the fact that however much they might boast in the nursery, they had no alternative but to obey orders.

Only once, when he was alone with Lucrezia, did Cesare cry out as he thumped his fist on his thighs so violently that Lucrezia was sure he was hurting himself: "Why should he go to Spain? Why should I have to go into the Church? I want to go to Spain. I want to be a Duke and a soldier. Do you think I am not more fitted to conquer and rule than he is? It is because our father loves him better than he loves me that Giovanni has cajoled him into this. I will not endure it. I will not."

Then he took Lucrezia by the shoulders, and his blazing eyes frightened her.

"I swear to you, little sister, that I shall not rest until I am free . . . free of my father's will . . . free of the will of any who seek to restrain me."

Lucrezia could only murmur: "You will be free, Cesare. You will always do what you want."

Then he laughed suddenly and gave her one of those fierce embraces which she knew so well.

She was anxious about Cesare, and that meant that she did not worry so much about her own future as she might otherwise have done.

MONTE GIORDANO

Adriana of the house of Mila was a very ambitious woman. Her father, a nephew of Calixtus III, had come to Italy when his uncle became Pope, because it seemed that under such benign and powerful influence there might be a great future for him. Adriana was therefore related to Roderigo Borgia, who held her in great esteem, for she was a woman not only of beauty but of intelligence. It was owing to these qualities that she had married Ludovico of the noble house of Orsini, and the Orsini was one of the most powerful families in Italy. Adriana had a son who had been named Orsino; this boy was sickly and, having a squint, rather unprepossessing, but on account of his position—as the heir to great wealth—Adriana hoped to make a brilliant marriage for him.

The Orsinis had many palaces in Rome but Adriana and her family lived in that on Monte Giordano, near the Bridge of St. Angelo. And it was to this palace that Lucrezia and Cesare were taken when they said good-bye to their brothers and their mother.

Here life was very different from what it had been in the house on the Piazza Pizzo di Merlo. With Vannozza there had been light-hearted gaiety, and the children had enjoyed great freedom. They had been allowed to wander in the vineyards, or to enjoy trips on the river; they had often visited the Campo di Fiore where it had given them great delight to mingle with all kinds of people. Cesare and Lucrezia realized that life had indeed been changed.

Adriana was awe-inspiring. She was a beautiful woman but always dressed in ceremonial black, insisting constantly that it must not be forgotten that this was a Spanish household even though it was in the heart of Italy. With its great towers and crenellations dominating the Tiber, the palace was gloomy; its thick walls shut out the sunshine and the gaiety of the Rome which the children had known and loved. Adriana never laughed as Vannozza had laughed, and there was nothing warm and loving about her.

She had many priests living in the palace; there were constant prayers, and consequently Lucrezia believed in those first years in the Orsini palace that her foster-mother was a very virtuous woman.

Cesare chafed against the discipline, but even he was unable to do anything about it, even he was overawed by the gloomy palace, the many prayers and the feeling that the palace was a prison in which he and Lucrezia had been incarcerated while Giovanni had been allowed to go in pomp and splendor to Spain and glory.

Cesare brooded silently. He did not rage as he had in his mother's house; he was sullen and sometimes his quiet anger frightened Lucrezia. Then she would cling to him and beg him not to be sad; she would cover him with kisses and cry out that she loved him best of all . . . better than anyone else in the whole world, that she would love him today, the next day and forever.

Even this declaration could not appease him, and he remained brooding and unhappy, but sometimes he would turn to her and seize her in one of those fierce embraces which hurt her and excited her. Then he would say: "You and I are together, little sister. We'll always love each other . . . best in the world . . . best in the whole world. Swear it to me."

And she swore it. Sometimes they would lie together on her bed or his. She would go there to comfort him, or he would come to her for comfort. Then he would talk of Giovanni and how unfair life was. Why did their father love Giovanni? Cesare would demand. Why should not Cesare have been the one who was chosen to go to Spain? Cesare would never go into the Church. He hated the Church, hated it . . . hated it.

His vehemence frightened her. She crossed herself and reminded him that it was unlucky to talk thus against the Church. The saints, or perhaps the Holy Ghost might be angry and come to punish him. She was afraid, she said; but she said it to give him the chance of comforting her, to remind him that he was great Cesare, afraid of none, and she was little Lucrezia who was the one to be protected.

Sometimes she made him forget his anger against Giovanni. Sometimes they laughed together and remembered the fun they had had on their jaunts to the Campo di Fiore. Then they would swear that no matter what happened they would always love each other best in the world.

But during those first months the children felt that they were prisoners.

RODERIGO VISITED THEM at Monte Giordano.

In the early days Cesare asked that they might go home, but Roderigo, fond father though he was, could be firm when he felt himself to be acting for the good of his children.

"My little ones," he said, "you have been running wild in the house of your mother. But to run wild is for little children, not for big ones. It is not meet that you should pass your time in that humble house. A great future awaits you both. Trust me to judge what is best for you."

And Cesare knew that when his father's face was set in those lines there was nothing to be done about it. He had to obey.

"Very soon," Roderigo told Cesare, "you will be leaving this house. You will be going to the university. There you will have great freedom, my son; but first I would have you know how to act like a nobleman, and although there is discipline here such as you have never encountered before, this is necessary to make you worthy of what you will become. Have patience. It is but for a little while."

And Cesare was mollified.

The head of the house of Orsini was Virginio, one of the great soldiers of Italy, and when he was at Monte Giordano, the palace resembled a military camp. Virginio shouted orders to all, and the serving men and maids scurried hither and thither, in fear of displeasing the great commander.

Strangely enough Cesare, who so longed to be a soldier, had no objection to this stern rule; and for the first time in her life Lucrezia saw her brother ready to bend to the will of another. Cesare rode behind Virginio, straight as a soldier, and Virginio would often watch him and do his utmost to hide the smile of approval which touched his lips. He would watch Cesare, bare to the waist, learning to wrestle with some of the best teachers in the whole of Italy; the boy gave a good account of himself.

"That boy for the Church!" said Virginio to Adriana and Ludovico her husband. "He's made for a military career."

Adriana answered: "Careers in the Church, my dear Virginio bring a man more profit than those of soldiering."

"'Tis a tragedy to make a prelate of him. What is Roderigo Borgia thinking of?"

"His future . . . and the future of the Borgias. That boy is destined to be Pope, I tell you. At least that is what Roderigo Borgia plans to make him."

Virginio swore his soldier's oaths and set the boy more arduous tasks, shouted at him, bullied him and Cesare did not object. He dreamed of being a great soldier. Virginio approved of his dreamings, and even went so far as to wish the boy was his son.

Thus that year was made tolerable for Cesare and, such was Lucrezia's nature that, seeing her brother reconciled, she could become reconciled too.

But by the end of the year Cesare had left the Orsini palace for Perugia, and Lucrezia wept bitterly in her loneliness. Then she suddenly began to realize that with Cesare absent she enjoyed a certain freedom, a certain lack of tension; she found that she could begin to consider what was happening to herself irrespective of Cesare.

Lucrezia was growing up and her religious education must not be neglected, since that formed the background of the education of all Italian girls of noble birth. Most of them went into convents, but Roderigo had given much anxious thought to this matter, for the behavior in convents was not always above reproach and he was determined to protect his Lucrezia. The Colonnas sent their daughters, it was true, to San Silvestro in Capite, and the convents of Santa Maria Nuova and San Sisto he believed were equally worthy; so he decided that it should be San Sisto's on the Appian Way to which Lucrezia should go for religious instruction. She was to stay there only for brief periods though, and she returned often to Monte Giordano where she was instructed in languages—Spanish, Greek and Latin—as well as painting, music and fine needlework.

It was not necessary, Roderigo had pointed out to Adriana, that his little daughter should become a virago (a term which in those days simply meant a learned woman). He wished his Lucrezia to be highly educated that she might be a worthy companion for himself. It was vital that she should be instructed in deportment, that she should acquire the airs and graces of a noblewoman and be able to take her place among Kings and Princes; he wished her to be modest in her demeanour. Her serenity of character gave her a charming graciousness which was apparent even at the age of seven, when she began this course of grooming; that, Roderigo wished to be preserved, for, as he saw his little daughter growing in beauty every day, he was becoming more and more ambitious on her account.

The nuns of San Sisto quickly learned to love their little pupil, not only for her pleasant looks and charming manners, but because of that eager desire within her to please everybody and be their friend; and perhaps also they remembered it was rumored that she was indeed the daughter of the great Roderigo Borgia, the richest of Cardinals and one who, it was said in high places, had every chance of one day becoming Pope.

When Lucrezia had been three years at Monte Giordano, Ludovico, Adriana's husband, died and the palace was plunged into mourning, Adriana covered herself with black veils and spent much time with her priests, and Lucrezia told herself then that Adriana was a very good woman.

One day when Lucrezia had returned from San Sisto's to Monte Giordano and sat at table with Adriana and Orsino she thought how sad it was that she and Orsino should eat and drink from silver utensils while Adriana, because she was a widow, mourning her husband in the Spanish manner, must do so from earthenware.

Lucrezia leaned on the table, the top of which was made of marble and colored pieces of wood, and said: "Dear Madonna Adriana, you are still very unhappy because you are a widow. I know, because my mother was unhappy when Giorgio di Croce died. She wept and talked of her unhappiness, and then she felt better."

Adriana straightened the long black veil which flowed over her shoulder. "I would not talk of my grief," she said. "In Spain we say it is ill-mannered to show one's grief to the world."

"But we are not the world—Orsino and I," persisted Lucrezia. "And my mother . . ."

"Your mother was an Italian woman. It will be well if you forget your Italian birth. In Spain to share a pleasure is a good thing because in sharing what is good one gives something worth having. To share one's sorrow is to beg that one's burden shall be partly carried by another. Spaniards are too proud to ask favors."

The matter was closed. Lucrezia blushed over her plate. She had much to learn, she realized. She was sorry she had spoken, and now she looked pleadingly at Orsino for comfort; but he was not looking at her. Orsino was one of the few people who did not admire her yellow hair and pretty face. She might have been one of the ornamental chairs, of which there were so many in the principal rooms of the palace, for all the notice he took of her.

Adriana was looking severe, and Lucrezia feared that she would always disappoint her because she was such a good woman and thought always of doing what was right.

Later that day, as she and Adriana sat together working on an altar cloth, Adriana said: "You will soon have a companion to share your dancing and music lessons."

Lucrezia dropped the gold thread and waited breathlessly.

"I am to have a daughter," said Adriana.

"Oh, but . . . a daughter! I thought . . ." Lucrezia at nine years of age was knowledgeable. She had seen certain sights from the house on the piazza; she had listened to the talk of her brothers and the servants. It seemed incredible that the pious widow could have a daughter.

Adriana was looking at her in surprise, and Lucrezia flushed again.

"My son is of a marriageable age," said Adriana coldly. "His bride will soon be coming here. She will live with us as my daughter until the marriage takes place."

Lucrezia picked up her needle and began to work, hoping to hide her embarrassment. "That will be pleasant, Madonna Adriana," she said, but she felt sorry for the girl who would be married to Orsino.

"Orsino," said Adriana as though reading her thoughts, "is one of the best matches in Rome."

"Is Orsino happy?" asked Lucrezia. "Is he dancing with joy because he is to have a bride?"

"Orsino has been brought up as a Spanish nobleman. They, my dear Lucrezia, do not jump for joy like any Italian shepherd on the Campo di Fiore."

"Assuredly they do not, Madonna Adriana."

"He will be happy. He knows his duty. He must marry and have sons."

"And the bride...."

"You will soon see her. I shall teach her as I do you."

Lucrezia continued to stitch, thinking of the companion she was to have. She hoped the bride would not mind too much . . . having to marry Orsino.

Lucrezia waited in the great dark room in which, because this was a special occasion, the tapestries had been hung.

They were gathered to greet the girl who was being brought to her new home, and Lucrezia wondered how she was feeling. She would quickly try to reassure her for she would be a little frightened perhaps. Lucrezia herself knew how alarming it could be to be taken from one's home to an entirely different place.

Orsino stood beside his mother. Adriana had talked severely to him of his duty and poor Orsino looked more sallow than ever in his Spanish black, and not at all like a bridegroom-to-be; his squint was more distressing than ever; it always seemed more pronounced at times of stress, and his mother's cold gaze was continually admonishing him.

Lucrezia was also in black, but there was gold and silver embroidery on her gown. She wished that they did not always have to follow the Spanish customs. The Spanish were fond of black for all ceremonial occasions and Lucrezia loved bright scarlet and gold and particularly that shade of deep blue which made her hair look more golden than ever. But black made a happy contrast to her light eyes and fair hair, so she felt she was fortunate in that.

And as she waited, Giulia Farnese entered the room. Her brother, Alessandro, a young man of about twenty, had brought her. He was proud, distinguished-looking and splendidly clad; but it was Giulia who held Lucrezia's attention and that of all those assembled, for she was beautiful, and her hair was as golden as Lucrezia's. She was dressed in the Italian fashion in her gown of blue and gold, and she looked like a Princess in a legend and far too beautiful for this world among the somberly clad Orsinis.

Lucrezia felt a twinge of jealousy. All would be saying: This Giulia Farnese is more beautiful than Lucrezia.

The girl knelt before Adriana and called her "Mother." When Orsino was pushed forward, he came shambling, and was fumbling and ungracious in his greeting. Lucrezia watched the lovely young face for a sign of the revulsion she must surely be feeling, and she forgot her jealousy in her pity for Giulia. But Giulia showed no emotion. She was demure and gracious—all that was expected of her.

THEY QUICKLY BECAME friends. Giulia was vivacious, full of information, and very ready to give her attention to Lucrezia when there were no men about.

Giulia told Lucrezia that she was nearly fifteen. Lucrezia was not quite ten; and those extra years gave Giulia a great advantage. She was more frivolous than Lucrezia and not so ready to learn, nor so eager to please. When they were alone she told Lucrezia that she thought Madonna Adriana too strict and solemn.

"Madonna Adriana is a very good woman," insisted Lucrezia.

"I don't like good women," retorted Giulia.

"Is that because they make us all feel so wicked?" suggested Lucrezia.

"I'd rather be wicked than good," laughed Giulia.

Lucrezia looked over her shoulder at the figure of the Madonna and child with the lamp burning before it.

"Oh," laughed Giulia, "there's plenty of time to repent. Repentance is for old people."

"There are some young nuns at San Sisto's," Lucrezia told her.

That made Giulia laugh. "I'd not be a nun. Nor would you. Why, look at you! See how pretty you are . . . and you'll be prettier yet. Wait until you're as old as I am. Mayhap then, Lucrezia, you'll be as beautiful as I am, and you'll have lovers, many of them."

This was conversation such as Lucrezia enjoyed. It brought back echoes of a past she could scarcely remember. It was four years since she had left the gaiety of her mother's house for the strict etiquette and Spanish gloom of Monte Giordano.

Giulia showed Lucrezia how to walk seductively, how to brighten her lips, how to dance. Giulia possessed secret knowledge which she allowed Lucrezia to coax from her.

Lucrezia was a little worried about Giulia; she was afraid that, if Adriana discovered what she was really like, she would send her away and this exciting companion would be lost to her.

They must not let Adriana see the carmine on their lips. They must not appear before her with their hair in the loose coiffure into which Giulia had arranged it. Giulia must never wear any of the dazzling but daring gowns which she had brought with her. Giulia giggled and tried to be prim before her prospective mother-in-law.

Orsino never troubled them, and Lucrezia noticed that he seemed more afraid of his bride than she was of him.

Giulia had a sunny nature; she told Lucrezia that she would know how to deal with Orsino when the time came. It was clear that all the low-cut dresses, the attention to her appearance which seemed to absorb Giulia, were not for Orsino's benefit.

Lucrezia felt that Giulia must be very wicked.

I believe, though, she said to herself, I also like wicked people better than good ones. I should be desolate if Giulia went away, but I should not care very much if Madonna Adriana did.

THERE WAS EXCITEMENT in the Orsini palace. It was one of those special days when Lucrezia must be more sedate than usual, when she must behave as a Spanish lady, and walk with the utmost grace, for Cardinal Roderigo Borgia was coming to Monte Giordano to visit his daughter, and Adriana was eager that he should not be disappointed in her.

Lucrezia wore her hair parted in the center and falling demurely over her shoulders. Giulia watched her Spanish maid prepare her, with great interest.

"Is he very solemn, the great Cardinal?" she asked.

"He is the most important man in Rome," boasted Lucrezia.

"Then," said Giulia, "you will have to pull down your lips in a sour expression because, when you do not, you look too happy, and you will have to be quiet and speak only when spoken to."

"My father likes to see me happy," said Lucrezia. "He likes me to smile, and he likes me to talk too. He is not in the least like Adriana. But she will be watching and I shall have to remember all she has taught me, since, as he sent me here to be taught by her, that is surely what he wished me to learn."

Giulia grimaced; and Lucrezia left her and went down to the intimate and pleasant little room where Roderigo was waiting for her.

The tapestries were hanging on the walls and the finest silver goblets had been brought out for this occasion.

Adriana stood by Roderigo while Lucrezia bowed in the Spanish fashion. Roderigo laid his hands on her shoulders and kissed her cheeks and then her forehead.

"But how she grows, my little one," he said tenderly. "Madonna Adriana has been telling me of your progress."

Lucrezia looked askance at Adriana whose expression was grim.

"It has not been as good as you hoped?" said Lucrezia timidly.

"My dear, who of us reaches perfection? You please me. That will suffice." Roderigo looked at Adriana, who bowed her head. He was asking that they be left alone.

When Adriana had gone she took all restraint with her, and Lucrezia threw herself into her father's arms telling him how wonderful it was to see him.

He kissed her with tenderness and passion, and brought a bracelet from his pocket, which he put on her wrist. She kissed it and he kissed it. He was always passionately sentimental when they were alone. He wanted to tell her of his love and to be assured of hers.

When these assurances were made they talked of Vannozza and of Cesare and Giovanni.

"Cesare does well at the university," said Roderigo. "I am proud of his scholarship and his prowess at sport. It will not be long, I swear before he becomes a Cardinal. And Giovanni does very happily in Spain. My Lucrezia is growing into a beautiful lady. For what more should I wish?"

"And Goffredo?"

"He grows in strength and beauty every day. Ah, we shall have to make plans for him before long."

Over her father's shoulder Lucrezia saw the door open slowly. Giulia, her face flushed, was peering round it.

Lucrezia shrank in horror. This was an unforgivable breach of etiquette. Giulia could not realize how very important the Cardinal was. To dare to come peeping thus . . . it was unthinkable. Giulia would be dismissed, and the marriage arrangements would be broken off, if Adriana discovered she had done such a thing.

Roderigo had sensed his daughter's dismay; he turned sharply and Giulia was caught.

"And who is this?" asked Roderigo.

"Giulia, you must come in now," said Lucrezia, "and I will present you to the Cardinal."

Giulia came, and to Lucrezia's consternation she was not wearing her most modest gown, and her lips were faintly carmined. Lucrezia prayed the Cardinal would not notice.

Giulia, reckless as she was, flushed and with her golden hair falling in tumbled curls about her shoulders, looked a little apprehensive as she came slowly toward them.

"My father," said Lucrezia quickly, "this is Giulia who is to marry Orsino. She meant no harm, I do assure you."

The Cardinal said: "I believe she did mean harm. She looks full of mischief."

"Oh no . . ." began Lucrezia; and then she stopped, realizing that her father was not at all angry.

"Come, my child," he said, "you do not need my daughter to speak for you. I pray you, speak for yourself."

Giulia ran to him and knelt. She lifted those wonderful blue eyes of hers to his face, and she was smiling that confident smile which said clearly that she did not believe anyone could really be annoyed with her, if only because of her enchanting presence.

"So you are to marry Orsino," said the Cardinal. "My poor child! Do you love the young man?"

"I love Rome, Your Eminence," said Giulia, "and the people I meet in Rome."

The Cardinal laughed. To Lucrezia's great relief she knew now that, far from being angry, he was pleased.

"On these occasions when I visit Lucrezia," he explained to Giulia as though she were one of his family, "there is no ceremony. I will have it thus. Come, you shall sit on one side of me, Lucrezia on the other, and we will talk to each other of Rome . . . and the people we meet in Rome. . . ."

"You are gracious to me, Your Eminence," said Giulia with a demureness which did not ring true. "I fear I have behaved very badly."

"My child, you are charming enough to dispense with that etiquette which others less fortunate must sustain."

Lucrezia noticed, as they sat together laughing and talking, that her father turned more often to Giulia than to herself.

She was too astonished to feel jealousy.

And it was thus that Adriana found them.

Strangely enough Adriana did not appear to be angry, and much to Lucrezia's relief and astonishment nothing was said about Giulia's alarmingly bold action.

Giulia herself seemed to change subtly; she was more subdued and, when Lucrezia tried to talk to her about Roderigo, Giulia seemed less communicative than usual. Yes, she replied to Lucrezia's insistence, she did think the Cardinal was a very fine man. The finest man she had ever seen? demanded Lucrezia, who always enjoyed hearing compliments about her family. It might well be so, admitted Giulia.

She would say no more than that and, during the whole of that day, she seemed to withdraw herself from Lucrezia so that the little girl could not help feeling uneasy.

And when on the following day, hearing the sound of horses' hoofs, she looked out from her window, and saw the Cardinal riding away from the palace, her first impulse was to call him, but that of course would be undignified. He had come alone, which was unusual, and he had not seen *her* which was more unusual still. For what reason would he come to Monte Giordano if it were not to see his little daughter?

It was bewildering. Then Lucrezia thought she understood. Certainly he could not allow Giulia's boldness of the previous day to go unpunished. Because he was gentle by nature and hated to be present when it was necessary to punish, he had not scolded Giulia but had pretended to be pleased by her company. That was entirely due to his courteous manners; but now he had come back to talk seriously to Adriana; he had come to complain and ask how such a minx as Giulia could possibly be a fit companion for his daughter.

Lucrezia's bewilderment turned to misery. She felt sure that very soon she would be deprived of Giulia's bright company.

GiuLia was gay. She was wearing a new necklace set with emeralds and rubies.

"But it is exquisite workmanship," cried Lucrezia. "You possessed such a treasure and did not show it to me before!"

"It is certainly exquisite," agreed Giulia; "and I should never have kept it from you for a day, sweet Lucrezia, if I had had it to show you. I have just received it."

"A gift! From whom?"

"That would be to tell, and to tell is somewhat unwise."

Giulia had seemed to grow up in a few hours. Full of coquetry, she seemed more like a girl of eighteen than one of fourteen. Her laughter was high and infectious; she sang gay Italian songs about love; and she was tantalizingly secretive. There was also the mystery of the necklace.

But Giulia was too young, too excited to keep up the secrecy for long. She wanted to share confidences; she wanted to flaunt her experience before Lucrezia. Lucrezia demanded: "What has happened? Why are you so pleased? You do not care that the Cardinal complained to Madonna Adriana of your forwardness—which may well mean that you will be sent away." Then Giulia laughed and retorted; "I shall not be sent away. And the Cardinal did not complain. I'll tell you something, Lucrezia. I have a lover."

"Orsino . . ."

"Orsino! Do you think I should ever take Orsino for a lover? Would you?"

"I . . . but I would never . . ."

"Mayhap you *are* over-young yet. For myself I shall be fifteen soon . . . and married to Orsino. Therefore what is there for me to do but take a lover?"

"Oh, have a care," begged Lucrezia. "What if Madonna Adriana should hear you talk thus? You would be sent away."

"I shall not be sent away. Oh no . . . no . . . no!"

Giulia laughed so much that the tears came to her eyes. Lucrezia gazed at her puzzled.

The Cardinal's visits to Monte Giordano became very frequent and he did not always come to see Lucrezia.

Giulia would dress very carefully before his visits—not in her most modest gowns—and sometimes Lucrezia would hear Giulia's high-pitched laughter when she was alone with the Cardinal. It was disconcerting.

But he always came to see *me!* Lucrezia told herself.

And then she began to understand.

Giulia had many rich presents. She was the loveliest girl in Rome, Lucrezia had heard the servants say. They had named her *La Bella*, and referred to her more often by that name than her own. The rich presents came from a rich lover, a lover whom Giulia was entertaining in the formal household of the Orsinis. It was some time before Lucrezia would allow herself to believe who that lover was.

Then she could keep her suspicions to herself no longer.

One night she slipped from her bed, took her candle, and went to Giulia's bedchamber. Giulia was asleep, and the light from Lucrezia's candle showed her the beauty of that perfect face. Giulia was indeed *La Bella*.

The candlelight playing on Giulia's face awoke her and she started up, staring in alarm at Lucrezia.

"What is wrong?" she demanded.

"I have to know," said Lucrezia. "The Cardinal is your lover, is he not?"

"Did you wake me up to tell me what everybody knows?" demanded Giulia.

"So it is true!"

Giulia laughed. "Think of it," she said, sitting up and hugging her knees. "He is fifty-eight and I am not yet fifteen. Yet we love. Is that not miraculous? Who would have thought a man so old could make me love him?"

"With him," said Lucrezia solemnly, "all things are possible."

That made Giulia emit one of her secretive laughs. "It is true," she said. "And I am happy."

Lucrezia was silent, looking at Giulia, seeing her afresh, trying to remember what she had been like before this astonishing thing had happened to her.

Then she said slowly: "If Madonna Adriana heard of this, she would be very angry."

Giulia laughed again, recklessly it seemed to Lucrezia.

"What you are doing should be kept secret," persisted Lucrezia. "I know we do not like Madonna Adriana, but she is a good woman and she would never allow you to live in her house if she knew."

Giulia stopped laughing and looked intently at Lucrezia.

"You will be cold, standing there," she said. "Come into my bed. You are no longer a child, Lucrezia. Why, you will soon be ten. You will soon have lovers of your own. There! That is better, is it not? Now, let me tell you this. The Cardinal is my lover. He says I am the most beautiful woman in the world. *Woman*, you understand, Lucrezia. And soon I shall marry Orsino. But who cares for Orsino! Not I. Nor the Cardinal."

"Madonna Adriana cares for him."

"Yes. Indeed yes. That is why she is contented that I should please the Cardinal. My family is contented also, Lucrezia."

"Contented! But how can that be when you are to marry Orsino?"

"Yes, yes. And it is a good match. The Farnese and the Orsini will be united, and that is good. One cannot marry a Cardinal . . . alas . . . alas!"

"If Cardinals could marry, my father would have married my mother."

Giulia nodded. Then she went on: "You must not be *sorry* for Orsino. I told you his mother is contented that I am the Cardinal's mistress. I told you that, did I not?"

"But she is a good woman. We have thought her harsh, but we must admit that she is good."

"Lucrezia, you live in a world of childhood and it is time you left it. Adriana is *glad* that the Cardinal loves me. She helps me dress when he is coming, helps to make me beautiful. And what does she say when she helps me dress? She says: 'Do not forget that you will be Orsino's wife before long. Get the Cardinal to agree to advance Orsino. He has great influence at the Vatican. Make sure that you squeeze the greatest good from this . . . for yourself and Orsino.' "

"So she is pleased that you and my father are lovers?"

"Nothing could delight her more. She makes everything easy for us."

"And you so soon to marry her son!"

Giulia laughed. "You see, you do not know the world. If I were to have a love affair with a groom . . . ah, then I should be beaten. I should be in disgrace, and he, poor fellow, would doubtless have a sword run through him one dark night, or be found in the Tiber with a stone about his neck. But my lover is a great Cardinal and when men of influence love as he loves me then all gather round to catch some of the prizes. That is life."

"Then Adriana with all her prayers and sternness, all her righteousness, is not a good woman after all!"

"Good and bad, little Lucrezia, what are they? It is only little children who have sentimental notions such as yours. The Cardinal is happy to love me; I am happy to be his mistress. And Orsino's family and my family are happy because of the great good I can bring to them. Orsino? He does not count, but one might say even he is happy because it means that he will not have to make love to me, which—unnatural monster that he is—I do not believe he is at all eager to do!"

Lucrezia was silent for a while, thinking more of Adriana than anyone else: Adriana solemnly on her knees before the Madonna and the lamp; Adriana, lips pursed, murmuring, "One must do this because, however unpleasant, it is one's duty" Adriana, who made one feel that the saints were continually on the watch, recording the slightest fault to be held against one at the day of Judgment, the good woman, who was willing to allow the illicit love affair, between a man of fifty-eight and her prospective daughter-in-law of fourteen, to be conducted in her house, and moreover connived at it and encouraged it because it could bring honors to her son.

Honors! It was necessary, Lucrezia realized, to make a reassessment of words and their meanings.

She was indeed a child; there was much that she had to learn; and she was very eager to grow out of childhood, a state in which it seemed innocence was synonymous with folly.

⚜👑⚜

Giulia HAD married Orsino, and the ceremony had taken place in the Borgia palace, the first of the witnesses to sign the marriage documents being Roderigo Borgia.

The married couple returned to Monte Giordano and life went on as before. The Cardinal paid frequent visits to the Orsini palace and no one now made any secret of the fact that he came chiefly to visit his mistress.

He was delighted to see his daughter also, and seemed content to spend a great deal of time in the company of the two young girls.

Giulia was exerting her influence on Lucrezia who was growing more and more like her. Giulia talked of the love between herself and the Cardinal and of many more trivial matters. She told Lucrezia that she knew how their hair could retain its bright yellow color; she had a recipe which would make it shine like pure gold with the sun on it. They washed their hair, tried the concoction, and congratulated themselves that their hair was more golden than ever.

Lucrezia began to long for the time when she would have a lover, for, always ready to be influenced by those who were near her, she was modelling herself on Giulia.

When she heard that her eldest brother, Pedro Luis, had died and that Giovanni was to become Duke of Gandia and marry the bride who had been selected for Pedro Luis, it seemed hardly important, apart from the fact that she wondered how Cesare would receive this news. He would surely want the dukedom of Gandia; he would surely want Pedro Luis' bride.

She was eleven when the Cardinal called at the palace and, after embracing her, told her that he was arranging a match for her.

It was to be a Spanish match because he believed Spain, which was fast rising to a power of first magnitude determined on the domination of the world, had more to offer his daughter than Italy.

Her bridegroom was to be Don Cherubino Juan de Centelles who was the lord of Val d'Ayora in Valencia, and it was a grand match.

Lucrezia was a little alarmed, but her father hastily assured her that, although the nuptial contract was drawn up and would soon be signed, he had arranged that she should not leave Rome for a whole year.

That was comforting. A year seemed a very long time to the young Lucrezia.

Now she could discuss her coming marriage with Giulia and it delighted her to do so, particularly as that event seemed so very far away in the distant future.

She was beginning to know the world, to accept with the utmost calm the relationship between her father and Giulia; to accept the mingling piety and callous amorality of Adriana.

That was life as it was lived in that stratum of society into which Lucrezia had been born.

She had learned this much; and it meant that she had left her childhood behind her.

ALEXANDER VI

During the following year Lucrezia really did grow up, and afterward it seemed to her that before Giulia had come into her life bringing enlightenment she had indeed been an innocent child.

Giulia was her dearest friend. Together they made many journeys to the Cardinal's palace where Roderigo petted them both, delighting that it was Lucrezia who brought him Giulia and Giulia who brought him Lucrezia.

And why should Lucrezia question the rightness of such conduct? She, Giulia and Adriana were all guests at the wedding of Franceschetto Cibo, a grand occasion when the whole of Rome had rejoiced and there were bonfires on all of the seven hills; Franceschetto was openly acknowledged as the son of Innocent VIII, and the Holy Father made no secret of this, for he was present at the banquet and caused the fountains to run with wine; moreover Franceschetto's bride was the daughter of the great Lorenzo de' Medici; so that it was not only Romans who honored the Pope's bastard.

So naturally it did not occur to Lucrezia to do anything but accept the conditions in which she lived.

Goffredo had now come to live at Monte Giordano, and she was happy to have her young brother with her. He wept a little to leave his mother, but Vannozza, while missing him sadly, was very glad to let him go for she saw in the arrangement an admission by Roderigo that he accepted Goffredo as his son.

It was during that year that Roderigo decided that Don Cherubino Juan de Centelles was not a satisfactory match for his daughter. It may have been the brilliant marriage of Franceschetto Cibo which decided him. It was true Franceschetto was the son of a Pope, but Innocent was ageing fast and who knew what the next months might bring forth? No! He would find a better match for his daughter.

He blithely dissolved the previous contract and made another more suited to his ambitious plans, choosing Don Gasparo di Procida, the count of Aversa, for Lucrezia's betrothed. This was because Don Gasparo was a connection of the House of Aragon which now ruled in Naples.

Lucrezia accepted the change placidly. As she had seen neither of her prospective bridegrooms she had no feelings in the matter. She had Roderigo's happy nature which made her believe that everything would come out well for her.

And then, in that August of the year 1492 when Lucrezia was twelve years old, there occurred that event which was to prove so important to the rest of her life.

Innocent was dying and there was tumult throughout Rome. The question on every lip was: Who shall succeed Innocent?

There was one man who was determined to do so. Roderigo was sixty. If he were going to achieve his life-long ambition he must do so soon. When he heard the news that Innocent was on his death-bed he determined, as he never had before, that he would be the next Pope.

Roderigo, gentle, courteous, seeming malleable, was a man of iron beneath the gentle exterior. Nothing was going to stand in his way. Unfortunately there must be a Conclave, and the Pope must be elected. Those days were days of real stress for Roderigo. He did not visit his mistress or his daughter during that period of decision, but the thoughts of everyone in the Orsini palace were with him at that time. They all prayed that the next Pope would be Roderigo.

Lucrezia was in a state of turmoil. Her father seemed to her godlike; tall, powerful; she could not understand why there should be any anxiety. Why did not everyone understand that there was only one thing they could do, and that was elect Cardinal Roderigo Borgia as their Pope?

She talked to Giulia, who was as tense and anxious as herself, for although it was exciting to be the mistress of the richest Cardinal in Rome, how much more so to be the mistress of the Pope. So Giulia shared Lucrezia's excitement, her enthusiasm and her fears. Little Goffredo sought to understand, and added his prayers to theirs; and Adriana saw a glittering future wherein she might cast aside her mourning and accompany her daughter-in-law to the Vatican; there she might live in state . . . if only Roderigo were elected Pope.

The heat was fierce in Rome during that fateful August. Each in his separate cell, the great Cardinals went into Conclave. Crowds were gathered in the streets, clustering about the Vatican, and there was continued and heated speculation as to the results.

In the beginning no one thought very highly of Roderigo's chances.

There were great rivalries, for Italy was at this time a country divided into small states and dukedoms, with the result that there were continual differences between them. Innocent had been weak but he had enjoyed the advice of his great ally, Lorenzo de' Medici, and it was largely due to this that the peninsula had been enjoying a period of peace. But Lorenzo had died and trouble was looming.

Ludovico Sforza, Regent of Milan, and Ferrante of Aragon, King of Naples, were the great rivals who threatened to plunge Italy into a state of war. The reason for this was that Ludovico's nephew, Gian Galeazzo, was the true heir of Milan; but Ludovico held this young man a prisoner and made himself Regent. His excuse was that the young Duke was not fit to rule; he, Ludovico, had brought about this unhappy state of affairs by arranging that the boy should be demoralized both mentally and physically with debaucheries which were arranged at Ludovico's instigation. Gian however had married an energetic princess of Naples, Isabella of Aragon, who was granddaughter of Ferrante. This was the cause of the trouble between Naples and Milan which threatened at this time to flare up into a war which could have involved all Italy.

Both Naples and Milan were afraid that the French would seek to invade their territory, for the French declared that they had a claim both to Naples and Milan—to Naples through the House of Anjou, and to Milan through the house of Orléans.

This meant that it would be very important for Ludovico and Ferrante to have a Pope at the Vatican who would favor them.

Rivalry was intense. Ascanio Sforza, brother of Ludovico, was the hope of Milan. Ferrante supported Giuliano della Rovere.

Roderigo, like a sly fox, waited.

He knew he had little to fear from Ascanio, as he was only thirty-eight and if he became Pope it would be the death-knell to the hopes of almost every living Cardinal. With such a young man elected, unless he died very young, there would be little hope of another Conclave for years. Moreover it was hardly likely that Ludovico's party would have much support. The Regency of Milan was known throughout the length and breadth of Italy as a usurper.

This was not the case with della Rovere, but although he was eligible, he had a bitter tongue which offended people. He might have supporters, but he also had many enemies.

The favorite was perhaps the Portuguese Cardinal Costa, who was eighty years of age. At such a time it was often felt to be advisable to elect a very old man, to give a short breathing space before there was another Conclave. If Cardinal Costa were elected, it would not be such a tragedy as the election of della Rovere or—the saints forbid it—Ascanio Sforza.

But Roderigo was determined that none should be elected but himself.

There was also among the several candidates Cardinal Oliviero Carafa whom Ascanio—feeling that on account of his youth he himself had a poor chance—was supporting because Carafa was an enemy of Ferrante.

Another candidate—Roderigo Borgia—did not seem to be in the running; but Roderigo was standing quietly, slyly waiting.

Roderigo was the richest of the Cardinals, and he knew what an important factor wealth was at such times. A little bribe here, a fat one there, a promise of gold and silver, a hint of what a man of his wealth could pay for votes—and who knew, the Papal throne might well be his while the others were wrangling amongst themselves.

The Cardinals were walled-up and the Conclave began. It was a period of intense strain for Roderigo yet he managed to conceal his feelings. As he attended morning Mass and Communion he was considering how he could win the votes he needed. At this time it seemed a hopeless task which lay before him, yet as he made his way to the Sistine Chapel lighted in readiness with candles on the altar and on the desk before each of the thrones, he seemed perfectly calm. He looked about him at his fellow Cardinals in their rustling violet robes and white *rochets*, and he knew that within none of them did the fire of ambition burn as fiercely as it did in him. He must succeed.

It seemed to him that the procedure was slower than it had ever been, but eventually the Cardinal-Scrutators were elected and he was sitting at his desk. There was no sound in the chapel but the scratching of many pens as each Cardinal wrote: "I, Cardinal . . . elect to the Supreme Pontificate the Most Reverend Lord my Lord Cardinal . . ."

Oh why, fumed Roderigo, could one not vote for oneself!

He rose with the rest and joined in the ceremonial walk to the altar. He knelt and murmured: "I attest before Christ who is to be my judge, that I chose him whom I think fittest to be chosen if it is according to God's will."

They placed their ballot papers on the shallow dish which covered the chalice, and tipped the paten until the paper slid into the chalice; then slowly and solemnly, each purple-clad figure returned to his throne.

At the first counting of votes Roderigo had seven, but Carafa had nine, Costa and Michiel, the Cardinal of Venice, also had seven, and della Rovere five. As for Ascanio Sforza he had none, and it was clear from the beginning that none of the Cardinals was ready to see a man so young on the Papal throne.

This was deadlock, for there must be a majority of two-thirds for one candidate before he was elected.

A fire was made and the papers burned; and all those waiting in St. Peter's Square to hear the result of the election, seeing the smoke, excitedly called each other's attention to it and knew that the first scrutiny had been ineffectual.

Roderigo now decided that he must act quickly. In his own cell he laid his plans and when he mingled with his fellow Cardinals, he lost no time in getting to work.

He began with Ascanio Sforza, begging him to walk with him in the galleries after the siesta. Ascanio, realizing he had no chance of being elected, hinted that he was ready to gain what he could. Roderigo could offer him bigger bribes than any.

"If I were elected Pope," Roderigo promised, "I would not forget you. Yours should be the Vice-Chancellorship and I would also give you the Bishopric of Nepi." It was a good consolation prize, and Ascanio wavered only a little before he agreed. And as with Ascanio, so with others who quickly realized that they were out of the running yet could come out of the Conclave richer men than when they went into it.

So while Rome sweated and waited for the results, that sly fox Roderigo worked quietly, stealthily and with the utmost speed within the Conclave. He had to. He had made up his mind that this time he must succeed, for how could he tell when there would be another chance.

It was August 11th, five days after the Conclave had begun. In the Piazza San Pietro people who had been waiting all through the night watched, their eyes on the walled-up window.

As the dawn lightened their eager faces there was a sudden shout and excitement was at fever-pitch for the bricks had begun to fall from the walled-in window.

The election was over. After the fourth scrutiny there had been an unanimous choice.

Roderigo Borgia had been elected Pope, and from now on he would be known as Alexander VI.

Roderigo stood on the balcony listening to the acclaim of the people. This was the greatest moment of his life. The crown, for which he had fought ever since his uncle, Calixtus III, had adopted him and his brother, was now his. He felt powerful as he stood there, capable of anything. Who would have believed five days ago that he would be the chosen one? Even his old enemy, della Rovere, had given him his vote. It was wonderful what a little persuasion could do, and who could resist persuasion such as a rich abbacy, the legation of Avignon and the fortress of Ronciglione? Not della Rovere. A great deal to pay for a vote? Not at all. He had bought power with the wealth he had accumulated over the years, and he was going to make sure that it became unlimited power.

He held out his hands and for a few seconds there was complete silence among the multitude.

Then he cried: "I am the Pope and Vicar of Christ on Earth."

There was loud acclamation. It was of no importance how he had reached this eminence. All that mattered was that it was his.

The Coronation of Alexander VI was the most magnificent Rome had ever seen. Lucrezia, watching from a balcony of a Cardinal's palace, was overwhelmed with pride and joy in this man who—apart from Cesare, whom she had not seen for so long—she loved best in the world.

This was her father, this handsome man, in his rich robes, sitting so straight on his white horse, blessing the multitudes who crowded about him, the center of all the pageantry, this man was her father.

Alexander was fully aware that there was nothing the people enjoyed more than pageantry, and the more brilliant, the better they liked it; and the more splendid it was, the greater would be the respect they had for him. Therefore he was determined to outdo all previous coronations. No expense must be spared, he had commanded; nor was it. The people of Rome were going to rejoice that day because Alexander VI was their Pope.

His Papal guards were so splendidly attired that even great Princes looked drab beside them; their long lances and shields glittered in the sunshine, and they looked like gods. Cardinals and high dignitaries who took part in the procession with their retinues, were all determined to outdo each other in their splendor, and so long was the procession that it took two hours for it to pass from St. Peter's to St. John Lateran. And in the center of it all was the Pope on his snow-white horse, the sixty-year-old Pope who seemed to have the vigor of a man of twenty. It was small wonder that the people—even as Lucrezia did—believed the new Pope to be more than human.

The procession was stopped here and there that Alexander's admirers and supporters—who now comprised the whole of Rome, it seemed—might pay their homage.

"*Vive diu bos, vive diu celebrande per annos,*

Inter Pontificum gloria prima choros," chanted one handsome boy on behalf of his noble family who wished to show they were wholeheartedly in support of the new Pope.

Others strewed flowers before him and cried: "Rome raised Caesar to greatness—and now here is Alexander; but one was merely a man, the other is a god."

Alexander received all this homage with a charm and courtesy which won the hearts of all who saw him.

What a moment of triumph! Everywhere was the emblem of the grazing bull. Alexander lifting his eyes saw it; he also noticed the golden-haired girl on the balcony, the only one of his children to witness this triumph. There was Giovanni in Spain, Cesare in his university of Pisa, and little Goffredo (whom he accepted partly because he loved the boy, partly because sons were so necessary to him) was too young to make an appearance. His children! They would all have their parts to play in his dream of power. Little Lucrezia standing there, eyes wide with awe and wonder, accepting him, as did these people in the streets this day, as a god among them, was the representative of his children.

The homage of the people, the shouts of acclamation, the intoxicating sense of power, they were the narcotic which lulled a man to sleep in which he dreamed of greatness; and all greatness must first take its shape in dreams.

"Blessings on the Holy Father!" cried the crowd.

Aye! thought Alexander. Let the blessings of the saints fall upon me, that I may realize my dreams and unite all Italy under one ruler; and let that ruler be a Borgia Pope.

SANTA MARIA
IN PORTICO

Lucrezia soon understood how much more gratifying it was to be the daughter of a Pope than that of a Cardinal.

Firmly on the Papal throne, Alexander made no secret of his intentions. Giovanni was to return from Spain that Alexander might put him in charge of the Papal armies; Cesare was to be made Archbishop of Valencia; as for Lucrezia she was to be given a palace of her own—that of Santa Maria in Portico. Lucrezia was delighted with this honor, and especially so because she might now move from the gloomy fortress of Monte Giordano into the center of the City.

Alexander had a double purpose in giving Lucrezia this palace; it adjoined the Church of St. Peter's and there was a secret passage which connected it with the church and continued into the Vatican. Adriana and Giulia were to be of Lucrezia's household; Orsino would accompany them, but of course he was of no account.

Lucrezia looked forward to the new life with zest. It was wonderful to be grown up. Her brother Giovanni would soon be in Italy and Cesare, so her father had told her, was to be recalled to Rome. He was only being kept away for a short while because Alexander did not want the people to think he was continuing his policy of nepotism since, before his election, he had promised to abandon it. Cesare was already an Archbishop, and Alexander knew that if his son were in Rome it would become very difficult not to shower more honors upon him. So, for the moment, Cesare should remain at Pisa—but it would only be for the present.

Lucrezia had a great deal to look forward to. She saw her father often, saw him in the midst of all his pomp and ceremony, and thus he seemed to grow more splendid, more magnificent.

All day she would hear the bells of St. Peter's; and while she worked at her embroidery or sat at her window watching the passing pageants, the scent of incense and the sound of chanting voices came to her seeming to promise her a wonderfully exciting future.

Adriana had put off her mourning and was as respectful to Lucrezia as she was devoted to Giulia, who had even more influence at the Vatican than Lucrezia had.

Lucrezia understood why. She was not surprised if, looking in on Giulia's bedchamber, she found the young girl absent. The sound of footsteps, late at night or in early morning, in that corridor from which led the secret passage to the Vatican, did not surprise her.

She agreed with Adriana that Giulia was indeed fortunate to be loved by one so magnificent as Alexander.

Many important visitors—ambassadors and other dignitaries from the various states—called at the palace of Santa Maria and, under Adriana's guardianship, Lucrezia knew how to receive them. None came without bringing gifts—some for Lucrezia, some for Giulia.

"How kind they are!" said Lucrezia one day when she was examining a beautiful set of furs. "None comes empty-handed."

Giulia laughed at her simplicity. "Do not be quite so grateful, dearest Lucrezia," she advised. "They only give because they hope to get in return something which means far more to them."

Lucrezia was reflective. "It spoils the gift," she said. "Indeed it makes no gift at all."

"Of course it is no gift. It is a payment for favors they hope to receive."

"The furs no longer seem so beautiful," sighed Lucrezia.

Giulia looked at her fondly and thought what a long time it took for her to grow realistic. If Lucrezia had been born poor what a good-hearted little simpleton she might have been!

Was she not aware that, as the Pope's beloved daughter, she had great influence with him?

Lucrezia did know, for she was quickly made aware of this. Adriana believed that Alexander did not want a simpleton for a daughter, therefore this simplicity, this generous open-heartedness of Lucrezia must be checked. Such qualities were foolish.

It was necessary for her to have many rich possessions, Adriana implied. Did she mean to rely entirely on her father for them? No, let her be subtle. Let her use her own shrewdness, so that the Pope realized that he had a clever little daughter and could be proud of her.

Did she love fine clothes? None more. Lucrezia had always been a little vain of her beauty, and what could show it to better advantage than beautiful furs and fine brocades? Then let her make those who sought her favors aware of this. Let them know that, if they made her presents which pleased her, she would show her gratitude by begging her father to give them the help they needed.

"Why," said Adriana, "Francesco Gonzaga will be coming to see you soon. He greatly desires that his brother Sigismondo should become a Cardinal."

"He comes to ask me this?"

"A word to your father from you would help his cause."

"But how could I who know so little of such matters influence my father?"

"Your father wishes you to show yourself to be a Borgia. He would be pleased to do what you ask of him, and he would like Gonzaga to know in what esteem he holds you. If Gonzaga brought you a valuable present and you could say to your father: 'See what Gonzaga has brought me!' why then His Holiness would be pleased at the honor done you and would be ready, I doubt not, to grant favors to one who had shown he knew how to pay for them."

"I see," said Lucrezia. "I did not know that these matters were arranged thus."

"Then it is time you learned. You love pearls, do you not?"

Lucrezia's eyes sparkled. She did love pearls. They suited her fair skin; when she put on the beautiful necklace which Giulia had been given by Alexander she was sure she looked as beautiful as Giulia.

"I will tell Gonzaga that you are excessively fond of pearls," said Adriana, smiling knowledgeably.

And it surely would be wonderful, thought Lucrezia, to possess pearls like Giulia's.

So this was the way a Pope's daughter lived. It was wonderfully exciting and very profitable. Who was Lucrezia—rather lazy Lucrezia, who more than most girls loved fine clothes and becoming ornaments—who was she to disagree with this mode of living?

𝕏 👑 𝕏

ALEXANDER RECEIVED HIS daughter in his apartments at the Vatican; with her, as companion, came Giulia. Alexander still doted on the latter and could scarcely let a day pass without seeing her.

When Alexander received these two beloved ones he liked to do so in the utmost intimacy, so he dismissed all his attendants when they arrived, and had the girls sit, one on either side of him that he might put an arm about each.

How beautiful they were, he thought, with their young smooth skins and their shining golden hair—surely two of the loveliest girls in Rome. Life seemed good when he at sixty had the vigor of a young man, and he was certain that Giulia was making no pretense when she showed so clearly that her passion for him was as great as his for her, and that her poor little squint-eyed husband, young as he was, had no charm for her.

Lucrezia nestling against her father was admiring the splendor of his apartments. The ceiling was gilded and the walls of delicate colors; there were oriental carpets on the floor, and the great artist Pinturicchio had begun the murals; but these did not yet cover the walls, and below them were hangings of the finest silk. There were many chairs, stools and cushions of silk and velvet in brilliant colors; and dominating all was the glory of the Papal throne.

All this belonged to this godlike person who, it seemed impossible to believe, was her tender and loving father, and who when he was alone with his beloved girls would seem to imply that his greatest joy in life was pleasing them.

"I have sent for you this day because I have something to tell you, daughter," he said. "We are going to cancel the arrangements we have made for your marriage to Don Gasparo di Procida."

"Is that so, Father?" she asked.

Giulia laughed. "She does not mind. She does not mind in the least."

The Pope caressed his daughter's cheek, and Lucrezia was reminded of the pleasure she had derived from Cesare's caresses.

"Father," she cried, "when shall I see Cesare?"

Giulia and the Pope laughed together and exchanged glances.

"You see I am right," said Giulia. "Poor Lucrezia! She has never had a lover."

It was hardly a frown which crossed the Pope's face; he rarely showed displeasure with his loved ones, but Giulia was aware that her remark had disturbed him. She was however too sure of her power to be afraid of displeasing. "It's true," she said almost defiantly.

"One day," said Alexander, "my daughter will find great joy in love, I doubt not. But she will wait until the time when she is ready."

Lucrezia took her father's hand and kissed it.

"She cares more for her father and brothers than for any others," said Giulia. "Why, she says of every man she sees: 'How insignificant he is beside my father ... or Cesare or Giovanni!' "

"Lucrezia is a Borgia," said Alexander, "and Borgias see great virtue in Borgias."

"They are not the only ones," said Giulia, laughing and holding his arm against her. "I pray you, beloved and Holy Father, tell us who will now be Lucrezia's bridegroom."

"A man of great importance. His name is Giovanni Sforza."

"Is he an old man?" asked Giulia.

"What has age to do with love?" demanded the Pope, and this time there was reproach in his voice.

But Giulia was quick with her soothing reply. "It is only gods who have the gift of remaining forever young. Giovanni Sforza, I'll swear, is but a man."

Alexander laughed and kissed her. "It is a good match. My beloved daughter will bless me for arranging it. Come, Lucrezia, are you not going to show your pleasure?"

Lucrezia kissed him dutifully. "But I have been betrothed so many times. I will wait until I see him and then until I am married to him before I am too grateful."

The Pope laughed. They amused him with their chatter and he was sorry to have to send them away because official matters must be settled.

Surrounded by their attendants they left the Vatican, and as they were crossing the square an unkempt vagabond peered at Giulia insolently and cried out: "Why, 'tis the bride of Christ!"

Giulia's eyes flashed, but the man lost no time in running as fast as his legs could carry him, and had disappeared before Giulia could send anyone after him.

"You are angry, Giulia," said Lucrezia, "angry at the words of a beggar."

"I do not care to be insulted," retorted Giulia. "You know what he meant."

"That you are my father's mistress. That is no insult. Think of all those who come to pay court to you because of that!"

"The common people consider it an insult," said Giulia. "I wish I could have that man put in prison. I'd have him punished."

Lucrezia shivered. She knew that often men who insulted those in high places had their tongues cut out.

She would not think of that. Perhaps she would have to learn to contemplate such things with indifference, as she had had to learn to accept the relationship between her father and Giulia and pious Adriana's acceptance of it, and as she had had to accept the fact that she must make herself rich and important by taking bribes. She doubted not that in time she would grow as indifferent as others to these matters; but there was a softness within her which made it difficult for her.

She must conform. She must be like those who lived about her. But for the time being she would refuse to think of the cruel things which could happen to men and women, merely because they spoke too freely.

She wanted to be happy; therefore she would not think of anything that might make her otherwise.

She turned to Giulia. "Perhaps I shall marry this man, this Giovanni Sforza. I like the sound of him. He has the same name as my brother."

"There are many Giovannis in Italy," Giulia reminded her.

"But I doubt not that something will happen to make my father choose another husband for me. Giulia, would it not be strange if I never married . . . because no sooner am I betrothed to one than I must marry someone who will be more grand, more suitable?"

"You will surely marry one day."

"Then I shall have a lover . . . even as you have."

"Husbands are not always lovers, my dear. And you have a long way to go before you are as I am."

Giulia put her face close to Lucrezia's and smiled her most secretive smile. "I will tell you a secret. The Pope is more than my lover. He is the father of the child I carry within me."

"Oh, Giulia! So you are to have a child!"

Giulia nodded. "That was why I was so angry when that vagabond said what he did. I believe it is becoming known. That means that some of our servants are more inquisitive than they should be . . . and too talkative."

"Do not punish them for that, Giulia," said Lucrezia. "It is natural that they should be so."

"Why should you care whom I punish?"

Lucrezia said: "I do not want to think of punishments. The sun shines so beautifully on the piazza, does it not, and were not my father's apartments quite beautiful? Cesare and Giovanni will soon be home, and I shall have a husband. There is so much to make me happy. It is merely that I do not wish to think of anyone's not being pleased."

"There are times," said Giulia, "when you seem so simple; and there are times when you seem so very difficult to understand."

Lucrezia was in her apartment at the Palace of Santa Maria, and her slaves and women were helping her to dress. One fastened the ribbon of her gown while another set a jeweled ornament in her hair.

The arrangements for her marriage had advanced considerably; Don

Gasparo, the rejected suitor, had been placated with a gift of three thousand ducats; and the whole of Italy was talking of the Borgia-Sforza alliance. Some saw in this a threat to their security, and della Rovere had decided he would be safer out of Rome. Ferrante of Aragon was disturbed by the alliance and waited apprehensively for what it would bring forth.

There was no doubt in Lucrezia's mind that this betrothal had reached a stage which none of the others had, and it seemed almost certain that she would marry Giovanni Sforza.

So, when a page knocked for admission and told one of her attendants that a noble gentleman had arrived at the palace and was asking to see her, Lucrezia immediately thought that Giovanni Sforza had come.

This was wrong of him, of course. He should not come informally; there would be a ceremonial procession into the city; the Pope's daughter and her betrothed husband could not meet like any serving man and maid; but it would be pleasant and so romantic to do so. She smoothed the folds of her brocade gown and looked at her reflection in the polished metal mirror. She was beautiful; she longed to partake of that sort of love about which Giulia talked.

She said: "Tell him I will receive him."

But even as she turned, the visitor stood in the doorway and the sight of him made Lucrezia forget the romantic longing she had had to see her future husband.

"Cesare!" she cried, and forgetting all ceremony she ran to him and threw herself into her brother's arms.

She heard his low laughter, laughter of triumph, of passion, of something she did not understand but loved. She took his hand and kissed it many times.

"You are happy to see me, Lucrezia?"

"It has been a long time," she cried.

"You thought of me now and then?"

"Every day, Cesare, every day of my life. I never knelt before the Madonna in my room without mentioning your name."

Cesare was looking impatiently at the women ranged about her. It was as though a new element was in the room, dominating all others; the women looked different; they stood like creatures who had been turned to stone. Yet they almost cringed. Lucrezia remembered how, long ago in the nursery in their mother's house, the slaves and serving men and women had been afraid of Cesare.

She said: "Leave us. My brother and I have much of which we wish to talk, and that is for our ears alone."

They did not need to be told twice.

Brother and sister twined their arms about each other and Cesare drew her to the window. "I would look at you," he said. "Why, you have changed, my Lucrezia."

There was anxiety in her eyes. "Cesare, you are not displeased with the change?"

Cesare kissed her. "It delights me," he said.

"But you must tell me of yourself. You have been out in the world. You are an Archbishop. That sounds strange. My brother Cesare, Archbishop of Valencia. I shall have to be very demure when I am with you. I must remember that you are a holy man of the Church. But Cesare! You do not look like an Archbishop! This doublet of yours! I declare it is stitched with gold. And what a little tonsure. A simple priest has more than that."

His eyes blazed suddenly; he clenched his fists, and Lucrezia saw that he was shaking with rage.

"Do not talk of these matters! Lucrezia, I demand that you stop. Archbishop of Valencia! Do I look like an Archbishop? I tell you, Lucrezia, I will not be forced to continue this life. I was never meant for the Church."

"No, Cesare, you were not, but . . ."

"But one of us must go into the Church. One of us, and that one must be myself. I am the eldest but I am the one who must stand aside for my brother. *He* will soon be home. One imagines the preparations there will be for him. Giovanni, Duke of Gandia! Our father cares more for his little toe than for the whole of my body."

"It is not true," she cried, distressed. "It is not true."

"It is true." His eyes seemed murderous as they were turned upon her. "Do not contradict me, child, when I tell you it is true. I will not remain in the Church, I will not. . . ."

"You must tell our father," said Lucrezia soothingly.

"He will not listen. By all the saints, I swear it." He went to the shrine and, lifting his hands as one who was about to take a solemn oath, he cried: "Holy Mother of God, I swear I will not rest until I am free to lead the life I wish. I will allow no one to bind me, to lead me. I, Cesare Borgia, am my own master from this day on."

He had changed, Lucrezia realized; he had grown more violent, and she was afraid of him.

She laid her hand pleadingly on his arm. "Cesare," she said, "you will do what you wish. No one shall lead you. You would not be Cesare if you allowed that."

He turned to her and all the passion seemed to have left him; but she saw that he still shook with the violence of his emotion.

"My little sister," he said, "we have been long separated."

She was anxious to turn the subject away from the Church. "I have heard news of you from time to time, how you excelled in your studies."

He touched her cheek gently. "Doubtless you have heard many tales of me."

"Tales of daring deeds."

"And foolish ones?"

"You have lived as men do live . . . men who answer to none."

He smiled tenderly. "You know how to soothe me," he said. "And they will marry you to that oaf from Pesaro, and doubtless they will take you away from me."

"We shall visit often, Cesare . . . all of us, you, Giovanni . . . Goffredo. . . ."

His face darkened. "Giovanni," he cried with a sneer. "He will be on his brilliant campaigns, subduing all Italy with his armies. He will have little time to be with us."

"Then you will be happy, Cesare, for you always hated him."

"And you . . . like the rest . . . worshipped him. He was very handsome, was he not? Our father doted on him—so much that he forces me to go into the Church when that is where Giovanni should go."

"Come, tell me about your adventures. You were a gay young man, were you not? All the women of Perugia and Pisa were in love with you, and you, by all accounts, were not indifferent to them."

"There was not one of them with hair as golden as yours, Lucrezia.

There was not one of them who knew how to soothe me with sweet words as you do."

She laid her cheek against his hand. "But that is natural. We understand each other. We were together when we were little. That is why, of all the men I ever saw, there was not one as beautiful in my eyes as my brother Cesare."

"What about your brother Giovanni?" he cried.

Lucrezia, remembering the old games of coquetry and rivalry, pretended to consider. "Yes, he was very handsome," she said; then, noticing the dark look returning to Cesare's face, she added quickly: "At least I always thought so until I compared him to you."

"If he were here, you would not say that," accused Cesare.

"I would, I swear I would. He'll soon be here. Then I'll show that I love you best."

"Who knows what gay manners he has picked up in Spain! Doubtless he will be irresistible to the whole world, as he now is to my father."

"Let us not talk of him, Cesare. So you have heard that I am to have a husband?"

He laid his hands on her shoulders and looked into her face.

He said slowly: "I would rather talk of my brother Giovanni and his beauty and his triumphs than of such a matter."

Her eyes were wide and their innocence moved him to a tenderness which was unusual with him.

"Do you not like this alliance with the Sforzas?" she asked. "I heard that the King of Aragon is most displeased. Cesare, perhaps if you are against the match and have good reason . . . Perhaps if you speak to our father . . ."

He shook his head.

"Little Lucrezia," he said quietly, "my dearest sister, no matter whom they chose for your husband, I should hate him."

It was hot June and everywhere throughout the city banners fluttered. The Sforza lion was side by side with the Borgia bull, and every loggia, every roof, as well as the streets, was filled to see the entry into Rome of the bridegroom whom the Pope had chosen for his daughter.

Giovanni Sforza was twenty-six, and a widower who was of a morose nature and a little suspicious of the bargain which was being offered him.

The thirteen-year-old child who was to be his bride meant nothing to him as such. He had heard that she was beautiful, but he was a cold man, not to be tempted by beauty. The advantages of the match might seem obvious to some, but he did not trust the Borgia Pope. The magnificent dowry which had been promised with the girl—thirty-one thousand ducats—was to be withheld until the consummation of the marriage, and the Pope had strictly laid down the injunction that consummation was not to take place yet because Lucrezia was far too young; and should she die childless, the ducats were to go to her brother Giovanni, the Duke of Gandia.

Sforza was no impetuous youth. He would wait, before congratulating himself, to see whether there was anything about which to be congratulated.

He had a natural timidity which might have been due to the fact that he came of a subordinate branch of the Sforzas of Milan; he was the illegitimate son of Costanzo, the Lord of Cotignolo and Pesaro, but he had nevertheless inherited his father's estate; he was impecunious, and marriage with the wealthy Borgias seemed an excellent prospect; he was ambitious, and that, could he have trusted the intentions of Alexander, would have made him very happy with the match.

But he could not help feeling uneasy when trumpets and bugles heralded his approach as he came through the Porta del Popolo, whither the Cardinals and high dignitaries had sent important members of their retinues to greet him and welcome him to Rome.

In that procession rode two young men, more magnificently, more elegantly attired than any others. They were two of the most strikingly handsome men Sforza had ever seen, and he guessed by their bearing who they must be. He was thankful that he could cut a fine figure on his Barbary horse, in his rich garments and the gold necklaces which had been lent to him for the occasion.

The younger of these men was the Duke of Gandia, recently returned from Spain. He was very handsome indeed, somewhat solemn at the moment because this was a ceremonial occasion and he, having spent some years at a Spanish Court, had the manners of a Spaniard. Yet he could be gay and lighthearted; that much was obvious.

But it was the elder of the men who demanded and held Sforza's attention. This was Cesare Borgia, Archbishop of Valencia. He had heard stories of this man which made him shudder to recall them. He too was handsome, but his was a brooding beauty. Certainly he was attractive; he would dominate any scene; Sforza was aware that the women in the streets, who watched the procession from loggia and rooftop, would for the most part focus their interest on this man. What was it about him? He was handsomely dressed; so was his brother. His jewels were glittering; but not more so than his brother's. Was it the manner in which he held himself? Was it a pride which excelled all pride; a certainty that he was a god among men?

Sforza did not care to pursue the subject. He only knew that if he had a suspicion of Alexander he felt even more uneasy regarding his son.

But now the greeting was friendly; the welcome warm.

Through the Campo di Fiore went the cavalcade, the young men in its center—Cesare, Sforza and Giovanni—across the Bridge of St. Angelo to pause before the Palace of Santa Maria in Portico.

Sforza lifted his eyes. There on the loggia, her hair shining like gold in the glittering sunshine, was a young girl in crimson satin decorated with rubies and pearls. She was gripping a pillar of the loggia and the sunlight rested on her hands adazzle with jewels.

She looked down on her brothers and the man who was to be her husband.

She was thirteen and those about her had not succeeded in robbing her of her romantic imaginings. She smiled and lifted her hands in welcome.

Sforza looked at her grimly. Her youthful beauty did not move him. He was conscious of her brothers on either side of him; and he continued to wonder how far he could trust them and the Pope.

THE PALACE OF Santa Maria was in a feverish state of excitement; there was whispering and shouting, the sound of feet running hither and thither;

the dressmakers and hairdressers filled the anteroom; Lucrezia's chaplain had been with her for so long, preparing her spiritually, that those who must prepare her physically were chafing with impatience.

The heat was intense—it was June—and Lucrezia felt crushed by the weight of her wedding gown heavily embroidered with gold thread and decorated with jewels which had cost fifteen thousand ducats. Her golden hair was caught in a net ornamented with glittering precious stones. Adriana and Giulia had personally insisted on painting her face and plucking her eyebrows that she might appear as an elegant lady of fashion.

Lucrezia had never felt so excited in the whole of her life. Her dress may have been too heavy for comfort on this hot day, but she cared little for that, for she delighted in adorning herself.

She was thinking of the ceremony, of the people who would crowd to see her as she crossed from the Palace to the Vatican, of herself, serenely beautiful, the heroine of this splendid occasion, with her pages and slaves to strew garlands of sweetsmelling flowers before her as she walked. She gave scarcely a thought to her bridegroom. Marriage was not, she gathered from what she had seen of those near her, a matter about which one should concern oneself overmuch. Giovanni Sforza seemed old, and he did not smile very often; his eyes did not flash like Cesare's and Giovanni's. He was different; he was solemn and looked a little severe. But the marriage was not to be consummated and, Giulia had told her, she need not be bothered with him if she did not want to be. She would continue to stay in Rome— so for Lucrezia marriage meant merely a brilliant pageant with herself as the central figure.

Giulia clapped her hands suddenly and said: "Bring in the slave that Madonna Lucrezia may see her."

The servants bowed and very shortly a dwarf Negress was standing before Lucrezia. She was resplendent in a gold dress, her hair caught in a jeweled net, and her costume was an exact replica of her dazzlingly beautiful mistress's. Lucrezia cried out in delight, for this Negress's black hair and skin made that of Lucrezia seem more fair than ever.

"She will carry your train," said Adriana. "It will be both amusing and delightful to watch."

Lucrezia agreed and turning to a table on which was a bowl of sweetmeats, she picked up one of these and slipped it into the Negress's mouth.

The dark eyes glistened with the affection which most of the servants—and particularly the slaves—had for Madonna Lucrezia.

"Come," said Adriana sternly, "there is much to do yet. Madalenna, bring the jeweled pomanders."

As Madalenna made for the door she caught her breath suddenly, for a man had entered, and men should not enter a lady's chamber when she was being dressed; but the lord Cesare obeyed no rules, no laws but his own.

"My lord . . ." began Adriana, but Cesare silenced her with a frown.

"Cesare, what do you think of my dress?" cried Lucrezia. "Tell me whether you admire me now."

Cesare ignored her and, looking straight at Adriana, said: "I wish to speak to my sister . . . alone."

"But, my lord, the time is short."

"I wish to speak to her alone," he repeated. "Do I not make my meaning clear?"

Even Adriana quailed before this arrogant young man of eighteen. Rumors of his life at the universities of Perugia and Pisa had reached her, and the strangeness of the stories had made her shudder. Accidents often happened to those who opposed this arrogant son of the Pope and she was not so powerful that she could risk offending him.

"Since you ask it, it shall be," she temporized, "but my lord, I beg of you remember that we must not arrive late at the Vatican."

He nodded his head, and Adriana signed to all the attendants to leave with her.

When they had gone Lucrezia cried: "Cesare, there is little time. I should be prepared. . . ."

"You should be prepared to give me a little of your time. Have you forgotten, now that you have a bridegroom, how you swore that you would never love any as you loved me?"

"I do not forget, Cesare. I never shall." She was thinking of herself crossing the square, imagining the cries of admiration; she could smell the incense and the scent of flowers.

"You are not thinking of me," said Cesare. "Who does? My father thwarts me, and you . . . you are as light-minded as any harlot."

"But Cesare, this is my wedding day."

"It is little to rejoice in. Sforza! Do you consider him a man? Yet I would rather see you married to him, than to some, for I swear he is little more than a eunuch."

"Cesare, you must not be jealous."

Cesare laughed. He came to her and gripped her neck in the gesture she remembered so well. She cried out in alarm because she was afraid for her jeweled net.

"The marriage shall not be consummated." He laughed. "I made our father see the wisdom of that. Why, who knows, if the scene changes these Sforzas may not be worthy of our friendship, and then it may well be that the Holy Father will wish he had not been so eager to get his daughter married."

"Cesare, why are you upset about this marriage? You know I have to marry, and it makes no difference to my love for you. I could never love any as I love you."

He continued his hold on her neck; his fingers would mark it—they always did—and she longed to beg him to release his hold, but she dared not. She enjoyed being with him as she always did, but now, as ever, that excitement which he aroused had its roots in a certain fear which she did not understand and which repelled her while it enticed.

"I believe that to be so," he said. "No matter what happens to you or to me . . . there will always be this bond between us. Lucrezia and Cesare . . . we are one, little sister, and no husband of yours, nor wife of mine could ever change that."

"Yes, yes," she said breathlessly. "It is true. I know it is true."

"I shall not be at the supper party after the ceremony," said Cesare.

"Oh, but you must, brother. I so look forward to dancing with you."

Cesare looked down at his Archbishop's robes. "It is not meet, sister, that men of the Church should dance. You will be dancing with your brother, the Duke of Gandia. He will make a splendid partner, I doubt not."

"Cesare, you will surely be there!"

"At your nuptial celebration. Certainly I shall not. Do you think I can bear to see you making merry at such a time?"

"Giovanni will be there, and mayhap Goffredo. . . ."

"One day, sister, you will understand that my feeling for you is stronger than anything Giovanni could feel for anyone."

There were shouts in the square and Cesare strode to the window.

Lucrezia stood beside him, but she could no longer feel the same pleasure in all the pomp which was being prepared for her, because she was deeply aware of the clenching and unclenching of Cesare's hands and the angry expression on his face.

"He comes," said Cesare. "The handsome Duke of Gandia."

"He is to conduct me to the Vatican," said Lucrezia. "I should be ready by now. Oh, we shall be late. Cesare, we must bring back Adriana and Giulia. Giovanni is here and I am not ready."

But Adriana, hearing the sounds of Giovanni's approach, decided that it was necessary for her to risk Cesare's anger, and she came into the room followed by Giulia and Lucrezia's attendants.

"The Duke is here," she said. "Come now, let me see if your net is in place. Ah yes, and where is the black dwarf? Here, dwarf. Take Madonna Lucrezia's train and stand there. . . ."

Cesare watched the preparations frowning, and Lucrezia aware of him felt that his jealousy was clouding this happy day.

Giovanni entered.

He had changed a great deal since he had gone to Spain. Tall and very elegant, he had led a life of debauchery but at seventeen this had left very little mark on his face. He wore a golden beard which softened the sensual cruelty of his mouth, and his eyes, pale, transparent and so like Lucrezia's own, though beautifully shaped and dark-lashed, lacked the serene gentleness of his sister's and were in contrast cold and hard. But he had that Borgia fascination which he had inherited from his father, and in his fine colorful garments, which consisted of a Turkish robe à la Française so long that it swept the floor, made of curling cloth of gold with immense pearls sewn into the sleeves and a cap adorned with an enormous gem, he was a magnificent spectacle. Jewels sparkled on his person and about his neck was a long necklace entirely composed of rubies and pearls.

Lucrezia caught her breath as she looked at him.

"Why, Giovanni," she cried, "you look magnificent."

For a moment she forgot Cesare glowering there. To him it seemed symbolic of his father's wish to humiliate him. Here before Lucrezia stood her two brothers, the rivals; and one, through the grace and bounty of their

father, could come like a prince while the other must wear the comparatively drab garments of the Church.

Cesare felt one of those moods of rage sweeping over him. When they
possessed him he wanted to put his hands about the throats of those who
fostered these moods, and squeeze and squeeze that he might soothe his
hurt vanity by their screams for mercy.

He could not squeeze that elegant throat. There had been a hundred
times in his life when he had longed to. One must not touch the Pope's
beloved. One day, he thought, I shall be unable to restrain myself.

Giovanni, understanding the mood of his brother, looked slyly from
him to Lucrezia. "Ah, my little sister, my beloved Lucrezia, you say I look
magnificent, but you . . . you are like a goddess. I do not believe you can be
my pretty little sister. No human being could possess such beauty. How
you sparkle! How you glitter! Even my lord Archbishop looks the brighter
for your closeness to him. I hear you are not coming to our father's party,
brother. Mayhap it is as well. The somber garb of you men of the Church
is apt to have a sobering effect, and there must be naught but gaiety this
night."

"Silence!" cried Cesare. "Silence, I say!"

Giovanni raised his eyebrows and Adriana cried: "My lord, we must
go. As it is, we shall be late."

Cesare turned and strode out of the room. His attendant, who had
been waiting outside the apartment, prepared to follow him. Cesare turned
to the boy—he was little more. "You smile," he said. "Why?"

"My lord?"

Cesare had the boy by the ear. The pain was almost unbearable.

"Why?" screamed Cesare. "I asked why."

"My lord . . . I do not smile."

Cesare knocked the boy's head against the wall. "You would lie then.
You have been listening, and what you overheard amused you."

"My lord . . . my lord!"

Cesare took the boy roughly by the arm and pushed him toward the
staircase. The boy lifted his hands as he fell and Cesare heard his screams
as he tumbled headlong down the stairs. He listened, his eyes narrowed,
his mouth slightly turned down. The cries of others in pain never failed to

soothe the pain within himself, the pain born of frustration and fear that there were some in the world who did not recognize him as of supreme importance.

Led by her brother Giovanni, Lucrezia entered the Pope's new apartment at the Vatican. The apartments were already crowded by all the most important people of Rome and representatives from the courts of other states and dukedoms.

Lucrezia had forgotten Cesare in the excitement of crossing the square, from the Palace to the Vatican; the shouts of the people were still in her ears and she could still smell the scent of the flowers which had been strewn in her path. And here on the Papal throne was her father, magnificent in his white and gold vestments, his eyes shining with love and pride as they rested upon her. Those eyes, however, quickly strayed to his beloved and beautiful Giulia who stood on one side of Lucrezia; on the other was another beautiful young girl, Lella Orsini, who had recently married Giulia's brother Angelo Farnese.

The bridegroom came forward. He looked almost shabby compared with the glory of that other Giovanni, the bride's brother. Giovanni Sforza, conscious of lacking the Spanish elegance of the Duke of Gandia, was remembering that even the necklace he wore about his neck was borrowed.

As for Lucrezia, she was scarcely conscious of him. To her, this marriage was nothing more than a brilliant masque. Sforza must be there because without him she could not play her part, and since there was to be no consummation for a long time she knew that life was going on exactly as it always had.

They knelt together on a cushion at the feet of Alexander and when the notary asked Sforza if he would take Lucrezia as his wife, the bridegroom answered in loud and ringing tones: "I will with a good heart!" And Lucrezia echoed his words. The Bishop put the rings on their fingers while a nobleman held a naked sword over their heads; and after that the Bishop preached a touching sermon concerning the sanctity of marriage, to which neither Lucrezia nor her husband paid a great deal of attention.

Alexander himself was impatient. There were too many such ceremonies in his life, and he was eager to proceed with the merrymaking.

Now celebrations began, and there were many churchmen present who wondered at the ease with which the Pope could cast aside his role of Holy Father and become the jocular host who is determined that all shall rejoice at his daughter's wedding.

None laughed more heartily than the Pope at the somewhat bawdy jokes which were circulated and which were considered to be a necessary part of wedding celebrations. A comedy was performed for the enjoyment of the company, obscene songs were sung; riddles were asked and answered, and all these had a sly allusion to the married state. Hundreds of pounds of sweetmeats were distributed among the guests—the Pope and all the Cardinals being served first, followed by the bride and bridegroom, the ladies, the prelates and the remaining guests. The fun was hilarious when the sweets were dropped down the bodices of the women's gowns and there were shrieks of delight as these were retrieved. When the company was tired of this game the remains of the sweetmeats were thrown from the windows and the crowds who were waiting below scrambled for them.

Later the Pope gave a dinner-party in the pontifical hall and, when the company had feasted, the dancing began.

The bride sat beside her husband, who glowered at the dancers; he disliked such entertainments and was longing for this one to end. Not so Lucrezia; she longed for her husband to take her hand and lead her in the dance.

She glanced sideways at him. He seemed very old, she thought, very stern. "Do you not like to dance?" she asked him.

"I do not like to dance," he answered.

"But does not the music inspire you to do so?"

"Nothing inspires me to do so."

Her feet were tapping, and her father was watching her; his face was a little flushed with so much feasting and merry-making, and she knew that he understood how she was feeling. She saw him glance at her brother Giovanni, who had interpreted the glance. In a moment he was beside her.

"Brother," he said, "since you do not partner my sister in the dance, I will do so."

Lucrezia looked at her husband, thinking that perhaps now she would have to ask his permission; she was a little apprehensive, knowing that neither of her brothers would allow any to stand in the way of what they wanted to do.

She need not have worried. Giovanni Sforza was quite indifferent as to whether his wife danced or stayed at his side.

"Come," said the Duke of Gandia. "A bride should dance at her wedding."

So he led her into the very center of the dancers and holding her hand, he said: "Oh, my sister, you are the fairest lady of the ball, which is as it should be."

"I verily believe, dear brother," she said, "that you are the handsomest of the men."

The Duke bowed his head and his eyes gleamed at her, amused and passionate as they had been in the nursery days.

"Cesare would be beside himself with envy if he saw us dance together."

"Giovanni," she said quickly, "you should not provoke him."

"'Tis one of the joys of my life," he murmured, "provoking Cesare."

"Why so, Giovanni?"

"Someone must provoke him, and everyone else, except our father, would seem to be afraid to."

"Giovanni, you are not afraid of anything."

"Not I," said Giovanni. "I would not be afraid of your bridegroom if he, being jealous to see his bride look so lovingly at me, should challenge me to a duel."

"He will make no such challenge. I fancy he is glad to be rid of me."

"By the saints, then perhaps I should run him through for his neglect of my lovely sister. Oh, Lucrezia, how happy I am to be with you once more! Have you forgotten the days in our mother's house . . . the quarrels, the dances? Ah, those Spanish dances. Do you remember them?"

"I do, Giovanni."

"And do you not think them more inspiring, more full of meaning than these of Italy?"

"Yes, Giovanni."

"Then we will dance them, you and I. . . ."

"Giovanni, dare we?"

"We Borgias dare anything, sister." He drew her to him and there was light in his eyes which reminded her of Cesare's. "Do not forget," he went on, "that though you have married a Sforza, you are a Borgia . . . always a Borgia."

"No," she answered, and she was breathless with sudden excitement. "I shall never forget it."

One by one the other dancers fell away from them, so that after a while there was none dancing but the Duke of Gandia and his sister. The dances were those of Spain—throbbing with passion, the sort of dances which a bride and bridegroom might have performed together, portraying love, desire, fulfillment.

Lucrezia's long hair escaped from its net in the abandonment of the dance; and there were many who whispered: "How strange that the sister and brother should dance thus while the bridegroom looks on!"

The Pope watched with benign affection. These were his best-loved children, and it did not seem strange to him to see them dance thus: Lucrezia expectant, on the brink of womanhood, and Giovanni with the light of a demon in his eyes, and a malicious glance over his shoulder for the dull bridegroom—and for another perhaps, another who wished he was present to watch this almost ritual dance with their sister.

Giovanni Sforza yawned in his indifference. Yet he was less indifferent than he seemed. Not that he had any deep feelings for the golden-haired child who was his wife; but it had occurred to him that the Borgias were a strange family, alien to Rome; their Spanish blood made them that; and he felt faintly uneasy sitting there, and although he was in a semistupor through too much food and wine, too much heat, too many celebrations, he was conscious of a warning voice within him: "Beware of these Borgias. They are a strange, unnatural people. One must be prepared for them to do anything . . . however startling, however strange. Beware. . . . Beware of the Borgias!"

LUCREZIA MARRIED

THOSE WEEKS WHICH FOLLOWED HER WEDDING were full of pleasure for Lucrezia. She saw little of her husband, and her brothers were constantly with her. The old rivalry was revived and, although Lucrezia was aware that there was now an even more dangerous element in this than there had been in nursery days, she could not help being stimulated by it.

It was an unusual situation; the bride and bridegroom indifferent to each other, while the bride's brothers strutted before her, as though they were trying to woo her, each trying to persuade her that he was a better man than the other.

The brothers invaded Lucrezia's apartments day and night; each planned spectacles in which he played the leading part and Lucrezia that of honored guest.

Adriana protested, but Giovanni ignored her, and Cesare's eyes blazed with anger. "The insolence of the woman is beyond endurance!" he cried, and there was a threat in his words.

Giulia remonstrated with Lucrezia.

"This is a strange mode of behavior," she declared. "Your brothers attend you as though you were something more than a sister."

"You do not understand," Lucrezia explained. "We were together in the nursery."

"Brothers and sisters often are."

"Our childhood was different. We sensed the mystery which surrounded us. We lived in our mother's house, but we did not then know who our father was. We loved each other . . . we were necessary to each other, and then we were parted for so long. That is why we love more than most families."

"I would rather see you take a lover."

Lucrezia smiled gently; she was too good-hearted to tell Giulia that she understood the reason for her concern; the Pope still doted on her and she remained his favorite mistress, but all lovers of members of the Borgia family must be jealous of that family's feelings for its own members. Giulia was thinking that, now Cesare and Giovanni were in Rome, the love their father bore them and his daughter far exceeded that which he had for herself, and she was frankly jealous.

Lucrezia was fond of Giulia; she understood her feelings; but the bond between herself and her brothers could not be broken by anyone.

Meanwhile the weeks passed. She would go to the Campo di Fiore to watch Giovanni joust; then Cesare staged a bull-fight in that same spot, himself acting as the brave matador. He arranged that there were crowds to watch, and in the place of honor, where she might miss nothing, was Lucrezia, to tremble when she saw him face death, to exult when she saw him triumph.

All her life Lucrezia would never forget that occasion; the moment of fear when she saw the bull charge and heard the deep sigh of the crowd; she herself had almost swooned with fear, in one terrible second visualizing a world without Cesare. But Cesare was supreme; light as a dancer he had stepped aside as the angry bull thundered past. How handsome he looked! How graceful! He might, thought Lucrezia, have been dancing the old *farraca*, that dance in which a man mimed his play with the bull, so unconcerned did he seem. She would never dance the *farraca* herself nor see others dance it without recalling this moment of fear and exultation; she would always remember the hot sun in the Campo di Fiore and the realization that Cesare was to her the most important person in the world.

She had sat there seemingly serene, yet she was praying all the time: "Madonna, keep him safe. Holy Mother of God, do not let him be taken from me."

Her prayers were answered. He killed his bull and came to stand before his sister, that all present should know that it was for her he fought.

She took his hand and kissed it and her eyes had lost their mildness as she raised them to his. She had never seen him look quite so happy as he did then. He had cast aside all resentment; he had forgotten that he was an Archbishop and Giovanni a Duke. The crowd was acclaiming him, and Lucrezia was telling him of the depth and breadth of her love for him.

Lucrezia planned a ball in honor of her brave matador.

"And what of the hero of the joust?" demanded Giovanni.

"For him also," said Lucrezia fondly.

She wanted them to be together; it was only when she was conscious of their intense rivalry that she could feel she was back in her childhood.

So at the ball she danced with Giovanni while Cesare glowered, and with Cesare while Giovanni looked on with smoldering jealousy. Often the Pope would be present on such occasions and there was astonishment among the spectators that the Holy Father could look on smiling while his sons and daughter danced the strangely erotic Spanish dances, and that he could witness the jealous passion of these two brothers—and the sister's pleasure in it—with such tolerant amusement.

Lucrezia would be seen riding between her brothers to Monte Mario to watch the noblemen trying out their falcons, laughing, laying wagers as to which of the birds would win the prize.

As for Giovanni Sforza, he lived like an outsider in this strange household. The marriage was not yet to be consummated. At that he shrugged his shoulders. He was not a man deeply interested in such pleasures, and his needs could be supplied by the occasional summoning of a courtesan. But there were occasions when he resented the continual presence of those two overbearing young men, and on one of these he ventured to protest to his wife. She had returned with her brothers from riding and when she went to her apartment he followed her there; he turned and waved a dismissal at her attendants. They obeyed the signal and did not enter the room.

Lucrezia smiled tentatively at him. Wishing to live on good terms with all, she was always polite to her husband.

Sforza then said to his wife: "This is a strange life you lead. You are constantly in the company of one of your brothers—or both."

"Is it strange?" she asked. "They are my brothers."

"Your conduct is talked of throughout Rome."

Lucrezia's eyes were wide with surprise.

"Do you not understand what is being said?"

"I have not heard it."

"One day," said Sforza, "you will be my wife in very truth. I would have you remember that that day must surely come. I would ask you to see less of your brothers."

"They would never allow it," said Lucrezia. "Even if I wished it."

There was a sound of laughter from without and the brothers entered the room. They stood side by side, legs thrust apart, and it was not their obvious strength and vigor which sent a twinge of alarm through Sforza. He felt then that there was something to fear which was as yet unseen, and that any normal man who made an enemy of them must certainly go in fear of his life.

They were not scowling, and Sforza felt it might have been better if they were. They were smiling, and Lucrezia and her husband might not have been in the room, for all the notice the brothers took of them.

Giovanni said, as his hand rested lightly on his sword: "This man our sister has married . . . it has come to my ears that he resents our presence in her house."

"He should have his tongue cut out if he has made such a monstrous suggestion," drawled Cesare.

"And doubtless will," added Giovanni, half drawing his sword from its sheath and letting it fall back again. "Who is this man?"

"A bastard son of the tyrant of Pesaro, I have heard."

"And Pesaro, what is Pesaro?"

"But a small town on the Adriatic coast."

"A beggar . . . little more, eh? I remember he came to his wedding in a borrowed necklace."

"What should we do to such a one if he became insolent?"

Giovanni Borgia laughed softly. "He will not become insolent, brother. Beggar he may be, bastard he is, but he is not such a fool as all that."

Then they laughed and turned to the door.

Lucrezia and Sforza heard them shouting and laughing as they went out. Lucrezia ran to the window. It was a strange sight to see the Borgia brothers walking together like friends.

Sforza was still standing where he had been when the door had opened. During the time when the brothers had been speaking he had felt unable to move, so strongly had he been aware of an overwhelming sense of evil.

Lucrezia had turned from the window and was looking at him. There was compassion in her gaze and the compassion was for him; for the first time since she had seen him Lucrezia was aware of some feeling for him, and he for her.

He knew that she too was conscious of that evil which had seemed to emanate from her brothers.

As the brothers walked away they knew that Lucrezia was at the window watching them.

Cesare said: "That will doubtless make the fool think twice before he speaks slightingly of us again."

"Did you see him quail before us?" said Giovanni with a laugh. "I tell you, brother, it was all I could do to prevent myself drawing my sword and giving him a prick or two."

"You showed great restraint, brother."

"You also."

Giovanni glanced sideways at Cesare. Then he said: "Strange looks come our way. Have you noticed?"

"We have rarely been seen walking thus amicably together. That is the reason."

"Before you begin to scowl at me, Cesare, let me say this: There are times when you and I should stand together. All Borgias must do this sometimes. You hate me as my father's favorite, for my dukedom and the bride I shall have. The bride is no beauty, if that is any consolation to you. She has a long horse-face. You would fancy her no more than I do."

"I would take her and the dukedom of Gandia in exchange for my Archbishopric."

"That you would, Cesare, that you would. But I will keep her, and my dukedom. I would not be an Archbishop even though the Papal throne was to be mine in the future."

"Our father has a long life before him."

"I pray Heaven that it is so. But, Archbishop ... nay, do not glower so ... Archbishop, let us continue this friendship just for one hour. We have our common enemies. Let us consider them as we did the Sforza a short while ago."

"And these enemies?"

"The accursed Farnese. Is it not a fact that that woman, Giulia Farnese, demands what she will of our father and it is granted her?"

"'Tis true enough," murmured Cesare.

"Brother, shall we allow this state of affairs to continue?"

"I agree with you, my lord Duke, that it would be well to put an end to it."

"Then, my lord Archbishop, let us put our heads together and bring about that happy state of affairs."

"How so?"

"She is but a woman, and there are other women. I have in my suite a nun from Valencia. She has beauty, grace and the charm of a nun. She has given me great pleasure. I think I shall put her to the service of my father. I have a Moorish slave also, a dusky beauty. They make a satisfactory pair—the nun and the slave; the one all vestal reluctance, the other ... insatiably passionate. We will go to our father, you and I, and we will tell him of the virtues of these two. He will wish to share ... and sharing, who knows, he may forget the beautiful Giulia. At least she will not be the sole playmate of his leisure hours. There is safety in numbers; it is when there is one—and rarely any other—that one sees danger ahead."

"Let us visit him now. Let us tell him of your nun and your slave. He will at least be eager to see them and, if they are all you say ... well, it might be that we can loosen the hold of the Farnese on our Holy Father."

The two young men went across the square to the Vatican while many eyes followed them, marvelling at this new friendship.

🐉👑🐉

It was said in the streets that one marriage begot another, and this was indeed the case. Giovanni was to make a Spanish marriage; Cesare was for the Church and could have no marriage; Lucrezia was married to Giovanni Sforza; now it was the turn of little Goffredo.

Vannozza, happy with her husband, Carlo Canale, was dizzy with joy. Often her children came to see her and nothing delighted her more than to give intimate little parties for their entertainment. Her talk was mostly of her children; my son, the Duke, my son, the Archbishop, my daughter, the Countess of Pesaro. And now she would be able to talk equally proudly of her Goffredo. He would be a Duke or a Prince very shortly as the Pope was to make a grand marriage for him.

This showed clearly, thought Vannozza, that Alexander no longer doubted that Goffredo was his son. But this was not so; Alexander continued to doubt. Yet he was of the opinion that the more brilliant the marriages he could make for his children, the better for the Borgias generally; he wished he had a dozen sons; therefore it was expedient to thrust aside all doubt and, at least in the eyes of the world, accept Goffredo as his.

The moment was propitious to arrange a new Borgia marriage. Ferrante, the King of Naples, had watched with concern the growing friendship between the Vatican and the Sforzas of Milan.

Alexander, sensualist though he was, was also a clever diplomat. He preferred to be on good terms with the rival houses of Milan and Naples. Moreover, Spain was naturally favorable to the ruling house of Naples, which was Spanish in origin and maintained the Spanish customs at the Court.

Ferrante was aware of the Pope's desire for friendship and had sent his son, Federico, to Rome with proposals to lay before the Holy Father.

Ferrante's elder son, Alfonso, who was heir to the throne of Naples, had a natural daughter, Sanchia, and Ferrante's suggestion was that Sanchia should be betrothed to the Pope's youngest son. That Goffredo was but eleven years and Sanchia sixteen was no handicap; nor was her illegitimacy, for illegitimacy was not considered an important stigma in fifteenth-century Italy, although of course legitimate children took precedence over natural ones. Goffredo himself was illegitimate; therefore it seemed a good match.

Little Goffredo was delighted. He came hurrying to Lucrezia, as soon as he heard the news, to impart it to her.

"I, sister, I too am to be married. Is not that great good news? I am to go to Naples and marry a Princess."

Lucrezia embraced him and wished him happiness, and the little boy ran about the apartment dancing with an imaginary bride, going through the ceremony which he had seen Lucrezia perform with her husband.

Cesare and Giovanni called on their sister, and Goffredo ran to them and told them the news. Lucrezia knew that they had already heard; she was aware of this because of Cesare's sullen looks. This was another reminder that he was the only one of them who must remain unmarried.

"What a bridegroom you will be!" said Giovanni. "An eleven-year-old bridegroom of a sixteen-year-old bride who is, unless rumor lies . . . but no matter. Your Sanchia is a beauty—a great beauty, my brother—so whatever else she may be she will be forgiven."

Goffredo began to walk about the apartment on his toes to make himself look taller. He stopped suddenly, his eyes questioning; then he looked toward Cesare.

"Everybody is pleased," he said, "except my lord brother."

"You know why he is ill-pleased, do you not?" cried Giovanni. "It is because as a holy man of the Church there can be no bride for him."

Goffredo's face puckered suddenly, and he went to Cesare. "If you wish for a bride, my lord," he said, "I would give you mine; for I should find no pleasure in her if by possessing her I should cause you pain."

Cesare's eyes glinted as he looked at the boy. He had not known until that moment how firmly Goffredo admired him. The little boy standing there clearly implied that he thought Cesare the most wonderful person in the world; and with Lucrezia and his young brother, to admire him thus, Cesare felt suddenly happy.

He did not care for Giovanni's taunts. He gloried in his rivalry with Giovanni because he had made up his mind that one day Giovanni was going to pay for every insult, just as any other man or woman would.

"You are a good boy, Goffredo," he said.

"Cesare, you believe I am your brother . . . entirely your brother, do you not?"

Cesare embraced the boy and assured him that he did; and Lucrezia watching saw all the cruelty and the hardness leave her brother's face. Like that, she thought, my brother Cesare is surely the most beautiful person in the world.

Lucrezia longed for peace between them all. They were all together now, and Cesare was delighted by the artless words of the boy. If Giovanni would only join then in their happy circle, they could dispense with rivalry; they could be as she longed to see them, in complete harmony.

"I will play wedding songs on my lute, and we will sing," she cried. "We will pretend we are already at Goffredo's wedding."

She clapped her hands and a slave brought her lute; then she sat on cushions, her golden hair falling about her shoulders; and as her fingers touched the lute she began to sing.

Goffredo stood behind her, and laying his hands on her shoulders sang with her.

The brothers watched them, listening; and for a short while peace was with them all.

❧♔☙

Now there was more merrymaking at the Vatican in honor of the formal betrothal of Goffredo and Sanchia of Aragon which took place in the Pope's apartments, Federico, Prince of Altamura and uncle of the bride, taking her place. This was conducted in the presence of the Pope with all the ceremony of a true marriage.

There was a great deal of merriment because little Goffredo as the husband looked so incongruous beside the Prince who was taking the place of the bride, and ribald comments soon broke out; nor were these checked by the presence of the Holy Father who in fact laughed more heartily than anybody and even added to the quips.

There was nothing Alexander liked better than what he called a good joke, and by good he meant bawdy. Federico, finding himself the butt of all the amusement and being something of an actor, then began to amuse the company by playing the part of bride with such fluttering of eye-lashes and coy gestures that what took place in the Vatican was more like a masque than a solemn ceremony.

Federico continued with his acting at the feasting and balls which followed; it was a joke of which no one seemed to tire, and the fun was increased when a member of Federico's retinue took an opportunity of whispering to the Pope that he would be even more amused if he had seen Sanchia.

"How so?" asked Alexander. "I have heard she is a beauty."

"She has beauty, Holiness, to make all others seem plain beside her. But our Prince behaves as a coy virgin. There is nothing coy about Madonna Sanchia . . . and nothing of the virgin either. She has had a host of lovers."

The Pope's eyes glistened with merriment. "Then this makes the joke even better," he said. He called Cesare and Giovanni to him. "Did you hear that, my sons? Did you hear what was said of Madonna Sanchia, our coy virgin?"

The brothers laughed heartily at the joke.

"I deeply regret," said Giovanni, "that young Goffredo is to go to Naples, and that Sanchia will not join him here."

"Ah, my son, I should not give much for poor Goffredo's chances if she set eyes on you."

"We should be rivals for the lady," said Cesare lightly.

"A pleasant state of affairs indeed!" said the Pope. "Mayhap since she is such an obliging lady she would be wife to three brothers."

"And to their father mayhap," added Giovanni.

This amused the Pope immensely, and his eyes rested fondly on Giovanni.

Cesare decided then that if ever Sanchia came to Rome she should be his mistress before she was Giovanni's.

Then his eyes narrowed and he said sharply: "So our little Goffredo is to be a husband. I myself am to be denied that pleasure. It is strange that Goffredo should be married before you, brother."

Giovanni's eyes flashed hatred, for he immediately understood Cesare's meaning.

Alexander was saddened. He turned to Giovanni. "Alas," he said, "you must soon return to Spain for your marriage, my dear son."

"My marriage will wait," said Giovanni sullenly.

"Ah, my son, time does not stand still. I shall be well pleased when I hear that your wife is the mother of a fine boy."

"In time . . . in time," said Giovanni shortly.

But Cesare was smiling secretly. Alexander's mouth was set along firm lines. When his ambition was concerned he could be adamant, and as Cesare had been forced to the Church so Giovanni would be forced to go to his Spanish wife.

It seemed to Cesare an even better joke than Federico's miming of Madonna Sanchia. Once he had longed to be in Giovanni's shoes that he might go to Spain to receive great honors including a Spanish dukedom; he had been forced to stay behind and enter the Church. Now Giovanni wanted nothing so much as to stay in Rome, and he would be forced to leave as certainly as Cesare had been forced into the Church.

Cesare laughed inwardly as he watched his brother's sullen looks.

Giovanni was angry. Life in Rome suited his temperament far better than the Spanish mode of living. In Spain a man of rank was stifled by etiquette; and Giovanni had no fancy for the pallid, long-faced bride, Maria Enriques, whom he had inherited from his dead brother. It was true that Maria was a cousin of the King of Spain and that marriage with her would forge a strong link with the Spanish Royal house and secure for him royal protection. But what did Giovanni care for that? He wanted to be in Rome, which he thought of as home.

He would rather be recognized as the son of the Pope than cousin, by marriage, to the King of Spain. He had felt homesick while he was away. He had imagined himself riding about Rome, and, cynic though he was concerning most things, tears would come to his eyes when he thought of entering the Porta del Popolo and watching the races to the Piazza Venezia in Carnival week. There seemed nothing like it in Spain—the Spanish were a melancholy people compared with the gay Italians. He had found great pleasure and sadness in thinking of the crowds, in the grand stand in the Piazza del Popolo, who had assembled to watch the race of riderless horses. How he had enjoyed those races, how he had shouted with glee to see the frightened beasts let loose, with pieces of metal tied to them to make a noise and frighten them still further as they galloped, the devilish type of spurs fastened midway between withers and shoulders, leaded and pear-shaped, the heavy end having seven spikes which prodded the horse at every step! The terrified horses, as they thundered along the Corso, provided a sight not to be missed. Yet in Spain he had sadly missed it. He had longed to wander along the Via Funari where the rope-makers lived, and the Via Canestrari where the basket-makers lived, to the Via dei Serpenti; to gaze at the Capitol and think of the heroes of Rome who had been crowned with glory there, and to see the Tarpeian Rock from which guilty men were thrown; to laugh at the old saying that glory was but a short way from disgrace, and to answer it with: Not for a Borgia; not for the son of the Pope!

All this was Rome, and Rome was where he belonged; yet he was so unfortunate as to be sent away from it.

He sought to postpone the hour of his departure. He threw himself madly into pleasure. He roamed the streets with a band of selected friends, and there was not a beautiful young woman—or man—who was safe, once Giovanni had set eyes on her or him.

He favored the most notorious of the courtesans. He roamed the Ponte district in their company. He liked courtesans; they were experienced, as he was; he liked also very young girls, and one of his favorite pastimes was seducing or forcing young brides before their marriage took place. Giovanni, he himself knew, would never be a brave soldier, and instinct told him that Cesare, who was no coward, was aware of that streak of cowardice in him, and that Cesare exulted because of it whilst raging at the unfairness which had made Giovanni a soldier and himself a man of the Church.

Giovanni sought to hide that streak of weakness within him, and how could he do this better, he thought, than by inflicting cruelty on those who could not retaliate? If he abducted a bride about to be married, who could complain against the beloved son of an all-powerful Pope? Such adventures lulled his fear of inadequacy and, he felt, made him appear as a lusty adventurer.

There was one person in whose company he found great delight. This was a Turkish Prince whom the Pope was holding as hostage in the Vatican.

Djem was of striking appearance; his Asiatic manners amused Giovanni; his Turkish costume was picturesque and he was more cunning and more coldly barbarous than anyone Giovanni had ever known.

Giovanni had struck up a friendship with Djem and they were often seen about the city together. Giovanni appeared in Turkish costume; it suited him, and Djem with his dark looks made a striking contrast to the golden beauty of Giovanni.

They were together in Alexander's cortège when it traveled from church to church; and it seemed strange to the people of Rome to see two prominent figures on a pair of matched horses, both dressed in turbans and colorful oriental costume.

Most people were horrified to see the Turk in this procession for the Turk was an infidel; but Giovanni insisted that his friend accompany them, and the Turk smiled at the horrified looks of the people in his slow indolent way which everyone knew was a veil to hide his barbarism. From him they looked to the handsome Duke of Gandia whose keen eyes were on the look-out for the most beautiful young women, marking the spot where they could later be found, and pointing them out to Djem, who would be planning that night's adventures.

In this Asiatic, who was capable of devising strange orgies of calculated cruelty and extraordinary eroticism, Giovanni had found a congenial companion.

Here was another reason why he had no wish to leave Rome.

As for Alexander, he knew of the complaints against Giovanni; he knew that the people were shocked by the appearance of the Pope's son in Turkish costume; but he merely shook his head and smiled indulgently.

"He means no harm," he said. "He is young yet, and it is merely high spirits which cause him to play his merry pranks."

And Alexander was as loth to let his beloved Giovanni leave Rome as Giovanni was to go.

※ ♛ ※

Lucrezia sat with Giulia; there was a piece of embroidery before her and she was smiling at it. She enjoyed working the beautiful pattern on silk in gold, scarlet and blue threads. Bending over the work she looked, thought Giulia, like an innocent child, and Giulia felt slightly impatient. Lucrezia was now a married woman, and though the marriage had not been consummated she had no right to look such a baby.

Lucrezia, thought Giulia, is different from the rest of us. Lucrezia is apart. She is like her father, yet lacking his wisdom and understanding of life; she has the same way of turning away from the unpleasant and refusing to believe in its existence; and she has a tolerance besides. I believe she makes excuses for the cruelty of people, almost as though she understands what makes them act cruelly; and that is part of her strangeness, for Lucrezia is never cruel herself.

All the same Giulia felt impatient in her company, for Giulia was uneasy. She hated Cesare and Giovanni; they had always made her uncomfortable, but now she knew that they were deliberately trying to oust her from her position. Sexually she was out of reach. She was, after all, their father's mistress and the bond between Giulia and the Pope was a strong one as he did not feel toward her as he would toward any light love of a night or so. Therefore his sons, while desiring her as they would desire any beautiful woman, were forced to respect her; consequently they were piqued about this, and it was part of their arrogance that they should dislike any who brought home to them the fact that they could not have all their own way in all directions. The Pope towered above his sons; he was the fount from whom all blessings flowed; and although he was the most indulgent of fathers, the most generous of benefactors, there were some bounds beyond which even they might not go.

Giulia's was a case which underlined this fact, and they resented her because of it. Accordingly they endeavored to destroy her influence.

She knew that they sought the most beautiful young people in Rome, and that they introduced the girls to their father. (Alexander had never been interested in their young male friends.) The Pope had been greatly taken with a certain Spanish nun whom Giovanni had brought with him in his retinue. The result was that the Holy Father had been too busy to see Giulia for some days. Giulia was furious, and she knew whom to blame.

Impetuous as she was, she wanted to storm into the Papal apartments and denounce Giovanni; but that would be folly. Much as the Pope liked to please his beautiful young mistress, and indeed found it difficult to refuse the request of any pretty young woman, there was one for whom he cared more than any woman—his precious Giovanni.

And if the Spanish nun was proving very delectable he might feel just a little more impatient than he would otherwise have done, if Giulia railed against Giovanni. Alexander might love various women in various degrees, but his love for his children never faltered.

Now Giulia, looking at the fair young face bent over the embroidery, said slyly: "Lucrezia, I am worried about Giovanni."

Lucrezia's innocent eyes were wide with surprise. "You are worried about him? I thought you did not like him."

Giulia laughed. "We banter . . . as brother and sister might. I would not say that I loved him as you do. I would never have that blind adoration for a brother which you have for yours."

"I think you are very fond of your brother Alessandro."

Giulia nodded. It was true. She was fond of Alessandro to the extent that she was determined to secure for him his Cardinal's hat before long. But that was different from this passionate attachment which seemed to exist between the Borgia brothers and their sister.

"Oh, fond enough," she said lightly. "But I was talking of Giovanni. There is a great deal of gossip in the streets concerning him."

"There is always gossip," murmured Lucrezia lightly, picking up her needle.

"That's true, but this is a time when gossip could be very harmful to Giovanni."

Lucrezia lifted her head from her work.

"On account of his marriage," went on Giulia impatiently. "I have heard it said, by friends who have come from Spain, that there is talk at the Court there of Giovanni's wild behavior, of his friendship with Djem, and how they spend their time. There is some displeasure in quarters where it could prove harmful to Giovanni."

"Have you told my father this?"

Giulia smiled. "If it came from me he would feel I was jealous of Giovanni. He knows that I am aware of the affection between them."

"Yet he should know," said Lucrezia.

Giulia was well pleased. It was easy to lead Lucrezia the way in which one wanted her to go.

"Indeed he should." Giulia looked out of the window to hide the sly smile playing about her lips. "If it came from you it would carry weight."

Lucrezia rose. "Then I shall tell him. I shall tell him at once. He would be distressed if aught should happen to prevent Giovanni's marriage."

"You are wise. I have it from a very reliable source that his future father-in-law is considering the annulment of the betrothal, and that if Giovanni does not claim his bride within the next few months another husband will be found for her."

"I will go to my father at once," said Lucrezia. "He should know of this."

Giulia followed her. "I will accompany you," she said, "and if the Holy Father feels disposed to see me, there I shall be."

ALEXANDER wept as he embraced his son.

"Father," cried Giovanni, "if you love me as you say, how can you bear that I should leave you?"

"I love you so much, my son, that I can let you go."

"Could not there be a more worthwhile marriage for me here in Rome?"

"No, my son. We have the future to think of. You forget you are Duke of Gandia and that when you are married to Maria you will have the might of Spain behind you. Do not underestimate the importance of this tie with the Spanish royal house."

Giovanni sighed, but the Pope put his arm about him. "Come, see what wedding presents I have for you and your bride."

Giovanni looked almost sullenly at the furs and jewels, and the chests which were decorated with beautiful paintings. In the last weeks all the best jewelers of Rome had been busy buying the best stones, and resetting them in exquisite ornaments for the Duke of Gandia. Alexander opened a chest and showed his son sables and ermine and necklaces of pearls and rubies until he made the young man's eyes glisten with eagerness to wear them.

"You see, my son, you will go to Spain in all the splendor of a Prince. Does not that delight you?"

Giovanni admitted grudgingly that it did. "But," he added, "there is still much I regret leaving."

The Pope embraced him. "Be assured, my beloved, that you do not hate going more than I hate to see you go." Alexander put his face close to his son's. "Marry your Maria," he said; "get her with child. Get yourself an heir . . . and then, why should you not come back to Rome? Rest assured none here will scold you for not remaining once you have done your duty."

Giovanni smiled. "I will do it, Father," he said.

"And remember, Giovanni, while you are in Spain you must behave as a Spaniard."

"They are so solemn."

"On ceremonious occasions only. I ask nothing more of you but this, my dearest boy: Marry, get an heir and conduct yourself in a manner not to offend the Court of Spain. Apart from that . . . do as you will. Enjoy your life. Your father would have you happy."

Giovanni kissed his father's hand and left him to join Djem who was waiting for him.

They rode out into the City on one of their adventures, more gay, more bizarre than ever. Giovanni felt he must cram as much excitement as possible into the short time left to him.

When his son had gone, the Pope sent for two men: Ginès Fira and Mossen Jayme Pertusa.

"You are making your preparations?" asked the Pope.

"We are ready to leave for Spain at a moment's notice, Most Holy Lord," answered Ginès.

"That is well. Keep close to my son and report to me everything that happens to him; however insignificant, I wish to hear of it."

"We are your servants, Holiness."

"If I should discover that you have withheld any detail—however small—I shall excommunicate you, and you may look forward to eternal damnation."

The men grew pale. Then they fell to their knees and swore that, as far as it was in their power, they would report every detail of the life of the Duke of Gandia; they had no wish on Earth but to serve his Holiness.

Lucrezia HAD BEEN riding out to Monte Mario to watch the falcons and, as she returned to the Palace, a slave ran to her to tell her that Madonna Adriana was looking for her.

Lucrezia made her way to the apartment where she found Adriana somewhat disturbed.

"The Holy Father wishes you to go to him," she said. "There is news of some sort."

Lucrezia's eyes widened and her lips fell slightly apart, a characteristic expression which, with her receding chin, made her look more like a girl of ten than one approaching fourteen.

"Bad news?" she asked, fear creeping into her eyes.

"It is news from Spain," said Adriana. "I know nothing else."

News from Spain must involve Giovanni. Indeed during the last months no one had been able to forget Giovanni. Alexander was preoccupied at all times by thoughts of his beloved son.

When bad news came from Spain he shut himself away and wept, and he would be quite unhappy for perhaps a day—which was a long time for him to grieve; then he would brighten and would say: "One cannot believe all one hears. Such a magnificent Prince must naturally have enemies."

The news had always been bad, so Lucrezia was fearful as she heard of the summons to go to her father.

She said: "I will take off my habit and go to him at once."

"Do so," said Adriana; "he is impatient for you."

She went to her apartments and Giulia followed her there. Giulia was pleased because she had regained all her old power over the Pope. She had learned that she must shrug aside his light preference for Spanish nuns or Moorish slaves; such desires passed. Lucrezia had told her of her mother's attitude toward her father's lighter loves; Vannozza had laughed indulgently, and he had always cared for Vannozza; he had given her two husbands, and Canale was treated as a member of the family; even Cesare had some regard for him out of respect for their mother. And look how the Pope had loved Vannozza's children, showering on them such loving care that could not have been exceeded even if he had been able to marry Vannozza and they were his legitimate offspring.

Lucrezia was right; and Giulia was determined that her little Laura should be treated with the same loving care. Alexander certainly doted on the little girl, and as a sign of his love of her mother had promised to bestow the Cardinal's hat on Alessandro Farnese. Her family could not tell her often enough how they admired her and depended on her.

But now Giulia wondered about this news which the Pope wished to impart to his daughter. In the old days she would have been rather piqued that he had not told her first, but now she was able to adapt herself and hide any resentment she felt.

"My father awaits me," said Lucrezia as her slave helped her to take off her riding habit.

"I wonder what fresh trouble there has been," said Giulia.

"It may not be trouble," said Lucrezia. "It could be good news."

Giulia laughed at her. "You do not change at all," she said. "You have been married nearly a year and yet you are the same as you were when we first met."

Lucrezia was not listening; she was thinking of all the preparations previous to Giovanni's departure. She knew how important Giovanni was to Alexander; she knew that he had gone to the utmost trouble to ensure that his son should please the Spanish Court; she knew about the Bishop of Oristano, into whose care the Pope had put Giovanni from the moment he stepped on to Spanish soil; she knew of the orders which had been issued to Ginès Fira and Pertusa. Poor men, how could they prevent Giovanni from disobeying his father's orders!

And poor Giovanni! Not to go out at night. Not to play at dicing. To keep his wife company and sleep with her every night until a child was conceived. To wear gloves all the time he was at sea because salt was harmful to the hands, and in Spain a nobleman was expected to have soft white hands.

And Giovanni, of course, had disobeyed his father. Letters came from Fira and Pertusa telling of these matters, and those letters plunged the Pope into gloom—temporary gloom, it was true—before he roused himself and said that in spite of everything he knew his dearest son would do all that was expected of him.

There had been gloomy letters from Giovanni. His marriage had taken place at Barcelona, and the King and Queen of Spain had been present, which was a great honor and showed in what esteem they held Maria; but wrote Giovanni, he had no taste for his wife; she was dull and her face was too long; she repelled him.

Lucrezia tried not to think of that day the letter came from Fira and Pertusa saying that Giovanni had refused to consummate the marriage and that, instead of sleeping with his bride, he took a few companions and prowled about the town at night looking for young girls to seduce or rape.

This was terrible, for if the Pope made excuses for his son, the King of Spain would not, and Giovanni's bride was of the royal house and must not be humiliated thus.

For the first time Alexander wrote angrily to Giovanni, and bade Cesare write on the same lines to his brother; this Cesare was only too eager to do.

Lucrezia was saddened by this state of affairs. She knew that her father was as worried as he possibly could be; it was not as much as most parents would have been, of course, but Lucrezia loved him so dearly that she could not bear to think of his being even mildly distressed.

She had wept in his presence and he had embraced her and kissed her passionately. "My darling, my darling," he had cried. "You would never hurt your father in this way, my sweet, sweet girl."

"Never, Father," she had assured him. "I would die rather than hurt you."

He had held her against him, called her his dear, dear love, and he could scarcely bear her to be out of his sight for a whole day.

But the storms passed and Alexander was soon his gay benign self again, for there was a letter from Giovanni declaring that by writing as he had his father had caused him great unhappiness—the greatest he had ever suffered.

At which Alexander wept and reproached himself.

He read Giovanni's letter aloud to Lucrezia, having sent for her on receipt of it.

"'I cannot understand how you can believe in such sinister reports which were written by malicious people who have no regard for the truth. . . .'"

"You see?" Alexander had cried jubilantly. "We have misjudged him."

"Then," said Lucrezia, "Fira and Pertusa have lied?"

Lights of fear came into the gray-blue eyes to disturb their mildness. She was afraid for those two men who had done, she knew, what the Holy Father had asked of them, and who might have to be punished to prove Giovanni right.

Alexander waved his hand. "No matter. No matter," he said. He did not want to discuss the two men whom he trusted to tell him the truth; he did not want to have to admit that he knew Giovanni's words to be lies. It was so much pleasanter to make believe that they were true.

"His marriage has been more than consummated," cried the Pope, continuing to read the letter. He burst out laughing. "Indeed it has. I know my Giovanni!"

Alexander went on reading:

"'If I have prowled at night, oh my Father, I did so with my father-in-law, Enrico Enriques, and other friends of His Most Catholic Majesty. It is the custom to take a stroll by night in Barcelona.'"

Then Alexander had walked about the apartment, talking about Giovanni, telling Lucrezia that he was always certain that his children would never fail him; but Lucrezia had been conscious of an uneasiness. And so, when this message came, she was afraid that there was further alarming news about her brother.

When she reached her father's presence she knew that she had been worrying unduly; she was taken into his arms and kissed fervently.

"My dearest daughter," cried the Pope; "here is the best possible news. We shall celebrate this with a banquet this very night. Listen to what I have to say, my darling: Your brother is soon to be a father. What do you say to that, Lucrezia? What do you say to that?"

She clasped her arms about him. "Oh Father, I am so happy; I can think of no words to express my joy."

"As I knew you would be. Let me look at you. Oh, how your eyes shine and sparkle! How beautiful you are, my daughter! I knew the joy this would give you; that is why I would let no other impart the news to you. I would tell none until you knew first."

"I rejoice for Giovanni," said Lucrezia. "I know how happy this will

make him; and I rejoice also for your Holiness, because I believe the pleasure it gives you is even greater than that which it will bring to Giovanni."

"So my little daughter cares deeply for her father?"

"How could it be otherwise?" demanded Lucrezia, as though astonished that he should ask.

"I loved you dearly since the first day when I held you in my arms,
a red-faced baby with a gleam of silvery down on your head; and I have
loved you steadily since. My Lucrezia . . . my little one . . . who would never
willingly cause me a moment's anxiety!"

She took his hand and kissed it. "'Tis true, Father," she said. "You
know me well."

He put his arm about her and led her to a chair.

"Now," he said, "we will see that all Rome rejoices in this news. You
and Giulia must put your lovely heads together and devise a banquet to
outdo all banquets."

Lucrezia was smiling when she returned to her apartments. She was
surprised to find her husband there.

"My lord?" she said.

He laughed. "It is strange to see me here, I know," he answered grimly.
"It should not be, Lucrezia. You are my wife, you know."

Sudden fear seized her. She had never seen Sforza thus. There was
something in his eyes which she did not understand.

She waited apprehensively. "You have been with his Holiness?" he
asked.

"Yes."

"I guessed it. Your radiant looks tell me and I know how matters stand
between you."

"Between my father and myself?"

"The whole of Rome knows that he dotes upon you,"

"The whole of Rome knows that he is my father."

Sforza laughed; it was an unpleasant laugh, but mildly so; everything
was mild about Sforza. "It is because all Rome knows him to be your

father that this affection...this more than doting...is so strange," he countered.

She stared at him, but already he had turned and was striding out of the apartment.

Cesare came to the Palace of Santa Maria in Portico. He was in a strange mood, and Lucrezia was unsure what it implied. Was he angry? Certainly he must be. Giovanni was now to be a legitimate father, and that was something, Cesare would be telling himself, that he could never be. How sad, thought Lucrezia, that the happiness of her father over Giovanni's wife's pregnancy must be a further cross for Cesare to bear.

She knew that he had never forgotten the vow he had made before the Madonna to escape from the Church; and she knew that he was as determined now to fulfill it as he had been when he had made it.

So now when he strode in, she wondered what could be the meaning of that glittering expression in the eyes, that tight tension of the lips.

She had heard rumors of his life at the universities. It was said that no vice was too degrading for Cesare to indulge in, if only experimentally. It was said that his father's money and influence had enabled him to set up a little court of his own and that he ruled his courtiers like a despotic monarch; one look was enough to subdue them and, if any failed to do his bidding, accidents quickly befell those people.

"Cesare," said Lucrezia, "has anything happened to anger you?"

He took her by the neck and bent back her head. He kissed her lips lightly. "Those beautiful eyes see too much," he murmured. "I want you to come riding with me."

"Yes, Cesare; with the utmost pleasure. Where shall we ride?"

"Along by the river mayhap. Through the city. Let the people see us together. They enjoy it. And why should they not? You are pleasant enough to look at, sister."

"And you are the handsomest man in Italy."

He laughed. "What," he said, "in my priest's robes!"

"You add dignity to them. No priest ever looked like you."

"A fact which doubtless makes all the Bishops and Cardinals rejoice mightily."

He is in a good mood, she thought. I was mistaken.

As they rode out another rider joined them. This was a lovely red-haired girl, magnificently, indeed over-dressed, glittering with jewels, her long red hair falling about her shoulders.

"Fiametta knows you well, sister," said Cesare, looking from the red-haired woman of the world to the golden innocence of Lucrezia. "She declares that I speak your name far too frequently when I am in her company."

"We are a devoted family," Lucrezia explained to the girl.

"Indeed it is so," said Fiametta. "The whole of Rome talks of your devotion—one to another; and it is hard to say who loves Madonna Lucrezia more, her brothers or her father."

"It is comforting to be so loved," said Lucrezia simply.

"Come," said Cesare, "we will ride together."

He rode between them, the sardonic smile playing about his lips as they went. People in the streets walked past them with lowered eyes but, when they had passed, stopped to stare after them.

Cesare's reputation was already such that none dared give him a hostile or critical look which he might see; but they could not help staring at him, riding through the streets with his sister and the other woman.

Cesare knew full well that he was shocking them by riding in daylight with one of the most notorious courtesans in Rome together with his sister; he knew that an account of this would be taken to his father and that the Pope would be displeased. It was what Cesare intended. Let the people look; let them gossip.

Fiametta was enjoying the jaunt. She was delighted that the citizens should know that she was the latest mistress of Cesare Borgia. It was a fillip to her reputation; and the longer she remained in favor with him, the better, for surely that must show that she was superior in her profession to her fellows.

They rode to the ancient Colosseum which never failed to fascinate Lucrezia and yet to fill her with horror as she thought of the Christians who had been thrown to the lions and killed for their faith.

"Oh," she cried, "it is so beautiful, and yet . . . disturbing. They say that if one comes here at night and waits among the ruins one hears the cries of the martyrs and the roar of the wild beasts."

Fiametta laughed. "'Tis a tale that is told."

Lucrezia turned questioningly to Cesare.

"Fiametta is right," he told her. "What you would doubtless hear would be someone taking away the stones and marbles to build him a house. These stories of ghosts are told in order to keep those away from the Colosseum who might disturb the thieves."

"Perhaps that is what it is. Now I no longer feel alarmed."

"But I pray you," said Cesare, "do not come here at night, sister. It is not for such as you to do so."

"Would you come here at night?" Lucrezia asked Fiametta.

Cesare answered for her: "At night the Colosseum is the haunt of robbers and prostitutes."

Fiametta flushed slightly, but she had learned to show no anger to Cesare.

Lucrezia, seeing her discomfiture and understanding its cause—for she realized to what profession Fiametta belonged—said quickly: "Pope Paul built his palace from these blocks of travertine. Is it not wonderful to contemplate that all those years ago the same marble, the same stone, was used and, although all the people who built it and lived in it are dead, fourteen hundred years later houses can still be built of the same material?"

"Is she not enchanting, my little sister?" said Cesare, and threw a kiss to her.

They galloped among the ruins for a while and then turned their horses back toward the Palace of Santa Maria in Portico.

Cesare told Fiametta that he would come to visit her later that day and went into Lucrezia's palace with her.

"Ah," he said, when they were alone—and whenever Cesare visited Lucrezia, her attendants always understood that he wished to be alone with her—"now you are a little shocked, confess it, sister."

"The people stared at us, Cesare."

"And you do not like poor Fiametta?"

"I liked her. She is very beautiful . . . but she is a courtesan, is she not; and should she have ridden in our company through the streets?"

"Why not?"

"Perhaps because you are an Archbishop."

Cesare brought his fist down upon his thigh in a well remembered gesture.

"It is precisely because I am an Archbishop that I rode through the streets with that red-headed harlot."

"Our father says . . ."

"I know what our father says. Have your mistresses—ten, twenty, a hundred, if you must. Amuse yourself as you will . . . in private. But in public remember, always remember that you are a son of Holy Church. By all the saints, Lucrezia, I have sworn that I will escape from the Church, and I will behave in such a way that our father will be forced to free me."

"Oh, Cesare, you will make him so unhappy."

"And what of the unhappiness he causes me?"

"It is for your own advancement."

"You listen to him rather than to me. I see that, sister."

"Oh no, Cesare, no. I would have you know that if there were aught I could do to free you from the Church, willingly would I do it."

"Yet you grieve for your father. You say with such sympathy: 'He would be made unhappy.' Not a word about my unhappiness."

"I know you are unhappy, dearest brother, and I would do everything in my power to put an end to that unhappiness."

"Would you, Lucrezia? Would you?"

"Anything . . . anything on Earth."

He took her by the shoulder and smiled down at her. "One day I may ask you to redeem that promise."

"I shall be waiting. I shall be ready, Cesare."

He kissed her ardently.

"You soothe me," he said. "Did you not always do so? Beloved sister, there is no one on Earth whom I could love as I love you."

"And I love you too, Cesare. Is that not enough to make us happy, even if we have other trials to bear?"

"No," he cried, his eyes ablaze. "I know my destiny. It is to be a King . . . a conqueror. Do you doubt that?"

"No, Cesare, I do not. I see you always as a King and a conqueror."

"Dear Lucrezia, when we were riding with Fiametta you looked at those old ruins and you thought of days long ago. There is one man glorious in our history. He conquered great countries. He lived before the Colosseum was built and he is the greatest man who—as yet—has come out of Rome. You know of whom I speak."

"Of Julius Caesar," she said.

"A great Roman, a great conqueror. I picture him, crossing the Rubicon and knowing that all Italy lay at his feet. That was forty-nine years before Christ was born, and yet there has never been another like him—as yet. You know what his motto was, do you not? *Aut Caesar, aut nullus.* Lucrezia, from this moment I adopt that as mine." His eyes were brilliant with megalomania; he was so certain of his greatness that he made her believe him. "But see, did they not call me Cesare! That was no mere chance. There was one great Caesar. There shall be another."

"You are right!" she cried. "I am sure of it. In years to come people will talk of you as they do of great Julius. You will be a great general. . . ."

Now his expression was ugly.

"And my father will make a Churchman of me!"

"But you will be Pope, Cesare. One day you will be Pope."

He stamped his foot with fury. "A Pope rules in shadow; a King in the full light of day. I do not wish to be Pope. I wish to be King. I wish to unite the whole of Italy under my banner and rule . . . myself and none other. That is the task of a King, not a Pope."

"Our father must release you."

"He will not. He refuses. I have begged. I have implored. But no, I am for the Church, he insists. One of us must be. Giovanni has his long-faced mare in Barcelona. Goffredo has his harlot of Naples. And I . . . I am to be wedded to the Church. Lucrezia, was there ever such crass folly? I feel murderous when I contemplate it."

"Murderous, Cesare! Against him!"

Cesare put his face against hers. "Yes," he said grimly. "I feel murderous . . . even toward him."

"He must be made to understand. He is the best father in the world, and if he but knew your feelings . . . oh Cesare, he would understand them. He would see that something was done."

"I have explained my feelings until I am weary. He loses all his benign looks then. I never saw a man so set on one thing as our father is when I talk of leaving the Church. He is determined that I shall stay."

"Cesare, what you have said causes me much pain. I cannot be happy knowing that you harbor such thoughts of our father."

"You are too soft, too gentle. You must not be so, child. How do you think the world will use you if you continue so?"

"I had not thought of how the world would use me. I think of you, dear brother, and how it has used you. And I cannot bear that there should be ill-feeling between you and our father. And Cesare . . . oh, my brother . . . you spoke of murder!"

Cesare laughed aloud. Then he was tender. "Set your fears at rest, *bambina.* I would not murder him. What folly! From him come all our blessings."

"Do not forget it, Cesare. Do not forget it."

"I am a man who is full of rage, but not of folly," he answered. "I revenge myself in my own way. Our father insists that I go into the Church, and I insist on showing how unsuitable I am for that calling. That is why I roam the streets with my red-headed courtesan—in the hope of making our father realize that he cannot force me to continue this life."

"But Cesare, what of the rumors we have heard concerning your marriage with a Princess of Aragon?"

"Rumors," he said wearily. "Nothing more."

"Yet our father seemed to be considering this at one time."

"It was diplomacy to consider it, child. Naples suggested it in order to alarm the Sforzas of Milan, and our father encouraged it for political reasons."

"But he gave such a warm welcome to the ambassador, and everyone knew that he had arrived here to discuss a possible marriage between you and the Princess."

"Diplomacy. Diplomacy. Waste no time on considering it. I do not. My only hope is to show our father how unsuitable I am for the Church, or to find a way of forcing him to release me. But there is little hope. Our father has determined to make me a Cardinal."

"A Cardinal, Cesare! So that is the reason for your anger." She shook her head. "I am thinking of all those who bring presents to me and to

Giulia because they hope we will influence our father in giving them the Cardinal's hat. And you . . . on whom he longs to bestow it . . . want none of it. How strange life is!"

Cesare was clenching and unclenching his hands. "I fear," he said, "that once I am in my Cardinal's robes there will be no escape."

"Cesare, my brother, you will escape," she told him.

"I am DETERMINED," said the Pope, "that you shall become a Cardinal."

Cesare had once more broached the subject of release and because he felt that his sister might have a softening effect on their father, he had insisted that she accompany him into his presence.

"Father, I implore you to release me from the Church before you take this step."

"Cesare, are you a fool? What man in Rome would refuse such honors?"

"I am as no other man in Rome. I am myself and myself alone. I refuse this . . . this questionable honor."

"You can say this . . . before Almighty God!"

Cesare shook his head impatiently. "Father, you know, do you not, that once I am a Cardinal it will be more difficult to release me from my vows?"

"My son, there is no question of releasing you from your vows. Let us discuss this no more. Lucrezia, my love, bring your lute. I should like to hear you sing that new song of Serafino's."

"Yes, Father," said Lucrezia.

But Cesare would not allow her to sing and, although the Pope regarded his son with mild reproach, he did nothing more.

"You cannot make me a Cardinal, Father," said Cesare triumphantly. "I am your son, but your illegitimate son, and as you know full well no man can become a Cardinal unless he is of legitimate birth."

The Pope brushed aside his argument as though it were not more than a wasp which provided a temporary irritation.

"Now I understand your anxiety, my son. It is for this reason that you have been reluctant. You should have spoken of your fears earlier."

"So, Father, you see that it is impossible."

"You . . . a Borgia to talk of the impossible! Nonsense, my dear boy, nothing is impossible. A little difficulty, I'll admit; but have no fears, I have thought of ways of overcoming such."

"Father, I implore you to listen to me."

"I would rather listen to Lucrezia's singing."

"I will be heard! I will be heard!" shrieked Cesare.

Lucrezia began to tremble. She had heard him shout thus before, but never in their father's presence.

"I think, my son," said the Pope coolly, "that you are overwrought. It is due to riding in the sun in company unfitted to your state. I would suggest you refrain from such conduct which, I assure you, my dearest boy, brings distress to those who love you, but could bring greater harm to yourself."

Cesare stood, biting his lips, clenching and unclenching his hands.

There was a moment of fear when Lucrezia thought he was about to strike their father. The Pope sat, smiling benignly, refusing to accept this as a major difference between them.

Then Cesare seemed to regain his control; he bowed with dignity and murmured: "Father, I crave leave to depart."

"It is granted, my son," said Alexander gently.

Cesare went, and Lucrezia stared unhappily after him.

Then she, who was sitting on a stool at her father's feet, felt his hand on her head.

"Come, my love, the song! It is a pleasant one and sounds best on your sweet lips."

As she sang, the Pope caressed his daughter's golden hair, and they both temporarily forgot the unpleasant scene which Cesare had created; they both found it very easy to forget when it was comforting to do so.

⁂

In the Pope's private apartments Cardinals Pallavicini and Orsini sat with him.

"A simple matter," said the Pope, smiling benignly, "and I am sure it will present no difficulty to you . . . this little formality of proving that he who is known as Cesare Borgia is of legitimate birth."

The Cardinals were astonished, for the Pope had openly acknowledged Cesare as his son.

"But, Most Holy Lord, this is surely an impossibility."

"How so?" asked the Pope with bland surprise.

Orsini and Pallavicini looked at each other in bewilderment. Then Orsini spoke. "Holy Father, if Cesare Borgia is your son, how could it be that he is of legitimate birth?"

Alexander smiled from Orsini to Pallavicini as though they were two simple children.

"Cesare Borgia," he said, "is the son of Vannozza Catanei, a woman of Rome. At the time of his birth she was a married woman. That dispenses with Cesare's illegitimacy, for a child born in wedlock is legitimate, is he not?"

"Holiness," murmured Pallavicini, "we were unaware that the lady was married at the time of his birth. It is generally believed that it was not until after the birth of her daughter Lucrezia that she married Giorgio di Croce."

"It is true that the marriage with Giorgio di Croce took place after the birth of Lucrezia, but the lady was married before that. Her husband was a certain Domenico d'Arignano, who was an official of the Church."

The Cardinals bowed. "Then that proves Cesare Borgia to be legitimate, Holiness."

"It does indeed," said the Pope, smiling at them. "Let a bull be made stating his parentage and his legitimacy." His expression was regretful; it saddened him to deny his son; yet such denial there must be in the name of ambition. He added: "Since I had taken this young man under my patronage I allowed him to adopt the name of Borgia."

The Cardinals murmured: "We will immediately obey your wishes, Most Holy Father."

But when they had left him the Pope immediately set about drawing up another bull in which he declared that he was the father of Cesare Borgia. It saddened him a little that this bull must be a secret one—for a while.

Cesare raged up and down Lucrezia's apartment, and in vain did she try to soothe him.

"Not content," cried Cesare, "with forcing me into the Church my father now allows it to be said that I am the son of a certain Domenico d'Arignano. And who is Domenico d'Arignano, I beg you tell me. Who has ever heard of Domenico d'Arignano?"

"They will hear of him now," said Lucrezia gently. "The whole world will hear of him. His claim to fame will be that he was named as your father."

"Insult after insult!" cried Cesare. "Humiliation after humiliation! How much longer must I endure this state of affairs?"

"My dearest brother, our father but wishes to advance you. In his opinion, it is necessary that you become a Cardinal, and this is the only way in which he can make you one."

"So he denies me!"

"It is only for a while."

"Never," cried Cesare, beating his fists on his chest, "will I forget that my father has denied me."

Meanwhile Alexander had called together a Consistory, that Cesare might be declared legitimate.

He had chosen this moment because so many had left Rome. The weather was hot and sultry and there had been reports of plague in various quarters. When pestilence crept into the city those who could invariably made an excuse to escape to their estates and vineyards in the country. This was such a time.

Alexander knew that there had been a great deal of opposition among the Cardinals on account of the favors he had bestowed on his family and friends; the matters he had to lay before them now concerned not only his son but the brother of his mistress, for although he had promised Giulia that her brother should have his Cardinal's hat it had not yet been bestowed upon him.

There were few Cardinals present at the Consistory, which pleased

Alexander. Better to deal with a few opponents than many. But those who were present were suspicious because they understood that this was a preliminary move and they feared what was to come. Alexander carried nepotism too far, they said to one another. It would not be long before every man in any position of importance was one put there to serve the Pope.

And their suspicions increased when Alexander folded his beautiful hands, smiled his most benign smile and declared: "My Lord Cardinals, make the necessary preparations. Tomorrow we elect the new Cardinals."

Then all was clear. Cesare had been declared legitimate that he might be made a Cardinal.

There was a faint murmur throughout the assembly, and many eyes were turned to Cardinal Carafa who had on previous occasions shown himself bold enough to oppose the Pope.

"Most Holy Lord," said Carafa, "has your Holiness given due consideration to the usefulness of making these nominations?"

Again that bland smile. "The question of creating these Cardinals concerns me alone."

"Holiness," said a voice from the assembly, "there are many among us who feel that it is not necessary to make new Cardinals at this time."

The smile disappeared from the face of the Pope, and for a moment all those assembled caught a glimpse of an Alexander who usually remained hidden.

Carafa boldly went on: "The point is, Holiness, that we know some of those names which you intend to propose, and we do not think they are suitable for the office, nor would we wish them to be our colleagues."

This was a direct reference to Cesare's reputation and a reminder that he had been seen in the city in the company of the courtesan, Fiametta. Cesare had deliberately flaunted his friendship with the woman, anticipating a scene such as this.

It was characteristic of Alexander that his anger should be not against Cesare but the Cardinals.

He seemed to grow in stature. The Cardinals trembled before him, for there was a legend in Rome that no man of Alexander's age could possess such virility, such amazingly good health, unless he was superhuman.

Those Cardinals felt that legend to be true as now their Pope faced them in his unaccustomed anger.

"You must learn who Alexander VI is," he cried. "And if you persist in your intransigence I shall annoy you all by making as many new Cardinals as I wish. You will never drive me from Rome, and any who try to, or oppose me in any way, will be very foolish men. You should really ponder on how foolish they will be."

There was a short silence while Alexander looked angrily at the crest-fallen Cardinals before him.

Then with the utmost dignity he went on: "Now we will nominate the new Cardinals."

And when the assembly saw that at the head of the list were the names of Cesare Borgia and Alessandro Farnese, and that all the thirteen proposed were men who could be trusted to work for the Pope against his enemies, they realized that there was nothing they dared do but agree to their election.

Alexander smiled at them, and the benevolent look had returned to his face.

WHEN THE CARDINALS had left the Pope's presence they discussed the situation.

Della Rovere, who always looked upon himself as a leader, recovered his belligerence although in the presence of the Pope he had been as subdued as the rest.

His one-time enemy Ascanio Sforza supported him. How long were they to endure the outrageous nepotism of the Pope? they asked each other. Not content with making a Cardinal of his illegitimate son, he had done the same for his mistress's brother. All the new nominees were his pawns. Soon there would be scarcely a man in an influential position to raise his voice against Alexander.

And what was Alexander's policy? To enrich his own family and friends? It seemed so.

There were rumors in the city that men were dying mysteriously.

Cesare Borgia's evil reputation was growing; it was now said that he was interested in and made a study of the art of poisoning; and that he had many malignant recipes which came from the Spanish Moors. But from whom would Cesare have learned this lore? From his father?

"Beware of the Borgias!" Those words were becoming more and more frequently heard throughout the city.

Alexander was aware of what was happening and, fearing a schism, he acted with his usual vigor. He made Ascanio Sforza almost a prisoner in the Vatican; and seeing what had happened to Sforza, della Rovere made haste to leave Rome.

Lucrezia's husband apprehensively watched the growing unrest. His relative and patron, Ascanio Sforza, was powerless in the Vatican. Moreover Giovanni Sforza knew that the Pope was less pleased with the marriage of his daughter than he had been, and that already he was on the look-out for a bridegroom who could bring him more profit.

The marriage had never been consummated; the dowry had never been paid. What sort of marriage was this?

He was beset by fears on all sides. He could not sleep easily for he was sure that he was spied on in the Vatican. He was afraid of the Orsinis who were allies of Naples and had always been the enemies of Milan. Would they, he wondered, now that he was out of favor at the Vatican, feel it to be a good opportunity to dispose of him? If he wandered across the bridge of St. Angelo, would they come sweeping down from Monte Giordano and run a knife through his body? And if they did, who would care?

Giovanni Sforza was a man who was sorry for himself; he always had been. His relatives cared little for him—as did the new connections he had acquired through his marriage.

His little bride—she seemed a gentle creature, but he must not forget that she was one of them—was a Borgia, and who would trust a Borgia?

He wished though, during that time, that he and Lucrezia had been husband and wife in truth. She had a sweet and innocent face, and he believed he could have trusted her.

But it was too late to think of that now.

There was a great spectacle taking place in Rome at this time. This was the departure of little Goffredo for Naples where he was to marry Sanchia of Aragon.

Cesare and Lucrezia watched their little brother set out for Naples; he was accompanied by an old friend of Cesare's, Virginio Orsini, who had made the boy's first year at Monte Giordano tolerable, and who was now Captain-General of the Aragonese army. Goffredo's tutor also accompanied the party to Naples; this was Don Ferrando Dixer, a Spaniard; and the Pope to show he did not forget the country to which he belonged, entrusted two caskets of jewels—presents for the bride and bridegroom—to this Spaniard.

And so the auburn-haired Goffredo, aged eleven, rode out of Rome to his bride, to be made Prince of Squillace and Count of Coriata and to receive the order of the Ermine, the motto of which was "Better die than betray."

There was one who watched the departure with mingling pride and sorrow. The maternal Vannozza's dream had come true. Her little Goffredo was accepted as the son of Alexander; he was to be a Prince, and she was happy.

But there were times when she wished that she were a humble Roman mother with her children about her; there were times when she would have given up her vineyards and her house with the water cistern to be that.

Giovanni Sforza's anxiety was increased by the new friendship between Naples and the Vatican which the marriage of Goffredo and Sanchia must foster.

He was afraid to show himself in the streets for fear of enemies of his family; he was afraid of enemies within the Vatican circle. He had a beautiful wife but he was not allowed to live with her; he was lord of Pesaro, a town on the Adriatic coast which seemed to him, particularly at this time, a very peaceful spot, shut away from all strife by the mountains which protected it and blessed by the cool waters of the Foglia River. With the sea on one side and the mountains on the other Pesaro offered a freshness in contrast with the fetid air of Rome; and Sforza longed for Pesaro.

He sought audience of the Pope, because he felt he could no longer stay in Rome.

"Well, Giovanni Sforza," said Alexander, "what have you to say to me?"

"Holy Father, everyone in Rome believes that Your Holiness has entered into agreement with the King of Naples who is an enemy of the state of Milan. If this is so, my position is a difficult one since, as a captain of the Church, a post in which through your benevolence I have been installed, I am in the pay of Your Holiness, and also in that of Milan. I do not see how I can serve two masters without falling out with one of them. Would Your Holiness, out of your goodness, define my position, that I may serve you as I am paid to do yet not become an enemy of my own blood?"

Alexander laughed. "You take too much interest in politics, Giovanni Sforza. You would be wise to serve those who pay you."

Giovanni writhed before the calm gaze of the Pope and wished with all his heart that he had never agreed to marry with the Borgias.

"Your questions are answered, my son," continued Alexander. "Leave me now, and I beg of you do not concern yourself overmuch with politics. They do not touch your duty."

Giovanni went away and immediately wrote to his uncle, Ludovico of Milan, telling him of what he had said to the Pope and declaring that he would sooner have eaten the straw under his body than have entered into the marriage. He was casting himself upon his uncle's mercy.

But Ludovico was not prepared to offer him asylum. Ludovico was intently watching the growth of the friendship between Naples and the Vatican; he was not convinced that the bond between those two was of such importance as might be thought in Naples; the Pope was wily and Ludovico preferred to remain aloof.

Giovanni was impatient.

The plague was increasing throughout Rome, and his fears increased with it. In the position he held at the Vatican he was free to leave Rome if he wished.

One day, surrounded by some of his men, he rode out of the city bound for Pesaro.

Lucrezia DID not miss him in the least. She had seen little of him, and it was only at special functions that they had appeared together.

Giulia laughed at her as they played with Giulia's little daughter Laura, who was now nearly two years old.

"One would think you had gained a lover rather than lost one," said Giulia.

"A lover! He was never that." Lucrezia was wistful. One grew up, and she was fourteen now. Giulia had been fourteen when she had become Alexander's mistress.

"Well, do not show your pleasure in his departure quite so openly," advised Giulia.

"Is my Holy Father coming to see me?" asked little Laura, tugging at her mother's skirts.

Giulia picked up the child and smothered her with kisses. "Soon, I doubt not, my darling. He could not stay away long from his little Laura, could he?"

Lucrezia watched them, still wistful, thinking of those days when the same father had delighted other children whose nursery he had visited. Alexander—as tender a father to little Laura as he had been to her and Cesare, Giovanni and Goffredo—remained as young as he had been when she and her brothers were in the nursery. Now they were no longer children, and it seemed that wonderful and exciting things happened to them all except herself. She had been married, but hers was no real marriage; and she could be glad because her husband had now run away. Whether he had run away from the plague or from her, it mattered not. Whatever he ran away from he was a coward. Yes, she was sure he was a coward.

She had dreamed of a lover as magnificent as her father, as handsome as her brother Giovanni, as exciting as Cesare—and they had given her a small man, a widower, a cold man who made no protest because the marriage was not consummated; they had married her to a coward who ran away from the plague and did not attempt to take her with him.

Not that she wanted to go. But, she told herself, if Giovanni Sforza had been the sort of man who insisted on taking me, I should have wanted to go.

"Giulia," she said, "do you think that, now Giovanni Sforza has left me, my father will arrange a divorce?"

"It will depend," said Giulia, smoothing her daughter's long fair hair from her forehead, "on how useful the Holy Father considers the marriage."

"Of what use could it be . . . now?"

Giulia left her little daughter and going to Lucrezia laid her hand on her shoulder.

"No use at all," she said. "Depend upon it the marriage will be dissolved and then you will have a fine husband . . . a husband who will declare he will have none of this marriage which is no marriage. Moreover, you grow up, Lucrezia. You are old enough now for marriage. Oh yes, it will be a handsome husband this time. A true marriage."

Lucrezia smiled. "Let us wash each other's hair," she said; and Giulia agreed. It was a favorite occupation, for their golden hair must be washed every three days because after that time it darkened and lost something of its bright color, so they spent a great deal of time washing each other's hair.

And while they washed they talked of the handsome husband who would be Lucrezia's when the Pope had freed her from Giovanni Sforza. Lucrezia saw herself in a gown of crimson velvet sewn with pearls. She was kneeling on a cushion at the feet of her father and saying: "I will with a good heart." And the man who knelt beside her was a shadowy figure, but he combined the presence of her father and the qualities she so admired in her brothers.

It seemed to her as though it were a Borgia who knelt beside her.

Lucrezia quickly ceased to dream, because when her father became aware that Giovanni Sforza had left Rome he was angry and recalled him at once.

But safe in Pesaro among his own subjects, far from the conflict of politics and the threat of plague, Giovanni could be bold. He ignored the orders.

There were threats and promises, for Alexander was afraid of what this son-in-law might do, once he was out of his control.

And then finally the Pope declared that if Giovanni Sforza would return to Rome his marriage should be consummated and the dowry paid.

All waited eagerly to see what Sforza would do then; Lucrezia waited . . . in trepidation.

PESARO

Even with such baits held out to him, Giovanni Sforza was reluctant to return to Rome.

There was unrest throughout Italy, and Sforza was fully aware of this. This time it was not warring states of the peninsula which cast a shadow over the land; there was a mightier enemy.

The King of France had renewed his claims to the throne of Naples and had informed Alexander that he was sending a mission to the Vatican that the matter might be discussed.

Alexander, with his clever diplomacy, received the French mission graciously; and his reception of them was viewed with such disfavor throughout Italy that there were rumors that before long Alexander would be deposed. Della Rovere was alert; he was determined that next time the Papal throne was empty he would sit on it.

Alexander however was not perturbed. He had infinite belief in himself and was sure that he could make the best of a situation however ominous it seemed. Ferrante of Aragon had died and his son Alfonso was now King. Alfonso determined at all costs to keep the Papal friendship, and offered great bribes to Alexander in order to cement it. It was not in Alexander's nature to refuse the bribes, so he now allied himself with Alfonso; meanwhile the French were dissatisfied and threatened invasion.

In his retreat at Pesaro Giovanni Sforza watched what was going on but could not make up his mind which road to take. Ludovico of Milan had shown him quite clearly that he could not be trusted to help his relative in an emergency. The Pope was obviously strong since Alfonso of Naples was suing so ardently for Papal friendship. Therefore Giovanni Sforza decided that he would return to Rome.

⚜ 👑 ⚜

Lucrezia was waiting. Her hair had been freshly washed, her body perfumed. At last she was to be a bride.

The Pope had welcomed his son-in-law as though his absence had been a natural one. He had embraced him warmly and declared that he was glad to receive him and that his nuptial couch was waiting for him.

There were banquets and the usual crude jokes. It was almost like another wedding, but Lucrezia could not enjoy the celebrations so lightheartedly as she had the real wedding. That had been a masque with herself in the principal part; this was reality.

Her husband's attitude had changed toward her; she sensed that. He took her hand and she felt his breath on her face. At last he had noticed that she was beautiful.

So they danced together, the dances of Italy, not the Spanish dances which she had once danced with Giovanni on that occasion which was so like this and yet so different.

And then to that nuptial couch.

He was quiet and said little. She was prepared for what must take place—Giulia had prepared her—but she knew that it was going to be very different from Giulia's experience.

She was a little frightened, but serene as always, and she knew that if she did not experience the ecstasy for which she had longed, at least she would be able to endure it.

When they were alone in the great bed she said to him: "Tell me one thing first, Giovanni. Why did you wait so long before you came back?"

"It would have been foolish to return," he mumbled. "There was plague and . . . matters were uncertain."

He turned to her, impatient after all the months of waiting, but she held aloof with the faintest sign of fear in her big light eyes.

"Did you come back for the consummation . . . or for the dowry?"

"For both," he answered.

It was strange, bewildering, as Giulia had said; and yet it was not as Giulia had said. She was aware of excitement, of the discovery of a new world which seemed to be opening before her, of delights undreamed of. She knew that with another it would have been different; but even with this man it was adequate.

Yet with some . . .

She lay back smiling.

SHE HAD GROWN up overnight. Alexander and Giulia, who had noticed it, discussed it together.

"I am sorry for her," mused Giulia. "My own experience was so different. Poor Lucrezia with that cold and nervous creature! Holiness, you should dissolve the marriage and give her a real man."

Alexander clicked his tongue playfully. "Such ways to talk of marriage! Oh, she is young yet. She has her whole life before her. I do not however shelve the idea of arranging a divorce, but divorces are not easy to arrange. The Church abhors them."

"But if the Holy Father decided, the Church would fall in with his wishes," Giulia reminded him.

"Ah, wicked one, you mock. I must devise a punishment for you."

"I will say ten 'I love yous' and throw myself in worship at your feet, and cry 'Do with me as you will, Holy Father, for my body and soul belong to you.'"

"My Giulia . . . my little love. What should I do without you! But you will look after my Lucrezia, will you not? You will advise her, wise woman that you are!"

"How to take lovers and deceive her husband. As I did."

"'Twas no deceit. Poor little Orsino, he was willing that it should be so—most willing."

They laughed together while she assured him that she loved Lucrezia as a sister and that she would look after her as such.

Giulia wished though to discuss other matters. She was eager that the Pope should arrange a grand marriage for Laura, since she wanted all Italy to know that the little girl was accepted as his daughter.

"I will do it. Dearest little Laura shall have as fine a husband as you could wish."

He kept her with him. He needed the relaxation his relationship with her could give him. There were dark clouds over Rome at this time and he did not care to think of them. So he would be gay with his Giulia; he would make love as a young man while they both rejoiced in his virility.

That was the very best antidote to trouble, he had discovered.

THey were in Lucrezia's apartment—Lucrezia and Giulia. Their hair was loose about their shoulders. Giulia's reached to her feet, and Lucrezia could sit on hers. They had been washing it once more.

"There is sun on the balcony," said Giulia. "Let us go there and dry it. Drying it in the sun should make it more golden than ever."

"Should we go on to the balcony?"

"Why not?"

"Could not infection reach us there?"

"Oh, Lucrezia, are you not tired of being shut in the Palace? We must not go out . . . not even for a minute. I am weary of it all."

"It would be more wearying still if we caught the plague."

"I suppose so. I shall be glad when the hot weather has gone. Perhaps it will take the pestilential air with it."

Giulia rose and shook out her damp hair. "I shall go on to the balcony."

"Did you not promise the Holy Father that you would not?"

Giulia grimaced. "I did not mention the balcony. I said I would not go out."

"He may have meant the balcony."

"Then let us pretend he did not. I am going out there now. I am going to sit in the sun and dry my hair."

"No, Giulia, you should not."

But Giulia had already gone.

Lucrezia sat down thoughtfully, looking at the figure of the Madonna and the lamp before it.

"Holy Mother," she prayed. "Let all be well soon."

There was much that was wrong, she knew. It was not only the plague; that was a frequent visitor. There were ugly rumors about her father. She had heard the servants whispering; she had not told anyone she had heard, because servants might be whipped or even more terribly punished for saying some of the things which she had overheard. They had said that the Pope's position was insecure and that there were many who wanted him to be removed and a new Pope set up in his place. Invasion was threatened by the French, and there were some who said that the Pope was a secret ally of Italy's enemy.

All these matters made her very uneasy. She did not know much about her husband's political feelings. They shared their bed now and she was in truth a wife, but a vaguely dissatisfied one. Giulia had said that he was cold; she had discovered that she herself was by no means so. She did not understand herself; desire—vague desire for someone unknown—was aroused in her, but it was not satisfied by Giovanni. She would lie beside him listening to his snoring and long to feel a lover's arms about her. Not Giovanni's. But there were times when she began to believe that any lover was better than none.

The love she experienced was very different from that which Giulia knew, but then Giulia's lover was that incomparable man, Alexander.

Somewhere in the world there would be the lover she desired, for there must be other men in the world who had the qualities of the Borgias.

But these were her own affairs and Lucrezia was rarely selfish, so that the affairs of others invariably seemed of as great importance—if not greater—to her than her own.

She could find time to think of poor Cesare, more furious than ever because now danger threatened and he was unable to act. He longed to have his own *condotta* in the army; here was a chance for military glory, and he was denied it. Adriana had become very pious again and spent a lot of time on her knees, so it was clear that she was very worried.

She heard shouting from the piazza and as she ran to the balcony to see what was happening, Giulia fell almost fainting into her arms.

There was blood on Giulia's forehead.

"What happened?" She looked from Giulia to the balcony.

"Do not go out there," said Giulia. "Am I bleeding? They saw me there. A crowd gathered in no time. Did you hear what they said of me?"

"I heard the shouting. Please sit down. I will bathe your forehead."

She clapped her hands and a slave came running.

"Bring me a bowl of water and soft cloths," she cried, "and tell none why you bring them."

Giulia looked at Lucrezia earnestly. "They called me lewd names," she said. "And they mentioned the Holy Father."

"They . . . they dare not!"

"But they *dared*, Lucrezia. That means that something more than we realize is happening in the city."

"Do you think they mean to depose him?"

"He'll never allow them to do that."

The slave came in with the water. Lucrezia took it and Giulia said: "I fell as I stepped on to the balcony and I have grazed my forehead."

The slave bowed and went away, but she did not believe Giulia.

They know of this trouble, thought Lucrezia. They know more than we have been allowed to.

※ ♔ ※

It was impossible to keep secret the news that stones had been thrown at the Pope's mistress who was on a balcony of Lucrezia's palace. When Alexander heard of it he came hurrying to them.

In spite of the dangerous position in which Alexander knew himself to be, his greatest concern at that moment was the safety of his mistress and daughter.

He embraced them tenderly and for the first time since the war clouds had appeared over his head he showed anxiety.

"But, my darling, let me see this wound. We must make sure there is no infection. Holy Mother of God, it might have been your eye. But the saints have preserved you, my precious one, and the wound is not great. And, Lucrezia, oh, my precious little daughter, you were unhurt. I thank the Virgin for that."

He held them both against him as though he would never let them go, and as each looked up into his face, she was aware of the conflict there.

"You must not be anxious, dearest Father," said Lucrezia. "We will take the greatest care. We will not venture on to the balcony until all this trouble is over."

The Pope released them and went thoughtfully to the figure of the Madonna. He stood beside it, his lips moving slightly. He was praying, and they were both aware that he was urging himself to make a decision.

Slowly he turned to them, and he was the old firm Alexander again.

"My darlings," he said, "I now have to do something which grieves me as nothing else could. I am going to send you away from Rome."

"Please do not do that, Father," begged Lucrezia. "Let us stay with you. We will promise *never* to go out. But to be away from you would be the worst that could befall us."

He smiled and laid a hand on her head.

"And my Giulia, what has she to say?"

Giulia had thrown herself at his feet and taken his hand. Giulia was thinking: Something more terrible than even the plague is threatening Rome. The French armies may invade us . . . they will set up a Pope of their own choosing, and who knows what will happen to Alexander?

Giulia had found Alexander a very satisfactory lover, accomplished and experienced; she did not doubt that she had been fortunate in having the best tutor in Rome. But part of Alexander's attraction had been his power; the knowledge, first that he was the richest Cardinal in Rome, and later the Pope himself. Such was Giulia's nature that all this had added to her pleasure. To imagine him without his glory, perhaps a humiliated prisoner of the French, made him appear a different person from the all-powerful, ever-indulgent and generous lover by whom it was an honor to be loved.

Giulia was therefore not entirely dismayed by the thought of retirement to a safe place until it had been settled whether or not Alexander was to retain his power.

She gave no sign of this; and Alexander who would have immediately detected duplicity in a statesman, was unaware of it in his mistress. This was partly due to that constant desire to see only that which he wished to see.

He was as devoted to Giulia as ever. The gap in their years made her seem, even now that she was a mother, a young and artless girl. Her passion had always seemed spontaneous; her joy in him as great as his in her. Therefore he believed that she would be as heartbroken to leave him as he would be to lose her.

"We will not leave you," said Giulia. "We will face anything, Holy Father, rather than do so. I would rather die of the plague or at the sword of foreign soldiers than . . ."

"Stop, I beg you," said Alexander wincing. "You know not what you are saying."

Giulia had recovered herself; she stood up and her face was as guileless as Lucrezia's. She said: "Tis true, is it not, Lucrezia? We would rather face . . . anything . . . anything . . ." She paused that Alexander might visualize the utmost horrors. . . . "Yes," she continued, "anything rather than leave you."

Lucrezia threw her arms about her father. "It is true, dearest Father," she cried; and she meant it.

"My darling girls!" murmured Alexander, and his voice was broken with emotion. "But it is because I love you as I do that I must be relentless in this matter. I cannot allow you to stay. I cannot imagine how dark my life will be without you; all I know is that it would be even darker if aught happened to you through my selfishness in keeping you here. The French are gathering their forces. They are a strong nation, and determined to have Naples. But they will not be content with Naples. Who can tell, we may see foreign soldiers in Rome. And my beloved, my Giulia, you think of death at the hands of foreign soldiers, but it is not always as simple as that. You are so young . . . so very beautiful. There were never two more lovely creatures in the world. And what would your fate be if you were to fall into the hands of brutal soldiery, think you? I will not think of it. I dare not think of it. I prefer to lose the brightness of your presence rather than think of it."

"Then let us go away for as short a time as is necessary to ease your mind," soothed Giulia.

"I hope it will not be too far from Rome," added Lucrezia wistfully.

"Rest assured, my precious ones, that as soon as it is safe for you to be here, I shall hold you in my arms again."

He embraced them both and continued to hold them against him.

"These are my plans, my dearest girls. Lucrezia shall visit her husband's domain of Pesaro. It is to Pesaro that I propose to send you both."

THere was one who was filled with delight at the prospect of leaving Rome, and that was Giovanni Sforza. He assured the Pope that his first care should be the two girls whom the Holy Father was placing under his protection, and he fervently agreed with His Holiness that Rome in this May of the year 1494 was no place for them.

So on a beautifully sunny day there was gathered in St. Peter's Square a crowd of babbling servants and excited slaves to complete the cortège which was to journey to Pesaro. Giulia declared that she could not travel without her hairdressers, dressmakers, and all the servants necessary to her comfort; Lucrezia, knowing how those of her retinue would grieve if left behind, was equally insistent that hers should accompany her. In vain did Giovanni Sforza point out that they would have less need of all their fripperies in quiet Pesaro; the girls would not listen; and Giovanni, eager only to escape from Rome as quickly as possible, gave way.

Adriana, with her priests and servants, was also in the procession; and the Pope stood on his balcony watching until he could see the last of those two golden heads which brought so much pleasure into his life.

When they had gone he retired to his apartments and shut himself away to mourn their absence. He gave himself up to the study of the political stiuation, determined that he would employ every ounce of energy he possessed to make Rome a safe place, so that he might bring back his beloved girls to brighten his life.

As they left Rome behind them Lucrezia was surprised to see how Giulia's spirits rose.

"One would think," she said, "that you are glad to leave the Holy Father."

"It is no use harboring melancholy which can do nothing but make further melancholy. Let us forget we are in exile from our Holy Father and our beloved city. Let us make the most of what we have."

"That will not be easy," said Lucrezia. "Did you not notice how sad he was?"

"He is the wisest man in Rome," Giulia assured her. "He will very soon cast off his sorrow. It is he who has taught me my philosophy of life. He'll soon be making merry. Therefore let us also make as merry as we can."

"That is certainly his philosophy," agreed Lucrezia.

"Then let us be gay . . . I wonder what kind of city this Pesaro is."

On they went northwards across the leg of Italy, and through every town they passed the people turned out to see the strangers from Rome. They marvelled at the two golden-haired beauties in their rich dresses; they stared at little Laura, who was with her mother, and marvelled because they had heard rumors that this child, like the golden-haired Lucrezia, was the Pope's own daughter.

They hung out banners of welcome, and the lords of the various towns through which they passed entertained them royally. Such entertainments amused the people and, as no one was sure yet that Alexander would be deposed, it would be unwise to offend, at this stage, one who, legend had it, was endowed with superhuman powers.

Giovanni Sforza's spirits rose as the distance between himself and Rome increased. He took on new stature; he even became something like the lover of whom Lucrezia had dreamed; and she, always ready to be contented, found that, as far as her married life was concerned, she had never been happier.

How Giovanni glowed with pride to see the banners displayed in their honor, to be treated as an equal by some of the lords such as those of Urbino who had previously thought themselves far above him.

Giovanni was realizing at last the honor which could come to him through his union with the Borgias, and that made him tender toward his wife and very eager to please her; and since she was ready to be pleased, the harmonious relationship between them continued all through that journey.

Sforza sent notice of their impending arrival to Pesaro and instructed his servants there that he wanted a welcome such as they had never given before; he wished flowers to be strewn in the streets and banners to be set up; he wanted verses to be written so that on their arrival they might be recited to him and his bride.

And so he was delighted as they made the arduous journey across the Apennines, and he congratulated himself on having a wife who was not only easy to arouse to ardor, who was not only a beauty, but the daughter of a man who, even if his power was threatened, most would agree, was the mightiest in Italy.

So he prepared for the triumphant entry into Pesaro.

Lucrezia and Giulia had not failed to wash their hair the night before the day of the entry. Lucrezia was to wear a rich gown embroidered with gold, and her golden hair was to be caught up in a net set with many jewels.

She lay beside her husband thinking of the next day, sleepily remembering the passion he had shown during the journey, passion of which she had not thought him capable. She wished that he would wake up and that there might be more lovemaking.

Then she wondered what was happening in Rome and whether her father had recovered from his unhappiness. Giulia did not seem to regret very much that they had left him, although it was certain that he would have found comfort with another woman.

Strange that Giulia did not care. But perhaps it was as well, for if Giulia had cared she would be unhappy, and as the Pope would undoubtedly find means of comforting himself, it was fortunate that Giulia should be reconciled to the parting.

The wind was rising, and she could hear the rain beating down.

She hoped the sun would be shining in the morning.

"Giovanni," she murmured, "do you hear the wind rising?"

He was not very handsome; he was not like the lover of whom she had dreamed; but she had always been ready to compromise. She would endow him with beauty and with qualities he did not possess, and think of him as she wished him to be, rather than as he was.

She touched his cheek lightly with her finger. His face twitched and he put up a hand as though to brush away a fly.

"Giovanni," she whispered.

But he only snored.

* * *

THey roDe into Pesaro in heavy rain and violent storm.

From the windows hung bedraggled banners; some had been blown down and lay neglected on the ground. The Lord of Pesaro had commanded that there should be banners, and banners his subjects provided; but the wind was cruel and obeyed no lord; so the entry into Pesaro was not the triumphal affair which its Lord had planned.

Giulia was angry; the rain had saturated her lovely hair so that it looked dark yellow instead of gold. Her beautiful dress was ruined.

"A curse on Pesaro!" cried Giulia, and wished herself in Rome.

Adriana murmured prayers as they rode. Her clothes were clinging to her uncomfortably, and the wind caught at her hair beneath its net; she felt undignified thus, and her dignity meant much to Adriana. Still she was calm and there was a certain triumph in her face. She was telling herself: "Anything will be better than Rome at this time."

Lucrezia's beautiful dress was ruined and her hair in the same state as Giulia's. One of her servants had found a large cape which she wrapped about her mistress so that all her glory was hidden to those few who had endured the wind and rain to watch the entry of the new Countess.

"I doubt not," she said to Giulia, "that the sun will shine tomorrow."

"As doubtless we shall be in bed, nursing fevers, that will matter little to us," grumbled Giulia.

They came to the Sforza palace and here, as ordered, were the poets waiting to read their verses of praises to their Lord and his bride.

So they must all stand in the rain and the wind whilst, huddled beneath the arches, the shivering poets read their verses welcoming their Countess to her home in sunny Pesaro.

Giulia sneezed, while Adriana silently prayed that the poets had kept their verses short, and Lucrezia, her beauty hidden by the great cloak, and her golden hair falling about her face in strands like dull yellow serpents, smiled as was expected of her, but her relief was obvious when the address was over.

What joy to be inside the palace, to dry and warm themselves by the great fire, to eat hot food and giggle with Giulia about the terrible journey to Pesaro which they would enjoy recalling because it was over.

But with the next day came the sunshine, and there was Pesaro before them in all its beauty.

Lucrezia, looking at the lovely expanse of Adriatic on which the town stood, the green hills surrounding it in a charming semi-circle at each end of which were the tall mountains of Accio and Ardizio, was delighted with her new home.

"Here," she told Giulia, "one feels shut away from the rest of the world."

"That is why we were sent here, to be safe until the conflict passes."

"I believe I could be happy," said Lucrezia, "if my father and my brothers were with me."

"Oh, Lucrezia, you will have to learn to be happy without your father and your brothers."

During the next days Lucrezia tried to be.

Giovanni's subjects had done their best to entertain their Countess in such a way that she would know how pleased they were to have her among them. There were banquets, dances, and carnival. The little streets of the town were full of laughing people, of clowns in grotesque costumes, and jugglers who had their tricks to perform in honor of Madonna Lucrezia. There had never been such gaiety in Pesaro, declared the people, and it was all in honor of the new Countess.

Lucrezia appeared among them and won their hearts, not only with her golden beauty, but with her obvious appreciation of all that they were doing for her.

Giulia and Lucrezia put their heads together and devised a program of merrymaking, determined to make the people of Pesaro see such magnificence as they had never seen before. They brought out their most splendid dresses that they might dazzle the provincials and give them a glimpse of how splendid Roman society was.

They were determined to outshine a local beauty, Caterina Gonzaga di Montevecchio, of whom they had heard so much, but they were a little apprehensive, as the fame of this woman's beauty had traveled as far as Rome.

They washed their hair, put on their jeweled nets, each assuring the other that she had never looked more beautiful; the dresses of silk and brocade set with gems which they were wearing were such as they would have worn for a state occasion in Rome. Thus magnificently dressed they set out, with Giovanni as their escort, for the Gonzaga ball.

It was an evening of triumph. They studied the far-famed beauty and discovered that although she had a beautiful skin and figure, her nose was fat, her teeth ugly and her hair was insignificant beside the long gold tresses of Guilia and Lucrezia.

Giulia became hilariously gay; Lucrezia more serenely joyous; and as soon as they arrived back at the Sforza palace they sat down to write to the Holy Father and tell him all about it, describing the appearance of Caterina, because they knew His Beatitude may have had the impression that she was more beautiful than she really was.

Giulia added that Lucrezia was satisfied with her new home and that she was in good health. The people of Pesaro were devoted to Sforza, she wrote, and there had been continual festivities, dancing, singing, and masques. As for herself, being absent from His Holiness, on whom all her happiness depended, she was unable to take any delight or satisfaction in the gaiety. Her heart was with one who was the treasure of her life. She trusted that His Holiness would not forget them but soon bring them back to him.

Such letters delighted the Pope. He demanded that they should write every day, and assured them that every detail of their lives was of the utmost importance to him.

This appeared to be so because, although the French were about to invade Italy and his enemies within the peninsula were seeking to depose him, he was quite happy when he received letters from his beloved girls.

And when some weeks later news reached him that Lucrezia was confined to her bed with a fever, he was thrown into an agony of fear for her life. He shut himself into his apartments, would see no one, blamed himself for allowing her to go away from him while he made feverish plans for bringing her back despite the dangers.

He wanted them with him. He could not enjoy life without them. He wrote that absence from Giulia aroused within him a demon of sensuality which could only be placated by her; of all his children, he realized now there was none he cared for as for his golden-haired little beauty. How could he have thought that the love he bore his sons could compare with that which a man such as he was must feel for one as delicately formed, as exquisitely beautiful, as his Lucrezia. They must return. They must not be parted again. Whatever the dangers they must face them together.

"Donna Lucrezia, my beloved daughter," he wrote in anguish. "You have given us days of deepest misery. There was evil news in Rome, bitter and terrible news that you were dead or that there was no hope for your life. You will understand the sorrow caused us on account of the great love we bear you which is greater than that which we have for anyone else on Earth. We thank God and our Glorious Lady that they have removed you from danger, but we shall not be happy until we see you in person."

So the letters traveled back and forth between Rome and Pesaro and, although it seemed to many that Alexander was on the edge of disaster, he refused to acknowledge this and declared that he would give all he had for the return of his darlings.

※ ♛ ※

Giovanni Sforza wanted nothing so much as to stay in Pesaro; there he believed he was sheltered from the disasters of invasion; the French would surely not cross the Apennines to take possession of such an insignificant Dominion. Moreover Lucrezia, removed from the influence of her father, was a contented and loving wife. Why should they not stay in Pesaro for the rest of their lives?

There was one drawback to this. On account of his post in the Church he was in the pay of the Pope; and although as a Sforza he worked for Milan, his kinsman Ludovico, preparing for invasion of which he knew he must be one of the first victims, had little time or money to spare for

Giovanni. Therefore Giovanni's income from Milan had not been paid for some time and, if he disobeyed the Pope by keeping his daughter from him, how could he expect his income from the Papacy to be paid?

Giovanni was a perplexed man during those weeks of festivities when Lucrezia and Giulia were flaunting their fine clothes and splendor at his provincial court.

Alexander understood his son-in-law perfectly. A meek man, a coward of a man, thought Alexander; the kind of man whom he despised. He knew that Giovanni was cowering in Pesaro, far from the impending conflict, and hoped to stay there keeping Lucrezia from her father.

That should not be; and, since if Giovanni decided to keep his wife at his side it would be a most delicate matter for the Pope to demand her return, Alexander arranged that Giovanni Sforza should be given a Neapolitan Brigade, and sent orders to Pesaro that he should at once set out to take over his command.

When Giovanni received this communication he was dumb-founded.

He strode into Lucrezia's apartment and demanded that she read the despatch from Rome.

"To leave at once . . . for Naples," read Lucrezia. "You . . . Giovanni . . . to go to Naples? But your family and the Neapolitans have always been enemies."

"That is so," cried Giovanni. "What is your father planning? Does he wish to destroy me?"

"How could he wish to destroy my husband when he declares his greatest pleasure is in pleasing me?"

"Perhaps he thinks that by destroying me he would not displease you."

"Giovanni!" Lucrezia's wide eyes were imploring him to say no more. She greatly feared scenes such as this.

"Oh yes," stormed Giovanni. "He wants you back with him. He cannot exist without you. Is that not what he says? Do you think I do not understand why? Do you think I am a fool?"

"He is my beloved father, it is true."

Giovanni laughed aloud. "Your beloved father! That is amusing. The whole of Italy laughs. The Pope is the beloved father of Madonna Lucrezia, and he yearns to shelter her beneath the apostolic robe."

"Giovanni, you are hysterical."

It was true. Giovanni was terrified. He saw himself caught in the Papal web. His relatives in Milan had no time for him; his father-in-law, the Pope, wished him out of the way; therefore he was to be sent to the enemies of his family. What would become of him?

"I shall refuse to obey the Pope's commands," he said. "Does he think I do not see what they mean?"

"Oh, Giovanni," said Lucrezia, "you would be ill-advised to disobey my father."

"You would advise me to obey, would you not! You would say 'Go to the Neapolitans. Accept this command with them. You are a Sforza and sworn enemy of the Neapolitans, but go, go . . . because my father wishes you out of the way, so that I may return to him . . . and that I may live close to him, and the rumors may grow and grow . . . and grow. . . .'"

He began to laugh, but his face was twitching with fear.

She sought to calm him; but he only shouted: "I shall not go—do you hear me? I shall not go."

❧ ♔ ❧

There was further trouble. News came from Capodimonte, Giulia's native town, that her brother Angelo was very ill and the family believed that he could not live.

Giulia was distraught. She was very fond of her family, particularly her brothers Angelo and Alessandro.

She came to Lucrezia, and never in the course of their friendship had Lucrezia seen Giulia so distressed.

"It is news from my home," Giulia explained.

"My dearest Giulia, how sorry I am!" cried Lucrezia. "We must pray that all will be well."

"I must do more than pray," Giulia told her. "I shall go to him. I cannot let him die without seeing him again."

"You remember my father's orders . . . We were not to leave Pesaro without his consent."

"My brother is dying, do you understand? What if Cesare or Giovanni were dying? Would you not go to them?"

"But it is not Cesare, nor Giovanni," said Lucrezia calmly. "It is only Angelo."

"He is as much my brother as Cesare and Giovanni are yours."

But Lucrezia could not concede that. Giulia did not understand the bonds which bound the Borgia family. And the Pope would be angry if Giulia left Pesaro to go to her family.

"Why," pointed out Lucrezia, "Orsino is at Bassanello, and that is not very far from Capodimonte. You know how my father dislikes you to be anywhere near your husband."

"I need not see Orsino."

"But he might come to you. Oh, Giulia, if you value my father's love, do not go to Capodimonte."

Giulia was silent. She was torn between her desire to see her brother and her wish to please the Pope.

Giovanni left for Naples. Lucrezia said farewell to him without any great regret. During the last days she had seen what a weak man she had married, and she longed for the strength which she had always admired in her father and brothers.

Giovanni, furious and humiliated, had decided that as he could not serve the enemies of his family he would pretend to do so and send information to his family as to the moves made by the Neapolitan army. He would be doing dangerous work, and if he were discovered, as a spy he would be in acute danger. But what could he do? How else could he reconcile himself with his family? He was a small ruler of a small community; he was a provincial lord who could not live without the support of his family and the Pope.

Gloom descended on the palace after Giovanni had left. There were no more entertainments; the girls had no inclination for them. They would sit in the apartment, Lucrezia amusing Laura while Giulia watched at the window for a messenger from Capodimonte.

There came a day when that messenger arrived, and the news he brought was grave. Angelo Farnese was on his death-bed; there was no doubt of that; he had expressed a desire to see his beloved sister Giulia who had brought so many honors to the family. That decided Giulia.

She turned to Lucrezia. "I am leaving at once for Capodimonte," she said. "I am determined to see my brother before he dies."

"You must not go," insisted Lucrezia. "My father will be displeased."

But Giulia was firm, and that day she, with Laura and Adriana, set out for Capodimonte.

Giovanni, Giulia, Laura and Adriana had gone.

What changes, pondered Lucrezia, as she was left in loneliness at Pesaro, were taking place all around her.

In the Orsini castle at Bassanello, Orsino Orsini was brooding.

Like Giovanni Sforza, he was a weak man. Giovanni could never forget that he belonged to a small branch of the Sforza family and was despised by his wealthier relations; Orsino could not forget that he was small in stature, that he squinted, and that not even humble serving girls were eager for his attentions.

Often he brooded on the way he was treated. It seemed that they had mocked him even more than was necessary by marrying him to one of the most beautiful women in Italy, one who had already become the Pope's mistress before she was his wife.

It was as though they said: "Oh, but it is only Orsino, and Orsino is of no account."

His mother even had played a prominent part in his humiliation. "Don't be silly, Orsino," she had reproved him. "Think what favors Giulia can make the Pope bestow on you. Riches! Land! They are more profitable than a wife. In any case if it's women you want there will be many at your disposal."

La Bella Giulia! She was notorious throughout Italy. The Pope's mistress! Mother of the Pope's child! And she was married to Orsino who was never allowed to go near her for fear of offending the Pope!

Orsino swore an oath.

"This is an end to my humiliation. She has left the Pope. She is at

Capodimonte and, by all the saints, I swear she shall be my wife in truth. I swear to take her from her lover."

From his castle he looked out on the little village clustered about the old church with its campanile, six stories high; he gazed at the quiet valley through which the Tiber flowed. About him, all seemed at peace. But if he did what they expected of him he would not long enjoy peace. His family were firm allies of the Neapolitans and he was in command of a brigade. Soon he would have to leave this place and join the Neapolitan camp. Then he would be far away from Giulia and, if the Pope heard she had come to Capodimonte to visit her dying brother, he would not be so disturbed as he would be if he knew that Orsino Orsini was in the neighborhood.

But why should one placate the Pope? Why was it so necessary now? The French were on the way with a mighty army, and it was said that one of their objects would be to depose Alexander. Well then, was there the same need to placate the Pope?

"By the saints, I will have what is mine!" vowed Orsino.

He sent for one of his captains, and when the man came to him he said: "You will take the troops to Umbria. I have orders that they are to proceed there."

The man acknowledged the order but Orsino saw the astonished look which came into his eyes.

"I am feeling unwell," Orsino explained. "I feel a fever creeping upon me. I cannot accompany you. I must remain behind for a while."

He was smiling slyly as he dismissed the captain.

Now he had taken the first step.

The Holy Father was about to lose a mistress, and he, Orsino Orsini, was about to gain a wife.

WHEN HIS MEN had left he set out for Capodimonte where both his mother and Giulia were surprised to see him.

"But what means this?" cried Adriana. "Should you not be with your men in camp?"

"I will be where I wish to be," said Orsino.

Giulia cried: "But we understood you had orders."

Orsino regarded her intently. It was not for nothing that she was known as La Bella throughout Italy. He was suddenly tortured by a hundred images of what her lovemaking with that connoisseur of love, the Holy Father, must have been; and he was maddened by mingled anger and desire.

He answered her: "The time has come when I have decided to order my own life."

"But . . ." began Giulia.

"And yours," said Orsino.

"This is madness," retorted Giulia. She looked at her mother-in-law, but Adriana was silent. She was thinking quickly. She did not believe that Milan would stand up against the onslaught of the French. She believed that very soon the foreigners would be in Rome. If they reached Rome, then Alexander's days as Pope were numbered. A woman as shrewd as Adriana did not go on placating a man about to fall. If Italy were invaded it would be families such as the Orsinis and Colonnas who would survive; and Orsino, squint-eyed though he might be, was a powerful Orsini. Let him show a little spirit and his physical deformity would be forgotten.

Adriana lifted her shoulders. "He is your husband when all is considered," she answered.

And she left them together.

Giulia, startled, faced Orsino.

"Orsino, do not be foolish," she said.

He had approached her, and seized her by the wrist.

"You know," she cried, "that the Pope has forbidden you to come near me."

He laughed, and gripping her by the shoulders shook her roughly. "Has it not occurred to you that it might be my place to forbid the Pope to come near you?"

"Orsino!"

"La Bella," he said, "you have brought great profit to your family. You have considered all the demands they have made upon you." His eyes were on her smooth white neck on which she wore the sparkling diamond necklace which had been a gift from her lover. He pulled the necklace and the clasp snapped. He flung it from him without looking where it fell. And it was as though, as his hands touched her warm flesh, he made a decision. There would be no more prevarication. Not even for a moment.

"If you touch me," she cried, "you will have to answer to . . ."

"I answer to none," he said. "I would remind you of something which you seem to have forgotten . . . now, as when you married me. You are my wife."

"Think carefully, Orsino."

"This is not the time for thinking."

She pressed her hands against his chest; her eyes were imploring; the lovely golden hair escaped from its net.

"Now!" he said. "This moment. . . ."

"No," she cried. "I will not. Orsino . . . I hate you. Let me go. At a time like this! My brother dying . . . and . . . and . . ."

"There should have been other times," he said. "A hundred times . . . a thousand times. I've been a fool, but I'm a fool no longer. Those times have passed. This shall not."

She was breathless, determined on escape. But he was equally determined; and he was the stronger of the two.

After a while she gave up struggling.

❧♔❧

ANGELO WAS DEAD. He had embraced his sister for the last time and told her that she must always thank the Virgin for her beauty and remember that through it she was able to lay the foundations of her family's greatness.

He did not know what was happening beyond the palace walls. He did not know what was happening within them. She was never free from Orsino. He was full of demands; he insisted on his rights; and he would take no refusal.

She herself was a sensual woman and as such was beginning to find a certain excitement in her encounters with Orsino.

Alexander would be furious, but she was powerless. She was a prisoner in Capodimonte at the mercy of a husband who had been kept away from her for years. Alexander was an accomplished lover, Orsino something of a boor, but the boor provided a stimulating change; and it amused her to submit to what was almost rape and yet was legitimate behavior for a married pair.

She was sorry Lucrezia was not with her, so that she might have confided in her.

As for the Orsini family, they naturally supported their kinsman. Orsino was within his rights in his demands, they declared. Her lover? They could laugh now at an old man in decline. He would not last long.

Adriana had changed too. "I must support my son," she declared. "It is the most natural thing in the world that he should insist on his wife's living with him."

News of what had happened eventually reached Alexander.

Never had anyone seen him so furiously angry as he was at that time. He paced up and down his apartments, threatening excommunications right and left. He would not leave Giulia in the hands of that boor, that cross-eyed idiot. She must be brought back to Rome at once.

Why had she been allowed to leave Pesaro? What of his daughter? Was she conniving at this plot against him?

He wrote to Lucrezia. It was bad enough, he wrote, that a daughter should be so lacking in filial love that she showed no wish to return to her father, but that she should disobey him passed all understanding. He was bitterly disappointed in one whom he had loved beyond everything on Earth. She was deceitful and indifferent to him, and the letters she was writing to her brother Cesare were not written in the same sly way as were those she wrote to him.

When Lucrezia heard thus from her father she was desperately unhappy.

There had always been quarrels between Giovanni and Cesare, but never between her and the other members of her family. And that her father should write to her in this way wounded her deeply.

Desperately lonely, she fell into a mood of melancholy. What had happened to the beloved family? They were all separated now. No wonder there was misunderstanding. Giovanni was in Spain, and Goffredo in Naples. Cesare was in Rome, wrapped up in his bitterness particularly now that war threatened. And most dire tragedy of all, her father loved her so little that he could vent his anger, at Giulia's betrayal, on her, his daughter Lucrezia.

She could only try to ease her sorrow by writing to her father. She implored him to believe that she had been unable to prevent Giulia's leaving Pesaro, and that she had done all in her power to stop her going. Her letters to him were as loving, as tender and as truthful as those she wrote to Cesare. He could always be sure of her love and devotion. "I long to be," she wrote, "at the feet of Your Beatitude, and I long to be worthy of your esteem, for if I am not I shall never know satisfaction and have no wish to live."

When Alexander received this letter, he wept and kissed it tenderly.

"Why did I doubt my beloved girl?" he asked. "My Lucrezia, my little love. She will always be faithful to me. It is others who disobey and deceive."

But what an unhappy man he was! The "demons of sensuality" were gnawing at him, and he could not shut out of his mind pictures of Giulia and the cross-eyed Orsino together.

THE FRENCH FLEET had a speedy victory over the Neapolitans at Rapallo. The French armies crossed the Alps and the Italians found themselves outmatched from the start. These armies under the white banners of the Valois were advancing through Italy. At Pavia Charles VIII found the poor half-demented Gian Galeazzo, the true Duke of Milan; and when his beautiful young wife Isabella threw herself at the feet of little Charles, the French King was so moved, because she was beautiful and had suffered so much, that he promised that he would do all in his power to restore her husband. However, Ludovico's friends hastily administered a posset to the young Duke, and within a few days he was dead. Ludovico was then declared Duke of Milan.

The news was bad for the Italians. Ludovico decided not to fight, and welcomed the French invaders as they swept through his land. The great captain Virginio Orsini also put up no fight, but issued the command that all were to give way to the invaders.

There was only one who seemed prepared to take a stand against the French: Alexander, the Pope.

He was contemptuous of the Italians. "They are despicable," he cried. "Good for nothing but parading in fine uniforms. The only weapons the French need to conquer Italy are pieces of chalk, that they may mark their billets."

He was determined that he would stand out alone if necessary against all his enemies.

Once again, as he had at the time of the death of Calixtus, Alexander showed the world the stuff of which he was made. No one could but admire that calm dignity, that assurance that he could not fail though all the world came against him.

The French King, *Re Petito* as the Italians called him, for he was deformed and made a strange sight riding in the midst of his stalwart troops, was a little disturbed about attacking a man who had the courage of Alexander. It seemed to him that there was a touch of divinity about the Pope after all. He therefore turned aside from the repeated prayers of Alexander's enemies in Italy to go ahead and depose him.

Harm must not come to the Pope from him, Charles decided; if it did, he might have the whole of Catholic France and Spain against him.

Cardinal della Rovere, Alexander's old enemy, who had allied himself with the French King, riding beside him and declaring that the French had come to deliver Italy from the yoke of Alexander, was dismayed. He saw once again that his plans to step into Alexander's shoes were to be foiled.

The French must pass through Rome on their way to the south, but Charles decided that all he would ask for in Rome was the Pope's permission for transit through the Papal states.

Meanwhile Alexander remained firm. He would resist the French demands, he said; a tremor of fear ran through all those who had been assuring themselves that Alexander's days of power were over. Adriana and the Orsinis in Capodimonte were the first to falter.

Adriana upbraided her son for disobeying the Holy Father, and other members of the Orsini family joined with her and urged Orsino to leave at once for his brigade and not risk infuriating Alexander further.

Consequently Giulia awoke one morning to find that the masterful manners of her husband had been only temporary, and that he had fled.

There came a letter for Giulia from the angry Pope.

"Perfidious and ungrateful Giulia! You tell us you cannot return to Rome without your husband's permission. Though now we know both the wickedness of your nature and those who advise you, we can only suppose that you wish to remain where you are so that you may continue relations with that stallion of a husband."

Giulia read the letter in alarm; the Pope had never written to her in quite the same manner before; her family were beginning to criticize her for having turned against her lover for her husband's sake, and the husband, who had been so bold, had fled at the first sign that Alexander's power was unshaken.

Trembling she held her daughter to her.

"We should never have left Rome," she said.

"Shall we go to see my father?" asked the little girl. She had refused to call the squint-eyed Orsino, Father; Father, to her, was a glorious god-like creature, tall, commanding, in beautiful robes with a deep sonorous voice, caressing hands and comforting affection.

"We shall," said Giulia, determination shining in her eyes. She laughed suddenly. After all, she was La Bella, she could win back all she had lost.

She sent a slave to ask Adriana to come to her at once.

"I am leaving for Rome," she told her mother-in-law as soon as she appeared.

"For Rome! But the roads are unsafe. The French invaders may be anywhere . . . before we reach Rome."

But Adriana was looking intently at her daughter-in-law, and Giulia realized that, dangerous as the road might be, it was even more dangerous to remain under the shadow of Alexander's displeasure.

* * *

So Giulia, Adriana and a small retinue set out from Capodimonte on their journey to Rome.

Giulia was in high spirits; so was Laura. Giulia was wondering how she could have been momentarily excited by the sudden masterful ways of Orsino who at the first hint of alarm had taken to his heels and fled. She was longing for reunion with her lover. Laura was prattling about going home and seeing her father again; Adriana was silently praying that the Holy Father had not been so angry toward herself and Giulia that he would never have the same feelings for them again. They were all eagerness to reach Rome.

The journey was long and tedious; the weather was not good, as it was November; but the gaiety of Giulia was infectious, and it was a merry party which traveled along the road to Viterbo.

Suddenly Laura pointed and cried out that she could see houses ahead of them. They pulled up to look, and there sure enough on the horizon was the town of Viterbo.

"It will not be very long now," cried Giulia. "More than half the journey is done. I shall write to His Holiness when we reach Viterbo and tell him that we are on the way."

"Listen!" said Adriana.

"What was that?" asked Giulia.

"I thought I heard the sound of horses' hoofs."

They waited. They could hear nothing, and Giulia laughed at her mother-in-law. "You are nervous. Did you imagine Orsino was galloping after us to take us back by force?"

Laura began to cry at the thought. "I want to see my father."

"And so you shall, my darling. Have no fear. We shall be with him shortly. Come, let us waste no more time but ride with all speed into Viterbo."

They started off, but this time it was Giulia who fancied she heard the sound of galloping horses.

They stopped again. This time there was no mistake. Giulia looked fearfully at her little party, mostly women.

"Let us go on with all speed," she said. "We do not know whom we might meet on these roads at such times."

They put spurs to their horses but it was not long before one of the women cried out that cavalry were advancing upon them.

They rode desperately on but nearer and nearer came their pursuers, and they were almost a mile from Viterbo when they were surrounded.

Adriana's lips moved in silent prayer; Giulia was horrified when she recognized the uniform of the French invaders.

It was a desperate moment as they were forced to stop while the men surrounded them, and Giulia felt several pairs of eyes fixed upon her, knowing too well what those looks meant.

"Fair lady," said the commander, "whither do you go in such a hurry?"

He spoke in French, and Giulia did not understand him very well. She turned to Adriana who was so terrified that she could only murmur prayers almost involuntarily while her mind ran on, visualizing the horrible things which could happen to the women at the hands of the invaders.

Laura, who was riding with her mother, suddenly cried out and flung her arms about Giulia as though to protect her from the strangers.

"By the saints," said one man, "she's a beauty!"

"Keep your eyes from her," answered another. "She'll be for the Captain. If you're wise you'll look more closely at one of the other girls—and be satisfied."

Giulia said imperiously: "I am Giulia Farnese, wife of Orsino Orsini. You would be wise to allow me to pass. The Pope is my friend."

One of the men pushed his way through to her and touched her golden hair wonderingly. She slapped his hand aside, and the man growled ominously.

Then someone said: "Look out. Here comes the Captain."

A tall handsome man came riding up, and Giulia's spirits rose at the sight of him, for he had an air of natural nobility about him, and there was a certain gentleness in his face which was very comforting at such a time.

"What have we here?" he cried.

The men, who had been handling some of the women, dropped back.

"A party of women and their servants, sir," said the man who had led the band. "One's a real beauty, sir."

The commanding officer looked at Giulia and said slowly: "So I perceive." Then he bowed and spoke in fluent Italian, with the faintest trace of a French accent.

"My lady, forgive my men's roughness. I trust they have not insulted you."

"But they have," said Giulia. "And I would have you know that I am Giulia Farnese, the wife of Orsino Orsini. You have doubtless heard of me."

He bowed again. "Who has not heard of the most beautiful woman in Italy? I see now that rumors have not lied. Madame La Bella, accept my apologies for what has passed. My name is Yves d'Allegre, at your service."

"I am pleased to see you here, Monsieur d'Allegre," said Giulia. "And now I am sure you will tell your men not to be foolish. We are in a hurry."

"Alas, alas," sighed Yves d'Allegre. "These roads are unsafe for beautiful ladies."

"Then accompany us to Viterbo, and there perhaps it can be arranged that we shall have soldiers to protect us. A message to His Holiness the Pope telling him of our plight will call forth an immediate response."

"I am sure it would," said the Frenchman, his gaze taking in the beauty of her exquisite figure. "There is not a man in Italy or in France who would not serve you."

Giulia's fear was rapidly disappearing. The man was so charming. The French were notoriously gallant and the Captain had even more than French gallantry to offer. She was beginning to enjoy the adventure.

"Alas," he went on, "your beauty is such, Madame, that it may so madden those who behold it that they forget the respect and honor due to a lady of your rank. I shall ask you to allow me to ride beside you into Montefiascone, when I shall protect you with my sword."

"I thank you," said Giulia. "But it is to Viterbo that we wish to go."

"Alas, I am a soldier, with duties to perform. What a hard taskmistress duty is when she conflicts with pleasure! A thousand apologies, but I must take you and your party into Montefiascone."

Giulia shrugged her shoulders. "Well then, when we are there, will you do this for me? Will you have a message sent to His Holiness to tell him what has befallen us?"

Yves bowed and said that he would certainly do that.

So, taking Giulia's horse by the bridle and placing it at the head of the little band, with her beside him he led the party toward Montefiascone.

Montefiascone was already in the hands of the French and, as they approached the place, soldiers hurried out to look at them. There were shouts of delight when they saw the women, and many eyes were on Giulia. But Yves d'Allegre shouted stern orders. His prisoner was no ordinary woman. Any laying hands on her or her party would suffer immediate and drastic punishment.

The men fell back. They thought they understood. The Captain had selected the beautiful captive for himself.

Giulia herself believed this to be so and, as she looked at the handsome man riding beside her, she shivered, not without a certain pleasure, wondering what lay before her.

Yves rode with her into the town and, after he had had a short conversation with his superior officers, Giulia and her party were received with the greatest respect and lodged in one of the most comfortable houses of the town.

Giulia sent Laura to rest in the care of her nurse, and went to the room which had been allotted to her. She took off her cloak and shook her hair out of its net. She lay on the bed, thinking of all the strange things which had befallen her since she left Rome. Her mind went with distaste to the episode with Orsino; she told herself that she had been forced to participate in that affair, and was glad it had come to an ignoble end.

This ... this would also be *force majeure.* The man was so charming, so handsome. . . .

But she waited in vain for the coming of Yves d'Allegre, for, while she was waiting, he was penning a note to the Pope telling him that La Bella Giulia was a captive in the hands of the French and that a ransom of 3,000 scudi was demanded for her safe conduct to Rome.

WHEN ALEXANDER HEARD the news he became frantic with anxiety that some ill might befall his mistress. He hastily collected the money, which was despatched at once. Then, trembling with anticipation, he found he could not wait patiently in the Vatican for the return of Giulia.

He must go to meet her. No matter if the French were at his gate; no matter if the whole world were laughing at an old man's passion (and that man a Pope) for a young woman, he could not remain in the Vatican. He must ride out to greet her.

He was like a man of twenty. He ordered that fine clothes be brought to him. He wore a black doublet with a border of gold brocade; about his waist was a beautiful belt of Spanish leather, in which was a jeweled sword and dagger. On his feet were Spanish boots, and he wore his velvet beret at a jaunty angle.

Thus he rode out to greet Giulia and bring her back to Rome.

Giulia was delighted to see him. She now felt humiliated by her encounter with Orsino and piqued by that with Yves d'Allegre, but here was Alexander, the most important man in Italy—despite all the evil rumors of late—and he was her passionate and most devoted lover.

"Giulia, my darling!" cried the Pope.

"Most Holy Lord!" murmured Giulia submissively.

And if there was laughter throughout Rome because the Holy Father, dressed as a Spanish grandee, had behaved like a young man of twenty with his mistress, little Alexander cared. His position was precarious, the French were almost in Rome, he had his crown to fight for—but that seemed little to a man of his immense genius for statecraft. His mistress was delighted to be back, turning away from younger lovers to be with him.

There remained one other thing necessary to his complete content. Lucrezia must be brought back to Rome.

ALONE IN HER husband's palace at Pesaro, Lucrezia eagerly waited for news. Sometimes a wandering friar would come begging for food and a night's lodging; sometimes a messenger would arrive with letters from her father; Lucrezia welcomed such visitors warmly, and listened eagerly to all they had to tell, for she felt shut away from the world behind the hills which encircled Pesaro.

She heard that the conflict was growing, that Charles of France was on his way to Rome; she heard of Giulia's capture and release, and of the ransom which the Pope had gladly paid. She heard that her father had ridden out to meet his mistress dressed like a young man, a gallant Spanish grandee, and how happy he was to have Giulia with him once more.

Others might sneer at her father's behavior. Lucrezia did not. She would sit at her window, looking out across the sea envying Giulia the affection and passion she inspired in the Pope, and thinking how different Alexander was from the cold man she had married.

But when she heard that the French were almost at the gates of Rome she trembled for her father.

❦ ♔ ❦

THERE WAS NO one in Rome who remained calmer than Alexander, as he considered the little King with his magnificent army, and the Italians who were eager to dress up and play at soldiers, but who were not so anxious to fight.

Cesare was with him at this time, sardonic because he had been denied the pleasure of defeating the French, losing no opportunity to point out to his father that had he been in charge of his *condotta* there would have been at least one company ready to hold back the invader.

He laughed scornfully and beat his fists against his chest.

"Oh, no! I must stay in the Church. I . . . who might have saved Rome, who might have saved Italy and would certainly have saved you from your present humiliating position, am not allowed to fight."

"My dear son," chid the Pope, "you are too impetuous. Let us not be so hasty. The battle is not over yet."

"Is Your Holiness aware," said Cesare, "that the French have stormed Civita Vecchia and that in a day or so they will be at the very gates of Rome?"

"I know it," replied the Pope.

"And you intend to remain here so that the King can make you his prisoner and present you with his terms, to which you will have to agree?"

"You go too fast, my son. I am not yet little Charles's prisoner. And I have no intention of being so. Wait awhile. See who, in a few months' time, is the victor of the campaign. Do not, I pray you, make the mistake of placing yourself among my enemies who, from the moment the first French foot stepped onto Italian soil, have been telling themselves and each other that I am a defeated man."

The calmness of Alexander had a soothing effect, even on Cesare.

But when the Pope saw the vanguard of the French army camping on

Monte Mario, he knew that he must immediately, with his family, take refuge in the fortress of St. Angelo.

⁂

THE entry into Rome of the French King was spectacular. It was growing dark when he and his army came marching into the City, and in the twilight they seemed more terrifying than they would by day. They came by the light of a thousand torches, and the Romans shivered to behold them. The Germans and Swiss, who earned their livelihood by fighting other people's wars, were all stalwart men, strong and rough, as was to be expected. The French were fine soldiers and so far they had met nothing but easy victory. There were numerous noblemen accompanying the soldiers, and these were decked out with many a glittering jewel, mostly plunder, which had been picked up on the way to Rome. The Army took six hours to march past; there were the archers from Gascony and d'Aubigny's Scotsmen whose pipers played stirring music as they marched; there were the macebearers and crossbowmen, and thirty-six bronze cannon. With the procession came the King, the least awe-inspiring of any. Surrounded by his victorious army, the deformed and stunted Charles looked pathetic in his golden armor.

Through the Via Lata went the column to the Palace of Saint Mark, where the King was to have his lodging; and the cannon were formidably drawn up in the piazza.

From his fortress Alexander and his entourage heard the shouts in the city of "Francia! Rovere!"

Cesare stood beside his father, clenching and unclenching his fists. He knew, as Alexander knew, that when night fell it would go hard with the citizens of Rome. There were tempting treasures in the houses—gold and silver plate, ornaments of majolica and pewter. And there were the women.

Rome, the eternal city, was about to be sacked.

And as they waited they heard the shouts, the screams, and the thousand tortured cries of a ravished city.

"There is my mother's house," said Cesare in a low voice.

"Grieve not for a house," said the Pope. "Your mother will not be in it."

"Where is my mother?" cried Cesare.

"Have no fear. I arranged that she should leave Rome with her husband some days ago."

How could he be so calm? Cesare wondered. The fate of the Borgias was in danger; yet he who had made the name great could stand there listening to the sounds of horror, serene, as though this was nothing but a passing thunder-storm.

Cesare cried: "I will have my revenge on those brutes who enter my mother's house."

"I doubt not that you will," said Alexander quietly.

"But what are you doing? Oh my father, how *can* you remain so calm?"

"There is nothing else to be done," said Alexander. "We must wait for a propitious moment to make terms with *il Re Petito*."

Cesare was astounded, for it seemed to him almost as though Alexander did not understand what was happening. But Alexander was thinking of another crisis in his life. Then his uncle had lain dying and the whole of Rome was crying out against the friends of Calixtus. Alexander's brother, Pedro Luis, had fled from Rome and consequently had never realized his great ambitions. Alexander had stayed, counting on his dignity and bold strategy; and Alexander had lived to succeed in his ambitions.

This was what he would do again.

❦ ♛ ❦

In the Borgia apartments of the Vatican the little French King fidgeted. He paced up and down looking out of the windows across the gardens, beyond the orange trees and pines to Monte Mario.

He felt somewhat aggrieved. He came as a conqueror. Should he be expected to wait for the conquered? But this was no ordinary victim of a conquering army. This was the Holy Father himself, the head of the Catholic Church throughout the world. Charles was Catholic, his country was devoutly so; and Charles would never be able to cast aside the respect he felt for the Holy Father.

At last the Pope had agreed to discuss terms. What else could he do? The north of Italy was conquered; Charles was in command of Rome, ready to fight his way south to Naples and achieve his country's great ambition.

The Pope had been forced to make terms. He had been besieged in Castle St. Angelo, but when a bullet had pierced the walls of that seemingly impregnable fortress, he had felt it was time to come out and talk peace terms. And those terms, decided the French King, would be *his* terms, for the Holy Father, a prisoner in his own city, would be forced to agree to them.

The January sun was shining on the gold and enamel of Pinturicchio's murals, as yet not completed, and here portrayed were members of the Borgia family. Charles was studying them when he heard a movement in the room and turning saw a splendid figure in a golden mantle. For a moment he thought he was in the presence of a supernatural being and that one of the paintings on the walls had come to life. It was Alexander who had entered through a low and narrow doorway, and as the Pope advanced into the room, Charles fell to his knees immediately conscious of that great dignity.

Alexander bade him rise; his manner was paternal and benign.

"So, my son," he said, "we meet."

And from that moment he was in command; Charles could not think of himself as the conqueror in this presence; he could only speak with the utmost respect to the Holy Father who spoke to his son, as though bidding him take courage in spite of the predicament in which he found himself.

It was quite ridiculous, but nevertheless Charles stammered that he wished free passage through the Papal States, and that he had come to demand it.

The Pope's eyebrows shot up at the word demand, but even as Charles was speaking he heard sounds of looting in the streets below and was brought back to reality, remembering that he was a conqueror and that the Pope was in his power.

"So you would ask for free passage," mused the Pope. He looked beyond the French King, and he was smiling serenely as though he were looking into the future.

"Yes, Holiness."

"Well, my son, we will grant you that, if you and your soldiers will leave Rome immediately."

The King looked at one of his men who had stepped forward—a bold soldier who would not be impressed by his surroundings or the majestic personality of Alexander.

"The hostages, Sire," he said.

"Ah yes, Most Holy Father," said the King, "we should need hostages if we left you free in Rome."

"Hostages. It seems a just demand."

"Right glad I am that Your Holiness agrees on this. We have decided on Cesare Borgia and the Turkish Prince Djem."

The Pope was silent for a while. Prince Djem, yes. They were welcome to him. But Cesare!

Outside he heard the piteous wails of women; he could smell smoke. Rome was being ravished. She was in flames and crying out to her Holy Father in her agony. He must save Rome through Cesare and Djem.

Looking out over the beautiful Adriatic Sea, Lucrezia felt her uneasiness growing. She knew that Giovanni was in a desperate situation; he was in the pay of the Pope and the Neapolitans, and was working for Milan. How could she blame him? Nothing would have induced her to work against her own family, so how could she blame Giovanni for what he was doing? Lucrezia characteristically tried not to think of her husband; he was an unpleasant subject.

But to brood on the affairs of her family seemed even more so. What was happening to the Borgias? When travelers arrived at the Sforza palace Lucrezia had them brought immediately to her; she would give them food and shelter and implore them to tell her what was happening to her father.

She tried to visualize the situation. The French in Rome; her mother's house pillaged; her father forced to receive the little King of France and listen to his terms. And Cesare—proud Cesare—to be forced to ride out of Rome, a hostage of the conquerors. That was the worst thing that could have happened. She pictured his rage, and as she sat brooding, trying to turn her mind from unpleasantness, working a little with her needle, idly playing her lute, she was aware of disturbance below and, putting aside her work, she hurried down in case it should be messengers with news.

The arrival turned out to be that of a friar, humble and hungry, who was calling on the Lady of Pesaro to tell her the news—great news from Rome.

Lucrezia found it difficult to show him how delighted she was. She clapped her hands for slaves to bring him water with which to wash his tired feet; they brought wine and food for him; but before he was refreshed Lucrezia insisted on his telling her whether the news was good or bad.

"Good, lady," he cried. "The best of good news. As you know, the French conqueror had audience with the Holy Father in the Vatican, and there it was necessary for his Holiness to come to terms."

Lucrezia nodded. "And I know the terms included the giving of hostages, and that one of these was my brother Cesare."

"'Tis so, Madonna. They rode out of Rome with the conquerors. The Cardinal Borgia and the Turkish Prince."

"How was my brother? Tell me that. Angry I know he must have been since his pride was brought so low."

"No, Madonna. The Cardinal was serene. All those who watched him marvelled—not only at his calmness but also at that of the Holy Father who could watch his son depart with what seemed like indifference. We did not understand then. The Cardinal took with him much baggage. There were seventeen wagons all covered with velvet, and this caused much amusement among the French. 'What sort of a Cardinal is this,' they asked each other, 'to be so concerned with his possessions!' And, as you will guess, Madonna, the Turkish Prince traveled with equal splendor."

"So he rode out to the jeers of our enemies," said Lucrezia, "yet he rode with serenity and dignity. Oh, but how angry he must have been."

"He surprised them when the soldiers encamped at the end of the first day. I have heard that it was a sight to behold when he threw off his Cardinal's robes and, stripped to the waist, wrestled with them and threw their champions."

Lucrezia clasped her hands and laughed. "That would have delighted him. I know it."

"They were astonished that a Cardinal should behave thus, Madonna. But the next night he had a greater surprise for them."

"Tell me quickly, I beg of you. I cannot endure the suspense of waiting."

"The second night they halted at Velletri, on the edge of the Pontine Marshes. All was quiet and none noticed when one of the muleteers rose and moved silently among the foreign soldiers. That muleteer made his way to a tavern in the town and there he found a servant waiting with horses. The muleteer mounted a horse, and he and the servant rode hotfoot to Rome."

"It was Cesare, my brother!"

"It was the Cardinal himself, Madonna. He has rejoined the Holy Father in Rome, and I heard that there is much laughter and merrymaking in the Vatican on this account."

Lucrezia laughed with pleasure.

"It is the best news I have heard for a long time. How he would have enjoyed that! And poor fat Djem, he did not escape?"

"Nay, the Prince remains with his captors. It is said that he lacked the stamina of His Eminence. He could not wrestle with the French; nor could he have managed to escape. He stays behind. But they have only one hostage where they wished for two; and the more important of the two—the Pope's own son—has escaped them."

Lucrezia rose to her feet and there before the friar danced a few steps of a Spanish dance.

The friar watched in astonishment, but Lucrezia only threw back her head and laughed as she whirled round and round until she was breathless.

Then she paused and explained: "I am carried away with joy. This is an omen. My brother has made a laughing stock of the French. It is a beginning. My father will rid Italy of the conquerors, and all men throughout the land will be grateful to him. This is the beginning, I tell you. Come! Now you shall eat your fill of the best we have in this palace. You shall drink the best wine. You must be merry. This night there shall be a banquet in the palace and you shall be our guest of honor."

"Madonna, you rejoice too soon," murmured the friar. "This is but the escape of a hostage. So much of Italy lies in the hands of the conqueror."

"My father will save all Italy," said Lucrezia solemnly.

But she was solemn only for a moment. Now she was calling to her slaves and attendants. She wanted them to prepare a banquet; there would be dancing and revelry in the palace this day.

Cesare had triumphed, and Cesare's triumphs were as important to her as her own.

Lucrezia was right. That was the beginning of brighter prospects. The French were furious at the hoax played on them by Cesare, but there was nothing they could do about it. A protest to Alexander made him shake his head sorrowfully. "The Cardinal has behaved badly, very badly," he murmured; and had to retire hastily to give vent to the laughter which shook him.

Fat little Djem could not stand up to the rigors of life with an army; he was stricken with fever and died. Thus in a short while the French were robbed of both their hostages.

However, they went marching on to Naples, where Alfonso, the King, hearing of their approach, hurried to Sicily leaving his kingdom in the hands of his son Ferrandino. But Ferrandino proved to be no soldier, and when he saw the French armies approaching, followed his father's example—choosing the island of Ischia for his refuge, whither he went with his court—leaving Naples open to the invaders.

This seemed good luck for Charles, but the French King had reckoned without the climate and the indolence of his soldiers. Italy lay behind them, a conquered country, and they were encamped in sunny Naples. The women were luscious, the brothels were numerous, and the soldiers determined to enjoy a rest from the march.

Meanwhile Alexander had not been idle. Messengers had been riding hard back and forth between the Vatican and Venice, to Milan, to the King of Spain and to the Emperor Maximilian.

Alexander pointed out that unless they quickly became his allies, Italy would fall completely under the dominion of the French, and that this would be to the advantage of none of them.

When the French King heard of the alliances which were being formed he became alarmed. His soldiers were in a debilitated condition; moreover they were becoming insubordinate, and many of them were sick. Charles was about to receive the crown of Naples, when it occurred to him that this crown would be of little use to him if he was to wear it but for a week or so before his enemies overcame him.

There was only one way out of his difficulty. He must leave Italy with all speed. But on his way he would see the Pope, whom he rightly suspected of organizing his, Charles's, enemies against him, and he would demand from him the investiture of Naples.

Charles left Naples and started the march northward, but Alexander, hearing of his approach, immediately left Rome for Perugia, so that when Charles reached Rome he found the Vatican deserted.

Fuming with anger, he could do nothing but continue his march.

He was bewildered. He had conquered the land with his victorious armies, and the rulers of states had fallen before him; then he had come to Rome, believing that the Borgia Pope was as much his vassal as those heads of states who had stood aside for him. It had seemed so. And yet . . . it was not so.

Charles went marching on, cursing the wily fox of the Vatican.

ALEXANDER FOUND LIFE amusing at Perugia. Once again he had proved his strategy to be sound. It was as it had been at the time of the death of Calixtus. He had waited then, as now, serene, accommodating; and now, as then, his enemies had played into his hands.

With him were Giulia and Cesare; but there was one whom he sadly missed; his dearest daughter.

"Lucrezia must come to us here," he told Cesare. "She has been parted from us too long."

Cesare smiled at the prospect of seeing his sister again. He was feeling happier. His father had been highly amused by his adventure. Was he beginning to see what an asset Cesare would be as a commander of the armies? It was not like a Cardinal to wrestle, as he had, with soldiers, and to accomplish such a spectacular escape.

Cesare was twenty; he was growing in stature; and the Pope, for all his miraculous virility, was sixty-four years of age.

Cesare began to think of the day when his father would turn to him for advice, and when he, Cesare, would make the decisions.

Now they were in perfect accord, for they had both determined that Lucrezia should come to them at Perugia.

❦ ♔ ❧

Giovanni Sforza, WHO was back in Pesaro, was not pleased by the message from the Pope.

He stormed into Lucrezia's apartment where she was giving orders as to the packing of her baggage.

"You shall not go," he said.

"Not go?" The light eyes were wide with incredulity. "But these are orders from my father."

"I am your husband. It is I who shall say where you may go."

"Giovanni, you cannot refuse to allow me to go."

"I can and I will."

He was bold; that was because he was thinking of the miles between Perugia and Pesaro. Poor Giovanni! thought Lucrezia. He is not a bold man.

But almost immediately she was alarmed, for she too remembered the distance between Pesaro and Perugia.

Giovanni was a weak man and as such he was always eager to show his strength when he thought he had a chance of doing so. Now he turned to her servants. "Take out the Countess's gowns," he said. "Put them back where they belong."

Then he turned and left her.

Lucrezia did not storm or rage. She was like her father and was aware of the efficacy of diplomacy. She was convinced that after a short delay, she would be on her way to Perugia. So she smiled regretfully and sat down to pen a letter to her father.

Giovanni had his price. He was learning the necessity of bargaining. He was kept poor and of no importance, but the Borgias must remember that although his wife was the Pope's daughter, as her husband he, Giovanni, had some control over her. Since she was so precious to them, they must show some respect to her husband.

He wanted to be freed from the invidious position into which they had thrust him. He wanted a new command; and since the Pope had made an alliance with Venice, why should he not be enrolled as a Captain in the Venetian army? The Pope could easily arrange this for his son-in-law; let him do it and, for such services, Giovanni Sforza would place no restrictions on his wife's movements.

When the Pope heard of Sforza's aspirations, he laughed aloud.

"Why," he said to Cesare, "there is some spirit in the poor thing after all. I will see what can be arranged with the Doge."

Cesare was scornful of his brother-in-law. He would have hated him, whoever he was, simply because he was Lucrezia's husband, but it seemed humiliating to him that his sister should have had to accept such a man.

"'Tis a pity," he said to his father, "that we cannot find some means of ridding Lucrezia of Sforza."

The Pope's gaze shifted a little. "Mayhap . . ." he murmured. "Sometime. . . . At the moment we will pass him to the Doge."

Giovanni stormed up and down his wife's apartments.

"So," he cried, "I am to have a *condotta* in the Venetian army!"

"And you are glad, are you not?" asked Lucrezia lightly. "Was not that what you wanted?"

"I should have equal treatment with your brother," shouted Giovanni.

"Is that not what you have? Giovanni Sforza and Giovanni Borgia both have commands in the Doge's army. Is that not so?"

"Yes, it is so. We both have commands. But there is a difference. Your father has seen to that. I am to get four thousand ducats . . . your brother thirty-one thousand!"

"But Giovanni," soothed Lucrezia, "if you had not heard what my brother was to have, you would have been happy with your four thousand."

"But I *have* heard!" Giovanni's veins stood out at the temples. "I am treated thus to show that I am of no importance beside your brother. Your father deliberately insults me. I shall not let you go."

Lucrezia was silent for a few seconds; then she said demurely: "If you do not, then even the four thousand ducats will not be yours."

Giovanni clenched his fists and stamped his foot. He looked as though he would burst into tears.

Lucrezia watched him dispassionately. She thought: Soon we shall set out for Perugia and when he has taken me there he will leave us.

She gave herself up to the pleasure of contemplating reunion with her father and Cesare.

CESARE

Lucrezia was embraced by her father and Cesare, and how warm, how passionate were those embraces!

"I cannot understand how we managed to live without you," declared the Pope.

"We have missed you more than we can tell," Cesare murmured.

She turned from one to the other, taking their hands and kissing them. "Oh my father, oh my brother!" she cried. "Why is it that all other men seem small and insignificant beside you?"

They made her turn about as they studied each detail of her appearance. She had changed, declared Cesare; and temporarily his brow darkened; he was remembering that her marriage had now been consummated.

"Our little one grows up," murmured the Pope. "I reproach myself. It would have been possible to have kept you with me, my dearest, through all the troubles."

"There were many uneasy moments," mused Cesare, "I think we should have suffered agonies of anxiety, Holiness, if our beloved one had been exposed to danger."

"You are right, my son. And why should we grieve over what is past. Let there be a banquet to welcome my dearest child, and let me see you two dance and sing together."

Cesare had taken her hand. "And what say you sister?"

"I long to dance with you. I long to show everyone how happy I am that we are re-united."

Cesare had taken her face in his hands and was studying it intently. "How have you changed, sister?"

"I am a little older, nothing more."

"More learned in the ways of the world," said the Pope fondly and almost archly.

Cesare kissed her. "I trust, dearest sister, your ordeal has not been too tedious?"

She knew what he meant, and she laughed. "No, it was well enough."

The Pope, watching them, laid his hand on Cesare's shoulder. "Let her go now. Let her women dress her for our banquet. Then I shall see you two dancing together and I shall feel so happy because I have two of my dear ones under the same roof as myself."

Lucrezia kissed her father's hand and both men watched her as she left them.

"How enchanting she is!" said Cesare.

"I am beginning to believe she is the loveliest girl in Italy," replied the Pope.

"I am sure of it," Cesare said.

He looked at his father quickly. Giulia was losing her hold on the Pope, for he had not forgiven her since she had lived with her husband. He had made the grand gesture of riding out to greet her when he had paid her ransom, but Cesare was fully aware that Giulia was no longer the Pope's favorite mistress, and he was glad. He had always been irritated by the rise to power of the Farnese family.

While he appeared to take frivolous pleasure in the revelries which were going on about him, Alexander was planning ahead. He now said to Cesare: "I hope it will not be long before we return to Rome. There is much we have to do if we are going to prevent near disasters arising such as that through which we have now passed. Cesare, we must concentrate on destroying the power of the barons who proved themselves to be so weak and feeble at the approach of the invader. I visualize a strong Italy."

"A strong Italy under the Papacy," agreed Cesare. "You need a strong army, Father, and good generals."

"You are right, my son."

Alexander saw the request rising to Cesare's lips: Release me. See what a general I will make.

It was not the time, Alexander realized, to tell Cesare that as soon as he was in Rome he intended to bring back Giovanni from Spain. Giovanni should have charge of the Pope's armies and he should go out and do battle against the Orsinis, who during the French invasion had shown themselves to be traitors to the Pope's interest. When he had subdued them, rival families would see how powerful the Pope had become; they would conform to the wishes of the Borgia Pope or suffer likewise.

He would have enjoyed talking of these matters with Cesare, but clearly they could only lead to one subject: the recall from Spain of Giovanni.

It was so pleasant to have his dear Lucrezia with him; it made him happy to see Cesare's delight in her and hers in him. Alexander did not want anything to spoil that pleasure, so deftly changed the subject.

"Our little Lucrezia . . ." he murmured. "I would we had found a husband more worthy of her."

"It maddens me to think of that oaf . . . that provincial boor . . . near my sister."

"We will arrange it so that he does not enjoy Perugia," suggested the Pope.

Cesare was smiling again. "We must send him with all speed to the Doge," he said. "Can it be arranged?"

"We must put our heads together, my son. Then we shall have Lucrezia to ourselves."

Lucrezia lay on her bed, her hair damp about her. She felt a strange excitement as she recalled the pleasures of the previous night. It had been a grand banquet in the palace of Gian-paolo Baglioni, who as a fief-holder of the Church had deemed it his duty and pleasure to entertain the Holy Father.

Baglioni was a fascinating man, handsome and bold. There were stories in circulation about his cruelty, and his slaves and servants trembled at a stern look from him. Cesare had told her as they danced that in the dungeons below the palace those who offended Baglioni were tortured without mercy.

It seemed hard to believe that such a fascinating man could be cruel; he had shown nothing but kindness to Lucrezia. If she had seen anyone tortured at his command she would have hated him; but the dungeons were a long way from the banqueting hall, and the cries of victims could not reach the revelers.

Baglioni had watched her and Cesare as they danced, and his eyes were full of malicious amusement. So were those of others.

"The Spanish dances, Cesare," she had whispered. "Our father would like to see us dance them."

And they had danced, she and Cesare together, danced as she had danced with her brother Giovanni at her wedding. She had recalled those wedding dances, but had not referred to them; she did not want to make Cesare angry on such a night.

Baglioni had danced with a very beautiful woman, his mistress.

He was tender toward her and, watching them, Lucrezia whispered to Cesare: "How gentle he is! Yet they say that he inflicts terrible torture on those who offend him."

Then Cesare had drawn her to him. "What has his gentleness toward her to do with his cruelty toward others?"

"Merely that it is difficult to believe that one who can be so gentle could also be so cruel."

"Am I not tender? Am I not cruel?"

"You . . . Cesare . . . you are different from anyone else on Earth."

That had made him smile; and she had felt his fingers gripping her hand so that she could have cried out in pain; but the pain inflicted by Cesare had always in some strange way delighted her.

"When we return to Rome," he had told her, and the expression on his face had made her shudder, "I will do such things to those who violated our mother's house as men will talk of for years to come. I will commit acts to equal those which take place in Baglioni's dungeons. And all the time I shall love you, my sister, with the same fierce yet gentle love which you have had from me since you were a baby in your cradle."

"Oh Cesare . . . have a care. What good can it do to remember what was done in the heat of war?"

"This is the good it can do, sister. It will show all those who took part that in future they must remember what they risk by daring to insult me or mine. Ah, you are right in saying that Baglioni loves that woman."

"She is his favorite mistress, I have heard; and there can be no doubt of it."

"Have you heard aught else concerning her, Lucrezia?"

"Aught else? I think not, Cesare."

He had laughed suddenly, and his eyes had grown wild. "She is indeed his beloved," he had said; "she is also his sister."

It was of this Lucrezia was thinking as she lay on her bed.

Her husband came into the room and stood by the bed looking at his wife. Then he waved his hands to the woman who sat close by, stitching at one of Lucrezia's gowns.

Lucrezia studied her husband through half-closed eyes. He seemed smaller, less imposing, here at Perugia than he had at Pesaro. There she had seen him as her husband and, being Lucrezia, she was ready to be contented with what life had given her; she had done her best to love him. It was true she had found him unsatisfying, cold, lacking in ardour. Her desires had been aroused, and she was constantly aware of their remaining unsatisfied.

Here at Perugia she saw him through the eyes of her brother and father; and it was a different man she saw.

"So," he cried, "I am to go. I am to leave you here."

"Is that so, Giovanni?" she asked languidly, making sure that he should not be aware of the faint pleasure which she was feeling.

"You know it!" he stormed. "It may well be that you have asked to have me removed."

"I? Giovanni! But you are my husband."

He came to the bed and took her roughly by the arm. "Forget it not," he said.

"How could I forget such a thing?"

"You might well do so now that you are with your family."

"No, Giovanni. We all talk of you constantly."

"Talk of how you can rid yourselves of me, eh?"

"Why should we wish to?"

That made him laugh.

"What fine bracelets you are wearing! Whence came they? Do not tell me—I'll guess: A present from the Holy Father. What fine presents for a father to give his daughter! He lavished nothing better on Madonna Giulia at the height of his passion for her. And your brother, he is equally attentive. He rivals his father, one might say."

She lowered her eyes; she let her long slender fingers play with the jeweled ornaments on her wrists.

She remembered her father's putting them there; the solemn kisses, the words of love.

"They do not want me here," shouted Giovanni. "I am an encumbrance. I am a nuisance. Am I not your husband?"

"I pray you, Giovanni, do not make such scenes," she said. "My brother might hear you."

She looked at him then, and saw the lights of fear come into his eyes. The mention of Cesare's name did that to many people, she knew.

His clenched fists had dropped to his sides. He took one look at the beautiful and seductive girl on the bed; then he turned away.

She was the decoy. He must be careful. He was like a careless fly who had flown into the Borgia web. The safest thing he could do was to escape while he had time. At the moment he was a mild irritation to them. Who knew what he might become?

He thought of her gentleness and of the first weeks in Pesaro when she had truly become his wife. She was young and seemingly innocent; she was also very beautiful, very responsive; indeed, perhaps too responsive; with his natural fear he had been a little afraid of something which had warned him of pent-up passion within that exquisitely formed yet frail body.

He wanted to say to her: Come away with me. Come secretly. Do not let them know, because they will never allow you to escape them.

But if she came with him, what would happen to the pair of them?

They would never be allowed to escape. He understood that. He realized now why they would not let her go.

The knowledge came to him when he had seen Baglioni and his mistress at their banquet. The Pope had blessed them both, Baglioni and his mistress, and the Pope had known about them.

Giovanni Sforza hesitated. Take her with you, urged a voice within him; she is your wife. As yet she is undefiled; she is gentle and there is kindness in her. They have not yet made her one of them . . . but they will. And she is your wife . . . yours to mold, yours to keep forever.

But he was a meek man. He had watched the look in her father's eyes as they had rested on her; he had seen the fierce possessiveness in those of her brother.

But Giovanni dared not, for he was a frightened man.

"I am to go," he cried out in sudden anger. "And you will stay. They are saying in Rome that there is ample shelter for you beneath the apostolic robe!"

She seemed to have forgotten he was there.

She was thinking of herself dancing with Cesare, and of Baglioni, sitting at the table caressing his beautiful sister.

Cesare had been right when he had said she had grown up. There were many things which she was now beginning to understand.

Lucrezia's slaves were combing her long hair. Freshly washed, it gleamed golden as it fell over her shoulders. She was growing more beautiful. Her face still wore the innocent look which was perhaps largely due to her receding chin and wide eyes; but in those eyes there was now an expectancy.

She was back in Rome after a brief visit to Pesaro, and her husband Giovanni was with her again, but soon he would be going away. He must return to his *condotta*. She was glad he was going. She was weary of Giovanni and his continual insinuations. At the same time she was conscious of her father's growing dislike of her husband, and of Cesare's firm hatred.

Cesare was the most important person in her life, yet still she retained her fear of him—that exquisite terror which he aroused in her and which she was beginning to understand.

Her life with Giovanni had taught her what she could expect from men, and it might have been that, because she now knew herself to be capable of passion even as were her father and brothers, she was eagerly waiting for what the future would bring her. From Giovanni she expected nothing; yet, because he was a coward, and because he was continually worried by his lack of dignity and the lack of respect paid to him, she was sorry for him; and she would be glad when he had left, because not only was she sorry for him, she was afraid for him.

Her women had fixed the jeweled net over her hair and she was ready for the banquet.

This was to be in honor of the conqueror of Fornovo, and her father had insisted that Gonzaga should be entertained at the Palace of Santa Maria in Portico, that all Rome might know in what esteem he held his beautiful daughter.

So she was indeed growing up. This night would be gathered in her house all the most notable people in Rome, and she was to be their hostess.

Giovanni Sforza would be angry, for it would be clearly shown that he was of little importance. He would be in the background and no one would take any notice of him; and when Gonzaga rode away, Giovanni would ride with him and there would be a brief respite from his company once more.

She was very lovely as she went to greet her guests, her tiny Negress holding the train of her dress which was of rich brocade and stiff with jewels. She had the gift of looking both younger and older than her sixteen years—at one moment an innocent child, at another a woman.

There assembled were her father, brother and members of the Papal Court, and among them the retinue of Francesco Gonzaga, the Marquis of Mantua.

The Marquis himself stood before her, a man of striking appearance and personality. He was very tall, thin and very dark; and his body, though graceful in the extreme, suggested an immense strength and virility. His dark eyes were brilliant, deep set, and their hooded lids gave them the appearance of being constantly half-closed; his lips were full and sensuous;

he was clearly a man who had enjoyed many adventures—both in love and war.

He bowed graciously before the daughter of the Pope.

"I have heard much of your charms, Madonna," he said in a voice which held a note of tenderness; "it gives me the greatest pleasure to kiss your hand."

"We have heard much of you here," murmured Lucrezia. "The story of your valor has traveled before you."

He sat beside her and told her of the battle, of how he reproached himself because the French King had escaped.

"He left behind him many prisoners," said Lucrezia, "so we have heard here, with many of the treasures which he had taken from the people of Italy."

It was true, agreed Gonzaga, and he went on to explain more details of the campaign, amazed at himself for talking thus to a beautiful girl. But this was merely a child. She was sixteen years old, but to him she seemed much younger.

As for Lucrezia, she wished this attractive man would talk of himself, which she knew would interest her far more than details of his battles.

They danced, and she felt a tingle of excitement run through her as their hands touched. She thought: If Giovanni Sforza had been such a man, how differently I could have felt toward him.

She lifted her eyes and smiled at him, but he still saw her as a child.

The Pope and Cesare watched them as they danced.

"A handsome pair," said the Pope.

Cesare looked uneasy. "Gonzaga is notorious for his attractiveness to women. He should not think that Lucrezia is for his taking before he passes on to the next conquest."

"Rest assured he does not," murmured Alexander. "He sees her as a pretty child."

There was another matter which Alexander would have to broach soon to Cesare, and he wished to choose the right moment for doing so. Giovanni Borgia would receive his father's letter very soon, and he had no doubt that the young Duke of Gandia would lose little time in returning to Rome.

And when he came, Alexander was going to put him in charge of his armies, which would infuriate Cesare.

They are my sons, pondered Alexander; is it not for me to command them?

Perhaps. But, as he looked at the glowering face beside him, he was uneasy. That dark and brooding side of Cesare's nature had become more pronounced of late. Cesare had had great devotion showered upon him; he had enjoyed many privileges. When he was at the universities the wealth and power of his father had enabled him to assemble a little court of his own, a court of which he was the despotic ruler. There were disquieting rumors regarding Cesare's powers and the methods he employed for ridding himself of his enemies.

Alexander would not believe that he, the all-powerful Pope, who had recently triumphed over his enemies, was afraid of his own son.

Yet now he hesitated to tell him that there was little doubt that his brother would soon be in Rome.

Instead he spoke of Goffredo, that younger son, whom he had also recalled.

"It is time," he said, "that Goffredo and Sanchia were with us. The rumors concerning that woman grow more and more interesting."

That made Cesare laugh; and there was nothing Alexander liked so much as to enjoy a little light-hearted gossip with the members of his family. It seemed very amusing to them both to contemplate little Goffredo with this wife of his, who was notorious for her amours.

"Such a woman," said Cesare lightly, "will be an interesting addition to Your Beatitude's household."

✿♔✿

Lucrezia stood with her father and Cesare on the balcony, watching the departure of Francesco Gonzaga. He rode at the head of that procession, the man who had stirred some feeling of regret within her because Giovanni Sforza was not such a man. Now Francesco was making his way to Naples and, as he passed through Italy, everywhere he would be honored as the man who, with the Holy Father, had done more than any to drive the invader from the land.

He had the appearance of a conqueror. The crowds shouted their acclaim; they strewed flowers in his path and the eyes of the women were for him alone in the vast procession.

Graciously he acknowledged the acclaim, his dark eyes lighting as they fell on some girl or woman outstanding for her beauty. A smile of admiration for the beauty, regret that he was but passing by, would touch his face momentarily changing its expression.

He turned and smiled his last farewell to the group on the balcony, and his eyes rested briefly on the daughter of the Pope, for she was such a pretty child with her glistening golden hair, but if the thought occurred to him that in a few years' time she would be worthy of a closer acquaintance, it was quickly forgotten. There was one other who rode in the procession and who turned to take a last look at the assembly on the balcony: this was Giovanni Sforza. He felt angry as his eyes rested on the golden-haired girl. There she stood between father and brother, and it seemed to Giovanni that she was their captive. They would take her from him; they would make her one of them, and very soon it would be impossible to recognize the docile girl who had been his wife during those months at Pesaro. He felt regretful for those months, for he knew that he would never again live in such harmony with his gentle Lucrezia.

Already she was changing. She was a young girl still, but she was a Borgia, and they had determined to stamp her with the mark of the Borgia. In a few years' time—perhaps less—she would be as they were ... that charming innocence lost, her sensuality enlarged so that she, too, would be ready to appease it at no matter what cost; they would tarnish that tenderness in her; they would supplant it with indifference.

He longed to turn back, to storm into the palace, to force her to leave them and come with him back to Pesaro where they would live away from the conflict of politics and the shadow of her scheming and unscrupulous family.

But who was he to dream such dreams? He was a small man; he was a coward who had always been afraid of someone or something, always trying to shake off the memory of humiliation.

No. It was too late. They had taken her from him and already she was estranged; already he had lost her.

Mists of anger danced before his eyes.

Francesco had turned to him.

"It grieves you," he said, "to leave the Lady Lucrezia."

Sforza laughed bitterly. "It does not grieve her," he said. "She is happy enough to settle under the apostolic mantle."

Francesco was looking at him oddly. Sforza, remembering past slights, could not stop himself from muttering savagely: "His Holiness is eager to be rid of me. He wishes to have the complete care of his daughter . . . he wishes to be husband as well as father."

There was silence. Francesco was looking ahead of him; the cavalcade rode on.

On the balcony the Pope was looking fondly at his daughter.

"So Gonzaga rides away," he said. "Now, my dearest, you must make preparations to greet your brother Goffredo and your sister-in-law Sanchia. It will not be long now before they are with us."

SANCHIA OF ARAGON

THE VOLUPTUOUS SANCHIA LAY ON HER BED NIBBLING sweetmeats. Sprawling on the bed, helping themselves now and then from the dish were her three favorite ladies-in-waiting: Loysella, Francesca and Bernardina.

Sanchia was telling them about last night's lover, for she enjoyed recounting details of her various love affairs, declaring that thus she acquired a double pleasure—first in actuality, then in memory.

Sanchia was strikingly beautiful, and one of her greatest attractions was the contrast between her dark hair, dark brows, olive skin and her startling blue eyes. Her features were bold, her nose aquiline and beautifully shaped; her mouth was soft and sensual. To look at Sanchia was to be reminded immediately of erotic pleasures; Sanchia knew this, and the frank sensuality of her smile suggested that she had made discoveries which were unknown to all others but which she would be delighted to impart to those at whom she was smiling, that they and they alone might share this secret.

Sanchia had had lovers for as long as she could remember and she knew that she would go on taking them until she died.

"I do not anticipate the journey with much pleasure," she was saying now. "But what fun it will be when we arrive in Rome. I am halfway in love with Cesare Borgia already, and I have not even seen him. Oh, what a great passion awaits us!"

"You will make the Pope jealous of his own son," suggested Francesca.

"I think not. I think not. I shall leave his Holiness to you, Loysella, or perhaps to little Bernardina. Together mayhap you will compensate him for his weariness of Madonna Giulia—she who is known as La Bella."

Loysella said: "Madonna, you should not talk thus of the Holy Father."

"He is but a man, my child. And do not look so shocked. It is not as though I suggest you should be bedfellow to that mad monk Savonarola."

Loysella shivered, but Sanchia's eyes were speculative. "I have never had a lover who was a monk," she mused. "Perhaps on our journey we shall pass by some monastery. . . ."

"Oh, you are wicked, Madonna," said Francesca with a giggle. "Are you not afraid to talk thus?"

"I am afraid of nothing," retorted Sanchia. "I confess and I do my penances. When I am old I shall reform my ways and doubtless enter a nunnery."

"It will have to be a monastery for you, wicked one," said Loysella.

"Nay, nay, although I would try a monk, it would be but for once. I do not ask for monk night after night . . . day after day."

"Hush!" said Francesca. "If our conversation were reported . . ."

"It matters not. No one attempts to make me change my ways. My father the King knew how I love men, yet what did he do? He said: 'She is one of us. You cannot grow oranges on pear trees.' My brother shakes his head and agrees; and even my old grandmother knew it was useless to try to reform me."

"His Holiness will reform you. It is for this reason that he sends for you."

Sanchia smiled wickedly. "From what I hear of His Holiness it is not to *reform* me that he invites me to Rome."

Loysella pretended to stop her ears because she would not listen to such profanity, but Sanchia merely laughed and bade Francesca bring out the necklace of gold and rubies which her latest lover had brought her.

She leaped up and putting on the necklace paraded before them.

"He said: 'Only the best is worthy to adorn that perfect body.'"

She grimaced and looked at the necklace. "I hope it is of the best," she said.

"The workmanship is exquisite," Francesca cried, examining it.

"You may try it on," said Sanchia. "All of you. Ah," she went on, "last night was wonderful. To-night perhaps will be as exciting, but perhaps not. It is the voyage of discovery which enchants me. The second night is like crossing a sea which has already been traversed. Not the same surprises . . . not the same discoveries. How I wish I had been here when the French soldiers were in Naples!"

Francesca pretended to shiver. "There have been such tales. You would not have escaped. They would have seized on you."

"That would have been exciting. And they say the French are good lovers, and so chivalrous, so gallant. To think that while we were cowering on that dull, dull island of Ischia, such exciting things were going on in Naples."

"You might have hated it," suggested Bernardina. "There was one woman who, pursued by soldiers, killed herself by leaping from the roof of her house."

"I can think of better resting places than the courtyard stones," said Sanchia. "Oh yes, I wish I had been here to meet the gallant French. I was angry . . . quite angry when we were hustled away to live in exile. That is why I must take so many lovers now. There is much time to be made up. You understand?"

"Our lady makes up for lost time very creditably," Loysella murmured.

"At least," said Sanchia, "the rumors have not lied. His Holiness writes to my father that accounts of my conduct, which have reached him in Rome, have most seriously disturbed him."

"Madonna . . . Sanchia, take care . . . take care when you reach Rome."

"Take care! Nay, I'll take Cesare instead."

"I have heard much talk of Cesare," said Loysella.

"Strange talk," put in Francesca.

"It is said," went on Loysella, "that when he casts his eyes on a woman and says 'Come hither,' she dare not disobey. If she does, she is taken by force and punished for having dared delay in obeying the lord Cardinal."

"I have heard," added Bernardina, "that he roams the streets looking for suitable virgins to fill his harem. I have heard that any who stand in his way die mysteriously; none knows how."

Sanchia clasped her hands at the back of her neck, threw back her rippling black hair and laughed. "He sounds more exciting than any man I have ever met. I long to see him face to face."

"Take care, Sanchia," begged Bernardina. "Take care when you come face to face with Cesare Borgia."

"I would have you take care," said Sanchia with a laugh. "I pray you keep my little Goffredo busy this evening. I do not want him strolling into my bedchamber when I am entertaining visitors. It is bad for the dear little creature's morals."

The girls laughed.

"Dear Goffredo. He's a darling, and so pretty. I long to pet him," declared Francesca.

"You may pet him all you wish," Sanchia promised her. "But I pray you keep him from my bedchamber. Where is he now? Let us have him come to us and tell us about his brother. After all, he knows more of Cesare Borgia than any one of us."

They helped Sanchia into her gown, and she was lying back on her pillows when Goffredo came in.

He was very pretty and looked younger than his years, for he was nearly fourteen.

He ran to the bed and threw himself down beside his wife. She put out an arm and held him against her while she stroked his beautiful hair, which was touched with tints of copper. His long-lashed eyes looked at his wife with admiration. He knew that he had married a woman who was said to be the most lovely in all Italy. He had heard her beauty compared with that of his sister, Lucrezia, and his father's mistress, Giulia; and most of those who had seen the three beauties declared that Sanchia had beauty to equal the others and something more—there was a witchery about

Sanchia, something which made her unique. She was insatiably sensual; she scattered promises of undreamed-of delight on all those of the opposite sex who came near her. Thus, although the golden beauty of Lucrezia and Giulia was admired, the dark beauty of Sanchia was more than admired; it was never forgotten.

"And what has my little husband been doing this day?" asked Sanchia.

He put up his face to kiss the firm white chin. "I have been riding," he said. "What a pretty necklace!"

"It was given me last night."

"I did not see you last night. Loysella said I must not disturb you."

"Wicked Loysella," said Sanchia lightly.

"You had a lover with you," stated Goffredo. "Was he pleasing?"

She kissed his head absently, thinking of last night's lover.

"I have known worse, and I have known better," she pronounced judgment.

Goffredo laughed and lifted his shoulder slightly, as a child does in pleasure. He turned to Loysella and said: "My wife has had more lovers than any other woman in Naples—except courtesans of course. You cannot include courtesans, you will agree."

"Agreed," said Francesca.

"Now," demanded Sanchia, "tell us about your brother. Tell us about the famous Cesare Borgia."

"You will never have known a man like my brother Cesare."

"All that we have heard leads us to believe it," Sanchia answered.

"My father loves him dearly," boasted Goffredo, "and no woman has ever said no to him."

"We have heard that women are punished for saying no to him," said Loysella. "How can that be, if none ever do?"

"Because they know he would punish them if they said no. They would be afraid to say it. Therefore they do not say no, but yes . . . yes . . . yes."

"It's logic," said Sanchia, "So must we all prepare ourselves to say yes . . . yes . . . yes."

She popped a sweetmeat into Goffredo's mouth; he lay back against her, sucking contentedly.

"Francesca," commanded Sanchia, "comb my little husband's hair. It is such pretty hair. When it is brushed it glows like copper."

Francesca obeyed; the other two girls stretched themselves out at the foot of the bed. Sanchia lay back sleepily, her arm about Goffredo. Occasionally she would reach for a sweetmeat and nibble a piece before putting it into Goffredo's mouth.

Goffredo, well contented, began to boast.

He boasted about Cesare—Cesare's prowess, Cesare's cruelty.

Goffredo did not know for whom his admiration was the greater: for his brother at whose name everyone in Rome trembled, or for his wife who had taken more lovers than any woman in Naples, except of course courtesans—which was an unfair comparison.

THE CAVALCADE WHICH made its way toward Rome was a merry one, for in its center rode the lovely Sanchia with her little husband and her three devoted ladies-in-waiting. Sanchia had the bearing of a queen; it might have been because she was the illegitimate daughter of the King of Naples that in public she assumed an air of royalty; this enhanced her startling attractiveness because, underlying the air of royalty, was that look of promise which was directed toward any personable young men she encountered, no matter if they were no more than grooms.

Her ladies-in-waiting laughed at her promiscuity; they themselves were far from prudish; lighthearted in their love affairs as butterflies on a sunny day, they flitted from lover to lover: but they lacked the stamina of Sanchia.

Sanchia had ceased to regret that she had not stayed behind in Naples during the French invasion. She had ceased to care because she had not been allowed to meet the French King. Cesare Borgia, she felt sure, would be a more amusing and exciting lover than poor little Charles.

In any case Sanchia was not one to repine. Life was too full of pleasure for such as she was; *her* kingdom was within her reach. Sad and terrible things might happen to those about her. Her father had been driven to exile and to madness. Poor Father! He had been heartbroken when the French took his kingdom.

Knowing of his anguish, Sanchia was determined not to set store on such treasures as those which delighted her father.

When she had heard that they were to marry her to a little boy—a Pope's bastard and not even a favorite bastard at that—she had at first been piqued. That was because the proposed marriage had shown her clearly that she was not of the same importance as her half-sister who was the legitimate daughter of King Alfonso.

Goffredo Borgia, the son of Vannozza Catanei and possibly the Borgia Pope—and possibly not! She knew that there had been suspicions as to her little husband's birth and that at times even the Pope had declared the boy to be no son of his. Should Sanchia, daughter of the King of Naples—illegitimate though she might be—be given in marriage to such as Goffredo?

But they had explained to her: Whether or not he is the Pope's bastard, the Pope accepts him, and that is all that matters.

They were right. The Pope sought alliance with Naples and it was for this reason that the marriage was arranged. But suppose there should be a time when the Pope fell out with Naples and no longer considered the marriage could bring him good?

She had heard how Giovanni Sforza had fallen out of favor with the Pope, and how shabbily he was treated in Vatican circles.

But that was different. Sforza was a man, not very attractive, not pre-possessing, and of a nature which could not be called charming. Sanchia would know how to take care of herself, as poor Giovanni Sforza had not.

So she had become reconciled to her marriage, and she had grown fond of the little boy they had brought to her; she had joined in the sly jokes about the marriage and there had been many, for the whole Court knew that she had her lovers, and they could not hide their amusement at the thought of their experienced and accomplished Princess with this young boy.

Such a pretty little boy he had been when they had brought him to her. And, when they had been put to bed and he had been a little frightened by those who had crowded about them with their crude jokes and lewd gestures, she had answered them with dignity; and when she was alone with her husband she had taken him in her arms, wiped away his tears and told him not to fret. There was nothing he need worry about.

Being Sanchia she had been glad of such a husband. It was so simple to leave him in the care of those devoted ladies of hers while she entertained her lovers.

Thus it was with Sanchia. Life would always be merry. Lovers came into her life and passed out of it; her reputation was known throughout Italy; and she believed there were few men who would not have been delighted to become the lover of Madonna Sanchia.

And so to Rome to become a member of that strange family regarding whom there were so many rumors.

In her baggage were the gowns she would wear when she visited the Pope in the Vatican; there was the gown in which she would make her entry. She must be beautiful for that because, if accounts could be relied upon, she had a rival in her sister-in-law, Lucrezia.

Rome was in a fever of excitement. All through the night the citizens had been congregating to line the streets. It would be a brilliant procession; the people were sure of that, for the Pope's youngest son was bringing his bride to Rome, and one of the greatest accomplishments of the Borgias was their ability to organize brilliant pageants.

In the Vatican the Pope waited with obvious eagerness. It was noted that he was absentminded concerning his duties, but that he was deeply interested in the preparations which were being made for the reception of his daughter-in-law.

Cesare was also eagerly awaiting the arrival, although he did not express his joy as openly as did his father.

In the Palace of Santa Maria in Portico, Lucrezia was more anxious than any, as she was a little afraid of all she had heard concerning her sister-in-law.

Sanchia was beautiful. How beautiful? Lucrezia studied herself anxiously in her mirrors. Was her hair as golden as it had been? It was a pity Giulia was scarcely seen nowadays; being no longer in favor she was a rare visitor at the Vatican and at Santa Maria. Giulia would have offered comfort at a time like this. Lucrezia was aware of a slight feeling of anger, which was alien to her nature, when she thought of how Cesare and her father talked constantly of Madonna Sanchia.

"The most beautiful woman in Italy!" She had heard that again and again. "She has but to look at a man and he is her slave. It is witchcraft, so they say."

Now Lucrezia was beginning to know herself. She was envious of Sanchia. She herself wished to be known as the most beautiful woman in Italy; she wished men to look at her and become *her* slaves; and she longed to be suspected of witchcraft because of her extraordinary powers.

And she was jealous . . . deeply jealous because of the attention Cesare and her father had given to this woman.

Now the day had arrived. Very soon Sanchia of Aragon would be riding up the Appian Way. Very soon Lucrezia would see whether rumor had lied.

She felt vaguely unhappy. She had not wanted to go to meet her sister-in-law, but her father had insisted: "But of course, my dearest, you must go to meet her. It is the respect due to your sister. And what a pleasant picture you will make—you and your ladies, she and hers. You two must be the most lovely creatures in the country."

"I have heard it said that she is. Do you not think that she will put me in the shade?"

The Pope pinched his daughter's cheek affectionately, murmuring: "Impossible! Impossible!"

But his eyes were gleaming and she, who had observed his absorption in Giulia at the beginning, knew that his thoughts were with Sanchia, not with his daughter.

Lucrezia wanted to stamp her foot, to shout at him: "You go and meet her, since you're so eager for her arrival." But being Lucrezia she merely bowed her head and suppressed her feelings.

So now she was preparing herself.

She stood in her apartment while her green and gold brocade dress was slipped over her head. There was a murmur of admiration from her women.

"Never, never, Madonna, have you looked so lovely," she was told.

"Yes, yes," she said, "here in the apartment among you all who are dressed without splendor. But how shall I look when we meet at the Lateran Gate? Suppose she is dressed more splendidly? How shall I look then, for they say she is the most beautiful woman in Italy, and that means in the world?"

"How can that be, Madonna, when you hold that title?"

Characteristically she allowed herself to be soothed; and indeed, when she looked at herself in green and gold, when her eyes went to the feathered bonnet which so became her, when she looked at her glistening golden hair, she was appeased. Nobody had hair like hers, except Giulia, and Giulia was out of favor.

Her train was ready and she had selected it with care. There were twelve girls in beautiful dresses—not beautiful girls but beautiful dresses; one did not want too much competition—and her pages wore mantles of red and gold brocade.

Lucrezia did not feel that she was going out to meet a sister-in-law, but a rival. She knew that while she murmured polite welcoming words she would really be thinking, Is she more beautiful than I? Are my father and my brother going to give all their attention to this newcomer and forget Lucrezia?

In the May sunshine, the retinues of the Cardinals were waiting for her, all splendidly clad, all glittering in the clear bright air; the ambassadors were present, and the palace guards were on duty.

The people cried out in admiration as Lucrezia with her twelve girls appeared. She certainly looked charming, her fair hair rippling about her shoulders beneath the feathered hat, and the green and gold brocade sparkling with jewels. But as they approached the Lateran Gate Lucrezia caught sight of the girl who had caused her so many jealous thoughts, and she realized that Sanchia was indeed a formidable rival.

Surrounded by the retinue which, as Princess of Squillace, Sanchia had brought with her—her halberdiers and equerries, her women and men, her slaves, her jesters—she rode with Goffredo at her side.

A quick look was enough to tell Lucrezia that Goffredo, although he had grown up a little, was still a boy. People might admire his pretty looks and his beautiful auburn hair, but it was toward the woman who rode beside him that every eye would be turned.

This was Sanchia, dressed solemnly in black—as was Goffredo—to remind all who beheld them that they were Spanish. Sanchia's dress was heavily embroidered and her sleeves were wide; her blue-black hair rippled over her shoulders and her eyes were brilliantly blue in contrast.

Suddenly the green and gold brocade seemed girlish—pretty enough, but lacking the elegance of an embroidered black Spanish gown.

Sanchia's dark eyebrows had been plucked a little, after the fashion, but they were still plentiful and her face was heavily painted; there were murmurings in the crowd that she looked older than nineteen.

Her manner was both royal and insolent. It was haughty, and yet as always there was that look of promise in her expression for every personable young man who caught her eye.

Lucrezia had drawn up her horse before that of her brother and sister-in-law, and their greeting was affectionate enough to satisfy all who beheld them.

Then they turned their horses and rode together toward the Vatican.

"I rejoice that we meet at last," said Sanchia.

"I also rejoice," answered Lucrezia.

"I am sure we shall be friends."

"It is my ardent wish."

"I have long desired to meet the members of my new family."

"Particularly Cesare," put in Goffredo. "Sanchia has asked endless questions about our brother."

"He is as eager to see you. Reports of you have reached us here in Rome."

Had she been alone with Lucrezia, Sanchia would have burst into loud laughter. As it was, she said: "Tales of you all have reached me. What beautiful hair you have, sister!"

"I must say the same of yours."

"I have never seen hair so golden."

"You will see it often now. The women of Rome are having silken wigs made, and we see them walking in the streets wearing them."

"In honor of you, dear sister."

"They are mostly courtesans."

"Beauty is their business, and they try to look like you."

Lucrezia smiled faintly but she was unable to hide the apprehension this young woman aroused in her.

She did not hear the whispers behind her.

"Madonna Lucrezia does not like to have a rival in the Vatican."

"And what a rival!"

❧ ♔ ❧

ALEXANDER HAD BEEN unable to wait with the Cardinals to greet the procession, as formality demanded. He had been in a room which overlooked the piazza, impatiently looking out, so eager was he for the first glimpse of this girl who was reputed to be more beautiful than any woman in Italy and as free with her favors as any courtesan.

Now as he saw her at the head of the procession, and riding beside her his golden-haired daughter—raven-haired and golden-haired—the sight enchanted him. How beautiful they were—both of them! What a contrast, a delightful contrast!

He must hurry down to be in his place to greet them when they arrived. He was all impatience to embrace the beautiful creature.

He stood beneath the golden vault, on which was depicted the story of Isis, as he waited for his daughter-in-law to come to him. About him were ranged the Cardinals, and Alexander knew a moment of great content. He reveled in all the pageantry, the ceremony, which as Holy Father he encountered at every hour of his daily life; he loved life; it had everything to offer him for which he craved and he was one of those rare beings who could be satisfied with each moment as it came. He was a happy man; and never happier than at moments such as this.

She was approaching now—beautiful, dark-haired, and so bold; her eyes were downcast, but she could not hide her boldness. She had all the arrogance of a woman who knows herself to be desired; she had all the charm of her sex for a man such as himself.

He was in a fever of excitement as she, with little Goffredo beside her, knelt to kiss his toe.

Now she had stepped back and the others came forward, those ladies of hers—all delicious, all worthy to be her handmaidens, thought Alexander. He studied them all in turn, and he felt anew his pleasure in having them with him.

Now they had taken their places; Goffredo was standing by Cesare, and Cesare had his speculative eyes on his brother's bride; and on the steps of the throne, kneeling on two red velvet cushions, were Lucrezia and Sanchia.

Oh, this is a happy moment, thought Alexander; and he wished quickly to dispense with solemn ceremony that he might talk with his daughter-in-law, make her laugh, make her understand that, although he was her father-in-law and head of the Church, he was none the less a merry man and one who knew how to be gallant to the ladies.

One of the Cardinals who watched turned to another and said: "Brother and father have eyes on Goffredo's wife."

Another whispered: "All have eyes on Goffredo's wife."

The answer came back: "Mark my words, Madonna Sanchia will bring trouble to the Vatican."

Sanchia came into Lucrezia's apartment and with her were her three handmaidens.

Lucrezia was a little startled by the intrusion. It was Whit Sunday, two days after the arrival of Sanchia and Goffredo, and Lucrezia was being dressed for the service at St. Peter's.

Sanchia had begun by ignoring all rules of etiquette and Lucrezia saw that she was determined to behave here in Rome as though she were at the lax court of Naples.

Sanchia's dress was black, but she looked far from demure; the blue eyes were almost cynical, thought Lucrezia; it was as though Sanchia was weaving plans, secret subtle plans.

"And how is my dear sister this day?" asked Sanchia. "Ready for the ceremony? I hear we are to listen to a Spanish prelate." She grimaced. "Spanish prelates are apt to be over-devout and therefore to deliver over-long sermons."

"But we must attend," Lucrezia explained. "My father will be present, and so will all the dignitaries of the Papal Court. It is an important occasion and . . ."

"Oh yes . . . oh yes . . . we must attend."

Sanchia, putting her arm about Lucrezia and drawing her to a mirror, looked at their reflections. "I do not look as though I am about to attend a solemn service, do I? And, when I look closer, nor do you. Oh Lucrezia, how innocent you look with your lovely light eyes and your golden hair? But are you innocent, Lucrezia? Are you?"

"Innocent of what?" asked Lucrezia.

"Oh, life . . . of what you will. Oh Lucrezia, thoughts go on inside that golden head, of which you say nothing. You look startled. But I am right, am I not? One as lovely as you are cannot be so remote from . . . from all that makes the world so interesting."

"I am afraid I do not understand."

"Are you such a child then? What of Cesare? He will be at this solemn service. Do you know, sister, I have longed to meet you all, and you are the only one with whom so far I have been alone."

"There have been so many ceremonies," murmured Lucrezia, uncertain of the girl who was so outspoken and who therefore said those things which embarrassed and would have been so much better left unsaid.

"Oh yes. Later I shall know you all very well, I doubt not. Cesare is not exactly as I would have imagined him. He is as handsome in person as rumor says he is. But there is a strangeness about him, a brooding resentment. . . ."

"My brother wished to be a great soldier."

"I see. I see. He does not take kindly to the robes of the Church."

Lucrezia looked uneasily about her. She said to her servants: "That will be enough. Leave us now."

She looked at Sanchia, expecting her to dismiss her women.

"They are my friends," said Sanchia. "I hope they will be yours. They admire you. Do you not?" she demanded of the trio.

"We all agree that Madonna Lucrezia is quite lovely," said Loysella.

"Now tell me about Cesare," insisted Sanchia. "He is angry . . . a very angry man. I know it."

"Cesare will always succeed in the end," said Lucrezia. "He will always do what he sets out to do."

"You are very fond of your brother?"

"It is impossible not to admire him more than anyone on Earth, as he excels all others."

Sanchia smiled knowledgeably. Now she understood. There was something in these rumors she had heard, of the strange and passionate attachments which existed in the Borgia family.

She knew that Lucrezia was suspicious of her, jealous because she feared Sanchia might attract the Pope and Cesare so that they ceased to be so eager for Lucrezia's company. It was a novel situation and one which appealed to Sanchia.

Moreover it was comforting to think that Cesare Borgia did not have all his own way. He hated the robes of the Church yet he was forced to wear them, and that was why she had seen that smoldering anger in his eyes. She, as the illegitimate daughter of the King of Naples, forced to take second place to her half-sister, understood his feelings. It drew her closer to Cesare, and his vulnerability intrigued her.

As they set out for St. Peter's she felt almost recklessly gay; she put her arm lovingly through Lucrezia's as they entered the church. How long the ceremony was! There was the Holy Father, seeming quite a different person from the jovial father who had been so affectionate during last night's banquet. She had been right about the Spanish prelate; his sermon went on and on.

"I am tired," she whispered to Lucrezia.

Lucrezia's pale face turned slightly pink. The Princess from Naples seemed to have no understanding as to how to conduct herself during a solemn ceremony.

Lucrezia said nothing.

"Will the man never end?"

Loysella smothered a giggle, and Bernardina whispered: "For the love of the saints, Madonna, be quiet!"

"But it is too long to stand," complained Sanchia. "Why should we not be seated? Look, there are empty pews."

Lucrezia said in an agonized whisper: "They are for canons when they sing the gospel."

"They shall be for us now," said Sanchia.

Several heads turned on account of the whispering voices, so many saw this beautiful young woman climb into the pews with a rustling of silk and the exposure of very shapely legs. Loysella, Francesca and Bernardina, who followed their mistress in all things, did not hesitate. Where Sanchia went, so did they.

Lucrezia, watching them for a second, was aware of a rising excitement within her. She knew that these girls lived colorful lives, and she herself longed for the sort of adventures which she knew to be theirs; she wanted to identify herself with them.

Without hesitation, she followed, climbing into the pews, settling down beside them with a rustle of garments, an unusually mischievous smile on her lips, the laughter rising within her.

They had settled down in their pews and Sanchia had forced a look of mock piety on to her face. Loysella dropped her head hurriedly to hide her mirth, and Lucrezia needed all her willpower to stop herself breaking into hysterical laughter.

They had shocked the Papal Court.

Never, complained the Cardinals, had such behavior been seen during a solemn service. The woman from Naples was clearly nothing more than a Court harlot. The glances she distributed confirmed the reputation which had preceded her.

Girolamo Savonarola declaimed long and loudly from the pulpit of San Marco in Florence that the Papal Court was a disgrace to the world, and the Pope's women behaved with great impropriety and were the disgrace and scandal of the people.

The Cardinals tentatively approached the Holy Father.

"Your Holiness will have suffered great sadness," said one. "The spectacle of those young women's behavior during the Whitsuntide ceremonies horrified all who beheld it."

"Is that so?" said Alexander. "I noticed many an eye glistened as it turned in their direction."

"With disgust, Holiness."

"I saw no disgust, but I did see some delight."

The Cardinals looked grim. "Your Holiness will doubtless deal adequately with the offenders?"

"Oh come, come, what offense is there in the pranks of girls? Young girls are by nature high-spirited. I for one would not have them otherwise. And who among you was not a little bored by our worthy preacher?"

"Nevertheless, to bring the manners of Naples to Rome!"

The Pope nodded placatingly. He would speak to the girls.

He did. He put an arm about Sanchia and another about Lucrezia, and composed his features into an expression of mock reproach. He kissed them tenderly and smiled benignly at Loysella, Bernardina and Francesca who stood before him, their heads bowed—but not so low as to prevent their glancing upwards occasionally at the Holy Father.

"You have shocked the community," he said, "and if you were not so beautiful, I should be forced to scold you, and so I am sure bore you as thoroughly as did your Spanish prelate."

"But you understand, Most Holy Lord," said Sanchia, looking at him from under her dark lashes with those bluest of blue eyes.

"I understand this," said the Pope, giving her a passionate look. "It gives me the greatest pleasure in the world to see so much brightness and beauty at my Court; and should I as much as frown on you I should be the most ungrateful man on Earth."

Whereupon they all laughed, and Sanchia said they would sing for him, for he was not only their Holy Father but their greatly beloved one.

So Sanchia sang to the accompaniment of Lucrezia's lute, and the girls ranged themselves about him, Loysella, Bernardina, Francesca on stools at his feet, raising wondering and admiring eyes, while Sanchia and Lucrezia leaned against his knees.

Scold these lovely creatures! thought Alexander. Never! Their little pranks could only amuse such a benevolent father.

※ ♛ ※

THAT NIGHT SANCHIA danced with Cesare. His eyes held hers and she was conscious of that smoldering resentment against the world which had afflicted herself. She was of a different temperament, and it was because of this that she had been able to shrug aside the slights and enjoy her life. But there was a bond between them.

For all his demonstrations of affection the Pope had not assigned to her that position at the Papal Court for which she longed. She was merely the wife of Goffredo, himself suspected of having a father other than Alexander; it would have been different had she been the wife of Cesare.

But her sensuous nature made it possible for her to forget all else in the pursuit of sexual satisfaction. That satisfaction dominated her life. It was not so with Cesare. He craved carnal pleasures but he had other desires as insistent. His love of power was greater than his desire for women.

She, who had known so many men that she read them easily, was aware of this, and she determined now to make Cesare forget his ambitions in his pursuit of her. They were both experienced, and they would find great pleasure in surprising each other by their accomplishments. Each was aware of this as they danced; and each was asking: Why delay longer? Delay was something which neither of them would tolerate.

"You are all that I heard you were," Sanchia told him.

"You are all that I hoped you would be," he answered her.

"I wondered when you and I would be able to talk together. This is the first time it has happened, and all eyes are on us now."

"They were right," said Cesare, "when they said you were the most beautiful woman in the world."

"They were right when they said there was something terrifying about you."

"Do you find me terrifying?"

She laughed. "No man terrifies me."

"Have they always been so kind?"

"Always," she said. "From the time I was able to talk, men have been kind to me."

"Are you not weary of my sex, since you know it so well?"

"Each man is different from all others. That is what I have found. Perhaps that is why I have always discovered them to be so fascinating. And none that I have ever known has been remotely like you, Cesare Borgia; you stand apart."

"And you like this strangeness in me?"

"So much that I would know it so well that it ceases to be strangeness and is familiar to me."

"What tales have you heard of me?"

"That you are a man who will never take no for an answer, that men fear your frown, and that when you beckon a woman she must obey, in fear if not in desire. I have heard that those who displease you meet ill fortune, that some have been discovered in alleys, suffocated or with knives in their bodies. I have heard that some have drunk wine at your table and have felt themselves to be merely intoxicated, only to learn that they are dying. These are the things which I have heard of you, Cesare Borgia. What have you heard of me?"

"That you practice witchcraft so that all men whom you desire fall under your spell, and that having once been your lover none can ever forget you."

"And do you believe these tales of me?"

"And do you believe the tales of me?"

She looked into his eyes and the flame of desire in hers was matched by that in his.

"I do not know," she said, "but I am determined to discover."

"Nor do I know," he answered; "and I think I am as eager to make my discoveries as you are."

His hand tightened on hers.

"Sanchia," he said, "this night?"

And she closed her eyes and nodded.

They were watched.

The Pope smiled affectionately. It was inevitable. How could it have been otherwise? Cesare and Sanchia! They were well matched, and from the moment Cesare had heard of her he had determined it should be so.

Now we shall have the tiresome scandalmongers whispering, mused Alexander, now we shall have the Cardinals raising shocked hands and voices; and Savonarola will be thundering from his pulpit of the vice which goes on at the Papal Court.

The Pope sighed, faintly envious of his son, laughing slyly to himself; he would prevail upon Cesare to give him a full account of the affair.

Goffredo watched delightedly. How handsome they looked dancing together. My wife and my brother. They are the two most distinguished people in the ballroom. All watch them. And they find each other delightful.

Cesare, great Cesare, will be grateful to me because I have brought him Sanchia. And Sanchia, she is clearly delighted to meet Cesare. All her lovers must seem so unworthy when she compares them with him!

Lucrezia watched.

So, she thought, Goffredo's wife has now determined to take Cesare as her lover. She knows how to lure him, how to please him.

Lucrezia wanted to bury her face in her hands and sob; and fervently she wished that Sanchia had never come to Rome.

THey lay together on Sanchia's bed.

Sanchia was smiling, glancing sideways at her lover. It is true, she thought exultantly, he is as no other man. He has the virility of two men; he is skilled and yet eager to discover; he is ardent and yet aloof, passionate and yet cold. In all her experience she had never known a lover such as Cesare Borgia.

She turned to him and said languidly: "They should have married me to you . . . not to Goffredo."

She saw the change creep into his face; the slack sensuality disappeared and in its place was sudden anger so intense that it shocked her even in her present mood of indolence.

He clenched his fists and she realized that he was fighting with himself to hold back his anger.

"My father," he said, "saw fit to send me to the Church."

"It is incomprehensible," she answered soothingly, and she laid her hand on his arm to draw him to her, once more to court desire.

But he was not to be seduced from his anger.

"I have two brothers," he said, "and yet I was the chosen one."

"You will be Pope," she told him; "and that need not prevent your enjoying adventures such as this, Cesare."

"I wish to command the armies," he said. "I wish to have sons . . . legitimate sons. I wish to cast aside my Cardinal's robe. I loathe the thing and all connected with it."

She sat up in bed, her long hair falling about her nakedness. Her blue eyes shone. She wanted now to turn him from his anger, to bring him back to making love. It was a challenge. Is his anger more important to him than I am? What sort of man is this to talk of his ambitions while he lies in bed with me?

She took his hands and smiled at him.

"I doubt not all that you desire will be yours, Cesare Borgia."

"Are you a witch?" he asked.

She nodded slowly and laughed showing her red tongue.

"I am a witch, Cesare Borgia, and I promise you this . . . a soldier's uniform, a wife and legitimate offspring."

He was looking at her intently; at least she had focused his attention on herself, even if it was the possible power of prophecy, rather than her body, which attracted him.

Her eyes were wide. "One of the family must go into the Church," she went on. "It should have been little Goffredo. Why should it not be Goffredo?"

He knelt on the bed beside her; he took her by the shoulders and looked into her wild blue eyes.

"Yes," she said. "Here is the answer. There should be a divorce. Little Goffredo should wear the Cardinal's robes and Sanchia and Cesare should be man and wife."

"By the saints!" cried Cesare, "it is a good plan."

Then he seized her and kissed her wildly.

She laughed. "I trust my lord likes me no less because I might one day be his bride. They say the gentlemen of Rome find the mistresses they discover for themselves more to their liking than the wives who are found for them."

"Have done," he said fiercely.

"First," she cried, "you must declare that you wish to be my husband. . . ."

She fell back laughing, and they struggled for a while.

"Cesare," she murmured blissfully, "you have the strength of ten men."

Lucrezia BEGGED AUDIENCE of her father.

Alexander studied his daughter anxiously. She looked pale and unhappy.

"What is it, my dearest?" he asked.

She lowered her eyes. She hated lying to him, yet she could not bring herself to tell him the truth.

"I feel unwell, dearest Father," she said. "There is plague in the air of Rome, and I think it affects me. I have suffered from a slight fever these last days and nights."

His cool jeweled hands were on her forehead.

"My blessed one," he murmured.

"I crave your pardon," said Lucrezia, "because I am going to ask something which I know you will not be anxious to grant me. I feel I need a change of air, and I would go for a short while to Pesaro."

There was silence.

Her husband would be there, thought the Pope; and he was becoming increasingly dissatisfied with his daughter's marriage. But Lucrezia looked wan, and he longed to make her happy.

She let her eyes linger on the red velvet cushion on which she knelt.

She felt that she was a strangely bewildered girl, who did not understand herself. She hated Sanchia—Sanchia with her bright blue eyes, wild laughter and deep, deep knowledge.

Sanchia treated Lucrezia as a child, and Lucrezia knew that in worldly matters she would remain a child while her emotions were such as she did not understand. She only knew that she could not bear to see Sanchia and Cesare together; that she hated the complaisance of Goffredo, the giggling of those three women who served Sanchia.

Often she had thought of Pesaro during the last weeks, when she had gone to Sanchia's apartments because she knew that Cesare would be there and that if she did not go she would miss seeing him that day.

Pesaro, that quiet little town with the hills which formed a semi-circle about it and the blue sea washing its shores, Pesaro, where she could live with her husband and behave as a normal wife. In Pesaro she had felt herself to be as other women, and that was how she wanted to be.

Her father's fingers were caressing her hair; she heard his voice, very gentle and tender, as though he understood: "My dearest, if it is your wish that you should go to Pesaro, then to Pesaro shall you go."

ALEXANDER MET HIS son in the Papal apartments.

"I have news for you, Cesare," he said.

Alexander was uneasy, but the news had to be broken soon, and Cesare was deep in a love affair with Sanchia which was proving to be an absorbing one. Alexander had no doubt of that. Therefore with Cesare satisfied, this was a good moment to tell him that which he had long wished to tell and which could not much longer be kept a secret from him.

Cesare answered: "Yes, Most Holy Father?"

"Giovanni is coming home."

Alexander quickly slipped his arm through that of his son; he did not want to see the blood rush into Cesare's cheeks; he did not want to see the angry red in his eyes.

"Yes, yes," said Alexander, walking toward the window and gently pulling Cesare with him. "I am growing old and I shall be a happy man to have all my family about me once more."

Cesare was silent.

No need yet, thought Alexander, to tell Cesare that Giovanni was being brought home to conduct a campaign against the Orsini who must be punished for going over to the French without a fight during the invasion. No need to say, When Giovanni comes I shall make him commander of the Papal forces. Cesare would have to know . . . but later.

"When he returns," said Alexander lightly, "we must recall little Lucrezia. I long for the day when I have every member of my beloved family sitting at my table, that I may feast my eyes upon them."

Still Cesare did not answer. His fingers twitched as he pulled at his Cardinal's robes. He did not see the piazza beyond the window; he was unaware of Alexander, standing beside him.

All he could think of was that Giovanni, the envied, the hated one, was coming home.

ROMAN CARNIVAL

The two brothers met at the Porta Portuense. Cesare, as tradition and his father insisted, set out at the head of that procession which was made up of the Cardinals and their splendid households, to greet the brother whom he hated more than anyone in the world.

They faced each other. Giovanni had changed a little since he had gone to Spain. He was more arrogant, more magnificent and the lines of cruelty about his mouth had deepened. Dissipation had marked his features, but he was very handsome still. His dress was more grand than anything Cesare had ever seen him wear before. His red velvet cape was decorated with pearls, and his waistcoat of the same material in a light shade of brown was ablaze with pearls and glistening jewels of all colors. Even his horse was made brilliant by golden ornaments and silver bells. Giovanni was a dazzling sight as he entered the city of Rome, and the citizens were astonished to behold him.

As they rode side by side to the Apostolic Palace, which was to be the

Duke's home, Giovanni could not help taking sly glances at his brother, letting him know that he was fully aware of the enmity which existed between them and that, now he was a great Duke with a son and another child shortly expected, now that he came home at their father's request to command their father's forces, he realized that Cesare's envy was not likely to have abated in the smallest degree.

THE POPE COULD not contain his joy at the sight of his best-loved son.

He embraced him and wept, while Cesare watched, standing apart, clenching his hands and grinding his teeth, saying to himself, Why should it be so? What has he that I lack?

Alexander looking toward Cesare guessed his feelings and, as he knew that Cesare must certainly feel still more angry when he understood in full the glory which was to be Giovanni's, he stretched out his hand to Cesare and said tenderly: "My two sons! It is rarely nowadays that I know the pleasure of having you both with me at the same time."

When Cesare ignored the hand, and strolled to the window, Alexander was uneasy. It was the first time Cesare had openly rebuffed him, and that it should have happened in the presence of a third party was doubly disturbing. He decided that the best thing he could do was to ignore the gesture.

Cesare said without turning his head: "There are crowds below. They wait, hoping to catch further glimpses of the splendid Duke of Gandia."

Giovanni strode to the window; he turned to Cesare, smiling that insolent smile. "They shall not be disappointed," he said, looking down at his bejeweled garments and back at Cesare. "A pity," he went on, "that the comparatively somber garments of the Church are all you have to show them, brother."

"Then you understand," Cesare answered lightly, "that it is not the Duke whom they applaud, but the Duke's jeweled doublet."

Alexander had insinuated himself between them, putting an arm about each.

"You will be interested to meet Goffredo's wife, my dear Giovanni," he said.

Giovanni laughed. "I have heard of her. Her fame has traveled even to Spain. Some of my more prudish relatives speak her name in whispers."

The Pope burst into laughter. "We are more tolerant in Rome, eh, Cesare?"

Giovanni looked at his brother. "I have heard," he said, "that Sanchia of Aragon is a generous woman. So generous indeed that all she has to bestow cannot be given to one husband."

"Our Cesare here, he is a fascinating fellow," said Alexander placatingly.

"I doubt it not," laughed Giovanni.

Determination was in his eyes. Cesare was looking at him challengingly, and whenever a challenge had been issued by one brother to the other it had always been taken up.

Giovanni Sforza rode toward Pesaro.

How thankful he was to be home. How tired he was of the conflicts raging about him. In Naples he was treated as an alien, which he was; he was suspected of spying for the Milanese, which he had. The last year had brought nothing to enhance his opinion of himself. He was more afraid, and of more people, than he had ever been in his life.

Only behind the hills of Pesaro could he be at peace. He indulged in a pleasant daydream as he rode homeward. It was that he might ride to Rome, take his wife and bring her back with him to Pesaro—defying the Pope and her brother Cesare. He heard himself saying: "She is my wife. Try to take her from me if you dare!"

But they were dreams. As if it were possible to say such things to the Pope and Cesare Borgia! The tolerance which the Pope would display toward one who he would believe had lost his senses, the sneers of Cesare toward one whom he knew to be a coward parading as a brave man—they were more than Giovanni Sforza could endure.

So he could only dream.

He rode slowly along by the Foglia River, in no hurry now that Pesaro was in sight. When he reached home he would find it dreary; life would not be the same as it had been during those months when he had lived there with Lucrezia.

Lucrezia! At first during those months before the marriage had been consummated, she had seemed but a shy bewildered child. But how different he had discovered her to be! He wanted to take her away, make her his completely and gradually purge her of all that she had inherited from her strange family.

He could see the castle—strong, seeming impregnable.

There, he thought, I could live with Lucrezia, happy, secure, all the days of our lives. We should have children and find peace in our stronghold between the mountains and the sea.

His retainers were running out to greet him.

"Our Lord has come home." He felt grand and important, he the Lord of Pesaro, as he rode forward. Pesaro might have been a great dominion; these few people might have been a multitude.

He accepted the homage, dismounted and entered the palace.

It was a dazzling manifestation of his dream, for she stood there, the sun shining on her golden hair which fell loose about her shoulders, and lighting the few discreet jewels she wore—as became the lady of a minor castle.

"Lucrezia!" he cried.

She smiled that fascinating smile which still held a child-like quality.

"Giovanni," she answered him, "I was weary of Rome. I came to Pesaro that I might be here to greet you on your return."

He laid his hands on her shoulders and kissed her forehead, then her cheeks, before he lightly touched her lips with his.

He believed in that moment that the Giovanni Sforza whom he had seen in his dreams might have existence in reality.

But Giovanni Sforza could not believe in his happiness. He must torture himself—and Lucrezia.

He was continually discovering new ornaments in her jewel cases.

"And whence came this trinket?" he would ask.

"My father gave it to me," would invariably be the answer. Or: "It is a gift from my brother."

Then Giovanni would throw it back into the box, stalk from the room or regard her with glowering eyes.

"The behavior at the Papal Court is shocking the world!" he declared. "It is worse since the woman from Naples came."

This made Lucrezia unhappy; she thought of Sanchia and Cesare together, of Goffredo's delight that his wife should so please his brother, of Alexander's amusement and her own jealousy.

We are indeed a strange family, she thought.

She would look across the sea, and there was a hope in her eyes, a hope that she might conform with the standards of goodness set up by such men as Savonarola, that she might live quietly with her own husband in their mountain stronghold, that she might curb this desire to be with her own disturbing family.

But although Giovanni had no help to offer her, and only gave her continual reproaches, she was determined to be patient; so she listened quietly to his angry outbursts and only mildly tried to assure him of her innocence. And there were occasions when Giovanni would throw himself at her feet and declare that she was good at heart and he was a brute to upbraid her continually. He could not explain to her that always he saw himself as a poor creature, despised by all, and that the conduct of her family and the rumors concerning them made him seem ever poorer, even more contemptible.

There were times when she thought, I can endure this no longer. Perhaps I will hide myself in a convent. There in the solitude of a cell I might begin to understand myself, to discover a way in which I can escape from all that I know I should.

Yet how could she endure life in a convent? When letters came from her father, her heart would race and her hands tremble as she seized on them. Reading what he had written made her feel as though he were with her, talking to her; and then she realized how happy she was when she was in the heart of her family, and that only then could she be completely content.

She must find a compensation for this overpowering love which she bore toward her family. Was a convent the answer?

Alexander was begging her to return. Her brother Giovanni, he pointed out, was in Rome, even more handsome, more charming than he had been when he went away. Each day he asked about his beloved sister and when she was coming home. Lucrezia must return at once.

She wrote that her husband wished her to remain in Pesaro, where he had certain duties.

The answer to that came promptly.

Her brother Giovanni was about to set out on a military campaign which was to be directed first against the Orsini, and which was calculated later to subdue all the barons who had proved themselves to be helpless against the invader. The rich lands and possessions of these barons would fall into the Pope's hands. Lucrezia knew that this was the first step on that road along which Alexander had long planned to go.

Now, his dear son-in-law, Giovanni Sforza, could show his mettle and win great honors for himself. Let him collect his forces and join the Duke of Gandia. Lucrezia would not wish to stay on at Pesaro alone, so she must return to Rome where her family would prepare a great welcome for her.

When Giovanni Sforza read this letter he was furious.

"What am I?" he cried. "Nothing but a piece on a chequer-board to be moved this way and that. I will *not* join the Duke of Gandia. I have my duties here."

So he stormed and raged before Lucrezia, yet he knew—and she knew also—that he went in fear of the Pope.

However, on this occasion he determined to try compromise. He gathered together his men but, instead of leaving with them, he wrote to the Pope and explained that his duties in his own dominion prevented his leaving at this time.

He and Lucrezia waited for the command to obey, the expressions of angry reproach.

There was a long silence; then from the Vatican came a soothing reply. His Holiness fully understood Giovanni Sforza's reasons; he no longer insisted that he should join the Duke of Gandia. At the same time he would like to remind his son-in-law that it was long since he had seen him in Rome, and it would give him the utmost pleasure to embrace Giovanni and Lucrezia once more.

The letter made Lucrezia very happy. "I feared," she told her husband, "that your refusal to join my brother would have angered my father. But how benevolent he is! He understands, you see."

"The greater your father's benevolence, the more I fear him," growled Giovanni.

"You do not understand him. He loves us. He wishes to have us in Rome."

"He wishes you to be in Rome. I do not know what he wishes for me."

And Lucrezia looked at her husband and shivered imperceptibly. There were times when she felt there was no escape from the destiny which her family was preparing for her.

Cesare HAD rarely been so happy in the whole of his life as he was at this time.

His brother Giovanni was helping to prove all that he, Cesare, had been at such pains to make their father realize. How angry he had been at that ceremony when Giovanni had been invested with the standard, richly embroidered, and the sword, richly jeweled, of Captain General of the Church! How the fury had welled up within him to see his father's eyes shining with pride as he beheld his favorite son!

"Fool!" Cesare had wanted to cry. "Do you not see that he will bring disgrace on your armies and the name of Borgia?"

And Cesare's prophecies were coming true. That was what gave him this great pleasure. Now surely his father must see the folly of investing his son Giovanni with military honors which he could not uphold, and the crass stupidity of preventing the brave bold Cesare from taking over the command which, in a fond father's folly, had been given to Giovanni.

Everything was in Giovanni's favor. The wealth and might of the Pope was behind him. The great Captain Virginio Orsini was still a prisoner in Naples and could not take part in his family's defense. To any with an ounce of military knowledge, so reasoned Cesare, the campaign should have been swift and victorious.

And at first it seemed as though it would be so, for, with Virginio a prisoner, the Orsinis appeared to have no heart for the fight, and one by one surrendered to Giovanni's forces as they had to the French. Castle after castle threw open its gates, and in marched the conqueror without the shedding of one drop of blood.

In the Vatican the Pope rejoiced; even in Cesare's presence, knowing how galling it was to his eldest son, he could not hide his pride.

That was why the new turn of events was so gratifying to Cesare.

The Orsini clan were not so easily overcome as the brash young Duke of Gandia and his doting father had believed. They had gathered in full force at the family castle of Bracciano under the leadership of the sister of Virginio. Bartolommea Orsini was a brave woman. She had been brought up in a military tradition and she was not going to submit without a fight. In this she was helped by her husband and other members of the family.

Giovanni Borgia was startled to come up against resistance. He had had no experience of war, and his methods of breaking the siege at Bracciano seemed to the experienced warriors on both sides, both childish and foolish. He had no wish to fight, for Giovanni was a soldier who had more affection for jeweled sword and white stick of office than for battle. He therefore sent messages to the defenders of the castle, first wheedling, then threatening, telling them that their wisest plan would be to surrender. It was uncomfortable, camping outside the castle; the weather was bad; and Giovanni's gorgeous apparel unsuited to it. His most able captain, Guidobaldo of Montefeltro, the Duke of Urbino, was badly wounded and forced to retire, which meant that Giovanni had lost his best adviser.

Time passed and Giovanni remained outside the stronghold of Bracciano. He was tired of the war, and he had heard that the whole of Italy was laughing at the Commander of the Pope's forces, and moreover he guessed how his brother was enjoying this turn of events.

The people of Rome whispered about the grand Captain: "How fares he now? Does he look quite so gorgeous as he did when he set out? The rain and wind will not be good for all that velvet and brocade."

Alexander was filled with anxiety, and declared he would sell his tiara if necessary to bring the war to a satisfactory conclusion. He could not bear the company of his elder son Cesare, for Cesare did not attempt to hide his delight at the way things were going. This hatred of brother for brother, thought Alexander, was folly of the first order. Had Cesare and Giovanni not yet learned that strength was in unity?

Cesare was with him when the news came to him that Giovanni was still waiting outside the castle and that Urbino had been wounded.

He watched the red blood flood his father's face and, as he stood there, exulting, Alexander swayed and would have fallen had not Cesare rushed forward to catch him.

Looking at his father, whose face was dark with rich purple blood, the whites of his eyes showing red, and the veins knotted at his temples, Cesare had a sudden terrible fear of a future in which there would be no Alexander to protect his family. Then did he realize how much they owed to this man—this man who hitherto had been renowned for his vitality, this man who surely must possess true genius.

"Father!" cried Cesare aghast. "Oh, my beloved father!"

The Pope opened his eyes and became aware of his son's anxiety.

"Dear son," he said. "Fear not. I am with you still."

Once again that exceptional vitality showed itself. It was as though Alexander refused to accept the ailments of encroaching age.

"Father," cried Cesare in anguish, "you are not ill? You cannot be ill."

"Help me to my chair," said Alexander. "There! That is better. It was a momentary faintness. I felt the blood pounding in my veins, and it seemed that my head would burst with it. It is passing. It was the shock of this news. I must control myself in future. There is no need to fret about that which has not yet happened."

"You must take greater care, Father," Cesare warned him.

"Oh my son, my son, do not look so distressed. And yet I feel happy to see that you care so much for me."

Alexander closed his eyes and lay back in his chair smiling. The astute statesman, always wilfully blind where his family was concerned, allowed himself to believe that it was out of affection for his father that Cesare was alarmed, not because he was aware of the precarious position he, with the rest of his family, would be in if the Pope were no longer there to protect them.

Cesare then begged his father to call his physician, that he might be examined; and this Alexander at length promised he would do. But the Pope's resilience was amazing and, a few hours after the fainting fit, he was making new plans for Giovanni's success.

Alas, eventually even Alexander had to face the fact that Giovanni was no soldier, for this became undeniable when help came to the Orsini from the French, and they were able to attack the besiegers of the castle.

Faced with real battle Giovanni proved himself to be a hopeless leader, and the engagement went badly for the Papal forces; the only man among them who distinguished himself was the Duke of Urbino who, recovered from his wounds, was taken prisoner by the Orsini. As for Giovanni, he was wounded, but slightly, and realizing that he was in a somewhat ridiculous position, from which above all things he longed to extricate himself, he declared that being wounded he was unable to carry on, and must leave his armies to finish the conflict under a new commander.

Now the whole of Italy was laughing at the adventures of the Pope's son. They remembered the ceremony at which he had been made head of the Papal armies; when he had led his armies out of Rome, he had marched like a conqueror.

This was very amusing to the Romans; and many people were pleased. This should teach the Pope that it was dangerous to his own interests to carry nepotism too far.

Cesare had recovered from his alarm over the Pope's fainting fit, for Alexander was as full of vitality as ever, and Cesare was not going to lose this opportunity of scoring over his brother.

He called his friends to him and together they devised brilliant posters which they set up on various important roads throughout the city.

"Wanted," ran the words on these posters, "those who have any news concerning a certain army of the Church. Will anyone having such information impart it at once to the Duke of Gandia."

Giovanni came home, where he was received with undiminished affection by his father, who immediately began making excuses for his son and assuring everyone that, had Giovanni not had the ill luck to be wounded, there would have been a different tale to tell.

And all who heard marvelled at the dissembling of Alexander who so delighted to deceive himself. But they were soon admiring his diplomacy, for it appeared that the Pope never lost a war. Defeated in battle he might be, but terms followed battle, and from these terms the Pope invariably emerged as the victor.

Cesare went to see his father, and found Giovanni with him.

As Cesare looked at his brother he could not prevent a sneer from curling his lips.

"So," he cried, "you have not rejoined your army, General."

"Cardinal, my army and I have parted company," said Giovanni lightly. "We wearied of each other."

"So I hear." Cesare laughed. "All Rome talks of it. There are even posters on the city's walls."

"It would be interesting to discover who put them there." Giovanni's eyes gleamed murderously.

"Be at peace, my sons," put in Alexander. "What is done is done. We have suffered ill-fortune and we will now make peace."

"We have to sue for peace!" Cesare's tone was grim. "A pretty pass."

"We'll make it a pretty pass in all truth," mused Alexander. "The Orsini are in no mood to continue the fight. I have offered my terms to them now and they will be accepted."

"Your terms, Holiness?"

"My terms and their terms," said Alexander lightly. "I shall allow them to buy back their castles. You will see that we shall lose nothing from this war."

"And Urbino?" asked Cesare. "He is a prisoner. What ransom will be asked for him?"

The Pope shrugged the question aside. "Doubtless his family are gathering together the ransom."

Cesare's eyes narrowed. This brilliant man who was their father was in actuality turning Giovanni's defeat into victory. Giovanni was watching his brother slyly.

He said: "Being weary of war, I rejoice that to-morrow the carnival begins."

There was hatred in Giovanni's eyes to match that in Cesare's. You have sought to disparage me in our father's eyes, Cesare Borgia, he was thinking; do not imagine that I shall allow you to attack me with impunity. Have a care, for I will find a way to turn the tables, my lord Cardinal!

It was with Cesare that the Pope discussed the peace terms. Giovanni was too busy contriving his costume for the carnival and planning his own revels. He missed Djem who had always had some bizarre and fantastic suggestion to make at such a time.

There must come a day, Cesare was thinking, when our father realizes that I am the one to stand beside him, to share his ambition. How can a man, so brilliant as he is, continue to risk our position through this blind and foolish trust in one son at the expense of the other?

At such times as this Cesare was almost happy. There was no need now to call attention to Giovanni's shortcomings; they must be perfectly obvious even to the besottedly devoted Alexander.

"My father," he said now, "you astonish me. We Borgias have just suffered defeat which would have proved disastrous to many, and you are fast turning that defeat into victory."

Alexander laughed. "My son, more is won at the council table than on the battlefield."

"That, I venture to suggest, Holiness, might depend on the soldiers. Had I been a soldier I would have carried my banner into the enemy stronghold. I would have placed my heel on the enemy's throat, and the terms I made would have been all my terms. Indeed, there would be no terms. I should have been conqueror of their estates and castles."

"Nobly spoken, my son."

Cesare was alert. Did he detect a certain speculative light in his father's eyes? Was Alexander going to be reasonable at last?

"But," went on the Pope, "we are in a certain position now, and we must extricate ourselves from it. The important point in the present case is speed. If *we* have been humiliated, my son, *they* are exhausted. They dread further fighting; that is why they are ready to make terms."

Cesare laughed in admiration. "And you have made them buy back their castles!"

"For 50,000 golden florins."

"But you would rather have kept the castles, Father; which you would have done had you defeated them completely."

"We are 50,000 florins the richer."

"This was to be a beginning. We but started with the Orsini. And now?"

"We shall resort to peace for a while."

"And the Orsini, when they have recovered from their weakness?"

The Pope looked straight at his son. "There is one clause in the treaty to which I have had to agree. Virginio Orsini was in prison in Naples during the conflict. . . ."

Cesare snapped his fingers. "And if he had not been, oh my father, that would have been very unfortunate for us."

The Pope agreed to this. Cesare was smiling; he was remembering those days long ago when he had left his mother's house and lived for a year in Monte Giordano. He remembered the coming of the great soldier to the Orsini stronghold, and how his young boy's heart had rejoiced in that man; he thought of the long rides, of Virginio's grim yet affectionate way with him. During that year one of the heroes of Cesare's life had been Virginio Orsini. Cesare had been proud when Virginio had wished that he had been his son; and if he had been, he would have made a soldier of him.

"You admire him, I see," said Alexander.

"He is a great soldier."

"Not so reliable when the French invaded Italy."

"Doubtless he had his reasons, Father. The Orsinis have made themselves allies of the French."

"Against us," said the Pope. "But this clause in the treaty. . . . The Orsini demand that Virginio be immediately released from his prison."

"I see, Father, that you do not wish to release Virginio."

"You have said yourself that it would have been a different state of affairs had Virginio been at hand to lead his family's forces. They are our enemies still. At this time they are exhausted by the recent conflict; they are without a true leader; but if they had such a leader . . ." The Pope shrugged his shoulders. "My son, it occurs to me that the Orsini may be so ready to agree to my terms, insisting only that Virginio be free, so that when he is among them again they may band themselves against us. Virginio must not be freed."

"Yet you say this is the clause they insist on."

"It is."

"And you have agreed to it?"

"I have."

"So Virginio will in a very short time *be free*."

"He should not leave his prison."

"Yet you have agreed. . . ."

"We have friends in Naples. There are a few days yet. Cesare, I charge you with this. You have always sought to show me your subtlety. Great commanders must be possessed, not only of courage, but resource."

"When I was a boy and lived at Monte Giordano I knew him well," said Cesare slowly.

"That was long ago, my son."

"Yes," said Cesare, "long ago."

The Pope laid his hand on his son's shoulder.

"You will know how to do what is best for our family," he said.

It was foolish to harbor sentimental feelings.

Cesare paced up and down his own apartments. It was unlike him to delay when he knew something must be done which would redound to his advantage. And yet, memories would keep recurring. He could see himself riding behind that stalwart figure; he could feel again the admiration he had known.

Virginio Orsini, the man who had made life at Monte Giordano tolerable; Virginio who had wanted to make a soldier of him.

There was no time for delay. A message must be taken at once to Naples. A small quantity of a white powder must be carried there and instructions given.

Virginio Orsini would soon be taking his last meal in the prison.

If it were another I would not hesitate, thought Cesare. I would not give the matter a second thought. But Virginio! Oh nonsense, nonsense! What was a boy's hero-worship?

Yet he had been kind.

Kind! What had kindness to do with Cesare Borgia?

Still he continued to pace up and down his apartment.

"Not Virginio," he murmured, "not Virginio Orsini."

In the streets the Carnival was at its height, and the people of Rome were bent on enjoying themselves. The Pope, with that mental dexterity which amazed all who came into contact with it, had once more brought diplomatic victory out of military defeat with the sleight of hand of a conjuror. The Orsinis had been the victors. But what had they won? A cessation of hostilities merely. They had paid heavily to regain their castles; and the head of their family, Virginio Orsini, although the Pope had granted his release, had died suddenly a few hours before he was due to leave his prison.

The people laughed at the wily ways of the Holy Father as they gave themselves up to enjoying themselves.

Men and women in masks and fancy dress filled the streets. Processions passed along, among which some carried grotesque figures held high over the heads of the revelers; others manipulated fantastic bizarre figures, puppets which performed lewd gestures to the immense amusement of the crowd. There was music, dancing and general revelry, and wars and political intrigue seemed far away.

From his apartment Cesare looked out on the revelers in the square and was angry with himself because he could not erase the memory of Virginio Orsini from his mind; when he slept he would awake startled, imagining that the tall stern figure stood at his bedside watching him reproachfully.

It was foolish, unlike him. He wanted entertainment. He wished Lucrezia was in Rome. He and his father must bring her back, and they must free her from that provincial boor, Giovanni Sforza. He hated the fellow. There was comfort in hating.

Now he would go along to Sanchia's apartment. He would indulge with her in such an orgy of sensuality that he would forget all the shadows which hung over him, the thought of Sforza and Lucrezia, the memory of Virginio Orsini.

He found Loysella alone in Sanchia's apartment and demanded to know where her mistress was.

"My lord," answered Loysella, throwing glances at him from under lowered lids, "the Princess went out some time since with Francesca and Bernardina to look at the carnival. Your lordship should not be dismayed. They were masked."

He was not dismayed; only slightly irritated.

He was in no mood to go out into that seething crowd to search for her.

He looked at Loysella; Loysella was hopeful.

Then suddenly he turned away in disgust. It was as though he were a boy again, and Virginio stood beside him, reproaching him for some breach of manners.

Abruptly he left the apartment; he went to his own and in vain tried to shut out the sounds of carnival.

SANCHIA'S MASK ONLY partially concealed her beauty. Through it her blue eyes regarded the scene about her. Her black hair escaped from the hood of her cloak.

Francesca and Bernardina were similarly masked; and they were giggling because they knew that as they left the palace they were being followed.

"What excitement! What a grand carnival!" breathed Francesca. "There were never such carnivals in Naples."

"Let us wait here and watch the crowds go by," suggested Sanchia, knowing that the three men were standing behind them.

She glanced over her shoulder and a pair of brilliant eyes beneath a mask met hers and held them.

"I think," she said, "that we were unwise to come out alone, unescorted by any gentlemen. Why, anything . . . just anything might happen to us."

Some passing revelers halted as they saw three girls, for there was that in their bearing which attracted immediate attention.

One young man, carnival-bold, approached Sanchia and seized her hand. "There is a very fair lady cowering beneath that mask, I'll swear," he said. "Come, fair one . . . join us."

Sanchia said: "I do not wish it."

"This is carnival, lady, and such as you must not stand aloof."

She screamed as he took her arm, and one of the men who had been standing behind her cried out: "Dispatch the insolent dog."

The young man who had first spoken to her turned pale under his mask as one of the trio stepped forward, his sword in his hand. The young man stammered: "'Tis carnival time. No harm was meant. . . ." Then as the other raised his sword and pricked his arm, he cried out and ran, followed by the members of his party.

"Shall I give pursuit, my lord?" asked he who had drawn his sword.

"Nay," said a languid voice. "It is enough."

Sanchia turned to him. "I thank you, my lord," she said. "I shudder to think what might have befallen me and my women had you not been at hand to save us."

"It is our great pleasure to save such as you," said the man.

He kissed her hand.

She knew him and she was fully aware that he knew her also. But this was a pleasant game they were playing; it had begun with his return from the wars. She was also aware that it was partly due to his hatred of Cesare that he was determined to pursue her; and although she had no intention of allowing herself to become a symbol between them, she was determined to make Cesare's brother her lover.

He was handsome—in his way handsomer than Cesare; his reputation was as evil but in a different way. She was going to teach the Duke of Gandia a lesson; she was going to show him that his need of Sanchia of Aragon would exceed his desire for revenge on his brother. That need was going to be the most important thing in his life.

But at the moment it pleased them to pretend, masked as they were, that they were unaware of each other's identities.

He kept her hand in his.

"Shall we join the revelers?"

"I am not sure that it would be fitting for us to do that," replied Sanchia. "We merely came out to watch from a distance."

"Impossible to watch carnival from a distance as you have learnt from the conduct of those insolent dogs. Come, let me show you the carnival. You need have no fear. I am here to protect you."

"We must keep together—my ladies and I," she murmured. "I should never forgive myself if aught happened to them."

She was smiling slyly. What she meant was: I do not trust to your protection, Giovanni. Were there danger, you might run away. But with your attendants close at hand I shall be happier."

"We will keep with our little party," said Giovanni. He signed to the two men, one of whom immediately took Francesca's hand the other Bernardina's. "Now," he went on, "whither shall we go? To the Colosseum? There will be great revelry there. Or to see the racing in the Corso?"

"Escort us whither you will," said Sanchia.

"Then may I suggest, my lord," put in one of the men, "that we find our way out of the crowd. These delicate ladies are in danger of being trampled underfoot by the plebs."

"You speak wisely," said Giovanni.

"There is a little *albergo* near the Via Serpenti. A place where we can be free of the clamor of the common people."

"Then to it," said Giovanni.

Sanchia turned to Francesca and Bernardina. "No," she said, "I do not think I and my ladies should accompany you to this inn. If you will take us to St. Peter's Square, we shall be safe enough and . . ."

"Come," said Giovanni, his eyes shining through his mask, "put yourself in my hands, fair lady. You will regret nothing."

Sanchia pretended to shiver. "I am a little uneasy. . . ."

But Giovanni had his arm about her and started off at a run, taking her with him. She looked fearfully over her shoulder, but Francesca and Bernardina were being similarly treated. They gave little shrieks of feigned horror, but their cavaliers ignored them as they followed Giovanni and Sanchia.

"Make way! Make way!" shouted Giovanni as he forced his way through the crowds. Many called after him; some attempted to stop him. Spirits and tempers ran high in carnival time.

But always those two men would be close to Giovanni, and was it something they said, or were they known? However, it was apparent every time that those who challenged them soon slunk away in fear.

Then Sanchia noticed that Giovanni's cloak was caught together by a brooch on which was emblazoned the grazing bull. His men carried the emblem too, one in his hat, the other on his doublet. Sanchia laughed inwardly. Giovanni would not venture into the streets masked at any time without some indication of who he was, prominently displayed on his person. There might be many to attack a young braggart who made himself unpleasant, but who would dare to raise an arm against a Borgia?

She was enjoying her evening. Cesare was to be taught a lesson. He had been far more interested in his brother's humiliation than in her, and such slights must be paid for. She knew of a way which would infuriate him more than any. That was the way in which Cesare should pay for the slights he had given her.

There had been understanding glances between herself and Giovanni during the last few days; but this was the most amusing way to allow those little innuendoes to reach their climax.

When they reached the Via Serpenti they hurriedly slipped through a maze of alleys. The noise of the merrymakers seemed muted now as one of Giovanni's men pushed open the door of an inn and they all went in.

Giovanni shouted: "Bring food. Bring wine . . . plenty of it."

The innkeeper came running to them. He bowed low and looked very frightened as his eyes rested on the brooch which Giovanni was wearing.

"Good sirs," he began.

"You heard us ask for wine and food. Bring it quickly," said Giovanni.

"With the greatest speed, my lord."

Giovanni sat on a couch and pulled Sanchia down beside him.

"I am determined," he whispered, "that you shall enjoy the hospitality . . . all the hospitality . . . which the innkeeper can offer."

Sanchia said: "My lord, I think I should tell you that I am no humble woman to be seized in carnival time."

"Your voice, your manner betray you," he said. "But women who venture into the streets at carnival time ask to be seized."

His men laughed, and applauded everything he said.

"We will drink wine with you and then we shall leave you here," declared Sanchia.

"We are eager to enjoy *all* the pleasures that the carnival can offer," ventured one of the men, keeping his eyes on Giovanni.

"*All,*" echoed Giovanni.

The innkeeper came hurrying in with wine.

"Is this the best you have?" demanded Giovanni.

"The very best, my lord."

"Then it should be good, and if it is not I may grow angry."

The innkeeper was visibly trembling.

"Now," cried Giovanni, "bolt all doors. We would be alone ... completely alone, you understand me?"

"Yes, my lord."

"As for food, do not bring it after all. I find I am not hungry. Wine will suffice. You have some comfortable rooms in your inn?"

"I can vouch for them," said one of the men with a snigger, "having already used them."

"Now leave us, fellow," said Giovanni. And turning to the ladies: "We will drink to the joy this day will bring us all."

Sanchia had risen.

"My lord..." she began. Giovanni put his arms about her and embraced her. She struggled, but Giovanni was fully aware that her struggling was feigned, that she knew who he was and that she had been as determined that this should happen as he was.

He put down his goblet and said: "At such a time, I have no need of wine." He picked up Sanchia in his arms shouting: "Landlord! Take me to the best of your chambers ... and delay not, for I am in a hurry."

Sanchia kicked prettily and ineffectually. Bernardina and Francesca clung together while their two prospective lovers seized them and Sanchia and Giovanni disappeared.

The room was small; its ceiling low; but it was as clean as could be expected.

"Not the couch I would have chosen for you, my Princess," said Giovanni. "But it will suffice."

"You should know who I am," Sanchia told him.

He took off her mask. "I was as wise before," he answered, "as you were. Why, sweet Sanchia, did you wish me to stage this pretty little show of rape? Mutual agreement to meet the inevitable would have been so much more comfortable."

"Considerably less amusing," she said.

"I have a notion," he challenged, "that you are afraid of Cesare."

"Why should I be?"

"Because you have been his mistress since you came into Rome, and he is reputed to be a jealous lover."

"I am afraid of no man."

"Cesare is unlike other men. Sanchia . . . insatiable Sanchia. You cannot look at a man without wishing to know him. I saw your looks . . . I saw your speculation. At the moment we first met I saw it. You were determined that we should be together thus, but you thought to play safe. 'Let Giovanni take all the blame,' you said. 'Therefore let it be rape.'"

"Do you think I care what my old lovers think?"

"Even you are afraid of Cesare."

"I will be dictated to by none."

"There you are mistaken. In this room, the door locked behind us, I shall be your dictator."

"You forget that a moment ago you accused me of arranging this."

"Let us not argue about that. Sanchia . . . Sanchia!"

She laughed. "How masterful you are! Why, if you had shown the same determination against the Orsini as you do toward three defenseless women . . ."

He caught her by the shoulders and shook her, temporarily angered. Then he laughed at her. "You do not want a gentle lover, Madonna Sanchia. I understand."

"I am thinking of Francesca and Bernardina."

"They will be in their lovers' arms by now. They have been watching each other for days; ever since you decided that you would change brothers, those four people have been waiting for this day. Come, why procrastinate?"

"Why, indeed!" she murmured.

Cesare was furious, for it was not long before his spies brought news to him that Sanchia and Giovanni were constantly together.

He went to Sanchia's apartments while her women were combing her hair. Bursting in upon them he found them giggling over their adventures with their lovers. He strode to Sanchia, swept the dish of sweetmeats from the table and, waving his arms, shouted to her women: "Get out!"

They left her fearfully, for they thought they saw murder in Cesare's eyes.

"So, you harlot," he said, "I hear that you are my brother's mistress."

Sanchia lifted her shoulders reflectively. "And does that surprise you?"

"That you give yourself to any who asks, no! But that you dare to arouse my anger, yes!"

"It surprises me that you have time to be angry with me . . . you who waste so much of it being jealous of Giovanni's dukedom, and Giovanni's favor with your father."

"Be silent. Do you think I shall allow you to insult and degrade me in this way?"

"I cannot see, Cesare, that you can do very much about it."

She had turned and was smiling at him, her blue eyes blazing with desire for him. When he had this mad rage upon him she found him more interesting than she did when he was an affectionate lover.

"You will see, Sanchia," he said. "I only ask you to have patience."

"I am not a very patient person."

"You are a harlot, I know, the most notorious harlot in Rome. One brother's wife, and mistress of the other two. Do you know that the whole of the city talks of your behavior?"

"And of yours, dear brother . . . and of Giovanni's . . . and of the Holy Father's. Yes, and even of Lucrezia's."

"Lucrezia is innocent of all scandal," he said sharply.

"Is that so?" she asked lightly.

Cesare strode to her and gave her a stinging blow on the side of her face, she caught his hand and dug her teeth into it, watching the blood spurt while she put her hand to her burning cheek.

It was as though the sight of blood maddened him. Anger leaped into his eyes as he caught her by the wrist, and she cried out in pain. "Do not think," he said, "that you can treat me as you may have treated others."

"Cesare, take your hands from me. You are causing me pain."

"It delights me to hear it. It is exactly what I intend." Again those sharp teeth were dug into his hand; he caught her by the shoulder and, as his grip on her wrist was released, she scratched his face. The excitement of battle was on them both. He tried to grasp her hands again; but she had him by the ear and was twisting it.

In a few moments they were rolling on the floor together, and inevitably, with two such people, desire and brutality mingled.

She resisted; not because she wished to resist but because she wished to prolong the battle. He called her bastard, harlot, every name that he could think of which would hurt one as proud as she. She retaliated. Was he not a bastard? she screamed. "Brute! Cardinal!" she sneered.

She lay panting on the floor, her eyes wild, her clothes torn, while she thought of fresh insults to hurl at him.

"All Rome knows of your jealousy of your brother. You . . . the Cardinal! You with your fine clothes and your mistresses. . . . I hate Your Eminence. I hate you, Cardinal Borgia."

He bore down on her; she kicked him; he cursed her; and after a while they were silent together.

She laughed afterward, rising from the floor to stare at her appearance in the polished metal of her mirror.

"We look like two beggars on the Corso," she said. "How shall I hide these scratches, these bruises you have given me, you brute? Ah, but you are well marked too. It was worth it though, was it not? I begin to think that the floor is as good a bed as any."

He was looking at her with hatred. But she liked his hatred. It was more stimulating than affection.

"Now," he said, "perhaps you will be more wary when you next meet my brother."

"Why so?" she asked.

"Because you have discovered that I am a man of some temper."

"I adore your temper, Cesare. You cannot ask me to forgo the pleasure of rousing it."

"You mean then that you will not give him up?"

She appeared to be considering. "We find such pleasure in each other," she said almost plaintively, longing to arouse him to a fresh frenzy.

But he had grown cold.

He said: "If you prefer one at whom all Italians are jeering, then continue to enjoy him."

And he went out, leaving her stimulated but a little disappointed.

THE POPE WATCHED the growing antagonism between the two brothers with uneasiness.

Little Goffredo was bewildered. He had been delighted that both his brothers found his wife so attractive; but when he discovered that their admiration for his beautiful wife caused dissention between them which was greater than anything ever had before, he began to be worried.

Giovanni rarely left Sanchia's side. He liked to ride out with her through the streets of Rome; he did his best to circulate rumors concerning their relationship and was very eager that they should reach Cesare's ears.

Then suddenly Cesare seemed to lose interest in Sanchia.

His father sent for him because Alexander had some matter of importance to discuss, and he was finding that it was with Cesare rather than with his cherished Giovanni that he wished to discuss matters of policy.

"My dear son," said Alexander, taking Cesare into his arms and kissing him, "there is a matter of some importance which I wish to discuss with you."

It delighted the Pope to see the frown on his son's face fade at such words.

"It is of Lucrezia's husband, this man Sforza that I wish to speak," said the Pope.

Cesare's lip curled in disgust and Alexander went on: "Your opinion of the man coincides with my own."

"It has caused me great grief," replied Cesare, "to think of my sister's spending her days in that remote town, far away from us all ... and Your Holiness giving him orders which he does not obey. I would that we could rid Lucrezia of the oaf."

"It is to discuss this matter that I have called you to me now. Cesare, I wish this to be a closely guarded secret."

"Between us two?" asked Cesare eagerly.

"Between us two."

"And Giovanni?"

"No, Cesare, no. I would not even trust Giovanni with this. Giovanni is light-hearted and not as serious minded as you are, Cesare. I wish this to be a matter closely guarded, so that is why I choose to confide in you."

"Thank you, Most Holy Lord."

"My dearest son, I am determined to rid my daughter of that man."

"And the means?"

"There is divorce, but divorce is not beloved of the Church; and as the Head of the Church I am expected to frown on it except in special circumstances."

"Your Holiness would prefer another method?"

Alexander nodded.

"It should not be impossible," said Cesare, his eyes shining. He was thinking, it had been sad to know that Virginio must die, but there would be no such sadness where Giovanni Sforza was concerned.

"Our first move," said the Pope, "would be to recall him to Rome."

"Then let us make it."

"Easier said than done, my son. The provincial lord entertains certain suspicions regarding us."

"My poor Lucrezia, how she must suffer!"

"I am not sure of that, Cesare. Her letters would seem to grow more distant. Sometimes I feel that the Lord of Pesaro is taking our Lucrezia away from us, that she is becoming more of a wife to him than a daughter to me or a sister to you."

"It shall not be. He will rob her of her charm. He will make her dull . . . insipid as he is. We must bring her back, Father."

The Pope nodded. "And Sforza with her. And when they come . . ." The Pope hesitated, and Cesare prompted him: "And when they come, Holiness?"

"We will disarm him with our friendship. That will be the first step, Cesare. We will tell him by our words, gestures and deeds that we are no longer estranged from him. He is the spouse of our dearest one, and as such we will love him."

"'Twill be a hard task," said Cesare grimly.

"Not when you remember to what it is leading us."

"When we have his confidence, we will ask him to a banquet," mused Cesare. "He will not die at once. His shall be a lingering death."

"You shall introduce him to the embrace of cantarella."

"With the utmost pleasure," said Cesare.

So to Rome came Lucrezia and with her rode her husband. Giovanni Sforza was reluctant; he grumbled continually throughout the journey.

"What do your family plan now? Why have they become so friendly toward me? I do not trust them."

"Oh, Giovanni, you are too distrustful. It is because they have so much regard for me, because they are delighted to see me as a happy wife, that they offer you their friendship."

"I warn you I shall be wary," declared Giovanni.

He was surprised by his reception.

The Pope embraced him, called him his beloved son, and said that as the husband of Lucrezia he was entitled to a high position at the Papal Court. Never had Giovanni enjoyed such prestige as he did during those weeks. He began to lose his fears. When all is considered, he told himself, I am Lucrezia's husband, and Lucrezia is well satisfied with me.

He confided in a certain retainer of his whom he liked to take with him wherever he went, for he felt that Giacomino, his handsome young chamberlain, was one of the few people whom he could trust.

"My lord," said Giacomino, "it appears that you are well received here, but have a care, oh my lord. They say that it is unwise to eat rashly at the Borgia table."

"I have heard such rumors."

"Remember the sudden death of Virginio Orsini, my lord."

"I think of it."

"My lord, it would please me if you ate food prepared only by me."

That made Giovanni laugh; but there were few people who had such a true affection for him as Giacomino had, and he knew it; he laid an affectionate arm about his servant's shoulders.

"Fret not, Giacomino," he said. "I can take good care of myself."

He told Lucrezia of Giacomino's anxieties.

"They are groundless," Lucrezia assured him. "My father has taken you into the family circle. He knows that you and I can be happy together.

But Giacomino is a good fellow, Giovanni; and I am glad he feels so deeply for you."

And in the weeks which followed, Giovanni Sforza acquired a new air of confidence.

I can make Lucrezia happy, he thought; and the Pope loves his daughter so dearly that he is ready to bless any who can do that. He began to believe that he had exaggerated rumor and that the Borgias were merely a family who, with the exception of Giovanni and Cesare, were particularly devoted to one another.

Carnival time came round again, and the Borgias found the revels irresistible. The Pope, watching the scenes from his balcony, called his applause for the lewdness, and gave his blessing at the same time. There had never been a man who was able to mingle his love for the lewd and the pious so happily together; there was never a man more ready to take his religion in a merry way. At carnival times, more than any other, the people were satisfied with their Holy Father.

Giovanni Sforza disliked the carnival, was embarrassed by the lewd scenes which were enacted and, finding no pleasure in the coarse jokes, he was already homesick for Pesaro.

He did not want to go out and mingle with the crowds in the streets, so Lucrezia went with her brothers and Sanchia, some of their men and Sanchia's and Lucrezia's women.

It was Giovanni Borgia's idea that they should dress as mummers and mingle more freely with the crowds.

This seemed great fun to Lucrezia who, unlike her husband, delighted in the gaiety of Rome and certainly did not sigh for quiet Pesaro.

Sanchia had decided to give her attention to Giovanni in order to arouse Cesare's anger, and Giovanni was nothing loth; in their mummers' dresses, masks hiding their faces, they danced through the streets, Sanchia and Giovanni leading the troupe, dancing in the Spanish manner, suggestively, and going through the motions of courtship to an end which seemed inevitable.

But Cesare was not thinking of Sanchia at this moment; he had plans which concerned Giovanni, but he was shelving those, for more pressing ones concerning another Giovanni obsessed him at this moment. Moreover Lucrezia was with him, and his lust for Sanchia had never been as great as his love for his little sister.

He could lash himself into a fury now, not because Sanchia was behaving amorously with Giovanni, but by thinking of Lucrezia's life with Sforza.

"Lucrezia, little one," he said, "you love the carnival."

"Oh brother, yes. Did I not always? Do you remember how we used to watch from the loggia of our mother's house and long to be among the revelers?"

"I remember how you clapped your hands and danced there on the loggia."

"And sometimes you lifted me, so that I could see better."

"We share many happy memories, beloved. When I think of the times we have been parted, I feel murderous toward those who parted us."

"Do not talk of murderous feelings on such a night as this, Cesare."

"It is such a night that takes my thoughts back to those weary separations. That husband of yours has deliberately kept you from us too long."

She smiled gently. "He is Lord of Pesaro, Cesare, and as such has his duties to Pesaro."

"And what think you, Lucrezia—will he soon be carrying you back to his dreary home?"

"I think that before long he will be impatient to return."

"And you want to leave us?"

"Cesare! How can you say so? Do you not realize that I miss you all so sadly that I can never be happy away from you?"

He drew a deep breath. "Ah! That is what I wished to hear you say." He put his arm about her and held her close to him. "Dearest sister," he whispered, "have no fear. It will not be long now before you are free of that man."

"Cesare?" She spoke his name in the form of a question.

The excitement of the dance was upon him. His hatred of Sanchia and his brother was overlaid by his love for this little sister. He felt a great longing to protect her from all unhappiness and, believing that she despised her husband, even as he and their father did, he could not lose another moment before telling her that she would soon be free of him.

"It will not be long, sweet sister," went on Cesare.

"Divorce?" she asked breathlessly.

"Divorce! Holy Church abhors it. Have no fear, Lucrezia. There are other ways of ridding oneself of an undesirable partner."

"You cannot mean . . ." she cried.

But he silenced her.

"Listen, my dearest. We'll not talk of these matters here in the streets. I have plans concerning your husband, and I can promise you that before next carnival time you will have forgotten his very existence. There, does that please you?"

Lucrezia felt sick with horror. She did not love Giovanni Sforza, but she had tried to; when she was in Pesaro she had done her best to be the sort of wife he wished for, and she had not been unhappy in her efforts. He was not the lover of whom she had dreamed, but he was her husband. He had feelings, aspirations; and if he was full of self-pity, she too had pity for him. He had been unfortunate so many times.

"Cesare," she said, "I am afraid. . . ."

His lips were close to her ear. "People watch us," he said. "We are not dancing with the others as we should. I will come to your apartment to-morrow in the afternoon. We will make sure that we are neither over-looked nor overheard. Then I will explain my plans to you."

Lucrezia nodded mutely.

She began to dance, but now there was no gaiety in her. Those words of Cesare's kept drumming in her ears. They are going to murder Giovanni Sforza, she told herself.

AFRAID AND UNSURE, that night she was sleepless, and next day disturbed.

Never in her life had she felt so closely bound to her family; never had she had to face such an important decision.

To her father and her brother she believed she owed complete loyalty. To betray their confidences would be to commit an unforgivable act. And yet to stand aside and allow them to murder her husband—how could she do that?

Lucrezia discovered that she had a conscience.

She was aware of her youth and inexperience of life. She realized that like her father she longed for harmony all about her; and unlike him she could not achieve it ruthlessly. She did not love Sforza; she understood now that she would not greatly care if she never saw him again; but what horrified her was that he should be led to violent death or even quiet death, and that she would be among those who led him there, which she must be if she did not warn him.

She was faced with two alternatives. She could remain loyal to her father and brother and let Sforza go to his death or she could warn Sforza and betray her family.

It was a terrible decision which she had to make. All her love and devotion was at war with her sense of rightness.

Murder! It was a hideous thing and she wanted none of it.

If I let him to go his death the memory of my betrayal would haunt me all my life, she thought.

And if she betrayed Cesare and her father! They would never trust her again; she would be shut out from the trinity of love and devotion on which she had come to rely.

So she lay, sleepless, asking herself what she must do, rising and going to the Madonna's shrine, falling on her knees and praying for help.

There was no help. What she did must be her own decision.

Cesare was coming in the afternoon to tell her of his plans, and she knew that before that time she must have decided which course she was to take.

❦ ♛ ❦

SHE SENT ONE of her women for Giacomino, Sforza's chamberlain.

As Giacomino stood before her she thought how handsome he was; there was an honesty in him which was apparent, and she knew that he was her husband's most faithful servant.

"Giacomino," said Lucrezia, "I have sent for you that I may talk to you for a while."

Lucrezia was aware of the little lights of alarm which had sprung into the young man's eyes. He believed that she found him attractive, for doubtless many women did, and she felt that she was making matters very difficult; but this was her plan and she must carry it out, since she saw no other way out of her dilemma. Giacomino stood before her with bowed head.

"Do you long to return to Pesaro, Giacomino?"

"I am happy to be where my lord is, Madonna."

"Yet if you could choose, Giacomino?"

"Pesaro is my home, Madonna, and one has an affection for home."

She nodded and went on to talk of Pesaro. She was thinking, He is bewildered, this good Giacomino, and I must go on talking, even though he may believe that I am seeking to make him my lover.

Giacomino had taken the stool she had indicated. He seemed to grow more miserable with every passing moment, as though he were already wondering how he, his master's most loyal servant, was going to repulse her. But at length she heard the sound for which she was waiting, and greatly relieved, sprang up, crying: "Giacomino, my brother is on his way here."

"I must go at once, Madonna," said the agitated Giacomino.

"But wait. If you leave through the door he will see you, and my brother would not be pleased to see you here, Giacomino."

What fear Cesare inspired in everyone! The young man had grown pale, his discomfort turning to terror.

"Oh Madonna, what shall I do?" stammered Giacomino.

"I will hide you here. Quick! Get you behind this screen and I will place these draperies over you. If you keep perfectly still you will not be discovered. But I implore you to be as still as you possibly can, for if my brother were to discover you in my apartments . . ."

"I will be still, Madonna."

"Your teeth are chattering, Giacomino. I see you realize full well the dangerous position in which you find yourself. My brother does not like me to receive young men in friendship. It angers him. Oh, do take care, Giacomino."

As she spoke she was pushing him behind the screen and arranging the draperies over him. She looked at her work with satisfaction; the chamberlain was completely hidden.

Then she hurried to her chair and was sitting there assuming a pensive attitude when Cesare came into the room.

"Lucrezia, my dearest." He took both her hands and kissed them, as he smiled into her face. "I see you are prepared for me, and have arranged that we should be alone."

"Yes, Cesare, you have something to say to me?"

"It was dangerous to talk last night in the streets, sister." He went to the window and looked out. "Ah, the revelries still continue. The mumming and masquing goes on. Is Giovanni Sforza out there in the streets this day, or is he moping in his apartment dreaming of dear dull Pesaro?"

"Dreaming of Pesaro," said Lucrezia.

"Let him dream while he may," cried Cesare grimly. "There is not much time left to him for dreaming."

"You refer to the plans you have made for him?"

"I do, sister. Oh, it has maddened me to think of you with that provincial boor. He deserves to die for having presumed to marry my sweet sister."

"Poor Giovanni, he was forced into it."

"You yearn for freedom, dearest sister, and because I am the most indulgent brother in the world, I long to give you all you desire."

"You do, Cesare. I am happy when I am with you."

Cesare had begun to pace the floor.

"Our father and I have not told you of our plans before. This is because we know you to be young and tender. You were ever one to plead for the meanest slave who was in disgrace, and ask that punishment be averted. It may be, we thought, that you would plead for your husband. But we know that you long to be free of him ... even as we long to see you free."

"What do you plan to do, Cesare?" asked Lucrezia slowly.

"To remove him."

"You mean ... to kill him?"

"Never mind how we do it, sweet sister. Before long he will cease to worry you."

"When do you propose to do this deed?"

"Within the next few days."

"You will ask him to a banquet or . . . will it be that he meets his assassins by night in some dark alley near the Tiber?"

"Our little Sforza is not without friends," said Cesare. "I think a banquet would suit him better."

"Cesare, there is talk of a poison which you use—cantarella. Is it true that the secret is known only to you and to our father, and that you are able not only to kill people but decide on the day and even hour of their death?"

"You have a clever brother, Lucrezia. Does it make you happy to know that he puts all his skill at your disposal?"

"I know that you would do anything in the world for me," she told him. She moved to the window. "Oh Cesare," she went on, "I long to go out into the streets. I long to mingle with the revelers as we did last night. Let us ride out to Monte Mario as we did in the old days, do you remember? Let us go *now*."

He came to her and laid his hands on her shoulders. "You want to feel the air on your face," he said. "You want to say to yourself, Freedom is one of the greatest gifts life can offer, and soon it will be mine!"

"How well you know me," she said. "Come, let us go now."

Only when they had left the Palace could she breathe freely. She was astonished at the cleverness with which she had been able to play her part.

Every minute had been fraught with terror that something would betray the presence of a third party in the room; and even more terrifying had been the constant thought: Cesare, my dearest, my beloved, I am betraying you.

Giacomino extricated himself from the draperies and made all haste to his master's apartments. He was breathless and begged Giovanni Sforza to see him privately.

"My lord," he stammered as soon as they were alone, "Madonna Lucrezia sent for me, I know not why, unless it was to give me some message to bring to you, but while I was in her apartments Cesare Borgia arrived and Madonna Lucrezia, fearing his anger, forced me to hide behind a screen. There I heard that he and the Pope are planning to murder you."

Sforza's eyes dilated with terror.

"I suspected it," he said.

"My lord, there is not a moment to spare. We must leave Rome with all speed."

"You are right. Go prepare the strongest horses we have. We will set out at once for Pesaro. Only there can I be safe from my murderous relations."

So Giacomino obeyed, and in less than an hour after the chamberlain had heard Cesare and Lucrezia talking together, he and Sforza were riding at full gallop out of Rome.

SAN SISTO

THE POPE AND Cesare were annoyed by Sforza's flight. Already the news was being whispered throughout Rome that he had fled because he feared the dagger or the poison cup which the Borgias were preparing for him.

"Let him not think to escape," raged Cesare.

Alexander was serene.

"Calm yourself, my dear son," he said. "The only matter which concerns us is his separation from your sister. He is suspicious of our feelings toward him. It would be dangerous now to go the way we planned. There is only one course left open to us. I do not like it. As a Churchman I find it distasteful. The other would have been so much more convenient. I fear, Cesare, that we are left with divorce."

"Well then, let us set about procuring it as soon as possible. I have promised Lucrezia her freedom and I intend her to have it."

"Then let us study this matter of divorce. There are two alternatives, as I see it. First we could declare that the marriage was invalid because

Lucrezia had never been released from a former entanglement with Gasparo di Procida."

"I fear, Father, that that would be difficult to prove. Lucrezia was released from that betrothal, and there would be many to point to the proof of this. We should have Ludovico and Ascanio coming to their kinsman's aid if we put forward such a reason."

"You are right there, my son. That leaves us the other alternative. We will ask for a divorce on the grounds that the marriage has never been consummated."

"But this is not so."

"My dear son, who shall say that it has been consummated? Is there a child to confirm it?"

"It is a barren marriage, Father, but consummation has surely taken place."

"Who shall swear to this?"

"Sforza. He will not wish his impotence to be proclaimed to the world."

"But Lucrezia will say what we wish her to."

"Sforza will protest, he will protest vigorously."

"We will protest with equal vigor."

"It is the answer. Truly, Father, you have genius."

"Thank you, my son. Are you beginning to realize that I know how to manage my family's affairs and do what brings my children the most good?"

"You have done much for Giovanni," said Cesare with a hint of sullenness; "and now I see that you will do what is best for Lucrezia."

Alexander patted his son's shoulder affectionately. "Send for the sweet creature," he said. "Let us tell her of the joy we are preparing for her."

Lucrezia came to them. She was full of fears but, because she was growing up and learning the art of dissimulation which they practiced so expertly, she managed to hide the state of her mind from their searching eyes.

"My dearest," said the Pope embracing her, "Cesare and I could not resist the pleasure of bringing you here. We have great news for you. You are to be freed from Sforza."

"In what way, Father?"

"There will be a divorce. We do not like divorce, but there are times when it is necessary. So we shall use it to free you from Sforza."

A feeling of relief swept over her. So they had abandoned their plans to murder him, and she had saved him.

The men noticed this relief and they smiled at one another. Their dear Lucrezia would be very grateful to them.

"Unfortunately," declared the Pope, "the Church is opposed to divorce, and my Cardinals will demand a very good reason if we are to grant it."

"It will be a simple matter," added Cesare, "as the marriage has not been consummated."

Lucrezia said quickly: "But it *has* been consummated."

"No, my child," contradicted the Pope, "it has not."

"Father, we have shared the same bed on countless occasions."

"Sharing a bed is not necessarily tantamount to consummation. My dear sweet innocent child, there is much you do not know. The marriage has not been consummated."

"But Father, I swear it has."

The Pope looked uneasily about him.

"All is well," whispered Cesare. "No one would dare remain within hearing when I have given orders that they should not."

"My child," went on the Pope, "consummation is not what you think."

"I know full well," persisted Lucrezia, "that my marriage has been consummated."

The Pope patted her cheek. "They may insist," he said to Cesare, "on an examination of the child. They are full of doubts and suspicions."

"Father, I must assure you that I . . ."

"Have no fear, my child," whispered the Pope. "Such examinations have taken place before. It is so easy. The virgin, veiled on account of modesty. You understand. You yourself need not submit. We shall find a suitable virgin, and all will be well. All you would have to do would be to swear before the jurists and Cardinals of a commission."

"Father, I could not so swear."

The Pope smiled. "You fret too much, my child. There are times when it is necessary for us to diverge from the truth, if not for the sake of ourselves, for the happiness of others."

She was aghast. She looked from one to the other of these two men whom she loved beyond all others in the world. She knew that whatever the future held she must continue to love them, that they must mean more to her than anyone else, that she was bound to them in more ways than she understood; she belonged to them, and they to her; she was bound to them by bonds of affection and a family feeling which was stronger than any other she had known; and she knew them to be dissemblers, treacherous liars and murderers.

She could not endure any more. She said: "Father, I pray you give me leave to retire. I would consider this matter."

They kissed her tenderly, brother and father; and she left them, talking together of their plans to overcome any opposition.

As to Lucrezia, they did not expect any trouble from her.

SHE WOULD not sign the monstrous document. It was a lie, a blatant lie.

Her father and Cesare pleaded with her. She must throw aside her scruples; she must remember what was at stake. Her brother Giovanni joined his pleas to those of Cesare and Alexander. It was degrading, he declared, that Lucrezia Borgia should remain married to such a man as Giovanni Sforza. Certainly her family wished to bring about her release. She was foolish to hesitate. What was the mere signing of a document?

"But it is a lie . . . a lie," cried Lucrezia.

The Pope was gentle in his explanations, but astonished, he said, that his little daughter—the best loved of all his children—should so grieve her father.

"It is not the lie, so much, Father," she tried to explain, "but the hurt it will give to my husband. He will be branded as impotent, and you know what humiliation that will cause him."

"You must not worry so much on account of others, my child. He will be free to marry again and prove himself."

"But who will wish to marry a man who, it is declared, cannot give children?"

"This is a little foolish, my child. Sign the document. It is so simple. Your name here . . . and in a short time all will be well."

But again and again she refused.

Meanwhile Giovanni Sforza, enraged at the terms on which the Pope intended to procure a divorce, protested loudly and vigorously.

It was a lie to say that the marriage had not been consummated, he declared. It had been consummated a thousandfold.

He decided that there was only one place to which he could go for help. He would ride with all speed to Milan and seek the aid of his Sforza cousins. They had not shown themselves very eager to help in the past, but surely a family must stand together when one of its members was so insulted.

Having his own worries Ludovico was not very pleased to see his cousin. It might be that the French would return to Italy, and if they did Milan would be one of their first targets. If such circumstances arose, Ludovico would need the help of Alexander; and for what could he hope if he opposed the Pope in this matter? Ludovico obviously could offer little help to poor Giovanni Sforza.

"My dear cousin," said Ludovico, "why do you not agree to the divorce? It would be quickly over and there would be an end to the matter."

"Do you not understand this monstrous suggestion?"

"I see that the Pope will allow you to retain Lucrezia's dowry if you agree. He also says you shall keep his goodwill."

"Dowry! Goodwill! I am to retain these if I allow him to bruit it abroad that I am impotent!"

"It was a handsome dowry, and Papal goodwill is not to be despised."

"Cousin, I ask you this: Had such a slur been thrown on *your* virility, how would you act?"

Ludovico was thoughtful for a few seconds, then he said: "Well, Giovanni, my cousin, there is a way in which you could prove the Borgia's allegations to be wrong."

"How so?" asked Giovanni eagerly.

"Prove it without doubt in the presence of our ambassador and the Papal Legate. Lucrezia could come to the castle of Nepi, and there you could show us publicly that you are capable of being a good husband."

Giovanni shrank from his cousin in horror at the suggestion.

"But my dear cousin," said Ludovico mildly, "it has been done before. And if Lucrezia refuses to come, why then I could arrange for several courtesans to be in attendance. You could take your choice, and I can assure you that our Milanese women are as desirable as any they have in Rome."

"It would be quite impossible."

"I have made the suggestion," said Ludovico, shrugging his shoulders. "If you refuse to consider it, then people will draw their own conclusions."

"I refuse to make a public spectacle of myself."

"It seems to me the only way to counter this charge."

"In the presence of the Milanese ambassador and the Papal Legate!" cried the outraged Giovanni. "And who is the Papal Legate? Another Giovanni Borgia, a nephew of His Holiness. Why, I doubt not that, whatever I did in his presence, he would swear I was impotent. He is another example of the incessant nepotism of the Pope! And the Milanese ambassador! Doubtless he would be bribed to speak against me, or threatened if he refused."

Ludovico looked at his relative sadly, but there was no other advice he could offer. Giovanni Sforza was an unlucky man; he had aroused the contempt and dislike of the Borgias. He was also a foolish man; because the Borgias wished to be rid of him, and he was making it difficult for them.

�✕

Lucrezia knew that she must sign. She could not hold out against them any longer. Each day they visited her or she was summoned to the Pope's presence. They all assured her that she must sign. There was her father, benevolent still but giving the faintest hints of losing patience; Cesare, growing angry with her now and then as he had never been before; Giovanni, telling her she was a stupid little girl who did not know what was good for her.

She did not know where her husband was. At first she had considered leaving Rome by stealth and fleeing to Pesaro, but when she had heard of the cruel things which Giovanni had said about her she no longer wanted to do that; for Giovanni Sforza, humiliated and angry, had declared that the Pope was eager for a divorce because he wanted his daughter to live in his immediate circle that he might take the place of her husband.

This was the first time that Lucrezia had heard this evil rumor concerning herself, and she shrank from the man who could spread it.

She had never felt so much alone as she did at that time. She longed to have someone like Giulia to confide in, but she never saw Giulia now; Sanchia was too immersed in her own affairs and the battle between Cesare and Giovanni for her favors which she was engendering.

And so there came the day when she signed the document which they had prepared for her, in which she declared that, owing to her husband's impotence, she was still *virgo intacta.*

THere was laughter in Rome.

A member of the most notorious family in Europe had declared her innocence. It was the best joke that had been heard in the streets for many years.

Even the servants, amongst themselves, could not refrain from sly titters. They had witnessed the passionate rivalry of the brothers for Lucrezia's affection; they had seen her embraced by the Pope. And there were many who could swear that Giovanni Sforza and Lucrezia had lived as husband and wife.

They did not do so, of course. They had no wish to be taken to some dark dungeon and return minus their tongues. They did not care to risk being set upon one dark night, tied in sacks and thrown into the river. They had no wish to drink of a certain wine and so step into eternity.

But at that time one of the most unhappy people in Rome was Lucrezia. She was filled with shame for what she had done, and she felt that she could no longer endure the daily routine of her life.

She thought longingly of those days of her childhood when she had lived so happily with the nuns of San Sisto, and everything within the convent walls had seemed to offer peace; and, very soon after she had signed that document, she left her palace for the convent of San Sisto.

There she begged to be taken to the Prioress and, when Sister Girolama Pichi came to her, she fell on her knees and cried: "Oh, Sister Girolama, I pray you give me refuge within these quiet walls, for I am sorely oppressed and need the comfort this place has to offer me."

Sister Girolama, recognizing the Pope's daughter, embraced her warmly and told her that the convent of San Sisto was her home for as long as she wished it to be so.

Lucrezia asked that she might see her old friends, Sister Cherubina and Sister Speranza, who so long ago, it seemed, had undertaken her religious teaching. The Prioress sent for them and, when Lucrezia saw them, she wept afresh and Sister Girolama told them to take Lucrezia to a cell where she might pray, and that they might stay with her as long as she needed their comfort.

WHEN HE DISCOVERED that Lucrezia had gone to the convent, Cesare was angry, but the Pope soothed him and begged him not to let any know how concerned they were at this unexpected move.

"If any should know that she had run away from us they would ask the reason," said the Pope, "and there would be many to question whether she had willingly put her name to our document."

"They will know soon enough that she has fled to the nuns to seek refuge from us."

"That must not be. This day I will send men-at-arms to bring her back to us."

"And if she will not come?"

"Lucrezia will obey my wishes." The Pope smiled grimly. "Moreover the nuns of San Sisto will not wish to arouse Papal displeasure."

The men-at-arms were dispatched. Lucrezia was with four of the nuns when she heard them at the gates.

She turned startled eyes to her companions and wished she were one of them, serene and far removed from all trouble. Oh, she thought, what would I not give to change places with Serafina or Cherubina, with Paulina or Speranza?

The Prioress came to her and said: "There are men of the Papal entourage below. They have come to take you back, Madonna Lucrezia."

"Holy Mother," said Lucrezia, falling on her knees and burying her face in the voluminous black habit, "I beg you do not let them take me away."

"My daughter, is it your wish that you should renounce all worldly things and stay here with us all the days of your life?"

Lucrezia's lovely eyes were full of bewilderment. "They will not permit it, Holy Mother," she said; "but let me stay awhile. I pray you let me stay. I am afraid of so much outside. Here I find solitude and I can pray as I cannot in my palace. Here in my cell I am alone with God. That is how I feel, and I believe that if you will but give me refuge for a little longer I shall know whether I must give up all outside these walls and become one of you. Holy Mother, I implore you, give me that refuge."

"We would deny it to none," said Girolama.

One of the nuns came hurrying to them to report that men were at the gates demanding to see the Prioress. "They are soldiers, Holy Mother. They are heavily armed and look fierce."

"They have come for me," said Lucrezia. "Holy Mother, do not let them take me."

The Prioress went boldly to the gates and faced the soldiers, who told her they were in a hurry, and had come, on the orders of His Holiness, to take Madonna Lucrezia with them.

"She has sought refuge here," said the Prioress.

"Now listen, Holy Mother, this is an order from the Pope."

"I regret it. But it is a rule of this house that none who asks for refuge shall be denied it."

"This is no ordinary visitor. Would you be so foolish as to offend His Holiness? The Borgia Pope and his sons do not love those who oppose them."

The soldiers meant to be kind; they were warning the Prioress that if she were a wise woman she would heed the Pope's request. But if Girolama Pichi was not a wise woman she was a brave one.

"You cannot enter my house," she said. "If you do, you commit an act of profanity."

The soldiers lowered their eyes; they had no wish to desecrate a holy convent, but at the same time they had their orders.

Girolama faced them unflinching. "Go back to His Holiness," she said. "Tell him that as long as his daughter craves refuge, I shall give it, even though His Holiness commands me to release her."

The men-at-arms turned away, abashed by the courage of the woman.

In the Vatican, the Pope and his two sons chafed in quiet anger.

They knew that in the streets it was whispered that Madonna Lucrezia had entered a nunnery, and that the reason was that her family was trying to force her to do something which was against her will.

Alexander came to one of his quick and brilliant decisions.

"We will leave your sister in her convent," he said, "and make no more attempts to bring her out. They cause gossip and scandal, and until the divorce is completed we wish to avoid that. We will let it be known that Madonna Lucrezia has been sent to San Sisto by ourselves, our wish being that she should live in quiet retirement until she is free of Giovanni Sforza."

So Lucrezia was left in peace; but meanwhile the Pope and her brothers redoubled their efforts to obtain her divorce.

Life for Lucrezia was now regulated by the bells of San Sisto, and she was happy in the convent where she was treated as a very special guest.

No one brought her news so she did not know that Romans continued to mock at what they called the farce of the divorce. She had never been fully aware of the scandals which had circulated about herself and her family, and she had no notion that verses and epigrams were now being written on the walls.

Alexander went serenely about his daily life, ignoring the insinuations. His one aim was to bring about the divorce as quickly as possible.

He was in constant communication with the convent, but he made no attempt to persuade his daughter to leave her sanctuary. He allowed the rumor, that she intended to take the veil, to persist, realizing that the image of a saintly Lucrezia was the best answer to all the foul things which were being said of her.

He selected a member of his household to take letters to his daughter and, as he was planning that after the divorce he would send her to Spain for a while in the company of her brother the Duke of Gandia, he chose as messenger a young Spaniard who was his favorite chamberlain.

Pedro Caldes was young and handsome and eager to serve the Pope. His Spanish nationality was on his side as Alexander was particularly gracious to Spaniards; his charm of manner was a delight to the Pope, who was anxious that Lucrezia should not become too enamoured of the nuns and their way of life.

"My son," said Alexander to his handsome chamberlain, "you will take this letter to my daughter and deliver it to her personally. Now that the Prioress knows that my daughter is in the Convent of San Sisto with my consent, you will be admitted to my daughter's presence." Alexander smiled charmingly. "You are to be not merely a messenger; I would have you know that. You will talk to my daughter of the glories of your native land. I want you to inspire within her a desire to visit Spain."

"I will do all in my power, Most Holy Lord."

"I know you will. Discover whether she is leading the life of a nun. I do not wish my little daughter to live so rigorously. Ask her if she would like me to send a companion to her—some charming girl of her own age. Assure her of my constant love and tell her that she is always in my thoughts. Now go, and when you return come and tell me how you found her."

So Pedro set out for the convent determined to make a success of his mission. He was delighted with it; he had often seen Madonna Lucrezia and had greatly admired her. She was the most beautiful of all the women, he thought, preferring her serene youthfulness to the more bold beauty of Madonna Giulia; as for the Princess of Squillace she was not to his taste at all, being nothing more than a brazen courtesan. It seemed to Pedro that, compared with such women, Lucrezia was wonderful.

He stood before the convent, at the foot of the Aventine, and looked up at the building. He felt then that this was a fateful moment in his life; he was to have a chance to win the friendship of Lucrezia, a chance which he had never thought would be his.

He was allowed to enter, and the nuns who passed him in the corridors hurried along with downcast eyes, scarcely looking at the stranger. He was conducted to a small room. How quiet it was!

He looked about him at the stone floor and the bare walls on which there was nothing but a crucifix. The furniture in the room consisted of a rough bench and a few stools. Outside the brilliant sun seemed far away for it was so cool behind those thick walls.

And suddenly Lucrezia came and stood before him. She was dressed in a long black robe, such as the nuns wore, but there was no covering on her head, and her golden hair streamed down her back. It was symbolic, thought Pedro. The display of all that golden beauty meant that she had not yet decided to take the veil. He would know when she had, because then he would not be allowed to see her golden hair.

He bowed; she held out her hand and he kissed it.

"I come from the Holy Father," he said.

"You have brought letters?"

"Yes, Madonna. And I hope to take a reply back to him."

"You are welcome." He noticed how eagerly she took the letters.

He hesitated, then said: "Madonna, it is the wish of His Holiness that I should linger awhile and talk with you, that you might ask me for news of the Vatican."

"That is kind of him," said Lucrezia with a dazzling smile. "I pray you sit down. I would offer you refreshment, but . . ."

He lifted a hand. "I want none, Madonna. And I could not sit in your presence unless you sat first."

She laughed and sat down facing him. She had laid the letters on the bench, but kept her hands on them as though her fingers were longing to open them.

"Tell me your name," she said.

"It is Pedro Caldes."

"I have seen you often. You are one of my father's chamberlains, and you come from Spain."

"I am honored to have been noticed by the lady Lucrezia."

"I notice those who serve my father well."

The young man flushed with pleasure.

"It is a double delight for me to be here," he said, "for not only has His Holiness entrusted me with the mission, but it is the pleasantest I ever undertook."

Lucrezia laughed suddenly. "It pleases me to hear a compliment again."

"There are rumors which have greatly disturbed your eminent father,

Madonna. Some are hinting that it is your intention to remain here for the rest of your life." She was silent, and there was alarm in Pedro's eyes as he went on: "Madonna Lucrezia, that would be wrong . . . wrong!"

He paused, waiting to be dismissed for his insolence, but there was nothing arrogant about Lucrezia. She merely smiled and said: "So you think it would be wrong. Tell me why?"

"Because," he said, "you are too beautiful."

She laughed with pleasure. "There are some beautiful nuns."

"But you should be gracing your father's Court. You should not hide your beauty in a convent."

"Did my father tell you to say that?"

"No, but he would be deeply wounded if you made such a decision."

"It is pleasant to talk to someone who cares what I do. You see, I came here for refuge and I found it. I wanted to shut myself away from . . . so many things. I do not regret coming here to dear Sister Girolama."

"It was a pleasant refuge, Madonna, but a temporary one. May I tell His Holiness that you are looking forward to the day when you will be reunited with your family?"

"No, I do not think you may. I am as yet undecided. There are times when the peace of this place overwhelms me, and I think how wonderful it is to rise early in the morning, and to wait for the bells to tell me what to do. Life here is simple and I sometimes long to live the simple life."

"Forgive me, Madonna, but you would deny your destiny were you to stay here."

She said: "Talk of other things, not of me. I am weary of my problems. How fares my father?"

"He is lonely because you are not with him."

"I miss him too. I long for his letters." She glanced at them.

"Would you wish me to leave you that you might read them in peace?"

She hesitated. "No," she said. "I will keep them. They will be something to look forward to when you have left. How are my brothers?"

Again Pedro hesitated. "All is much as it was when you left them."

She nodded sadly, thinking of them and their passion for Sanchia of which they were making another issue on which to build their hatred.

"Will you return to Spain one day?"

"I hope so, Madonna."

"You are homesick?"

"As all must be who belong to Spain and leave her."

"I fancy I should feel the same if I were forced to leave Italy."

"You would love my country, Madonna."

"Tell me of it."

"Of what shall I tell you—of Toledo which is set on a horse's shoe of granite, of the Tagus and the mighty mountains? Of Seville where the roses bloom all through the winter, of the lovely olive groves, of the wine they make there? It is said, Madonna, that those whom God loves live in Seville. I should like to show you the Moorish palaces, the narrow streets; and never did oranges and palms grow so lush as they do in Seville."

"You are a poet, I believe."

"I am inspired."

"By your beautiful country?"

"No, Madonna. By you."

Lucrezia was smiling. It was useless to pretend that she did not enjoy the young man's company, that she did not feel revived by this breath of the outside world; she felt as though she had slept long and deep when she needed sleep, but now the sounds of life were stirring about her and she wanted to wake.

"I long to see your country."

"His Holiness hinted that when the Duke of Gandia returns to Spain he might take you with him."

To Spain! To escape the gossip, the shame of divorce! It seemed a pleasant prospect.

"I should enjoy it . . . for a while."

"It would be for a while, Madonna. His Holiness would never allow you to stray long from his side."

"I know it."

"And so solicitous is he for your happiness that he is concerned to think of you here. He asks: 'Is your bed hard? Do you find the food tasteless? Do the convent rules irk you?' And he wonders who combs your hair and washes it for you. He says he would like to send you a companion, someone whom he would choose for you. She would be young, a friend as well as a servant. He asks me to bring him word as to whether you would like him to do this."

Lucrezia hesitated. Then she said: "I pray you convey my deep devotion to my father. Tell him that the love he bears me is no more than that I bear him. Tell him that I pray each night and morning that I may be worthy of his regard. And tell him too that I am happy here, but that I have enjoyed your visit and look forward to receiving one whom he will send me to be my servant and companion."

"And now, Madonna, you would wish me to retire and leave you with your letters?"

"How kind you are," she said. "How thoughtful!"

She extended her hand and he kissed it.

His lips lingered on her hand and she was pleased that this should be so. The nuns were her good friends, but Lucrezia bloomed under admiration.

She was still safe in her refuge; but she had enjoyed that breath of air from the outside world.

※♛※

THE POPE sent for the girl whom he had chosen to be Lucrezia's companion in the Convent of San Sisto.

She was charming, very pretty and small, with brilliant dark eyes and a dainty figure. Alexander had thought her charming when he first saw her. He still thought so, but at the moment he admired red hair such as that of his favorite mistress.

He held out his arms as the girl approached. "Pantisilea," he said, "my dear child, I have a mission for you."

Pantisilea lowered those wonderful eyes and waited. She was afraid that the Holy Father was going to send her away. She had been dreading this. She had known that their relationship could not continue indefinitely; the Pope's love affairs were fleeting, and even that with Giulia Farnese had not lasted forever.

Pantisilea had had dreams. Who in her place would not? She had pictured herself as a lady of substance like Vannozza Catanei or Giulia Farnese.

Now she was beginning to understand that she had been lightly selected to charm a weary hour or two.

"You are trembling, my child," said Alexander kindly.

"It is in terror, Holy Lord, of being sent away from you."

Alexander smiled kindly. He was always kind to women. He fondled the dark curls absentmindedly; he was thinking of his red-headed mistress.

"You shall not go far from us, my dear; and, when you hear for what mission I have selected you, you will rejoice, knowing that I could give this task—not only to one I loved, but one whom I respected and trusted."

"Yes, Holiness."

"You are going to the Convent of San Sisto, there to attend my daughter Lucrezia."

Pantisilea's relief was obvious. The lady Lucrezia was a gentle mistress, and all those who served her considered themselves fortunate to do so.

"There," said the Pope. "You are delighted, for you are aware of the honor I do you."

"Yes, Holiness."

"You must be prepared to leave this day. My daughter is lonely, and I want you to comfort her, and be her friend." He pinched the girl's soft cheek tenderly. "And at the same time, my sweet child, you will constantly let her know how grieved her father is because he does not have her with him. You will wash her hair for her and take some of her fine clothes and jewels with you. You will persuade her to wear them. Pantisilea, my dear, it is said that my daughter wishes to become a nun. I know this to be but talk; but my daughter is young and impressionable. It is your task to remind her of all the joys outside a convent walls. Girls' chatter, gossip, fine clothes! My Lucrezia loved them all. See, my child, that she does not lose that love. The sooner you bring her from that place, the greater will be your reward."

"Holy Father, my ambition is to serve you."

"You are a good child. You are beautiful too."

The Pope took her into his arms in a farewell embrace which was one of mingled approval and passion.

❧ ♛ ❧

Lucrezia was ready to be very fond of Pantisilea. She was excited to have someone who laughed readily, and enjoyed gossiping. Serafina and the others were too sober, believing that there was something sinful in laughter.

Pantisilea opened trunks and showed Lucrezia the dresses she had brought with her.

"These become you far more than that black habit, Madonna."

"I have no heart for them in this quiet place," Lucrezia explained. "They would look incongruous here, Pantisilea."

Pantisilea appeared bitterly disappointed. "And your hair, Madonna!" she persisted. "It is not as golden as it used to be."

Lucrezia looked slightly alarmed. It was sinful to care for worldly matters such as the adornment of her person, the sisters had told her; and she had tried not to regret that her hair was left unwashed.

She explained to Pantisilea that the sisters would not have approved of her washing her hair as often as had been her custom. They would accuse her of vanity.

"Madonna," said Pantisilea slyly, "they have not golden hair like yours. I pray you let me wash it, only to remind you how it will shine."

What harm was there in washing her hair? She allowed Pantisilea to do so.

When it was dry, Pantisilea laughed with pleasure, took strands of it in her hands and cried: "But look, Madonna, it is pure gold again. It is the color of the gold in your green and gold brocade gown. Madonna, I have the dress here. Put it on."

Lucrezia smiled at the girl. "To please you, little Pantisilea."

So the green and gold dress was put on and, as Lucrezia stood with her golden hair about her shoulders, one of the nuns came to tell her that Pedro Caldes had arrived at the convent with letters from the Pope.

Lucrezia received him in the cold bare room.

He stared at her, and she watched the slow flush creep up from his neck to the roots of his hair. He could not speak, but could only stare at her.

She said: "Why, Pedro Caldes, is aught wrong?"

He stammered: "Madonna, it would seem that I am in the presence of a goddess."

It was so pleasant to be wearing beautiful clothes again, and to sense the admiration of this young man. He was personable and she had been too long without admiration.

After that she did not wear her black habit again and her hair was always gleaming like gold.

She could never be sure when Pedro would call, bringing messages from her family; and she was determined that this young man, who so admired her, should always see her at her best.

🙰 ♛ 🙰

Pantisilea was a merry companion, and Lucrezia wondered how she had endured the long days before the coming of this bright girl.

They would sit together in rooms allotted to them and work at a piece of embroidery, although Pantisilea liked better to sing to the accompaniment of Lucrezia's lute. Pantisilea had brought the lute with her; she had also had some tapestry sent so that the bare walls were hung with this and it no longer seemed like a cell. She continually talked of the outside world. She was amusing and a little indiscreet; and perhaps, thought Lucrezia, that was what made her company so exciting; she felt now that she would go to sleep in that of the kindly but somber sisters.

Pantisilea, delightedly shocked, gossiped about Cesare's anger against his brother and how Sanchia was alternately the mistress of each. There had never been anyone at the Papal Court like Sanchia, she declared. The brothers visited her openly, and the whole of Rome knew that they were her lovers. And there was little Goffredo too, delighted that his wife should be causing so much controversy, and helping his brother Cesare prevail over his brother Giovanni.

She had a story to tell of a lovely girl from Ferrara who was betrothed.

"His lordship of Gandia set eyes on her and greatly coveted her," said Pantisilea; "but her father was determined on her marriage, for it was a good one. She had a big dowry and that together with her beauty, was irresistible. But the Duke of Gandia was determined to make her his mistress. It is all very secret, Madonna; but now the marriage has been postponed and there are some who say that the masked companion who is seen often with the Duke of Gandia is this lady."

"My brothers are alike in that what they want they are determined to have."

"Indeed it is so, and there is much gossip throughout Rome concerning the Duke's mysterious love affair."

"And the masked one is this girl?"

"No one can be sure. All that is known is that in the company of the Duke of Gandia there is invariably a masked figure. They ride together—sometimes pillion. The clothes worn by the Duke's companion are all-concealing, so that it is impossible to say whether it is man or woman."

"How like Giovanni to attract attention to himself thus. And my brother Cesare? Has he a masked mistress?"

"No, my lady. The Lord Cardinal has not been seen except at the church ceremonies. There is talk that he no longer cares for Madonna Sanchia, and that because of this, harmony has been restored between the two brothers."

"I trust it is so."

"They have been seen, walking together, arms linked like true friends."

"It does me good to hear it."

"And, Madonna, what will you wear? The green velvet with the pink lace is becoming to your beauty."

"I am well enough as I am."

"Madonna, what if Pedro Caldes should come?"

"What if he should?"

"It would be wonderful for him to see you in the green velvet and pink lace."

"Why so?"

Pantisilea laughed her merry laugh. "Madonna, Pedro Caldes loves you. It is there in his eyes for anyone to see—but perhaps not for anyone. Not for Sister Cherubino." Pantisilea made a wry face that was a fair imitation of the good sister. "No, she would not recognize the signs. But I do. I know that Pedro Caldes is passionately but hopelessly in love with you, Madonna."

"What nonsense you talk!" said Lucrezia.

He was in love with her.

She knew that Pantisilea was right. It was in every gesture, in the very tone of his voice. Poor Pedro Caldes! What hope was there for him?

But she looked forward to his visits, and was taking as much interest in her appearance as she ever had.

The merry serving-maid was an intrigante. Frivolous and sentimental, it seemed to her inevitable that Lucrezia should indulge in a love affair. Continually she talked of Pedro—of his handsome looks, of his courtly manners.

"Oh, what a tragedy if the Holy Father decided to employ another messenger!" she cried.

Lucrezia laughed at her. "I believe you are in love with this young man."

"I should be, were it of any use," declared Pantisilea. "But his love is for one and one only."

Lucrezia found that she enjoyed these conversations. She could grow as excited as Pantisilea, talking of Pedro. There in their little room, which was becoming more and more like a small chamber of one of the palaces, they sat together gossiping and laughing. When Lucrezia heard the bells, when she looked out of her window and saw the nuns passing to the chapel, and when she heard their singing of Complines, sometimes she would start guiltily out of her reverie. Yet the sanctified atmosphere of the convent made the visits of Pedro seem more exciting.

One day when she went into the cold bare room to receive him, she noticed that he was quiet, and she asked him if anything had happened to sadden him.

"Madonna," he said earnestly, "I am sad indeed, so sad that I fear I can never be happy again."

"Something very tragic has happened to you, Pedro?"

"The most tragic thing that could happen to me."

She was at his side, touching his sleeve with gentle and tender fingers. "You could tell me, Pedro. You know that I would do all in my power to help."

He looked down at her hand resting on his sleeve, and suddenly he took that hand and covered it with kisses; then he fell on his knees and hid his face against her billowing skirts.

"Pedro," she said softly. "Pedro, you must tell me of this tragic thing."

"I can come here no more," he said.

"Pedro! You are weary of these visits. You have asked my father to send another in your place." There was reproach in her voice, and he sprang to his feet. She noticed the shine in his eyes and her heart leaped with exultation.

"Weary!" he cried. "These visits are all that I live for."

"Then Pedro . . ."

He had turned away. "I cannot look at you, Madonna," he murmured. "I dare not. I shall ask His Holiness to replace me. I dare not come again."

"And your tragedy, Pedro?"

"Madonna, it is that I love you . . . the saints preserve me!"

"And it makes you sad? I am sorry, Pedro."

He had turned to her, his eyes blazing. "How could it make me anything but sad? To see you as I do . . . to know that one day the order will come, and you will return to the Vatican; and when you are there I shall not dare to speak to you."

"If I returned to my palace it would make no difference to our friendship, Pedro. I should still ask you to come and see me, to entertain me with your conversation and tales of your beautiful country."

"Madonna, it is impossible. I crave leave to depart."

"It is granted, Pedro," she said. "But . . . I shall expect you to visit me still, because I should be so unhappy if any other came in your place."

He fell on his knees and, taking her hands, covered them with kisses.

She smiled down at him, and she noticed with pleasure how the fine dark hair curled on his neck.

"Oh yes, Pedro," she said. "I should be very unhappy if you ceased to visit me, I insist that you continue to do so. I command it."

He rose to his feet.

"My lady is kind," he murmured. Then he looked at her with a hunger in his eyes which enthralled her. "I . . . I dare stay no longer," he said.

He left her, and when he had gone she marvelled that in this convent of San Sisto she had known some of the happiest hours of her life.

Cesare rode to his mother's house to pay her one of his frequent visits. He was thoughtful, and those about him had noticed that of late there had been a certain brooding quietness in his demeanor.

He had ceased to court Sanchia; he had ceased to brood on his sister's voluntary retreat to the convent; he had become quite friendly with his brother Giovanni.

When Vannozza saw her son approaching, she clapped her hands vigorously and several of her slaves came running to do her bidding.

"Wine, refreshment," cried Vannozza. "I see my son, the Cardinal comes this way. Carlo," she called to her husband, "come quickly and greet my lord Cardinal."

Carlo came running to her side. Carlo was well satisfied with his lot, which had brought marriage with the Pope's ex-mistress and mother of his children. Many privileges had come his way, and he was grateful for them. He showed his gratitude by his profound respect for the Pope and the Pope's sons.

Cesare embraced his mother and his stepfather.

"Welcome, welcome, dearest son," said Vannozza with tears of pride in her eyes. It never ceased to astonish her that these wonderful sons of hers should visit their comparatively humble mother. All her adoration shone in her eyes, and Cesare loved her for that adoration.

"My mother," murmured Cesare.

Carlo declared: "It is a great day for us when my lord Cardinal honors our house."

Cesare was gracious. He sat with his mother and his step-father, and as they drank from the silver goblets which had been hastily taken from the *credenza*, Vannozza was regretting that she had not been warned of her son's coming and had not had time to hang the tapestries on the walls and bring out the majolica and pewter ornaments. They talked of Lucrezia and of the impending divorce.

"Your father will do what is best for you all," said Vannozza. "Oh, my son, I would that I were not such a humble woman and could do more for you."

Cesare laid his hand over hers and smiled at her; and when Cesare smiled his face was beautiful. It was real affection which he had for his mother; and Vannozza, because she knew how others feared him, valued that affection the more.

After they had refreshed themselves, Cesare asked that she would show him her flowers, of which she was justly proud, and they went into the gardens.

They wandered among her plants, Cesare's arm about her waist; and since he was so affectionate, Vannozza found courage to tell him how pleased she was that he and his brother Giovanni seemed to be better friends.

"Oh, Mother, how senseless quarrels are! Giovanni and I are brothers. We should be friends."

"They were merely brotherly quarrels," soothed Vannozza. "Now you are growing older you realize the futility of them."

"It is so, Mother. I want the whole of Rome to know that Giovanni and I are now friends. When you next give a supper party let it be an intimate one . . . for your sons only."

Vannozza stood still, smiling delightedly. "I shall give the party at once," she said. "For you and Giovanni. It is too hot in the city. It shall be an alfresco supper in my vineyards. What think you, Cesare, of that idea?"

"It is excellent. Make it soon, dearest Mother."

"Say when you wish it to be, oh my beloved, and it shall be then."

"Tomorrow is too soon. The day after that?"

"It shall be so."

"Mother, you are my very good friend."

"And should I not be, my best beloved son who has cherished and honored me at all times?"

She closed her eyes and remembered what Cesare had done to all those who, he had been able to discover, had taken part in the raiding of her house during the French invasion. He had been brutal and many had suffered, and Vannozza was a woman who did not care to see great suffering; but this showed the measure of Cesare's love for her. "Nothing," he had cried, "nothing . . . is too severe for those who sought to dishonor my mother by desecrating her house."

"You will be glad to see Giovanni with me at your supper party," said Cesare. "You love him too, remember. It is a pity Lucrezia will not be with us."

"I should take great pleasure in seeing my daughter, and I agree that I shall be happy to have Giovanni with me. But, my son, of all my children there is one who delights me as none other could. It is you, my dearest."

He kissed her hand with that extravagant show of love which the family displayed toward each other.

"I know you speak truth, dear Mother. I swear to you here and now that no harm shall ever come your way while there is power in this body to prevent it. I will inflict torture and death on any who dare whisper a word against you."

"My dearest, do not be so vehement on my poor account. I need nothing to make me happy but to see you often. Bless me with your presence as frequently as is possible—although I know that you have your destiny, and I must not let my selfish love interfere with that—and I shall be the happiest woman on Earth."

He held her against him, and then they continued their walk among the flowers, planning the supper party.

❧♛☙

Cesare walked through the streets, his cloak concealing his fine clothes, his mask hiding his features, so that none would have guessed his identity. Reaching the Ponte district he sauntered into a narrow street, slipped into another and paused before a house. Looking about him to make sure that he was not followed, he walked through the open door shutting it behind him, and descending the stone steps to a room with wooden panelling and flagstone floor, clapped his hands as he did so.

A servant appeared, and when Cesare removed his mask the man bowed low.

"Your mistress is here?" asked Cesare.

"Yes, my lord."

"Conduct me to her at once."

He was led to a room which was typical of many such rooms, furnished with a canopied bed, wooden chairs with carved backs, and the statue of the Madonna with the lamp burning before it.

A very beautiful young girl, tall and slender, who had risen at Cesare's entry, fell on her knees before him.

"My lord," she murmured.

"Rise," said Cesare impatiently. "My brother is not here?"

"No, my lord. He comes two hours from now."

Cesare nodded.

"The time has come for you to fulfill your duty," he said.

"Yes, my lord?"

Cesare looked at her shrewdly. "You are beloved by my brother. What are your feelings for him?"

"I serve one master," she said.

His fingers closed about her ear. It was a gesture both tender and threatening. "Remember it," he said. "I reward those from whom I demand service, and the reward depends on the nature of their service."

The girl shivered, but she repeated firmly: "I serve one master."

"That is well," said Cesare. "I will tell you quickly what is required of you. You will present yourself at the vineyard of Vannozza Catanei at midnight on a date which I shall give you. You will be cloaked and masked as usual when you ride with my brother. You will leap on to his horse and ride away with him."

"Is that all, my lord?"

Cesare nodded. "Except this one thing. You will insist on taking him to an inn which you have discovered, and where you will tell him you have planned to stay until morning."

"And this inn?"

"I will give you its name. It is in the Jewish quarter."

"We are to ride there after midnight!"

"You have nothing to fear if you obey my instructions." He took her face in his hands and kissed her lingeringly. "If you do not, my beautiful one . . ." He laughed. "But you will remember, will you not, that you serve one master."

🌊👑🌊

Vannozza, still a very beautiful woman, greeted her guests in her vineyard on the summit of the Esquiline. The table was heavily laden with good food, and the wine was of the best. Carlo Canale was beside her to do honor to the distinguished guests.

"You think we shall be merry enough with only your sons' cousin, the Cardinal of Monreale, and a few other relations?"

"When my sons come to me they like to escape from all the pomp which usually surrounds their daily life."

Canale kept sipping the wine to assure himself that it was of the very best; Vannozza nervously surveyed her table and shouted continually to the slaves; but when the guests arrived she gave all her attention to them.

"My dearest sons," she murmured, embracing them; but the embrace she gave Cesare was longer than that she had for Giovanni, and Cesare would notice this.

The warm summer night was enchanting; they could look down on the city, while the cool sweet air and the scent of flowers from the meadows about the Colosseum wafted up to them.

A perfect night, thought Vannozza.

Conversation about the table was merry. Cesare teased Giovanni in the pleasantest way.

"Why, brother," he cried, "you expose yourself to danger. I have heard that you ride among desperadoes with none but a groom to protect you— you and your masked friend."

"None dare harm my father's son," said Giovanni lightly.

"Nay, but you should take care."

"I have taken most things in my life," laughed Giovanni, "but rarely that."

"Yes, my son," said Vannozza, "I beg of you take greater care. Do not go to those parts of the city where danger lurks."

"Mother, I am a baby no longer."

"I have heard," said Cesare, "that he was seen riding in the Jewish quarter late one night. That is foolish of him."

"Foolish indeed, my son," scolded Vannozza.

Giovanni laughed and turned to Canale. "More wine, Father. 'Tis good, this wine of yours."

Canale, delighted, filled his stepson's goblet, and the conversation turned to other matters.

It was past midnight, and they were preparing to leave when Cesare said: "Why look, who is that lurking among the trees?"

The company turned and looking saw that cowering in a clump of bushes was a slender masked figure.

"It would appear that your friend has called for you," said Cesare.

"It would appear so," answered Giovanni, and he seemed to be well pleased.

"Must your friend come even to our mother's house?" asked Cesare.

"Perhaps," laughed Giovanni.

"This friend is very eager for your company," said Cesare. "Come, we will not delay you. Farewell, dear Mother. It has been a night I shall long remember."

Vannozza embraced her sons and watched them mount their horses. When Giovanni was in his saddle, the masked creature sprang up behind him in order to ride pillion.

Cesare was laughing and calling to the few attendants, whom he had brought with him, to follow him; and he broke into a song, in which the others all joined, as they rode down the hillside and into the city.

When they reached the Ponte district Giovanni drew up and told his brother that he would be leaving him there. He called to one of his grooms: "Hi, fellow, you come with me. The rest of you . . . go to your beds."

"Whither are you bound, brother?" asked Cesare. "You are surely not going into the Jewish quarter?"

"My destination," retorted Giovanni arrogantly, "is my own concern."

Cesare lifted his shoulders with an indifference which was unusual.

"Come," he said to his followers and to those of Giovanni's servants who had not been commanded to accompany him, "home to the Borgo."

So they left Giovanni, who, with the masked figure riding behind him, and the groom a little distance in the rear, went on into the narrow streets of the Jewish quarter.

That was the last time Cesare saw Giovanni alive.

THE NEXT DAY, Alexander, waiting to receive his beloved son, was disappointed by his continued absence. All that day he waited, but still Giovanni did not put in an appearance.

He sent to Giovanni's household. No one had seen him. He had not visited Sanchia.

Alexander chuckled. "I doubt not that he has spent the night in the house of some woman, and he fears to compromise her by leaving in daylight."

"Then he is showing himself unusually discreet," said Cesare grimly.

But that day brought no news of Giovanni, and toward the end of it, a messenger hurried to the Pope to tell him that the young Duke's groom, who had been seen to accompany him, was found stabbed to death in the Piazza degli Ebrei.

All Alexander's serenity vanished. He was frantic with anguish.

"Send out search parties," he cried. "Examine every street . . . every house . . . I shall not rest until I hold my son in my arms."

When the search had gone on for several days and there was no news of Giovanni, the Pope grew desperate, but he would not believe any harm had come to his son.

"It is a prank of his, Cesare," he kept repeating. "You will see, he will come bounding in on us, laughing at us because he so duped us. Depend upon it."

"It is a prank of his," agreed Cesare.

Then there was brought before the Pope a Dalmatian boatman who said that he had something to say, and he would say it only to the Holy Father because he believed it concerned the missing Duke of Gandia.

Alexander could scarcely wait to see the man, and he was immediately brought before the Pope who, with Cesare and several high officials of the Court, waited eagerly for him.

His name, he said, was Giorgio and he slept in his boat which was tied up on the shores of the Tiber.

"My duty, Holiness," he said, "is to guard the wood pile near the church of San Gerolamo degli Schiavoni close to the Ripetta bridge."

"Yes, yes," said the Pope impatiently. "But do not waste time. Tell me what you know of my son."

"I know this, Holiness, that on the night when the Duke of Gandia disappeared I saw a man riding a white horse, and on this horse he carried what could well be the body of a man. There were two other men, holding the body as the horse came down to the river's edge. When the horse came to the water the rider turned so that the horse's tail was to the river; then the two men pulled off that which could well be a body, Holiness, and it fell into the river."

"Can we trust this man?" demanded the Pope. He was fearful. He did not want to believe him. While the man had spoken he had visualized that limp body on the horse, and it was the body of his beloved son.

"We have no reason to doubt him, Most Holy Lord," was the answer.

"Holiness," said Giorgio. "I can tell you more. The body slipped into the water, and it was held up by what seemed to be his cloak, so that it floated and began to drift down stream. Then the man on the horse said something to the others and they began throwing stones at the floating cloak. They pitched the stones on to it again and again until it sank with the weight and disappeared. Holiness, they stood watching for some time and then they rode away."

"You saw this happen," said Cesare, "and you told no one! Why not?"

"Why, bless Your Eminence, I live by the river, and living there see countless bodies thrown into the water. There seemed nothing especial to report about this one, save that it happened on the night about which the gentlemen were asking."

The Pope could bear no more. A terrible melancholy had come to him.

He muttered: "There is nothing to do but drag the river."

THUS THEY FOUND Giovanni. There were wounds in his throat, on his face and his body; the mud of the river clung to his fine clothes on which the jewels still remained; his purse was full of ducats, and his rings, brooches and necklace, worth a fortune, had not been taken.

When Alexander was told he went out and stopped those who carried the corpse as it was brought into the castle of St. Angelo. He threw himself on to the body, tore his hair and beat his chest, while he cried out in his grief.

"To those who have dealt thus with him, so they shall be dealt with!"

he cried. "Nothing shall be too bitter for them to endure. I'll not rest, beloved son, most beloved of all, until I have brought your murderer to justice."

Then he turned to those who carried the ghastly corpse and said to them: "Take my beloved, wash him, perfume him, put on his ducal robes; and thus he shall be buried. Oh Giovanni, oh my beloved son, who has done this cruel deed to you . . . and to me?"

He was washed and dressed in his ducal robes, and at night by the light of one hundred and twenty flares he was carried from Castle St. Angelo to Santa Maria del Popolo.

The Pope did not accompany him, and as he sat at the window of Castle St. Angelo, looking down on the winding cortège lit by those flares, he could not contain his grief.

"Oh Giovanni, Giovanni," he moaned, "best loved of all, my dearest, my beloved, why have they done this to thee and me?"

Pedro Caldes came to the convent to see Lucrezia. He was very agitated when she received him, falling on his knees and kissing her hands.

"There is news, terrible news. You will hear of it before long, but I wished to break it gently. I know how you cared for him. Your brother . . ."

"Cesare!" she cried.

"No. Your brother Giovanni."

"He is ill?"

"He disappeared, and now they have discovered his body. It was in the Tiber."

"Giovanni . . . dead!"

She swayed uncertainly, and Pedro put his arms about her.

"Madonna," he murmured, "dearest Madonna."

She sat down and leaned against Pedro.

She lifted her eyes to his face; they were bewildered and filled with misery. "My brother Giovanni . . . but he was so young, so full of health."

"He was murdered, Madonna."

"Who . . . ?"

"None knows."

She covered her face with her hands. Giovanni, she thought. Not you. It is not possible. She saw him strutting about the nursery, asserting his rights, fighting with Cesare. Fighting with Cesare!

Not Cesare, she told herself. It could not be Cesare who murdered him.

Such thoughts must not be spoken.

Pedro kept his arms about her. He told her the story, beginning with the supper party at Vannozza's vineyard, while Lucrezia stared blankly before her, picturing it all.

Cesare had been there, and the masked person had lurked in the bushes. Evil thoughts kept coming into her mind. Who was the masked person?

"Did they discover the masked one?" she asked.

"No. None knows who it was."

"And my father?"

"He is overwhelmed with grief. None has ever seen him so distressed, so unlike himself."

"And . . . my brother, my brother Cesare?"

"He does all he can to soothe your father."

"Oh Pedro, Pedro," she cried, "what will become of us?"

"Madonna, do not weep. I would die rather than see you unhappy."

She touched his face lightly. "Sweet Pedro," she murmured. "Sweet and gentle Pedro."

He took the fingers which caressed his cheek, and kissed them frantically.

"Pedro, stay with me," she begged. "Stay here and comfort me."

"Madonna, I am unworthy."

"There was never one more gentle and kind to me and therefore more worthy. Oh Pedro, I thank the saints that you came to me, that you will help me bear my sorrows, that you will help stay my fear, for Pedro, I am desperately afraid."

"Of what, Madonna?"

"I know not, I only know I am afraid. But when you put your arms about me, dear Pedro, I am less afraid. So . . . do not talk of leaving me. Talk only of staying with me, of helping me to forget these evil things which happen all about me. Pedro, sweet Pedro, talk no more of unworthiness. Stay with me, Pedro. Love me . . . for I love you too."

He kissed her lips this time, wonderingly, marvelling, and she returned his kisses.

There was a wildness about her.

"Pedro, I keep seeing it. The pictures come to me. The party . . . the masked figure . . . and my brother . . . and then Giovanni. Oh Pedro, I must shut them out. I cannot bear them. I am frightened, Pedro. Help me . . . help me, my loved one, to forget."

ALEXANDER HAD GIVEN orders that a search was to be made to find the murderers of his son, that they might be brought to justice, and there were rumors implicating various people, for Giovanni had had a host of enemies.

It was said that Giovanni Sforza had planned the murder; that he resented the affection between his wife and her family; and Giovanni Borgia had shared that affection with her brother Cesare and her father.

Giovanni Sforza and other suspects quickly established their innocence; there was one name, however, which none dared utter.

The Pope was too unhappy to voice his fears; nor would he face them. He was shut in his rooms alone because he feared someone might give voice to the terrible suspicion which at this time he was unable to face, even in his own thoughts.

This was the greatest tragedy of Alexander's life and when, a few days after Giovanni's body had been discovered, he stood before the Consistory, he mourned openly for the death of his beloved son.

"A worse blow could not have fallen upon us," he declared, "since we loved the Duke of Gandia above all others. We would give most willingly seven tiaras if we could bring him back. We have been punished by God for our sins, for the Duke did not merit this terrible death."

To the astonishment of all present, Alexander went on to declare that the way of life at the Vatican should be reformed and there should be no more pandering to worldly interests. He would renounce nepotism and begin the reforms in his own household.

The Cardinals were aghast. Never had they thought to hear Alexander make such utterances. He was a changed man.

Cesare sought audience with his father afterward, and looking at that stricken face he was filled with sharp jealousy as he asked himself: Would he have felt such grief for me?

"Father," said Cesare, "what meant you by those words you spoke before the Cardinals?"

"We meant exactly what we said," replied the Pope.

Cesare felt as though icy hands were gripping his body, realizing that his father would not meet his eyes.

"Then," pursued Cesare, who could not leave this subject, once he had started it, "do you mean that you will do nothing to help me, to help Goffredo, Lucrezia and the rest of our family?"

The Pope was silent.

"Father, I beg of you, tell me what is in your mind."

The Pope lifted his eyes to his son's face, and Cesare saw there what he had dreaded to find. They held an accusation.

He suspects! thought Cesare. He knows.

Then he remembered those words which the Pope had spoken when he heard of Giovanni's death. "To those who have dealt death to him so shall they be dealt with. Nothing shall be too bitter for them to endure."

"Father," said Cesare, "we must stand together after a tragedy such as this. We must not forget that, whatever happens to any of us, the family must go on."

"We would be alone," said the Pope. "Go from us now."

Cesare went uneasily.

He sought out Sanchia. "I would Lucrezia were here," he said. "She might comfort our father. But he did not ask even for her. He does not seem to want any of us now. He thinks of nothing but Giovanni."

But Cesare could find no peace with Sanchia. He must go to his father once more. He must know whether he had read aright the accusation in those eyes.

He went to the Pope's apartments, taking Sanchia and Goffredo with him, and after a long delay they were admitted.

Sanchia knelt at Alexander's feet and lifted her beautiful blue eyes to his face. "Father, be comforted," she said; "it is double grief to your children to see you so."

The Pope looked at her with cold eyes. He said: "They quarrelled over you—he and his brother. Go from me. I am arranging that you shall leave Rome. You will be departing shortly, with your husband, for Squillace."

"But Father," began Sanchia, "we would comfort you in your bitter loss."

"You comfort me most by removing yourself from my presence."

It was the first time Cesare had seen his father unmoved by beauty.

"Please go now, you and Goffredo," he said to Sanchia. Then, turning to Cesare, he went on: "I would have you stay."

When they were alone they looked at each other, and there was no mistaking the meaning in Alexander's eyes.

His voice broke as he said: "They shall search no more. I would not have them discover my son's murderer now. I could bear no further misery."

Cesare knelt and would have taken his father's hand, but Alexander removed it. It was as though he could not bear to be touched by the hand which had slain Giovanni.

"I wish you to go to Naples," he said. "You are appointed Cardinal Legate for the coronation of the new King."

"Father, another could go," protested Cesare.

"It is our wish that you should go," said the Pope firmly. "Now, I pray you leave me. I would be alone with my grief."

PEDRO PRESENTED HIMSELF daily at the convent. When Sister Girolama suggested his visits were too frequent he had his explanations: His Holiness was prostrate with grief; his one comfort was derived from his daughter's messages. He did not wish her to return to the Vatican which was deep in mourning, but to stay where she was that he might write to her and she to him. He wished to hear details of her daily life. That was why Pedro called so frequently at the convent.

This was not true, but it was a good enough excuse. It might have been that the sisters had realized that the beautiful girl would never be one of them. Perhaps they sensed her innate worldliness and made no effort to combat it.

Lucrezia lived in her cells which she had converted into comfortable rooms, and if Pedro visited her there instead of in the cold bare room at first assigned to them, that was a matter between the Pope's daughter and her visitor. Her maid would act as chaperone and, although the maid was a very frivolous creature, she was one who had been selected for the post by the Holy Father, and it was not for the Prioress to complain.

Lucrezia had changed, but the nuns were not conscious of physical appearances, and it was left to Pantisilea to tell her that her eyes were brighter and that she was a hundred times lovelier than she had been when she, Pantisilea, had first come to attend her.

"It is love," said Pantisilea.

"It is such a hopeless love," murmured Lucrezia. "Sometimes I wonder where it can lead us."

But when Pedro was with her she ceased to ask herself such practical questions. All that mattered to Lucrezia was the fulfillment of her love, for she was fully alive now to her own sensuality.

That love had begun in sorrow. She remembered well the day when the terrible shock of Giovanni's death had made her turn to Pedro. It was then, when he had put his arms about her, that she had realized how deeply in love with him she was.

Love! It was a precious thing. It was worth facing danger for the sake of love; and she had discovered this about herself: She would never again be one to deny love.

Love filled her life, filled the cell at the convent, touching austerity with a roseate light.

Sorrow passed, she found, for news came that even the Pope had come out of retirement, that he was no longer heard weeping and calling for Giovanni.

On the day when Pedro brought the news that the Pope had taken a mistress, they were all very lighthearted in Lucrezia's room. Only Pantisilea was a little regretful, wishing she had been the one chosen to comfort the

Pope. But her place was with Lucrezia whom she hoped never to leave. Nor should she; Lucrezia had promised her that.

"You shall always be with me, dear Pantisilea," Lucrezia told her. "When I leave this place you shall come with me. No matter where I go I shall take you with me."

Pantisilea could be happy, for when they left this place she would still live close to His Holiness, and there was always hope that he might notice her again.

Weeks passed. The Pope seemed to have forgotten his grief completely. Cesare was on his way home from Naples, and Alexander was preparing a welcome for him.

Giovanni, the beloved son, was dead, but that was in the past, and the Borgias did not grieve forever.

Cesare stood before his father, and now the Pope looked full into his son's eyes.

"My son," he said brokenly.

Cesare kissed his father's hands; then turned his appealing eyes upon him.

Alexander had been too long alone, and having lost one son he did not intend to lose another.

Already, because he was Alexander, to him Giovanni had become a shadowy figure, and Cesare was here beside him, young, ambitious, strong.

He is the stronger of the two, mused Alexander. He will do great deeds before he dies. With him at its head, the house of Borgia will prosper.

"Welcome home, my son. Welcome home, Cesare," said the Pope.

And Cesare exulted, for all that he had done, he now knew, had not been in vain.

Lucrezia and Pantisilea were working on a piece of embroidery when Lucrezia dropped the work and let her hands lie idly in her lap.

"Does aught ail you, Madonna?" asked Pantisilea.

"What should you think?" asked Lucrezia sharply.

"I thought you seemed . . . over-pensive, Madonna. I have noticed it of late."

Lucrezia was silent. Pantisilea was looking at her in some alarm.

"You have guessed," said Lucrezia.

"It cannot be, Madonna. It must not be."

"It is so. I am to have a child."

"Madonna!"

"Why do you look so shocked? You know that it can easily happen when one has a lover."

"But you and Pedro! What will your father say? What will your brother do?"

"I dare not think, Pantisilea."

"How long?"

"It is three months."

"Three months, Madonna! So it happened in the beginning."

"It would seem so."

"June, July, August," counted Pantisilea. "And it is now the beginning of September. Madonna, what shall we do?"

"I do not know, Pantisilea. I think mayhap I shall go away some- where in secret. These things have happened before. Perhaps Pedro will come with me." Lucrezia flung herself into the arms of Pantisilea. "Lucky one!" she cried. "If you loved you might marry; you might live with your husband and children, happy for the rest of your life. But for one such as I am there is nothing but the marriage which will bring advantage to my family. They betrothed me twice and then they married me to Giovanni Sforza." Now that she loved Pedro she shuddered at the memory of Giovanni Sforza.

"They will soon divorce you from him," soothed Pantisilea. "Mayhap then you will marry Pedro."

"Would they allow it?" asked Lucrezia, and all the melancholy had left her face.

"Who knows . . . if there is a child? Children make so much difference."

"Oh Pantisilea, how you comfort me! Then I shall marry Pedro and we shall go away from Rome; we shall have a house like my mother's and I shall have my *credenza* in which I shall store my silver goblets, my majolica. Pantisilea, how happy we shall be!"

"You will take me with you, Madonna?"

"How could I manage without you? You shall be there, and mayhap I'll find a husband for you. No, I shall not find you one. You shall find your own and you must love him as I love Pedro. That is the only way to marry, Pantisilea, if you would live happily."

Pantisilea nodded, but she was apprehensive.

Lucrezia had yet to be divorced, and she was to be divorced because she was *virgo intacta* on account of her husband's being unable to consummate the marriage. Pantisilea believed that Lucrezia would have to appear before the Cardinals, perhaps submit to an examination. "Holy Mother of God," thought Pantisilea, "protect us."

But she loved Lucrezia—how she loved her! No one had ever been so kind to her before. She would lie for Lucrezia; she would do anything to make her happy. To be with Lucrezia was to share her philosophy of life, to believe that everything must come right and that there was really nothing about which to worry oneself. It was a delightful philosophy. Pantisilea planned to live with it for the rest of her life.

"Pantisilea, should I go to my father, should I tell him that I am to have Pedro's child? Shall I tell him that Pedro is my husband in all but name and that he must let us marry?"

When Lucrezia talked thus, Pantisilea felt herself jerked roughly into reality.

"His Holiness has had a shock, Madonna. The death of your brother is but three months away. Let him recover from one shock before he is presented with another."

"This should mean happiness for him. He loves children and he longs for us to have them."

"Not the children of chamberlains, Madonna. I beg of you, take the advice of Pantisilea. Wait awhile. Choose the right moment to tell His Holiness. There is time yet."

"But, people will notice."

"The sisters? They are not very observant. I will make you a dress with voluminous petticoats. In such a dress your child could be about to be born and none know it."

"It is strange, Pantisilea, but I am so happy."

"Dearest Madonna, you were meant to have children."

"I think that is so. When I think of holding this child in my arms, of showing him to Pedro, I am so happy, Pantisilea, that I forget all my troubles. I forget Giovanni. I forget my father's grief, and I forget Cesare and . . . But no matter. It is wrong of me to feel so happy."

"Nay, it is always right to be happy. Happiness is the true meaning of life."

"But my brother so recently murdered, my father bowed down with grief, and myself a wife already to another man!"

"The time passes and the grief of His Holiness with it. And Giovanni Sforza is no husband to you and never was . . . so the Pope would have it."

Pantisilea did not press that subject. She knew that Lucrezia would have to appear before the gathering of Cardinals and declare herself a virgin. The petticoats would have to be very wide.

THE POPE AND his elder son were often together now. It was said in the Vatican: "His Holiness has already forgotten his vow to end nepotism; he has forgotten his son Giovanni, and all the affection he had for him is now given to Cesare."

There was a new relationship between Alexander and Cesare; the shock of Giovanni's death had shaken Alexander; Cesare was exultant because he believed that his father would never be the same again, that their positions had shifted, very slightly it was true; but there was an indication of what they would one day be to each other.

Alexander had lost a little of his authority; Cesare had gained that little. At the time of his great grief Alexander had seemed like an old man; he had recovered, but he had never regained that air of a man in his prime.

Cesare had learned something of great importance: I may do what I will and it makes no difference. There is nothing I cannot do, and he will help me to achieve my ambitions.

Now the Pope said to him: "My son, this divorce of your sister is long delayed. I think we should arrange for her to appear before the assembly."

"Yes, Father. She cannot be too quickly freed from the man."

"You were not idle while you were in Naples, Cesare? You sounded the King on the question of a possible husband for your sister?"

"I did, Holiness. Alfonso, the Duke of Bisceglie was suggested."

The Pope murmured: "Illegitimate."

Cesare shrugged his shoulders.

"And," went on Alexander, "Sanchia's brother."

"He is like his sister in appearance only," Cesare said.

The Pope nodded. He could forgive Cesare for bringing about the death of Giovanni, because he was a Borgia and his son; but he found it harder to forgive Sanchia for being one of the causes of jealousy between Cesare and Giovanni.

He considered the marriage. Alliance with Naples would be good at this juncture; and if the marriage became irksome there were always ways of ending it.

"I have been approached by the Prince of Salerno on account of his son Sanseverino."

"I doubt not that the King of Naples had heard of it, and that is why he was so anxious for you to consider Alfonso of Bisceglie. He would not wish to see such a firm ally of the French joined with us by such a marriage."

"Francesco Orsini is another; and there is the Lord of Piombino and Ottaviano Riario."

"Dear Lucrezia—although she is not yet rid of one husband, she has many waiting for her. Fortunate Lucrezia!"

"You are thinking that you are denied marriage, my son."

Cesare's eyes were now alight with eagerness. "Oh my father," he said, "Carlotta of Aragon, the King's *legitimate* daughter who is being educated at the Court of France, is marriageable. It was hinted that were I free she might be my wife."

There was a brief silence. This seemed to Cesare one of the most important moments of his life, for it was as though the Pope were struggling to regain his old supremacy.

Then, after what seemed a long time to Cesare, Alexander spoke. He said slowly: "Such a marriage would be advantageous, my son."

Cesare knelt in sudden emotion. He took his father's hand and kissed it passionately.

In this son, thought Alexander, I shall forget all my grief. He shall achieve such greatness that in time I shall cease to regret the loss of his brother.

❧ ♔ ❧

Life for Lucrezia in the Convent of San Sisto had been an alternation of joy and terror.

She and Pedro indulged in feverish pleasure which was the more intense because they both knew that it could not last. They were two people who must snatch at every moment of happiness, savoring it, cherishing it because they could not know when it would be their last together.

Pantisilea watched them, sharing vicariously their joys and sorrow; her pillows were often wet at night when she lay awake trying to look into the future.

There came that day when Pedro brought an inevitable message from the Pope. Lucrezia was to prepare herself to appear before an assembly of Envoys and Cardinals at the Vatican. There she should be declared *virgo intacta*.

Lucrezia was terrified.

"But what can I do?" she demanded of Pantisilea.

The little maid tried to comfort her. She should try on the dress Pantisilea had made for her. It was winter-time and she would be expected to wear many petticoats, as it was cold in the convent. She would hold her head high and impress them all with her innocent appearance. She must.

"How can I do it, Pantisilea?" she cried. "How can I stand before those holy men and act this lie?"

"You *must* do it, Madonna dearest. The Holy Father commands it, and it is necessary that you should be freed from Giovanni Sforza. On what other grounds could you be divorced?"

Lucrezia began to laugh hysterically.

"Pantisilea, why do you look so solemn? Do you not see what a joke this is? I am six months pregnant, and I am to go before the assembly and swear that I am *virgo intacta*. It is like a tale told by Giovanni Boccaccio. It is a joke . . . or it would be if it were not so serious . . . if it might not end tragically."

"Dear Madonna, we will not let it end tragically. You will do what your father asks of you, and when you are free you will marry Pedro and go away to some place where all will be peace and happiness for you."

"If only that could be so!"

"Remember it when you stand before those men, and that will give you courage. If you act this lie convincingly you will gain your freedom; and it is, after all, not the child of Giovanni Sforza that you carry. Your happiness—and that of Pedro—depend on how you act before the assembly. Remember that, Madonna."

"I will remember it," said Lucrezia firmly.

PANTISILEA DRESSED HER with care. Cunningly she arranged the velvet flounces, and when she had finished she was pleased with her work.

"None will guess . . . I swear it. But, Madonna, how pale you are!"

"I feel the child moving within me as though to reproach me for denying it."

"Nay you are not denying it. You are making a happy life for it. Do not think of the past, Madonna. Look to the future. Look to happiness with Pedro, and all that will come out of this day."

"Pantisilea, my dear little maid, what should I have done without you?"

"Oh Madonna, none ever had a sweeter mistress. If I could not serve you, life would be dull for me. Anything I have done for you has been repaid a thousandfold."

They clung together, two frightened girls.

And so she came to the Vatican, and there in the presence of her father and the members of the assembly she listened to the reading by one of the Cardinals of the document which declared that her marriage to Giovanni Sforza had not been consummated and that as a result Lucrezia was *virgo intacta*. This being no true marriage they were gathered together to pronounce its annulment.

She stood before them and never had her innocent looks served her so well.

The Cardinals and Envoys were impressed by her beauty and her youthful appearance; they needed no other proof of her virginity.

She was told that she was no longer married to Giovanni Sforza, and she answered with a speech of thanks which was so disarming that all present were charmed with her.

There was a moment when, feeling the child move within her, she felt dizzy and swayed slightly.

"Poor child!" murmured one of the Cardinals. "What an ordeal for one so young and innocent to endure!"

THE POPE WAS waiting for her in his private apartments; Cesare was with him.

"My dearest," said the Pope, embracing her warmly, "at last I hold you in my arms again. This has been a trying time for us all."

"Yes, Father."

Cesare added: "And to have you shut away from us . . . that has been the most trying of all."

"I needed the refuge," she answered, not daring to meet their eyes.

"I trust," said the Pope, "that you found little Pantisilea a good servant?"

Lucrezia replied passionately: "I love the girl. I do not know what I should have done without her. Thank you a thousand times, Father, for sending her to me."

"I knew she would serve you well," answered Alexander.

"The time has come for you to begin a new life, dear sister," Cesare murmured. "Now that you are rid of Sforza you will find life sweet again."

She did not answer. Desperately she was seeking for courage to tell them of her condition, to explain why they must put aside all thought of a grand marriage for her, how she loved Pedro and that he was the father of the child she carried.

She had imagined herself telling them, again and again as she lay in her converted cell and, although it had seemed a great ordeal which lay before her, it had not seemed impossible. Facing them, she found that she had underestimated the fear and awe in which she held them, the power which they held over her.

Alexander's smile was almost roguish. "There are many clamoring for your hand, daughter."

"Father . . . I do not wish to think of them."

Cesare had moved swiftly toward her and put an arm about her. "What ails you, Lucrezia? You look ill. I fear you have suffered privation in your convent."

"No . . . no. I have been comforted there."

"It is no place for such as you are."

"But you are pale and you look exhausted," said the Pope.

"Let me sit down a moment," Lucrezia begged.

Both men watched her intently. Only Alexander realized how frightened she was, and he motioned her to a stool.

Cesare told her of the men who were eager to marry her. "Francesco Orsini . . . Ottaviano Riario . . . and there is Sanchia's brother, the little Duke of Bisceglie."

Alexander said suddenly: "This has been an ordeal for the child. She needs rest now. Your apartments have been prepared for you, my dear. You shall go to them at once."

Cesare was about to protest, but the Pope was his old firm self. He was clapping his hands and slaves were appearing.

"Madonna Lucrezia's women should conduct her to her apartments," he said.

WHEN HE WAS alone, Alexander stood before the shrine in his apartments. He was not praying; he was staring at it, and there were furrows in his brow and the rich purple blood stained his face, while in his temples a pulse throbbed visibly.

It was impossible. But it was not impossible at all. What had been happening in the convent all these months? He had heard stories of what could and did happen in convents. But not that of San Sisto.

He had not dared voice his supicions before Cesare. Oh yes, he was afraid of his son. If Cesare had guessed what was in his mind he might have done anything, however reckless. Cesare must not know yet . . . if it were true. But this monstrous thing which he suspected must not be true.

He thanked the saints that Cesare's mind was so constantly on his own affairs that he had failed to be as perceptive as his father. Cesare had been dreaming of release from the Church and marriage to Carlotta of Naples, even as Lucrezia stood before them, and he had not noticed how complete was the change in Lucrezia. Could all those months of quiet life at San Sisto's have wrought such a change? Not they alone.

But he must be careful. He must remember his fainting fits. It would not do for him to be ill now, because if what he suspected were true he would need all his wits to deal with it.

He must wait. He must recover his equanimity; he must remind himself that he was Alexander, who had emerged triumphant after the death of Calixtus—Alexander who on every occasion turned defeat into victory.

At length he made his way to his daughter's apartment.

Lucrezia was lying on her bed, and only Pantisilea sat beside her. There were tears on Lucrezia's cheeks, and the sight of them filled Alexander's heart with tenderness.

"Leave us, my dear," he said to Pantisilea; and the girl's dark eyes were fearful and yet adoring as they met his. It was as though she implored him, out of his great tenderness, his power and understanding, to save her dear mistress.

"Father!" Lucrezia would have risen, but Alexander put a hand on her shoulder and gently forced her back on to the pillows.

"What have you to tell me, my child?" he asked.

She looked at him appealingly, but she could not speak.

"You must tell me," he said gently. "Only if you do, can I help you."

"Father, I am afraid."

"Afraid of me? Have I not always been benevolent to you?"

"The kindest father in the world, Most Holy Lord."

He took her hand and kissed it.

"Who is he?" he asked.

Her eyes opened wide and she shrank against her pillows.

"Do you not trust me, child?"

She sprang up suddenly and threw herself into his arms; she began to sob wildly; never had he seen his serene little Lucrezia so moved.

"My dearest, my dearest," he murmured, "you may tell me. You may tell me all. I shall not scold you whatever you have to tell. Do I not love you beyond all else in the world? Is not your happiness my most constant purpose?"

"I thank the saints for you," sobbed Lucrezia.

"Will you not tell me? Then must I tell you. You are to have a child. When, Lucrezia?"

"It should be in March."

The Pope was astounded. "That is but three months hence. So soon! I should not have believed it."

"Pantisilea has been so clever . . . oh, such a comfort, Father. Thank you for sending her. I could not have had a dearer friend. I shall always love her . . . as long as I live."

"She is a dear creature," said the Pope. "I am glad that she comforted you. But tell me, who is the father of your child?"

"I love him, Father. You will permit our marriage?"

"It is difficult for me to deny my daughter anything."

"Oh Father, beloved Father, would I had come to you before. How foolish I was! I was afraid. When you were not with me, I did not see you as you really are. I saw you as the powerful Pope determined to make a politically advantageous marriage for me. I had forgotten that the Holy Father of us all was first my own dear father."

"Then it is time we were together again. The name of the man?"

"It is your chamberlain, Pedro Caldes."

The Pope rocked her to and fro in his arms.

"Pedro Caldes," he repeated. "A handsome boy. One of my favorite chamberlains. And he visited you in your convent, of course."

"It was when he brought me news of Giovanni's death, Father, and I was so unhappy. He comforted me."

The Pope held her fiercely against him; for a moment his face was distorted with rage and anguish. My beloved Giovanni murdered, he was thinking; my daughter pregnant with the child of a chamberlain!

But when Lucrezia looked at him, his face wore its habitual expression of tenderness and benignity.

"My dear child," he said, "I will confess that I am startled."

She took his hands and covered them with kisses. How appealing she was, looking at him with those adoring yet frightened eyes; she reminded him of her mother at the height of their passion.

"Father, you will help me?"

"Do you doubt it . . . for one moment? Shame, Lucrezia! But we must be cautious. You have been divorced in the belief that your husband is impotent and you are a virgin." In spite of the Pope's horror at the situation with which he was confronted he he could not refrain from smiling. It was a situation which, in any circumstances, must seem to him essentially humorous. "What will our good Cardinals say, think you, if they discover that the charming innocent young virgin, who appeared before them so decorously, was six months pregnant? Oh Lucrezia, my clever one, my subtle one, it would not do at all. We might even have Sforza claiming the child and swearing it was his. Then where would be our divorce? We have to act now with the utmost caution. The matter must be kept secret. Who knows of it?"

"None but Pedro and Pantisilea."

The Pope nodded.

"None must know, my child."

"And Father, I may marry Pedro? We want to go away from Rome to live quietly and happily somewhere together, where no one concerns themselves with us and what we do; where we can live peaceful happy lives, as ordinary people may."

The Pope smoothed her hair from her hot face. "My beloved," he said, "you must leave this matter in my hands. The world shall know that the ordeal through which you have passed has been a trying one. You will stay in your apartments at Santa Maria in Portico and, until you have regained your health, none shall wait on you but the faithful Pantisilea. In the meantime we will discover what can be done to make you happy."

Lucrezia lay back on her pillows, and the tears slowly ran down her cheeks.

"In truth," she said, "Alexander VI, you are not a man; you are a god."

Madonna Lucrezia was ill. For two months since she had left the convent she had been confined to her apartments, and only her maid Pantisilea and the members of her family were allowed to see her.

The citizens of Rome laughed among themselves. What did this mean? What had Madonna Lucrezia been doing during her stay in the convent? They remembered that she was after all a Borgia. In a few months' time would there be a child at the Vatican, a little infant whom the Pope in his benevolence had decided to adopt?

Cesare heard the rumors, and declared he would be revenged on those who repeated them.

He went to his father's presence and told him what was being said.

"It is inevitable," said the Pope. "There are always such stories concerning us. The people need them as they need their carnivals."

"I'll not have such things said of Lucrezia. She must come out of her seclusion. She must show herself."

"Cesare, how could she do that?"

The Pope was looking at his son, marvelling at the egoism of Cesare, who was waiting for that day when he would be released from the Church to marry Carlotta of Naples and take charge of the Papal armies. That image in his mind was so big that it obscured all others. Thus it must have been when he arranged for the murder of Giovanni. The grief of his father was as nothing beside his own grandiose ambitions. Even Lucrezia's predicament was not known to him, which seemed fantastic because, had he given the matter a moment's thought, it would surely have been obvious.

"By appearing among them," Cesare replied.

It was time he realized the true state of affairs. At the end of the month, or the beginning of next, Lucrezia's child would be born. He would have to know.

"That," said Alexander, "would be but to confirm the rumors."

Now Cesare was really startled. The Pope watched the hot blood rush into his handsome face.

"'Tis true enough," went on Alexander. "Lucrezia is with child. Moreover the birth is imminent. Cesare, I wonder you did not realize this."

Alexander frowned. He understood how terrified Lucrezia would be of Cesare's discovering her condition. She and little Pantisilea would have been doubly careful when Cesare visited her.

"Lucrezia . . . to have a child!"

The Pope lifted his shoulders. "These things happen," he said lightly.

"While she was in the convent!" Cesare clenched his fists. "So that was why she was so contented there. Who is the father?"

"My son, let not our tempers run high. This is a matter wherein we need all our cunning, all our calm. It is unfortunate, but if this marriage we are planning for Lucrezia is to be brought about, it will not help us if it should be known that, while she stood before the Cardinals declaring herself *virgo intacta*, she was in fact six months pregnant. This must be our little secret matter."

"Who is the father?" repeated Cesare.

The Pope went on as though he had not spoken. "Listen to my plan. None shall attend her but Pantisilea. When the child is born it shall be taken away immediately. I have already been in contact with some good people who will take it and care for it. I shall reward them well, for remember, this is my grandchild, a Borgia, and we have need of Borgias. Mayhap in a few years' time I will have the child brought to the Vatican. Mayhap I will watch over its upbringing. But for a few years it must be as though there was no child."

"I wish to know the name of this man," insisted Cesare.

"You are too angry, Cesare. I must warn you, my son, that anger is the greatest enemy of those who allow it to conquer them. Keep your anger in chains. It was what I learned to do at an early age. Show no anger against this young man. I shall not. I understand what made him act as he did. Come, Cesare, would not you and I in similar circumstances behave in exactly the same manner? We cannot blame him." The Pope's expression changed very slightly. "But we shall know how to deal with him when the time comes."

"He shall die," cried Cesare.

"All in good time," murmured the Pope. "At the moment . . . let all be peaceful. There is my little Pantisilea." The Pope's tone was regretful, and his smile tender. "She knows a great deal. Poor child, such knowledge is not good for her."

"Father, you are wise. You know how to deal with matters like this, but I must know this man's name. I cannot rest until I do."

"Do nothing rash, my son. His name is Pedro Caldes."

"Is he not one of your chamberlains?"

The Pope nodded.

Cesare was shaking with rage. "How dare he! A chamberlain, a servant . . . and my sister!"

The Pope laid a hand on his son's shoulder, and was alarmed by the tremors which shook Cesare.

"Your pride is great, my son. But remember . . . caution! We shall know how to settle this matter, you and I. But at the moment our best method is caution."

Caution! It was not in Cesare's nature to be cautious. The rages which had come to him in boyhood were more frequent as he grew older, and he found it becoming more and more difficult to control them.

His mind was dominated now by one picture: His sister with the chamberlain. He was obsessed by jealousy and hatred, and there was murder in his heart.

The Pope had urged caution, but he no longer obeyed the Pope. After the death of his brother he had learned his father's weakness. Alexander did not remember to mourn for long. He forgot the misdeeds of his family; he ceased to regret the dead and gave all his attention to the living. The great affection of which he was capable—evanescent though it might be—was intense while it lasted; and it had to be directed toward someone. Cesare had taken the affection his father had given to Giovanni, as though it were a title or estate. Cesare knew he need not fear the loss of his father's affection, no matter what he did. That was the great discovery he had made. That was why he felt powerful, invincible. Alexander was lord of Italy, and Alexander would bend to the will of his son.

So when Alexander said Caution, why should Cesare heed that warning unless he wished to?

One day he came face to face with Pedro Caldes in one of the ante-rooms leading to the Papal apartments, and Cesare's anger flared up to such an extent that he was drained of all memories of his father's warning.

"Caldes, halt!" cried Cesare.

"My lord . . ." began the startled chamberlain, "what would you have of me?"

"Your life," said Cesare, and he drew his sword.

The startled young man turned and fled toward the Pope's apartments. Cesare, grasping his sword, followed.

Pedro, breathless and terrified, could hear the cruel laughter of Cesare close behind him; once Cesare's sword touched his thigh and he felt the hot blood run down his leg.

"You waste time in running," Cesare cried. "You shall die for what you have dared do to my sister."

Fainting with fear, Pedro reached the Papal throne, on which Alexander was sitting; with him were two of his chamberlains and one of the Cardinals.

Pedro cried: "Holy Father, save me . . . save me before I die!" And he flung himself at Alexander's feet.

Cesare was upon him. Alexander had risen, his expression horrified and full of warning.

"My son, my son, desist," he cried. "Put away your sword."

But Cesare merely laughed and thrust at the chamberlain, as Alexander stooped forward to protect him, so that the blood spurted up and stained the Pope's robes, and even splashed his face.

Those who had been with the Pope stood back aghast, while Alexander put his arms about Pedro and looked up into his son's glowering face.

"Put away your sword," he said sternly, and there was a return of the Alexander who, benevolent as he was, had always known how to quell his sons. "Bring not your quarrels to our sacred throne."

Cesare laughed again, but he felt once more that awe of his father which he was surprised to discover he had not quite overcome.

He obeyed as he said truculently: "Let him not think that this is the end of our quarrel."

Then he turned and strode out of the apartment.

Alexander murmured: "The hot blood of youth! He does not mean to be so rash. But who of us was not rash in youth? Have this young man's wounds attended to and . . . for his own safety let him be kept under guard."

Pantisilea leaned over the bed.

Lucrezia murmured: "It is beginning, Pantisilea."

"Lie down, Madonna. I will send a message to the Holy Father."

Lucrezia nodded. "He will take care of everything."

Pantisilea despatched a slave to the Vatican with a signet ring which the Pope had given her and which was to be a sign between them that

Lucrezia was in need of a midwife. In this affair, the Pope had decided, no word should be written. When he received the ring he would know its purpose, and for no other reason must it be sent to him.

"How blessed I am in such a father," murmured Lucrezia. "Oh, Pantisilea, why did I not go to him at once? If I had, Pedro and I might have been married now. How long it is since I saw Pedro! He should be close to me now. How happy I should be if he were! I shall ask my father to bring him to me."

"Yes, Madonna, yes," soothed Pantisilea.

She was a little uneasy. She had heard rumors concerning the disappearance of Pedro Caldes, but she had not told Lucrezia of this. It would upset her with her confinement so near.

"I dream, you know," said Lucrezia. "I dream all the time. We shall have to leave Rome. That will be necessary for a while, I doubt not. We shall live quietly for a few years in some remote place—even more remote than Pesaro; but I do not think my father will allow us to be away from him forever. He will visit us; and how he will love his grandchild! Pantisilea, do you think it will be a boy?"

"Who can say, Madonna? Let us not pray for a boy or a girl, but that it will bring you great happiness."

"You speak like a sage, Pantisilea. And look, your cheeks are wet. You are crying. Why are you crying?"

"Because . . . because it is so beautiful. A new life about to begin . . . the fruit of your love. It is beautiful and it makes me weep."

"Dear Pantisilea! But there are the pains to be endured first, and I confess I am frightened."

"You should not be, Madonna. The pains come and then . . . there is the blessing."

"Stay with me, Pantisilea. All the time stay with me. Promise."

"If it is permitted."

"And when the child is born, when we have our little home, you will be with us. You must not make the baby love you too much, Pantisilea, or I shall be jealous."

Pantisilea's answer was to burst into stormy tears.

"It is because it is so beautiful," she repeated. "Almost too beautiful to be true."

The midwife came. She was masked and accompanied by two men, also masked. They waited outside the door of Lucrezia's room and the midwife came to the bed.

She examined Lucrezia and gave orders to Pantisilea. The two men remained outside the door during Lucrezia's labor.

Lucrezia awoke from exhaustion, and asked for the child. It was placed in her arms.

"A little boy," said Pantisilea.

"I feel I shall die of happiness," murmured Lucrezia. "My own child. I would that Pedro were here. He should be eager to see his son, should he not? Pantisilea, I want you to bring Pedro to me."

Pantisilea nodded.

"I want you to bring him at once."

The midwife had come to the bed. She said: "The Madonna is weary and needs to rest."

"I want to hold my baby in my arms," said Lucrezia, "and when his father is here with me I shall feel completely at rest."

"Your maid shall be sent at once for the child's father. It has been arranged," said the midwife. She turned to Pantisilea. "Put on your cloak, and prepare to go at once."

"I do not know where to find him," began Pantisilea.

"You will be taken to him."

Lucrezia smiled at Pantisilea, and the little maid's eyes were wide with joy.

"I will not delay a moment," she cried. "I will go at once."

"You will be conducted there. You will find your guide waiting at the door."

"I shall not be long, Madonna," said Pantisilea; and she knelt by the bed and kissed Lucrezia's hand.

"Go, Pantisilea," murmured Lucrezia. "Go with all speed."

Lucrezia's eyes followed Pantisilea to the door. Then the midwife stooped over the bed.

"Madonna, I will take the baby from you now. He must sleep in his cradle. You need rest. I have a draft here which will send you to sleep. Take it and sleep long and deep, for you will have need of your strength."

Lucrezia took the draft, kissed the child's fair head, gave him to the midwife and lay back on her pillows. In a few minutes she was asleep.

One of the men who had been waiting outside the door of Lucrezia's apartment stepped forward as Pantisilea came out.

"Follow me," he said, and together they went out of the palace to the courtyard, where a horse was waiting for them.

It was evening and there was only moonshine to light the streets as Pantisilea rode pillion with her guide away from the palace. They went from the populous quarter and down to the river.

When they were near the bank, the horseman stopped.

He said: "'Tis a beautiful night, Pantisilea."

She looked at the pale moonlight on the water and thought it wonderful. All the world looked beautiful because she was happy. Her mistress safely delivered of a fine boy, herself on the way to bring Pedro to Lucrezia. She had been thinking of their future as they rode along.

"Yes," she said, "it is beautiful. But let us not tarry. My mistress longs to see Pedro Caldes."

"There is no hurry," said the man. "Your mistress will have a long sleep. She is exhausted."

"I would rather proceed at once to our destination."

"Very well, Pantisilea."

He leaped down from his horse.

"Whither are you going?" she asked.

His answer was to lift her from the horse. She looked about her for some dwelling where Pedro might be sheltering, but she could see none.

The man said: "How small you are, Pantisilea, and so young."

He bent his head and kissed her lips.

She was astonished, but not displeased. It was long since a man had caressed her.

She laughed softly and said: "It is not the time. I wish to be taken at once to Pedro Caldes."

"You have spoken, Pantisilea," said the man.

He put his hands tenderly on her head and moved them slowly down to her ears, caressing them. She looked up into his face; he was not looking at her; he seemed to be staring at the moonlit river. His eyes were fixed and glassy, and suddenly a terrible fear took hold of Pantisilea.

For in a moment of blinding understanding she knew, even before it happened.

Then she felt the hands slide down to her throat.

Lucrezia awoke. It was daylight.

She had been dreaming. She was in a beautiful garden in the country; her baby boy lay in his cradle, and she and his father were bending over it looking at the child.

A happy dream, but only a dream. And here was the day, and she was awake.

She was not alone in her room; a man sat on either side of her bed, and she was conscious of the dull thudding of her heart. Pedro had been promised her; and he had not come; and where was Pantisilea?

She struggled up.

"You should rest," said Alexander. "You need your strength, my dear."

"Father," she murmured; and then she turned to that other figure. "And Cesare," she added.

"We have come to tell you that all is well," said Cesare. He spoke in stern clipped tones, and she knew that he was angry. She shrank from him toward her father. Alexander's voice had been as kind and tender as it ever was.

"I want my child," she said. "Father, it is a boy. You will love him."

"Yes," said the Pope. "In a few years he shall be with us."

She smiled. "Oh, Father, I knew I could rely on you to look after me."

The beautiful white hand patted hers. "My little one," murmured Alexander. "My wise little one."

She took his hand and kissed it.

"Now," said Alexander briskly, "there is nothing to worry about. Everything has been settled. You will in a short while resume your normal life, and this little affair, although there have been some ugly rumors, will have been forgotten."

"Father, Pedro . . ."

"Do not speak his name," said Cesare harshly.

"Cesare, dearest brother, understand me. I love Pedro. He is the father of my child and soon to be my husband. Our father has arranged that it shall be so."

"My dearest," said the Pope, "alas, that cannot be."

She struggled up in her alarm.

"My dear daughter," murmured the Pope. "It is time you knew the truth."

"But I love him, Father, and you said . . ."

Alexander had turned away and put a kerchief to his eyes.

Cesare said almost viciously: "Pedro Caldes' body was recovered from the Tiber yesterday. You have lost your lover, sister; lost him to death."

She fell back on her pillows, her eyes closed. The Pope leaned over her lovingly. "It was too sudden," he said. "My sweet, sweet child, I would I could bear your pains for you."

A smile of sarcasm twisted Cesare's lips as he looked at his father.

He wanted to shout: "At whose orders was the chamberlain murdered? At mine and yours. Rightly so. Has she not disgraced our name enough by consorting with servants!"

Instead he said: "There is another who has joined him there . . . your maid Pantisilea. You will never see her face again."

Lucrezia covered her face with her hands; she wanted to shut out the sight of this room and the men who sat on either side of her. They were her guardians; they were her jailors. She had no life which was not designed by them. She could not take a step without them; if she attempted to do so, they arranged that she should meet only disaster.

Pedro in the river! She thought of him with the wounds on his body or perhaps the bruises on his throat; perhaps neither. Perhaps they had poisoned him before they had given him to the river.

Pedro, the handsome boy. What had he done but love Lucrezia?

And little Pantisilea. Never to see her again. She could not endure it. There was a limit to the sorrow one could suffer.

"Go . . . go from me," she stammered. "Have my child brought to me . . . and go . . . go, I say."

There was silence in the room. Neither Cesare nor Alexander moved.

Then Alexander spoke, still in those gentle soothing tones. "The child is being well looked after, Lucrezia. You have nothing to fear on his account."

"I want my son," she cried. "I want my baby. I want him here . . . in my arms. You have murdered the man I love. You have murdered my friend. There is nothing I want now of you but to give me my child. I will go away. I will live alone with my child . . . I want never to see this place again. . . ."

Cesare said: "Is this Lucrezia speaking? Is this Lucrezia Borgia?"

"Yes," she cried. "It is I, and no other."

"We have been wrong," said Alexander quickly. "We have broken this news too sharply. Believe me, dearest daughter, there are times when one sharp cut of the knife is best. Then the healing can begin at once. It was wrong of you—a Borgia, our own beloved daughter—so to conduct yourself with a servant. And that there should be a child, was . . . criminal. But we love you dearly and we understand your emotions. We forgive them as we would forgive all your sins. We are weak and we love you tenderly. We have saved you from disgrace and disaster, as we always should. You are our dearest treasure and we love you as we love none other. I and your brother feel thus toward you, and together we have saved you from the consequences of great sin and folly. Those who shared this adventure are no more; so there is no danger of their betraying you. As for the child, he is a beautiful boy and already I love him. But you must say good-bye to him— oh, only for a short while. As soon as it can be arranged I shall have him brought back to us. He is a Borgia. He kicked and screamed at me. Bless him. He is in the best of hands; he has a worthy foster-mother. She will tend him as her own—nay better. She'll not dare let any harm come to our little Borgia. And this I promise you, Lucrezia: in four years . . . nay, in three, we'll have him with us, we'll adopt our lusty boy, and thus none will be able to point a finger at him and say, 'There is the bastard of Lucrezia and a poor chamberlain.'"

She was silent. The dream had disappeared; she could not grasp the reality. Not yet. But she knew she would. She knew that she could do no other.

Cesare had taken her hand, and she felt his lips touch it.

"Dearest," he said, "we shall arrange a grand marriage for you."

She shivered.

"It is too soon to talk of such things," reproved Alexander. "That comes later."

Still she did not speak.

They continued to sit there. Each held one of her hands and now and then would stoop to kiss it.

She felt bereaved of all happiness; and yet she was conscious of a vague comfort which came to her through those kisses.

She was growing aware of the inevitability of what had happened. She was beginning to realize how foolish her dreams had been.

THE SECOND
BRIDEGROOM

Lucrezia was being dressed for her wedding. Her women stood about her, admiring the dress, heavy with golden embroidery and sewn with pearls. Rubies glittered about her neck, and the design on the dress was the mingling arms of Aragon and the Borgias.

It was but a few months since she had given birth to her son, yet now she had recovered her outward placidity; and as she stood in her apartment while she was dressed in her finery, she appeared to have no thought for anything but the ceremony about to take place.

Sanchia was with her.

Lucrezia turned slowly and smiled at her sister-in-law. Who would have thought that it should be Sanchia who would bring such comfort in her misery?

It was Sanchia who had talked of her numerous love affairs, who had explained that in the beginning one felt so intensely. Did not one remember one's first ball, one's first jewels? Thus it was with love affairs. Did not Sanchia know? Was not Sanchia a connoisseur of love?

Sanchia had talked of her little brother. He was gentle; he was beautiful; and all loved him. Lucrezia would bless the day that she had taken Sanchia's brother, Alfonso Duke of Bisceglie, to husband.

Sanchia was excited at the prospect of her brother's arrival in Rome, and inspired Lucrezia with that enthusiasm. Oh, thought Lucrezia, how glad I am to have Sanchia with me at this time!

She was a Borgia. She must not forget it. Everywhere she looked she was confronted by the emblem of the grazing bull. We must not dream of simple love and marriage, she told herself. That is for simple people, people without a great destiny.

She was the beloved of her father and brother. It was as though they had forgotten she had ever attempted to defy them. Somewhere in Rome—perhaps not even in Rome—a little boy was being brought up by his foster-parents, and in a few years he would come to the Vatican. He was all that remained of that brief idyll which had given him life and brought such suffering to his mother, and death to two who had loved her dearly.

As a Borgia one did not brood. The past was as nothing, the present and the future all-important.

She was ready now to go to her bridegroom.

LIGHT ON LUCREZIA

A NOVEL OF THE BORGIAS

AUTHOR'S NOTE

After delving into the lives of the Borgias it is difficult to understand why Lucrezia has been given such an evil reputation. It could have been because many of the writers of the past believed, with reason, that lurid sensationalism was more acceptable than truth. To the more intelligent reader of today, this is not so; and a bewildered girl, born into a corrupt society, struggling to maintain her integrity, is, I think, a more interesting and convincing figure than an evil and sordid poisoner.

What, I asked myself, is the solution to the enigma of Lucrezia? Did that unnatural devotion to father and brother really exist? Why was it that, when she left her family for Ferrara, she appeared to lead an almost exemplary life, and there was so little scandal about her? It is true that there were two love affairs after her marriage to Alfonso d'Este, but one of these seems to have been almost entirely platonic, while the other was carried on in the glamorous glow of secret correspondence; and considering the licentious nature of the times, such affairs would not be considered of any special significance. Where was the evil poisoner—depicted in such works as the Donizetti opera—hiding in this serene and gentle girl?

So I have thrown this light on Lucrezia and what I have found is set out in this book.

In my search for the true Lucrezia I have been considerably helped by the undermentioned works.

An Outline of Italian Civilization. Decio Pettoello, Ph.D.

History of the Italian Republics in the Middle Ages. J. C. L. Sismondi. (Recast and supplemented in the light of historical research by William Boulting.)

France. William Henry Hudson.

The Old Régime in France. Frantz Funck-Brentano.

The Life and Times of Lucrezia Borgia. Maria Bellonci. Translated by Bernard Wall.

Lucrezia Borgia. A Chapter from the Morals of the Italian Renaissance. Ferdinand Gregorovius.

The Marriage at Ferrara. Simon Harcourt-Smith.

Lucrezia Borgia. Joan Haslip.

Alma Roma. Albert G. MacKinnon, M.A.

Hadrian the Seventh. Fr. Rolfe (Frederick Baron Corvo).

Isabella d'Este, Marchioness of Mantua, 1474-1539, A Study of the Renaissance. 2 Vols. Julia Cartwright.

Lucretia Borgia, The Chronicles of Tebaldeo Tebaldei, Renaissance Period. Algernon Swinburne, with commentary and notes by Randolph Hughes.

Memoirs of the Dukes of Urbino, Illustrating the Arms, Arts and Literature of Italy from 1440-1630. 3 Vols. James Dennistoun of Dennistoun.

Cesare Borgia. Charles Yriarte. Translated by William Stirling.

Cesare Borgia. William Harrison Woodward.

The Life and Times of Roderigo Borgia, Pope Alexander VI. The Most Reverend Arnold H. Mathew, D.D.

Chronicles of the House of Borgia. Frederick, Baron Corvo.

Life of Cesare Borgia. A History and Some Criticisms. Rafael Sabatini.

J.P.

I

THE BRIDEGROOM

FROM NAPLES

At the head of the cavalcade which was traveling northward from Naples to Rome, rode an uneasy young man of seventeen. He was very handsome and richly dressed. His doublet was embroidered with gold and he wore a necklace of rubies; those who rode with him showed a deep respect when they addressed him, and it was obvious that he was of high rank.

Yet his mood was reflected in his followers who did not sing or shout to one another as they habitually did; there was among them an atmosphere of reluctance, almost of dread which indicated that although they rode steadily on, they were longing to go back along the road they had come.

"We cannot be far from Rome now," the young man called to a member of his guard.

"Less than a day's ride, my lord," came the answer.

The words seemed to echo through the company like a distant rumble of thunder.

The young man looked at his men, and he knew that there was not one of them who would wish to change places with him. What did they whisper to one another? What was the meaning of their pitying glances? He knew. It was: Our little Duke is riding straight into the net.

Panic possessed him. His fingers tightened on the reins. He wanted to pull up, to address them boyishly, to tell them that they were not going to Rome after all; he wanted to suggest that as they dared not return to Naples they should form themselves into a little band and live in the mountains. They would be bandits. The King of Naples would be their enemy. So would His Holiness the Pope. But, he would cry, let us accept their enmity. Anything is preferable to going to Rome.

Yet he knew it was useless to protest; he knew that he must ride on to Rome.

A few months ago he had had no notion that his peaceful life would be disturbed. Perhaps he had stayed too long in childhood. It was said that he was young for his seventeen years. Life had been so pleasant. He had hunted each day, returning at night with the kill, pleasurably exhausted, ready to feast and sleep and be fit for the next day's hunting.

He should have known that a member of the royal house of Aragon could not go on indefinitely leading such a pleasant but, as his uncle the King would say, aimless life.

There had come that day when he had been summoned to the King's presence.

Uncle Federico had welcomed him in his jovial way and had been unable to suppress his smiles, for he was fond of a joke; and what he had to tell his nephew seemed to him a very good one.

"How old are you, Alfonso?" he had asked. And when Alfonso had told him, he had continued to smile. "Then, my boy," he cried, "it is time you had a wife."

There had been nothing very alarming in that statement. Alfonso had known that he would soon have a wife. But Uncle Federico, the joker, had not told all. "You are not sufficiently endowed, my nephew, to satisfy the bride I have in mind for you," he went on. "Oh no! A bastard sprig, even of our noble house, is not good enough. So we shall ennoble you. Alfonso of Aragon, you shall be Duke of Bisceglie and Prince of Quadrata. What say you to that?"

Alfonso had declared his delight in his new titles. But he was eager, he said, to know the name of his bride.

"All in good time, all in good time," murmured Federico, as though he wanted to keep the joke to himself a little longer. Alfonso remembered, although he had only been a very little boy at that time, how Uncle Federico—not King then but only brother of the King—had come to Naples from Rome and told how he had stood proxy for Alfonso's sister Sanchia at her marriage with Goffredo Borgia, and how he had amused the company vastly—and in particular the Pope—by his miming of a reluctant virgin as the bride. As all knew that Sanchia had been far from a reluctant virgin for quite a long time before her marriage to little Goffredo, that was a great joke; it was the sort of joke which Uncle Federico, and doubtless others, reveled in.

Alfonso then wondered whether it was a similar joke which was now amusing his uncle.

"You are seventeen," said Federico. "Your bride is a little older, but only a little. She is eighteen, nephew, and reputed to be one of the loveliest girls in Italy."

"And her name, sire?"

Federico had come close to his nephew and put his mouth to his ear. "Nephew," he said, "Duke of Bisceglie and Prince of Quadrata, you are to marry His Holiness's daughter, Lucrezia Borgia."

From the moment his uncle had spoken the dreaded name Alfonso had known no peace. There had been many evil rumors concerning that family, and his future bride had not escaped them. All feared the Pope. It was said that he was possessed of supernatural powers, and this must be so for at sixty-seven he had the vigor of a young man. His mind was alert and cunning as it had ever been; and it was rumored that his mistresses were as numerous as they had been in the days of his youth. But it was not the Pope's vigor or diplomatic skill which was to be feared.

Rumors concerning the mysterious deaths of those who crossed the Pope's will were continually being circulated throughout Italy. He and his son Cesare had formed, it seemed, an unholy partnership, and whenever their names were mentioned, men lowered their eyes and were afraid, for it was said that as little as a look could bring down the wrath of the Borgias, and that wrath could mean the assassin's knife, a final plunge into the Tiber, or what was perhaps even more dreaded, an invitation to sup at the Borgia table. Those who lived within the shadow of the Borgias could never relax their vigil; they must be continually on the alert, watching, waiting and wondering.

It was to this shadow that his uncle was condemning young Alfonso, and not to its edge where he might exist in a certain amount of obscurity, but to its very heart.

His new brother-in-law would be that Cesare Borgia whose hands were so recently stained with his own brother's blood. There were rumors concerning his relationship with Lucrezia, and it was said that he loved her with a love which went beyond what a brother should feel for his sister. The rumor added that he hated all those on whom his sister's affection alighted, and sought to destroy them; so Cesare's cold vicious eyes would at once and inevitably be directed toward Lucrezia's bridegroom.

And Lucrezia? How did this young bridegroom picture her as he rode toward Rome?

A bold and brazen woman. The stories concerning her relationship with her father and her brother were shocking. Giovanni Sforza, her divorced husband, had many a tale to tell of the wicked and incestuous woman who had been his wife. Giovanni Sforza, it was true, was an angry man because the Pope had branded him with the stigma of impotency. It was natural, Uncle Federico had said, that Sforza should want his revenge, and how could he better take it than by slandering the wife whose family had insisted she divorce him? But was it true that Lucrezia, when she had stood before the Cardinals and Envoys in the Vatican declaring herself to be *virgo intacta*, had really been six months pregnant? Was it true that the child she had borne three months later had been smuggled out of the Vatican, her lover murdered, her faithful maid, who had shared Lucrezia's secrets, strangled and thrown into the Tiber?

If these stories were true, what manner of woman was this to whom his uncle was sending him? At the moment the Pope and his terrifying son were eager for the marriage, but what if in time to come they found it not to their liking? Giovanni Sforza, it was said, had escaped death by running away, but he had escaped with his life, only to be branded as impotent.

What fate was in store for the newly made Duke of Bisceglie?

Nearer and nearer they came to Rome, and as the distance decreased so his fears grew.

THOSE FEARS WOULD have been allayed in some measure if he could have seen his future wife at that moment. She was in her apartments with a piece of needlework in her hands, her golden hair, freshly washed, damp about her shoulders. She looked very young and immature; she was pale, and in the last months had grown thin, and there was a look of intense tragedy in her expression as she bent over her work.

Her women who sat with her were chattering together, trying to disperse her melancholy thoughts. They were talking of the imminent arrival of the Duke of Bisceglie.

"I hear he is a very handsome man."

"Madonna Sanchia is beside herself with pleasure at the thought of his arrival."

Lucrezia let them talk. What did it matter? Nothing they said could make her happy. She did not care if he was the handsomest man in the world. There was only one husband she wanted, and he would never be hers. Three months ago they had taken his body from the Tiber.

"Pedro, Pedro," she whispered to herself, and with a supreme effort she prevented the tears falling from her eyes.

How could she break herself of this unhappy habit, this preoccupation with the past? Until recently she had had the gift, inherited from her father, of never looking back. Now when she saw one of her father's chamberlains in the apartments of the Vatican, or perhaps from the window of this Palace of Santa Maria in Portico, she would believe for one ecstatic second that it was but a nightmare which haunted her, and that it was truly Pedro whom she saw, Pedro, young and beautiful as he had been in the days when they had loved and dreamed of a life they would have together. When she saw a woman carrying a child, or heard the cry of a baby, the anguish would return.

"I want my baby," she whispered to herself. "Now . . . here in my arms . . . I want him now. What right have they to take him from me?"

The right of might, was the answer. She had been powerless in their hands. While she lay helpless they had lured Pedro to his death; she, a woman weak from childbirth, lay exhausted, and they had stolen her baby from her.

There was a commotion without and one of her women said: "It is Madonna Sanchia coming to visit you, Madonna."

And there was Sanchia with her three constant attendants, Loysella, Bernardina, and Francesca; Sanchia merry and vivacious, Sanchia from Naples who snapped her fingers at Roman etiquette.

Lucrezia never looked at Sanchia without astonishment, for Sanchia was the most arrestingly beautiful woman Lucrezia had ever seen. Lucrezia with her golden hair, pale eyes, delicate skin, serene expression and that slightly receding chin which gave her a look of perpetual innocence, was considered to be a beauty, but beside black-haired, blue-eyed Sanchia she seemed colorless. It was said of Sanchia that she dabbled in witchcraft, and that was why she was possessed of that extraordinary beauty which men found irresistible. Lucrezia could believe that Sanchia would be capable of anything.

But during recent months there had grown a bond between them, for it was Sanchia who had comforted her as no one else could. Lucrezia had found it strange to discover unsuspected depths in Sanchia's character. Sanchia, who had a host of lovers, could smile at Lucrezia's tragic relationship with Pedro, and her advice was: "Take more lovers. That is the way to forget."

They were different though. Sanchia must understand that.

Sanchia was now frowning at the needlework in Lucrezia's hands.

"You sit there stitching, when at any moment my brother may be here."

Lucrezia smiled gently. "One would think it was your husband who was coming, rather than your brother."

Sanchia grimaced; she sat on one of the high-backed chairs and her three women drew up stools and sat at her feet. Lucrezia's women had withdrawn themselves, yet hoping that they would not be dismissed for Sanchia's conversation was invariably racy and indiscreet; so if Lucrezia forgot to dismiss them—and she had been absentminded of late—they might stay and garner much interesting news.

"Ah, my husband!" said Sanchia. "Do not mistake me, dear sister. I love your brother, my little Goffredo, but I am a woman who asks more of a husband than that he should be a pretty little boy."

"My brother is happy to be your husband," murmured Lucrezia.

"But he is so young. Far too young for me."

"He is sixteen now."

"But I am twenty-one and he still seems a child to me. You know he has never been a husband to me. . . ."

Sanchia's voice was low but penetrating. She was aware of the listening women. She wanted them to hear her; she wanted the news spread throughout Rome that her marriage had not been consummated. It was not true, and unfortunately for Sanchia, that consummation had been witnessed by the King of Naples and a Cardinal. However, Sanchia's thoughts were on divorce, and she knew that if it was declared firmly enough that the marriage had not been consummated then such declaration could be accepted.

"Poor little Goffredo," said Lucrezia.

Sanchia dismissed the subject abruptly. "How brightly your hair shines. Smile, Lucrezia. It would seem that you are contemplating a funeral rather than a wedding."

"It is because she has not yet seen the Duke," said Loysella.

"When you have seen him you will be enchanted," Sanchia told her. "He is very like his sister in appearance." Sanchia laughed. "Now you are hoping that our resemblance is in appearance only. That's so, is it not?"

"Oh Sanchia," said Lucrezia, and she put out her hand and touched that of her sister-in-law. Sanchia looked at her in alarm. Poor Lucrezia! she thought. She has suffered too much over that affair of Pedro Caldes. She must stop brooding. Alfonso will be here perhaps this day; he must not find a sad Lucrezia brooding on the death of her murdered lover.

"I would talk to Madonna Lucrezia alone," she said on impulse.

"Alone!" Loysella, Francesca and Bernardina looked at her reproachfully.

"Yes," Sanchia told them firmly, "I mean alone."

Sanchia, illegitimate daughter of a King of Naples, could suddenly put on the dignity of royalty, and when she did this her intimate women knew that she expected immediate obedience, so they rose and left the apartment, Lucrezia's attendants following them.

"Now," said Sanchia, "they are gone and we can speak freely. Lucrezia, stop grieving. Stop grieving, I say."

Lucrezia shook her head and said in a broken voice: "How can one . . . at will?"

Sanchia ran to her and put her arms about her. "Lucrezia, it is so long ago."

"Three months," Lucrezia's smile was a twisted one. "We swore to be faithful forever, and you say three months is long."

"All lovers swear eternal fidelity," said Sanchia impatiently. "It means 'I will be true to you as long as our love lasts.' That is the most that can be expected."

"Our love was different."

"All loves are different. Had your Pedro lived, you would have forgotten him by now. It is because they murdered him . . . because they made a martyr of him . . . that you remember."

"I would remember him all my life, no matter what had happened."

"Lucrezia, he was your first lover. That man they married you to—Giovanni Sforza!" Sanchia wrinkled her nose with disgust. "You never loved him."

"It is true," said Lucrezia. "I never loved him, and now . . . I think I hate him."

"He is no friend of yours. Who could expect it? He is branded as impotent. He'll never forgive you that, Lucrezia. He'll be your enemy for life."

"I lied," said Lucrezia. "I signed the document because they insisted and I was weak. Perhaps God punishes me because of the lie I told."

Sanchia shook her head impatiently. "You had no alternative but to sign the document. Had not His Holiness and Cesare determined that you should sign?"

"But I should have stood out against them. Our marriage was consummated . . . many times."

"Hush! It is something we know but never mention. And you are divorced now, sister, free of Sforza. Never say aloud those words, never admit your marriage was consummated. But Lucrezia, do stop grieving. Pedro is dead; nothing can bring him back, and that is an episode which is over. Learn to forget. He was your first love, I know, and you remember. But when you have had many lovers you will find it hard to remember what he looked like."

"You forget—you, Sanchia, who have had lovers since you were a child, who have known so many that you cannot remember them all—you forget that we planned to marry, that we have a child."

"You should not grieve for the child. He will be taken good care of."

"Don't you understand, Sanchia? Somewhere a baby lives . . . my baby.

Some strange woman feeds him and soothes him when he cries. He is my baby . . . my own son—and you ask me to forget him!"

"You should not have had the child, Lucrezia." Sanchia laughed suddenly. "I cannot help it. I think of you, standing before the dignitaries, solemnly swearing that your marriage to Sforza had not been consummated, and as a consequence you were *virgo intacta*, when actually you were pregnant . . . and in three months' time your child would be born."

"Do not speak of it, Sanchia; it is more than I can bear."

"Dear sister, it is because you are young that you suffer so deeply. I tell you this, that when my brother comes it will be a different story. Oh, why is he not here! Shall I weary you with the stories of his many virtues, and how he and I were such good friends when we were very young? Shall I tell you how we escaped to the island of Ischia at the time of the French invasion? But I have told you of these matters before. I will tell you something else, Lucrezia. Yes, I will talk of myself, that you may forget your own sorrows. I and Goffredo are to be divorced."

"That cannot be so."

Sanchia's blue eyes sparkled. "Oh, but it is! That is why I sent the women away. It is not yet the moment to let them into this secret."

"Goffredo will be heartbroken. He worships you."

"His future is being taken care of, and he'll be pleased to pass me over to my new husband."

"And why so?"

"Because my new husband is to be one whom he adores: Cesare."

"But that is not possible," said Lucrezia quickly.

"If the Pope and Cesare decide that they desire it, it will be done."

"Cesare has long wished to leave the Church, and always our father has opposed it."

Sanchia came a little closer to Lucrezia and spoke in a whisper: "Do you know who is the master now?"

Lucrezia was silent. Sanchia had done what she had set out to do; she had diverted Lucrezia's thoughts from her own unhappiness.

"I have noticed often," said Sanchia, "how His Holiness defers to Cesare, how he seeks always to please him. It seems that Cesare is loved even more than Giovanni Borgia was ever loved. Have you not noticed it? Cesare wants a wife, and who is more suited to be his wife than I?" Sanchia laughed slyly, her eyes looking beyond Lucrezia so that the younger girl knew that she was thinking of many passionate encounters with Cesare, the strongest and most feared personality in Rome, the most fascinating of men, the only one whom Sanchia considered worthy to be her husband.

"Do you mean," said Lucrezia, "that they are seriously considering this matter?"

Sanchia nodded.

"But my father always wished one of his sons to follow him to the Papal chair. That was what Cesare was to do."

"Well, there is Goffredo."

"The Cardinals will never agree."

"Do you not know your family yet, Lucrezia?"

Lucrezia shivered. She did know them: she knew them too well, for the murderers of her lover had been her father and her brother.

Sanchia stretched herself like a cat in the sunshine, and the gesture was erotic and expectant.

Lucrezia, watching, felt renewed fear of the future.

In his apartments at the Vatican the Pope received his son Cesare, and when his attendants had bowed themselves out and father and son were alone, Alexander laid his hand on Cesare's shoulder and, drawing him close, murmured: "My son, I think our little plan is going to work out in a manner which will be pleasing to you."

Cesare turned and gave his father a dazzling smile which warmed the Pope's heart. Since the mysterious death of his son Giovanni, Alexander had redoubled his devotion toward Cesare. Giovanni had been Alexander's favorite son, yet, although Alexander knew that Cesare was his brother's murderer, this son of his had been given that affection which had previously been Giovanni's, together with the honors which had substantiated it.

There was a bond between these Borgias which seemed incomprehensible to those outside the family. No matter what its members did, whatever suffering they brought on one another, the bond was not slackened. Between them all was a feeling so strong—in most cases it was love, but in that of Giovanni and Cesare it had been hate—that all other emotion paled before this family feeling.

Now Alexander looked at this son of his who was known as the most vicious man in Italy, and had no wish to please him. Cesare was handsome—all the Pope's children were handsome—and his hair had the auburn coloring which was shared by Goffredo. His features were bold, his body graceful, his manners those of a king; his skin at this time was slightly marred—the aftermath of an attack of the *male francese.*

Cesare wore his Cardinal's robes with an arrogant disdain; but there was now a light in his eyes because he had great hopes of discarding those robes before long. And Alexander was happy because he was going to make Cesare's wish come true.

"Well, Father?" said Cesare, the faintest hint of impatience in his voice.

"I am beginning to feel that it was a happy event when French Charles decided he would watch a game of tennis after his dinner." The Pope smiled. "Poor Charles! I picture him with his Queen at Amboise. Who would have thought that such an innocent diversion as watching a game of tennis could have been so important to him . . . and to us?"

"I know," said Cesare, "that he went into the fosses of the castle at Amboise and passed through the opening in the gallery and that it was very low—that opening—and our little Charles struck his head against the arch."

"Such a little blow," went on the Pope, "that he scarce felt it, and it was only afterward when he was returning to his apartments in the castle that he collapsed and died."

"And now Louis XII is on the throne, and I hear he is as determined to win back what he calls French claims in Italy as his predecessor was."

"We have rid ourselves of Charles. So shall we of Louis if need be," said Alexander. "But Louis, I believe, is going to be very useful to us. I have decided that Louis shall be our friend."

"An alliance?"

The Pope nodded. "Speak low, my son. This is a matter to be kept secret between us two. King Louis XII wishes to divorce his wife."

"That does not surprise me."

"Oh come, she is a pious woman, a good creature, and the people of France revere her."

"Hump-backed, ugly and barren," murmured Cesare.

"But pious withal. She is ready to denounce her throne and retire to a convent at Bourges. That is, of course, if a divorce is granted King Louis."

"He'll need a dispensation from Your Holiness if he is to gain that," said Cesare with a grin.

"He asks much. He would marry his predecessor's wife."

Cesare nodded. "I have heard Anne of Brittany is a pretty creature, though a little lame, but they say that her wit and charm more than make up for her lameness."

"Her estates of Brittany are vast and rich," added the Pope. "So . . . Louis hungers for them—and for her."

"And how does Your Holiness feel regarding the granting of his requests?"

"That is what I wish to discuss. I shall send a message to the King of France that I am deeply considering the possibility of granting that dispensation. Then I shall tell him of my son—my beloved son—who desires to leave the Church."

"Father!"

There were tears in Alexander's eyes. It delighted him to bring such pleasure to his loved one.

"I doubt not, my dearest son, that before long you will find yourself enabled to cast off the purple for which so many crave and from which you so long to escape."

"You understand my feelings, Father. It is because I know my destiny does not lie within the Church."

"I know, my dearest son, I know."

"Father, bring about my release and I'll promise you shall not regret it. Together we will see all Italy united under the Borgia Bull. Our emblem shall shine forth from every town, every castle. Italy must unite, Father; only thus can we take our stand against our enemies."

"You are right, my son. But do not talk to others of these matters as you talk to me. Our first task is to free you from the Church, and I shall demand Louis' help in exchange for his divorce. But I shall ask more than that. You shall have an estate in France and . . . a wife."

"Father, how can I show my gratitude?"

"Let there be no such talk between us," said the Pope. "You are my beloved son, and my greatest wish is to bring honor, glory and happiness to my children."

"This talk of a divorce between Sanchia and Goffredo?"

The Pope shook his head. "On the grounds of the non-consummation of the marriage! I like it not. People will be talking of Lucrezia's divorce from Sforza, and we shall have that scandal revived. I hope soon to have the little boy brought to me here, and I long for that day. No, as yet there shall be no divorce. And you, my son, with the titles which will come to you when you leave the Church, will not wish for marriage with your brother's divorced wife. Why should you? Oh, Sanchia is a beautiful woman, well skilled in the arts of love; but do you need marriage to enjoy those? Not you, my son. You have been enjoying all you could get as Sanchia's husband, these many months. Continue in your pleasure. I would not have you curb it. But marry Sanchia! A Princess, I grant you, but an illegitimate one. What say you to a legitimate Princess of Naples, Cesare?"

Cesare was smiling.

Holy Mother of God, said the Pope to himself, how beautiful are my children and how my heart trembles with the love I bear them.

❧♔❧

ALƒONSO DUKE Oƒ Bisceglie rode quietly into Rome. There were no crowds to line the streets and strew flowers in his path. He came unheralded. The Pope had wished that there would be no ceremonial entry. The scandal of Lucrezia's divorce was too recent, having taken place only six months previously, and since during that time Lucrezia had borne a child—and how was it possible, however many precautions were taken, to keep these matters entirely secret?—it was better for the new bridegroom to come unheralded.

So Alfonso apprehensively came to Santa Maria in Portico.

Sanchia, awaiting his arrival was with Lucrezia. She guessed what his feelings would be. She knew he would come reluctantly, and she was fully aware of the tales he would have heard regarding the notorious family into which he was to marry. He did not come as a respected bridegroom, as a conquering prince, but as a symbol of the desire of Naples for friendship with the Vatican.

"Have no fear, little brother," murmured Sanchia. "I will take care of you."

She would demand of Cesare that he be her brother's friend; she would make it a condition for Cesare was her lover. If Cesare showed friendship for young Alfonso—and Cesare could be charming when he so desired—others would follow. The Pope, whatever he was planning, would be gracious; and Lucrezia, however much she mourned Pedro Caldes, would be gentle with Alfonso.

Sanchia was longing to show her brother the power she held at the Vatican. Her love for other men waxed strongly and waned quickly, but her love for her young brother was constant.

Lucrezia, with Sanchia and their women, went down to greet her betrothed; and as soon as she saw him her interest was stirred, and it was as though the idealized shadow of Pedro Caldes receded a little. Alfonso was such a handsome boy. He *was* very like Sanchia, having the same vivid coloring, but he appeared to lack Sanchia's wantonness, and there was about him an earnest desire to please which Sanchia lacked and which was endearing.

Lucrezia was moved by the way he clung to his sister and the display of emotion between them.

Then he was standing before his bride, those beautiful blacklashed blue eyes wide with a surprise which he found it impossible to suppress.

"I am Lucrezia Borgia," said Lucrezia.

It was easy to read his thoughts, for there was a simplicity about him which reminded her that she was his senior, if only by a little. He had heard evil tales of her and he had expected...What had he expected? A brazen, depraved creature to strike terror into him? Instead he found a gentle girl, a little older than himself but seeming as young, tender, serene, gentle and very beautiful.

He kissed her hands, and his lips were warm and clinging; his blue eyes were filled with emotion as they were lifted to her face.

"My delight is beyond expression," he murmured.

They were not idle words; and in that moment, a little of the dark sorrow which had overshadowed her during the last months was lifted.

SANCHIA WAS RECLINING on a couch, surrounded by her ladies, when Cesare was announced.

She had been telling them that before long they would have to say good-bye to little Goffredo, because he would no longer be her husband. The method employed in the Sforza divorce had been so successful that His Holiness was tempted to repeat it.

"But I," she was saying, "shall not be six months pregnant when I stand before the Cardinals and declare my marriage has not been consummated."

Loysella, Francesca, and Bernardina laughed with delight. Their mistress's adventures were a source of great pleasure to them and were emulated by them to the best of their ability.

She had made them swear to secrecy, and this they had done.

"Your future husband is at the door," whispered Loysella.

Sanchia tapped her cheek playfully. "Then you had better leave me. I asked him to come. I demanded that he should."

"You must get him accustomed to obedience," laughed Bernardina.

But Cesare was already in the room and even their frivolity was stemmed. He looked at them imperiously, not assessing their obvious charms as he sometimes did, but impatiently as though they were inanimate objects which offended his eyes. They might joke about him when he was not present, but as soon as he made his appearance they were conscious of that power within him to strike terror.

They curtsied hurriedly and went out of the room, leaving him alone with their mistress.

Sanchia lifted a hand. "Come, Cesare," she said, "sit beside my couch."

"You wished to see me?" he asked, sitting down.

"I did. I am not very pleased with you, Cesare."

He raised his eyebrows haughtily, and her blue eyes shone with sudden anger as she went on: "My brother is in Rome. He has been here a whole day and night, yet you have ignored him. Is this the courtesy you have to show to a Prince of Naples?"

"Oh ... but a bastard," murmured Cesare.

"And you ... my fine lord ... what are you, pray?"

"Soon to be the ruler of Italy."

Her eyes flashed. It would be so. She was sure of it, and she was proud of him. If any could unite Italy and rule it, that man was Cesare Borgia. She would be beside him when he reigned supreme. Cesare Borgia would need a queen, and she was to be that queen. She was exultant and intensely happy, for there was one man to whom she longed to be married, and that was this man,

Cesare Borgia. And it would be so. As soon as she was divorced their marriage would take place, and the whole of Italy would soon have to recognize her as its Queen.

He was looking at her now, and she held out her arms. He embraced her, but even as she put her arms about his neck she sensed his absentmindedness.

She withdrew herself and said: "But I demand that you pay my brother the respect due to him."

"That have I done. He merits little."

She brought up her hand and slapped his face. He took her by the wrist and a smile of pleasure crossed his face as he twisted her arm until she squealed with the pain.

"Stop," she cried. "Cesare, I implore you. You will break my bones."

"'Twill teach you not to behave like a beggar on the Corso."

Freed, she looked angrily at the marks on her wrist.

"I ask you," she said sullenly, "to call on my brother, to welcome him to Rome."

Cesare shrugged aside her request.

"If," she went on, "he is to be your brother in very truth . . ."

"I never looked on Lucrezia's first husband as my brother. Nor shall I on her second."

"Jealous!" snapped Sanchia. "Insanely jealous of your sister's lovers. It is small wonder that there is scandal concerning your family throughout Italy."

"Ah," he said, smiling slowly, "we are a scandalous family. I fancy, my dear Sanchia, that scandal has not grown less since you joined us."

"I insist that you welcome my brother."

"It is enough that my father sent for him and that he is here."

"But Cesare, you must do him some small honor. You must show the people that you do so—if not because he is to be Lucrezia's husband, then because he is my brother."

"I do not understand," said Cesare with cruel blankness.

"But if I am divorced . . . if I am free of Goffredo and we are married . . ."

Cesare laughed. "My dear Sanchia," he said, "I am not going to marry you."

"But . . . there is to be a divorce."

"His Holiness is not eager for another divorce in the family. The Church deplores divorce, as you know. Nay, you shall stay married to your little Goffredo. Of what can you complain in him? Is he not a kind and complaisant husband? As for myself, when I am free of these garments, I shall seek me a wife elsewhere."

Sanchia could not speak; it seemed to her that her fury was choking her.

"Moreover," went on Cesare, savoring her efforts to keep that fury under control, "when I acquire my titles—and I can assure you they will be mighty titles—I must look farther than an illegitimate Princess, Sanchia. You will readily understand that."

Still she could not speak. Her face was white, and he noticed her long slender fingers plucking at the skirt of her dress. He could still feel the sting of those fingers on his cheek; he could still see the mark of his on her wrist. Their relationship had always been a fiery one; they had inflicted their passion on one another, and many of their most satisfactory encounters had begun with a fight.

"My bride," went on Cesare, flaying those wounds he had laid open with the whip of humiliation likely to cause most pain, "will doubtless be a near relative of yours: the daughter of your uncle, the King of Naples, his legitimate daughter, the Princess Carlotta."

"My cousin Carlotta!" cried Sanchia. "You deceive yourself, Cardinal Borgia! Bastard Borgia! Do you think my uncle the King would allow *you* to marry his daughter?"

"His Holiness and I have very good reason to believe that he is eager for the match."

"It is a lie."

Cesare lifted his shoulders lightly. "You will see," he said.

"See! I shall not see. It will never come to pass. Do you think *you* will have Carlotta? My uncle will want a prize for her."

"It might be," Cesare retorted, "that he will be wise enough to see in me what he seeks for her."

In the ante-room her women, hearing Sanchia's wild laughter, trembled. There was something different about this encounter. This was surely not one of those violent quarrels which ended in that fierce lovemaking which set their mistress purring like a contented cat while they combed her hair and she told them of Cesare's virility.

"I can tell you," screamed Sanchia, "that you will never have Carlotta."

"I beg of you, do not scream. You will have your women thinking I am murdering you."

"They could easily suspect it. What is one more murder in your life? Murderer! Liar! Bastard! Cardinal!"

He stood by the couch, laughing at her.

She sprang up and would have scratched his face, but he was ready for her; he had her by the wrist, and she spat at him.

"Is it the time for you to think of marriage?" she cried. "By the marks on your face I should think not."

He shook her. "You should control your temper, Sanchia," he warned her.

"Are you so calm, Cesare," she demanded.

"Yes, for once I am."

"Do not think you may come here and treat me as your mistress while you make these plans for Carlotta."

"I had not thought of it," he said. "You weary me, Sanchia. With your ambitions you weary me."

"Get out of here," she cried.

And to her astonishment he threw her back on to her couch and left her.

She stared after him. She was bitterly wounded for he had hurt her where she was most vulnerable.

Her women came in and found her weeping quietly. They had never seen her quiet; they had never before seen her so unhappy.

They coaxed her, combed her hair, smoothed unguents into her hot forehead, told her she must not cry so and spoil her beautiful eyes.

And at length she ceased to cry and, springing up, swore revenge on Cesare Borgia, swore that she would use all her powers to prevent his marriage with her cousin. She would make a wax image of Cesare; she would stick red-hot pins into its heart. Evil should come to him because he had wounded her deeply and had exulted in the wounding.

"By all the saints!" she cried. "I will be revenged on you, Cesare Borgia."

THIS WAS LUCREZIA's wedding day—her second wedding day.

That other, which had taken place five years before when she was thirteen, seemed now like some haunting scene from a nightmare—horrible and unreal. She did not want to think of it. Then she had been too young to consummate the marriage, and the man beside her had been grim and unattractive, a widower who had seemed quite unimpressed by her beauty.

She wanted to be happy. She realized now how like her father she was. She knew how bitterly he had suffered when Giovanni, his best-loved son, had been murdered. Thus had she felt when the news had been brought to her that Pedro Caldes' body had been taken from the Tiber. Then she had cried to the saints: "Out of your goodness, let me die." Alexander must have uttered similar words.

He had recovered quickly. He had turned from memories of the dead to delight in the living. He was wise; she believed him to be the wisest man on Earth; his conduct in crises had always been an example. Now she understood more than she ever had before that she needed to follow his example.

She wanted to love her bridegroom. Was it very difficult? He was young and handsome and, although they had first met but three days ago, he was already becoming ardent. He had had fears of what he would find; those fears were dispersed. Thus should her misery disappear. In the arms of Alfonso, her legitimate lover, she would forget that passion for Pedro Caldes which had been doomed from its beginning.

How glad she was that he had come unceremoniously to Rome, thus enabling them to make each other's acquaintance before the wedding day. She was delighted when Alfonso had whispered to her: "You are so different from the wife I expected to find waiting for me."

"You are pleased with what you find?" she had asked, and he had answered: "I am bemused with delight."

She believed that he spoke with the sincerity of youth rather than with the flattery of a courtier.

Lucrezia was right. Alfonso was happy; he was thinking only of her. He knew that Cesare hated him because he was to be Lucrezia's husband, and he did not seem to care. The Papal guards made bets on how long it would be before the Pope decided that his new son-in-law was useless to his aims, and how long after that Alfonso would cease to exist; for a second divorce would provide something of a scandal, and indeed might be difficult even for the wily Alexander to procure. Still, Alfonso did not care. He was to marry Lucrezia, and that was all he had time to think about.

Her women were dressing Lucrezia in a gold-colored gown which was heavy with pearls comprising the mingling arms of Borgia and Aragon. About her neck were priceless rubies, and the lustrous emerald which adorned her forehead gave some of its color to her pale eyes. She looked very little older than she had on the day she married Giovanni Sforza.

She was conducted with her attendants to the Pope's private apartments in the Vatican, to that room, which she knew so well, with the Pinturicchio murals and the ceiling on which was carved the gilded bull and the papal crown.

Here Alfonso was waiting for her and, as she looked at him in his magnificent wedding garments, there was no doubt in her mind that he was the most handsome man in Italy.

The Pope smiled benignly at the young couple, and he was amused because of what he saw in their eyes.

They knelt before the Papal throne and the wedding ceremony took place and, in accordance with the ancient custom, a naked sword was held over the heads of the bride and groom. This duty fell to a Spanish captain, Juan Cervillon, and as he stood very still, his sword held high above this beautiful pair, many eyes were turned to that gleaming blade, and the question was in many minds: How long before it will descend on our little bridegroom?

THE ceremony was over, and it was time for the feasting and celebration. Lucrezia walked by her husband's side and even her dress, stiff with embroidery and pearls and heavy with jewels, could not impair her grace. Dainty and elegant, as she was, she seemed aloof from the coarse jests, which were encouraged by the Pope. Her bridegroom was enchanted with her and he and she seemed apart from the company. All noticed their absorption in each other, and the Pope pointed it out to all who came near him.

"What a delightful pair!" he cried. "Did you ever see a more beautiful bride and groom? And I declare that they are so eager for each other that they are wishing the feasting and dancing over. The marriage will be consummated before long, I have no doubt."

And as they came into the apartment where the banquet was in readiness, one of Sanchia's suite, who had heard that his mistress had been bitterly humiliated by Cesare and was determined to show his loyalty, stuck out his foot while one of Cesare's suite was passing and the man went sprawling on the floor. This caused much amusement among Sanchia's suite and several leaped on to the fallen man and began belaboring him. Hot-blooded Spaniards, servants of Cesare, were not prepared to see one of their number so treated; they pushed into the fray and soon there was pandemonium throughout the apartment.

Cardinals and Bishops sought to make peace, calling on the protagonists to desist for fear of the Pope's displeasure; but there was too much noise for them to be heard, and hot-tempered Spaniards and Neapolitans continued to fight.

One Bishop was felled to the ground; another was bleeding at the nose; and Alexander, who could not help laughing inwardly at the sight of his Bishops without their dignity, delayed for a few seconds before, in an authoritative voice, he put an end to the skirmish by threatening terrible punishment to all concerned in it unless they desisted at once.

There was quiet and those who a moment before had been defending and attacking with vigor crept back to their places while Alexander led the bride and the bridegroom to the banqueting table.

But the fight was an omen. There were several present who knew what it indicated. The rumors of a possible marriage between Cesare and Sanchia had been well circulated. It would seem that Sanchia's supporters had a score to settle with those of Cesare. Could this mean that Cesare, when he obtained his release from the Church would look elsewhere for a bride?

Sanchia's angry looks supported this theory; as did Cesare's sly contented ones.

Now the Pope called for music and entertainment behaving as though nothing unusual had happened.

There followed the songs, the dancing and the theatrical performances. During these Cesare appeared dressed as a unicorn, and such was his beauty and dignity that the Pope's eyes glistened with pride and even Lucrezia turned from her bridegroom for a moment and had eyes for none but her brother.

As Lucrezia danced with her bridegroom, there was an ecstatic air about them both, and not since they had told her of Pedro's death had she known such pleasure.

Alfonso said as they danced together: "This is the happiest night of my life."

"I am glad," Lucrezia told him. "We shall be happy together, you and I, Alfonso."

"Whatever happens to us we shall have our happiness to look back on," he said, sober suddenly.

"We shall see that it is always with us," she told him. "There shall be no looking back . . . only forward, Alfonso." She smiled at him tenderly. "You were afraid when you heard you were to marry me, were you not?"

"I had heard tales," he confessed.

"Evil tales of me. There are always evil tales of my family. You must not believe them."

He looked into her clear light eyes. He thought: Does she not know? She cannot. And how could she understand . . . she who is so young and innocent?

"Alfonso," she continued, "I want you to know that I have been unhappy, so unhappy that I never thought to laugh again. You have heard me laugh, Alfonso, this day. It is the first time for many months, and it is because you have come."

"You make me so happy."

"You must make me happy, Alfonso. Please make me happy."

"I love you, Lucrezia. Is it possible that in three short days one can love so deeply?"

"I hope so. For I think I am beginning to love you too, and I want to be loved . . . deeply I want to be loved."

"We will love each other then, Lucrezia . . . all the days of our lives."

He took her hand and kissed it; and it was as though they had made a vow as solemn as that which they had taken before the Papal throne.

The Pope, watching them, chuckled and remarked to one of his Cardinals: "It is a shame to keep them from the nuptial bed. Did you ever see two lovers more eager?"

I I

DUCHESS OF BISCEGLIE

THOSE CARDINALS WHO HAD ASSEMBLED FOR THE Consistory were uneasy. They were wishing that they had followed the examples of their fellows and pleaded some excuse which would keep them from Rome at such a time.

The Pope, from his Papal throne, had greeted them with his accustomed benevolence, but those who knew Alexander well were aware of the determination beneath the benignity. Once again they would be presented with one of those outrageous demands such as Alexander made from time to time for the sake of his family; they would be faced with the knowledge that they were in honor bound to oppose the Borgia wish, and they knew that they would lack the courage to do so.

They remembered with chagrin the recent divorce when so many of them had been deceived by the innocent looks of Lucrezia Borgia. They were fully aware that the Pope and his family were going to score another triumph over them.

Alexander watched Cesare as he took his stand before the assembly, and did his best to subdue the pride within him. Cesare was right. He was the man made to rule Italy, and he could best achieve his ambitions in freedom from the Church.

In his slender fingers Cesare held the scroll on which Alexander and he had spent so much time, while he begged his fellow Cardinals to give him their attention.

Cesare's voice was gentle. Alexander had warned him to be humble and, astonishingly, Cesare was obeying his father in this respect. Alexander was a man who must have his way but who always sought to have it peaceably if possible. There he differed from Cesare who was so impatient to achieve his desires that he often did not care how he did so.

"It was not of my own free will that I entered the Church," he was saying now. "I have never had a vocation."

Aware that many eyes were turned upon him, Alexander let his head fall on to his chest in an attitude of dejection as though what his son was saying caused him the utmost pain. In spite of his display of surprise and anguish, all knew of course that it was Alexander's wish that Cesare should be released, and that he had composed the very words which Cesare was now uttering. They also knew that those Cardinals who refused to act in accordance with his wishes should beware of reprisals.

"My conscience demands that I lay these facts before you," went on Cesare, "for I see no other course than to appeal to your mercy and goodness, and I trust that in your compassion you will see fit to release me from my vows."

There was silence. The Cardinals had once more turned their gaze upon the Holy Father, who had now lifted his face so that all could see the concern thereon.

Cesare appealed to the Pope. "Were I free," he cried, in loud and confident tones, "my life should be dedicated to my country. I would visit the French—from whom we all stand in great danger—and I would give my life to save our country from invasion, and bring peace to the land."

Alexander spoke then. "That which is asked by the Cardinal Cesare Borgia of Valencia is a grave matter. It demands deep thought and deliberation from this assembly, so that a reply cannot at once be given."

Cesare retired while the Cardinals discussed his case. There was not a man among them who did not regard the whole procedure as farcical. The Borgia Pope desired Cesare to be released from his vows; and who dared oppose the Borgia Pope?

Cesare went away with a light heart, knowing that before the week was out he would have achieved a lifelong ambition. He would be a soldier leading his armies, free of the restricting influence of the Church.

He came to his sister's apartments where she was with her husband. Alfonso, the happy bridegroom, involuntarily moved closer to his wife as his brother-in-law came in.

"Ha!" cried Cesare. "The happy pair. Why sister, why brother, all Rome talks of your pleasure in each other. Do they speak truth?"

"I am very happy," Lucrezia told him.

"We are happy in each other," added Alfonso.

Cesare smiled his slow sardonic smile and as he looked at the handsome boy, a momentary anger possessed him. Such a boy! Scarce out of the nursery. Smooth-cheeked and pretty! Cesare's once beautiful skin was marred now and would doubtless remain so for the rest of his life. It was strange that he, who felt that it would not be long before the whole of Italy was at his feet, should thus feel envy of the smooth cheeks of a pretty boy.

"Why," he cried, "you do not seem pleased to see me!"

"We are always pleased to see you," said Lucrezia quickly.

"Do not allow your wife to speak for you, brother," put in Cesare, a faint sneer turning up the corners of his mouth. "You should be master, you know."

"Nay," said Alfonso, "it is not thus with us. I wish to please my wife, nothing more."

"Devoted husband!" murmured Cesare. "Lucrezia, we are going to have days of celebration. Prepare yourself. What sort of fête shall I arrange for your pleasure?"

"There have been so many celebrations," said Lucrezia. "Alfonso and I are happy enough without them. We have our hunting, our dancing and music."

"And other pleasures in each other's company I doubt not. Oh, but you are so newly wed. Nevertheless there shall be celebrations. Do you know, Lucrezia, that before long I discard my Cardinal's robes?"

"Cesare!" She ran to him and threw herself into his arms. "But I am so happy. It is what you have wanted for so long. And at last it has come. Oh dearest brother, how I rejoice with you!"

"And you are ready to dance with me at a ball I shall give. You are ready to watch me kill a bull or two?"

"Oh Cesare . . . not that. It frightens me."

He kissed her tenderly, and putting his arm about her he drew her to an embrasure; he stood looking at her, his back turned to Alfonso who, as Cesare intended he should, felt himself to be excluded.

Alfonso stood awkwardly, watching; and suddenly all his fears returned to him and he found he could not control his shivers. He could not take his eyes from them—the most discussed brother and sister in Italy, so graceful, both of them, with that faint resemblance between them, yet that vivid contrast. There was Cesare fierce and frightening, determined to dominate, and Lucrezia slender and clinging, wishing to be dominated. Seeing them thus, all Alfonso's doubts and suspicions returned, and he wanted to beg Lucrezia to leave this place which now seemed to him evil. He wanted to rescue Lucrezia who, although she was born of them, was not one of them; he wanted to take her right away from her family and live in peace with her.

He heard their voices. "But you would not have me stand aside while others killed the bulls?"

"I would. Indeed I would."

"But my dearest, you would then be ashamed of your brother."

"I should never be ashamed of you. And you risk your life with the bulls."

"Not I. I'm a match for any bull."

Cesare turned and drew her to him and over her head smiled for a second of triumphant mockery at Alfonso. Then he released her suddenly and cried: "But we have forgotten your little bridegroom, Lucrezia. I declare he looks as though he is about to burst into tears."

Alfonso felt the blood rush to his face. He started forward but Cesare stood between Lucrezia and her husband, legs apart, his hand playing with the hilt of his sword; and although Alfonso wanted to draw his own sword and challenge this man here and now to fight, and fight to the death if need be, he felt as though his limbs would not move, that he was in the presence of the devil, who had laid a spell upon him.

Cesare laughed and went out; and when he was no longer there Alfonso's courage came back to him. He went to Lucrezia and took her by the shoulders. "I like not his manners," he said. Lucrezia's eyes were wide and innocent. "He . . . he is too possessive. It is almost as though . . ." But he could not say it.

He had not the courage. There were questions he wanted to ask, and he was afraid to ask them. He had been so happy, and he wanted to go on being happy.

Lucrezia put her arms about his neck and kissed him in that gentle way which never failed to be a source of excitement to him.

"He is my brother," she said simply. "We were brought up together. We have shared our lives and it has made us good friends."

"It would seem when he is by that you are unaware of any other."

She laid her head against his chest and laughed. "You are indeed a jealous husband."

"Lucrezia," he cried, "have I cause to be?"

Then she lifted her face to his and her eyes were still full of limpid innocence. "You know I want no other husband," she said. "I was unhappy, desperately unhappy, and I thought never to laugh in joy again. Then you came, and since you came, I have found happiness."

He kissed her with increasing passion. "Love me, Lucrezia," he pleaded. "Love me . . . only."

They clung together, but even in the throes of lovemaking Alfonso could not rid himself of the memory of Cesare.

Cesare was in the ring. The assembled company watched him with admiration, for he was the most able matador in Rome. His Spanish origin was obvious as, lithe and graceful, he twisted his elegant body this way and that, springing from the path of the onrushing bull at that precise moment in time when death seemed inevitable.

Alfonso, sitting beside Lucrezia and watching her fingers twisting the embroideries on her dress, was aware of the anxiety she was experiencing. Alfonso did not understand. He could have sworn that she was glad because Cesare would soon be leaving for France; yet now, watching his antics in the bullring, he was equally sure that she was conscious of no one but her brother.

Alfonso murmured: "God in Heaven, Holy Mother and all the saints, let him not escape. Let the furious bull be the instrument of justice—for many have died more horribly at his hands."

Smiling coolly Sanchia watched the man who had been her lover. She thought: I hope the bull gets him, tramples him beneath those angry hoofs . . . not to kill him . . . no, but to maim him so that he will never walk or run or leap again, never make love to his Carlotta of Naples. Carlotta of Naples! Much chance he has! But let him lose his beauty, and his manhood be spoiled, so that I may go to him and laugh in his face and taunt him as he has taunted me.

Among those who watched there were others who remembered suffering caused them by Cesare Borgia, many who prayed for his death.

But had Cesare died that day there would have been three to mourn him with sincerity—the Pope who watched him with the same mingling of pride and fear as Lucrezia's; Lucrezia herself; and a red-headed courtesan named Fiametta, who had sought to grow rich by his favors and found that she loved him.

But, for all the wishes among the spectators in the ring that day, Cesare emerged triumphant. He slew his bulls. He stood the personification of elegance, indolently accepting the applause of the crowds. And he seemed a symbol of the future, there with his triumph upon him. His proud gestures seemed to imply that the conqueror of bulls would be the conqueror of Italy.

The Pope sent for his son that he might impart the joyful news.

"Louis promises not to be ungenerous, Cesare," he cried. "See what he offers you! It is the Dukedom of Valence, and a worthy income with the title."

"Valence," said Cesare, trying to hide his joy. "I know that to be a city on the Rhône near Lyons in Dauphiné. The income . . . what is that?"

"Ten thousand *écus* a year," chuckled the Pope. "A goodly sum."

"A goodly sum indeed. And Carlotta?"

"You will go to the French Court and begin your wooing at once." The Pope's expression darkened. "I shall miss you, my son. I like not to have the family scattered."

"You have your new son, Father."

"Alfonso!" The Pope's lips curled with contempt.

"It would seem," muttered Cesare, "that the only member of the family who is pleased with its new addition is Lucrezia."

The Pope murmured indulgently: "Lucrezia is a woman, and Alfonso a very handsome young man."

"It sickens me to see them together."

The Pope laid his hand on his son's shoulder. "Go to France, my son. Bring back the Princess Carlotta as soon as you can."

"I will do so, Father. And when Carlotta is mine I shall stake my claim to the throne of Naples. Father, no one shall prevent my taking that to which I have a claim."

The Pope nodded sagely.

"And," went on Cesare, "if I am heir to the crown of Naples, of what use to us will Lucrezia's little husband be?"

"That is looking some way ahead," said Alexander. "I came through my difficulties in the past because I did not attempt to surmount them until they were close upon me."

"When the time comes we shall know how to deal with Alfonso, Father."

"Indeed we shall. Have we not always known how to deal with obstacles? Now, my son, our immediate concern is your own marriage, and I shall not wish you to appear before the King of France as a beggar."

"I shall need money to equip me."

"Fear not. We'll find it."

"From the Spanish Jews?"

"Why not? Should they not pay for the shelter I have given them from the Spanish Inquisition?"

"They will pay . . . gladly," said Cesare.

"Now my son, let us think of your needs . . . your immediate needs."

They planned together, and the Pope was sad because he must soon say good-bye to his beloved son, and he was fearful too because he had once vowed that Cesare should remain in the Church, and now Cesare had freed himself. Alexander felt suddenly the weight of his years, and in that moment he knew that that strong will of his, which had carried him to triumph through many turbulent years, was becoming more and more subservient to that of his son Cesare.

THE DAYS OF preparation were over. The goldsmiths and silversmiths had been working day and night on all the treasures which the Duke of Valence would take with him into France. The shops of Rome were denuded of all fine silks, brocades, and velvets, for nothing, declared the Pope, was too fine for his son Cesare; the horses' shoes must be of silver, and the harness of the mules must be fashioned in gold; Cesare's garments must be finer than anything he would encounter in France, and the most magnificent of the family jewels must be fashioned into rings, brooches and necklaces for Cesare. Nothing he used—even the most intimate article of toilet—must be of anything less precious than silver. He was going to France as the guest of a King, and he must go as a Prince.

He left Rome in the sunshine of an October day, looking indeed princely in his black velvet cloak (cut after the French fashion) and plumed hat. Beneath the cloak could be seen his white satin doublet, gold-slashed, and the jewels which glittered on his person were dazzling. Because he hated any to remember that he was an ex-Cardinal he had covered his tonsure with a curling wig which gave him an appearance of youth; for those who watched in the streets could not see the unpleasant blemishes, the result of the *male francese*, on his skin.

He was no longer Cardinal of Valencia, but Duke of Valentinois and the Italians called him Il Valentino.

The Pope stood on his balcony with Lucrezia beside him, and as the calvacade moved away and on to the Via Lata, the two watchers clasped hands and tears began to fall down their cheeks.

"Do not grieve. He will soon be with us once more, my little one," murmured Alexander.

"I trust so, Father," answered Lucrezia.

"Bringing his bride with him."

Alexander had always been optimistic, and now he refused to believe that Cesare could fail. What if the King of Naples had declared his daughter should never go to a Borgia; what if it were impossible to trust sly Louis; what if all the Kings of Europe were ready to protest at the idea of a bastard Borgia's marrying a royal Princess? Cesare would still do it, the Pope told himself; for on that day, as he watched the glittering figure ride away, in his eyes Cesare was the reincarnation of himself, Roderigo Borgia, as he had been more than forty years earlier.

WITH THE DEPARTURE of Cesare a peace settled on the Palace of Santa Maria in Portico, and the young married pair gave themselves up to pleasure. Alfonso forgot his fears of the Borgias; it was impossible to entertain them when the Pope was so affectionate and charming, and Lucrezia was the most loving wife in the world.

All commented on the gaiety of Lucrezia. She hunted almost every day in the company of Alfonso; she planned dances and banquets for the pleasure of her husband, and the Pope was a frequent participator in the fun. It seemed incredible to Alfonso that he could have been afraid. The Pope was so clearly a beloved father who could have nothing but the warmest feelings toward one who brought such happiness to his daughter.

Lucrezia was emerging as the leader of fashion; not only were women wearing golden wigs in imitation of her wonderful hair, they were carefully studying the clothes she wore and copying them. Lucrezia was childishly delighted, spending hours with the merchants, choosing materials, explaining to her dressmakers how these should be used, appearing among them in the greens, light blues and golds, in russet and black, all those shades which accentuated her pale coloring and enhanced her feminine daintiness.

Lucrezia felt recklessly gay. This was partly due to the discovery that, contrary to her belief, she could be happy again. Whole days passed without her thinking of Pedro Caldes, and even when she did so it was to assure herself that their love had been a passing fancy which could never have endured in the face of so much opposition. Her father was right—as always. She must marry a man of noble birth; and surely she was the happiest woman on Earth, because Alfonso was both noble and the husband she loved.

The household heard her laughing and singing, and they smiled among themselves. It was pleasant to live in the household of Madonna Lucrezia; it was comforting to know that she had given up all thought of going into a convent. A convent! That was surely not the place for one as gay and lovely, as capable of being happy and giving happiness, as Lucrezia.

They knew in their hearts that the peace of the household was due to the absence of one person, but none mentioned this. Who could doubt that an idle word spoken now might be remembered years hence? And Il Valentino would not remain forever abroad.

The days passed all too quickly, and when in December Lucrezia knew that she was going to have a baby, she felt that her joy was complete.

ALfonso was ridiculously careful of her. She must rest, he declared.
She must not forget the precious burden she carried.

"It is soon yet to think of that, my dearest," she told him.

"It is never too soon to guard one's greatest treasures."

She would lie on their bed, he beside her, while they talked of the child.
They would ponder on the sex of the child. If it were a boy they would be
the proudest parents on Earth; and if a girl, no less proud. But they hoped
for a boy.

"Of course we shall have a boy," Alfonso declared, kissing her tenderly.
"How, in this most perfect marriage could we have anything else? But if she is
a girl, and resembles her mother, then I think we shall be equally happy. I see
nothing for us but a blissful life together."

Then they loved and told each other of their many perfections and how
the greatest happiness they had ever known came from each other.

"One day," said Alfonso, "I shall take you to Naples. How will you like
living away from Rome?"

"You will be there," Lucrezia told him, "and there will be my home.
Yet . . ."

He touched her cheek tenderly. "You will not wish to be long separated
from your father," he said.

"We shall visit him often, and perhaps he will visit us."

"How dearly you love him! There are times when I think you love him
beyond all others."

Lucrezia answered: "It is you, my husband, whom I love beyond all others.
Yet I love my father in a different way. Perhaps as one loves God. He has always
been there, wise and kind. Oh Alfonso, I cannot tell you of the hundred kind-
nesses I have received at his hand. I do not love him as I love you . . . you are
part of me . . . I am completely at ease with you. You are my perfect lover. But
he . . . is the Holy Father of us all, and my own tender father. Do not compare
my love for him with that I have for you. Let me be happy, in both my loves."

Alfonso was reminded suddenly of the loud sardonic laughter of Cesare,
and he had an uncanny feeling that the spirit of Cesare would haunt him all

his life, mocking him in his happiest moments, besmirching the brightness of his love.

But he did not mention Cesare.

He, like Lucrezia, often had the feeling that they must hold off the future. They must revel in the perfect happiness of the present. It would be folly to think of what might come, when what was actually happening gave them so much pleasure. Did one think of snowstorms when one picnicked on warm summer evenings in the vineyards about the Colosseum? One did not spoil those perfect evenings by saying: "It will be less pleasant here two months hence."

Sanchia was restless. She missed her passionate meetings with Cesare. She assured herself that she hated him, and she had taken many lovers since his departure, but none satisfied her.

She constantly thought of him in France, courting Carlotta, the legitimate daughter of her uncle; and the humiliation she suffered was intense. She, who had been accused of witchcraft because of her power over men, she who had never yet been deserted by a lover, was insulted, and openly so because everyone had known that at one time it had been the intention of Cesare to marry her.

Now with his French dukedom and his French estates and riches, he found himself too important for marriage with an illegitimate princess, and sought a higher prize.

She might rage before her women; in the secrecy of her apartments she might at midnight stick pins into his waxen image, but at the same time she wept for a lost lover, knowing that no other man could so enthrall her.

Sanchia might feign gaiety in public, seeking to hide her chagrin, but many at the Papal Court were aware of her feelings, and there was one who sought to turn the situation to his advantage.

Cardinal Ascanio Sforza, brother of Ludovico, Duke of Milan, and cousin of that Giovanni Sforza from whom Lucrezia had been recently divorced, watched Sanchia closely and believed that he could use her in the political game he intended to play. The Sforzas had been very uneasy since it had become apparent to them that the bonds between France and the Papacy were being made more secure. The Sforzas had never trusted Alexander, and now with Il Valentino a French Duke hoping to marry a Princess who, although she was the daughter of the King of Naples, had a French mother and was being brought up at the French Court, it seemed that before long there would be an alliance between France and the Papal State. It was only logical to suppose that French ambitions had not abated with the death of King Charles, and that one day there would be another French invasion. If this happened, Milan—to which the French believed they had a claim through the House of Orléans—would be the first target. Ludovico had lost his kingdom once and was eager not to do so again; therefore the Sforzas were uneasy to see Cesare Borgia going to France as the guest of their foremost enemy.

Women had a great influence on the Pope. It was inevitable in the case of a man who, shrewd diplomatist though he was, had been known as the most carnal man in all Italy. He had always found feminine appeals irresistible, so with Cesare away, it seemed to Ascanio Sforza that the Pope might be reached through the women of his Court.

He therefore called on Sanchia and was soon able to test to the full the measure of her rancor against Cesare.

"I understand," he began slyly, "that your uncle is overwhelmed by the honor about to be done to him by Il Valentino!"

Sanchia was unable to control her anger. "Honor!" she cried. "My uncle will not look upon his aspirations as such. He may ask for Carlotta's hand, but he'll not get it."

"The Borgias have a way of asking which can be irresistible."

"Not when it comes to the marriage of my uncle's daughter."

"But it is a mighty alliance—this of France and the Papacy."

Sanchia's eyes blazed. "An unholy alliance!" she cried. "It is not long since the French were invading Italy. I remember well how they took possession of Naples and turned my father off his throne. He went mad because of it. I remember how we had to take refuge on the island of Ischia. It seems a strange thing that there should be this friendship between Il Valentino and those who brought so much misery to Italy."

"A very strange thing, a very unhappy thing," murmured Ascanio. "It is something which those who are most affected should do all in their power to hinder. Do you not agree?"

"I agree with all my heart," said Sanchia.

"We Sforzas of Milan are uneasy."

"And well you may be!"

"And you of Naples have suffered also from the French."

Sanchia agreed.

"Naples and Milan have been enemies in the past," said Ascanio, "but old differences should be forgotten when a mighty enemy threatens both."

It was true. Sanchia wanted to fill her days with intrigue, and that intrigue was to be directed against her faithless lover. She was excited, realizing that Ascanio Sforza could do more toward bringing about the downfall of Cesare Borgia than those incantations she muttered while sticking pins into a figure of wax.

She had a new interest. Ascanio Sforza was a constant visitor.

🎭 👑 🎭

Lucrezia and Alfonso now had their own little court, and there was gaiety in the apartments in Santa Maria in Portico. Alfonso and Lucrezia had discovered a mutual love of music and poetry, and their encouragement of poets and musicians meant that an intellectual group was beginning to form about them.

One day Sanchia came to their *soirée* bringing Cardinal Ascanio Sforza with her.

Lucrezia received him graciously but she was surprised to see him in the company of Sanchia, for the enmity between Milan and Naples was of long standing. Lucrezia, however, gave no indication of her feelings, and, while she was playing the lute for the Cardinal's pleasure, Alfonso took his sister aside and asked her what had possessed her to bring Cardinal Sforza to them, for the Sforzas were not only the enemies of the Aragonese but one of them had been Lucrezia's first husband, and in view of the slander he had spread about her, it seemed tasteless to bring a relative of his here as a guest.

Sanchia smiled affectionately at her brother, as she explained: "Alfonso, you love Lucrezia dearly, and Lucrezia loves you. You are happy and at peace. Have you forgotten your feelings as you rode into Rome not so long ago?"

"That was before I knew Lucrezia."

"It was not only Lucrezia you feared."

"The Pope has been my good friend, and Cesare is no longer here."

"The Pope's moods are variable, brother, and Cesare will not remain forever in France. He plans to marry our cousin Carlotta. And when he has done so, he will return."

Alfonso shook his head impatiently. He was loath to have his pleasure spoilt, and the thought of Cesare's return could spoil it. "He'll not be allowed to marry Carlotta."

"No," cried Sanchia. "But he'll be back, and when he comes, mayhap he'll bring the French with him. Alfonso, have you forgotten our flight to Ischia? Do you remember our return to Naples? Do you remember what we saw ... the tales we heard? If the French come, that will happen again and Cesare Borgia might well march with them, the ally of the French."

"The Borgias against Naples ..."

"Against Naples and Milan, and all Italy. They are treacherous, and Cesare does not love you, brother."

"Oh, forget him. Mayhap he'll have an accident in France. I cannot believe the French will love him."

"You are not a child, Alfonso. Face the truth. We have to stand against Cesare. Naples, Milan ... and as many states as we can find to help us. That is why Ascanio Sforza comes to these apartments. He is our new friend and there will be others. Alfonso, this shall be their meeting place. Here, while there is dancing and music and reading of poetry, we shall gather our friends together and we shall be firm and ready should the time come when it is necessary to break the Borgian and French alliance."

"These are politics," murmured Alfonso. "I dislike them. Why should there be this talk of war and fighting when there are poetry and music and love?"

"Idiot brother!" chided Sanchia. "If you will continue to enjoy the good things of life you must learn to protect them."

Alfonso was frowning. He did not want to think of unpleasantness, yet Sanchia's words reminded him of all he had feared as he had ridden along the road to Rome.

"And what think you His Holiness will say when he knows that men and women assemble here, not to talk of music and poetry, but of politics ... dangerous politics?"

"Why should he know?"

"Because he might be here when such things are talked of."

"We would not be so foolish as to talk of them when he was here."

"His spies would carry tales to him."

"That is where we shall outwit him. We shall tell our secrets only to those who are with us. That is why we must be careful with Lucrezia. She would be loyal always to the Pope and her brother. That family have a devotion to each other which would be past belief if we did not see it every day. We must be careful of Lucrezia."

"But this is her palace. I am her husband. You are asking me to have secrets from her!"

"Come out of your lover's dream, foolish brother. Do you want them to take Lucrezia from you? They will, if you are of no use to them; and if there should be a French invasion and the Pope were friendly with the French, what do you think would happen to you? They would scarcely say your marriage had not been consummated. You have made it obvious how you spend your nights. No, you would not escape with divorce, brother."

Alfonso began to tremble; she was bringing back all his terrors. At the beginning of his marriage he had suffered from nightmares, waking in a cold sweat to clutch Lucrezia and beg for comfort. He had dreamed that the naked sword which had been held over them during their wedding was slowly descending, and that the hand which held it was that of Cesare, and that the Pope looked on smiling his affectionate and benign smile which in its strange way was commanding Cesare to murder him.

Sanchia was bringing back all his fear of the Borgias.

"But Alfonso, my dear brother, we have a period in which to work. If we stand together, we can defeat the French. They would never have come against us if the whole of Italy had been united. They were victorious because the small kingdoms stood aloof while, one by one, each was swallowed up by the French monster. We are going to work together; we shall make a strong party and we will follow closely all that happens between France and Rome. We will have our spies in the Vatican who will keep us informed. And Milan and Naples shall stand together against this alliance which, to gain French estates and our cousin Carlotta, Cesare Borgia is making with the French."

"But what am I to do?" asked Alfonso in despair.

"Work with us. Talk to Lucrezia when you are alone. Gradually make her one of us, lightly, subtly, so that she does not know she is working against her father. She might be induced to ask certain favors of His Holiness. You know he can deny her nothing."

Alfonso winced, and Sanchia laughed at him.

"We'll be bold, Alfonso. Life is good, eh? But remember how quickly it can change, how quickly it once changed for us. We will not let it change again. We will keep that which we have. You are beginning to understand, I think?"

Alfonso nodded.

Lucrezia was calling him. She wanted him to sing to her accompaniment on the lute; and as he smiled and went to her Sanchia was pleased to see how he was able to hide his uneasiness.

Alfonso realized the wisdom of his sister's words; in the weeks which followed he talked now and then with Lucrezia, touching very lightly on the excellent qualities of Ascanio Sforza who was not to be blamed for the short-comings of his relative Giovanni. He talked of the desirability of friendship between Naples and Milan, and the possibility of union, so that, should there be another French invasion, they would stand together.

"There will be no French invasion," Lucrezia had said, "because my brother Cesare is the friend of the French King, and it is to prevent such a calamity that he has primarily gone to France."

Alfonso repeated then what Ascanio had whispered.

Cesare had been long in France and there was no news of his marriage. It would be well not to say such things to the Pope, for all knew how he doted on his son, but might it not be that the French looked upon Cesare as a hostage as, although he was apparently fêted in France, the wily French King seemed as though he wanted to keep him there.

Lucrezia was truly alarmed, and Alfonso felt a rising resentment because of her immediate preoccupation with her family.

Now she would be worrying about Cesare, thinking of her brother perhaps held against his will in France, instead of the love and passion which they shared.

Was Cesare always to be a shadow across their married life?

But she had seen his point about not alarming the Pope and she, who loved peace all around her, was very ready to believe that friendship between Naples and Milan would be advantageous.

It was thus that during those months Lucrezia's apartments became the focus of a new party, the main object of which was to unite the states of Milan and Naples against the French—while the Papacy was the friend of France.

In the great hall the marriage festivities were in progress. At the head of the table sat the King of France, content because the woman he had desired to marry was at last his wife. Beside him was Queen Anne herself, young, beautiful, her shrewd eyes showing her satisfaction.

She, the widow of dead King Charles, had shown no great desire to become the wife of reigning King Louis; but all were aware of the satisfaction she must be feeling at finding herself twice Queen of France.

She was a rich woman, and some might say that her estates of Brittany were the prize Louis sought. But that was not all. Poor humpbacked Jeanne had not only been plain and dull but—unforgivable sin in royalty—infertile.

Anne knew herself for a prize and was proud of it. At twenty-three she was in the full flush of her charms and hoped to give Louis the sons he needed. She was optimistic about their future, for Louis, although he seemed older, was but thirty-seven, and there were many years before them for the begetting of children.

Among the guests was that strange man, Cesare Borgia, known in France as the Duc de Valentinois. He was a dangerous man, this Valentinois; and perhaps because of this Louis had decided to treat him with caution. Louis was a cautious man; he was often jeered at for what was called his miserliness, but Louis said that he would rather make his courtiers laugh at his stinginess than his subjects weep for his extravagance. Thus it was that even at his wedding he had scarcely the look of a King, and the most magnificently clad and bejeweled man in the company was the Duc de Valentinois.

Cesare was hopeful on this night, more so than he had been since he had begun to understand the French attitude toward him, for Carlotta was at the ball tonight and when he lifted his eyes he could see her—young, adequately pretty with something about her to remind him of Sanchia. Brought up at the court of Anne of Brittany she was prudish according to Cesare's standards, but he found that aspect of her intriguing. He had little doubt that once he was allowed to meet the girl he would sweep her off her feet; he would marry her no matter what opposition he was called upon to meet.

He distrusted the French. They were subtle, clever people, and it was a new experience to be among those who showed no fear of him. He had been made to realize as soon as he had stepped ashore at Marseilles that he was in a country where the emblem of the grazing bull did not strike immediate terror into all who beheld it. His reputation had gone before him; these people knew him as a murderer and a politically ambitious man; but they did not fear him.

Now as he watched the shabby King, contented with his newly married wife, he remembered again the journey into this country, himself so splendid with his magnificent retinue and silver-shod horses, with his dazzling clothes—brocade and velvet slashed with satin, his cloth of gold and jewels, each of which was worth a fortune. More than all this splendor he had carried with him the Bull of Divorce, which he in person was to hand to Louis—a gift from his Holiness. No, not a gift, a favor for which Louis must pay dearly.

But the people had come out of their farms and cottages to stare at him as he rode by. He believed that they laughed behind his back at his haughty looks, and he heard murmurs which he knew he was intended to hear.

"All these riches, and for a bastard!"

"Is it to provide jewels for the Pope's bastard that we have rewarded our priests? Have we paid for our indulgences that these jewels might be bought?"

"What splendor! Our mighty King is as a beggar beside this one—and he a petty Duke of Valence!"

They were hostile. He should have come more humbly, had he wished to impress the French.

Cesare felt from the first moment that they were sneering at him, that Louis' old wool cloak and stained beaver hat were worn to call attention to the tastelessness of the upstart Duke—who was but a bastard. Cesare was among foreigners and he was made to feel it.

He vividly remembered his first meeting with the King at Chinon where the French Court was at that time. Louis was too clever to reproach him for his splendor or to show that he had noticed it; but he told Cesare that Carlotta of Naples was with Anne of Brittany and it would depend on the future Queen when they would be allowed to meet.

Cesare suspected treachery, and withheld the Bull of Divorce.

Was it not a business arrangement? Was not the price of the Bull, marriage as well as French titles and estates?

That was not so, Louis pointed out when Cesare continued to withhold the Bull; for he was a man to keep his word, and how could he bargain with that which was not his to offer? Cesare had his estates. He was indeed Duke of Valence; and he had what Louis had promised, his permission to seek marriage with Carlotta. Louis had paid in full; he now demanded the Bull of Divorce.

It was then that Cesare began to respect these people, and to realize that he must be more discreet in his demands. There was nothing to do but hand over the Bull to Louis, who, delighted with what he had got, set about making plans for his marriage, and told Cesare that he too was free to go ahead with his courtship.

But the months had passed and opportunities were denied Cesare. Anne of Brittany had promised him nothing, she implied. She did not greatly desire marriage. It was the King who was the ardent suitor.

Cesare did not doubt that, once he had a chance to woo the girl, she would soon be his wife. He was conscious of the whispering that went on around him; he guessed what was being said in Rome, and that his enemies there, who would not have dared to mention his name while he was in Rome, would now be writing their epigrams on the walls.

Carlotta was conscious of him now. Her eyes often strayed in his direction. He smiled at her and brought into full play all that fascination which had been wont to bring Italian women at his bidding.

She sat eating, pretending to be absorbed in her food and the conversation of the man at her side. How insulting of the King and Queen to let her sit beside that man! And who was he? He was fair-haired and smooth-skinned. Cesare was conscious nowadays of others' skins, because his had never regained its youthful smoothness, and this defect, although mitigated by his strikingly handsome features, irritated him.

He demanded of his neighbor: "Who is that man seated next to the Lady Carlotta?"

The answer was a lift of the shoulder. "Some Breton baron, I believe."

Clearly, thought Cesare, a man of no importance.

And when the feasting was over and there was dancing, the Queen evidently remembered her obligations, for she called Carlotta to sit beside her and when she was seated there she sent for Cesare to come to her.

Carlotta of Naples looked at the man of whom she had heard so much, Cesare Borgia whose scandalous behavior with her cousin Sanchia had been spoken of even in France. She compared him with the gentle Breton baron, and she said to herself: "Never . . . never! I'd rather die."

Cesare bowed over her hand. His eyes would have alarmed her had she not been in this crowded ballroom and felt the cool protectiveness of the Queen.

"Have we Your Majesty's permission to dance?" asked Cesare of the Queen.

Anne replied: "My lord Duke, you have mine if you have the lady's."

Cesare took Carlotta's hand and almost pulled her to her feet. Carlotta was too astonished to protest; Cesare clearly did not understand the etiquette of the French Court. No matter. She would dance with him, but never, never would she marry him.

He was graceful; she had to admit that.

He said: "These French dances, how think you they compare with our Italian ones—or our Spanish ones?"

"*Your* Italian ones! *Your* Spanish ones!" she answered. "I have spent so long in France that I say *my French* ones."

"Do you not feel that it is time you left France and returned to your home?"

"I am happy here. The Queen is kind to me and I love her dearly. I have no wish to leave her service."

"You lack the spirit of adventure, Carlotta."

"Perhaps," she said.

"But that is wrong of you. There is so much in life to be enjoyed if you go out to seek it."

"I am fortunate in having found so much that I do not have to seek," she answered.

"But you are so young. What do you know of the adventures and pleasures which the world has to offer?"

"You mean such as those you enjoy with my cousin?"

"You have heard stories of me then?"

"Your fame has reached France, my lord Duke."

"Call me Cesare."

She did not answer but appeared to be concentrating on their steps.

"You know why I am here," he said.

"Yes. You come to collect your dues—the price asked for the King's divorce!"

"How French you are! All decorum one moment; all impetuosity the next. I confess I find the combination fascinating."

"Then, as my frankness does not offend you, I will be even more so. I know your intentions concerning myself."

"That pleases me. Now we can dispense with a long courtship."

"My lord Duke, I have had no word from my father that I may look upon you as a suitor."

"We shall soon have that."

"In that you are mistaken."

"You do not know me. I do not flinch at a little opposition."

"Yet you, my lord, who feel such devotion toward legitimacy—for if you do not, why did you not wait for my cousin Sanchia who is so much more beautiful than I and for whom, if rumor does not lie, you have already some affection—seem to have so little regard for the same devotion in others."

He flushed angrily. The girl, for all her prudery, had a sharp tongue and he was in no mood for a protracted wooing; he had dallied long enough, and he was becoming a laughing stock—which he found intolerable—both in France and in Italy.

"Legitimacy," he retorted, "is invaluable to those who lack qualities which make it unimportant."

"And you, my lord, are richly endowed with such qualities?"

He gripped her hand and she winced. "You will soon discover how richly," he retorted.

He relaxed his grip on her hand and she murmured: "You scowl, my lord Duke. I pray you do not. It will appear that you are not satisfied with your partner. If that is the case, I beg of you, conduct me to the Queen."

"I'll do no such thing," he answered, "until I have had an opportunity— for which I have been waiting ever since I set foot in this country—of talking to you."

"Then, my lord, I pray you talk."

"My first purpose in coming to France is to make you my wife."

"You forget, my lord, that I am a Princess of Naples and that you should not speak thus to me unless you have first obtained the consent of my father."

"It is the wish of His Holiness."

"I did not mean the Holy Father. I mean the King, my father."

"He knows it is the Pope's wish that our marriage should take place."

"Nevertheless, my lord, I have received no instructions that I may listen to you."

"They will come."

"My lord will understand that, as an obedient daughter, I must wait for those instructions."

"You are clearly a lady of strong character. I can see that you are one who would make up her own mind."

"You are right. I have made up my mind to wait for my father's instructions. I see that the Queen signs for me to return to her. Will you conduct me to her?"

"No," said Cesare.

She had, however, disengaged herself and, dropping a curtsey, she turned slowly and walked back to the Queen.

Cesare stood for a few seconds glowering after her; then he realized that amused eyes were watching him. He found a bold-eyed girl and turned his attentions to her, but all the time he was seething with rage which he was finding it difficult to hide for he was still conscious of Carlotta who was being much more charming to the insignificant Breton nobleman than she had been to him.

Louis summoned Cesare to his presence. The shrewd eyes of the French King took in the elaborate doublet, the jewels which glittered on hands and neck. Cesare found it difficult to suppress irritation when he was in the presence of the King of France. That determined lack of expression was more galling than jeers would have been. Cesare believed that the King's mild appraisement of his finery meant: We understand why you must deck yourself so, my bastard Dukeling. These gewgaws would seem very precious to a bastard, who has just escaped from his Cardinal's robes.

In France Cesare had had to learn restraint, and that was not easy for one of his temperament.

He knelt before the King, and he fancied that Louis took a sly delight in keeping him on his knees longer than he would another.

At length he was bidden to rise. Then Louis said: "The news is not good, my lord Duke, and deeply I regret that it should be my task to impart it."

Louis' expression was commiserative but Cesare could not rid himself of the idea that behind it was a certain pleasure.

"It's from Naples," he went on. "Federico stubbornly refuses to consent to your marriage with his daughter."

"Why so, Sire?" demanded Cesare, and the imperious tones sent the royal eyebrows up a fraction.

There was silence, then Cesare added: "I pray Your Majesty, tell me on what grounds the King of Naples objects to my marriage with his daughter."

"On the grounds of your birth."

"My birth! I am the son of the Pope."

Louis' mouth lifted slightly at the corners. "It is a sad but nevertheless logical conclusion, my lord, that the sons of Popes must be illegitimate."

Cesare clenched his right fist and banged it into the palm of his left hand. He found it difficult to refrain from taking this man by the shoulders and shaking him, King though he was.

"This is folly," he cried out.

The King nodded sadly.

"And," went on Cesare, "I doubt not, in Your Majesty's power and determination to fulfill your contract with my father, you will ignore the objections of this petty monarch."

"My lord Duke, you forget that I have carried out my part of the bargain. I gave you your estate and title and my consent for you to woo the lady. I cannot take a father's place when she has a father living."

"We could be married here, Sire, and then what could her father do?"

Louis allowed a profoundly shocked expression to cross his face. "You would ask me to come between a daughter and her father? No, not even for my friends could I do it. Moreover I have received protests from all over Europe. There is one here from my brother of England—King Henry VII. He sends word that he is deeply shocked that there is a possibility that bastardy should be linked with royalty, and that a son of His Holiness should marry with the legitimate daughter of a King." Louis smiled. "I fancy our brother of England is a little shocked that His Holiness should even possess a son—but that is beside the point."

"And he a Tudor!" cried Cesare, his rage refusing to be controlled. "Can the Tudors feel so certain of their own legitimacy?"

Again the King's eyebrows were raised, and his expression was so cold that Cesare was immediately made aware that he might be a hostage in a foreign land.

"I could not discuss my brother's affairs with you," said Louis sharply. He waved his hand to indicate that the interview was over.

Cesare angrily left the apartment. His attendants, who had been waiting for him at a respectful distance, followed him. He looked at them sharply. Did they know that he had been humiliated?

He resisted an impulse to take one of the men by the ear, to drag him to his apartments and there order that his tongue be cut out. He was determined that none should carry tales back to Rome of what he had suffered in France. First to be flouted by that foolish girl; then to be treated as a man of no account by the King! And what the King did today his friends would do tomorrow.

But caution restrained him. A moment ago he had had a glimmer of understanding as to what his position was. What if he decided to leave France at once? Would he be allowed to go? Was he going to marry Carlotta when it seemed that the whole of France and Europe was against him? Was he going to return to Rome, a laughing stock?

He had to be careful, never forgetting for an instant that he could not behave in France as he did in Italy.

Therefore he noted the face of that man who he fancied had been amused to see his master humiliated. He would remember; but the man must be allowed to keep his tongue while they remained on French soil.

Now that she was to have a child, Lucrezia told herself that this was the happiest time of her life. She refused to look back; she refused to look ahead. The present was all-satisfying.

Each day her love for her husband seemed strengthened; and the Pope, seeing that love, seemed eager to assure her that he also had a great affection for his son-in-law.

In the apartments at Santa Maria in Portico, Cardinals and men of letters continued to assemble; there were whisperings and insinuations, and the political intent of those meetings grew more insistent. The anti-Papal and anti-French party was growing and, since the meetings took place in Lucrezia's apartments, Alfonso would appear to be one of the leaders of it.

But like Lucrezia, Alfonso quickly wearied of politics. He was barely eighteen and there were so many more interesting things in life than intrigue. He was faintly impatient of men such as Ascanio Sforza who must continually— or so it seemed to him—be watching the behavior of others for slights, insults, innuendoes. Life was good. Enjoy it. That was Alfonso's motto.

The Pope was so charming, so solicitous of their happiness. None had been more delighted than he to learn of Lucrezia's pregnancy, and it astonished Alfonso to see this amazing man turn from the dignities of his holy office to the tender care of his daughter. He would walk with the pair in the Vatican gardens and make plans for their child, and he would talk to them in that rich musical voice, so that Alfonso could almost see the wonderful little boy playing in the gardens there in the years to come.

It seemed incredible that anyone would want to be the enemy of such a man; and as long as Cesare remained in France Alfonso was sure he would be completely happy.

One day the Pope said to him: "You and I in company with two of my Cardinals will go on a hunting expedition toward Ostia, for the woods there are full of game and we shall find good sport." He had laughed to see Alfonso's expression. "As for Lucrezia, she must stay quietly behind for a few days and rest. I fancy she looks a little tired lately, and we must think of the child. And, my son, all the time you are enjoying the hunt you will be looking forward to the pleasure of reunion with Lucrezia! Oh, you are a fortunate young man."

Lucrezia had declared he must go, for she knew how he enjoyed a long hunt and he would only be away for a few days. So Alfonso went in the company of the Pope and Cardinals Borgia and Lopez; and he saw yet another side of the character of this man who was his father-in-law, the sportsman and hunter; and he began to believe in those rumors he had heard which declared that Alexander VI was possessed of magical powers; what he believed he now learned was that these did not come from the Devil but from God.

Alfonso would never forget the return from that hunt, the joy of riding into Rome in pale February sunshine and seeing Lucrezia on the balcony watching for their approach.

She ran down to greet them and stood among them, slender and golden-haired, for two months' pregnancy was not apparent; and there, among the stags and wild goats and other booty of that hunt, he embraced his wife with tenderness and delight which brought tears to the eyes of the Pope and his Cardinals.

Alfonso had cried out: "I am happy . . . happy to be home."

And he marveled, realizing what he was now calling his home was that City to which, but a short while ago, he had come with no little dread.

SHE HAD MISSED him, she told him when they were alone. She had been counting the hours to his return.

"Did you ever believe there could be happiness such as this?" asked Alfonso.

"No," she told him. "I did not believe it." It was true, for during her love affair with Pedro Caldes she had always known that they could never enjoy delights such as this. She had dreamed of a small house far from Rome in which she, Pedro and their child would live; she had known that if she had gained her happiness with Pedro she would have lost much of that which she shared with her father. Now she had lost nothing. She was completely happy; she was sure that when her baby was born she would cease to dream about that other child who had once been as much to her as the one she now carried.

She said to Alfonso: "No, I did not think there could be such happiness, but now I believe there can be even greater happiness than this. That will be on the day when I hold our child in my arms."

They lay sleeping, arms entwined; and in their sleep they looked like two innocent children.

THE NEXT DAY brought realization to Lucrezia of what a flimsy thing happiness could be.

Sanchia came to her apartments in the morning.

"It is going to be a sunny day," she said. "We should prepare for the journey to the vineyards of Cardinal Lopez."

Lucrezia remembered. Last night the Cardinal had issued the invitation to the ladies, and they had accepted joyfully.

"Why," said Sanchia, "pregnancy suits you, Lucrezia. You look more beautiful than you did two months ago."

"It is happiness that suits me," Lucrezia answered.

"You are not disappointed in my little brother?" Sanchia asked.

"You know my feelings for him."

"Take care of him, Lucrezia. Take care of him when Cesare comes home."

"You have news of Cesare?"

"I know that he is not going to marry Carlotta, but I knew that before he went."

Lucrezia smiled sadly at her sister-in-law. Sanchia had been jealous, she knew, and she was sorry for Sanchia's unhappiness.

Sanchia said fiercely: "He went in October. It is now February. Yet he remains unmarried. I tell you this, Lucrezia: Cesare is nothing more than a hostage of the French. The bonds are silken, shall we say, but they are nevertheless bonds. Why does Cesare not marry? Because the King of France wishes to keep him in France!"

"You mean he is so attached to Cesare . . ."

Sanchia laughed. "Do you think the whole world loves your brother as you do? No! The King of France is planning an attack on Italy, and if he holds the Pope's beloved son as hostage he can be sure that he will be free from Papal interference when he makes the attack."

"Cesare . . . a hostage!"

"Why not? He was once before, remember. He escaped at Velletri and thus inflicted humiliation on the French which they will not easily have forgotten. Mayhap they remember it still."

"But the King of France greatly honors my brother. We constantly hear of the entertainments he gives for his pleasure."

Sanchia put her face close to Lucrezia's and whispered: "One of those who accompanied Cesare to France has written that the honors paid to Cesare are like those paid to Christ on Palm Sunday, when less than a week later there were cries of 'Crucify him.' "

"Sanchia! You mean Cesare is in danger!"

"I doubt not that he will know how to look after himself. But he'll not get Carlotta." Sanchia lifted her shoulders. "Come, which bonnet will you wear?"

Lucrezia tried to turn her attention to the bonnets. She would not believe that Cesare was in any danger. If he did not marry Carlotta, then he would have someone else. Soon he would be home. She was not going to let fears for her brother cloud her happiness.

So they set out for the vineyards of Cardinal Lopez. They were very beautiful in the pale February sunshine and Lucrezia was determinedly merry, eager to banish the uneasy thoughts which Sanchia had set in motion.

Cardinal Lopez and his household had prepared a feast for the visitors, and they sat watching races or joined in the outdoor games which he had arranged for their entertainment. There was much laughter, but every now and then Lucrezia felt a longing to be with Alfonso that she might tell him of Sanchia's words which had made her a little uneasy, and seek reassurance. She would not tell her father because, although he would dismiss the rumors, he might in the secrecy of his mind brood on them; but Alfonso, she was sure, would dismiss them as ridiculous because he would know that was what she wanted him to do.

Longing to be with Alfonso, she cried out as they were walking down one of the sloping paths to the stables: "Do hurry. Let us race!"

Bernardina, who was close behind her, gave a whoop of joy and, pulling at Francesca's gown, shouted: "Come along. I'll be at the stables first."

Lucrezia cried: "Not you!" And sped away.

She was leading when her foot tripped over a stone and, as her ankle twisted under her, she fell; Bernardina unfortunately was too close on her heels to pull up and, as Lucrezia went down, fell on top of her. Francesca fell over Bernardina and for a few seconds the pair lay on Lucrezia, their full weight pressing her to the ground. They were laughing as they leaped to their feet; then suddenly they stopped, for Lucrezia had not moved. She was lying, her body twisted and still, exactly as she had fallen.

THE POPE SAT by his daughter. They had carried her back to her palace, and put her to bed; then they had taken the news to the Vatican that there had been an accident and that the doctors feared the consequences might be serious. Lucrezia lay white and still; she had lost the baby.

It was comforting, when she opened her eyes, to see her father beside her. She put out a hand and he took it. She knew immediately what had happened, because she was aware of the sorrow in his eyes. The loss of a grandchild could make him more unhappy than the news that the French were at the outskirts of Rome.

"Dearest Father . . ." she began.

Now he was smiling, ready to soothe her.

"You will get better, my daughter," he murmured. "Your weakness will pass."

She whispered: "My baby . . ."

"Oh, but it is an unfortunate accident, nothing more. Two people in love, such as you and Alfonso are, will get many more children. As for this one . . . we do not even know that it was a boy."

"Boy or girl, I loved it."

"Ah, we loved it. But it was not to be." He leaned over the bed. "And dearest daughter, you are safe. Soon you will be well. I praise the saints for that mercy. Shall I grieve because of an unborn grandchild, when my dearest is spared to me? When they brought me the news of your accident terrible fears beset me, and I cried out that if aught happened to my Lucrezia I would have no more interest in life. I prayed for your life as I never prayed before; and you see, Lucrezia, my prayers have been answered. My beloved is safe. And the child . . . But I tell you there will be more children."

"Father," she said, "stay near me. Do not leave me yet."

He smiled and nodded.

She lay back and tried to think of the children she and Alfonso would have; when they had a child, a living child, she would cease to mourn for this one; she wanted to think of the future; she wanted to forget the uneasy words she had heard concerning her brother Cesare.

Meanwhile Cesare remained unsatisfied in France. He was wishing that he had never set out on the French adventure. He had been humiliated, he considered, as he never had been before in all his life. Carlotta of Naples hated him, and she had declared to all her friends, who had made sure that her comments should reach his ears, that she would never be known as Madame la Cardinale, as she surely would if she married the Borgia.

When they met, which they did frequently, she would endeavor to appear guileless and imply that he must not blame her for his lack of success in his courtship; she merely obeyed her father who was upheld in his determination by all the royalty of Europe—except of course the King of France.

It was a galling position, but Cesare must control his anger and pretend that he was not perturbed, not growing more and more worried with every passing week.

The King sent for him one day. His Queen was with him and he did not dismiss those few ministers who stood near his throne; which Cesare felt to be an added insult.

"I have grave news for you, my lord Duke," said Louis, and Cesare was aware that some of those men about the throne were hard pressed to hold back their smiles.

"Sire?" said Cesare, fighting for control with all his might.

"Two of our subjects have married," said Louis, "and I fear this is not going to please you."

"Have I any special interest in these subjects of Your Majesty?" asked Cesare.

"A great interest. One is the Princess Carlotta."

Cesare felt the uncontrollable twitch in his lips; the hot blood flooding his face; he was clenching his fists so tightly that his nails, which were buried in his palms, drew blood.

He heard himself stammering, and his voice seemed to begin in a whisper and end in a roar. "Married, Your . . . Majesty?"

"Yes, the minx has married her Breton nobleman." The King lifted his shoulders. "Of course, she had her father's consent to the marriage, and the Queen and I consider that in these circumstances the matter was out of our hands."

"His Majesty, the King of Naples, seems very pleased with his daughter's match," said Anne of Brittany quickly.

Cesare's fingers itched to seize his sword and attack the royal pair there and then. They were his enemies; they had arranged this. And to think that it was he who had brought them the Bull which enabled them to marry! They were deliberately insulting him, telling him that the King of Naples did not object to a Breton nobleman of no great importance, whereas he would not accept Cesare Borgia, son of the Pope, as his son-in-law.

It was unendurable. They were asking him to suffer too much humiliation.

Perhaps Louis realized this, because he said quickly: "Ah, my lord Duke, there are other ladies at our Court. Perhaps they would be less capricious."

"Holy Mother," prayed Cesare, "keep me calm. Stop this mad racing of my blood which bids me murder."

He managed to say: "What lady has Your Majesty in mind?"

Louis smiled pleasantly. "This is a bitter disappointment. But I have a good match in mind for you. My kinsman, the King of Navarre, has a fair young daughter. What say you to marriage with young Charlotte of Navarre?"

Cesare felt his heartbeats quicken. He had set his heart on Carlotta, but Charlotte was no mean alternative.

"Alain d'Albret," went on the King, "come forth, cousin, and tell us what you would say to a match between our good friend the Duke of Valentinois and your little Charlotte."

The King of Navarre came and stood before the King of France. His looks were sullen. He said: "It does not seem meet to me, Sire, that a Cardinal has a right to marry."

"The Duke is no longer a Cardinal," the King reminded him.

Cesare cried: "I have been freed from my vows. I am as fit and able to marry as any man."

"I should need to be sure that a man who had once been a Cardinal was free of all ecclesiastical ties, before I gave him a daughter of mine," said Alain d'Albret stubbornly.

Cesare cried out: "You are a fool! The whole world knows I am free."

There was silence all about him. Louis' looks were cold. This foreigner had forgotten the strictness of Court etiquette in France.

Cesare said quickly: "I crave pardon. But these matters could be proved to you."

"They would *need* to be proved," said rough Alain.

"You must forgive his caution," added the King, looking from Alain to Cesare. "He is a father with a father's feelings."

"Your Majesty can explain to him that I am free."

"We will give him full proof," said the King. "But this will take a little time."

"I shall need the utmost proof, Your Majesty," declared Alain.

The King rose and going to Alain put his arm through his; then he turned and beckoned to Cesare, and linking his other arm through Cesare's he walked with the two of them to an embrasure where he spoke in whispers while those who had watched the previous scene talked among themselves, respecting the King's wish for privacy.

"The proof will come," said the King to Alain. "His Holiness will lose no time in supplying it." He turned to Cesare. "Charlotte's brother Amanieu will be your brother, my lord Duke. He has long desired his Cardinal's hat. A Cardinal's hat, Alain! I feel that, if you saw your son in possession of that, you would hasten your decision, would you not?"

"Proof, Sire," said Alain. "I must have proof . . . proof for myself, and a Cardinal's hat for my son; and then . . . I should not be averse to accepting a husband for my daughter."

Cesare was silent. He must have a bride. He could not face the humiliation of returning to Rome without one. And Charlotte d'Albret was the daughter of a King, even as Carlotta was.

He saw in this marriage a means of saving his face, but at the same time he was wary.

Was it true, that which was being whispered throughout the Court: "The King keeps Cesare Borgia here as a hostage"?

Had he suggested this marriage to delay Cesare's departure from France, to make him a willing visitor rather than an unwilling one? Cesare believed that Louis was even now planning an attack on Milan. Was he, the great Cesare, to be put in the humiliating position of hostage once more?

Yet marriage with a kinswoman of France would serve him well.

He determined then to marry Charlotte as quickly as possible.

THE COURT OF France was at Blois, and the occasion was the wedding of Cesare Borgia, Duke of Valentinois, and Charlotte d'Albret.

The King was delighted. He was invariably delighted to be in this beautiful château on the banks of the Loire, so grand yet so exquisite, built as it was on different gradients which made it both picturesque and majestic. Louis loved Blois best of all his châteaux because it was here that he had been born one June day in the year 1462, and it was in the same château on an April night as recent as 1498 that a messenger had brought news to him of the death of King Charles, and kneeling before him had cried: *"Le Roi est mort! Vive le Roi!"*

Blois had very special memories for him.

Therefore he was pleased that this marriage should take place at Blois. His armies were ready to march against Milan, and he had succeeded in detaining the Pope's beloved son on French soil for seven months. His marriage would keep him here for several more months as he would not leave France until his wife was pregnant. Moreover the Borgias were now bound by marriage to the French Royal House—a great honor for them, which they would most certainly recognize.

When Louis was ready to invade Italy he would find that he had the mighty influence of the Pope on his side, and he could congratulate himself on a diplomacy to equal that of Alexander VI. He had obtained his divorce and the support of the Pope—all for Alain d'Albret's daughter and a paltry estate and title.

So he felt satisfied and benign as he watched the celebrations. And what celebrations these were! Let the Borgia pay. He wanted splendor, so let him have it. His father was one of the richest men in the world. Let these Borgias parade their wealth before the eyes of French cynics. Better for them to spend it on wedding festivities than on armies to hold out against the French.

The weather was warm and sunny and the fields about the castle delightful. It was acclaimed as an excellent idea to have the celebrations out of doors, and tapestries embroidered with flowers were set up in the fields forming square tents without any top covering, so that the clear blue sky was visible. These tapestried walls made a palace of the meadows with a great banqueting hall and ball-room—grass for carpet and the sky for a ceiling.

The Pope, delighted with the arrangements, had sent caskets of jewels for the bride; and little Charlotte, who had been brought up simply, was dazzled.

She was sixteen and young even for her years. She was a quiet little bride and, as her frightened eyes met his, even Cesare was moved by her simplicity. He realized too that she would be ready to admire him, as he seemed very splendid to her and, shut away from the world as she had been, she had not heard of his reputation.

As Cesare sat beside her at the banquet and danced with her under the blue sky in the tapestry-enclosed ball-room, he decided to make her happy while he was with her, for he had already made up his mind that as soon as she was pregnant he would return to Rome.

His ambitions were as strong as ever. He had his plans for conquering Italy. He would get her with child and leave her as chatelaine of his French estates; then he would return to make himself conqueror of his native land and perhaps of the world.

But he did not tell her this, and as he danced, looking very handsome in his wedding garments, he fascinated the simple girl with his witty conversation and his tender looks. Those who knew him well marveled at the change in him, and for a while forgot to be sorry for little Charlotte d'Albret.

As for Charlotte, she was far from sorry for herself. She was the bride of one of the most discussed men in the world, and she had found him charming, gay yet sentimental, tender yet passionate.

So under that May sky at Blois, the bride and bridegroom dreamed of their future, and the bride would have been surprised had she known that in the dreams of this witty yet tender husband she figured scarcely at all.

Lucrezia was by this time pregnant once more, and visiting her father every day.

When Cesare's messenger Garcia came hot-foot to Rome with the news that the marriage had indeed taken place Alexander was as excited as though it were his own marriage. He sent for Lucrezia immediately and had Garcia brought at once to him although the poor man, exhausted with the fatigue of the journey, collapsed at the Pope's feet.

Alexander, seeing his condition, had a comfortable chair brought for him, sent for wine and food to refresh him, but would not let him out of his sight until he had recounted what was happening in Blois.

"The marriage has been celebrated, Most Holy Lord," gasped Garcia.

"And the consummation?"

"That also, Holiness. I waited until morning that I might bring news of this."

"How many times?" asked the Pope.

"Six, Holiness."

"A worthy son of his father," Alexander cried, laughing. "My beloved boy, I am proud of you."

"His Majesty the King of France congratulated my lord Duke on his prowess, Holiness."

That made Alexander laugh still more.

"Saying, O Most Holy Lord, that my lord Duke had beaten His Majesty."

"Poor Louis! Poor Louis!" cried the Pope. "Did he expect Valois to rival Borgia!"

Then he must hear every detail of the ceremony, going on to the consummation of which he liked to hear again and again.

He was heard murmuring for days afterward: "Six times! Not bad . . . not bad at all, my son."

He enjoyed telling the story. He repeated it again and again to any who had not heard, and often to those who had, embroidering here and there, multiplying the jewels and the splendor and never leaving out that "six times"; and laughing aloud until the tears came to his eyes.

It was wonderful, thought Lucrezia, to see him so contented. It was but a month since the conception of her child, but she was feeling completely happy again. Her father was delighted; Cesare had a wife; and she had her beloved Alfonso, and they were to have a child. What more in the world could she want?

***

Sanchia was uneasy. She waylaid her brother as he came from his wife's apartments.

Alfonso was humming a gay tune which Lucrezia often played on her lute, and the sight of his contented—almost ecstatic—expression irritated Sanchia.

"Alfonso," she cried, "come into this little room where we can be quiet. I must talk to you."

Alfonso opened his beautiful eyes, so like her own, in surprise, and said: "You sound disturbed, Sanchia."

"Disturbed! Of course I'm disturbed. So would you be if you had any sense."

Alfonso was a little impatient. Sanchia had changed since Cesare had gone away. None of her lovers pleased her and she was continually dissatisfied.

"Well," said Alfonso stubbornly, "what ails you?"

"The French are planning an invasion."

Alfonso wanted to yawn; he suppressed the desire with an effort.

"It is no use turning away from what I have to say because you find it unpleasant, Alfonso. You must listen to me. Ascanio Sforza is alarmed."

"He is always alarmed."

"Because he is a man of sound sense with his ears attuned to what is going on about him."

"What goes on about him?"

"Intrigue."

"Of a truth, Sanchia, you were always a lover of intrigue. I confess it was more amusing when they were intrigues of love."

"What is going to happen when Cesare comes back?"

"I'll swear he'll be your lover in spite of his French wife."

"He is now firmly allied with the King of France, and the French have always wanted Milan and . . . Naples. We belong to Naples. Do not forget it, Alfonso. Cesare will never forgive our uncle for refusing him Carlotta. He will band with the French against Uncle Federico. I would not care to be in Naples when Cesare enters with his troops."

"We are of Naples," said Alfonso, "and are the son and daughter-in-law of His Holiness, who is our friend."

"Alfonso, you fool . . . you fool!"

"I am weary, Sanchia."

"Oh, go to your wife," cried Sanchia. "Go . . . and revel in your love, for what little time is left to you. Alfonso, be warned. You must take great care when Cesare returns to Italy."

"He has just got him a wife," cried Alfonso, his brow wrinkling.

"All husbands are not as devoted as you, brother. Some have ambitions beyond making love." She caught his arm suddenly. "You are my brother," she said, "and we stand together, as we always have."

"Yes, Sanchia, indeed yes."

"Then . . . do not be lulled into false security. Keep your ears and eyes open, brother. There is danger near us ... danger to our house ... and do not forget, although you are Lucrezia's husband, you are also a Prince of Naples."

GOFFREDO, WHO WAS now seventeen, was aware of the tension and determined not to be left out. The Pope showed great delight in the marriage of Cesare and the pregnancy of Lucrezia, and it seemed to Goffredo that he had little time to be interested in his younger son. People were often less respectful to him than they had ever dared be to Cesare and the dead Giovanni. Goffredo knew why. It was because many declared he was not the son of the Pope, and Goffredo had an uneasy feeling that Alexander himself was inclined to take the same view.

Goffredo admired the Borgias with an intensity of feeling which he could feel for no one else. He believed that if he were not accepted as one of them, life would have no meaning for him.

He determined therefore to draw attention to the similarity between himself, Cesare and the late Giovanni, and took to roaming the streets after dark in the company of his attendants, entering taverns, seeking out women and causing brawls among the men. This had been a particularly favorite pastime of Giovanni before he had died, and Goffredo longed to hear people say: "Oh, he is going the way of his brothers."

One night as he and his men were roystering on the Bridge of St. Angelo, the guard called to them to halt.

Goffredo, a little alarmed, but determined to acquit himself like a Borgia, swaggered forward, demanding to know what this low fellow thought he was doing in obstructing the pleasure of a Borgia.

The guard drew his sword and two of his soldiers came quickly to his side. Goffredo would have preferred to retire, but that was something which neither Cesare nor Giovanni would ever have done.

The guard, however, was a brave man; moreover it was well known throughout Rome that the Pope was not so fanatically devoted to Goffredo as he was to the other members of his family. Cesare was in France; Giovanni was dead; and the guards of the City of Rome had decided that they would not allow this youngest member of the family to strike terror into the hearts of good Roman citizens, and he should be taught a lesson.

"I ask you, my lord," said the man civilly, "to go quietly on your way."

"And I ask you," blustered Goffredo, "to mind your manners."

"I mind my duty," retorted the guard, "which is to defend the citizens of Rome."

Thereupon Goffredo had no alternative but to fly at the man in a rage which he hoped matched that so often displayed by Cesare; but the guard was waiting for him. His sword pierced Goffredo's thigh and the young man fell groaning to the ground.

WHEN SANCHIA SAW Goffredo carried home she thought he was dying. His wound was bleeding profusely as he lay inert on a hastily constructed bier, his face without color, his eyes closed.

Sanchia demanded to know what had happened, and was told that the guard had attacked her husband because he refused to go quietly on his way.

"Why," declared one of his men, "had there not been so many of us to surround him and protect him he would doubtless have met the same fate as his brother, the Duke of Gandia, and we should have had to dredge the Tiber for his body."

Sanchia was incensed. First she called the physicians to attend her husband, and when she was assured that his life would be saved she gave vent to her anger. None would have dared attack Cesare or Giovanni as they had Goffredo. It was a sign that her husband was not accorded the respect due to the Pope's son.

She determined therefore that the guard who had attacked Goffredo should be severely punished as a warning to all who might think they could ill-treat her husband with impunity.

She sought an early audience with Alexander, and was immediately angered because of his lack of concern in the fate of Goffredo. He did not dismiss his attendants nor did he give her that warm and tender smile which he habitually bestowed on all beautiful women.

"Holiness," cried Sanchia, "is nothing being done to bring this fellow to justice?"

The Pope looked astonished.

"I refer," went on Sanchia, "to this soldier who dared attack my husband."

The Pope looked sad. "I regret that little Goffredo is wounded. It is a sorry matter. But the guard who attacked him was but doing his duty."

"Duty to strike my husband! To wound him nigh to death!"

"We know full well that Goffredo was acting in an unseemly manner, and that when he was politely asked to go quietly on his way, he refused and in his refusal made ready to attack the guard. To my mind there was only one thing for our man to do. He must defend himself . . . and the peace of Rome."

"Do you mean he is to go unpunished?"

"Punishment has already been meted out. Goffredo was the offender; his was the punishment."

"This is your own son!"

The Pope lifted his shoulders and allowed a doubtful expression to creep across his face, which infuriated Sanchia. That he should deny the paternity of her husband, here before others, was intolerable. She lost control of her feelings.

"He is your bastard!" she cried.

"It is a matter of which there has always been some doubt."

"Doubt! How can there be doubt? He looks like you. He behaves like you. How like a Borgia to roam the streets in search of women to rape!"

"My dear Sanchia," said the Pope, "we know you are only part royal, and that only as a bastard; but I pray you do not expose your base blood in unseemly brawling."

"I will speak the truth," cried Sanchia. "You may be Pope, but you are the father of countless children. It ill becomes you to deny the rights of any of them; but one as close to you as Goffredo . . ."

The Pope silenced her. "I ask you to go, Sanchia."

"I'll not go!" she cried, although she was aware of the amazement and acute interest, perhaps delight, of all those within earshot. "You did not despise my birth when you married me to Goffredo."

"You are a fitting bride for Goffredo," said the Pope. "I am uncertain who his father was. It may be that your mother was not certain who yours was."

"I am the daughter of a King of Naples."

"So says your mother. A little divergence from the truth has been known to take place on certain occasions, and from your conduct it might seem that this was one of them."

Sanchia's blue eyes blazed. This was an insult to her birth and her beauty.

Never before had the Pope been known to show such anger toward a beautiful woman.

He said coldly now: "Will you leave me of your own accord?"

It was a threat and, looking round at the two stalwart men who were coming forward, and having no desire to further her humiliation by being hustled from the Pope's presence, she bowed coldly and retired.

Feeling calmer in her own apartments she told herself that this was an indication of the acute danger in which her country stood. The Pope must intend to stand firmly with the French. She had been insulted; what fate was there in store for her brother? Even Lucrezia would not be able to save him. Had she saved Pedro Caldes?

Very shortly after her interview with the Pope, Ascanio Sforza came to see her.

News of her encounter with the Pope had reached him and he, like Sanchia, was filled with misgivings.

"It is certain," he said, "that invasion is imminent."

Sanchia agreed. "What should I do?" she asked.

"For yourself, stay where you are, discover all you can. Remain the friend of Lucrezia, for through her it may be possible to learn what is happening here in Rome. I shall leave as soon as possible for Milan. My brother Ludovico must begin his preparations immediately, and I will be there to help him. As for your brother . . ."

"Yes," said Sanchia eagerly. "What of my brother?"

"It is difficult to guess what fate they have in store for him."

"The Pope is full of affection toward him at this moment."

"And ready to insult his sister before members of his suite."

"It may be that I goaded him. I was very angry."

"No, he would not have treated you as he did if he cared for the goodwill of Naples. Do not trust his friendship for your brother. When the French come Cesare will be with them, and when Cesare is in Rome they will seek to dispose of your brother. Cesare always hated Lucrezia's husbands, and the fact that Lucrezia is really devoted to this one will not make Cesare hate him less."

"You think my brother is in immediate danger?"

Ascanio nodded slowly. "He will be when it is known that I have left for Milan. The Pope knows of our meetings; it would be impossible to keep them secret from him. He has his spies everywhere, so he will know that we are on the alert. From the moment I leave Rome, Alfonso's danger will be increased."

"Then the wisest thing would be for him to leave at once for Naples?"

"Try to persuade him to leave without delay."

"It will not be easy. He'll find it difficult to tear himself from Lucrezia."

"As you love him," warned Ascanio, "bid him fly for his life."

Lucrezia was lying on her bed while her women combed her hair. She was nearly six months pregnant and was easily exhausted.

But she was happy. Three months, she told herself, and our child will be born. She was planning the cradle she would have.

"Is it too soon?" she asked her women. "Why should I not have the pleasure of seeing it beside me when I wake, so that I may say to myself: 'Only eighty-four days ... eighty-three days ... eighty-two days....'"

Her women hastily crossed themselves. "It would seem like tempting Providence, Madonna," said one.

"All will be well this time," Lucrezia said quickly.

Then she was back on one of those unhappy journeys into the past. She saw herself six months pregnant as now, dressed in the voluminous petticoats which Pantisilea, the little maid who had attended her in her convent, had provided for her, standing before the Cardinals and Envoys and swearing that she was *virgo intacta* in order that she might be divorced from Giovanni Sforza.

"Perhaps," she told herself, "I am unlucky. My first child unknown to me, being brought up in the care of some woman in this city! (Holy Mother, make her kind to my little one.) And then that little one who was lost to me before I knew whether it was girl or boy."

But this was different. This child should be given the greatest care. It was alive within her—lively and strong; and everything indicated that this was a healthy pregnancy.

"My lord is late," she said. "I had expected him before this."

"He will be with you before long, Madonna," she was told.

But she waited and he did not come. She dozed. How tired this healthy little one within her could make her feel; she touched her swollen body lightly and smiled tenderly.

"This time all will be well. It is a boy," she murmured, "certainly a boy. He shall be called Roderigo after the best and most loving father a woman ever had."

She heard voices in the ante-room, and sat up to listen. Why was it possible to tell by the tone of voices that something was wrong?

"The Madonna is sleeping. Wait until she wakes."

"She would want to know at once."

"No . . . no. She is happier in ignorance. Let her sleep out her sleep."

She rose and putting a robe about her went to the ante-room. A group of startled people stared at her.

"Something has happened," she said. "I pray you tell me quickly."

No one spoke immediately, and she looked appealingly at them.

"I command you to tell me," she said.

"Madonna, the Duke of Bisceglie . . ."

Her hand went to the drapery of her throat, and she clutched it as though for support. The faces of those people seemed to merge into one and recede, as one of her women ran to her and put an arm about her.

"He is well, Madonna. No harm has come to him," the woman assured her. "It is merely that he has left Rome."

Lucrezia repeated: "Left Rome!"

"Yes, Madonna, he rode out with a small party a few hours ago; he was seen riding South at full speed."

"I . . . I understand," she said.

She turned and went back into her room. Her women followed.

THere was a letter from Alfonso.

It was brought to Lucrezia an hour after she had heard the news of his departure. She seized it eagerly; she knew that he would not willingly have run away from her without a word.

She read it.

He loved her. His life had no meaning without her. But he had been forced to leave her. News had reached him of plots to take his life. He knew that if these plots succeeded they would bring the greatest unhappiness in the world to her, and he was more concerned for the unhappiness his death would inflict on her than for anything else, since if he were dead of what consequence would anything be to him? He was unsafe in Rome, as he had always known he must be, but he had allowed his happiness to blind him to his danger; now that danger was so close that he dared wait no longer. It broke his heart to leave her, but they should not long be separated. He implored her to ride out from Rome, as he had done, and join him in Naples. There they would be safe to pursue their idyll of happiness.

Lucrezia read the letter through several times; she wept over it; and she was still reading it when the Pope was announced.

He would not let her rise; he came to her bedside and taking her in his arms, pressed passionate kisses upon her.

He dismissed her women, and then she saw how angered he was by the flight of Alfonso.

"He is a young fool, a frightened young fool," stormed Alexander; and Lucrezia was aware then that Alexander had lost some of that magnificent calm which had been his chief weapon in the days of his early triumphs. "Why does he run away from a young and beautiful wife like you?"

"He has not run from me, Father."

"All will say he has run from you. Giovanni Sforza will be amused, I doubt not, and make sure that the whole world is aware of his amusement. And you to have his child in three months! The young idiot has no sense of the position he holds through marriage into our family."

"Father, dearest and Most Holy Father, do not judge him harshly."

"He has hurt you, my child, I would judge any harshly who did that."

"Father, what do you propose to do?"

"Bring him back. I have already sent soldiers after him. I trust that they will soon restore the foolish boy to us."

"He is uneasy, Father."

"Uneasy! What right has he to be uneasy? Has he not been treated as one of us?"

"Father, there is trouble brewing. Cesare's friendship with the French . . ."

"My little Lucrezia, you must not bother this golden head with such unsuitable matters. It was meant to delight the eye, not muse on politics. This husband of yours has wandered into a maze of misunderstanding because he thought he understood matters which are beyond his comprehension. It is that sister of his and her friends, I doubt not. I trust they have not contaminated *you* with their foolish notions."

"Would these notions be so foolish, Father, if there were war with the French?"

"Have no fear. I would always protect you. And I will bring your husband back to you. This is what you want, is it not?"

Lucrezia nodded. She had begun to cry and although she knew that the Pope hated tears she could not suppress hers.

"Come, dry your eyes," he begged; and as she moved to obey him, Alfonso's letter, which had been beneath the bed covering, was exposed and the Pope saw it.

He picked it up. Lucrezia hastily took it from him. Alexander's expression showed that he was a little hurt, and Lucrezia said quickly: "It is a letter from Alfonso."

"Written since he went away?"

"He wrote it before he went and sent a messenger back with it. It explains why he has gone and . . . and . . ."

The Pope clearly longed to lay hands on the letter, and waited for his daughter to show it to him; but when Lucrezia did not, he was too clever a diplomatist to demand it and perhaps be refused. He did not want any unpleasantness with Lucrezia, and he knew now that her husband considered himself his enemy; therefore Lucrezia would be urged in two directions. The Pope was determined to keep his hold on his daughter and knew that he could best do this by continuing to be her benevolent and understanding father.

"I wonder he did not take you with him," said Alexander. "He professes to love you dearly, yet he leaves you."

"It is because of the child I carry. He feared that the journey must be made in such haste that harm might come to me and the child."

"Yet he decides to leave you!"

"He wants me to join him as soon as possible in Naples."

The hardening of the Pope's mouth was not perceptible to Lucrezia. Alexander was determined Lucrezia should never be allowed to leave her father for her husband.

He hesitated for a few seconds, then he said: "He cannot be as anxious for your condition as I am. But perhaps he is young and does not realize that child-bearing can be a hazardous experience. I should not allow you, my dearest, to travel so far until your child is born."

Their eyes met, and Alexander knew then that Lucrezia was no longer a child, and that he had underestimated her. She knew of the existence of rivalries; she was fully aware of the possessive nature of his love for her, and that Alfonso had every reason to mistrust his intentions toward him.

Lucrezia began to cry once more. She could not stop the tears. They were tears of misery and helplessness.

And Alexander, who could not bear tears, kissed her forehead lightly and went quietly away.

Alfonso reached Naples and, in spite of the fact that the Pope demanded that he return at once, he refused to do so; nor would his uncle, King Federico, give him up.

This infuriated the Pope who knew that the whole of Italy would be aware that Alfonso had good reason for being afraid, since he was prepared to leave a wife with whom, it was common knowledge, he was deeply in love.

Alexander had been suffering from fainting fits more frequently during the last year, and there were occasions when the purple blood would flood his face, when the veins would knot at his temples and he would find it difficult to regain that composure which he knew was one of his greatest assets.

This was one of the occasions when he found it impossible to remain calm.

He sent for Sanchia and told her that she might prepare to leave at once for Naples; since the King was determined to retain her brother he could have her also.

Sanchia was astounded. She had no wish to leave Rome, and she immediately made this clear to the Pope.

He did not look at her, and his voice was cold. "We are not discussing your wishes, but mine," he told her.

"Holiness, my place is here with my husband."

"Your place is where I say it shall be."

"Most Holy Lord, I beg of you, consider this."

"I have already considered, and this is my decision."

Sanchia lost her temper. "I refuse to go," she said.

"Then," reiterated the Pope, "it will be necessary to remove you by force."

Gone was the urbane charmer of women. Her beauty meant nothing to him. She had never believed this would be possible.

She cried out in humiliated rage: "If I go, I shall take Goffredo with me."

"Goffredo remains in Rome."

"And Lucrezia!" she cried. "I shall take Lucrezia and Goffredo with me. They'll come. Lucrezia longs to join her husband. If my place is in Naples, then so is hers."

And with a certain satisfaction, for she saw that she had alarmed him, she left him.

Outside the Palace of Santa Maria in Portico a brilliant cortège was preparing to leave. There were forty-three coaches, and among them a splendid litter with embroidered mattresses of crimson satin and a canopy of damask. This was to carry Lucrezia, and had been designed by the Pope himself to afford the utmost comfort to a pregnant woman during a long and tedious journey.

Now Lucrezia was reclining in the litter, and Goffredo had mounted his horse; together at the head of the cortège they would ride out of Rome for Spoleto.

Standing in the Benediction loggia was Alexander himself, determined to see the last of his daughter before she left Rome; his smile was tender and full of affection and he raised his hand three times to bless them before they departed.

Lucrezia was glad to leave Rome. The past few days had been very uneasy. Sanchia had been forced to return to Naples very much against her will, and Lucrezia was aware that this journey to Spoleto was being undertaken because her father feared that Lucrezia and Goffredo might escape him and join their husband and wife in Naples.

They were in benign and tender custody; there was no doubt of it. Surrounding them were attendants who had sworn they would not let them out of their sight, and who would have to answer to the Pope if they escaped.

The Pope had told Lucrezia of this journey she was to make to Spoleto. She was his beloved daughter, he said, and he wished to do honor to her. He was going to make her Governor of Spoleto and Foligno, a position which usually fell to the lot of Cardinals or high-raking priests. But he wanted all the world to know that he respected his daughter as deeply as he loved her; and that was why he was going to invest her with this duty.

Lucrezia knew that this was but half the reason. He was afraid she would run away, and he could not have borne that; he did not wish to make her his prisoner in Rome. So he made her his prisoner in Spoleto. There she would live in what was tantamount to a fortress, and Spoleto—being a hundred and fifty miles north—put a greater distance between Lucrezia and Alfonso than there would have been had she remained in Rome.

She knew too that her continual tears wearied him. He wanted her to laugh a great deal, to sing to him, to amuse him; he could not endure tears.

The journey was arduous, and it took six days to reach Spoleto. There was much discomfort to be faced for one in her condition, even in her crimson mattressed litter and the satin palanquin which the Pope had had the foresight to equip with a footstool.

Yet she was happier than she had been since she heard of Alfonso's departure, because her father had told her that he would do all in his power to bring her husband to her, and he doubted not that he would bring about this happy state of affairs within a few weeks by sending Alfonso along to Spoleto to keep her company.

It was impossible to doubt Alexander's ability to achieve what he set out to do, and she believed that before long Alfonso really would be with her.

And when they crossed the meadows and she saw the great castle, dour and formidable, standing high above the town, she felt as though she were going to a real prison; but, she told herself, if Alfonso should join her there, she would be a very happy prisoner.

In the town the citizens were waiting to greet her; they had crowded into the streets to see her entry in her litter under the canopy of gold damask. They were all eagerness to gape at this Lucrezia Borgia of whom they had heard such tales, both shocking and romantic.

Smiling she was carried under the arches of flowers, and listened with intent pleasure—in spite of her weariness—to the speeches of welcome. Although it was early in the afternoon when she reached Spoleto she did not pass between the Torretta and Spiritata Tower until the sun was about to set.

Inside the castle she was taken into the court of honor with its many arcades, where she handed the briefs, given her by the Pope, to the dignitaries assembled there. She listened to more speeches; she was acclaimed as Governor of Spoleto; and while she listened and smiled so charmingly on all, she was praying: "Holy Mother of God, send Alfonso to me here."

She would stand at a window, looking down on the town or across the ravine to Monte Luco, watching for Alfonso.

Several weeks passed; August was over. It was September, and in November her baby was due to be born.

She thought of Alfonso constantly; she longed for him. And one day in the middle of the month her women aroused her from her sleep, and she heard the trills of joy in their voices. She had not time to rise from her bed before the door was flung open and Alfonso had her in his arms.

They clung together, speechlessly, while Lucrezia's trembling hands examined his face as though to assure herself that he was Alfonso in the flesh and not some phantom, conjured up in a dream.

"Alfonso," she murmured at last. "So . . . you have come."

He was a little shamefaced at first. "Lucrezia, I don't know how I could have left you, but I thought it best. I thought . . ."

She was never one for recriminations. "Perhaps it was for the best," she said; and now that he was with her, she wanted to forget that he had ever left her.

"Lucrezia, I thought you would join me. Had I known we should be separated so long I would never have gone."

"It is over. We are together again," she told him. "Oh, Alfonso, my beloved husband, I believe I shall never again allow you to pass out of my sight."

Food was brought to them and eaten on Lucrezia's bed. There was laughter in the apartment. Some of the noblemen and ladies came in and danced there, and while Lucrezia played her lute, Alfonso sang. They were together again, their hands clinging at odd moments, as though they were determined never more to be parted.

THE LOVERS WERE happy in Spoleto. Alfonso was with her and it was not in either of their natures to alarm themselves by thought of what the future might hold. The Pope had made it possible for them to enjoy this happiness and they accepted him as their loving father.

They consequently did not allow the fact that the French had invaded Italy to worry them. They heard that Ludovico, unable to get help from his ally Maximilian Emperor of Austria, who was fighting the Swiss, had fled from Milan, taking his brother Ascanio with him, and leaving Milan open to the French. Brilliant politician though Ludovico was, he was no fighter, as he had shown during the previous invasion; he could plan, but he needed military leadership if those plans were to be carried out. It seemed as though Louis was going to have a victory as easy as that of Charles a few years earlier.

There came news which did arouse the lovers from their passionate devotion. Cesare was in Milan.

"I shall soon see my beloved brother again," cried Lucrezia. "I long to hear about his adventures in France. I wonder his bride could bear to part with him."

And Alfonso, listening, felt again that cold shadow over his life. It had always been Cesare who had alarmed him more than any.

But it was so easy to forget. Lucrezia would bring out her lute; Goffredo would sing with them and they would call in the men and women for the dancing.

ALEXANDER FELT ELATED. Cesare was home, and it would not be long now before he held his beloved son in his arms. The French were in possession of Milan and the Neapolitans were alarmed; but the Pope in the Vatican was well content. Cesare was a kinsman of the King of France, and the French and the Borgias would now be allies.

Alexander had already formed his plans for the future Borgia kingdom which would be his. The time was at hand when it should be seized; Milan, Naples, Venice, all the Italian States and kingdoms would be concerned with protecting themselves from the French. Now was the time for Cesare to step in with the Papal armies. Now was the time to form the State of Romagna. Towns such as Imola, Forlì, Urbino, Faenza and Pesaro (oh yes, certainly Pesaro; they would be revenged on Giovanni Sforza for the rumors he had circulated concerning the Borgia family) should all fall to Cesare. And here *was* Cesare, in Italy with his French allies, waiting to seize his Kingdom.

There was only one thing which irked Alexander at this time; this was his separation from his daughter. So he sent messages to Spoleto commanding Alfonso to take his wife to Nepi (that town which, at the time of his election to the Papal Chair, he had given to Ascanio Sforza in exchange for his support, and which he had since retaken from him) where he, Alexander, would join them.

Why should not Cesare ride to Nepi from Milan? There he and Alexander could discuss their plans for the future.

✸♛✸

Cesare set out from Milan, eager for the reunion with his family. He longed to see Lucrezia again—even though he would have to see her husband as well; he wanted to bask in the warmth of Goffredo's admiration; but chiefly he wished to hear his father's plans for his advancement.

At last Cesare was doing what he had always made up his mind to do: he was a soldier, and the Papal forces were to be at his command.

It was exhilarating to feel the Italian air on his face again. In France he had always been conscious that he was in a strange land and that he was continually watched. The French had disliked him; they had inflicted many humiliations on him, and Cesare was not one to forget humiliations.

As he rode along the road from Milan to Nepi he thought of what he would like to do to the students of the Sorbonne, if it were only in his power to punish them. They had staged a comedy based on Cesare's marriage, and they had taken particular delight in defaming Cesare and the Pope. Louis had declared his wish that this should be stopped, for the comedy, performed many times, was the talk of Paris; he had even sent two of his officials to the capital to prevent its presentation, but the students, six thousand strong, had refused to stop their performance, and Louis himself had at length gone to Paris to prohibit this insult to one who should have been an honored guest.

Cesare could not be revenged on the students, but he would on others. He had a mental dossier of all those who had offended him, even if it was but by a slighting word or a look. They should all die—in one way or another—for it was Cesare's doctrine that none should insult him and live.

But revenge must wait. First he had his kingdom to conquer, and the great dream of his life had to be realized.

Lucrezia was watching for him as he rode to the castle of Nepi, and was the first to greet him. She was large with child—the birth was a few weeks away—and this irritated him even as he embraced her, as it reminded him of Alfonso, her husband, and all the rumors he had heard of the affection between these two.

"It has been so long, Cesare, so very long," she cried.

He took her face in his hands and studied it intently. Her face at least had changed little.

"You had your husband and this child to think of," he told her.

"Do you think anything would stop me thinking of you?"

It was the answer he expected; the sort of answer she had learned to give in nursery days.

The Pope was ready to greet him, taking him in his arms, kissing him fondly, his face quivering with emotion.

"My beloved son, at last . . . at last!"

"Father, I would it had been earlier."

"No matter, now you are here, and we are contented."

Cesare had nothing more than a curt greeting for his brother-in-law; Alfonso was taken aback, the smile of welcome freezing on his face. He glanced quickly at Lucrezia, but Lucrezia, with whom he had shared all emotions since he had rejoined her at Spoleto, was unaware of him. He was conscious of the pride shining in her eyes, pride in this brother of hers.

THE POPE AND Cesare were closeted together. They bent over maps as they sketched in the kingdom of Romagna.

"One by one these towns should fall to us," said the Pope. "No doubt some, terrified of war, will surrender without a fight."

"I shall know how to terrify them," Cesare told him.

"The Italians are a pleasure-loving people," went on the Pope. "Charles's invasion taught us that. They like to parade in fine uniforms; that is beauty and color, and they are great lovers of beauty and color. They love carnivals, mock-battles; they like the parade of conquering heroes . . . but the true battle . . . no! I do not think our task will be difficult."

"I shall accomplish it with ease."

"You are confident, my son."

"Should not all generals be confident before the battle? To believe in defeat is to court disaster."

"You are going to be a great general, my son."

"Did I not always tell you so? Do not forget, Father, that I have much time to make up for." His gaze was accusing, and the Pope flinched, feeling suddenly old, as though he had given over the reins to this headstrong son of his and bidden him drive their chariot.

Alexander looked down at the map and traced a line with his finger.

"We shall subdue all the Roman barons," he said. "They shall all come under Papal authority. You are Gonfalonier of the Church, my son."

Cesare's brilliant eyes looked into those of his father. Yes, Romagna would be under Papal control and, as the Pope would be under the control of his son, Cesare would soon be ruler of those States. Nor would his ambition end there.

Cesare intended to unite all Italy and rule as King.

In their bedroom at Nepi Alfonso and Lucrezia lay together. It was early morning and Lucrezia was conscious of the restlessness of her husband.

"Alfonso," she whispered. "What ails you?"

"I cannot sleep," he answered.

"Why not, Alfonso?"

He was silent; she raised herself on her elbow and, although she could not see his face, she touched it lightly with her fingers. He took her hand and kissed it passionately. His was trembling.

"What ails you, Alfonso?" she asked again.

He hesitated. Then he lied. "I know not. It must have been some nightmare."

She kissed him again and lay down beside him.

He knew how deeply she loved her brother—too deeply, so many had said—and he could not bring himself to say to her, "It is the presence of your brother here at Nepi. While he is here I find it impossible to be at peace. It is as though the castle is full of shadows—fantastic, grotesque and horrible—that hang over me. There are warning shadows and threatening shadows. And I dream of Cesare, standing over me with the naked sword in his hand and that half-smile on his face which mocks me and is so cruel."

᯽ ♛ ᯽

THere was rejoicing throughout the Vatican, for Lucrezia had come safely through childbirth and the baby was a boy.

He was to be called Roderigo after the Pope, and no one seemed more delighted than the child's grandfather, who immediately inspected the baby and declared that the little one resembled him in more than name. Pacing up and down Lucrezia's chamber with young Roderigo in his arms he seemed to have regained all his lost youth. He was already making plans for the boy's future, and demanded of all those present if they had ever seen a more healthy boy than this grandson of his.

Lucrezia lying back in her magnificent bed in Santa Maria in Portico, content in her child though she was, was exhausted for her labor had been long and arduous. Alfonso remained by her bed, her hand in his, smiling his delight to see the Pope's pleasure in the child.

Cesare had not accompanied them on their return to Rome, and Alfonso could forget those nights of terror now Cesare was far away.

Outside in St. Peter's Square were the sounds of soldiers at their drill, for the Papal armies were preparing to march; and although the Pope showed himself enchanted with this new baby, his soldiers were the enemies of the child's paternal relatives.

Sanchia was in Rome, as Lucrezia had begged the Pope to allow her sister-in-law to return; and unable to deny his daughter her whims Alexander placed no obstacle in the way of Sanchia's return, and when she came back treated her as though there had been no differences between them.

Lucrezia was delighted to have her with her; Alfonso was more than delighted; he was relieved. He could not have too many friends about him and he trusted his sister completely.

This was the day of the christening of the infant Roderigo, and there was great ceremony in the Palace of Santa Maria in Portico. No one would have guessed that so recently the Pope had declared that the lords of Pesaro, Forlì, Urbino, Imola and Faenza had forfeited their rights to these dominions because they had failed to pay their tithes to the Church, and that this declaration was the sign for Cesare to begin his series of attacks.

All was gaiety in Lucrezia's palace for the christening of her baby boy. She was too weak to be up, so she lay in her bed among her pillows of red satin embroidered with gold; and the room in which she lay had been hung with velvet of that delicate blue made fashionable by Lucrezia herself and called Alexandrine blue.

Guests came to her bedside—all the most important men and women of Rome; they brought gifts and compliments, and they all declared their good wishes for the baby's health and prosperity.

Lucrezia was very tired, but she sat up on her cushions bravely smiling while her father looked on with approval. This was his way of showing his love for her child, of telling her that this little Borgia should have his share of that indefatigable love and devotion which Lucrezia knew so well because she had shared it.

Many Cardinals had gathered in the chapel, and when the time for the christening drew near they went in a splendid procession from the palace chapel to the Sistine Chapel which was adorned with Botticelli's Daughters of Jethro and Perugino's Handing over of the Keys.

Holding the baby was Juan Cervillon, the brave Spanish Captain whom Lucrezia had come to look upon as her friend; and very splendid was the little Roderigo in his ermine-edged gold brocade.

At the altar the Archbishop of Cosenza (Francesco Borgia) took the baby from Cervillon and carried it at the font while Cardinal Carafa performed the baptismal ceremony.

It had been the Pope's wish that after the ceremony the baby should be handed to a member of the Orsini family, that all present might take this as a sign of his desire for friendship with them.

The effect was spoilt when the young Roderigo, having behaved perfectly from the moment he left Santa Maria in Portico and all through the ceremony in the Sistine Chapel, set up a wail of anguish as the Orsini took him, and continued to cry fiercely until he was taken into another pair of arms.

An evil omen, said the watchers. The Orsinis should beware of the Holy Father and he of them.

THE DAYS WHICH followed the baptism were uneasy, and even Lucrezia and Alfonso could not escape the tension.

Lucrezia's friend, Juan Cervillon, came to her the day after the baptism and told her that he had been long from his home, and wanted to return to Naples that he might see his wife and family.

"You must go, Juan," Lucrezia told him. "It is not to be expected that you should be separated from them for so long."

"I have asked the permission of His Holiness," he told her.

"And it has been given?"

"Yes, but somewhat reluctantly."

Alfonso, who had joined them and stood listening, said: "That is to be understood. You have served him well."

"I shall never forget," said Lucrezia, "that it was you, Juan, who persuaded King Federico to allow my husband to come to me at Spoleto."

"I was merely the ambassador of His Holiness."

"But you worked well for us, I know, dear Juan. Do not slip away without saying good-bye to us; and when you say good-bye I shall want you to promise that you will not stay long away from us."

He kissed her hand. "I promise that," he said.

That day Cesare came home. He was eager to raise more money for his campaign, and spent long periods shut in with the Pope discussing his plans.

He came to see Lucrezia, told her that she looked wan, and was curt to Alfonso as though he blamed him for Lucrezia's fragility; and he scarcely looked at the baby.

It was reported to Lucrezia that he had cut short the Pope's eulogies on his grandson.

"He is jealous," said Alfonso to Lucrezia, and she noticed that the fear was back in his eyes and that when Cesare was near he was a changed man. "He is jealous of my love for you and yours for me, of your father's love for you and our child."

"You are wrong," soothed Lucrezia. "He is over-anxious because I have taken so long to recover from little Roderigo's birth. We have always been such an affectionate family."

"An affectionate family!" cried Alfonso. "So affectionate that one brother murders another."

She looked at him with that hurt expression in her eyes which made him hasten to soothe her. "I spoke without thinking. I repeated idle gossip. Forgive me, Lucrezia. Let us forget I have spoken. Let us forget everything but that we love and are together."

But how was it possible to forget those fears when a terrible tragedy occurred two days later.

Alfonso heard of it and came pale-faced and trembling to Lucrezia.

"It is Juan Cervillon," he stammered; "he will never go home to Naples now. His wife and children will never see him, as they hoped. He was stabbed to death late last night when leaving a supper party."

"Juan . . . dead! But it was only yesterday that he was with us."

"Men die quickly in Rome."

"Who has done this terrible thing?" cried Lucrezia.

Alfonso looked at her but did not answer.

"They will bring his murderers to justice," Lucrezia said.

Alfonso shook his head and said bitterly: "People recall the death of your brother, the Duke of Gandia. He died after he left a supper party. Juan has already been buried in Santa Maria in Transpontina in the Borgo Nuovo, and it is said that none was allowed to see his wounds."

Lucrezia covered her face with her hands. Alfonso went on almost hysterically: "He was heard, shortly before he died, talking scathingly of the affair of Sanchia and your brother Cesare, and it is said that he knew too many Papal secrets to be allowed to take them out of Rome."

Lucrezia kept her face hidden. She did not want to see the haunting fear in her husband's.

The death of Juan seemed to be the beginning of a new terror. There were several deaths—from stabbing, in alleys after dark; some bodies were recovered from the river; and there were many who passed mysteriously away and in such a manner that none could say how they had died. They were attacked by sicknesses of varying symptoms; some seemed to become intoxicated and die in their sleep. There was one fact which was the same in the cases of many mysterious deaths; those who suffered from them had supped at the Borgia table not long before their deaths.

The Borgias had a new weapon; all Rome knew what it was: Poison. They had their special apothecaries working for them, compounding and perfecting from their poisons recipes, it was said, which they had brought with them from Borja, their native town on the borders of Aragon, Castile and Navarre; and these secrets they had learned from the Moors. Spanish Moors and subtle Italians, a formidable combination, and from it was concocted Cantarella, that powder which was becoming feared by all whose daily life brought them into contact with the Borgias.

Ferninando d'Almaida, the Portuguese Bishop of Ceuta, was the next victim of note. He had been with Cesare in France, and it was said that he had seen Cesare humiliated more than once. He died mysteriously in camp with Cesare.

Meanwhile Cesare's military operations were going forward with the utmost success, and he was now ready to turn his attention to Forlì which was in the hands of the Countess of Forlì, Caterina Sforza, reputed to be one of the bravest women in Italy.

She was fully aware that she could not hold out against Cesare. Imola, Caterina's first stronghold, had already fallen to his troops, and she sent messengers from Forlì to Rome imploring the Pope for mercy.

The Pope had no intention of granting mercy since Forlì must fall to Cesare, and was chosen to be an important part of the Kingdom of Romagna; so he had the messengers arrested, and when they were tortured they "confessed" that the letter they brought to the Pope had been treated with a poison which was intended to bring about his speedy death.

There was consternation in the Vatican. When Lucrezia heard the news she ran to her father and burst unceremoniously into his presence. She flung herself into his arms and kissed him again and again.

"There, there!" soothed Alexander, stroking the long golden hair. "What is there to feel so excited about?"

"They might have killed you!" cried Lucrezia.

"Ah," said Alexander, "it is worth the risk to see how much my beloved daughter cares for her father."

"Father, life without you would be intolerable."

"And you a wife! And you a mother!"

His eyes were alert, watching. The desired answer was: What are these to me without my beloved, my sacred Holy Father, my affectionate earthly father?

She kissed his hands and he felt her warm tears on them. Such tears did not displease him.

"All is well, my dearest," he murmured. "All is well. We are too wily for them, we Borgias."

"That they should dare!" she cried.

Then she stopped, as she remembered the rumors she had heard of how men supped at the Borgia tables and said good-bye to life. She thought of poor Juan Cervillon, who had been so gay and happy one day, anticipating his return to his family, and whose body was in the grave less than twenty-four hours later.

Cesare marched on Forlì, determined to revenge the threat to his father's life. He would have no mercy on Forlì, whose Countess had dared attempt to give the Borgias a dose of their own medicine. She must understand the might of the Grazing Bull.

From the battlements of her castle Caterina watched the soldiers encamped below. Her case was hopeless but she was not going to give way until she had inflicted great damage on the enemy. It was not in Caterina's nature to give way without a fight. She was the illegitimate daughter of Duke Gale-azzo Maria Sforza, and thus her ancestor was the famous *condottiere*, Francesco Sforza. She had been only sixteen when she was married to Gerolamo Riario, nephew of Pope Sixtus who made him Count of Forlì. This man had been notorious for his cruelty and, shortly after his marriage to Caterina, the people had risen against him, entered his castle, stripped him and thrown his naked body from the towers. She was afterward married to Giacomo de Feo who met a similar fate at the hands of the mob; but this time Caterina was older and, determined on revenge, assembled her soldiers and pursued her husband's murderers to their village, where she ordered that every man, woman and child in that village should be hacked to pieces; and this was done. That was the sort of woman Caterina had become.

Now she stood in the forefront of the battle directing her soldiers, fight-ing till the last, extracting every sacrifice from Cesare and his men, knowing that in the end, because of their superior weapons and numbers, they must defeat her.

When Cesare broke through and forced his way into the castle she was waiting for him, her long hair falling in disorder about her shoulders, a mature woman but a tempestuous and beautiful one.

"I surrender," she said with dignity.

"Having no alternative," Cesare reminded her.

Cesare came close to her and stood watching her; their eyes met and his were full of latent cruelty.

This was the woman who had attempted to poison his father, so her messengers had said when the Question was applied to them. He would let her see what befell those who thought they could oppose the Borgias.

Caterina measured her opponent. She had heard stories of the chivalry of the French, and she remembered that when Giulia Farnese had fallen into the hands of Yves d'Allegre, that gallant French captain, she had emerged unscathed.

"I demand," she went on, "that I be handed over to the French."

"Why so?" said Cesare. "Are you not my prisoner? Do not imagine that I shall let you go."

Caterina thought in that moment how glad she was that she had sent her children away. For herself, she was a woman who had enjoyed many adventures and it had been said with some truth that since the death of her husbands she had surrounded herself with men who would work wholeheartedly for her, their only reward being a share of her bed.

She understood the meaning in those eyes of his. She was not alarmed; in fact she was excited; although she would not let him know this. His very cruelty and the rumors she had heard of his barbarism made an appeal to her wild nature.

"What would you have of me?" she asked, putting out a hand to ward him off.

He struck down the hand and she winced.

"I demand the *droit de seigneur.*"

Caterina's eyes flashed. "Not content with the rape of my city you would rape my person?"

"I see you understand your predicament perfectly," said Cesare.

"I ask you to leave me."

"It is not for you to ask, but to submit," said Cesare, his eyes glowing with sudden lust as he seized her by the shoulder. She would fight, this wild woman, and he would enjoy an encounter such as those he had shared with Sanchia.

He called aloud: "You may all leave me with the Countess."

She sought to evade him, and the struggle began.

Cesare's laughter was demoniacal. She would fight, and she must surely be the loser. She should remember that he had stormed the castle; she should know that every stronghold must fall before him.

It was more than a sexual adventure, this; it was a symbol.

Cesare was returning to Rome. He came as a conquering hero, and the Pope was preparing a magnificent ceremony that all might realize his pride in his son.

In truth Cesare was returning in a far from triumphant mood. It was merely to raise money and change his plans that he had been forced to return to Rome, for unexpectedly, Ludovico, being helped by Maximilian of Austria, had reconquered Milan and the French had found it necessary to recall all their troops to the troubled area of Lombardy. As Cesare had been fighting his battles with the help of his French allies he suddenly found his armies so denuded that he had scarcely enough men to leave guarding the towns which he had conquered. Accordingly there was nothing he could do but return to Rome.

But he was not eager for the world to know how much he had relied on the French; therefore Cesare must return in triumph as the victorious Romans had done in the past.

Cesare's motto was *Caesar aut nihil.* He was determined to hold what he had gained and gain still more.

Soon after the capture of Forlì, Cardinal Giovanni Borgia had come to the town in order to congratulate his kinsman on his victory; he had however been suddenly seized with a violent sickness, and died within a few hours of being taken ill.

There were whispers of Cantarella and, although there seemed to be little motive, Cesare was suspected of murdering his kinsman. It was known that

Cesare needed little motive—a look would suffice to annoy him and bring him to the decision that the one who had given it was unfit to live.

On account of the Cardinal's death, Cesare decided to enter Rome in mourning. It was an effective spectacle and the people who watched it did so in silence. The carriages—one hundred of them—which came in advance of the soldiers were draped in black; there were no drums nor fifes, and the only sound heard in the streets of Rome was the tramp of feet and the roll of carriage wheels. The Swiss guards wore black velvet, and the great black plumes in their hats made them look like menacing birds of prey as they marched.

Cesare himself was a somber figure in black velvet, its darkness accentuating the bright auburn of his hair and beard. Beside him rode his brother Goffredo with Alfonso who, on the Pope's instructions, had gone to the gates of the city to ride with Cesare.

Above the soldiers, floated the banners with their emblems of the Grazing Bull and the Golden Lilies of France.

Lucrezia, watching from the balcony, could not take her eyes from the three men—all of them so handsome—Cesare in the center, aloof in his black velvet doublet from the brilliantly clad and bejeweled young men on either side of him.

Lucrezia saw that her handsome husband was nervous. There was in his eyes that expectancy, that furtive horror, which she had noticed before when he was in the company of her brother Cesare.

Cesare HAD arriveD in Carnival time, and the people were given a subject for their revelry which was certain to please the Pope. There were masques depicting Cesare's victories over his enemies; poems and songs were written of his brilliant soldiery and his daring campaigns.

Cesare was in good spirits. He had no doubt that he would achieve his destiny. He danced with Lucrezia in the presence of his father and their dances were those of Spain. He had renewed his pursuit of Sanchia, and it was reported throughout Rome that they were lovers again. Goffredo worshipped his brother and sought to copy him in everything; he was delighted that his wife pleased the great Cesare, and took to himself great credit for having

married her that he might provide Cesare with the best mistress he had ever
had.

As for Sanchia, her feelings toward him were mingled; she hated him yet
she found him irresistible; and as before, her hatred increased her passion.

But there was one thing which struck Cesare during this time. Lucrezia
was no longer a child, no longer so pliable; and he realized with a shock that
her loyalty to her husband might prove greater than that which she had for him.

Lucrezia had been present at those occasions when members of the Neapolitan and Milanese factions had put their heads together and plotted against
Cesare Borgia. Lucrezia, his own sister, might be working against him!

Cesare noted the Pope's devotion to his grandson. If the baby was in the
Vatican gardens, Alexander would find some pretext for going out to him. He
was becoming almost foolish in his adoration of his grandchild, and this was
to a certain extent the measure of his love for Lucrezia.

With growing suspicion Cesare began to reassess the state of affairs in the
Vatican. His sister's husband was his enemy and had great influence with his
sister, who in her turn had great influence with the Pope.

There was only one person who must be allowed to dominate the Pope;
and there was only one whom his sister must serve: Cesare Borgia.

He began to make plans concerning that very handsome but very weak
boy to whom they had married Lucrezia.

He found it difficult to be polite to the young fool, and increasingly
irksome to see them together, to witness a hundred little signs of their fond
and foolish love. The thought of their eagerness for each other drove Cesare
to something like a madness, from which even the inordinate sensuality of
Sanchia could not relieve him.

He would sit in his rooms above the Pope's in the Vatican, for on his
return to Rome he had not gone to his own palace, and there he would make
plans. He would look out over Rome, of which he was now master, as his
troops were camped all around the city and in their hands was the law. If any
committed a misdemeanor—and a misdemeanor could be an idle word spoken
in a tavern against Cesare Borgia—they would not repeat it. The gallows on
the St. Angelo's Bridge was well supplied with hanging corpses, a lesson for
all to see.

He was lord of Rome. He was Cesare.

So why should he allow an insignificant and foolish youth to irritate him?

THUNDER AND LIGHTNING rent the darkness over the eternal city. It was the Feast of St. Peter, and there was not a soul to be seen in the streets, for all had scuttled to safety as the first great raindrops had begun to fall. The rain splashed down in the streets and danced back as though in fury. Overhead the sky was black; and in their houses the people trembled.

Alexander was in his apartments with the Bishop of Capua and his chamberlain, Gasparre, executing some formal and unimportant business.

"How dark it is!" he said, looking up. "I cannot see to read."

"The storm grows fierce, Most Holy Lord," said the Bishop.

"We shall have to have lights," replied the Pope. "And see, the rain is coming in through the windows."

Gasparre was on his way across the apartment to call for lights and the Bishop had gone to the window when the roof immediately above the Papal chair collapsed.

Gasparre cried out in alarm and he and the Bishop, choking with the dust which filled the air, ran to that spot where the Pope had been sitting.

They could not lift the heavy beams, so they ran from the apartment shouting for help.

"The Pope is dead," cried Gasparre. "The roof has collapsed and he in the chair is buried beneath the masonry."

Guards and officials were running into the apartments; and it was not long before the news was spreading through Rome: "The Pope is dead. This is the work of God. He has been struck down because of his evil deeds. God has taken his life, as he and his son have taken the lives of so many."

The people were preparing to riot, as they invariably did on the death of the Pope. The wise ones barricaded themselves in their houses; and guards were placed at the gates of the Vatican.

IN THE POPE'S apartment men worked hard to lift the fallen masonry.

"He cannot be alive," they said.

They crossed themselves; they believed that what they saw was the work of God. They were astonished though that God had not taken Cesare with his father. Cesare's rooms above the Pope's had been hit; his floor had collapsed and it was under this that the Pope now lay buried; but Cesare had left his apartments only a few moments before the lightning had struck a chimney and a thunderbolt had crashed through the roof.

Cesare heard the news and came hurrying to his father's apartment.

He was horrified. In those moments he realized that he needed his father as much now as he had needed him all his life. If the Pope died there would be a new Pope, and what of Cesare's grandiose plans then? How could he carry them out without the help of the Holy Father? Who would respect him without the might of his father behind him?

"Oh my father," he cried. "You must not die. You shall not die."

Calling for shovels and axes, he tore at the masonry, his hands bleeding, the sweat pouring down his face.

"My lord," gasped Gasparre, "His Holiness cannot be alive."

Cesare turned and struck the chamberlain across the face.

"Work harder!" he shrieked. "He is under there and he is not dead. He is not dead, I tell you."

Under his orders the men obeyed; sweating and panting they lifted the great beams and at length Cesare discovered a corner of the Pope's cloak. He seized it with a shout of triumph and in a few breathless minutes Alexander, unconscious and bleeding from cuts, was exposed to their view. Cesare shouted orders. "Help me carry him to his bed. Send for physicians. Let no one delay. If my father dies, so shall you all."

Alexander was very weak, but he was not dead and, when Cesare knelt down and called aloud his thanks to God and the saints for his father's escape, he opened his eyes and smiled at his son.

"Oh my father," cried Cesare, "you are still with us. You must not leave us. You must not."

His voice had risen to a hysterical cry which the Pope seemed to interpret as a call for help; slowly he smiled, a beautiful smile of reassurance; and those watching said: "These Borgias are not human. They have powers of which we know nothing."

The doctors said that the Pope had sustained a great shock, that he was suffering from an acute fever, and that there must be more bleeding.

"Then bleed him," cried Cesare. His eyes glinted threateningly. "His life is in your hands. Forget it not, for I never will."

He sent for Lucrezia and they sat together in the sickroom, their arms about each other, fearful for the life of the beloved man in the bed.

"You will nurse him, Lucrezia; you only," insisted Cesare; his eyes wide with fear; for he believed that there might be some to seize this opportunity and attempt to do that to the Pope which he and his son had done to so many. Cesare put his face against his sister's. "You, I . . . and our father . . . we are as one," he went on. "We must be together . . . always. Therein lies our strength and our happiness."

"Yes, Cesare," she answered.

"Do not forget it, sister. We may be Pope . . . we may be General . . . we may be wife and mother . . . but first—always first—we are Borgias."

She nodded, and she was afraid. She had seen lights in Cesare's eyes which terrified her.

But at this time there must be no thought in her head but that of her father's well-being. It would be her duty and her pleasure to nurse him back to health.

ALEXANDER was a Titan. A few days after the accident, which would have proved fatal to most men of his age, he was sitting up in bed, as merry as he had ever been, with the members of his family about him, his intellectual powers undiminished, receiving ambassadors, conducting matters of Church and State with a vigor which would have been astonishing in a man twenty years his junior. His eyes dwelt more fondly on one member of the family than on any other: his beloved daughter Lucrezia. Cesare was conscious of this.

Alexander had been aware of Cesare's alarm and grief but he knew the reason for his hysterical emotion was in a large measure due to fear of the loss of that great protective canopy of Papal influence under which Cesare was sheltering. Cesare knew, as did every head of state in Italy, that once that canopy was removed, Cesare and all his brilliant triumphs would not last four days. Cesare had every good reason to keep his father alive.

But the fear in Lucrezia's eyes was not for her own future. Dear improvident child! she did not think of that. She had laid her hands against his chest and wept in her emotion of love. She had said: "Most beloved, Most Holy Father, how could I endure my life without you!"

It was gratifying to know that his son realized the worth of his father's protection; but the knowledge of his daughter's disinterested love was more precious than anything in Alexander's life at this time.

He loved her more deeply than ever before. His eyes followed her about the room, and he was uneasy when she was not there.

He declared: "I will have none but my daughter to nurse me."

And when she threw herself beside his bed and declared with tears in her eyes that she would be near him night and day, they mingled their tears, and then because the Pope had never encouraged tears in himself or his family, he held her to him and cried: "For what do we weep? We should laugh, daughter, sing songs of joy, for what father in this world was ever blessed with such a daughter, and what daughter ever had such love from a father as I give to you?"

She must leave Santa Maria in Portico and stay in the Vatican. An apartment must be made ready for her next his own. Then he would rest easily knowing that at any hour of the day or night he had only to call to bring her to his bedside.

There were two who watched with dissatisfaction. Cesare because he could see that his sister's influence with their father could at any moment outstrip his own; Alfonso because Lucrezia had moved to the Vatican where he was not allowed to join her, and this meant that he must, temporarily, give up his wife to her father.

Alfonso fretted and spent a great deal of time with his friends, those men and women with whom he had associated in Lucrezia's apartments before the French invasion. They were mostly Neapolitans, who were on the alert, measuring the extent of the alliance between the Borgias and the French.

Cesare, knowing this, told himself that Alfonso was more than an irritation. He was a danger. Lucrezia was devoted to him; what might he not ask of her, and knowing her influence with the Pope, what might come of it?

It seemed to Cesare that Alfonso—insipid youth though he was—was one of his most dangerous enemies.

During that July of the Jubilee year 1500 there were many pilgrims in Rome. Christians were arriving from every part of Europe and many of them, either because of poverty or piety, spent their nights sleeping against the walls of St. Peter's.

It was a night of moonshine and starlight, and Alfonso was taking supper with Lucrezia in her apartments of the Vatican. They were alone together and Alfonso, saying his last farewell complained bitterly of the need to leave her.

"Very soon, dearest, my father will be recovered," said Lucrezia. "Then I shall be with you in Santa Maria."

"He is well enough now for you to leave him," retorted Alfonso sulkily.

"He needs me here . . . for a little longer. Be patient, my dear husband."

Alfonso kissed her. "I miss you so much, Lucrezia."

She touched his face tenderly. "As I do you."

"Dearest Lucrezia, the nights seem long without you. I dream still . . . !"

"Your nightmares, dearest? Oh that I were there to comfort you and tell you there is nothing to fear. But soon, Alfonso . . . perhaps next week."

"Next week, you think?"

She nodded. "I will speak to my father."

"I long for next week."

They embraced and, as it was approaching midnight, he left her.

With his gentlemen-in-waiting, Tomaso Albanese and his squire, he left the Vatican and came into the Square. It was very quiet, as the place was deserted except for a group of pilgrims who huddled on the steps of St. Peter's.

"It may well be," said Alfonso to Albanese, "that this time next week we shall no longer have to make these journeys. My wife will be with me in Santa Maria."

"I rejoice, my lord," answered Albanese.

They had moved a little nearer to the group of pilgrims. Alfonso scarcely glanced at them because they were such a common sight; but as he walked on there was a sudden movement, a rustle, the sound of quick footsteps and, startled, Alfonso and his two men suddenly found themselves surrounded.

It happened in a few seconds. The pilgrims had thrown back their ragged cloaks, and their swords were poised ready for action. Alfonso realized that he had been ambushed and that his life was in imminent danger. But he was young and strong, and expert with the sword.

"On guard," he shouted, and drew his sword, but even as he gave the order his shoulder was pierced, and the hot blood was streaming down the gold embroidery of his doublet.

Albanese and the Squire had drawn their swords and were giving a good account of themselves against the attackers; but the latter had the advantage in numbers, and Alfonso was already faint from loss of blood.

A sword of one of his assailants pierced his thigh, and with a groan he fell fainting to the ground. Two of the "pilgrims" then tried to pick him up and hustle him to a waiting horse, but the gallant Albanese and the Squire, while calling loudly for the Papal Guards, threw themselves into an attack against those who were seeking to remove Alfonso.

There was a shout from the precincts of the Vatican followed by the sound of running feet.

"Disperse!" cried one of the attackers, and they all leaped on to their horses and galloped away as the first of the Papal Guards made his appearance.

"We have been attacked!" cried Albanese. "Our master is in urgent need of attention."

They picked up Alfonso and, with the help of the guards, carried him into the Vatican.

"My wife..." murmured the fainting Alfonso. "Take me to my wife... and no other."

Lucrezia was with her father, sitting on one side of his bed while Sanchia sat on the other, and thus it was into the Pope's bedchamber that Alfonso was carried.

Lucrezia gave a cry of horror as they laid Alfonso on the floor, and then with Sanchia she rushed to him and knelt beside him.

"Alfonso... my dearest!" cried Lucrezia.

Alfonso's eyes were glazed. He looked appealingly into Lucrezia's face. "Save me, Lucrezia," he murmured. "Do not let him come near me..."

Sanchia gave orders to the men: "Call the physicians without delay. Some of you help us to get him to a bed. Bring hot water and bandages! Oh my brother, have no fear. We will save you."

But he kept his eyes on Lucrezia as he said distinctly so that all could hear: "I know who has sought to kill me. It is your brother... Cesare!"

Then he closed his eyes; and all those in the room believed that he would never open them again.

ALfonso lay in the Borgia Tower, in a room the walls of which had been decorated by Pinturicchio. Sanchia was with him; so was Lucrezia; they had cut away his doublet and staunched the flow of blood while they waited for the physicians to come and dress his wounds.

"Together and alone we will nurse him," said Sanchia to Lucrezia. "It is the only way if he is to live."

Lucrezia agreed. She was conscious now of the reality of that terror which had overshadowed Alfonso's happiness and she was determined to nurse him back to health. She knew against whom she had to protect him, and she was determined to do this.

"I will have beds made for us in this room," she said.

"Beds for both of us," added Sanchia. "Lucrezia, if he lives after this night's outrage, we alone must prepare his food, and we must not leave the room together. One of us must always be here."

"It shall be so," said Lucrezia.

They were interrupted by the arrival of the Neapolitan ambassador.

"How fares my lord?" he asked.

"We cannot say yet," answered Sanchia.

"His Holiness is insistent that I remain while the physicians dress his wounds."

Sanchia nodded.

"Why are the doctors so long in coming?" cried Lucrezia. "Do they not understand that delay is dangerous?"

Sanchia put her arm about Lucrezia. "My dear sister," she said, "you are overwrought. They will be here soon . . . and if he lives through this night . . . we will save him. You and I together."

When the physicians came Sanchia drew Lucrezia to a corner of the room while Alfonso's wounds were dressed and the ambassador looked on.

Sanchia's voice was cold and angry as she whispered: "Lucrezia, you understand what this means . . . all that this means?"

"I heard his words," Lucrezia replied.

"We have to fight *him!* We have to fight your brother and my lover for Alfonso's life."

"I know it."

"They would have taken him to the Tiber, as they did your brother Giovanni. It is the same method . . . so successful before. Thank God it failed this time."

"Thank God," whispered Lucrezia.

"There will be other attempts."

"They shall not succeed," declared Lucrezia fiercely.

"The Pope understands. That is why he insists on the Neapolitan ambassador's watching the dressing of the wounds. He does not want it said that poison was inserted into his blood by the Papal doctors. You love him, do you not? He is your husband and should be more to you than any other. Can I trust you with my little brother?"

"Can I trust *you* with my husband?"

Then they began to cry and comforted each other, until Sanchia said: "It is not the time for tears. If he recovers we will have a stove brought into this room, and all that he eats shall be prepared by us. We will stand guard over him, Lucrezia . . . my little brother, your beloved husband."

"It is wonderful, Sanchia," said Lucrezia, "at such a time to have someone whom one can trust."

"I feel that too," answered Sanchia.

In the streets the people stood in little groups, discussing the attempt on the life of Alfonso of Bisceglie. In the Vatican there was much whispering and hurrying to and fro.

In the sick-room Alfonso hovered between life and death, and two women with a fierce fanaticism in their eyes stood guard over him. In a corner of that room two beds had been placed, although they were not occupied at the same time. When Sanchia slept Lucrezia was on guard and Lucrezia slumbered while Sanchia watched Alfonso. They had had a field-stove brought into the apartment in readiness, to prepare his food.

Sanchia had demanded that the guards placed outside the apartment should be those whom she was sure she could trust—members of her own household and her brother's. She sent messages to her uncle, King Federico, telling him what happened, and as a result Messer Galeano da Anna, a noted

Neapolitan surgeon, arrived in the company of Messer Clemente Gactula, Federico's own physician.

By this time it seemed almost certain that Alfonso would live, and now that he was well enough to realize that either Lucrezia or Sanchia was constantly with him and that his doctors were those sent by his uncle, he felt a new confidence and with this came a new strength.

The Pope was a little irritated by his daughter's desertion of his own sick-room for that of her husband. He hinted that it was a little melodramatic of the two women to watch over Alfonso as though his life were still in danger.

But Alexander was worried. He was fully aware who was responsible for the attack, and this meant that he could only pretend that he wanted his son-in-law's would-be murderers brought to justice.

It was said in the Vatican and in the streets that if Alfonso recovered from this attack it would not be long before he met with another, for it was clear that Cesare Borgia, the dreaded Il Valentino, was behind this attempt on his life.

They were very anxious days for Lucrezia. How could she help recalling that period of great anguish when she had learned that her lover's body had been found in the Tiber? She knew who had arranged poor Pedro's death. It was the same one who had tried to strike down Alfonso.

Sometimes Alfonso would call out in his sleep and she would rush to his bedside to soothe him. She knew that his nightmares were always of threatening danger, and there was one name which he never failed to whisper—Cesare!

Lucrezia decided that she must see her brother; she must make him understand how devotedly she loved Alfonso. Cesare loved her. Had they not always been close? Surely he could not continue to plot Alfonso's death if he understood how much she loved her husband.

She left Sanchia with Alfonso and went to Cesare's apartments.

Her brother's eyes shone with mingled affection and speculation. "My dearest sister, it is rarely that you have given me this pleasure of late."

"I have been nursing my husband."

"Ah, yes. And how fares he?"

"He will live, Cesare, if his attacker does not make another and successful attempt."

"How could that be while his two guardian angels watch over him?" said Cesare lightly. "You look tired, my beloved. You should rest. Or better still, ride with me. What say you . . . out to Monte Mario?"

"No, Cesare. I must go back to my husband."

He took the back of her neck in his hands and squeezed gently. "Have you no time for your family?"

"Our father is well again," she said; "you do not need me, and my husband has been wounded nigh to death. Oh Cesare!" Her voice broke suddenly. "There is a great deal of scandalous talk. People say . . ." She faltered, and his hands on her neck tightened. He put his face close to hers, and the gleam in his eyes frightened her.

"What do people say?" he demanded.

"They say that he who was behind the killing of the Duke of Gandia was behind the attempted killing of Alfonso."

She lifted her face and forced herself to look into his eyes.

"Cesare," she insisted, "what have you to say to that?"

She saw his mouth tighten; she was aware of the intense cruelty in that face, as he answered brutally: "If it was so, there is no doubt that he had his reasons; and I am certain that your little husband deserved his wounds."

She had been trying to tell herself, against her better judgment, that it could not be Cesare, but she found it impossible to deceive herself longer.

Cesare pulled her to him, his fingers still on her neck, and she suddenly felt that he saw her as a kitten, a pretty playful kitten whose charming ways delighted him when he deigned to be amused by them. He kissed her. "You must not tire yourself," he said. "But I shall not insist on your riding with me today. I would have you come of your own free will."

"That will be when Alfonso is quite well," she answered firmly, disengaging herself.

"In the meantime," he said, "you and the militant Sanchia will guard him well, knowing that what fails at noon may be successful at night."

She lowered her eyes and did not answer. Her throat was constricted with an emotion which she ascribed to fear.

Back in the apartment she consulted Sanchia.

"I have been with Cesare, and I know that he will not rest until he has killed Alfonso."

"I know it too," replied Sanchia.

"He will make another attempt, Sanchia. What can we do?"

"We are here to prevent that attempt."

"Is it possible, Sanchia?"

"I do not think," said Sanchia, "that while you and I are near any will come to attack him. Cesare is suspect. If any were taken in the act and put to the Question they might confess. A confession involving Cesare would not please him."

"But, knowing Cesare is involved, my father would never allow the murderers to be brought to justice."

"It would be difficult to murder Alfonso here in the Vatican itself. No, I believe they will wait until he is well, and then they will lure him to some lonely spot. They will attack then. It is later that we have to fear such an attack. What we must guard against now is poison."

"Sanchia, I am frightened. I see shadows all about me. It is like being alone in the dark when I was very young and peering into the shadows, waiting for wild beasts and ghosts to spring at me."

"There is a vast difference," said Sanchia grimly. "These are not ghosts."

"Sanchia, we must get him out of Rome."

"I have been turning over plans in my mind for days."

"Can we do it?"

"We will. As soon as he is well we will have him smuggled out of Rome. We'll disguise him as one of the chamberlains and send him with a letter which I will write to my uncle Federico. We will do it, Lucrezia."

"Thank you, Sanchia, thank you for all you have done for my husband."

"Who," Sanchia reminded her, "is also my brother. Listen, Lucrezia. When the doctors come tomorrow we will consult with them. You know that little hunchback from Alfonso's household?"

"He who loves Alfonso so much, and has waited outside this room ever since it happened?"

Sanchia nodded. "We can trust him. He will be able to have horses ready, and as soon as Alfonso's wounds are healed, he shall escape. Tomorrow we will begin preparations to put the plan into action."

SHE SAT BY Alfonso's bed, holding his hand. He had just awakened from one of his nightmares.

She put her face close to his. "Alfonso, my dearest, all is well. It is I . . . Lucrezia."

He opened his blue eyes and she felt a surge of tenderness, for he looked very like little Roderigo.

"Lucrezia," he murmured, "stay close."

"I am here. I shall remain here. Try to sleep, my darling."

"I am afraid of sleep. I dream, Lucrezia."

"I know, my love."

"He is always there ... in my dreams. He bends over me ... that cruel smile on his lips ... that gleam in his eyes, and his sword raised. There is blood on that sword, Lucrezia. Not my blood. His brother's blood...."

"You distress yourself."

"But he will not rest until he is rid of me, Lucrezia. He is your brother and you have loved him. You have loved him too much. Your father protects him. You all protect him."

"I have one thought only, Alfonso—to protect you, to make you well. Listen, my dearest, there are plans afoot. As soon as you are well enough you are going to slip away from Rome."

"And you?"

"I shall follow you."

"Come with me, Lucrezia."

"And our baby?"

"We must all go together. No more separations."

She thought, the three of us to escape; that would not be easy. But she would not disturb him now by pointing out the difficulties. Let him dream of their escape. Let him replace his nightmare with that happy dream.

"The three of us," she said. "We will go together."

"I long for that night. 'Twill be at night, will it not? You and I ... and the child, riding away to safety, Lucrezia. When ... *when?*"

"When you are well enough."

"But it will take so long."

"No. Your wounds are healing. You are very healthy, they tell me. Your blood is good. Few would have recovered as quickly as you have. It will not be long now. Think of it, Alfonso. Think of it all the time."

He did think of it; and when he slept there was a happy smile on his lips.

Alfonso was now able to walk about the apartment. He would sit on the balcony overlooking the Vatican gardens, and feel the warm sun on his face. The doctors said that he would soon be ready to sit his horse.

He was longing for that day.

Sanchia or Lucrezia had first held his arm as he tottered about the apartment, and it was a great day when he walked unaided to the balcony.

"Soon," Lucrezia whispered.

"We must wait," Sanchia said, "until he is strong enough to endure a long journey."

So he took exercise, and waited, and longing began to take the place of fear in Alfonso's blue eyes.

The little hunchback, whom he had befriended and who was ready to give his life for him if need be, was constantly in attendance and one day, when he, Alfonso, was sitting on the balcony, he called to the little fellow to bring him a cross-bow so that he could discover whether he had strength to shoot a bird in the gardens.

The cross-bow was brought, and he tried it.

He missed the bird and sent the hunchback down into the gardens to retrieve the bolt.

Cesare was walking in the gardens with Don Micheletto Corella, one of his Captains, when he saw the hunchback running swiftly across the grass to retrieve the bolt.

"Is that not the servant of my brother-in-law?" he asked.

"It is indeed, my lord, and do you not see your lord-ship's brother-in-law at the window now, the cross-bow in his hands?"

"By all the saints!" cried Cesare. "We have narrowly escaped death."

The Captain returned his master's smile. "Had the bolt pierced one of our hearts, my lord, we should indeed not be alive."

"So . . . he would attempt my life!"

"None could blame your lordship if, in the circumstances, you demanded his."

Cesare laid his hand on the man's shoulder; they smiled. It was the opportunity they had been waiting for.

It was afternoon and many were sleeping in the August heat. Alfonso was resting on his bed. The exercise of the morning had tired him. Lucrezia and Sanchia sat on either side of the bed. They were dozing lightly.

Suddenly there was a commotion outside the room, and Sanchia went to see what was happening, Lucrezia following her. At the door they saw soldiers arresting the guards.

"What is this?" demanded Sanchia.

"If it please the Madonna," explained Captain Micheletto Corella, "these men are all accused of a plot against the Pope."

"It is not possible," cried Lucrezia.

"These are my orders, Madonna," was the answer.

"What is this plot?" demanded Sanchia.

"I do not know, Madonna. I merely obey orders." He looked at them with respectful kindness, as though he were disturbed to see two such beautiful ladies in distress. He went on: "His Holiness is but two doors away. Why do you not go to him and ask him to release these men, if you are so sure of their innocence?"

Lucrezia and Sanchia ran toward the Pope's apartments.

He was not there.

Then suddenly they looked at each other and, without a word, ran back as fast as they could to Alfonso.

They were too late.

Alfonso lay across his bed. He had been strangled by the cruel hands of Micheletto Corella.

III

THE CASTLE OF NEPI

THE cortège made its dismal way to the little church in the shadow of St. Peter's. It was dusk and the light of twenty flares showed the way to Santa Maria delle Febbri. Mingling with the shuffling footsteps of the friars were their low voices as they chanted prayers for the soul of the dead man.

The apartments of Santa Maria in Portico were filled with the gloom of mourning. Red-eyed servants spoke in whispers, and silent-footed slaves passed one another with downcast eyes.

And in the rooms of Madonna Lucrezia there could be heard the sound of weeping voices as she and her sister-in-law reproached themselves while seeking to comfort each other.

✥

Sanchia, her beauty impaired by the signs of her sorrow, paced up and down Lucrezia's apartment, storming with rage one moment, collapsing on to Lucrezia's bed in misery the next.

"How could we have been such fools!" she demanded.

Lucrezia shook her head. "We should have known it was a trap."

"All the care we took . . . cooking his meals, watching over him, never leaving him for a moment without one of us with him . . . and then . . . to be such fools!"

Lucrezia covered her face with her hands. "Oh Sanchia, I have an unhappy feeling that I bring tragedy to all who love me."

"Have done with such talk," cried Sanchia. "They would not have dared, had we not left him alone. It is not some evil luck you must curse, but your own—and my—stupidity."

"It was such a short way to go."

"But we left him long enough for that brute to put his fingers at his throat and strangle him."

"He said that Alfonso suffered from a haemorrhage when he got up too quickly as they entered the room."

"Haemorrhage!" cried Sanchia. "Did we not see the bruises on his throat? Holy Mother, shall I ever forget?"

"Don't, I beg of you, Sanchia."

Loysella came hurrying into the apartment, fear in her eyes. "Il Valentino comes this way," she cried. "He will be with you, very, very soon."

Loysella dropped a curtsey and hurried out. She no longer had any wish to watch with coquetry the coming of Cesare Borgia.

"That he should dare!" cried Sanchia.

Lucrezia was trembling. She did not want to see him; she was afraid her feelings would get beyond restraint when she must look at this beloved brother—this once-beloved brother?—whom the whole of Rome knew as the murderer of her husband.

There was the sound of soldiers' footsteps on the stairs and, when the door was flung open, two of them stood on guard as Cesare came into the room.

Lucrezia had risen. Sanchia remained seated, her blue eyes flashing hate and scorn.

"Cesare . . ." stammered Lucrezia.

He looked at her coldly, marking the signs of her grief with distaste.

Sanchia cried out: "Murderer! How dare you come here to violate our grief?"

Cesare was looking at Lucrezia, talking to Lucrezia. "Justice has been done."

"Justice?" said Lucrezia. "That murder of one who did no harm to any!"

Cesare's voice was more gentle. "That he did no harm was no fault of his; he tried hard enough. He acted so that it was clear that it should be my life or his. I had no alternative but to make sure that it was not mine."

"He would never have hurt you," said Lucrezia. "He would never have hurt me by hurting you."

"You are too gentle, sister. You know not the ways of ambition. Why, shortly before he died he attempted to take my life. I saw him at his window, the cross-bow in his hand."

"He but shot idly to amuse himself and test his strength," said Lucrezia.

"Little thinking," cried Sanchia, "that it would give you the excuse you sought."

Cesare ignored Sanchia. He said: "There have been plots . . . plots against me . . . plots against the Papacy. Dearest sister, you have been an innocent dupe. They have been concocted in your own apartments; while you chatted of art and music, of poetry and sculpture, your late husband and his friends made their plans. His death was just."

"You admit to the murder?" said Sanchia.

"I admit to the justifiable killing of Alfonso of Bisceglie; and so shall die all traitors. Lucrezia, I come to you to say this: Dry your tears. Do not grieve for one who was your family's enemy, who plotted against your father and your brother." He came to her and took her by the shoulders. "Many members of your household are being placed under arrest. It is necessary, Lucrezia. My little one, do not forget. Have you not said that, whatever else we are, we are Borgias first of all."

He was trying to make her smile, but her expression was stony.

She said: "Cesare, leave me. I beg you, I implore you . . . go from me now."

He dropped his hands, and turning walked abruptly from the room.

※ ♛ ※

THE POPE SENT for his daughter, and received her with a certain amount of reserve; her blank expression and the marks of grief on her face vaguely irritated him. Alfonso was dead; no amount of grief could bring him back.

She was twenty, beautiful, and he was going to see that a worthy marriage was arranged for her. Why should she continue to grieve?

He kissed her and held her against him for a few seconds. The gesture was enough, in Lucrezia's emotional state, to set her weeping.

"Oh, come, come, my daughter," protested Alexander, "there have been tears enough."

"I loved him so much, Father," she cried. "And I blame myself."

"You . . . blame yourself! Now that is foolish."

"I had sworn to watch over him . . . and I left him . . . I left him long enough for my brother's murderers to kill him."

"I like not such talk," said the Pope.

She cried out: "It's true, Father."

"Your husband, my child, was a traitor to us. He received our enemies and plotted with them. He brought his own death upon himself."

"Father . . . *you* can say that!"

"My dear, I must say what I believe to be true."

"In your eyes Cesare can do no wrong."

He stared at her in amazement.

"My child, you would criticize us . . . your brother and your father . . . and all because of this infatuation for . . . a stranger!"

"He was my husband," she reminded him.

"He was not one of us. I am shocked. I am amazed. I never thought to hear you talk thus."

She did not run to him and beg his pardon, as she would have done a few months before. She stood still, her expression stony, caring little for the disapproval of her family so great was her grief, so overwhelming her sense of loss.

"Father," she said at length, "I pray you to give me leave to retire."

"I beg of you, retire at once, since it is your wish," said the Pope, and never before had he spoken so coldly to his daughter.

Alexander was growing more irritated. The position was a delicate one. The King of Naples was demanding to know how his kinsman had died. All the states and kingdoms were considering this matter of the murder of the Bisceglie. The murder of Giovanni, the Duke of Gandia, was recalled. "Cesare Borgia has murdered his brother and now his brother-in-law," it was said. "To whom will Il Valentino turn next? It would not be safe to enter that family."

And, mused Alexander, it is now necessary to find another bridegoom for Lucrezia; but this will have to be delayed until some of the more virulent rumors have died down.

But who would ever forget that disgrace of Lucrezia's first husband, the murder of her second?

The old Alexander would have blamed Cesare for his rash action in having had his brother-in-law murdered in such a way that it was obvious who was the murderer. The new Alexander did no such thing; he used his shrewd mind to fabricate excuses for his son.

He called Cesare to him, and they discussed the matter.

"We are being watched by every state and kingdom in the land," he began. "It is being said that there was no plot against us, and the murder was one of spite and hate, and that Alfonso was an innocent man."

"What care we for their opinions?"

"It is always better to lay a cloak of benevolent intentions and sound good sense over one's actions, my son. Alfonso was a foolish boy but he was a Prince of Naples."

Cesare snapped his fingers. "That for Naples and their bastard princelings!"

"We have the future to think of, Cesare. Do not let it be said that a Prince of Naples ... or Milan ... or Venice ... may visit us here in Rome, displease us in some way, and then lose his life. That may mean that, when we wish to receive such Princes in Rome, they will be chary of coming ... which could be an inconvenience. No. These people must understand that Alfonso was plotting here against you ... and you merely had him killed before he could kill you. You have imprisoned members of his household?"

"They are in Castel St. Angelo now."

"There let them stay. Now you must make an inquiry into these plots and send some account of it to Naples ... to Milan. Circulate it throughout Italy."

"The matter is done with," growled Cesare.

"Nay. No such matter is ever done with while there are men and women to remember that it took place."

"Very well. I will do it ... in good time."

"That is well, my son. And do it promptly, for before long you will be leaving us to rejoin your armies."

Cesare stood up suddenly and began hitting the palm of his left hand with the clenched fist of his right. "And to think," he said, "that my own sister should be making this more difficult for us!"

"She is a wife who loved her husband."

"She loved our enemy!" cried Cesare.

"It is sad to contemplate that she can forget our interests in her grief for his loss," admitted the Pope.

Cesare looked artfully at his father. A short while ago Lucrezia was his favorite child, and Cesare could have sworn that she had enjoyed more favor at the Vatican than any. Now the Pope was less pleased with his daughter. It was strange that Cesare should have had to commit a murder in order to oust his sister from first place in their father's esteem. Foolish Lucrezia! She had ruled by her love for her father—her gentle disinterested love. Now she had been unwise enough to show that her grief in the loss of her husband overshadowed her love for her father; and Alexander, who always turned from the unpleasant, disliked to see the grief of his daughter, and was irritated at the signs of tears on her face.

"This husband of hers, it seems, bewitched her," went on Cesare. "We were of little consequence to her when he was alive. Now that she has lost him she mourns him so bitterly that all Rome knows it. She has not appeared in public since it happened, but servants carry tales, and it may be that passers-by have seen her in loggias or on the balconies—a white-faced grieving widow. The people—the stupid sentimental people—are ready to weep with her and cry vengeance on those who rid Rome of a traitor because in so doing they brought tears to his widow's eyes!" Cesare's voice had risen to a scream. "Sanchia and she . . . they are together all the time, talking of his perfections, lashing each other to more displays of grief, crying out against his murderers. And this, oh my father, is Lucrezia Borgia—my sister, your daughter—so far forgetting that she is one of us that she—if only in her secret heart—calls down vengeance on her brother."

"She would never cry for vengeance on you, Cesare. She loves you dearly . . . no matter what passing fancies afflict her."

"I tell you at this time she has no thought for any but her dead husband. Separate them, Father, because they brew mischief. Send Sanchia back to Naples. And Lucrezia—send her away from Rome. No good can come of keeping her here."

The Pope was silent for a few seconds.

He was thinking: There is good sense in this. Let her go away from us. Let her quietly brood on her sorrow. She is a Borgia at heart. She is one of us. She will not long mourn him who cannot be brought back, however many tears are shed. A short stay in a quiet place, and she will pine for the pleasures of Rome, the affection of her family. Has she ever been happy for long without them?

Then he spoke: "You are right, my son. Sanchia shall go back to Naples. As for Lucrezia, she also shall leave Rome. I think a short stay in the castle of Nepi would be beneficial to her health."

So Lucrezia came out of Rome and traveled north along the Via Cassia through Isola Farnese, Baccano, Monterosi, to the dismal castle of Nepi.

Nepi, bleakly situated on a plateau surrounded by deep ravines through which flowed little streams, seemed the appropriate place in which to nurse a sorrow. Lucrezia however was unimpressed by its air of aloof solitude; she had no wish but to be alone.

From the peperino casements she would be able to look out across that strange country from the city walls of dark red tufa to the rushing water in the deep chasms, to the oak forests, black and forbidding on the horizon. From the topmost turret of the castle she could see the great volcanoes and the mountains of Viterbo; she could see Soracte and the sloping plateau which led down to the gleaming Tiber; and beyond, in a mist of blue haze, the Sabine mountains.

There was one comfort in her life now—her little Roderigo; and she rejoiced that he was too young to appreciate his loss.

All her attendants who accompanied her to Nepi were subdued, and behaved in accordance with the Spanish custom of mourning, which was more ceremonious than that of Italy.

Lucrezia dressed herself in black and took her meals off earthenware plates. She would shut herself into her apartment for hours and mentally reconstruct those happy two years which she had spent with Alfonso, reliving little details—the first time they had met, their wedding ceremony, the birth of Roderigo. And all the time she was trying not to remember that horrifying moment when she and Sanchia had returned from the Pope's apartment to find him lying across the bed . . . murdered.

But how could she shut out the memory? It was ever present. She would wake from sleep, thinking he was beside her. She would call his name and put out a hand to feel for him. The loneliness was unbearable.

The sorrow was with her every waking hour, and when she signed her letters she called herself The Unhappy Princess of Salerno.

$Giovanni$ $S\int orza$ was watching the march of events with horror. He knew that what had happened to Lucrezia's second husband might so easily have happened to her first. Disgruntled as he was, continually cursing the Pope, who had placed upon him the stigma of impotence, he realized that he had some reason to rejoice, for at least his life had been spared.

But even so, it was in danger.

Cesare Borgia was intent on setting up the Dukedom of Romagna for himself, and one of his strongholds would be the town of Pesaro, of which Giovanni Sforza was the Lord.

He knew, that September day, that Cesare was marching relentlessly forward. He knew that he would be powerless against him. And what would await Giovanni Sforza when he came face to face with Cesare Borgia? Giovanni had been the husband of Cesare's sister, and Cesare, who had murdered her second husband and had planned to murder her first, would not hesitate when he had that first husband within his power. And what sort of death could he expect at the hands of Cesare Borgia? The tales of the scandalous life led by the Borgias, many declared, had been started by Giovanni Sforza. It was true there had always been murmurings against them, but he had added plausibility to those tales.

If they had branded him as impotent, he had retaliated by branding them with the stigma of incestuous conduct.

Clearly, with Cesare's armies closing in, Pesaro was no place for him.

Whither could he go?

To Milan? The French had recaptured Milan once more, and his relative, Ludovico Sforza, was Louis' prisoner. He thought then of the Gonzagas of Mantua, as his first wife had been the sister of Francesco Gonzaga, that Marquis of Mantua who had won the victory at Fornovo which had been responsible for driving the armies of Charles VIII out of Italy after the previous French invasion.

So to Mantua went Giovanni Sforza, and there he was welcomed by Isabella d'Este who was the wife of Francesco Gonzaga.

Francesco was a great soldier who had won renown for his bravery, but his wife Isabella was a strong-minded woman with such a high opinion of her family, the Estes, that she deemed all others inferior to them. She was clever, politically acute, cultured and handsome; but there was in her a cold determination to dominate all who came within her sphere of influence.

When she had married him ten years before, Francesco bad adored her. She had seemed to him quite wonderful, combining handsome looks with a clever brain. As for herself, she tolerated him. She considered him far from prepossessing, for although he was tall and had a good figure he bore unmistakably the mark of his German ancestors; and the Hohenzollern features did not appeal to Isabella's sense of beauty. His nose had the appearance of being flattened out; his eyes looked sleepy; his forehead immense. His charm did not touch Isabella, and she was surprised that other women should be deeply conscious of it.

It was necessary to Francesco to indulge in love affairs outside his marriage as he was a deeply sensual man and, in any case in his time, men who did not so indulge were often accused of impotence.

What did it matter what mistresses he took, Isabella asked herself, as long as she produced sons for the glorification of her family and his?

Rumor had it that when, immediately after the birth of one of her children, she discovered it to be a girl, she rose from her bed and removed it from the elaborate cradle which had been prepared, as she pointed out, for a male child.

She was a strong woman, accustomed to rule, sharp-tongued, witty, elegant, admired and respected, but loved by few.

She had heard much about the women who were beloved by the Pope, and she was envious of them; therefore she was ready to grant asylum to Giovanni Sforza, when he came riding to Mantua to beg it, and received him with as much warmth as he could expect from a woman of her character.

"My dear Marchesa," he said, bowing over her hand, "I come to you as a beggar, knowing that the brother of my dear dead Maddalena would not turn me away."

"Certainly he shall not turn you away," said Isabella. "Certainly you shall have refuge here. There must be some place where those who have suffered at the hands of these outrageous Borgias should find rest."

"How happy I am that I came!"

Isabella looked at him with some scorn, since he was a weak man and she despised weakness. On the other hand she was looking forward to talking with him at her little court, and drawing from him further scandalous stories concerning the infamous Borgias.

So Giovanni was made welcome, and he found the cultured court of Mantua to his taste. Here wars were not considered of the greatest importance. Literature was discussed; matters of the mind. The Duke, with his military glory, might be an outsider, but let him go to his stables where he was breeding those horses which were fast becoming known as not only the best in Italy but in the world.

There was nothing which delighted Isabella more than to gather about her the wittiest people of Mantua and many of those from all parts of Italy who visited her court. She wished to be known, not as the virtual governor of Mantua only, but as patroness of the arts.

Conversation in her apartments must be witty; and she must reign indisputably queen—she, Isabella d'Este Gonzaga. Her father, the Duke of Ferrara, and her brothers all respected her political genius; they always had; and thus she had habitually visualized herself as the most brilliant member of the most important family in Italy. It was small wonder that she felt piqued to see the rise of another family and the power which the women of that family seemed to possess over its head.

Now with Giovanni Sforza in her salon she led the conversation to the affairs of the Borgias and declared that Giovanni Sforza, who had intimate experience of that strange family, would be able to tell them whether those tales they heard of the scandalous Borgias were really true.

So Giovanni told the stories which Isabella wished him to tell.

He had been forced to divorce Lucrezia! Why? Because His Holiness was so enamored of his daughter that he could not endure her having a husband. The marriage had not been consummated! Lies . . . all lies. It had been consummated a thousand times. And the golden-haired, innocent Lucrezia, who had stood before the assembly so demurely and declared herself still a virgin was then truly pregnant. But the child was not his.

The apartments of Mantua rang with laughter. Old scandals were revived; and Giovanni felt his vanity soothed in some measure. He could not fight the Borgias with arms, but he could with his tongue.

Lucrezia, SHUT in her apartments in the castle of Nepi, bent over the cradle of her child. Each time she looked at him she must be vividly reminded of all the wonderful plans she and Alfonso had made together; and she would weep afresh, telling herself that this little one would never know his father.

Her women had given up trying to comfort her; they wished that Madonna Sanchia were with them. She had been stricken in her grief also; but the two ladies would have done much to comfort each other.

And then suddenly one of the pages came running to Lucrezia's apartments to tell her that soldiers were approaching the castle.

Lucrezia threw back her hair which was less bright than usual (she had forgotten to wash it so frequently); her gown was black and plain; and she looked unlike the gay Lucrezia who had taken such pride in the elegant garments which she had worn in Rome.

She ran to her window that she might see who these soldiers were who had come to disturb the peace of Nepi.

A brilliant sight met her eyes as she looked down on the advancing men. They were singing as they came; and there was laughter in their ranks. Ahead of them were carried the yellow and red banners; and as she looked the heralds blew triumphal notes on their silver trumpets, and there was in those notes a joyous sound which seemed to shatter the melancholy of Nepi.

And then she saw him; he was riding at their head—the *condottiere* in his brilliant uniform—and her heart leaped with pride to behold him thus; and, for the first time in the six weeks since the most tragic day, Lucrezia smiled.

Then she hurried down to greet her brother.

He had leaped from his horse, throwing the reins to one of his men; he ran to her, picked her up in his arms and laughed into her face.

She looked at him for a moment; then she took his face in her hands and cried: "Cesare . . . oh, Cesare!"

But almost immediately it was as though Alfonso was with her, and she recalled that apartment in the Borgia Tower and Alfonso's limp body lying across the bed.

"Cesare," she said, "why have you come?"

"A strange question, sister. How could I pass within a few miles of your stronghold and resist the temptation of seeing you?"

"I had thought you would not come here," she answered dully.

He had put her on her feet and, placing his arm about her, he said: "I am hungry. We are all hungry. Can you not feed us?"

"We are unprepared," she said. She called to one of the dwarfs who stood watching the scene with astonishment. "Go to the kitchens. Bid them cook all they have. It would seem we have an army to feed."

The dwarf disappeared, and Cesare turned to one of his captains and gave him orders to look after the men, and find suitable billets in the town. He would stay the night at the Castle of Nepi.

When his captain had departed, he asked her to take him to that room where she spent most of her time, and she did so. They stood side by side, looking out on the awe-inspiring scenery.

"How are you faring in your battles?" she asked.

"So well," he replied, "that soon I shall be in possession of my kingdom."

"Did I not always say you would achieve your desires?"

"You did, sister."

"I remember so well how you railed against your Cardinal's robes."

"You see," said Cesare earnestly, "all such irritations pass. Like grief they loom large when they are close; they are infinitesimal in the distance. Look at the Sabine mountains . . . nothing but a chain of blue mist from this window. But stand beneath those towering peaks; there is a different story."

She smiled in agreement, and he put his hand under her chin and turned up her face to his.

"Thus it will be with you, sister."

She shook her head and would not meet his eyes, and for a moment anger shone in them. "Are you still moping here, Lucrezia?" he demanded. "Oh, it is wrong of you."

"I loved my husband," she answered. "You, who have never loved a wife as I loved him, cannot understand why his death should affect me as it does."

He laughed suddenly. "Before I leave here," he said, "you shall be gay once more."

"I heard you say you were staying but one night."

"Nevertheless, before I go you shall cease to think of your husband. Stop thinking of him, Lucrezia. Stop now."

She turned away. "Cesare," she said, "you cannot understand."

He changed the subject. "We will order food to be brought to us here . . . here in your room of shadows. Here we shall eat alone, you and I. What say you to that, Lucrezia?"

"I would rather that than sit down with your men."

He began to pace up and down the apartment. "I had pictured it differently . . . yourself eagerly greeting me . . . singing for me and my men . . . giving us a gay and happy evening, a memory which we could carry with us when we go into battle."

"I am in no mood for merrymaking, Cesare," she said.

Then he came to her again and took her by the shoulders. "Yet before I leave, I swear, your mood shall be changed."

She allowed her eyes to rest upon his face. She thought: Once I should have been frightened of Cesare in this mood; now I no longer care. Alfonso, my love, is dead; and when he died, I ceased to care what happened to me.

THE SMALL TABLE was laid in the room which overlooked the Sabine Mountains; there was a silver dish for Cesare, and an earthenware one for Lucrezia.

Cesare, frowning, called to a servant: "What means this? What is this from which you ask your mistress to eat?"

The servant was overcome by that fear which Cesare never failed to inspire. "If it please your lordship, it is the wish of Madonna Lucrezia to eat from earthenware as a sign of widowhood."

"It is ugly," said Cesare.

Lucrezia addressed the servant. "Leave the dish. It is my desire to eat from earthenware while I mourn my husband."

"You shall not eat from earthenware while you sit at table with me, sister."

"I am a widow, Cesare. I observe the custom of mourning."

"It is well to mourn when there is someone to mourn for," said Cesare. He called to the servant. "Bring a silver dish to replace this hideous thing."

"Nay . . ." began Lucrezia.

But Cesare had picked up the earthenware dish and thrown it at the servant. "A silver dish," commanded Cesare with a laugh.

And a silver dish was brought.

What did it matter? thought Lucrezia. Nothing could matter again. Could eating from an earthenware dish bring Alfonso back? Could it do him any harm if she ate from a silver dish?

They sat down and Cesare ate, but Lucrezia could swallow little.

"It is small wonder that you are looking frailer than ever," said Cesare. "I shall not have a good report to take to our father."

"I beg of you do not disturb him with tales of my ill health."

"And I beg you to regain your health and spirits. You will never do that while moping in this place. How can you be content here?"

"I can be as contented here as anywhere."

"Lucrezia, discard your mourning. The boy is dead. There are others in the world. I demand that you eat. Come . . . the food is good. You have an excellent cook here. I command you to eat. I shall insist, Lucrezia; so you must learn obedience."

"We are not in the nursery now," she said.

And she thought: No! Those days are far away. And it was as though the ghost of Giovanni, her murdered brother, came and stood at the table with the ghost of Alfonso.

If she were disturbed by these ghosts, Cesare was not. He had murdered her husband and their brother, yet he showed no signs of any qualms of conscience. It was necessary to Cesare to remove people, and he removed them. When they had gone he ceased to think of them.

"Then we will pretend we are," he said.

She answered boldly: "Then Giovanni would be here."

"There were happy days," he retorted, "when you and I were alone. Let us imagine one of those days."

"I cannot," she cried. "I cannot. When I think of nursery days I remember

Giovanni, even as I shall remember Alfonso, my husband, every minute of my life."

"You are talking like a hysterical woman, Lucrezia. It is not what I expect of you. Come, be my sweet sister. Lucrezia, *I* am here. I, Cesare. I have come here with the express purpose of making you forget your grief. Now . . . we will begin by eating and drinking together. Come, Lucrezia, be my sweet sister."

He was gentle suddenly, appealing to her love, and for a while she forgot that his hands were stained with the blood of her husband; and then she marveled at herself for forgetting.

She began to eat and, with his eyes upon her, she swallowed the contents of her silver dish.

He filled a goblet with wine and toasted her.

"To you, my love! To your future! May it be great and glorious."

"And to you, Brother."

"To our future then, which is one and the same. How could it be otherwise?"

He came to stand beside her at the table; he put his arm about her and drew her to him.

She thought: He is the greatest man in Italy. One day all will acclaim him; and he is my brother, who loves me . . . no matter what he does to others. He loves me . . . and no matter what he does to me, how can I stop loving him?

She was conscious of the old spell, and he knew it even as she did; he was determined that tonight he would carry her across the bridge which spanned the chasm between past and present; when she was safely over, he would make her look back and see that the past was vague and as shadowy as the Sabine Mountains seen from the castle of Nepi.

THey sat talking after the meal was over.

He wanted her to return to Rome. This was no place for her. She was young—only twenty—and was she going to spend the rest of her days pining for what could never be?

"I wish to stay here for a while," she told him. "Here I have solitude."

"Solitude! You were meant for company. Go back to Rome. Our father misses you."

"He does not like to see me with my grief upon me."

"Then he shall see you without it. He yearns to see you thus."

"He cannot. So I will remain here where I may nurse my sorrow as I wish to."

"You shall no longer nurse a sorrow for a worthless man," cried Cesare.

She rose, saying: "I will not listen to such words."

He barred her way. "You will," he said. He took a strand of her hair in his hands. "It is less golden that it was, Lucrezia."

"I care not," she said.

"And this gown," he went on, "is like a nun's habit. Where are your pretty dresses?"

"They do not interest me."

"Listen, my child, you will have a new husband soon."

"Do you think to tempt me with husbands as you would tempt a child with sweetmeats!"

"Yes, Lucrezia. And speaking of children, where is this child of yours?"

"He is sleeping."

"I have not seen him."

There was fear in her eyes. Cesare noticed it and exulted. He knew now that if he could not bend her through anything else he would through the child.

"You have no interest in the child," she said quickly.

Cesare's eyes were sly. "He is the son of his father."

"His grandfather . . . adores him."

"His grandfather's affection can be blown by the wind."

"Cesare," cried Lucrezia, "do not attempt to harm my child!"

He put his hand on her shoulder and grimaced as it touched the black stuff of her gown. "So ugly!" he said. "So unbecoming to my beautiful sister. Have no fear. No harm shall come to your son."

"If any tried to kill him, as they killed his father, they would have need to kill me first."

"Nay, do not excite yourself. Alfonso was a traitor. He sought to take my life, so I took his. But I do not concern myself with babies. Lucrezia, be serious. Be sensible. You will have to come back to Rome; and when you return you must be our merry Lucrezia. Let joyous Lucrezia come home and leave the weeping widow behind her."

"I cannot do it."

"You can." Then insistently: "You shall!"

"None can force me to it."

His face was close to her own. "I can, Lucrezia."

She was breathless; and he was laughing again, quietly, triumphantly. The fear of years took on a definite shape; she clung to fear, loving fear even as she loved him. She did not understand herself; nor did she understand him. She knew only that they were Borgias and that the bonds which bound them were indestructible while life lasted.

She was almost fainting with fear and with anticipated pleasure. In her mind two figures were becoming confused—Cesare, Alfonso; Alfonso, Cesare.

She could lose one in the other and, when she did that, she would lose the greater part of her misery.

She was staring at Cesare with wide-open eyes; and Cesare was smiling, tenderly, passionately, reassuringly, as though he were taking her hand and leading her toward the inevitable.

✦👑✦

He HAD gone and she was alone.

Everything had a different aspect now. The landscape was less harsh; she gazed often toward the misty Sabine Mountains.

Cesare had ridden away to fresh conquests. He would go from triumph to triumph, and his triumphs would be hers.

There were times when she wept bitterly; and times when she was triumphant.

How could she have thought that she could stand alone? She was one of them; she was a Borgia, and that meant that she loved the members of her family with a passion which she could give to no other.

Yet she was afraid.

She passed through many emotions. She washed her hair and ordered that her beautiful dresses might be brought to her: but when she examined her face in the mirror she was shocked by what she saw. She thought she saw secrets in her eyes and they frightened her.

She wanted to be in Rome with her father. Cesare would return to Rome some day.

She thought of their family relationship as something infinitely tender, yet infinitely sinister. She longed to be bound so tightly by those family ties that she could not escape; and then she was conscious of a longing to escape.

There were times when she thought: I shall never be at peace again unless I escape. I want to be as other people. If only Alfonso had lived; if only we had gone away together, right away from Rome; if only we had lived happily, normally!

She would tremble when she contemplated the future. Cesare had come to her at Nepi; he had disturbed the mournful solitude, the sorrowing peace.

With a shock she would remember that he was not only her brother; he was the murderer of her husband.

Then she knew she must escape the web into which she was being more closely drawn. She felt like a fly who has been caught on those sticky threads, caught and bound, but not so securely that escape was impossible.

Less than a month after Cesare's visit to Nepi she called her attendants to her and said: "I have my father's permission to return to Rome. Let us make our preparations and leave as soon as we may. I am weary of Nepi. I feel I never wish to see this place again."

※❦※

WHEN LUCREZIA ARRIVED in Rome, the Pope treated her as though her stay in Nepi had been merely a pleasant little holiday. He did not mention Alfonso, and was clearly delighted to have young Roderigo back.

Cesare's army was achieving its objectives, and the Pope was in a benign mood.

He walked with Lucrezia in the Vatican gardens and discussed the topic which was nearest his heart at the moment.

"My dearest," he said, "you cannot remain unmarried forever."

"I have been unmarried a very short time," said Lucrezia.

"Long enough . . . long enough. There is something which irks me from time to time, daughter. I cannot live forever, and I would wish to see you happily settled in a good marriage before I left you."

"A good marriage one week may be an unsuitable one the next, and marriage would seem, from my experience, a very unstable state."

"Ah, you are young and beautiful and you will have many suitors. Cesare tells me that Louis de Ligny would most willingly become your husband."

"Father, I would not willingly become his wife . . . nor any man's."

"But, my child, he is a cousin of the King of France and a great favorite of the King's. His future is rosy."

"Dearest Father, would you have me leave you to live in France?"

The Pope paused, then said: "I confess that has occurred to me as the great disadvantage of this match. Also the man wants an enormous dowry and makes fantastic demands."

"Then we'll have none of him, Father. I'll stay in peace with you awhile."

He laughed with her and declared he would snap his fingers at Louis' friend. He would never consent to giving his daughter to any who would take her miles away from her father.

But it was not long before he spoke to her of another offer. This time it was Francesco Orsini, the Duke of Gravina, who was very eager for the match and had most ostentatiously given up his favorite mistress that all the world should know how seriously he contemplated marriage.

"It is a pity he has given her up," said Lucrezia. "It was so unnecessary."

"He would be a good match, daughter. Like others he is greedy, of course, demanding offices in the Church, with good benefices to go with them, for his children by his previous marriage."

"Let him ask, Father. What matters it? There is no need for you to listen to his demands, for I shall not. Why do these men seek my hand in marriage? Have they not yet learned that my husbands are unlucky men?"

"You are so beautiful, so infinitely desirable," said Alexander.

"No," she answered; "it is simpler than that. I am the daughter of the Pope."

"Soon," went on Alexander, "Cesare will be home again. It makes me happy to have my children about me."

Cesare will be home! Those words rang in her ears. She thought of

Cesare's return, riding at the head of his men, the gay *condottiere* who would conquer all that lay before him. She felt that she was firmly caught in the web; and she could see no escape from it.

But perhaps there was one way of escape. If she married a ruler of some distant state she would be forced to leave her home and live with her husband.

It would be a bitter wrench, but she would be free, free from the Borgia might, from the Borgia stain; she would be free to be herself, to forget, to live as, deep down in her heart, she knew she had always wanted to live.

Thus it was that, when the name of Alfonso d'Este was mentioned as a possible suitor, she listened with some eagerness.

Alfonso d'Este was the eldest son of the Duke of Ferrara, and if she married him she would leave Rome and live with her husband in Ferrara, which as his father's heir he would one day govern.

That way lay escape.

IV

THE THIRD MARRIAGE

Wहेन Ercole, Duke of Ferrara, heard of the Pope's desire for a marriage between Lucrezia and his son Alfonso, he was incensed.

The old Duke was an aristocrat, and he considered this plan to foist a bastard on to the noble house of Este was an impertinence.

Now that he was sixty he knew that he had to contemplate that day when his son Alfonso would be head of the house, and he did so with a certain amount of misgiving. Ercole was a man of taste; he was deeply religious, and had at one time been a friend of Savonarola; he extended hospitality to the religious and the misconduct of the Borgias had filled him with horror.

He wished Ferrara to be apart from the rest of Italy and he had made it a center of culture. He encouraged literature and art, and his passions were music and the theater. He had offered hospitality to the great architect, Biagio Rossetti, and the result was apparent in the streets of Ferrara.

There was only one favorable aspect of the proposed marriage as far as Ercole was concerned; The Borgias were rich and, if he should ever demean himself and his family by agreeing to the match, he would be able to demand an enormous dowry. Ercole was a man who enjoyed hoarding money and hated to spend it.

Not, he brooded, that his son Alfonso was one who would be perturbed by the evil reputation of the family which was planning to marry into his. Alfonso was a coarse creature, and it was beyond Ercole's comprehension how he could have begotten such a son. Alfonso seemed to have no desire but to spend his days in his foundry experimenting with cannon, and his nights with women—the more humble the better. Alfonso had never cared for ladies of high degree; he preferred a buxom serving girl or tavern wench; his adventurers in low company were notorious.

Apart from a love of music which he had inherited from his father he did not seem to belong to the Este family. His brother Ippolito would have made a better heir; but Ippolito, as a second son, wore the Cardinal's robes, and in this he had something in common with Cesare Borgia—he hated them.

Where was Alfonso now? wondered Ercole. Doubtless in his foundry, testing his cannons. Perhaps one day they would be useful in war. Who could say? Perhaps he should go to Alfonso and tell him of this monstrous suggestion. But what would be the use? Alfonso would grunt, shrug his shoulders, and be quite prepared to spend half the night with the girl and doubtless soon get her with child, as he did half a dozen mistresses.

Duke Ercole decided he would not be able to discuss the matter with Alfonso.

His children, he was beginning to realize, were becoming unmanageable. Was that a discovery which must be made by all old men? Ippolito, elegant and handsome, was chafing against his Cardinal's robes. Ferrante, his third son, was wild, and he could never be sure what mad adventure he would undertake. Sigismondo was quiet, seemed to lack the ambition of his brothers and was clearly the one who should have worn the Cardinal's robes. Then there was Giulio of the wonderful dark eyes, his natural son—gay and handsome—a prime favorite with women. Ercole sighed. He had done his best to procure a high position in the Church for Giulio, but Giulio was not eager and had early in his life discovered a method of getting his own way.

There was also a daughter—Isabella—who had married Francesco Gonzaga and was now Marchesa of Mantua. Isabella should have been a man. Ercole would have enjoyed having her with him now to discuss this proposed marriage. Doubtless she had heard of it in her castle, on the Mincio; and how furious she would be. He pictured her with pride . . . there in her castle which contained some of the best sculpture in Italy together with paintings, books, and any object which had claim to beauty. Isabella was what Ercole had wished all his children to be—intellectual. She should have been a man of course. Still, she ruled Mantua, it was said, as any man might, governing her husband and their subjects; and she was referred to as "the first woman of her age." Isabella called attention to herself all the time. She made it known that her court was a refuge for artists; she must be unique; even her clothes were different from those worn by others, being designed by herself and made in the finest and most brilliantly patterned cloth. These clothes were copied, but by that time Isabella had discarded them.

Yes indeed, Ercole wished that Isabella was in Ferrara to give her opinion of the proposed marriage.

But she was not; so he must perforce go to the foundry to discuss it with Alfonso.

He made his way there. Alfonso was not in the building; he was lying out in the shade, eating a hunk of bread and an onion. His workmen lay beside him, and as he approached Ercole shivered with disgust, for it was impossible to tell which of those men was the heir of Ferrara and which his workmen. Alfonso was laughing heartily, possibly at some crude joke, and was fully at ease. But then he was always at ease. He did not care if the courtiers considered his manners crude; they were as Alfonso wished them to be and he made no apology for them. He would not even think of them. But at the same time he was clearly happier with the common people.

At the approach of the old Duke the workmen scrambled to their feet, and stood shambling and shuffling, not knowing how to act.

"Why, 'tis my father," cried Alfonso. "Have you come to see the cannon fired, Father?"

"No," said the Duke. "I have come to talk to you." He waved a white and imperious hand at the workmen, who glanced sheepishly at Alfonso and, on receiving a nod from him, moved off.

"Come Father, sit here in the shade," said Alfonso, patting the ground beside him.

The Duke hesitated, but he was hot and tired; and there was something endearing about this great bear of a man who was his eldest son, little as they had in common.

He looked about him for a moment and then sat down on the grass.

Alfonso turned his face toward him and as Ercole shrank from the strong odor of onion, he noticed that Alfonso's hands were grimy, and there was a rim of thick dirt under his nails.

"If ever an enemy came to Ferrara," he said, "I'd blast him out with my cannon."

"I trust it would be effective," said the Duke, flicking at a fly which had alighted on his brocade sleeve. "I have heard from the Pope. He hints that a marriage between you and his daughter would be desirable."

Alfonso went on chewing onion, quite unperturbed. His mind was on his cannon.

How insensitive! thought the Duke. What would a bride think of him? What had his first wife thought of him? Poor Anna Sforza! But perhaps he should not have said Poor Anna. Anna had known how to take care of herself. She had not been to Alfonso's taste. Not a feminine woman, but big and handsome. She had not had a chance against the greasy sluts of serving-girls who had claimed Alfonso's attention. Had she turned shuddering from those grimy hands, from that onion-tainted breath, from a husband who was full of animal desire and completely without the niceties of refined living? Alfonso never wasted his time wooing; he saw a girl, seduced her and, if the experience pleased him, repeated the performance. Otherwise the affair was forgotten. Alfonso was a hearty, virile man.

Anna Sforza had not really been disturbed. She had her own tastes and, although as wife to the heir of Ferrara, she had been ready to bear him children, she was clearly glad when Alfonso spent his nights with a humble mistress and left her to dally with that pretty Negress whom she adored.

But Anna oddly enough, in an attempt to do her duty, had met her death. She had died in childbed. Not the first nor the last woman to do so; yet in Anna's case it seemed doubly tragic.

"Well, Alfonso, what have you to say?"

"There has to be a marriage," murmured Alfonso absently.

"But with the Borgias!"

Alfonso shrugged.

"And she a bastard!" went on Ercole.

"You'll doubtless get a good dowry with her, Father," said Alfonso with a grin. "That should please you."

"Not for the biggest dowry in the world would I wish to see the house of Ferrara joined with that of the Borgias. Yet, if we refuse, we'll have the Papacy against us. You realize what that will mean in these days of unrest."

Alfonso's eyes were shining. "We'll use the cannon on any who come this way."

"Cannon!" cried Ercole. "Of what use are your cannon against the Pope's armies? And yet . . . and yet . . ."

"You'd be surprised if you saw them in action, Father."

"The Pope's armies . . ."

"No, no! My cannon. In days to come the cannon I shall make will have first place on the battlefield."

"It is of this marriage that I wish to talk. Oh Alfonso, have you no sense of the fitness of things?"

It was the old cry. Some years ago this son of his had been wagered that he would not walk through the streets of Ferrara naked, with a sword in his hand. He had accepted the wager and done this thing. He had not understood that the people who had watched his progress would never forget what the heir of Ferrara had done.

Oh, why was not Ippolito the eldest son? But Ippolito might have made trouble. Or Ferrante? Ferrante was reckless. Sigismondo? One did not want a priest to rule a dukedom. Giulio was a bastard and Giulio had been spoilt because of his beauty. But what was the use of railing against these sons of his? Alfonso was the eldest and for all his crudeness he was at least a man.

"Well, you do not seem in the least perturbed," said the Duke.

"There'll be compensations, I doubt not," murmured Alfonso. His thoughts were back in the foundry; at this time of day—unless some luscious girl crossed his path—cannons were so much more interesting than women.

"Oh, there might be compensations," agreed the Duke, rising, "but none would be great enough for me to welcome union with that notorious family."

He rose and walked away and, as he did so, he heard Alfonso, whistling— in the coarsest possible manner—to his men.

It was carnival time in Urbino, and Guidobaldo di Montefeltre, the Duke found himself forced to entertain Cesare Borgia while he was waiting for the surrender of the town of Faenza.

The Duke was not pleased, but he dared do nothing else. Cesare, who had now assumed the title of Duke of Romagna, was an enemy to be feared, as none was entirely sure in which direction his armies would turn next.

So to the castle came the newly made Duke of Romagna, and it was necessary for the Duke and his proud wife, Elizabetta Gonzaga (who was sister to Francesco Gonzaga, husband of Isabella d'Este) to receive Cesare with all honor.

Elizabetta hated the Borgias; she had a score to settle with them. Her husband had been prematurely struck down with gout and found walking difficult and he who had once been a great soldier was now a victim of periodic immobility. But the Duke was of a kindly nature and ready to forget the past. Elizabetta, proud, haughty, looking on herself as an aristocrat, resented the Borgias and the treatment her husband had received at their hands, for it was Guidobaldo who had been with Giovanni Borgia when war had been waged against the Orsinis at Bracciano; and forced to obey the unwarlike commands of Giovanni Borgia, Guidobaldo had been wounded and taken prisoner. It was during the months in a French prison that he had contracted his gout and his health had been impaired forever; during that time the Borgia Pope had made no effort to have him released, and it was his own family who had been hard pressed to find the necessary ransom.

Such matters rankled with a proud woman like Elizabetta; only one as gentle as Guidobaldo could forget.

Now they were forced to entertain Cesare, and, as in the ball-room, Cesare was looking about him for the most attractive of the women. Elizabetta watched him, her lips tight. She deplored the necessity to entertain one whose reputation was so evil.

Elizabetta, dressed in black velvet which she considered decorous, insisted that all her ladies wear the same, and Cesare, accustomed to the splendor of the Roman ladies felt his spirits flag.

He was wishing that he had not come to Urbino. The gouty old Duke and his prim wife were not companions such as he would have chosen, but he did enjoy a certain amount of fun by watching their apprehension.

"Yours is an attractive domain," he told them, and he let them see the glitter in his eyes.

They did not want trouble with the Pope, this Duke and Duchess; and they knew that the might of the Pope was behind his son.

Let them tremble in their shoes. If they could not give Cesare the entertainment he desired, at least let him enjoy what he could.

But Cesare suddenly discovered among the assembly a beautiful girl, and he immediately demanded of Elizabetta who she was.

Elizabetta smiled triumphantly. "She is a virtuous girl—Dorotea da Crema. She is staying here for a while but is on her way to join her future husband."

"She is enchanting to the eye," said Cesare. "I should like to speak with her."

"It might be arranged," said Elizabetta. "I will call her and her duenna."

"Is the duenna the plump lady in black? Then I pray you do not call her."

"My lord, even for you we cannot dispense with custom."

"Then," said Cesare lightly, "to enjoy the company of the beauty I must perforce put up with the dragon."

Dorotea was charming.

Cesare asked if he might lead her in the dance.

"I fear not, my lord," said the duenna. "My lady is on her way to join her future husband and, until she is married, she is not allowed to dance alone with any man."

"Alone . . . here in this ball-room!"

The duenna pursed her lips and held her head on one side with the air of one who has come up against an insurmountable obstacle. Cesare's anger flared up, but he hid it. The limpid eyes of the girl were on him for a second, before she lowered them.

"It is a senseless custom," said Cesare furiously.

No one answered.

He turned to the girl then. "When do you leave here?"

"At the end of the week," she answered.

She was very innocent, afraid of him, and yet a little attracted. Perhaps she had heard of his reputation; perhaps he seemed to her like the devil himself. Well, even the most innocent of virgins must be a little excited to be pursued by the devil.

"I leave tomorrow," he told her. "And that is as well."

"Why so?" she asked.

"Because, since I am not allowed to dance with you, it is better that we should not meet. I find the desire to dance with you overwhelming."

She looked eagerly at her duenna, but that lady was not glancing her way.

"What a bore is etiquette!" murmured Cesare. "Tell me, who is the most fortunate man in the world?"

"They say that you are, my lord. They talk of your conquests and say that every town you approach falls into your hands."

"It's true, you know. But I was referring to the man you are to marry. Remember that I am not allowed to dance with you; so I am not as fortunate as you had thought me."

"That is a small matter," she answered, "compared with the conquest of a kingdom."

"That which we desire intensely is never small. What is the name of your husband?"

"Gian Battista Carracciolo."

"Oh happy Gian Battista!"

"He is a Captain in the Venetian army."

"I would I were in his shoes."

"You . . . jest. How could that be so—you who are Duke of Romagna?"

"There are some titles which we would give up in exchange for . . . others."

"Titles, my lord? For what further title could you wish?"

"To be the lover of the fair Dorotea."

She laughed. "This is idle talk, and it does not please my duenna."

"Must we please her?"

"Indeed we must."

Elizabetta watched with satisfaction. She said to the duenna: "It is time your charge retired. We must not have her fatigued while she is with us. A long journey lies before her and travel can be so exhausting. Remember you are in my charge and I must consider your comfort."

The duenna bowed and Dorotea took her leave of Elizabetta. Her eyes lingered for a second on the figure of the Duke of Romagna. She shivered faintly, and was thankful that she was in the charge of her sometimes tiresome duenna.

Cesare felt angry and frustrated when she had gone. He was no longer interested in the entertainment, for the women seemed dull and prim to him, and he was filled with an urgent desire—which was fast becoming a necessity—to make the lovely Dorotea his mistress.

Dorotea rode out from Urbino surrounded by her friends and attendants.

They were all chatting about the ceremony and the clothes they would wear and how soon they would enter the Venetian Republic and there find Gian Battista Carracciolo waiting to greet them.

They were close to Cervia when a band of cavalry came galloping toward them. They were not alarmed; it did not occur to them that these horsemen would do them any harm; but as they came nearer it was seen that they were masked, and Dorotea was sure there was something familiar about their leader who shouted to them to halt.

The wedding party drew up. "You will not be harmed," they were told. "We seek one of your party; the rest may travel on unharmed."

Dorotea began to tremble, because she understood.

Her duenna said in a shaking voice: "You are mistaken in us. We are simple travelers on our way to Venice. We are going to attend a wedding."

The masked man who had seemed familiar to Dorotea had ridden up to her, forced her duenna aside and laid a hand on her bridle.

"Have no fear," he whispered. Then leading her horse after him, he moved away from the crowd while one of his men seized the youngest and prettiest of Dorotea's maids and the men galloped away taking the girls with them.

"How dare you!" cried Dorotea. "Release me at once."

Her captor only laughed, and there was something devilish in his laughter which filled her with terror.

She looked back; she could see the group on the road, the soldiers surrounding her party, preventing pursuit; and she knew that the masked man who had abducted her was Cesare Borgia; she knew the meaning of this and that Gian Battista Carracciolo would wait in vain for his bride, for Cesare Borgia had seen her, desired, waylaid her that his lust might be satisfied.

Isabella d'Este, when she heard of her brother's proposed marriage with Lucrezia, was furious.

She wrote at once to her father, Duke Ercole, and told him that on no account must Lucrezia Borgia join the family. It was preposterous. These upstart Borgias . . . who were they to think of mingling their blood with the best in Italy?

She could tell him a great deal about the Borgias. Giovanni Sforza, Lucrezia's first husband, had been staying in her court and the tales he had to tell would have been past belief if they had not concerned the Borgias.

The divorce had been arranged, so said Isabella, because the Pope was jealous of Lucrezia's husband and wanted her all to himself. Incredible? But these were Borgias. It was said that Lucrezia had been the mistress of all her brothers. That too seemed absurd. Must she remind him again that these were Borgias? Had he heard the latest scandal? Dorotea da Crema, on her way to meet her bridegroom, had been waylaid by Cesare Borgia and taken off to be raped. The poor girl had not been heard of since. And it was a member of that brute's family to whom her father was thinking of marrying the heir of Ferrara!

Isabella was right, mused Ercole. He wanted no Borgia in his family; but he must be very careful how he worded his refusal to the Pope.

There had been a time when a marriage between Alfonso and Louise d'Angoulême had been suggested. Therefore Ercole wrote, greatly regretting having to refuse the offer made by the Pope, but explaining that his son Alfonso had already made promises to this lady and was consequently not in a position to consider the brilliant marriage with His Holiness's daughter which the Pope so generously offered.

Ercole settled down in peace. Alfonso must marry soon. But it should not be with a Borgia.

WHEN ALEXANDER RECEIVED Ercole's letter he became pensive. It was clear to him that Ercole was not eager to ally his house with the Borgias. Then he grew angry.

There were other matters which gave cause for thought. The abduction and rape of Dorotea was arousing indignation throughout Italy, and even Louis of France had added his protest to the rest, sending, as a gesture of disapproval, Yves d'Allegre to Cesare to protest. Louis had been really angry, because the heartbroken bridegroom, Carracciolo, declared his intention of leaving Venice and searching through the whole country until he found his bride. As the Venetian army was under his command and there was fear of an invasion from Maximilian of Austria, there was great consternation among the French at the prospect of Carracciolo's desertion in order to conduct his purely personal affairs.

Cesare, confronted by the envoys of the King of France, denied all knowledge of the whereabouts of Dorotea.

"I have as many women as I want," he retorted. "Why should I cause such trouble by abducting this one?"

Many pretended to accept his word, realizing that to appear to doubt it would do little to help; but Carracciolo vowed vengeance on the Borgias, being certain that the man who had robbed him of his bride was Cesare.

In the Vatican, the Pope loudly proclaimed Cesare's innocence in the affair of Dorotea; but he was very perturbed by the refusal of the Duke of Ferrara to accept Lucrezia as a bride for his son.

He pondered on the Duke, whose main characteristic he deemed to be his meanness. Ercole would go to great lengths to avoid spending money; but if there was anything he would hate to part with more than money it was a single yard of the territory over which he ruled.

The Pope wrote to Ercole that it saddened him to think Alfonso was already engaged with another lady; but he was sure that great good could come to their houses by a marriage which would unite them, and he thought they should not lightly dismiss the plan. Alfonso was not available; Ippolito was a man of the Church; so he would give Lucrezia to Ferrara's third son, Ferrante. Now his daughter was very rich, and he must have a kingdom for her. It was his suggestion—and his wish, he implied—that Ferrante should be given that portion of Ferrara known as Modena, which could be made the State of Modena and ruled over by Ferrante and Lucrezia.

"Carve up Ferrara!" was the old Duke's comment. "Never!"

But he feared that the Pope would be adamant. He was certain of this when, appealing to the French for help (Ferrara had been an ally of the French for many years) he was told by Louis that a marriage between Este and Borgia was not displeasing to the French, and Louis' advice was to continue with negotiations.

Ercole knew then that Louis wished for the Pope's help in conquering Naples; France was the ally of the Vatican and as a consequence, Ferrara must suffer.

When Ercole received that intimation from the French he knew that he had to accept that which he hated.

But he would never carve up Ferrara. It was better to forget old contracts with Louise d'Angoulême. It was better for the marriage—since marriage there must be—to be between Alfonso and Lucrezia.

The Pope, walking with Lucrezia in the gardens of the Vatican, kept his arm in hers as they strolled among the flowers.

"It makes me happy to see you yourself again," he was telling her. "Lucrezia sad was like another being, not my bright daughter. And now I know you are pleased with this marriage which your loving father has arranged for you."

"Yes, Father," she answered, "I am pleased."

"I grieve that you must go so far from home."

"But you will visit me, and I you, Father. We shall never be separated for long."

He pressed her arm tenderly.

"You will be Duchess of Ferrara, my precious one. From the moment of the marriage the title will be yours. Fortunately old Ercole has no wife living, so you will be entitled to call yourself Duchess of Ferrara."

"Yes, Father."

"A fine title which will make you equal with the Princesses of Italy. That was what I always wanted for my little girl."

She was silent, thinking: How strange that I should look forward to this marriage. How strange that I should want to go away from my home.

This elation within her was due to the fact that escape was imminent. She was about to tear herself free from the bonds. She had imagined them like the threads of a spider's web, but they were made of flesh and blood and the wrenching apart would be painful.

And this husband of hers? She had seen his picture. He was big; he looked strong; but what had appealed to her most on examining that picture was the certain knowledge that he would not be a man to disturb her innermost self. She would give him children, and that would satisfy him; he would never want to know how much she had cared for his predecessors, how much she had suffered when that other Alfonso was murdered; he would never seek to discover the secret of that strange relationship between herself and Cesare, herself and her father. He was a practical man; he had his workshop and a host of mistresses. Many of the children in the villages of Ferrara were begotten by him. He was unrefined, he was called crude, yet, oddly enough, all that she heard of him pleased her. She would know her duty and she would perform it; and her secret life would be left inviolate. She would be alone in Ferrara, able to ponder on her life, to understand herself.

It was not the marriage to which she was looking forward; it was to freedom, to what she scarcely dared to think of as escape. But she let the Pope believe that it was the marriage which pleased her.

"They have made a hard bargain with us, Lucrezia," mused Alexander. "A dowry of 100,000 ducats and treasure worth 75,000 ducats, as well as the castles of Pieve and Cento."

"It is a great deal to ask of you, Father, for ridding you of your daughter."

"Ah!" laughed Alexander. "But it is the marriage I always wanted for you. Duchess of Ferrara, Lucrezia, my love! Alfonso, your husband, the legitimate heir of his father. It is a fine match, a grand match. And my beloved is worthy of it."

"But it is a high price for it."

"There is more than that. They insist on their tithes being reduced—4,000 ducats to 100. What impudence! But wily old Ercole knows how I have set my heart on this match. He is also asking for further honors for Ippolito. And this will not be all."

"It is too much."

"Nay. I'd give my tiara for your happiness, if need be."

She smiled at him, thinking: It is true. You would give much to buy me a grand marriage. But you could not mourn with me one hour when my husband was murdered.

Little Roderigo, in the gardens with his nurse, came toddling toward them.

"Ho!" cried Alexander, and picked up the little boy, and swung him above his head. Roderigo's fat hand reached for Alexander's not inconsiderable nose and tried to pull it. "Such impudence! Such sacrilege!" went on Alexander. "Do you know, young sir, that that is the sacred nose you mishandle so, eh?"

Roderigo crowed with pleasure, and Alexander, in a sudden passion of love, held the boy tight against him, so tightly that Roderigo set up a noisy protest. Alexander kissed him and put him down. He smiled at the nurse, a pretty creature, and murmuring a blessing, he let his hand rest on her soft hair.

"Take care of my grandson," he said tenderly. He would visit the nursery this evening. There he would find a double pleasure—the company of the boy and his nurse.

Lucrezia, watching, thought it was like the old pattern she remembered so well. Alexander did not change; thus had he visited that nursery on the Piazza Pizzo di Merlo, where she and her two brothers had eagerly awaited his coming, even as young Roderigo would wait now. Had there been a pretty nurse then to catch his attention? Perhaps not; Vannozza, their mother, would have made sure that there was not.

"You will miss Roderigo when we leave for Ferrara," said Lucrezia.

There was a short silence, and Lucrezia was aware of a sudden fear.

Alexander said gently: "If it were necessary for you to leave him behind, you would know he was receiving the best of care."

So it had been arranged. She was to leave Roderigo behind her. It was hardly likely that they would have allowed her to take him. The Estes would not want this child of a former marriage. Why, oh why, had this not occurred to her before she had shown her willingness for the match!

The Pope was looking at her anxiously. Her face, she guessed, showed her misery, and he would remember the weeks when she had mourned the murdered Alfonso. He was afraid now that she was going to be sad and he wanted her so desperately to be gay.

"Oh Father," she said impulsively, "perhaps after all this marriage will bring no happiness to me."

He caught her hand and kissed it. "It will bring great happiness, my Duchess. You have nothing to fear. You can trust me to care for Roderigo, for is he not your son! Does he not belong to us?"

"Father . . ." she faltered.

But he interrupted her. "You think that perhaps I shall not always be here."

"Do not speak of such a thing. It is more than I can bear."

He laughed. "Your father is an old man, Lucrezia. He is close to seventy years of age. Few live as long, and those who do cannot hope for much longer."

"We cannot think of it," she cried. "We dare not think of it. When we were little, it was you ... Uncle Roderigo then ... from whom all blessings flowed. It has not changed. Father, if you died, what would become of us? We should be only half alive, I believe."

He enjoyed such talk. He knew that it was not flattery; there was no hyperbole ... or perhaps but a little. They did need him—now as they always had. His delicate Lucrezia, his strong Cesare.

"I am strong and have much life in me yet," he said. "But, my dearest, to satisfy you, the little one shall have another guardian besides myself. What think you of our kinsman, Francesco Borgia? The Cardinal is gentle; he loves you; he loves the child. Would you feel happier then, Lucrezia?"

"I would trust Francesco," she said.

"Then so shall it be."

He took her hand and noticed that it was trembling. "Lucrezia," he said, "you are no longer a child. I shall be making a short tour of the territories very soon. I am going to leave you in charge, to take over my secular duties."

She was aghast. "But ... I am a woman, and this is a task for your most important Cardinals."

"I would show them all that my daughter is equal to any task with which, as a Borgia, she may be faced."

She smiled tremulously; she knew that he understood her fears of the new life which was stretching out before her. He wanted her to prove herself; he wanted to inspire her with the courage she would need.

He loved her with a devotion as great as he could feel for any and she loved him. She loved him fiercely, passionately; and she asked herself then: Is there some curse on us Borgias, that our love must be of such an intensity that there comes a point in our lives when we must turn from it, fly from it?

Rome was gay; the streets were crowded, everyone in the City wished to catch a glimpse of Lucrezia on her way to Santa Maria del Popolo, where she was going to give thanks because the Duke of Ferrara had at last signed the marriage contract between herself and his heir, Alfonso.

The Pope had wanted to make a grand occasion of this and, with that

Borgian love of showmanship, he had arranged a pageant to dazzle even the eyes of Romans. As with all these spectacles the occasion was not only serious but gay, not only a solemn ceremony, but a masquerade. The cannons of St. Angelo were booming, and the bells were ringing all over the seven hills of Rome. Lucrezia, glittering with jewels, her dress trimmed with gold and precious stones, the net which held her hair being composed of gold and jewels, rode in triumph through the streets; with her were the ladies and noblemen of her court, three hundred in all, together with the ambassadors of Spain and France.

The people crowded about the doorway of the church as Lucrezia entered and made her way to Alexander's impressive marble tabernacle where she knelt to thank God for bringing this great honor to her.

Her secular regency during Alexander's absence had been a great success; she had dealt with all matters which were not ecclesiastical, and the Cardinals had all been astonished by her gravity and grasp of affairs.

For the first time in her life Lucrezia had been aware of responsibility, and she enjoyed the experience. Cardinal Giorgio Costa, who was eighty-five, had made himself her adviser in particular and delighting in her youth had done a great deal to make the regency a success. It seemed impossible for these Cardinals, when they contemplated this serenely beautiful girl who so desired to please and listened so gravely to their advice, to believe those evil rumors they had heard concerning her. When the Pope returned he was immediately aware of the respect she had won, and knew that it had been a masterly stroke of his to appoint Lucrezia Regent.

Now she came out of the church. It was growing dusk and as she rode back to the Vatican the people shouted: "Long live the Duchess of Ferrara! Long live Alexander VI!"

As soon as it was dark the firework display began; and Lucrezia's dwarfs, all brilliantly clad, ran through the crowds, shouting "Long live the Duchess of Ferrara!" and singing songs about her virtue and her beauty.

The people, who loved a spectacle of this nature more than anything, were quite ready to forget old scandals and cry aloud "Long live the virtuous Duchess of Ferrara!"

The Pope was in the center of the celebrations, presiding over the banquet, making sure that the ambassadors and all those emissaries from foreign courts should know how he esteemed his daughter; this was a mark of his affection; it was also a warning to the Estes of how great his wrath would be if they attempted to slide out of their agreement or, when his daughter arrived in Ferrara, they did not give her all the respect due to their Duchess.

And the next day, after the traditional custom, Lucrezia gave her dress to her jester, who put it on and rode through the city, shouting "Hurrah for the Duchess of Ferrara!" The crowds followed him, shrieking with delight to see the fool so clad, making obscene gestures to the "bride"; all of which was watched by Lucrezia and the Pope with great amusement.

Now that the marriage agreement was signed by Ercole there was one matter which the Pope had long wished to settle and at this time felt he was able to do so. He sent for Lucrezia one day and, when she came to him and he had received her with his usual affection, he dismissed all attendants and said to her: "My daughter, I have something to show you!"

She was expecting a jewel, some piece of rich brocade, some article which was to be yet another wedding present for her, but she was mistaken.

The Pope went to the door of an ante-room and spoke to someone who was waiting there. "You may go," he said. "I will take the child."

Then he returned to Lucrezia and he was holding by the hand a beautiful little boy aged about three years.

As Lucrezia stared at the child she felt the blood rush to her face. Those beautiful dark eyes were like a pair she had once known, and memory came rushing back to her. She was in the convent of San Sisto where a dark-eyed Spaniard had visited her—handsome, charming, passionate.

"Yes," said the Pope, "it is he."

Lucrezia knelt down and would have taken the boy into her arms, but he drew back, watching her solemnly, a little distrustful, bewildered.

Lucrezia thought: And how could it be otherwise? It is three years since he was born . . . and all those years he has not seen his mother.

"Come, my little man," said the Pope. "What have you to say to the beautiful lady?"

"She is beautiful," said the boy, putting out a brown finger to touch the jewels on Lucrezia's fingers. He put his face down to those hands and made little clucking sounds of pleasure. He liked the smell of musk with which she scented her hands.

"Look at me, little one," said Lucrezia, "not at my trinkets."

Then the solemn eyes surveyed her cautiously, and she was unable to resist taking him into her arms and covering his face with kisses.

The Pope looked on, benign and happy. His greatest joy was in bringing pleasure to his loved ones; and this little boy—like most children and especially those who had Borgia blood in their veins—had immediately captivated him.

"Please," said the boy, "I do not like being kissed."

That amused the Pope. "Later you will, my son," he cried. "Later you will not spurn the kisses of beautiful women."

"Don't like to be kissed," reiterated the boy.

"Have you not been kissed much?" asked Lucrezia.

He shook his head.

"I think I should be tempted to kiss you often," she told him; which made him move hastily away from her and closer to the Pope.

"Little Giovanni likes his new home, does he not?" asked the Pope.

Little Giovanni's eyes lighted as he looked up into the impressive countenance, which might have been terrifying, but which was redeemed by that beautiful expression which enchanted young and old.

"Giovanni wants to stay with the Holy Father," he said.

Alexander's lips twitched with pleasure and emotion; the white hands caressed the child's thick curly hair. "Then you shall, my son, you shall, for His Holiness is as delighted with Giovanni as Giovanni is with His Holiness."

"Holiness, Holiness," chanted Giovanni.

"Come," said the Pope, "tell the lady your name."

"It is Giovanni."

"Giovanni what?"

"Giovanni Borgia."

"Borgia indeed! Never forget that. It is the most important part. There are thousands of Giovannis in Italy, but few Borgias; and that is the name you will be proud to bear."

"Borgia . . . !" repeated Giovanni.

"Oh Giovanni," cried Lucrezia, "did you mind leaving your old home?"

Giovanni's eyes clouded slightly. "This is a better one," he said.

"Of a certainty it is," said the Pope. "It contains His Holiness and the beautiful Madonna Lucrezia."

"Madonna Lucrezia," murmured the boy almost shyly.

Alexander picked him up and kissed him.

"There," he said. "You have seen him."

"He is to stay here now?"

The Pope nodded. "He shall stay with his Holy Father who loves him, for that is what he wishes."

Giovanni nodded gravely.

"Now we will return him to his nursery, and then you and I will have a little talk. I would wish you to see how happy he is there, and how well he gets on with his little friend and kinsman."

So, carrying young Giovanni, the Pope led the way to the nursery, where little Roderigo was seated on the floor playing with bricks which he was trying to build into a tower. When he saw Lucrezia he got to his feet and came stumbling toward her.

She lifted him in her arms and he showed no resentment at her kisses. Then he pointed to Giovanni and said: "Giovanni."

Lucrezia's voice was broken with emotion as she said: "So you love little Giovanni?"

"Big Giovanni," Roderigo reminded her; then his attention was caught by the great ruby she wore in her necklace, and his fingers closed over it and his big eyes started in wonder.

She hugged him and felt the tears rushing to her eyes.

Alexander saw them and said: "Let us leave the children with their nurses. I have something to say to you."

So they left the nursery and Alexander put his arm about her as he led her back to his apartment.

"You see," he told her. "I kept my promise. I have sent for him that he may be brought up as one of us."

"Thank you, Father."

"I fear I let this break upon you too suddenly. I should have prepared you. But I hoped to give you a great pleasure, and I could not keep the treat hidden any longer. He is a beautiful boy—already I see the Borgia in him."

She turned to him suddenly and threw herself into his arms. "I'm sorry, Father, but it brings it all back . . . so vividly."

He stroked her hair gently. "I know, my beloved. I saw that in your face. And these tears of yours are tears of joy, are they not. You see the boy has been well looked after. You need never worry on that score. I shall give him an estate and titles. He shall be as one of us. Have no fear for his future, Lucrezia. It is in my hands."

She kissed those hands. "The kindest and most capable hands in the world," she murmured.

"Their greatest joy is in making happiness for my dear daughter."

"But Father, he is my son, even as Roderigo is, and it saddens me to have to leave them."

"True, you cannot take them with you into Ferrara; but you know they are safe here."

"You wanted your children to grow up round you, Father. I want the same."

He was silent. "I know this." Then he smiled brilliantly. "Why should you not have them with you . . . in time, eh, Lucrezia? I know that you are full of wiles; you are charming and beautiful. When you wanted something of me, did you not invariably get it? Why? Because you were enchanting and I loved you so much that I could not refuse. I doubt not that you will soon learn to get what you want from your husband, as you do from your father."

"You mean in time I may persuade him to let me have the boys with me."

He kissed her tenderly. "I doubt it not," he said.

❦

It was impossible for the arrival of little Giovanni Borgia to go unnoticed, and the new child at the Vatican became the main source of conversation in certain circles. Who is Giovanni Borgia? was the question of the day. He was given a new title, the *Infante Romano*.

Alexander was faintly perturbed. The marriage with Ferrara would appear to be settled, but this was not so. Ercole had shown quite clearly that he was not enthusiastic for the marriage; he had bargained for his ducats and honors like a merchant; and Alexander believed he would choose the first opportunity to slide out of the agreement. It was only fear of the Papacy and the present unrest in Italy which made him agree; the arrogant aristocrat thought his family too good for that of the Borgias; in his prim way he recoiled from alliance with a family which had provoked more scandals than any other in Italy. Therefore it was a pity that there should be at this time another scandal—and that concerning a three-year-old child.

Who is the *Infante Romano?* It was impossible to escape from the question.

Isabella d'Este would be writing to her father, telling him of her belief as to the parentage of the mysterious child. If Lucrezia's name were mentioned in connection with the child, Ercole might consider he had ample reasons for breaking the marriage agreement.

Alexander then drew up a Bull, the prime motive of which was to legitimize little Giovanni, for he wished this healthy little boy with the flashing dark eyes to be known as a true Borgia, and legitimization was the only means of doing so. The child was, he declared, the son of Cesare, Duke of Valentinois, and a woman of Rome. Cesare, father of so many illegitimate children, would not mind accepting responsibility for another.

The *Infante Romano* then was the son of Cesare Borgia, and this accounted for the delight the Pope found in the child.

But Alexander was perturbed. He must consider the future, those days when he might not be there to protect the interests of the child. He wished to leave him certain properties; he accordingly drew up another Bull which should remain secret at least for as long as he lived. In this he declared the child to be his own by a woman of Rome. But for the moment he had stifled the rumors. He had given to the world his explanation of his love and care of the child, and the mystery would seem to be solved. The anxious Ercole at least could not use it as an excuse for canceling the wedding plans.

Meanwhile the King of France was planning his attack on Naples. He knew that, although he might conquer the land, he could not hold it without an investiture and for this reason he wished to placate the Pope. Therefore he had helped Cesare to conquer Romagna, and Cesare was to be his ally in the march on Naples.

Louis had made another shrewd move by forming an alliance with Spain. For certain concessions (the acquisition of Apulia and Calabria) the Spaniards had agreed to stand aside and leave their Aragonese kinsmen of Naples to fight alone.

Louis demanded that Cesare should leave garrisons in the towns he had conquered and join him in the conquest of Naples—which Louis declared was part of their contract. Cesare was furious, for he had been made to see how little his triumphs had been due to himself. He was realist enough to understand that he was under the Papal influence and that of France, and that should these be removed he would stand naked to his enemies.

There was disturbing news from Maximilian who was not pleased by the Franco-Spanish alliance and demanded to know who these Borgias were who had set themselves up as dabblers in European politics. He let it be known that he was considering coming into Italy himself and that he would smash through this petty kingdom of Romagna if only for the pleasure of making it clear to the Borgias that they were nothing but an insignificant family, a member of which happened to have been elected Pope.

It was humiliating, yet there was no help for it but to obey the French and march to Naples. Federico in panic surrendered before the arrival of the soldiers, and Louis offered him exile in France which he gratefully took. Thus, when the French with Cesare and his soldiers came into Naples, there was no battle; Naples was theirs to command, and the people came into the streets to welcome the conquerors.

Humiliation was turned to triumph and Cesare rode in glory through Naples.

Federico was now an exile—that Federico who had refused to allow his daughter to marry a Borgia! It was a moment for which Cesare had yearned for a long time. Moreover there were many who were fascinated by him, and in the processions of victory more eyes were turned on Cesare Borgia than on Louis of France.

There were balls and banquets, and Cesare was the center of attraction at these. There were many women eager to be noticed by him, although news of the massacre of Capua had reached them, and it was said that there had never been such barbaric savagery as that displayed by Cesare Borgia in the Neapolitan campaign, and that many French Captains who had prided themselves on their chivalry had made it known that they did not wish to be thought of as allies of such a man.

Cesare was always at his most brutal when he believed his dignity had been insulted; and every cruelty he perpetrated during that campaign was meant to soothe those wounds inflicted by Princess Carlotta and her father, Federico.

At Capua he had ridden through the town forcing his way into houses wherever he had heard there were beautiful young girls. He was insistent that they should be virgins; therefore it was necessary that they should be of a tender age. He discovered forty of them and demanded that they be taken to Rome, housed in his palace, and kept there to form a harem for his pleasure. His rule was barbaric. Men whom he suspected of insulting him, even by a word, had their tongues cut out, hands cut off and were exposed to public view until they died.

He set about amusing himself but so promiscuously did he do this that it was not long before he was again smitten with that disease which he had contracted in his early youth, from which he suffered periodic attacks and which was known throughout Italy as the *male francese.*

This sickness, exhausting him physically as it did, never failed to have its effect on his mind. His wildness increased with it; his anger was even more easily aroused; suffering pain as he did, he seemed to be filled with a demoniacal desire to inflict it on others.

There was a shiver through the whole of Rome when Cesare returned to recuperate and join in the celebrations of his sister's coming marriage.

Alfonso d'Este, working in his foundry by day and amusing himself with his countless mistresses by night, was the least disturbed member at his father's court.

"All this fuss about a marriage!" he guffawed. "Let us get the matter done with."

His brothers, Ippolito, Ferrante and Sigismondo who would travel to Rome to escort Lucrezia back to Ferrara, argued with him. He scarcely listened. There were continual arguments in the family, which was perhaps not so surprising when there were so many brothers, all of different opinions.

Ippolito, the fastidous Cardinal who longed to wear jewels and tasteful garments and had even designed a Cardinal's robe of his own, declared that he was all eagerness to see the bride. He had heard such stories about her. She was reputed to be beautiful with wonderful yellow hair which was probably dyed or brightened in some way. He felt that a woman with such a history would be interesting.

Ferrante declared that he was longing to see her. An incestuous murderess would make life exciting in Ferrara!

Sigismondo crossed himself hastily and said that they should go down on their knees and pray that no harm should grow out of the marriage.

Alfonso laughed at them. "Have done," he said. "This is a woman like ten thousand others."

"There you are wrong, brother," said Ferrante. "She is a seductress, and it is said that her brother, Cesare Borgia, murdered his brother and her husband out of desire for her."

Alfonso spat over his shoulder. "I could find a dozen like her any night in any brothel in Ferrara." He yawned. He was going back to his foundry.

Ercole called Ippolito to him. It was no use talking to Alfonso. Now more than ever he found it difficult to believe Alfonso was his son. It was distressing to witness his low tastes, his animal sexuality. Ercole had prided himself that the Este court was the center of culture. How could it continue so when he was dead and Alfonso ruled in his place? He himself had lived as chastely as a man of his time could have been expected to live. His wife, Eleanora of Aragon, had been virtuous; she had borne him six children, and four of these had been sons. His daughters had been a credit to him—his dear Isabella, who now ruled in Mantua, and Beatrice who had been the wife of Ludovico of Milan but was unfortunately now dead. He himself had only two mistresses (having fewer he would have been suspected of impotence) and one of these had borne him a daughter named Lucrezia, and the other—beautiful Isabella Arduino—had presented him with his beloved son Giulio who was admired throughout the court for those wonderful flashing dark eyes of his, so like his mother's that he was a continual reminder of past passion.

Ercole was a cultured gentleman; Alfonso, apart from his one talent for playing the viol, was a boor.

So it was to Ippolito that he must talk of this marriage, and as he talked, regretted, as he had so many times before, that Ippolito was not his eldest son.

"I do not despair altogether," he said, "of foiling the Pope's plans."

Ippolito was surprised. "At this late stage, Father?"

"Until the woman is actually here, there is hope. The Pope is urging that you set out for Rome at once. Thus you will reach the city before the winter." Ercole laughed. "I am delaying. I am telling him that the dowry must be paid in large ducats and not chamber ones, and he is protesting."

"You think that will hold up matters?"

Ercole chuckled. "I do indeed. Then the winter will be upon us, and who knows what will have happened by the spring?"

"Father, what arrangements are you making for the traveling of Sister Lucia's nuns?"

Ercole's face lengthened. Ippolito had introduced a subject which involved the spending of money, and such subjects always upset Ercole.

"It will be an expensive matter to transport them from Viterbo to Ferrara," went on Ippolito. "And I fear, my dear father, that you will be asked to pay for the journey."

Ercole was thinking of Sister Lucia da Narni whom he cherished here in Ferrara. Being very interested in theological matters he had been always impressed by miracles, and any who could provide them was sure of a welcome at his court. Some years ago Sister Lucia, who was in a Dominican convent in Viterbo, had begun to see the stigmata forming on her hands. This phenomenon appeared every Friday, and Ercole had been so impressed by what he heard of this miracle and so certain that Sister Lucia must be a very holy woman, that he had wished her to leave Viterbo and come to Ferrara.

Sister Lucia was not unwilling, but her superiors would not allow her to leave them, for they saw that she would bring much gain and glory to them. However, the sister was put in a basket, smuggled out of the convent, and brought to Duke Ercole who, delighted with his acquisition, installed her in a convent of her own, visited her frequently, looking upon the stained rags which she produced on Fridays as holy relics.

But she wished to have those nuns about her with whom she had lived at Viterbo, and after many negotiations it was agreed that certain of the nuns should come to share the Ferrara convent with Sister Lucia.

It was the transportation of these nuns which was now causing Ercole some concern. And Ippolito, watching his father slyly, said suddenly: "The nuns would have to pass through Rome. Why should they not travel with the bride and her company?"

Ercole was looking at his son speculatively.

Ippolito went on: "Why then, Father, they could travel at her expense."

"It is a good idea, my son," said Ercole.

"And think, Father, if you successfully oppose the match, in addition to all those ducats you will lose, you will have to pay for the nuns' journey yourself. You stand to lose, my father, if you do not accept Lucrezia."

Ippolito was filled with secret laughter as he watched avarice and family pride grapple with one another.

Cesare souɢʜt ʜɪs sister. She was surrounded by her women, and there were rolls of beautiful material in the apartment. Lucrezia was draping some of this about one of them and indulging in one of her favorite occupations— designing her own dresses.

The brocade of that shade of deep crimson, which had a hint of blue in it and which was called morello, fell from her hands as she saw Cesare. She felt the blood leave her face and she appeared to be without life, unable to move. Every time she saw him, she seemed to sense change in him. She was moved by pity, by fear and by admiration. There was no one like him in the world, no one else who could ever have the same power to move her, to hurt her, to fill her with tenderness and with fear.

"Why Cesare . . ." she began.

He smiled sneeringly at the fine materials. "So," he said, "you are preparing for the wedding."

"There is a great deal to do," she said. She waved her hand and the women were only too ready to leave her.

"My brother," she said, "it makes me happy to see you back in Rome."

He laughed, and touched his face with beautiful slender fingers, so like his father's. "The reason for my return does not make me happy."

"You suffer so. I trust the cure has done its work."

"They tell me it has, but I wonder sometimes whether the foulness will ever leave me. If I but knew who brought it to me this time . . ." His eyes were cruel, and she shuddered. Stories of his barbaric cruelty to the Neapolitans had reached her and she, who deplored cruelty and whose great desire was to live in peace with all around her, longed for him to curb his violence.

"Well, sister," he said, "you do not seem pleased to see me."

"Then it is because I see you not looking as well as I would wish to see you."

He took her by the arm, and she tried not to show that his grip hurt her.

"This man to whom they are marrying you," he said, "he is a boor, I hear. Alfonso. Alfonso the Second! He will bear no resemblance to the first Alfonso . . . that little one who so delighted you."

She would not look at him. She whispered: "It is our fate to marry when we are told to marry, and accept the partners chosen for us."

"My Lucrezia!" he said. "Would to God . . ."

She knew what he meant but she would not let him say it. She interrupted quickly: "We shall meet often. You shall visit me in Ferrara; I shall visit you in Romagna."

"Yes," he said. "That must be so. Nothing should part us, Lucrezia. Nothing shall, as long as there is life in this body." He put his face close to hers. He whispered: "Lucrezia . . . you tremble. You are afraid of me. Why, in the name of all the saints? Why?"

"Cesare," she answered him, "soon I have to leave Rome. Soon . . . I must go to my marriage. . . ."

"And you are afraid . . . afraid of the brother who loves you. Afraid because he is your brother . . . Lucrezia, I will not have you afraid. I will have you welcome me . . . love me . . . love me as I love you."

"Yes, Cesare."

"For love you I do, as I love no other. Always, no matter whom I am with, it is Lucrezia I love. All others are dull . . . they tire me. They are not Borgias. Lucrezia . . . Lucrezia . . . I would give so much . . . years of my life if . . ."

"No," she said fiercely, "no!"

"But I say Yes," he told her.

His hand was at the nape of her neck. She thought in that moment that he was going to kill her because he was imagining her with her new husband, and could not bear to see such images.

Then suddenly he released her. He laughed, and his laughter was bitter.

"The Borgia in you, Lucrezia, is hidden by the gentle serenity of the woman who would wish to be like all others . . . the gentle Lucrezia who longs to be a wife and mother . . . meek and mild—Lucrezia who would deny her Borgia blood for the sake of peace. You shall come to my apartments tonight. There shall be a supper party. Our father will be there and others. And this party shall be for your delight."

"I shall come with the greatest pleasure," she said.

"Yes, Lucrezia," he told her, "you shall come."

In Cesare's apartments there took place that night an orgy which would be remembered as long as the name of Borgia would be.

It was of Cesare's own invention; and his apartments were lighted by many brilliant candelabra and therein he had set up a Papal throne, elaborately covered with the finest brocade. Upon it was seated the Pope, and next to him Lucrezia, and on her other side Cesare himself.

There was feasting, and the conversation was lewd. Cesare set the pace, and he was fresh from the campaign in Naples, during which his barbarism and love of orgiastic spectacle had become intensified. The Pope was expectant. There was nothing he liked better than what he called goodly company, and he was not the man to turn from lewd talk nor from lewd behavior.

Cesare had ordered that fifty courtesans be brought to the apartment, and they came, some of the most notorious in Rome, ready to do whatever they should be asked, providing they received adequate payment; and payment or not, none would dare offend Cesare Borgia.

The payment for this night's work was to be very high indeed, and in addition they had the honor of working for Cesare and entertaining the Holy Father and the bride-to-be.

They began by dancing, and as the music grew wilder, so did their dancing. There was one theme: seduction and fulfillment; and this they stressed again and again. Cesare watched intently. He had placed on a small table a selection of dresses made of the finest silk, leather shoes and hats; and these he said were prizes which he wished Lucrezia to distribute. She must watch carefully, for he wished her to bestow the prizes on those whom she thought most worthy.

The Pope applauded the dances, and laughed with hilarity when the prostitutes began to discard one item of clothing after another.

Lucrezia sat very still, trying not to glance sideways at her father and brother, trying to set a fixed smile on her face.

Brought up as she had been in her particular age she was not shocked to see these naked women. She had seen suggestive dances many times; she had listened to bawdy plays. She could only apply the standards of her age to such; but this entertainment was symbolic. This was Cesare's way of telling her that she was one of them; she belonged to them; and that even when she was living with the prudish Este family, she would remember this night.

"Now," said Cesare, "the contest begins."

"I am all interest," said the Pope, his eyes on a plump dark-haired woman who discarded the last of her garments.

Cesare clapped his hands and a bowl of hot chestnuts was brought to them.

"We shall scatter these, and the ladies will retrieve them," he explained. "And each will hold a lighted candelabrum in her hand as she does so. It will be no easy feat in the state they are in."

"Your wine was potent. I declare I should not feel inclined to scramble for chestnuts," said the Pope, taking a handful and throwing them at the dark-haired courtesan.

Now all in the room, except Lucrezia, were rocking with laughter at the antics of the drunken prostitutes. Some shrieked as the lighted candles in the shaking hands of others touched them. Some fell to the ground, and rolled about on the floor in pursuit of the nuts.

This was the sign for Cesare's servants to gratify that lust which the sight of the women had aroused in them, and at the given signal they proceeded to do so.

The Pope was helpless with laughter, pointing to this one and that.

Cesare laid his hand over his sister's. "Take good note," he said. "It is for you to award the prizes to those who get on best together."

And she sat there, the fear upon her; the desire to escape never greater than at this hour of shame.

She felt that she did not belong to these Borgias and she longed to escape. They terrified her, and yet she was conscious of that strong feeling within her which she had for them and which she could have for no others. Was it love? Was it dread? Was it fear?

She did not know. All she did know was that it was the strongest emotion in her life.

She was tainted, and Cesare had determined that the stain should be indelible. "You shall not escape!" That was what he was telling her. "You are blood of our blood, flesh of our flesh. You cannot wipe the Borgia stain from yourself, because it is part of you."

It was over at last. She felt sick with revulsion and loathing mingling with fear. Yet she did as she was bidden. She selected the winners and gave the prizes.

She knew then that she would always do as she was bidden. She knew that the only escape was in flight.

"Holy Mother of God," she prayed, "send me to Ferrara. Let them come for me . . . soon . . . Oh, let it be soon, before it is too late."

SHE was waiting, and still they did not come.

The Pope fumed with rage.

"What now?" he demanded. "What should they want now? An appointment in the Church for the bastard Giulio. Something involving no labor and a goodly income. He'll not get it. A Cardinal's hat for his friend, Gian Luca Castellini da Pontremoli? He'll not get that either. What is he waiting for? For the weather to become too bad?"

Lucrezia was beside herself with anxiety. Cesare was ill, but he would recover. She was frightened; the web was tightening about her.

She wrote to her future father-in-law, telling him that she would with the utmost delight arrange to bring the nuns with her when she traveled to Ferrara.

The letters she received from her future husband were kindly, but still no move was made.

What shall I do? she asked herself. Can it be that they have decided not to come?

It was November and surely the journey would be almost impossible in a few weeks' time. He was deliberately delaying.

The Pope, seeing her downcast looks, sought to cheer her up and, when two mares were put into the courtyard with four stallions, he insisted on her watching from the windows of the Apostolic Palace to see the excitement below.

Several people had gathered to watch the spectacle, and Lucrezia was seen there with her father; this was talked of throughout the city, and Lucrezia believed that it would most certainly reach the ears of those who sought to defame her in the eyes of the old Duke of Ferrara.

Shall I never escape? she wondered.

Then she marveled that she could have thought of it as escape—leaving the home and family which she had loved so much!

She was determined to please her new family. She was in truth begging them not to close her way of escape.

Roderigo had been a matter of great concern to Duke Ercole; he did not want the expense of keeping a child of Lucrezia's by another marriage. Lucrezia publicly put the boy into the care of her old cousin, Francesco Borgia, who was now Cardinal of Cosenza, and bestowed on him Sermoneta so that the Este family might have no fear that the child would be an expense to them.

And still they did not come.

Lucrezia in desperation declared: "If there is no marriage with Ferrara I shall go into a convent."

And those who heard this marveled that the young girl who had been so gay, so happy in the possession of her beauty, so careful of its preservation, so enthusiastic in the designing of fine garments, could contemplate giving up her gay life for the rigors of a convent.

They did not know of the fear that had taken possession of Lucrezia.

❦♛❦

It was December before the cortège set out and, headed by the three brothers, Ippolito, Ferrante and Sigismondo, made its way toward Rome. The weather was bad and the rain incessant, but there was an easing of that fear in Lucrezia's heart, for she was certain now that in a few weeks she would be leaving Rome.

Alexander was as excited as a boy. He would burst into Lucrezia's apartment and ask to see the latest addition to her trousseau; he would exclaim with pleasure as he examined the dresses—the brocades and velvets in shades of blue, russet and morello, all encrusted with jewels and sewn with pearls; he could not refrain from calculating the number of ducats represented by these fine clothes, and would point out to the women: "That hat is worth 10,000 ducats, and the dress 20,000."

Cesare was to ride out to meet the cavalcade and conduct it into Rome, and fortunately a day before the entry into the capital the weather cleared and the sun shone.

Cesare, splendid on a magnificent horse, surrounded by eighty halberdiers in Papal yellow and black, and soldiers numbering four thousand, met the cavalcade from Ferrara at the Piazza del Popolo and placed himself at the head beside Ippolito. Nineteen Cardinals met them at the Porta del Popolo and many speeches of welcome were delivered. The guns at Castel Sant' Angelo thundered out as they rode on to St. Peter's Square and the Vatican.

Here Alexander was waiting and, when the ceremonial greeting was over and he had received countless kisses on his slipper, he put aside ceremony and embraced the Este brothers, telling them with tears of joy in his eyes, of the great delight he had in beholding them.

Then it was Cesare's duty to lead the distinguished guests to the Palace of Santa Maria in Portico where Lucrezia was waiting to receive them.

She stood at the foot of the staircase in readiness. At intervals on the staircase torches were blazing; the setting was dramatic, for Lucrezia possessed all the showmanship of the Borgias and, no matter how great was her fear at any time, she could usually spare thought for her appearance.

She had chosen to support her, for her escort, a very old Spanish noble-man, dignified, gray-bearded and grizzled, and there could not have been a greater contrast to her feminine fragility. Her brocade dress in her favorite morello color was stiff with gold and jewels; her velvet cloak was lined with sable, and on her head she wore an emerald-colored net lavishly decorated with pearls, while on her forehead a great ruby shone.

The three Este brothers, who had been so eager to see this woman whom they had so often heard called an incestuous murderess, gasped with astonish-ment as they came forward to kiss her hand.

Ippolito thought her delightful; Ferrante was half way to falling in love with her, and even Sigismondo assured himself that the stories he had heard of her could not be anything but lies.

※ ♔ ※

Now the celebrations, which were to precede and follow the marriage by proxy, began.

The Pope was determined to give entertainments such as had never been seen before, even of his devising. He took a puckish delight in displaying his splendor before the Este Princes. He fervently wished that he had their old miserly father in Rome so that he could shock him thoroughly. He would teach them how to enjoy wealth. It was the lavish spenders who did that, not the misers of this world.

He would take the brothers aside and call attention to the beauty of Lucrezia. "Is she not charming? Not a blemish. She is not lame. She is perfect, perfect I tell you."

He would ask them questions about the Duke and the bridegroom. "How tall is your father the Duke? Tell me, is he as tall as I am?"

"He is tall," Ippolito explained, "but I think perhaps Your Holiness has a slight advantage."

That delighted the Pope. "And my son, the Duke of Romagna, is he taller than your brother Alfonso? Tell me that."

"Our brother is tall, Holiness, but so is the Duke of Romagna. It is not easy to say, but perhaps the Duke is the taller of the two."

They were the answers the Pope wanted, and he was as pleased as a child. He was delighted with the marriage of his daughter into one of the oldest and most aristocratic families in Italy, but he did not want anyone to forget that the Borgias were more powerful than any, and if he was pleased, the Duke of Ferrara should be doubly so.

He whispered to Ippolito: "I long to see the Este jewels which you are to bestow on my daughter."

Ippolito was uneasy, for his father had warned him that the famous Este jewels were not to be given to Lucrezia as a gift to a bride. She would be allowed to wear them for her wedding celebrations, but she must not think they passed into her possession. They were worth a fortune, and to contemplate their passing out of the Este family was more than old Duke Ercole could bear.

Ippolito explained to the Pope as tactfully as he could; Alexander smiled ruefully, but he was not seriously perturbed. He was rich enough to snap his fingers at the 70,000 ducats which the jewels were said to be worth. The most important matter was to get Lucrezia married and, now that the embassy was in Rome, that would not be long delayed.

At the end of December the marriage was celebrated. Escorted by Don Ferrante and Don Sigismondo, Lucrezia was led across St. Peter's Square with a dazzling train to accompany her. She had fifty maids of honor and twenty pages, all exquisitely dressed, and these last carried the standards of Este side by side with the emblem of the Grazing Bull.

Lucrezia in crimson velvet and gold brocade lined with ermine was very beautiful, and the people who had assembled to watch gasped with admiration as she was led into the Vatican. The ceremony was not held in the intimate Borgia apartments but in the Sala Paolina. Lucrezia had asked the Pope's permission for this, as she did not feel that she could endure this marriage by proxy kneeling where she had knelt during the ceremony which had made her wife of that other Alfonso.

Here Alexander, Cesare and thirteen Cardinals were waiting for her, and the ceremony began.

Lucrezia had quickly seen that Sanchia was not present, and she was relieved. Sanchia, like herself, would be thinking of Alfonso of Bisceglie. It was as well that she was absent from this occasion.

The Bishop of Adria opened the proceedings and began to deliver a sermon which threatened to be of long duration. The Pope, however, was impatient to get on with the important part of the ceremony; he wanted to see his daughter in truth married; he wanted to watch the Este jewels being handed to her.

"Enough! Enough!" he murmured, waving a white hand impatiently, and the Bishop's sermon came to an abrupt end.

Then Ferrante stepped forward and placed the ring on Lucrezia's finger. "In the name," he proclaimed, "of my brother Alfonso."

The jewel box was then brought and ceremoniously handed to Lucrezia, and the Pope was almost beside himself with laughter on hearing the carefully chosen words of Ippolito. It required great tact to hand over a present which was not in truth a gift, but the dandified Ippolito managed very successfully: and after all it was not jewels which the Borgias sought. They could easily have acquired jewels such as those if they had wanted them.

Lucrezia when accepting the jewels commented rather on the exquisite workmanship which had gone into their making than on the gems themselves.

"And now to feasting and celebration!" cried the Pope.

And thus was Lucrezia married for the third time.

THE CELEBRATION CONTINUED. Lucrezia married, though by proxy, to the heir of Este now seemed possessed of a wild abandon. She remembered that her days in the Vatican circle were numbered, and another great fear took possession of her. In a few days she must say good-bye to her father, and she knew that this was constantly in his thoughts. Every time they were together he talked with almost feverish excitement of the visits she would pay to him, and he to her, in the years to come. He would enumerate all the good points of this marriage as though he were trying to convince himself that it was worth while, even though it was going to take his beloved daughter from him.

Cesare was silently angry, brooding on the marriage, hating it yet realizing that alliance with Ferrara was good for the Papacy and Romagna. But Cesare was young; Cesare would make sure that his duty took him near Ferrara. They would meet again and again.

And now that she had taken the step she was unsure. She plunged as feverishly as any of them into the festivities, taking great pains to dazzle the company with her magnificent clothes, washing her hair every few days so that it shone like gold and won the admiration of her new brothers-in-law.

She chattered with her women concerning this dress and that, which jewels she should wear, whether she should have her hair curled or hanging like a cloak about her shoulders. She tried to pretend that these matters were the most important in the world to her; and each day when she rose from her bed she remembered that the parting was coming nearer; each day brought her closer to a new life with a husband whom she did not know, with a family which she sensed, in spite of the charm of her brothers-in-law, was hostile.

Amongst her attendants was her young cousin, a very beautiful fifteen-year-old girl named Angela Borgia, who was excited to be with Lucrezia at this time and overjoyed because she was to accompany her into Ferrara.

Angela, gay and high-spirited, was determined to get all the fun she could out of life, and, watching her, Lucrezia tried to see everything through the young girl's eyes and thus feel young again.

Angela was with her while she was dressing for a party which was to be given in the Pope's apartments, and the irrepressible child was holding one of Lucrezia's gowns about her—a glorious creation, designed by Lucrezia herself, of gold and black striped satin with cascades of lace falling from its slashed sleeves. She was dancing about the apartment, pretending that she was being married and haughtily deigning to receive the ring from one of the women whom she had made take the part which Ferrante had taken at the wedding.

They were all helpless with laughter. There was that about Angela to inspire mirth. She was so wild and so lighthearted, so outrageously indifferent to etiquette, that at times she reminded Lucrezia of Sanchia who, though in Rome, took little part in the celebrations.

"Have done, child," said Lucrezia, "and come and help fasten my dress."

The dress was a mulberry velvet with gold stripes, and Angela cried out: "Oh... what would I not give for a dress like that! Twenty years of my life... my honor... my virtue..."

"You do not know what you are saying," said Lucrezia.

"You do not know how beautiful you look. If I had a dress like that, *I* should look fair enough."

Lucrezia smiled at the saucy young face. "You have pretty dresses."

"But not so grand. Lucrezia, dearest cousin, do you remember your blue brocade gown... the one with the slashed sleeves and the golden lace? That becomes me greatly."

"I have no doubt," said Lucrezia.

"You designed that dress for yourself, cousin, but you might have designed it for me."

Lucrezia laughed. "You want to wear it at the party tonight?"

Angela leaped up and threw her arms about her cousin's neck. "May I, dearest cousin? May I?"

"Well, perhaps," said Lucrezia.

"You are the dearest cousin in the world. I would rather die a thousand deaths than not accompany you into Ferrara."

"You cannot contemplate dying once, let alone a thousand times. Get the blue dress, and let us see if it fits you."

"It does. I have tried it."

So she was helped into the dress, and paraded before them, mimicking Lucrezia in many moods: Lucrezia at her wedding, Lucrezia dancing with Ippolito, with Ferrante and with Cesare.

And so amusing was she, so full of vitality, that Lucrezia could not help laughing and felt her spirits lifted by this young girl.

Ippolito stood in a corner of the Pope's apartments idly watching the dancers. He had a great deal about which to write home. He and his two brothers had written many letters, as requested, to their father, to Alfonso and to their sister Isabella. It was very necessary to write to Isabella; she had always considered herself the head of the family. Ippolito's lips curled. He took a delight in telling Isabella of the charm, beauty and grace of this newcomer to their family, for overbearing Isabella was going to receive a shock when she read those letters. Isabella would be furiously jealous; she considered herself the most attractive and charming, as well as learned woman in Italy. Isabella also considered herself the most elegant. She was going to be hard put to it to compete with Lucrezia's amazing collection of elaborate gowns. He knew that Ferrante was writing ecstatically of Lucrezia; and that Sigismondo was doing the same, although he knew how disturbing the eulogies would be to Isabella. Sigismondo wanted to please his sister but he was deeply pious and must tell the truth. Isabella knew this. That was why Sigismondo's accounts were going to disturb her more than those of Ippolito whom she knew might be malicious, and of Ferrante who was impressionable.

A very elegant, richly-clad figure had moved toward him, so heavily masked that the face was completely hidden; but Ippolito knew that it was Cesare, for that haughty bearing, that fine elegant figure, those rich garments, could belong to no one else.

There was a bond between Ippolito and Cesare. Ippolito was a reluctant Cardinal; Cesare had been an even more reluctant one; Cesare was attracted by the Cardinal's robes of Ippolito, which he had designed himself and which were therefore different from those of other Cardinals. They proclaimed his fastidiousness and his contempt for the role he had been called upon to assume.

"This is a gay gathering, my lord," said Ippolito.

"The gayest we have had so far."

"There would seem to be a hint of sadness in the laughter of His Holiness."

"He is reminded that before long my sister will go away."

Ippolito looked sharply at Cesare. "It is a matter of grief to you also?"

Cesare did not answer; his eyes behind the mask had grown angry suddenly, and Ippolito went on: "I wish you would tell me how you escaped from the purple."

Cesare laughed. "It took me many years to do it."

"I doubt I ever shall."

"You, my dear Ippolito, are not the son of a Pope."

"Alas! My father will do nothing to help me escape the destiny into which I have been thrust."

"My friend, let it not restrain your natural bent. When I was a member of the Sacred College I did not allow it to do so to me. I had many adventures then—amusing adventures—very similar to those which I enjoy today."

"I understand."

"You too have your adventures?"

"I do; and I believe I am on the brink of one at this very moment."

Cesare looked about the room.

"The enchanting creature in blue," Ippolito explained.

"Ha!" laughed Cesare. "My young cousin Angela. She is scarce out of the nursery, but I grant you she has a charm."

"She is delightful," said Ippolito.

"Then you must make haste in your adventure, my friend, for in a few days Angela will be leaving with my sister and, although you are to accompany them out of Rome it will be only for part of the way, since you are to return as a hostage for your family's good behavior to Lucrezia."

"I know it," said Ippolito. "And she is so young . . . and for all her look of witchery, inexperienced, I should say."

"So much the better," said Cesare. "But make haste, my friend. Time flies."

"Tell me which of the ladies here tonight are the most seductive and the most accommodating."

Cesare did not answer. Apparently he had not heard the question; and following his gaze, Ippolito saw that it was on his sister.

※♔※

Ippolito led Angela in the dance. She was enchanting, so young and gay, very eager to enjoy a flirtation with the handsome Cardinal. He told her she was beautiful; she replied that she found him tolerably handsome.

He could look at no one else from the moment she had entered the room, he said. Angela was coquettish. Clearly, thought Ippolito, I shall be her first lover; the first of many mayhap, but the first.

The thought delighted him.

He whispered: "Could we not go away somewhere where we could be alone . . . where we could talk?"

"Lucrezia would notice and send someone to look for me."

"Is Lucrezia your duenna?"

"After a fashion. I am in her charge and I am going to Ferrara with her." His hand tightened on hers; his eyes glowed.

"You enchant me," he said.

"You shock me," she retaliated. "You . . . a Cardinal!"

He grimaced. "Do not be deceived by my cloth."

"I will not. I know enough of Cardinals to know that one must be as wary of them as of any men."

"You are very wise doubtless."

"Far too wise to be taken in by the light words of . . . even a Cardinal."

Ippolito was regretful. She was undoubtedly charming; but she was not sweet and gentle as he had imagined she might be; she would need a long wooing. A pity; since there were not many days left to him.

She cried: "Lucrezia beckons me. Doubtless she does not care to trust me with a rake Cardinal."

He was scarcely listening, for a woman had entered the apartment who was in truth the most beautiful he had ever seen. Her hair was black, her eyes startlingly blue. He had heard of the charms of Sanchia of Aragon, but had not expected them to be so magnificent. She was quite different from the girl whose youth had attracted him. Sanchia was all-knowing, all fire and passion. There would be no long wooing needed with Sanchia. She would know at once whether a man attracted her and, if he did, there would be no delay.

He said: "Since the Duchess, your cousin, beckons you, we must needs obey."

"We could look the other way and pretend we don't see," suggested Angela.

"That," he said sternly, "would be a most ungracious act toward a gracious lady."

And he took the child firmly by the arm and walked with her to Lucrezia. He bowed over Lucrezia's hand and chatted for a while. Then Ferrante came to them, and he asked Ferrante to dance with Angela. Cesare too had come to his sister's side, and Ippolito moved off toward Sanchia of Aragon.

※ ♛ ※

Cesare said: "Lucrezia, you and I will dance."

They went to the center of the floor; she in the mulberry velvet with the dazzling stripes of gold, her hair in its net of jewels, and Cesare, elegantly dressed in cloth of gold looking like a god who had momentarily descended to Earth.

"A fig for these dances!" cried Cesare. "Let us dance as we did in our childhood. The old Spanish dances. You will not have an opportunity of dancing them in Ferrara. They are very prim there, we hear. Let us dance the *jota* . . . the *bolero* . . . the *baile hondo.*"

He towered over her and she felt frail and in his power, yet she knew that she possessed a certain power over him. She was reminded vividly of nursery days and the jealousy which she had inspired between him and their brother Giovanni.

"Lucrezia . . . Lucrezia . . ." he murmured, and his hands were warm and possessive upon her, "you are going away . . . far away. How shall we bear that . . . our father and I?"

"We shall meet," she said desperately. "Often we shall see each other."

"You will go away from us . . . become a member of a family which is not like ours."

"I shall always be of our family."

"Never forget it," he said. "Never!"

The Pope, seeing his son and daughter dancing together, could not bear that any others should be on the floor. He clapped his hands and signed for them all to leave the two dancers alone together. He signed to the viols and flutes, and they understood that he wanted Spanish dances.

So they danced alone, as Lucrezia had on another occasion danced at her own wedding but with another brother. The music grew wilder, more passionate and all marveled at the expression which these two could infuse into the old dances of Spain.

They were watched by many, and there was a whisper in the ballroom that the tales which were circulated about these two seemed to be true.

One of the few who did not watch them was Angela Borgia. She could see handsome Ippolito exchanging passionate glances with Sanchia of Aragon, and she knew that he had forgotten the young girl who had amused him for a moment or two. Her first taste of splendor in Lucrezia's beautiful dress was spoilt for her, and she wanted to run away and cry.

The Pope kept drawing attention to the beauty of the dancers. "Such exquisite grace! Did you ever see such dancing?"

He applauded loudly; he laughed hilariously; but those who were close to him detected a note of hysteria in his voice. Some predicted that, when it was time for his daughter to leave Rome, he would make all sorts of excuses to keep her with him.

THE DOWRY WAS being carefully counted by those officers from Ferrara who had been sent to collect it. There was much haggling about the size of the ducats, and at times it seemed that in spite of the fact that the marriage celebrations had taken place there would be some hitch and Lucrezia would not leave for Ferrara after all.

The nuns were giving Lucrezia a great deal of trouble. The women were terrified, never having traveled before. Some of them were very young and not without attraction. The lusty soldiers who were to accompany the cortège were already joking together and making bets with one another as to who would be the first to seduce a nun.

Lucrezia appealed to the Pope, who was inclined to laugh the matter off.

Let the women be seduced, was his suggestion. It would be something for them to think about for the rest of their days.

But Lucrezia was determined to please her new family, and she believed that if aught amiss befell the nuns, her father-in-law would blame her for it. She knew that Giovanni Sforza had been given shelter by Isabella the Marchesa of Mantua, and that her new sister-in-law would be ready to believe the worst of her. The three brothers had given her some indication of the temperament of the lady, and Lucrezia was already suffering qualms on her account. She must therefore placate Duke Ercole; she knew that she had to live down an evil reputation; she knew that Isabella was going to find fault with her wherever possible; so she determined that Ercole's band of nuns should arrive in Ferrara as virtuous as when they came to Rome.

Therefore she arranged that they should travel in carriages and leave several days in advance. She even arranged at some expense to herself that the carriages should have a covering, so that the nuns would be protected from the weather.

Thus she felt she would show her new father-in-law that she intended to be a good and docile daughter.

Meanwhile in the counting houses the 100,000 golden ducats were changing hands.

THere were tHe last farewells.

Lucrezia visited her mother in her vineyard outside the city.

Vannozza embraced her daughter fondly, but she could not hide her pleasure. This golden-haired beauty was a Duchess, and Duchess of Ferrara, now a member of one of the oldest families in Italy, a real aristocrat. And such a thought could not give Vannozza any feeling but pleasure.

If it had been Cesare who was going away she would have wept bitterly, but in Lucrezia's glorious departure she could feel nothing but pride.

"I shall be in the streets, my daughter," she said, "to watch you leave Rome."

"Thank you, Mother."

"I shall be proud . . . so proud."

Lucrezia kissed her mother, and her emotion was as slight as Vannozza's.

It was different saying good-bye in the nurseries. That was heartrending. Little Giovanni, the *Infante Romano,* in the few weeks he had been at the Vatican, had learned to love her. He had quickly forgotten his previous home, for he was only three years old; and it seemed to him that he had always lived in the splendor to which he had now become accustomed.

He was a little uneasy however to learn that Lucrezia was going away.

Fortunately little Roderigo, being only a year old, was too young to understand.

She embraced the little boys in turn as well as she could; their stiff little figures in rich brocade and the harness, which was worn by children of high degree, to make them grow straight and prevent rickets, stopped her from embracing them as she would have wished.

And at length she must face the most poignant farewell of all. Alexander received her in his private apartments and they were alone.

The Pope took his daughter into his arms and their tears mingled.

"I cannot let you go," he cried. "I will not."

"Oh my Father," she answered him. "Most Holy, most sacred and most loving Father, what will our lives be without each other?"

"I know not. I know not."

"But Father, you will come to Ferrara."

He forced himself to picture it. The journey was long for an old man to undertake, but he would undertake it. He was no ordinary man. He could only endure this parting if he believed that at any time he could set out for Ferrara and she for Rome.

"Yes," he said, "we shall meet often . . . often. How could it be otherwise with two who love as we do? You will write to me, my darling."

"Every day, Father."

"No matter what duties there are? Can you do that, my beloved one?"

"Yes, Father. I shall write every day."

"I wish to know everything, my sweet child. Every detail. The compliments they pay you, the dresses you wear, when you wash your hair, all about your friends; and if any should annoy you, then I wish to know that too, for I tell you this, Lucrezia, oh my love, if any so much as hurt one of these beautiful golden hairs it will go ill with them . . . very ill indeed."

"Did any woman ever have such a loving father?"

"Never, my daughter. Never."

Outside in the square the cavalcade was waiting, the horses pawing the ground, and the soldiers and members of the household were swinging their arms to keep warm in the cold January air.

Cesare came to the apartment and looked sadly from his father to his sister.

"You feel this, even as I do, my son," said the Pope.

Cesare placed his arm about his sister. "She is going from us, Father, but it is not good-bye. She will come to Rome before long. Ferrara is not all that distant from us."

"That is right, my son. I am in need of comfort."

The three of them spoke together then in the Valencian tongue, which they delighted to use when together. It enclosed them in a cozy intimacy and ensured that any, who by chance overheard, would not understand.

"Within the year," said Alexander, "I shall be in Ferrara."

"And," added Cesare, "woe betide any there who does not treat my sister with respect."

Alexander smiled proudly from son to daughter. "Cesare will protect you and your rights, dearest," he said. "You have not only a father who loves you, but a mighty brother, and your welfare is his greatest concern."

Then Cesare embraced her, and he cried out like an animal in pain: "How can we let you go! How can we! How can we!" His eyes were wild. "Let us keep her here, Father. Let us make a divorce. I will take an army against Ferrara if need be. But we cannot part with her."

The Pope shook his head sadly, and Cesare drew Lucrezia passionately into his arms.

Now Alexander became brisk and businesslike, as he knew he must at such times. Slyly he reminded Cesare of the advantages of the match; he discussed the welfare of little Roderigo and Giovanni.

"You, Cesare," he said, "have a little longer with her than I, since you are to ride with her part of the way."

The Pope drew her gold-colored mantle about her and touched its soft ermine lining.

"Keep this mantle wrapped well about you, dearest," he said. "Outside the snow is falling." He drew the hood up so that her face was almost hidden. "Protect this sweet face and this beloved body from the rigors of the journey."

Then he held her to him for the last time, and released her abruptly as though he could bear no more.

He accompanied her then to the waiting cavalcade. He watched her mount her mule, and he called aloud to her so that all might hear: "God go with you, daughter. The Saints preserve you. Though you are far away from me, I shall do as much for you as though you were here at my side."

All knew that that was an assurance for Lucrezia, a threat to themselves. If any do harm to my daughter, the wrath of the Vatican will descend upon him.

Slowly the cavalcade moved out of St. Peter's Square, followed by the 150 carts which contained Lucrezia's gowns and treasure.

Alexander, from a window of the Vatican, watched Lucrezia on her mule and would not move until she was out of sight.

Then he turned away from the window and shut himself into his private apartments.

"I may never see her again," he whispered, and for a short while gave himself up to an agony of grief such as he had experienced at the time of Giovanni's death.

At length he roused himself, shook off his forebodings, and called to his attendants.

"Ferrara," he said, "is not so very far from Rome."

V

INTO FERRARA

In her castle which overlooked the River Mincio, Isabella d'Este was growing more and more uneasy with every report which reached her.

She had placed in the retinue which had left Ferrara for Rome a spy whom she could trust, a man who had at one time been a priest. His letters to her were signed El Prete, and he had sworn before he left that he would attach himself to the suite of the lady Lucrezia and that nothing which concerned her should escape his watchful attention. He would send details of every dress she wore, of every word she spoke, so that Isabella should know as much as if she were present.

Isabella soundly rated all her women; during these weeks of preparation her temper, always uncertain, had been more difficult than usual and they had been at their wits' end to placate her.

Isabella was furious that the Borgia match was to take place; she was also desperately afraid that this girl, of whose attractions her brothers—even pious Sigismondo—wrote so consistently, was going to prove a rival.

"She has dresses such as you have never seen," wrote Ferrante. And there were El Prete's descriptions of mulberry velvets, blue brocades and slashed sleeves from which cascades of lace flowed like waterfalls.

Where did she get such dresses? Who made them? she demanded. The lady Lucrezia took great pleasure in planning her own dresses, she was told, and superintended the making of them.

Isabella had looked upon herself as the most elegant lady in Italy. The King of France had asked her to send him dolls wearing exact replicas of her designs. And here was Ferrante writing that she could never have seen such splendid dresses as those worn by the lady Lucrezia!

"I will show her what elegance means!" cried Isabella.

She summoned all her dressmakers to the castle. Rich stuffs were delivered for her approval. There was not a great deal of time if she was to be at the wedding with a wardrobe to put that of the Borgia woman in the shade.

Night and day she kept her sewing women busy while she designed garment after garment. Pearls were sewn on to rich brocade and capes of cloth of gold were lined with blonde lynx. Satins lay draped over tables, in the richest colors procurable.

Isabella paced up and down the great workroom reading extracts from the letters of her brothers and the priest.

"And what is she like?" she cried. "It would seem they are so bemused by her that they cannot write clearly. 'She is tall and slender and greatly do the gowns she designs herself become her.'"

Tall and slender! Isabella ran her hands over her somewhat ample hips.

Her women pacified her as best they might. "She cannot be more slender than you, Marchesa. If she is, she must be hideously thin."

Isabella's dark eyes flashed with anger and apprehension. It was bad enough to bring a Borgia into the family, but to have to accept her as a rival—a successful rival—even in only one of the talents at which Isabella excelled, was going to be intolerable.

Although her courtiers might tell her that she was ethereal, that she was slender as a young girl, she knew better. Therefore she began work on dresses which would make her appear taller and more slender than she was.

Ippolito wrote of the graceful manner in which Lucrezia danced. So Isabella must summon a dancing master to the castle and practice dancing.

Lucrezia played charmingly on the lute which accompanied her sweet singing voice. Very well, Isabella must play her lute, practice her singing more constantly than ever.

There was one who looked on with aloof amusement at all these preparations. This was Isabella's husband, Francesco Gonzaga, Marquis of Mantua.

The man irritated Isabella. Lazy as he was, there had been occasions when he had reminded her that he was ruler of Mantua, and she never forgot them; and, feeling herself to be his superior, the fact that she was forced on such occasions to acknowledge his supremacy was galling. Many people in Italy considered him a great soldier, a man of some importance; but to Isabella there was only one important family in Italy—her own, the Estes—and the rest should consider themselves highly honored to mate with them. Her dislike of the Borgia marriage had its roots in this belief, and lazy Francesco was fully aware of her feelings.

He understood her too well, this soldier husband; and to see his supercilious smiles at her fear of Lucrezia was decidedly irritating.

She stormed at him: "It is very well for you. What do you care! I tell you this, I do not enjoy seeing my family so demean itself."

"You should be pleased to see it so enrich itself, my dear," said gentle Francesco.

"Ducats! What are they in exchange for this . . . this misalliance?"

"Ask your father, Isabella. He has a mighty respect for the ducat. And ducats are ducats, whether they come from the Papal coffers or those of Ferrara."

"You mock me."

His expression softened a little. He remembered the first days of their marriage, his pride in her who had seemed to tower above all other women. Had he in those days accepted her own estimation of herself? Perhaps. But she had been handsome; she had been sprightly and intelligent. Ah, if Isabella had been more humble, what an enchanting person she might have been!

"Nay," he said. "I do not mean to mock."

"You have seen this girl. Tell me what she is like. These brothers of mine, and all those who report on her, seem to have been bemused by a display of velvet, brocade and fine jewels."

"So you hope to dazzle by an even more splendid display of velvet and brocade, with finer jewels?"

"Tell me, when you saw the girl did she dazzle you?"

Francesco thought back to that day when he had passed through Rome as the hero of Fornovo—that battle which had driven the French from Italy and had later proved to be far from decisive. He remembered a pleasant creature; a child she had been then. He had heard that she was sixteen but he would have thought her younger. He conjured up a vague vision with long golden hair and light eyes, very striking because not often seen in Italy.

"I remember her but vaguely," he answered. "She seemed a pleasant child."

Isabella looked sharply at her husband. The "child," if rumor did not lie, had been far from innocent even then. Isabella would have been interested to know what *she* had thought of Francesco who oddly, so it seemed to her, was so attractive to women. She could understand Ippolito's popularity, or Ferrante's and that of her bastard brother Giulio. But they were Estes. The fascination of her ugly husband was beyond her comprehension.

She shrugged aside such thoughts, for there was no time to think of anything but the coming wedding.

She said: "I must write at once to Elizabetta. I hear that the cortège will spend a little time at Urbino. I must put your sister on her guard against the Borgias."

Francesco thought of his prim sister Elizabetta, who had married the Duke of Urbino, and he said: "The bride is not very old. She will be coming to a strange country. I doubt not that she will be filled with apprehension. If you write to Elizabetta, ask her to be kind to the girl."

Isabella laughed. "Kind to Borgia! Is one kind to vipers? I shall certainly warn Elizabetta to be on her guard."

Francesco shook his head. "You will hatch some scheme between yourselves to make her days in Ferrara as uncomfortable as you can, I doubt not."

Francesco turned and strode away. Isabella looked after him. He seemed quite moved. Could he have felt some tender feeling for the girl when he had seen her? Impossible. It was so long ago and they had not met since. There was no doubt that this Lucrezia Borgia, in spite of her evil reputation (which Isabella was certain had been deserved), appealed to the chivalry in men.

But there was no time to think about Francesco's foolish gallantries and his sympathy with the Borgia girl. He should know better than seek to champion such a woman who had no right to marry into the aristocracy of Italy. She wrote at once to her sister-in-law, the Duchess of Urbino. Poor Elizabetta! she would be expected to entertain the upstart, and Elizabetta should be prepared. She should treat the girl with disdain. It was the only possible attitude in the circumstances.

A messenger brought a letter from her father.

She read it through quickly. It was the formal invitation to the wedding, and strangely enough it did not include Francesco.

There was a private letter in which the old Duke explained. He did not trust the Borgias. The marriage could have been arranged for the purpose of luring great lords to the wedding so that their domains might be left unprotected, for Cesare Borgia was eager to make a kingdom for himself, and Ercole thought they should be wary of the Duke of Romagna; therefore Francesco would be wise to stay at home in order to guard Mantua should the need arise.

Isabella nodded. She and her father had the same sagacious minds, and this suggestion was worthy of him.

Moreover she was rather pleased. She was determined to do everything in her power to make Lucrezia uncomfortable, and it would have been somewhat irritating to have to do so under Francesco's critical eyes. Now she would go without her husband to Ferrara, and there she would enjoy herself without restraint, for she had no doubt whatever that in a conflict between herself and Lucrezia, she would be the victor.

When she showed Francesco her father's letter, he was thoughtful.

"It is sound good sense, is it not?" she asked.

"Yes," he said. "It is sound good sense. Any man would be a fool to leave his domain while Cesare Borgia is seeking to enlarge his."

She slipped her arm through his and laughed up into his face. "I see that your kindness is all for the sister, and does not extend to the brother."

"The brother," he said, "is my affair."

"It's true, Francesco. Therefore the sister should be left to me."

THe journey to Ferrara was slow. There were so many to welcome them on the way, and stage pageants for their amusement. When Cesare said good-bye and rode back to Rome, a sense of freedom from the past came to Lucrezia, but it was not without its apprehensions for the future. Ippolito had said good-bye, for he too must return to Rome—a hostage from Ferrara. Angela Borgia had behaved with haughty indifference toward the elegant Cardinal, who had been slightly piqued and faintly amused, but his thoughts had mainly been on riding back to Rome where he could renew a most exciting friendship with Sanchia.

Riding beside Lucrezia was Adriana Mila, with whom Lucrezia had spent so much of her childhood. Adriana was in charge of Lucrezia's attendants and it was comforting to have her there; Lucrezia was grateful also for the company of her two cousins, young Angela and Girolama Borgia who was the wife of Fabio Orsini. It was very comforting, when going to a strange land, to have old friends about one.

And now the time had come to say good-bye to Francesco Borgia, the Cardinal of Cosenza, in whose kind hands she was leaving the care of her little Roderigo.

She could not prevent herself from weeping before them all when she said her good-bye to the old man, imploring him once more to care for her little boy; and this he again swore he would do. She knew that he would keep his promise for, although he was a Borgia (he was a son of Calixtus III) he lacked that overwhelming ambition which was possessed by her father and brother. In his hands Lucrezia felt she could best leave the welfare of her son, and this she told him while he assured her that her trust should not be misplaced.

Sorrowfully she watched him ride away, realizing that yet another link with the past had broken. Now they must continue the journey, since the Duke and Duchess of Urbino were waiting to receive them.

At the gates of the town of Gubbio in the territory of the Duke of Urbino, the Duke and his wife Elizabetta were waiting to greet Lucrezia.

Elizabetta was filled with an anger which she could not entirely suppress. Her husband had assured her that it was necessary to do honor to Lucrezia Borgia; Cesare had turned his eyes on rich Urbino and any excuse would be enough for him to descend upon it. Therefore they must give him no opportunity for enmity, and must offer his sister all the honors they would give to a visiting aristocrat.

Elizabetta, who had been in close correspondence with her sister-in-law, Isabella d'Este, found it difficult to compose her features as she waited.

She thought—as she had a thousand times—of all the misery the Borgias had brought into her life. When her husband Guidobaldo had been called into service to go into battle with the Pope's son, Giovanni Borgia, their troubles had begun. For one thing, Guidobaldo (acknowledged to be, with her brother Francesco Gonzaga, one of the greatest soldiers in Italy), had been obliged to serve *under* the Borgia. Of all the incompetent commanders who had ever dared command an army Giovanni had been the most incompetent, and as a result of obeying his orders, Guidobaldo had been wounded, taken prisoner by the French and kept in a dark dank prison while his family had strained all their resources to provide the ransom demanded for his release. The Borgia Pope could have paid that ransom, but he had been too busy slyly making his peace terms with the French and covering up the follies of his son.

And when Guidobaldo had returned home he was a different man from the husband Elizabetta had known. He was crippled with rheumatism and suffered piteously from gout. A young man had left his home in the service of the Papal armies; the wreck of that young man had returned. He walked slowly and there were days when he could scarcely walk at all; he was bent double, his face yellow and lined.

Elizabetta had grown bitter. Guidobaldo might forgive the Borgias, for he had a sweet and gentle nature which was the result of an inability to see evil until it was right upon him. Elizabetta would never forgive them.

She looked at him now crouched painfully on his horse, ready to bestow on the daughter of the man who was responsible for his present state that courtesy for which he was famous. He would be telling himself, if he even remembered past injuries: It was not this girl's fault. It would be churlish of me to show by look or word that I remember her father's ill-treatment of me.

But I, thought Elizabetta, shall do all in my power to show these upstarts that we accept them only because it is expedient to do so.

And here was the girl, looking fragile and very feminine, gentle and pretty, so that it was difficult even for one determined to hate her, to believe the evil stories concerning her.

The Duke bowed over her hand; his Duchess was gracious but Lucrezia, looking up into the prim face under the black broad-brimmed hat, at the black velvet garments which were not designed for decoration, was conscious of the Duchess's dislike.

She realized then that this was but a foretaste of what might be waiting for her in her new home; she had to fight prejudice; she had to win the affection or at least tolerance of people who had made up their minds before they met her that they would dislike her.

�│👑│🙐

Guidobaldo had put his castle at the disposal of Lucrezia, and he had planned masques, banquets and lavish entertainments; he was courteous and kind; but Lucrezia was constantly aware of the disapproval of Elizabetta; and it was with Elizabetta that she must travel to Ferrara, as it had been arranged (and it was the Pope's urgent desire that this should be so) that she and Elizabetta should share the magnificent litter.

Alexander had warned his daughter that she must spend as much time as possible in the company of Elizabetta and Isabella. She must study their clothes, their manners, their gestures; she must remember that they were aristocratic ladies belonging to the most noble families in Italy.

"Nothing will delight me more," Alexander had said, "since I cannot have my dearest daughter with me, than to think of her in the company of these Princesses. Do as they do. Speak as they speak. For, Lucrezia, my beloved, you have become a Princess even as they are."

So Lucrezia, lying side by side with Elizabetta in the litter, was determined to be as serene, as aloof as her companion; and thus Elizabetta lost one opportunity of snubbing Lucrezia as she had intended. The Borgia girl, she was forced to admit, had grace and charm, and to be in her company was to believe her to be almost as noble as oneself.

But Elizabetta did not forget. This girl had been brought up at the Papal Court. She had no doubt heard stories of Guidobaldo's impotence since he had returned from the prison in which the Pope had allowed him to languish. The Borgias had always appreciated the coarsest jokes. Elizabetta was not going to forget merely because this girl had a quiet grace and a serene dignity. The Borgias were loathsome; and if they appeared in the guise of charming girls they were even more deadly.

So Elizabetta continued cool and unhelpful, and Lucrezia was conscious that her companion was hoping all the time that she would commit some social error. Adriana Mila hated Elizabetta and was unable to avoid showing it. This hatred delighted the Duchess of Urbino. She would sit smiling her aloof superior smile as they continued the journey, thinking of all she would have to tell her dear friend and sister-in-law, Isabella, when they met in Ferrara.

Elizabetta was slyly amused when they came to Pesaro. She watched the wilting of Lucrezia's spirits as they entered the town. The girl must remember those months she had spent here as the wife of Giovanni Sforza who had been Lord of Pesaro before Cesare had taken it from him.

She must be remembering all the details of the scandalous divorce, and surely she must feel some shame.

Elizabetta said as they came into the town: "This must seem very familiar to you."

"I have been here before."

Elizabetta laughed lightly. "Of course, with the first of your husbands. But then you were so young, were you not. He could not have seemed like a husband to you. After all, it was no true marriage, was it? There was no consummation."

Lucrezia stared straight ahead, and there was a faint flush in her pale cheeks.

"Giovanni, who has been at the court of my sister-in-law, swears that the marriage was consummated," went on Elizabetta. "Poor Giovanni! He has lost so much . . . his lands . . . his wife . . . even his reputation as a man. I pity Giovanni Sforza."

Lucrezia still said nothing; she too pitied Giovanni.

"The people here will remember, doubtless," pursued Elizabetta. "They have long memories. They will remember when you came here as the bride of the Lord of Pesaro. Odd . . . that now you should come here as the bride of another, although their lord—I should say he who was their lord—still lives, still declares himself to be your husband!"

"I do not know how that can be," said Lucrezia, "since there was a divorce."

"On the grounds of non-consummation! But if the marriage *was* consummated, the grounds for divorce would disappear and . . . if there was no reason, how could there be a divorce? I do not know. Your father, who is wise in these matters, no doubt could tell us. Why, look! The people are eager to see you. You *must* show yourself, you know."

And Lucrezia, who had hoped to enter quietly into Pesaro of many memories, must leave the litter, and ride her mule, so that all might see her.

Elizabetta rode beside her, maliciously hopeful. If she could have incited those people to shout abuse at Lucrezia she would have done so.

But here was Ramiro de Lorqua, the Spaniard whom Cesare had set up to rule Pesaro in his absence, and Ramiro, knowing the esteem in which Lucrezia was held by his master, was determined that such a welcome should be given her as was never before seen in Pesaro. He could count on the cooperation of the people, for Ramiro was the most brutal of overlords and they dared not oppose him.

It may have been fear of Ramiro, it may have been because the slender girl with her long golden hair falling about her shoulders seemed to them so gentle and so charming, but there was no abuse; there were only cries of "Duca! Duca! Lucrezia!"

And although Lucrezia's misgivings did not abate during the time she was in Pesaro, Elizabetta was disappointed.

🐚👑🐚

It was Ramiro's duty to escort Lucrezia through the territory of Romagna, and this he did, making certain that in her brother's domain she should be fêted wherever she went. Banquets were arranged in her honor; in the captured towns the citizens displayed banners of greetings. Cries of welcome followed her wherever she went.

The Duke of Ferrara was growing uneasy, for the journey was taking longer than he had anticipated and as many of the wedding guests were already at Ferrara he was groaning at the expense of feeding and entertaining them.

He sent instructions that the journey must be speeded up. There must not be these long halts at various towns. He was all impatience to receive his daughter-in-law.

But Lucrezia showed a certain determination. She would not hurry. Every few days her hair must be washed, and she felt too fatigued to spend day after day in the saddle or even in the litter.

So the Duke fumed and counted the cost of entertaining his guests, while Lucrezia continued with her slow progress.

Ferrante was enchanted by her; he was writing the most eulogistic letters which were dispatched by special messenger to his sister Isabella, throwing that lady into a passion of jealousy.

"She and I opened the ball last night, sister. I have never seen her look more lovely. Her hair was more golden than ever. She had washed it that day. It was necessary that it should be washed every few days to preserve its gold. Her dress was of black velvet, and she looked more slender, more fair than ever before; on her head was a small gold cap, and it was difficult to see which was cap and which was hair; on her forehead there was an enormous diamond. Her Spanish dwarfs are amusing creatures. They dance in the ballroom when she dances, following her round, calling attention to her beauty. They are quite vain and like to parade in brilliant clothes to match those of their mistress. They gesture obscenely and make bawdy jokes—even about their mistress. No one seems to object. The manners of Rome are different from those of Ferrara or Mantua. I wonder, my dear sister, what you would say if your dwarfs made such jokes and gestures as they followed you round the ballroom. Lucrezia accepts it all in the utmost good humor, and since we left Pesaro—where I confess she seemed somewhat depressed—she has been full of high spirits."

When Isabella received that letter she was furious.

"Idiot!" she cried. "The young fool writes like a lover. From what we know of her reputation, mayhap he already is."

She would show the letter to Alfonso, try to rouse some indignation in his sleepy mind.

While Lucrezia was at Rimini, that town where she had opened the ball with Ferrante, one of the servants rode into the castle with disquieting news.

Ferrante was the first person he saw, and he fell at the young man's feet, declaring that Madonna Lucrezia was in terrible danger.

"How so?" asked Ferrante.

"Because, my lord, outside the town a company of men are waiting for her. These are led by Carracciolo."

"Carracciolo!" cried Ferrante.

"May I refresh your lordship's memory? Carracciolo was betrothed to Dorotea da Crema who was abducted by Cesare Borgia and has never been heard of since."

"You mean that this man seeks to abduct Madonna Lucrezia?"

"It would seem so, my lord. Aye, and do to her what Cesare Borgia did to *his* betrothed."

Ferrante lost no time in hurrying to Lucrezia, and telling her what he had heard. Lucrezia was terrified, for the thought of violence alarmed her.

Ferrante threw himself on his knees and declared that he would protect her with his life. She was not listening; she was thinking of Dorotea, who had set out on a journey very similar to this one she was making, and who had never reached her destination. She thought of Cesare, and she shivered.

She understood the feelings of this man Carracciolo. She knew what would happen to her if she fell into his hands.

Elizabetta came in, startling Ferrante from his knees.

He at once blurted out what he had heard.

Elizabetta shrugged her shoulders. "Doubtless it is merely some tale," she said.

But she could not hide the expression of pleasure which briefly flitted across her face. She hates me, thought Lucrezia. She hopes I shall fall into Carracciolo's hands.

She was horrified as much by the malice of this woman as by the fears this story had conjured up.

She thought then: I am a Borgia. The sins of my family are my sins. Can it be that now . . . they are catching up with me, that there is no real escape?

Lucrezia HAD spent a sleepless night. All through those hours as she tossed and turned she had expected to hear shouts of triumph from below, harsh voices demanding her surrender.

A thick fog lay over the town in the early morning, and she insisted that they slip away under cover of it. She was terrified of this place and could not bear to spend another hour in it.

So they left as quickly and as silently as they could, traveling along the Via Emilia toward Bologna.

When the fog lifted they were able to see the open country for miles round and there was no sign of a pursuing force.

Lucrezia's relief was apparent, but Elizabetta was determined that she should not enjoy it.

"I have news for you," she said. "Giovanni Sforza is coming to the wedding."

"Oh, but he can't do that!"

"He can. He has announced his intention of so doing. I have heard that he has already set out for Ferrara."

Lucrezia looked sharply at her companion, and she believed then that Elizabetta and her friend Isabella, whom she had now realized was also an enemy, had arranged that Giovanni Sforza should be at the wedding so that she would be embarrassed.

Looking forward to her new life she saw that it would be peopled with those who wished to destroy her.

THEY came to Bologna where members of the reigning family, the Bentivoglio, set out to meet her; and she was led in triumph to their beautiful house on the outskirts of the town.

Great fires were burning, and it was with immense relief that Lucrezia and her entourage warmed themselves. Entertainments had been prepared, but Lucrezia had begged that they should be postponed. She and her fellow travelers were very fatigued and longed to rest for this first day.

It was pleasant to be within these frescoed walls, to stretch out before a blazing fire, to call for hot water, that the dust of the journey might be washed from her hair.

Angela and Girolama helped with her toilet, chatting excitedly, reminding her that they were on the very borders of Ferrara and very soon would reach their journey's end.

Angela had been a little subdued since her encounter with Ippolito, but she was no less lovely for that.

They were talking of the receptions they had received, of the banners in morello and gold which had been hung out by the people, who knew how she favored these colors.

"It would seem, Lucrezia," said Angela, "that the whole of Italy loves you. Surely only love could inspire such enthusiasm."

"Love . . . or fear," said Lucrezia grimly.

Girolama said: "I hear their voices in my sleep. I hear the chanting: 'Duca! Duca! Duchessa!' It goes on and on."

"They loved you as soon as they saw you," persisted Angela. "They take one look at you and catch their breath with wonder."

"Rather is it surprise," said Lucrezia, "because my hair is not serpents and I have not the eye of the Gorgon."

"They love you the better because of the false rumors they have heard. You look . . . angelic. There is no other word for it."

"You look at me with the eyes of a Borgia, little cousin; and I have come to believe that in Borgian eyes Borgias are perfect. Try looking with the eyes of others."

Adriana came bustling in.

"Hurry!" she cried. "There is unexpected visitor. Oh . . . but look at your hair. Take off that robe quickly. Where is your striped morello? Oh, we shall never have time."

"Who is it?" demanded Lucrezia, terror seizing her. She thought of Carracciolo, furious on account of the rape of his betrothed, vowing vengeance on the Borgias; she thought of Giovanni Sforza humiliated and insulted, determined on revenge.

Adriana was so excited she could scarcely find the words. "I had no notion that this would happen. Come . . . girls . . . quickly. Oh dear . . . oh dear . . . that we should be caught like this!"

"But Adriana, be calm. Pray tell us who the visitor is."

"Alfonso is here. Your bridegroom is determined to see you before you make your state entry into Ferrara."

"Alfonso . . . !" Lucrezia had begun to tremble.

She was aware of the distracted Adriana, searching for the right dress, of Angela, running a comb through her wet hair.

Then there were heavy footsteps outside the room, there was a deep voice commanding someone to stand aside.

The door was flung open and Alfonso d'Este stood looking at his bride.

🜚👑🜚

He was tall and broad, his eyes gray-blue in color, his nose fiercely aquiline, and there was about him an air of brutal strength.

Lucrezia hastily rose to her feet and curtsied.

Those watching thought they had never seen her look so fair and fragile as she did beside her future husband.

"My lord," she said, "if we had had news of your coming we should not have received you thus."

"Ha!" he said. "'Twas my plan to surprise you."

"You find me with my hair wet. We have but recently arrived here with the grime of the journey upon us."

"I'm not so shocked by grime as are most." He took a strand of the hair in his hand. "I had heard it shone like gold," he said.

"It does so when it is dry. I am grieved that it should be wet when you first meet me."

He twisted a handful of it and pulled it gently. "I like it," he said.

"I am glad it pleases you. As *I* hope to...."

He was looking at her, and she knew him for a connoisseur of women; each detail of her body was considered, and now and again she would hear that short dry laugh of his. He was not displeased.

He looked at Adriana and the two girls.

"Leave me with Madonna Lucrezia," he said. "I have business with her."

"My lord," began Adriana in alarm.

He waved his hand at her. "Have done, woman," he said. "We have been married, if only by proxy. Begone, I say." And as Adriana hesitated, he bellowed: "Go!"

Adriana curtsied and went, the girls following her.

Alfonso turned to her. "They will learn," he said, "that I am a man who likes instant obedience."

"*I* have already seen that."

He came closer to her and laid his hands on her shoulders. He was not fully at ease in her company; he never was in the presence of well-bred women. He preferred the girls he met in taverns or in the villages. He looked; he beckoned; and because they would not dare disobey—nor did they want to—they came at his bidding. He was not a man who wished to spend a lot of time in wooing.

She looked fragile, but she was not inexperienced, he knew that much. He had sensed that sensuality in her which appealed to his own.

He seized her roughly and kissed her on the mouth. Then he picked her up in his arms.

"It was for this I came," he said, and carried her through the apartments to her bedchamber.

She was barely aware of the scuffling movement, the hasty departure of the girls, who had been waiting there for her.

All through the house they would be talking of Alfonso's visit. She did not care. Nor did he.

When Isabella heard that Alfonso had paid an unceremonious visit to the bride she was furious.

She stormed into Alfonso's apartments and demanded to know how he could have committed such a breach of etiquette.

"How!" cried Alfonso, who saw everything literally. "By taking horse and riding there."

"But you are expected to greet her standing by the side of our father at the ceremonial entry."

"I shall do so."

"But to go ahead like some lovesick apprentice!"

"All men have some curiosity about the woman they are to marry, whether they are dukes or apprentices. If you want to blame someone for this, blame yourself."

"Myself!"

"Certainly yourself. If you had not painted her so dark, made such a monster of her, I might have been ready to wait. As it was I had to satisfy my curiosity."

"And, knowing you, I imagine it was not only your curiosity which was satisfied."

Alfonso burst out laughing. "Would you have her fancy she had another Sforza for a husband?"

"Sforza was not as the Pope made him out to be."

"He should have proved otherwise."

"What, before witnesses?" Isabella laughed. "You would not have been diffident about proving your manhood, I am sure, no matter how many witnesses were mustered."

"It is hardly likely that mine would have been in question."

"Indeed not, when half the children in Ferrara have a look of you!"

"The people like to know a man is a man."

"You are almost licking your lips."

"She was adequate."

"As any woman would be, for you."

"Not any woman. I would not fancy one who sought to rule me as you rule Francesco."

Isabella angrily flounced out of the apartment and went to ask her father's permission to go ahead of the main party to greet Lucrezia.

"It will be a courteous gesture," she explained. "Alfonso has already been to see her. Now your daughter should go. For, as you have no wife, your daughter must act as hostess."

Ercole agreed because he knew it was no use doing otherwise.

"I will take Giulio with me," said Isabella, "since she should be met by one of your sons. And as Alfonso has already behaved like a yokel at a fair, and Ippolito is a hostage of the Borgias, and Ferrante and Sigismondo are with the travelers, there is no one but Giulio."

"Giulio will enjoy the journey, I doubt not," said Ercole.

Lucrezia stepped on to the barge which was to carry her along the river into Ferrara. This was the flat land, the land of mists in the valley of the Po. Ercole had followed his ancestors in draining much of the land and making it fertile; there were no hills, and the climate was cold compared with that to which Lucrezia was accustomed. Many times she had been grateful for her fur-lined cape and remembered her father's instructions to protect her face and body.

It seemed that when the wind was not blowing there were the fogs to contend with. There was a great deal in this new land to which she would have to resign herself.

But she had met her husband. She smiled, remembering that encounter. Few words had been exchanged. Alfonso made it clear that he had not come to talk. There was something brutal about him; the consummation with him had been quite unlike that with either of the other two husbands. With Sforza it had been shuffling and shameful because that was how Sforza had thought of it. With her first Alfonso, the Duke of Bisceglie, it had been a romantic fulfillment; with the man who was now to be her husband it was a quick and natural animal desire which without finesse or forethought must be immediately satisfied.

She believed she would satisfy him.

As she stood on the deck of the barge peering at the river bank, there was a cry, and looking ahead she saw a great golden galley coming toward them. It obviously belonged to some very rich person as it was decorated with cloth of gold.

Adriana came running to her.

"It is the *bucintoro* of the Marchesa of Mantua. She has come on ahead to welcome you to Ferrara." Adriana's eyes were anxious. She knew of the enmity which Isabella d'Este felt toward Lucrezia, and she wondered whether she should warn her charge.

The barges were tied and Isabella came aboard. She had scored the first victory as Lucrezia had not yet put on the ceremonial dress in which she intended to greet the old Duke of Ferrara. And there was Isabella, catching every eye and dazzling it, in green velvet ablaze with jewels and a long cloak of black velvet lined with blonde lynx.

Lucrezia bowed and Isabella took her into her arms and kissed her cheeks; there was patronage, resignation and hatred in those kisses, and Lucrezia was shocked by their vehemence.

"Welcome to Ferrara," said Isabella.

"I am honored by your coming to see me."

"I wished to see you," said Isabella. "My brother has been misguided enough to visit you already, it seems."

Lucrezia smiled at the memory.

Brazen! thought Isabella exulting. She will soon learn that Alfonso's passion is for every kitchen slut.

She had seen Elizabetta and turned to embrace her.

"My dearest, dearest sister! Elizabetta! How it delights me to see you!"

"Dear Isabella!"

"And the journey?" asked Isabella.

Elizabetta cast a glance in Lucrezia's direction. "Exhausting . . . most exhausting."

Lucrezia knew in that moment that Elizabetta and Isabella were allied against her. But she had caught sight of a very handsome young man who had leaped on the barge. He came to her, holding out both hands.

"Welcome! Welcome!" he cried. "We could not wait for you to come to us. We must perforce come to you." She saw the mist on his brows and curling lashes. His enormous dark eyes were the handsomest she had ever seen. "I am Giulio," he said with a smile. "The Duke's bastard son." His smile was so warm and admiring that she forgot the threatening hostility of Isabella.

She said: "These are my cousins, Girolama . . . Angela. . . ."

"Enchanted, enchanted," murmured Guilio.

His eyes rested on Angela, and Angela's on him.

Why, mused Angela, did I think Ippolito handsome? Only because I had not seen his bastard brother.

Isabella, realizing what was happening, came hurrying forward. They must not forget that she was in charge, so she gave orders that the barge was to proceed, as the Duke of Ferrara was waiting on the towpath a short distance away, to greet his new daughter.

The barge moved slowly forward; then through the mist Lucrezia saw figures take shape on the towpath. The barge stopped and she alighted.

She was led to the old Duke who stood erect to receive her. She fell to her knees on the damp grass; and, looking down on her golden head and wondering what sharp words Isabella had bestowed on her, the old Duke was momentarily sorry for her, she seemed so young and she was among strangers in a strange land.

"Come, rise, my dear," he said, "you must not kneel on this wet grass." He embraced her and went on: "We will not stand about; my barge is waiting here."

But Alfonso was at his father's side to greet her, and the smiles which he exchanged with her were those of two who had shared an experience after which they could no longer be strangers.

She boarded the Duke's barge with him, her husband and his attendants. Isabella was not pleased by her father's courteous care of the newcomer, but there was nothing she could do to prevent it.

She had to content herself with devising the little insults she intended to bestow during the wedding ceremonies.

And so the barge went on into Ferrara, while Alfonso's cavalry rode beside it along the river bank; and as they came near to the Este villa on the outskirts of Ferrara there was a sudden booming of her husband's cannon to welcome her.

Alighting, being received by that other Lucrezia, the illegitimate daughter of Ercole, and being conducted to her apartments where she was to spend the night before making her formal entry into Ferrara the next day, Lucrezia felt bewildered, wondering how she was going to fit herself into the new life which lay before her.

The next day dawned fine and bright, which was pleasing to everyone, as there had been much apprehension that the rain or mist would mar the entry into Ferrara.

Lucrezia was dressed in her wedding dress. Adriana was giving flustered commands to Girolama and a very lovely young girl named Nicola, who seemed more nimble-fingered than Angela, for Angela had fallen into one of her pensive moods since setting eyes on Giulio.

Lucrezia looked beautiful when she was dressed in the mulberry colored satin with the wide gold stripes; the dress did not follow the Spanish fashion of which she had always been so fond, but was cut after the French style. The Pope had impressed upon her the need to show the utmost respect for their French allies as without them Cesare would not have made such a speedy conquest of Romagna, and it was possible that but for French pressure Ercole would have held out against the marriage. Moreover, it had been arranged that the French ambassador was to be her escort at many of the functions which would ensue. She must therefore continually think of placating the French, so it was a pretty gesture to favor their fashion in the most important dress in her trousseau. The wide sleeves, lined with ermine were French; so was the overcoat of cloth of gold. She wore the Este jewels—diamonds and rubies to form a headdress—and for this occasion her hair, seeming more brilliantly golden than ever, was unrestrained and flowed freely about her shoulders.

Her gray horse had been decorated to make a worthy charger for such a glittering bride. Caparisoned in velvet of deep crimson, its harness of gold, it was a spirited creature, a gift from Ercole. Lucrezia did not know it, but Isabella had chosen the horse. It was one of the most beautiful in Ercole's stables, but it was for its wildness that Isabella had chosen it, telling herself that Lucrezia would have to be a very good horsewoman if she could ride the creature into Ferrara without some mishap.

When Lucrezia entered the city, after having been greeted by the French ambassador, a canopy of red satin was held over her and she was accompanied by the ambassadors and their retinues and those of the various noblemen and their households, all vying with each other to call attention to the splendor which they could parade before the eager eyes of the Ferrarese.

Alfonso, the bridegroom, had joined the procession, so plainly dressed in a gray doublet on which were traced fish scales in gold, a white feather the only ornament in his black hat, that he was the most modestly attired person in the assemblage and was noticeable for this very reason. Lucrezia was feeling a certain relief as she entered the city, although she was aware of the strict scrutiny which she must undergo, and she knew too that those who watched her every move with such eagerness were hoping to find fault. The relief was due to the fact that Giovanni Sforza had thought better of attending the wedding. He must, thought Lucrezia, have realized that, in endeavoring to humiliate her he might bring down scorn on his own head; he had therefore stopped short of Ferrara and turned back.

Nicola had brought her the news while she was dressing. She had had it, she said, from Don Ferrante who had expressed his delight and was eager that she should carry the news immediately to her mistress.

Thankful for this small blessing, Lucrezia rode on, her whole attention demanded by the spirited horse which reared and pranced from side to side and was clearly displeased with his burden.

Lucrezia was at home in the saddle, and she believed she could have mastered the creature if she had been on the slopes of Monte Mario or galloping across the meadows; it was a very different matter being the center of pageantry and forced to restrain him.

Isabella, looking startling in a dress of her own design, which was calculated to outshine Lucrezia's wedding dress, and watching Lucrezia's expert handling of the gray horse, grudgingly admitted to herself that Lucrezia was a horsewoman; and what was more to the point although she must be feeling uncomfortable, being forced to ride such a horse at such a time, her serene smiles were undiminished and if she was a little alarmed she gave no sign of it.

But when the fireworks display began, the terrified horse reared suddenly and there was a cry of alarm. Isabella watched exultantly until she realized that it was not Lucrezia who had cried out, but one of the spectators.

"It is dangerous!" cried a voice in the crowd. "No fit horse for the bride."

Alfonso spoke to his men, and a mule, almost as splendidly caparisoned as the gray horse, was brought forward and Lucrezia was urged to change mounts for the sake of the crowd.

With infinite grace she leaped from the horse and mounted the mule. There was a gasp of admiration in the crowd, for the person least perturbed by the incident seemed to be Lucrezia.

Disgusted, Isabella turned her horse away from the procession and with some of her women rode by a different route to the castle. She was no longer interested in Lucrezia's ride now that the bride was on a safe mule, and wanted to place herself in the most prominent position at the foot of the great staircase so that she, in her magnificent gown which was embroidered with quavers and crotchets and which she had called "pauses in music," might receive the guests and do everything in her power to assure everyone that she was the most important woman that day in the castle of Ferrara.

❧♔❧

THE tiring DAY was over. Lucrezia's women clustered about her to help her undress. They removed the mulberry and gold gown and the jeweled headdress; they combed the long golden hair.

There were those who wanted to play the familiar old jokes, indulge in crude wedding customs; but Lucrezia was anxious that they should not do so, and made her wishes clear.

Isabella and Elizabetta who, had she wished for horseplay, would have called her vulgar, now chose to be shocked by her aloof attitude and lack of humor.

But this was Lucrezia's wedding night. She feared that the jokes as arranged by Isabella might include references to her previous marriages. She was adamant, and such was her quiet dignity that her wishes were respected.

Alfonso entered. Unconcerned as to whether they were subjected to the usual crude practical jokes or not, he was ready to spend half the night with his bride.

So this wedding night was very different from that which she had shared with another Alfonso; but she had reason to believe that her husband was not displeased with her.

She would be glad when the night was over, for she was disconcerted by the presence of all those who, the Pope had insisted, should watch the nuptials so that he could be assured that the marriage had been well and truly consummated.

❧♔❧

Very SHORTLY AFTERWARD—in as short a time as a messenger could ride from Ferrara to Rome—Alexander was reading accounts of the wedding.

The details were explained to him: the entry into Ferrara, the magnificence of his daughter in mulberry and gold, her expert management of a frisky horse, the honor which was done to her.

Duke Ercole was now writing enthusiastically of his daughter-in-law. Her beauty and charm surpassed all he had heard of her, he wrote to the Pope. "And our son, the illustrious Don Alfonso, and his bride kept company last night, and we are certain that both were very well satisfied."

The Pope was delighted. He summoned his Cardinals and attendants that he might read the letters to them. He dwelt on the charm of Lucrezia and shook his head sadly because he had not been there to see her.

There were other letters, less restrained than Duke Ercole's.

"Three times," he said, shaking his head with a laugh. "Cesare did better, but then this illustrious Don Alfonso is not a Borgia. Thrice is well enough for an Este."

He was in great good humor. One of his mistresses was pregnant. This showed great virility for a man of seventy-one.

Contemplating this and the triumphs of Cesare and Lucrezia, it seemed to him possible that the Borgias were immortal.

THe morning after the wedding, Lucrezia awoke to find that Alfonso was not with her. It was true then, what she had heard of him. He had, even at such a time, arisen early either to go to some mistress or to his foundry.

What did it matter? She did not love him. This was quite different from her second marriage. She remembered that awakening with a pang of longing which she hastily dismissed, reminding herself of all the misery that marriage had brought her because she had loved too well.

She would not love in that way again. She would be wise. She now bore the title of Duchess of Ferrara, which was one of the grandest in Italy; and she would enjoy her position; she hoped she would bear sons; but she would not be in the least put out by her husband's mistresses.

She looked about her and saw that those who had remained in the apartment to watch the consummation were now missing; they must have retired with Alfonso. She clapped her hands, and Angela and Nicola appeared.

"I am hungry," she said. "Have food brought to me."

They ran away to do her bidding, and after a while came back with food for her. She ate hungrily, but when she had finished she made no attempt to move.

Throughout the castle the wedding guests were stirring, but still she lay in bed chatting with her women.

Angela reported that Isabella and Elizabetta were already up and were wondering why she did not join them.

"I need a little respite from their constant attention," she said.

"Hateful pair!" cried Angela.

"I am determined to rest for the whole morning in my bed," Lucrezia told them. "There will be dancing and festivities for days to come; and, as these will extend far into the night, I intend to rest during the day."

"What will Donna Isabella say to that?" asked Nicola.

"She may say what she will."

"Giulio said," ventured Angela, "that she has always been used to having her own way."

"Ferrante says," added Nicola, "that she rules Mantua when she is in Mantua, and Ferrara when she is in Ferrara."

"And," said Lucrezia, looking from one lovely face to the other, "it is clear to me that what Giulio and Ferrante say is in the opinion of Angela and Nicola absolutely right."

Nicola flushed slightly; not so Angela. She had recovered her spirit and had entered into a relationship with the bold and handsome Giulio, which Lucrezia feared might already have gone beyond a light flirtation. Was there any reason why Angela and Giulio should not marry? Angela had been promised to someone else but, as Lucrezia well knew, such arrangements could be broken. In Nicola's case it was different. Ferrante was the legitimate son of Duke Ercole; there could be no *marriage* with him for Nicola.

These affairs must—as they most certainly would—settle themselves; but she would at an appropriate moment drop a word of warning to Nicola.

Adriana came in to say that Donna Isabella was coming up to Lucrezia's apartments ostensibly to bid her good morning but in reality to study her face for what was called signs of "the battle with the husband." With her came her brothers and some of their young attendants.

Lucrezia knew that, cheated of their horseplay and crude jokes last night, they were determined to enjoy them this morning.

She cried out: "Lock the doors. They shall not come in."

Adriana looked at her questioningly. "Lock the doors against Donna Isabella and Donna Elizabetta?"

"Certainly," said Lucrezia. "Make haste and lock all doors."

So they came and called to her, but she would not let them in.

Isabella, fuming against the arrogance of the upstart Borgia who dared lock an Este door against her, was forced to go away, vowing that she would be revenged.

In his castle beside the Mincio, Francesco Gonzaga read accounts of the wedding.

From his wife Isabella he heard that Lucrezia was quite pleasant to look at but far from the beauty they had been led to expect. The poor girl looked wan and fatigued when she arrived, and was a great disappointment to all who beheld her. She would have been well-advised to have made her entry into Ferrara after dark. She would have looked so much more charming by the flare of torches.

One of his wife's ladies wrote in similar strain, stressing Ferrara's disappointment with the girl, who had turned out to be quite plain after being heralded as a beauty. "It would have been so much better if she had not defied the clear light of day. Everywhere one heard the comment: 'Compare her with Donna Isabella! There is true beauty. And her garments lack the style and dazzling delight of those of Donna Isabella.'"

But Francesco heard reports from other quarters which were not inspired by the malice of his dominating wife.

"Lucrezia Borgia is very pretty indeed; her eyes are light in color and adorable. Her hair is as golden as it is said to be. She is full of vitality, yet serene withal. And although she might appear to be a little too slender this but adds to her grace. She is extremely fragile, wholly feminine and a delight to look upon."

Francesco grimaced when he read that.

He was remembering the young girl he had met when she was in her early teens. He recalled her dainty charm. He was glad that she was beautiful. He hoped she would prove a match for Isabella.

During the next few days Lucrezia realized the depth of that enmity which Isabella felt toward her, and it seemed to her that her only friends were those women she had brought with her. Ferrante and Sigismondo were charming to her, but Ferrante was frivolous and Sigismondo was very much under the influence of his family. Duke Ercole had not wanted the match and was anxiously counting the cost of feeding the wedding guests; he was amazed by Borgia extravagance and ready to listen to Isabella's stories concerning his new daughter-in-law. She might have expected support from Alfonso, but uxorious as he was for part of the night, he was indifferent during the day and seemed scarcely aware of his wife. Lucrezia realized that if she asked for his support against his sister she would receive scant sympathy from him. His thoughts were on his foundry; all she had to concern herself about was getting with child. Alfonso had a horror of sterile women; he could not rid himself of the idea that he was virile enough to overcome infertility, and his favorite mistresses were his fruitful ones.

It was, on the whole, a hostile household, and Lucrezia was glad of her experience and upbringing which was helping her to steel herself against it, and to produce a mood almost of indifference.

She rose late, which was a habit Isabella deplored. She refused to be roused to anger, since she realized that it was her serenity which infuriated Isabella almost as much as her beauty and good taste in clothes.

Each day Lucrezia appeared among the guests in some dazzling gown of her own design which, brilliant as it was, accentuated her elegance; and beside her Isabella seemed coarse and overdressed.

Isabella, furious, determined to discountenance Lucrezia, and during the performance of a comedy, *Miles Gloriosus*, Isabella began to titter, and her attendants—who always sprang slavishly to do her bidding—joined in the tittering so that it was impossible to hear the actors speak. This was meant as an insult to Lucrezia, for the play was being given in her honor.

Lucrezia sat upright during the performance, looking at the players as though she was unaware of the disturbance.

And, when on the next night the somewhat bawdy *Casina* was performed, Isabella declared herself to be so shocked by the choice of the play that she would not allow her women (who were notorious for their lechery) to see it; so again Lucrezia sat through the play laughing heartily at the parts which would have amused her father, and seeming quite unaware of Isabella's disapproval.

But Lucrezia was unhappy, understanding how her sister-in-law was determined to hate her. Her father or Cesare would have gone wholeheartedly into the battle; they would have sought victory over Isabella. Not so Lucrezia, who longed to be loved and had no wish to be anyone's enemy.

There was yet another disturbing element. Isabella was giving Lucrezia's Spanish dwarfs costly materials, velvets and brocades, from which garments could be made. She knew how vain the dwarfs were; they were continually longing to wear clothes as fine as their mistress. This, Isabella pointed out to them, they could do; and there would be more presents for them if they would shout "Long live Donna Isabella" instead of "Long live Donna Lucrezia."

A few days after the wedding Lucrezia declared that she would spend the day in her own apartments, as her hair must be washed and there were letters to be written. Isabella was delighted, for this gave her a chance to win the French ambassador to her side.

She invited him to dinner; she played the lute and sang to him; and before he left she took off one of her scented gloves and gave it to him.

Philippe de la Roche Martin was susceptible, and Isabella was considered to be a very beautiful woman.

This would teach the sly creature to shut herself away, washing her hair! thought Isabella grimly. She was determined to parade her triumph that evening at the ball of torches.

During such balls each lady carried a torch which she gave to her partner of the evening and, when Lucrezia appeared, her hair freshly golden and her eyes sparkling with that vitality which was entirely her own because it was so serene, she looked more delightful than ever in her favorite morello and gold lined with ermine.

She had heard from Angela, who was turning out to be a perfect and reliable little spy for her mistress, of Isabella's encounter with the French ambassador, and she knew that Isabella was determined to lure him from her. So, with a charming smile she handed her torch to Philippe de la Roche Martin, and after such a gesture the gallant Frenchman was so charmed that he had eyes only for Lucrezia, seeming scarcely aware of Isabella's presence, and all were declaring that at last Lucrezia had scored a victory over her rival.

Thereafter Lucrezia kept the Frenchman at her side, which was a triumph indeed, as the French were more feared than any and it was important for all to be on good terms with Louis' ambassador.

The French were subtle; one could never be sure what meaning lurked behind their words and actions. Even those wedding presents which Philippe de la Roche Martin brought from his master seemed to have some subtlety attached to them for those who could understand the dry humor of the King of France. There was an engraving of St. Francis on a gold medal for the Duke; was that meant to imply: What a pious man is Duke Ercole! Here is an image of St. Francis for him to pray to, but if there is one thing he admires as much as the saints it is gold. For Lucrezia there was a rosary of golden beads, but when these beads were opened they were seen to contain musk. Did that mean: She is outwardly demure but what lies within? For Alfonso there was a recipe for casting cannon and a figure in gold of Mary Magdalene. Was Louis slyly reminding the bridegroom of the scandals he had heard concerning his bride?

With the French no one could be sure. That was why it was necessary to be on good terms with the French King's ambassador. That was why Angela, Adriana, Nicola and all those whom Lucrezia had brought with her rejoiced, and Isabella and the rest of the Ferrarese looked on in dismay.

THE CELEBRATIONS WENT on. Each day there was some spectacle to be witnessed. Each day Isabella in company with Elizabetta planned some fresh insult for Lucrezia, each day Lucrezia realized more and more how difficult it was going to be to live in harmony with her relations.

Alfonso continued passionate by night, indifferent by day; Duke Ercole continued to count the cost; letters went to and fro between Rome and Ferrara, but no one yet dared tell the Pope that his daughter had her enemies in the Este stronghold.

The Ferrarese were now being deliberately insulting to Lucrezia, laughing at her as she passed, mocking her graceful walk and her beautiful clothes. She gave no sign at the time that she noticed their rudeness, but she told those ladies who had been selected by Duke Ercole to be her attendants that she had no more use for them and refused to allow them into her apartments. She remained in bed during the greater part of the morning, chatting with her ladies, discussing dresses, attending to her toilet; in her imperturbable way she was behaving as she would in her home at Santa Maria in Portico.

She appeared at the balls and banquets serenely lovely. Once at a ball her own ladies played Spanish tunes on their lutes and, selecting one of the very pretty girls who had come with her to Ferrara, Lucretia danced with her, their skirts whirling, the castanets in their hands; and so enchanted was the company that there was a hushed silence all about them, and Isabella's attempts to start a conversation on some entirely different subject were defeated.

When the dancing was over, and the applause ringing out, Angela demanded of Isabella: "Do you not think Madonna Lucrezia dances like an angel, Donna Isabella?"

"An angel? I was thinking of a Spanish gypsy. Donna Lucrezia dances with fire and spirit, as I hear they do."

Angela was furious, but Giulio was beside her, laying a restraining hand on her arm.

There was talk and laughter throughout the company—and Angela cried to Giulio: "Are you all afraid of her . . . this sister of yours?"

But Lucrezia was sitting back in her chair, while one of her Spaniards fanned her. She was smiling, as though she had not understood the malice behind Isabella's remarks.

That night Alfonso and Giulio danced together for the enjoyment of the company, and later Alfonso played his viol.

It was strange to see his somewhat clumsy fingers, the foundry grime still on them, making such music. Lucrezia began to wonder then whether there was a side to her husband which she had not yet discovered.

ISABELLA WOULD SOON return to Mantua, and she was determined that she must leave some lasting memory of her visit behind for Lucrezia.

She sought out her father. Ercole was pondering over his accounts.

"Do you know, daughter," he said, "that there are still more than four hundred guests in the castle? What do you think it costs me to feed them?"

Isabella, never having time for other people's problems, ignored the question.

"Your daughter-in-law will make Este into a Spanish Court before she has been here long."

"She will do no such thing," retorted Ercole.

"And how can you be sure?"

"Because I would never permit it."

"It will creep in subtly before you realize it. Oh, she is so calm, so smug. There are no tantrums with Madonna Lucrezia. She merely looks like a fragile flower and says 'I want this. I want that.' And because no one takes her seriously and tries to stop her she gets it."

"I have no time for your women's quarrels. Over four hundred guests! Calculate the food that means! And four hundred guests is not all. What of their horses?"

"Those dresses of hers are half-Spanish. All that gold. It is Spanish, I tell you. Spanish! Do you know she wears zaraguelles?"

"What is that?"

"Zaraguelles. Those silk pantaloons, all richly embroidered. She wears them beneath her dresses. It is a Spanish custom. It should be stopped. Father, you will have no peace with that woman and her Spanish attendants."

"Oh, let her be and help me devise a means of ridding myself of these guests who are making of me a poor man."

"Father, if you sent away her Spanish attendants you would have fewer mouths to feed. She has too many attendants."

The Duke was thoughtful, and Isabella smiled. She had made her point.

The loss of her friends was going to hurt Lucrezia more than any of the pin-pricks which Isabella had been able to inflict. She wished she could rob Lucrezia of her more intimate circle—that watchful Adriana, sly Nicola and the saucy Angela. But to go so far as that would certainly bring down the wrath of the Pope. For the moment she must content herself with banishing the Spaniards.

She wrote to Francesco telling him that she was tired of Ferrara and was longing for Mantua. She wished to be with her husband and her little son Federico.

Reading the letter Francesco laughed.

He guessed that the young Lucrezia was holding her own against Isabella, and wondered why he should feel so pleased.

At last the ceremonies came to an end and the guests began to depart. The ambassadors came to make their farewell speeches to Lucrezia, but Isabella contrived to be present with Elizabetta, and it was she who answered them, Elizabetta following her, although the thanks and good wishes of the ambassadors had been directed at Lucrezia.

Lucrezia did not attempt to stop them, but when they were over she offered a few modest and well-chosen words as though she had not been ousted from her rightful place.

The ambassadors thought her meek and nervous, but there were some among them who believed that she considered the open animosity of her sister-in-law too foolish for her attention.

These too were Lucrezia's thoughts; she was also reminding herself that Isabella had a home in Mantua. She could not desert that forever. And it was a happy day when Isabella and her retinue set out for Mantua. Lucrezia could not hide her pleasure.

But, as she went on her way, Isabella was smiling, well satisfied; she knew her parsimonious father would soon deprive Lucrezia of her Spanish attendants, and that Lucrezia's patience was going to be strained to the limit by life in Ferrara.

VI

IN THE LITTLE ROOMS
OF THE BALCONY

W HEN THE GUESTS HAD DEPARTED Lucrezia relinquished the apartments in which she had lived in state and prepared to settle in the "little rooms of the balcony" (*gli camerini del poggiolo*) which had been reserved for her own special use.

She examined them in the company of Angela and Nicola, and all three were delighted with the cozy intimacy of the place. Here, Lucrezia realized, she could shut herself away from the main castle, receive her friends and make of the rooms a little corner of Rome in Ferrara.

Angela bounced on the bed to test it and as she did so there came the sound of tearing material. She saw that the bed covering had split; she touched it and tore it still further.

"It is perished," she said. "It must be hundreds of years old." She looked at her hands black with dirt; the grime of years was on them.

Lucrezia pulled back the coverlet. The sheets, she found, when she touched them, might have been made of paper.

"It is as though they made my bed a hundred years ago and it has been waiting for me all this time!"

Nicola had shaken the velvet hangings and a cloud of dust emerged to hang in the air.

"They are in tatters," she cried.

In despair Lucrezia sat down on a stool and the brocade on its seat split as she did so.

"So these are the little rooms which Duke Ercole so magnanimously gives me," she said.

"It is characteristic of your welcome," cried Angela. "Lavish enough on the surface, full of enmity beneath. If I were you, cousin, I would go at once to your miserly father-in-law and demand to know what he means by giving you such miserable quarters in his castle."

Lucrezia shook her head. "I doubt that would do me any good."

"I should write at once to the Holy Father," suggested Nicola. "He will send orders that you be decently housed."

"I wish to live in peace," explained Lucrezia. "If I complain of this it will only make trouble. No. We will strip off these ancient furnishings and put new ones in their place. We'll have it gay and brilliant. We'll have upholstery in morello and gold, and until it is finished I shall go back to the apartments I have occupied so far."

"So you will do it at your own expense?" murmured Nicola.

"My dear Nicola, how else could I get what I want in Ferrara?"

Angela took Lucrezia's hand and kissed it. "You look like an angel," she said, "and verily I believe you must be one. Your husband spends his days and half his nights with other women; yet you greet him with a smile when he visits you. Your father-in-law insults you by offering you the dust and grime of ages, and you smile sweetly and say you will refurnish your apartments at your own expense. As for that demon, Isabella d'Este, your sister-in-law, she behaves to you like a fiend, and you behave—outwardly at least—as though you respect her. Nicola, what do you think of my cousin? Is she not an angel?"

"I think," said Nicola, "that she is wise, and when you have to live on Earth it is doubtless better to be wise than an angel."

"I trust I am wise," said Lucrezia. "I have a strong feeling within me that I have need of wisdom."

While she was making her plans for the little rooms of the balcony she received the first blow.

Duke Ercole visited her.

He said: "I see you have not yet occupied the rooms of the balcony which I allotted to you."

"They are in sore need of refurnishing," she told him. "When that is done I am going to find them quite delightful. I am grateful indeed to you for having given me such charming rooms."

"Refurnish them!" cried the Duke aghast. "That is going to cost good ducats."

"I have already decided on my color scheme. And refurnishing is necessary. It must be years since it was done."

"The wedding has cost me a great deal," grumbled the Duke.

"I know. *I* intend to pay for the refurnishing of these rooms."

The Duke looked somewhat placated. He went on: "I have come here to tell you that on account of the great cost of the wedding I can no longer afford to feed and house so many of your attendants, so I am sending your Spaniards back to Rome tomorrow."

Lucrezia felt a cold touch of fear. These were her friends, and he wanted to deprive her of them.

She said: "They need cost you nothing. There is, I believe, a clause of the agreement between us which provides that I pay my own household expenses."

"There is," agreed the Duke quickly. "But you must keep within your income here. Moreover Spaniards do not fit well into Ferrara. I have decided they shall go."

She was fighting for control. She had been able to face the hostility all about her because she had been surrounded by her friends. Was this a plot to rob her of them one by one? A terrible feeling of longing swept over her. The Vatican seemed far away and how different was this grim hostile old man—her father-in-law—from the benign all-loving father who had shielded her during all those years which had preceded her journey to Ferrara.

She would not let him see how deeply moved she was. She had dropped her head. He must have thought the gesture one of submission, for he rose and laid a hand on her shoulder. "You will soon learn our ways," he said. "The Spaniards are an expense you cannot afford, and we do not like extravagance in Ferrara."

To whom could she appeal? There was, of course, her husband. He visited her nightly, so he must be pleased with her, and surely she might ask some favor of him.

She lay in the bed waiting for him. He would arrive soon; he had visited her every night since she had been in Ferrara. She guessed she was different from the women with whom it was his custom to associate, and that difference evidently provided a fillip to his passion.

He came singing, as he so often did. Surprisingly he had a good voice. She had not yet ceased to marvel that one, in other ways so insensitive, should have such a good ear for music and an apparent love of it.

He never wasted time in conversation, and there were nights when scarcely a word passed between them. He would undress, leap into the bed beside her, indulge in his animal passion and be gone when she awoke in the morning; but this night she was determined to talk to him.

She sat up in bed. "Alfonso, I have something to say."

He looked surprised, raising those heavy brows as though reproving her for suggesting conversation at such a time.

"We scarcely ever speak to one another, let alone indulge in conversation. It is simply not natural, Alfonso." He grunted. He was not giving her his full attention, she realized. "But tonight," she went on, "I am determined to talk. Your father has said that my Spanish attendants are to leave Ferrara in the very near future. Alfonso, I want you to stop that happening. These are my friends. Do not forget that although I am your wife I am a stranger here. It is difficult to live in a strange land even when one's friends are about one. There are different customs to which I must adjust myself. Alfonso, I beg of you, speak to your father. Alfonso, you are listening?"

"I did not come to talk," said Alfonso reproachfully.

"But are we never to talk? Are we always to meet like this and nothing else?"

He looked at her in some surprise. "But what else?" he asked.

"I do not know you. You visit me at night and are gone in the morning. During the day I scarcely see you alone."

"We do very well," he said. "You'll be with child before long. Perhaps you already are."

There was a flash of spirit in Lucrezia's voice as she retorted: "In that case would you not be wasting your time?"

"We can't be sure yet," said Alfonso speculatively.

Lucrezia felt hysterical. She began to laugh suddenly.

"You are amused?" asked Alfonso.

"It would seem I am a cow . . . brought to the bull."

Alfonso grunted. He was ready now. He blew out the candle and got in beside her. She felt his heavy body suffocating her, and she wanted to cry out in protest.

But there was no one who would heed her cries.

The next day when the Spaniards left Ferrara, she did not protest. She accompanied the Duke and his court on a hunting expedition, which he had had the good taste to arrange for her so that she should not see the actual departure of the Spaniards.

She was docile, and Ercole, watching her, believed that he had discovered how to treat his daughter-in-law.

WHEN THE SPANIARDS reached Rome they went straight to the Vatican where Alexander received them immediately.

"What news of Ferrara?" he cried. "What letters do you bring me from my daughter?"

While they gave him letters, they warned him that life was not as glorious for his daughter in Ferrara as he would wish.

He listened eagerly to the tales of Lucrezia's first days there, of the arrogance of Elizabetta and Isabella and the serenity of Lucrezia which had astonished all who beheld it.

The Pope's face darkened. "None shall insult her with impunity," he declared. "So the Duchess of Urbino received her coldly. That was a foolish thing to do. My son Cesare will not be pleased when he hears of that, and his temper is quick. He lacks his father's calmer and more forgiving nature."

He listened to an account of the festivities, of how Lucrezia had shone at them, her beauty dazzling all who beheld it, with everywhere women desperately trying to copy her dresses.

"We were dismissed, Holiness, and the Lady Lucrezia wept at our going."

"It must have been sad, and I am sure she misses you, but tell me—what of her husband?"

"Holiness, he spends his nights with Madonna Lucrezia—at least part of his nights. His mistresses are numerous, and he has not deserted one of them even now that he has a wife."

The Pope laughed. "But he visits his wife's bed every night?"

"Every night, Holiness."

"Then I swear she'll be with child by Easter."

"Yet, Most Holy Lord, her husband spends much time with other women."

"Ah, youth!" said the Pope regretfully. "What a glorious thing is youth. So Alfonso has mistresses, eh, many of them. Well, that is as it should be. I would not want another impotent husband for my daughter. Why, as soon as Lucrezia is with child, Alfonso must come to Rome. I will make him very welcome."

And the Spaniards went sorrowfully away, realizing that the Pope did not attach much importance to their dismissal from Ferrara.

Lucrezia HAD refurnished the little rooms, and they were now charming, opening as they did on to the balcony in which beautiful flowers were growing. There were three rooms—her bedroom, another room in which she entertained, and a third which was for her ladies. Here they seemed cut off from the rest of the castle; and if Lucrezia did not quarrel with the Ferrarese in her suite, she let them know that their allegiance, first to Isabella and then to Duke Ercole, had been noted by her and she did not trust them as her friends.

There were whole days when she would not emerge from the little apartments, and the sound of laughter and singing would be heard coming from them. Spanish customs prevailed in the little rooms, it was said. Lucrezia rarely left her bed until noon. Then after Mass she would eat a leisurely meal and chat with her women about the dresses she possessed and the new ones she would have. They sang songs and read poetry. There was of course her hair to be washed; and she liked to bathe her body in scented water. Often when she, Angela, Nicola and Girolama found themselves alone they could call to the little maid, Lucia, to bring in a great bath of scented water; then they would undress, put their hair into nets and leap into the bath, laughing and splashing each other, washing each other's backs, while little Lucia kept heating more water which she perfumed and added so that they could lie in the bath in scented comfort for as long as they wished.

Then they would get out, vigorously dry each other's bodies and put on silk shirts of the Moorish fashion which had been made for this purpose. They would stretch themselves out on couches and talk of poetry and love, of fine materials, of new styles in dresses and jewels, through the long afternoons, while Lucia burned sweet-scented incense in the braziers.

Lucrezia did not know that little Lucia was bribed with bonbons by El Prete, and that she gave detailed descriptions of what happened in the apartments to him, which he in turn passed on to his mistress Isabella.

"It is pagan, quite pagan!" stormed Isabella from Mantua; and she declared that she would write to her father about the extraordinary behavior of his new daughter-in-law.

Ercole read those letters from Isabella, and it hurt him so much to think of money being wasted so lavishly that he felt he must curb Lucrezia's extravagance. It was no use speaking to Alfonso who declared that his duties began and ended in the bed, and defied any to suggest he did not perform those with zeal.

Ercole had to act. He would not allow Spanish customs to be brought to Ferrara. He therefore forbade the wearing of *zaraguelles*, and there was now a law that the police might arrest any woman wearing these. But how, since these garments could be completely hidden by a gown, were the police to know they were worn? It would be possible, it was pointed out to Ercole, for women to defy the law under the very eyes of the police.

Ercole was in a difficulty. The law had been made and must be carried out, but he was not the man to give his police a chance of behaving lewdly. He could not allow them to arrest women suspected of wearing these strange garments and submit them to a search. Then how could it be ascertained whether or not a woman was wearing *zaraguelles?*

Ercole then declared that the police might discover by examination whether women were wearing the forbidden garments; but if they put an innocent woman to the test, if they were to submit her to the search only to discover she was without the offending garment, then the hand which had made the search was to be cut off. It was the only curb Ercole could put on possible immorality—which would offend him even as much as the introduction of Spanish customs to his court.

In the little rooms there was laughter. Lucrezia and her ladies continued to wear their *zaraguelles* of softest silk delicately embroidered; for what man was going to risk the loss of his hand to discover what was worn beneath a woman's gown?

THE LAW AGAINST *zaraguelles* had been made to placate Isabella. But there was something else on Ercole's mind.

He made his way to the little apartments one day.

There was an immediate scuffle when he was known to be approaching, for fine materials had to be put away, aromatic baths concealed.

Lucrezia received him graciously, but inwardly she smiled to notice his dismay at the lavish decoration of her apartments.

"Welcome, my lord Duke," she said, and gave him her scented hand to kiss.

Musk! thought the Duke. The price of musk today is high and of what use is scent? What purpose does it serve?

"I pray you sit beside me," said Lucrezia. "I would make you comfortable. Will you drink some wine?" She clapped her hands.

"I am in no need of wine," said the old Duke, "being fully refreshed. My dear daughter, you are more than comfortable here."

"I have made these rooms very like those I occupied in Santa Maria in Portico."

"They must have been very richly decorated."

"They were comfortable enough."

"You live extravagantly here, daughter, and it is for this reason that you and I must have a talk. We do not like debts in Ferrara."

"Debts! But I have my money . . . my own money. I ask nothing of Ferrara!"

"But surely you cannot afford to live as you are living on 8,000 ducats a year."

"8,000 ducats a year! But certainly I could not live on 8,000 ducats a year."

"It is a goodly sum, and it is what I have decided shall be your income."

"My lord Duke, you joke."

"I am in great earnest."

"I could not live on 8,000 ducats a year. I must have at least 12,000, and I should not consider that princely."

"You have been brought up very extravagantly, I fear," said the Duke sternly.

"Moreover," said Lucrezia with spirit, "my father has paid you a handsome dowry. This was to enable you to give me an income which would compare with that to which I have been accustomed."

"Ferrara is not Rome, my daughter. I am not a rich man as your father is. In Ferrara we consider 8,000 ducats a goodly income. I pray you, adjust your ideas and consider it so, for it is all you will get."

"I cannot accept it," said Lucrezia. "It would be penury."

"I doubt it not, if there must be so many gowns, so much costly scent. You have many of these luxuries. Be more careful with them, and they will last you a very long time."

Lucrezia's expression was blank. She said: "I am and my household cannot live on 8,000 ducats a year."

"How vulgar is this talk of money," sighed the Duke. "Now that you belong to our noble family you should learn that we speak only of such matters with discretion."

"I have heard you speak of them with fervor many times," retorted Lucrezia.

The Duke looked pained. "Then I beg of you, let us drop the subject."

"That," said Lucrezia, "I cannot do until you agree to give me at least 12,000 ducats a year. It is the least I can live on."

The Duke rose abruptly and left her. He was murmuring something about upstart families who married into the aristocracy.

It was an open break.

Lucrezia very soon became certain that she was pregnant. She called her women to her and imparted the news.

They were delighted.

"Now," said Angela, "you will be in a position to bargain with the mean old Duke. He will surely not deny the income she deserves to the mother of his grandchild!"

"I doubt it," cried Adriana. "He is a miser, that man; and he is even now wondering how he can best rid the court of us."

"I'd die rather than leave," declared Angela, thinking of handsome Giulio, who was her lover.

"I'll not let you go," declared Lucrezia. "Moreover I shall not accept a ducat less than 12,000."

Alfonso was delighted when he heard the news. He strutted about the castle declaring that he would have been very surprised if she had remained barren longer.

His habits changed slightly; having achieved his object he no longer came so regularly to her by night.

The old Duke was, as had been anticipated, delighted with this early proof of Lucrezia's ability to bear sons for Ferrara, and he relented a little. "I think," he said, "that we might allow you an income of 10,000 ducats."

But Lucrezia was unimpressed. She told him firmly that she could not possibly live on less than 12,000 and she considered even that beggarly.

The Duke stumped away in anger, reiterating that this preoccupation with money was downright vulgar.

One would need to be insensitive, thought Lucrezia, to endure meekly this new state of affairs in the Este palace. The continual haggling with the old Duke over money was indeed undignified; it was being made perfectly clear to her that she had been accepted into the family merely because her wealthy father was willing to buy her position; Alfonso, now that she was pregnant, showed clearly that he preferred his low-bred mistress. There was continual bickering between her intimate attendants and the Ferrarese, and the little rooms of the balcony became like a separate court.

Lucrezia then decided that she would do what she had done once before when she had found her position intolerable.

It was Easter week and she decided to find refuge in the quiet of convent life; there she could be at peace; she could meditate on her position; she could look at her life clearly and make up her mind how she should act.

So, a few weeks after her wedding, she entered the Convent of the Poor Clares, and in the quiet cell allotted to her and among the gentle nuns she considered her problems.

It was not possible for the wife of the heir of Ferrara to remain shut away, and Lucrezia's spell of peaceful contemplation with the Poor Clares was brief.

Soon she was back in the rooms of the balcony to find that nothing had been changed by her absence. There were still the same conflicts between her attendants and the Ferrarese; her husband's visits remained spasmodic and he showed quite clearly that he had no intention of trying to smooth out matters between herself and his father; and that his duty, which was to get her with child, had been expeditiously performed.

The Duke visited her in his somewhat ceremonious fashion but he did not come to discuss her income. He had, he considered, been quite magnanimous when he offered 10,000 ducats a year; he implied that, if he had taken a great deal from her father, it was because Este dignity was impaired by accepting a Borgia into its intimate family circle, and for this a great price must naturally be demanded.

But he came with further complaints.

"My daughter," he said, "there are two maids of yours whose levity is giving some cause for scandal in my court."

"And who are these?" she asked.

"Your cousin, Angela Borgia, and Nicola the Sienese."

"I beg of you, my lord Duke, tell me in what way these ladies have offended."

"My sons, Ferrante and Giulio, are enamored of them, I hear, and these two ladies are less virtuous than they should be."

"It is to be hoped," said Lucrezia, "that they are not as lacking in virtue as their two admirers, or I should tremble for the consequences."

"Ferrante and Giulio are men. There is a difference, you must understand.

There could be no marriage between my sons and these ladies. I would prefer that there should be no scandal either."

"You forbid them to meet? Then, my lord, I must ask you to tell your sons of your displeasure. You have more authority in this respect than I could possibly have."

"I have already made my wishes clear. They are not to visit these apartments each night, as they have been doing."

"So you would forbid them to come here."

"I do not forbid. I have told them that they may come here not more than twice a week, and then only when others are present."

"I will respect your wishes as far as is in my power," said Lucrezia. "But you must understand that while I may command my ladies I have no power over your sons."

"I know it," said the Duke. "But I ask you not to encourage their frolics." Lucrezia bowed her head.

The Duke took one look at the extravagant hangings, and Lucrezia could see that he calculated the cost as he did so. She smiled ruefully and bowed him out of the apartment.

It was impossible to restrain the young princes in their love affairs. Giulio was particularly ardent and Angela was by no means discouraging. How far had that affair gone? Lucrezia asked herself. She dared not ask Angela; nor did she wish to pry. It was not in her nature to administer strictures which were going to bring unhappiness to lovers. So she turned aside from asking awkward questions and let matters take their course.

She herself was thinking a great deal about the child she would have. It was in the early days of pregnancy yet, but she longed for a child. She often thought of Giovanni and Roderigo in Rome and wondered when she would be allowed to have them with her. The thought of suggesting such a thing filled her with bitterness. Duke Ercole was not eager to support *her*; what would he say if she asked permission to bring her sons to Ferrara? That project must wait. So she gave herself up to contemplating the new child.

To the little rooms of the balcony came some of the most interesting people in Ferrara. Writers and musicians felt that the atmosphere of those rooms was more congenial than that of the main apartments of the castle; and among those who came was a man who aroused Lucrezia's immediate interest. This was Ercole Strozzi. Strozzi was a member of a Florentine family of great riches. They had been bankers who had come to Ferrara some years before, and they had found great favor with Duke Ercole.

This was probably due to the fact that they were experts with money. They knew how to make it, how taxes could be levied; and since they proved to be an asset to Ferrara, Duke Ercole was ready to lavish titles on them. Tito Vespasiano Strozzi was a poet in addition to being a brilliant money-maker, and this doubly endeared him to Duke Ercole, so he was ready to be gracious to his son, Ercole Strozzi.

Alfonso was paying one of his rare evening visits to Lucrezia's apartments when Ercole Strozzi first came. Alfonso had been sitting at Lucrezia's side, playing the viol with that touch of near genius which seemed so incongruous in a man of Alfonso's kind. The company was listening entranced when Ercole Strozzi slipped into the room with the friend who wished to make him known to Lucrezia.

There was about Ercole Strozzi an air of distinction. He was not handsome but elegant; he was crippled and walked with the aid of a crutch.

Lucrezia's eyes held his as Alfonso continued with his playing. Ercole Strozzi gave her that startled look of admiration which she had received from others yet which seemed different on Strozzi's face. He bowed and stood perfectly still where he was, for ceremony was not observed in the little rooms, and art was all-important.

When Alfonso ceased playing, Strozzi came forward and taking her hand bowed over it.

He said: "The greatest moment in my life, Duchessa."

"Then, my friend," sneered Alfonso, "yours must have been a singularly unexciting life."

Strozzi smiled lightly and condescendingly. His favor with the Duke absolved him from paying much respect to his uncouth son. It was true that one day Alfonso would be Duke of Ferrara, but it was no use Strozzi's trying to curry favor with him; he would never achieve it however much he tried. He and Alfonso were so very different in outlook that there could never be harmony between them.

"I would not call it that," said Strozzi, still keeping his eyes on Lucrezia, "yet would I insist this is its greatest moment."

Alfonso guffawed. "Strozzi's a courtier, or fancies he is. Poet too. Do not take his words too seriously, Lucrezia. Well, Strozzi, what are your latest verses, eh? Ode to a red rose or a pale primrose?"

"You are pleased to mock," said Strozzi. "And while you may mock me as much as you wish, I confess it grieves me that you should speak slightingly of poetry."

"I am an uncouth fellow, as you know full well," said Alfonso. He looked round the company. "So elegant, these ladies and gentlemen! These artists! What right have I to be here among them with the odor of the foundry upon me?"

"You are very welcome here," said Lucrezia quickly. "We should be gratified if you came more often."

He chucked her under the chin, for he took a great delight in calling attention to his crude manners in such company. "Come, wife," he said, "let us have the truth. You'll be glad to see me gone. Truth is more interesting to a plain man like me than your precious poetry."

He put a hand on Strozzi's shoulder with such force that the poet almost lost his balance and was forced to lean heavily on his crutch.

"It is not so," began Lucrezia, but he interrupted her.

"Adieu, wife. I'll leave you to your art. I'm off to those pastures more suited to my animal tastes and spirits. Adieu to you all." And, laughing, he left the apartment.

There was a brief silence which Strozzi was the first to break.

"I fear my coming is the cause of his departure."

"You must not blame yourself," said Lucrezia. "I blame no one. He rarely comes here and, apart from the time when he plays his viol, seems to have little interest in what goes on."

"He will never like me," said Strozzi.

"It may be because he does not know you."

"He knows much of me which he does not like. I am a poet for one thing. A cripple for another."

"Surely he could not hate you for these reasons?"

"To a maker of cannons poetry seems a foolish thing. He is strong, never having known a day's sickness in his life. He regards with horror any person who is not physically perfect. It is often so with those who have physical perfection and something less in their mental powers."

A faint smile twisted the handsome lips, and Lucrezia was aware of a stab of pity, which was what Strozzi intended. Strozzi was not in the least sorry for himself; he would not have changed places with Alfonso. Strozzi was so mentally brilliant that he had quickly learned to turn his physical disability to advantage. His love affairs were conducted with a finesse which would have seemed incomprehensible to Alfonso d'Este, but they were as numerous and satisfactory as he wished. He had come now to charm Lucrezia and to win for himself a Cardinal's hat.

He stayed at her side throughout the evening, and he was not long in assuring Lucrezia that in him she had found a friend who would compensate her for all the hostility she had met with at the Este court.

He could not dance. He indicated his crutch.

"I was born with a deformed foot," he told her. "In my youth this caused me pain and discomfiture. It no longer does, because I have realized that those who would despise me for my deformity are not worthy of my friendship. I think of my deformity as a burden which for a long time I carried on my back, until I suddenly realized that through it I had developed other qualities; then it was as though the load had burst open to disclose a pair of wings."

"You are a philosopher, as well as a poet," said Lucrezia. "And I like your philosophy."

"Have I your permission to come to your apartment often? I feel that you and I could have a great deal to say to each other."

"I shall look for you tomorrow," Lucrezia told him.

When Alfonso visited her that night, he was unusually talkative. She was in bed when he entered the apartment in his brisk manner.

"So the Strozzi has found his way to your apartments, eh?" he said. "The greatest moment of his life!" Alfonso burst into loud laughter. "You understand what that means, eh? At last he has a chance—so he thinks—to get his Cardinal's hat. The Pope's own daughter! How could he get nearer the Pope than that?" Alfonso wagged a finger at her. "Mark you, he'll be asking for the hat before long."

"I think you are wrong, Alfonso," she said. "You judge everyone by . . . by the people you know here. There was a delicacy in his manner."

That made Alfonso laugh still more. "He knows how to manage the ladies, eh? Not the women . . . but the ladies. Strozzi wouldn't look at a mere serving-woman. What good could she bring to him? I tell you a Cardinal's hat means more to him than any of your gracious smiles. He wouldn't as much as *see* a kitchen girl. He wouldn't see what she could offer. He'd only know she hadn't Cardinals' hats to give away."

"It might be more comfortable for us all if you were less interested in the gifts of kitchen girls," began Lucrezia. "It might be that if you made some pretence of living a life more in keeping with your rank . . ."

But Alfonso was in bed and no longer interested in conversation.

UNDER THE COVER of music Strozzi talked.

"I make no secret of the fact, my dear Duchessa, that it has been the ambition of my life to possess a Cardinal's hat."

"It is a worthy ambition," Lucrezia told him.

"And knowing of the love your father bears you, I feel that, should you consider me worthy, you would be able to convince His Holiness that I should not disgrace the Sacred College."

"I am certain that you would grace the Sacred College," Lucrezia assured him.

Strozzi bent nearer to her. "I would be willing to spend as much as 5,000 ducats to attain my desire."

"It is a great sum," said Lucrezia.

"My family is rich, and I feel that I must go out into the world. I have my life to live in places beyond Ferrara."

"I will write to my father. I believe the friendship that you have shown to me will please him more than 5,000 ducats."

"I am grateful." His beautiful eyes were eloquent. She smiled at him. She was realizing that, in spite of her chilly reception in Ferrara, she was at last making her own court, and life was becoming interesting.

"How you must miss Rome!" he said suddenly.

"More than I can say."

"Ferrara seems dull to you doubtless?"

"It is so different from Rome. In Rome there was so much to do. There were so many shops full of wonderful things."

"So you think the shops of Rome the best in Italy?"

"Indeed yes. Those of Naples are exquisite, but I think Rome holds the palm."

"You have not seen the shops of Venice?"

"No."

"Then I must tell you they have goods therein . . . jewels . . . cloth . . . to outshine anything you ever saw in Rome."

"Is this really so?"

"Indeed yes. Venice is the traders' center. They congregate there from the north and the south; and all that is best in their merchandise is bought by the merchants of Venice and displayed in the shops there. I see that you have exquisite taste. May I say that I have never seen gowns of such style? Your velvets and brocades are very beautiful; I have never seen better outside Venice."

He continued to tell her of the beauties of Venice, of its culture and riches. Strozzi had many friends in that city but there was none other who held the place in his esteem which belonged to Pietro Bembo. Lucrezia knew of Pietro Bembo, of course. He was the greatest humanist in Italy and one of the finest poets. The friendship was treasured by Strozzi, he declared, and he felt himself honored by it.

"I know his work well," said Lucrezia. "I agree with you that it could only come from a fine mind. Now I envy you your visits to Venice more than ever. There you will be with your poet friend. You will be together in that beautiful city; you will search the merchants' treasures. Oh yes, I greatly desire to explore Venice."

"You are a beautiful woman and nothing should be denied you. I could bring Venice to you, in some measure. I shall of course speak of you with my friend Pietro Bembo; I shall tell him of your charm and delicacy. I will make you known to him and him to you. With your permission I will search the shops of Venice for the finest velvets and brocades, and I will bring back the most exquisite, the most delicately embroidered, that they may be made into gowns worthy to be worn by you."

"You are kind, my friend. But I could not buy these stuffs. Since I have been in Ferrara I am no longer rich."

"You are the Pope's daughter. I shall but mention that, and there is not a merchant in Venice who would fail to give you all the credit you desire."

"You are a very good friend to me," she told him.

He lifted her hand and kissed it. "To be the best friend you ever had, Madonna, is the greatest ambition of my life."

"I thought that was to wear a Cardinal's hat," she answered.

"No," he said slowly. "I have suddenly discovered that I no longer desire that hat."

"You speak seriously?"

"I do indeed. For of what use to me would a place in Rome be when my Duchessa must remain in Ferrara?"

Ercole Strozzi was possessed of an inner excitement. His thoughts were constantly of Lucrezia. Her entirely feminine quality appealed to him in such a way as to present a challenge. Lucrezia seemed to demand to be dominated. He wished to dominate. He did not seek to be her lover; their relationship must be of a more subtle nature. The bucolic Alfonso satisfied Lucrezia's sexual appetite, and Ercole would have considered a physical relationship between them crude and ordinary; he had been the lover of many women and there was no great excitement to be gleaned from a new love affair.

The lameness of Strozzi had filled him with a desire to be different from others in more important ways. There was in his nature a streak of the feminine which betrayed itself in his love of elegance, in his exquisite taste in clothes and his knowledge of those worn by women. This feminine streak impelled him to show his masculinity. The artist in him wished to create. It was not enough to write poetry; he wished to mold the minds of those about him, to guide their actions, to enjoy, while he suffered his infirmity and was conscious of the feminine side of his nature, the knowledge that those he sought to mold were in some respects his creatures.

Lucrezia, gentle, all feminine, so eager for friendship in this hostile land, seemed to him an ideal subject whose life he could arrange, whose character he could mold to his design.

He could advise her as to her dresses; he could show her the charm of a fashion she had hitherto ignored. He was now going to Venice to choose rich stuffs for her. Her outward covering would be of his creation; as in time the inner Lucrezia should be.

She was sensitive; she was fond of poetry. It was true that they had not educated her in Rome as Isabella d'Este, for instance, had been educated. He would remedy that; he would encourage her to become more intellectual;

he would increase her love of poetry, he wished to be the creator of a new Lucrezia.

Thus he reasoned as he came into Venice, as he went through the stocks of the merchants and bought exquisite patterned satins and velvets of varying shades of color.

"They are for Lucrezia Borgia, Duchess of Ferrara, and daughter of the Pope," he explained; he had come from Ferrara on a visit to Venice, and she had entrusted him with these commissions.

There was not a merchant in Venice who was not prepared to bring out his most treasured stock for the daughter of the Pope.

When Strozzi had made these purchases he visited his friend, the poet Pietro Bembo, who welcomed him with great pleasure. Pietro was handsome and thirty-two years of age; but his attraction did not only lie in his handsome looks. His reputation throughout Italy was high; he was known as one of the foremost poets of his time, and because of this there was always a welcome for him in Ferrara, Urbino or Mantua, should he care to visit these places.

Pietro was a lover of women, and experience was necessary to him. He was in love at this time with a beautiful woman of Venice named Helena, but the love affair was going the way of all his love affairs, and Pietro, finding it difficult to write under the stress, longed for a quiet refuge. He and Strozzi had been fond of each other since they had met some years before in Ferrara; they admired the same poetry; they were passionately devoted to literature in any form; and they shared a detestation of the commonplace.

"I feel angry with Helena," said Strozzi. "I fancy she is the cause of your long stay in Venice."

"I am thinking," said the poet, significantly, "of leaving Venice." Strozzi was pleased to hear this.

"I have been buying fine materials here in Venice," he said. "Such silks, such tabbies! You never saw the like."

"Silks and tabbies? What do you want with such fripperies?"

"I have been buying them on behalf of a lady—the new Duchess of Ferrara."

"Ah! Lucrezia Borgia. Tell me, is she a monster?"

Strozzi laughed. "She is the daintiest, most sensitive creature I ever set eyes on. Exquisite. Golden-haired, eyes that are so pale they take their color from her gowns. Delicate. Quite charming. And a lover of poetry."

"One hears such tales!"

"False. All false. It is an ill fate which has married her to that boor Alfonso."

"She feels it to be an ill fate?"

Strozzi's eyes were thoughtful. "I do not entirely understand her. She has learned to mask her thoughts. It would seem that Alfonso perturbs her little; and when I think of him—uncouth, ill-mannered—and her—so sensitive, so delicate—I shudder. Yet there is a strength within her."

"You are bewitched by your Duchess."

"As you would be, had you seen her."

"I admit a certain curiosity as to the Borgia."

"Perhaps one day you will meet."

The poet was thoughtful. "A delicate goddess married to Alfonso d'Este! One would say Poor Lucrezia, if one did not know Lucrezia."

"You do not know Lucrezia. Nor do I. I am not certain that Lucrezia knows herself."

"You are cryptic."

"She makes me thus."

"I see she absorbs you. I have never known you so absentminded before. I declare you are longing to go back to Ferrara with your silks and tabbies."

Strozzi smiled. "But let us talk of you. You are restless. You weary of Helena. Why do you not go to my Villa at Ostellato?"

"What should I do there?"

"Be at peace to write your poetry."

"You would come and see me there?"

"I would. Mayhap I would induce Lucrezia to ride that way. It is not far from Ferrara."

The poet smiled, and Strozzi saw that the exquisitely lovely Duchessa of such evil reputation, whom he had described as sensitive and unformed, was catching at Pietro's imagination as she had caught at his.

Strozzi was pleased. He wished to mold those two. He wished to put them together in his great villa at Ostellato and watch the effect they had on each other.

WHEN Strozzi returneD to Ferrara he found that the heat of the summer was proving very trying to Lucrezia. She was suffering a great deal of discomfort in her pregnancy, and her relations with Duke Ercole had worsened.

She was delighted with the velvets, silks and tabbies which Strozzi had brought her, and they did lift her spirits for a while. She was interested too in his account of the poet, Pietro Bembo, and she gave a party during which Strozzi read the young man's newest verses.

But these were isolated incidents, and Strozzi saw that she was suffering too much discomfort to feel really interested in either fine materials or absent poets.

She ordered a handsome cradle to be made in Venice so that she could have it well before the baby was due. "It is a great extravagance," she said, "and I know full well that the Duke will be shocked when he sees it. But I care not. I have come to think that the only pleasure I have in this heat is from shocking the Duke."

Alexander had now heard of Duke Ercole's offer of 10,000 ducats as his daughter's annual income, and he was incensed.

"My daughter cannot be expected to live on a pittance," he cried, and reminded that old Duke of the 100,000 ducats he had received as dowry, besides all other benefits.

The Duke retorted that marriage into aristocratic families could not be attained by those of lower status without high costs; this infuriated Alexander, and all benefits from the Papacy immediately ceased.

Alexander wrote that he had heard that Lucrezia had been treated with scant respect at the time of the wedding, and he would like Duke Ercole to know that he was far from pleased.

But from the stronghold of Ferrara the Duke snapped his fingers at the Papacy; Lucrezia declared that she would rather starve than accept the miserly 10,000 ducats a year. She gave a banquet for the Duke in her apartments and at this she used the goblets and silver-ware which were marked with the emblem of the Grazing Bull, the arms of Naples and those of the Sforzas. She wished the Duke to know that she was not dependent upon him. She had the relics of a less penurious past, and the Grazing Bull was much in evidence.

The Duke's reactions were that, as she had so much, he need not worry about her. He was content to save his money.

And after that, when he visited her, he found the doors of the little rooms closed against him.

But he did not wish them to be so obviously bad friends, and these little quarrels were patched up, although he remained adamant—and so did Lucrezia—about money.

Lucrezia was finding this pregnancy more exhausting than the others. She lost a little of her sweet temper and although she did not keep up the intense hostility between herself and the Duke, she was less forgiving than previously.

She spent a few weeks at the Este palace of Belriguardo and when she left this palace to return to Ferrara, the Duke, who was becoming disturbed by the spreading rumors of hostility between them, set out to meet her on the road.

Knowing that he was coming to greet her, Lucrezia deliberately delayed so that the Duke was kept waiting in the heat of the sun. When she came, fresh and cool from having rested in the shade, and expressed little concern to see him hot and angry, he realized that there was another side to the soft and gentle Lucrezia.

Guidobaldo di Montefeltre, Duke of Urbino, sat in the convent gardens outside the city walls. It was June and delightful to sit in the shade. He was suffering less pain than usual and was thinking how pleasant it was to enjoy that freedom from discomfort, to sense the peace all about him.

Elizabetta, his wife, was visiting Mantua. She and Isabella, he guessed, would put their heads together and discuss the latest Borgia scandal. Isabella was urging her father to stand firm and not to give the bride a ducat over 10,000 a year.

How those two hated the bride of Ferrara! He could understand Elizabetta in some measure, but in Isabella's case it was jealousy. He had urged Elizabetta to forget her rancor before she set out on her visit to Mantua.

"I suffer the fortunes of war," he had said. "It is wrong to blame young Lucrezia for what happened to me."

Then Elizabetta had cried out: "You went away young and healthy. You came back crippled. Alexander could have brought you back to me . . . as you went away. But he let you stay in that filthy prison. It was no concern of his, he said. You were no longer of use to him. Do you think I shall ever forget that?"

"Still, Elizabetta," he had said, "it is wrong to blame the girl."

"I blame them all. I would like to see all Borgias suffer as they have made us suffer."

Guidobaldo now shook his head, remembering. What joy was there in life if one nursed hatreds? To live peacefully one must forget past insults and injuries; and that was what he had tried to do. Even at this moment Cesare Borgia was passing through Urbino on his way from Romagna to Rome. He had asked permission to do so. Elizabetta would have refused, even though she knew that to have refused would have plunged Urbino into war. She would have cried: "I'll not give one concession to these Borgias, however small. Let him make a long march round Urbino. Let him know that we do not forget. He has laughed at you for your lost manhood, yet he must know that it was his father who destroyed it." Then he would have had to placate her, to tell her that to refuse would mean war. He was glad therefore that she was in Mantua and that they had avoided one of those unpleasant emotional scenes during which he was reminded how much his infirmity meant to her.

Sipping his wine he wondered where this would end. Would it happen, as some prophesied, that as the territory of Il Valentino grew so would his longing to make it bigger? Would he rest content until the whole of Italy was his?

Wretched thoughts. There had been too much war. The old soldier was weary, no longer being fit for battle. Thus he could enjoy the good wine, the pleasant shade and the thought that Elizabetta was away in Mantua.

He dozed and was awakened by the clatter of horses' hoofs. He heard voices in the distance.

"The Duke! He is here? Then I pray you take me to him at once."

Did he guess during those brief seconds before the messenger reached him?

Elizabetta was right when she said a man was a fool to trust a Borgia. He had laid his territory open to the Borgia, and at this moment Il Valentino and his ruthless troops might be in the city itself.

The messenger was kneeling before him. "My lord, there is not a moment to lose. Il Valentino has entered Urbino. He has taken possession of the city. He is sacking the palace. He is sending his soldiers to find you, and he knows that you are here. To horse . . . my lord Duke. Fly for your life!"

So Guidobaldo di Montefeltre, twice deceived by the Borgias, took horse and rode toward Mantua with all the speed his crippled body would allow.

He found that the news had preceded him. Elizabetta had retired to her apartments worn out with grief and worry. Isabella and Francesco consoled him, making him very welcome and insisting that he must rest.

"A curse on these Borgias!" cried Isabella.

But when she was alone with her husband, Francesco saw the speculative look in her eyes.

"Guidobaldo was a fool to allow Il Valentino free entry into Urbino," she declared. "What has come over him?"

"He is war-weary. He is no longer young. That is what has happened to Guidobaldo."

Isabella stalked up and down the apartment. She was visualizing the Urbino palace and Elizabetta's wonderful collection of statues which she had always envied. She had asked Michelangelo to make something similar to his Sleeping Cupid for her, but artists would not work to order. It was the same with Leonardo da Vinci; he could not be induced to produce anything beautiful at this time, being concerned with a new drainage system which he was sure would be the means of disposing of many of the causes of periodic plague. At least, thought Isabella, the Borgia would not *destroy* anything which was beautiful.

Francesco watched her, that wise expression in his sleepy eyes.

She turned on him in her rage. "How can you smile? Do you not realize what this means to Guidobaldo and Elizabetta?"

Francesco became serious. "Too well," he said. "I smiled because I thought of what it might mean to you."

"I do not understand you. What could it mean but a share in their grief?"

"It could also mean a share in their treasures."

She wanted to slap his face. He was too clever, with his habit of reading her thoughts.

She was loud in her denunciation of Cesare Borgia, but at the same time she secretly dispatched messages to Urbino, and her attitude would appear to be friendly. She had heard—she wrote—that Cesare had taken possession of the Urbino palace, and there was a statue there which she coveted beyond all others. She had longed to possess it and now, if Il Valentino were kind, she had a hope of doing so. It was the Sleeping Cupid which Michelangelo had made. She and Cesare were related since his sister's marriage to her brother. If he could find it in his heart to grant her this request, she doubted not that they could be friendly as relations should be.

The message was dispatched; she set about comforting Elizabetta and poor Guidobaldo, and her denunciation of the Borgias rang through the Castle.

Cesare was not one to give friendship lightly. He found the Sleeping Cupid and its beauty moved him deeply; it surely was one of the most exquisite pieces of workmanship in Italy, and it was small wonder that Isabella wanted it. Should he send it to Lucrezia? That would infuriate Isabella.

Cesare laughed aloud. His first impulse was to despatch the cupid to Ferrara, but he hesitated. He was the ruler of his own dominion now, and he dreamed of extending that dominion. He must not therefore give way to stupid whims. Isabella of Mantua was important in his schemes because she was a clever woman of wide influence, and at this time it was better to be friends with such as she.

He began to see the significance of this beautiful object. It was beyond price.

If he gave such a gift, what should he ask in return? The Duke and Duchess of Urbino were now sheltering in Mantua. They must be banished. Cesare's daughter by Charlotte d'Albret should have a husband. The heir of Mantua was reputed to be one of the loveliest little boys in Italy. He knew that poor Charlotte's child was ill-favored because he had read between the lines of all the reports that had come to him. She was intelligent enough, but her nose, young as she was, was ill-shaped and over-large. If she grew up ugly, a very large dowry might be demanded for her. Better to get her settled now while she was still a baby. And why should she not marry into one of the aristocratic families of Italy; why not the heir of Mantua?

Isabella had despised the Borgias and had shown this during the wedding at Ferrara. He would avenge Lucrezia and secure a prize for himself at the same time.

Smiling at the cupid, he assured himself that his terms would be accepted: The banishment from Mantua of the Duke and Duchess of Urbino; the betrothal of his daughter to handsome little Federigo, the heir of Mantua. And for that, Isabella should have her cupid.

Lucrezia HAD Left her scented bath and was lying on a couch in her Moorish shirt when the news was brought to her.

Angela, who was with her, watched her with startled eyes, for she received the news without a word, and when the messenger had gone she lay still, staring before her.

Angela ran to her and embraced her. "Why should you grieve?" she demanded.

"They gave me hospitality," answered Lucrezia. "The Duke was kind to me."

"His Duchess was not. Hateful creature! In her black velvet hat and black velvet gown, she was like an old crow."

"He asked for free passage through Urbino," said Lucrezia, "and it was given. And when there was no one to defend the place . . . he took it. Oh, why does he do such things? Why does he make me cringe in shame?"

"You are too sensitive. This is war, of which we know nothing."

"But we do know. I know that my brother's ambition is like a wild animal let loose. It attacks, destroys . . . destroys all . . . men, women, children—and self-respect. I would I had never gone to Urbino."

"The Duke and Duchess are safe. Your sister-in-law Isabella will look after her dear Elizabetta."

Lucrezia confined herself to her apartments. She would see no one, and there was no longer music or laughter in the little rooms. She was ashamed and unhappy.

Angela, Adriana, Girolama and Nicola all sought to comfort her.

"They are safe at least," they repeated. "They reached Mantua. There they will find refuge."

They had not yet heard that the Duke and Duchess of Urbino were being requested to leave Mantua for Venice. They did not know that the little heir of Mantua was being betrothed to Cesare's daughter.

Meanwhile Isabella stood looking at the exquisite work of art, and its beauty brought tears to her eyes.

Francesco watched her and murmured: "It is indeed beautiful. It should give you great pleasure. You paid a very big price for it, Isabella."

It was the middle of July and the heat was intense.

There was plague in Ferrara and, to the horror of all within the palace, one of the maids went down with it. Angela Borgia caught it, but mildly, and Lucrezia was in great fear. They might isolate the patient but the damage was done.

Ceccarella, one of Lucrezia's maids, died shortly after taking it and another, Lisabetta, was smitten with a serious attack.

Then Lucrezia caught it.

When the news reached Rome there was panic throughout the Vatican. The Pope became hysterical with fear. He paced up and down his apartment calling to the saints to watch over his beloved child and swearing to take a punitive expedition into Ferrara if she did not survive. He also sent her several physicians in whom he had great confidence.

He dispatched further messages to Cesare, begging him to add his prayers to those of his father that the greatest calamity which could befall them both might be averted.

Lucrezia's condition was aggravated by her pregnancy which had already given some cause for alarm, and the doctors shook their heads over her. They feared the worst would happen.

"The burden of the child will be too much for her to bear," was their verdict. "The best thing that could happen would be a still-birth; then we might reduce the fever."

Lucrezia herself, tossing on her bed, was barely conscious. The old Duke visited her and wept over her condition. If she would recover, he declared, he would meet her wishes as to her income. She should have her 12,000 ducats a year. "But part of it shall be in goods," he added quickly.

Lucrezia smiled vaguely at him; she was not fully aware who he was.

Furious messages came from Rome.

"The Duke of Ferrara has brought about my daughter's low condition by his meanness," cried the hysterical Alexander. "If aught happens to my beloved daughter I shall know whom to blame."

The Duke grew anxious. The recent conquest of Urbino had been alarming; where would Cesare Borgia turn next? everyone was asking.

Alfonso had been on a mission to Pavia where Louis of France was installed. The heir of Ferrara had gone there as his father's ambassador in order to placate the French King; and, Francesco Gonzaga had said, they must placate the French and with the French, Louis' ally, Il Valentino, for if they did not they would be hanged one after another and be unable to do anything about it. They could only hope that their territory was not the next on the list for invasion.

Duke Ercole sent an urgent message to Alfonso that his wife was near to death and he must return at once; and as soon as Alfonso arrived in Ferrara he hurried to the bedside of his wife.

Alfonso was ill at ease in the sick room. The sight of Lucrezia, pale and wan, her eyes glazed and unrecognizing, filled him with dismay.

He could think of nothing to say to her. He knelt by the bed and took her hands in his. Hers were dry and feverish.

"You'll be well," said Alfonso. "You'll get better. We'll have a big family . . . handsome boys . . . even if you lose this one."

But Lucrezia only looked at him with unseeing eyes, and Alfonso rose hopelessly to his feet.

She was dying, it was whispered throughout the castle. Her pregnancy had been a difficult one from the start, and now she had contracted this fever, what hope was there for her?

Furious and sorrowful messages came from the Pope. He was imploring them to save his Lucrezia's life and at the same time threatening them.

My daughter's death will not suit the Borgias at all, he wrote; and the Este family should be very careful how they acted, for he, Alexander, did not think it was going to suit them very well either.

The old Duke harangued his doctors. They must save his daughter-in-law. It was imperative that they do so. They must take every precaution, apply every cure—no matter how expensive—but they must not let her die.

In the draughty corners of the castle men and women whispered together. If she dies, the Borgias will come against us. More than all their possessions the Pope and Il Valentino love this girl.

But each day Lucrezia's condition worsened, and it was said: "She cannot last the night."

As she lay unconscious, half dead, unaware of what was going on about her, there was suddenly heard the sound of galloping horses.

A little band of riders was seen, and at the head of them rode a tall and elegant man who leaped from his horse, flung the reins to a groom and called: "Take me at once to the Duchess of Ferrara."

One of the servants ran out to this man and cried: "It is impossible, my lord. The Duchess lies near to death and there is plague in the castle. If you value your life you should not come here."

"Stand aside," was the answer, "and if you value *your* life conduct me with all speed to the bedchamber of your Duchess."

Others came running forward, and there were some who recognized the newcomer. One man threw himself on his knees and cried: "My lord, there is plague in the castle."

He was brutally kicked aside and a voice of thunder cried: "Must I fight my way to my sister?"

Then all fell back, and the man who had been kicked now whined: "My lord Duke, follow me; I will take you to her with all speed."

A shiver of fear ran through the castle. Voices shook as they whispered one to another: "Il Valentino is here!"

He knelt by the bed and took her into his arms.

"My love, my dearest, I am here. Cesare is here . . . come to cure you."

And she, who had recognized none, now opened her eyes; and those watching saw the change which came to her face as she whispered: "Cesare . . . Cesare . . . my beloved . . . so it is you."

He had his arms about her. He called for pillows that she might be propped up; he smoothed the damp hair back from her face.

"I am here now." His arrogant voice rang through the apartment. "You will be well now."

"Oh Cesare . . . it has been so long."

He had taken her hands and regardless of the risk was covering them with kisses. "Too long . . . too long, my precious one."

She was almost fainting on her pillows, but all were aware of the new life in her.

He shouted to them: "Leave us. Leave us together."

And none dared disobey.

⁂

THey waiteD outsiDe the room. It was a miracle, they whispered; she had been close to death, and he was bringing her back to life.

He called for wine—wine to revive her—and when it was brought, those who saw her marveled at the change in her, for it was as though this vital man breathed new life into her.

It is not natural, was the verdict. These Borgias are something more than human. They have power over life and death. They deal death and they raise from the dead.

The strange incomprehensible words which passed between them—for they spoke in the Valencian tongue—sounded like incantations to those listening ears. They remembered all the slights they had inflicted on Lucrezia since her arrival in Ferrara, and they trembled lest Il Valentino knew of these.

Lucrezia was saying: "You should not have come to me, Cesare, you who are so busy with your victories."

"Too busy to come to my dearest one when she is sick unto death! Never that, beloved. We must send a message at once to our father."

"He will be overjoyed when he knows you have been here."

"He will only be overjoyed if I can tell him that you are well again. Lucrezia, you must not die. Think of it! What would life mean to us . . . our father and myself . . . if we lost you!"

"But you have *your* life, Cesare. All your ambitions are being realized."

"They would be of no account to me if I lost you."

He embraced her and she wept a little. "Then I must get well. Oh Cesare, I have thought so much of you . . . and our father. I have thought of you and your conquests. I have thought of you in Urbino."

He was quick to sense the tremor in her voice and, because there were times in their lives when they were so close—and this was one of them—that they read each other's thoughts, he was aware of her unhappiness on account of his conquest of Urbino.

"Lucrezia, dearest," said Cesare. "It is necessary that I establish my kingdom. Do not think that I work for myself alone. Everything I have gained belongs to us all. Do not think I ever forget that. You ... our father ... our children ... shall all benefit from my conquests. I will give one of my new towns to your little Giovanni. What say you to that? The little *Infante Romano* is a Borgia, and he must not be forgotten."

"You comfort me," she said. "Often I have thought of my children."

"Grieve not, dearest. You have nothing to fear on their account while our father and myself are alive to care for them."

He could see that he had comforted her. He laid his hand on her hot forehead. "It is time you slept, beloved," he said. "I will remain at your bedside and, although I must leave you soon, it shall not be for long. I must go, Lucrezia, but I shall return."

So she slept and he remained on watch. When he left, the next day, all were talking of the miracle, for it now seemed that Lucrezia would recover.

✦✦✦

A FEW WEEKS later when Lucrezia, still weak, was reclining on her bed surrounded by her women, she cried out in sudden fear. "My pains are beginning," she said; and as the child was not expected for another two months there was consternation throughout the palace.

Doctors came hurrying to her bedside, and all those fears which had been dispersed with the coming of Cesare were revived.

How could Lucrezia emerge alive from a seven-months birth after her recent illness? It seemed impossible.

Alfonso came to his wife's bedchamber and knelt by her bed. Lucrezia smiled at him wanly, but he had no elixir of life to offer her comparable with that which, so all were certain, flowed from Il Valentino.

"Do not grieve, Alfonso," she said. "If I die you will marry again ... a woman who mayhap will be able to give you children."

"Do not speak of dying," cried Alfonso. "You must not die. You must live, Lucrezia. If you are spared I ... I will make a pilgrimage to Loreto."

She smiled. She realized that he was offering a great sacrifice in exchange for her recovery.

"On foot," added Alfonso.

"Oh, Alfonso," she murmured. "That is noble of you. But you must not grieve. I fear our child will be lost. They tell me that there is little hope that it will be born alive."

"Let it not disturb you," said Alfonso. "We are young, are we not? We will get more children. Boys . . . many of them."

Now the sweat was on her forehead and the pains were growing more frequent. She cried out in her agony, and shortly afterward her daughter was born, dead.

※♕※

ALL THROUGH THE night they waited, while Lucrezia lingered between life and death, and with the morning Cesare came riding once more to the castle. Hope soared at the sight of him for all believed in his supernatural powers, and that what he had achieved once he would achieve again.

Ercole and Alfonso greeted him with delight.

"I beg of you," cried Alfonso, "save my wife. It would seem that you alone can do it."

So Cesare went to the sick-room, and as Lucrezia's dull eyes fell upon him they brightened. She knew him, although she had been unaware of those at her bedside until he came.

He knelt by the bed and embraced her; he demanded that they be left alone. He was instantly obeyed and when he eventually called to all those who were hovering at the door, he demanded that the doctors come forward to bleed his sister.

"No more," moaned Lucrezia. "Let me rest. I am weary of remedies. I want only now to go in peace."

Cesare answered her reproachfully in the Valencian language and, turning to those about the bed, said that his sister should now be bled.

The leeches were applied while Cesare watched; he held Lucrezia's foot and talked to her while the bleeding took place. Although none knew what he said, it must have been amusing for from time to time Lucrezia would laugh, as those in the Este castle had thought never to hear her laugh again.

So Lucrezia recovered; and went for peace and a change of scene to the Convent of Corpus Domini. The people of Ferrara crowded about her litter as she was carried thither from the castle, and wished her a complete return to health.

Meanwhile Alfonso set out on his pilgrimage to the Virgin of Loreto. He had sworn to go on foot, which would have taken up much valuable time when all heads of states should be looking after their dominions, and Alfonso wished he had not been so rash in making his vow. However, now that his daughter had recovered, the Pope felt benevolent to all the world and declared that Alfonso should have a dispensation, releasing him from part of his vow. He must go to Loreto, but he might make the journey on horseback.

In Corpus Domini Lucrezia began to think of returning to life, and to long for fine clothes and music, for the company of her friends, and a lover who was less crude than Alfonso.

VII

THE GREAT CALAMITY

When Lucrezia returned to the little rooms
of the balcony Ercole Strozzi was waiting for her. Lucrezia had
regained her fragile beauty, the hair-washings had been resumed and it was as
golden as it had ever been, but she herself had changed subtly. She was more
spirituelle.

She seemed pleased that Alfonso was not in the castle. After his return
from the pilgrimage he was making a tour of the military fortifications of Ferrara, and as he probably felt that until Lucrezia was completely well again there
would be small chance of getting a healthy heir for Ferrara, he would therefore
be better occupied with the military and his stray mistresses.

Lucrezia was by no means unhappy at being left alone. The musical evenings continued. There was a truce between herself and the old Duke. She had
sent to Rome for Jacopo di San Secondo, who was one of the most famous
players of the viol in Italy; and the Duke often came to her apartments to hear
the music of this man.

Strozzi continued to bring exquisite materials from Venice, and displayed great interest in the making up of these. He could discuss clothes for hours and make suggestions which delighted Lucrezia.

He would read poetry to her and very often these verses were the composition of Pietro Bembo. He talked often of Pietro.

"Poor Pietro, he lives a lonely life now in my villa at Ostellato. It is good for his work, however. He speaks of you often."

"That is because you have often spoken of me to him."

"How could I help that? My thoughts of you occupy a large part of my waking life."

"My dear Ercole, I cannot tell you what your friendship has meant to me. Knowing you has changed my life here in Ferrara."

"There are many jealous of my favor with you."

"There will always be those to watch my actions and hate me for them."

"There is one who envies me more than any other. Can you guess who? No, you will not, I see. It is Pietro Bembo. I will confess something. Those verses I read to you today—they were written for you."

"But he has never seen me. How could he write such verses for one he has never seen?"

"I have talked of you so much that he has a clear picture of you. If you visited him he would know you at once."

"I cannot believe it."

Ercole Strozzi looked at her slyly. "Why not put it to the test?"

"Call him to Ferrara!"

"Then he would know you at once. No, I mean visit him at Ostellato."

"How could I do that!"

"It is simple. A short journey by barge. There is peace and solitude in my villa at Ostellato. Why should you not make the journey? Surprise him."

She laughed. "I should enjoy seeing our poet," she answered. She turned to Strozzi. "I believe you are continually trying to plan pleasures for me."

Strozzi smiled. He wanted to see them together—the amorous poet with his neo-Platonic leanings; this Lucrezia, fresh from the pains of childbirth and fever, whose husband could never give her anything but physical satisfaction.

It would be interesting to watch the reaction of these two; so interesting that Strozzi had long planned it, for he knew it would be irresistible.

BEMBO WAS WEARYING of the quiet life, although it was true that when he was in Venice he had longed for it. He had come here on Strozzi's invitation mainly to escape from his Helena. She was charming but she was demanding, and he was satiated with physical love. Handsome and famous, sought after by courtiers and rich women, he had felt the solitude of the country to be inviting.

He would stay until Strozzi came again, and then he would explain to him his feelings. It would be churlish not to explain in person to his friend after he had offered him the hospitality of his villa.

He was sitting in the shade, murmuring verses to himself, when he heard the sound of voices. There was music too, and feminine laughter. A party was sailing down the river. He did not bother to go and look, and suddenly he was aware of her coming toward him. She was dressed in cloth of gold and there was an emerald on her forehead; her long golden hair was caught in a net which was sewn with pearls.

She said: "Good day to you, poet. You know me?"

He knelt at her feet, took her musk-scented hand and kissed it. "There is only one who could look thus, Duchessa."

"Strozzi said you would know me. I have so enjoyed your poems. I could not resist the opportunity of telling you so."

"You have come with friends?"

"Some of my women and other attendants. They await me in the barge."

"Then you have come in simplicity. I am glad. For I live simply."

"I know. Strozzi told me."

"He has told you much about me?"

"So much that I cannot believe we are now meeting for the first time. I also know you through your works."

"I am so overwhelmed that I forget the duties of a host. You will take refreshment?"

"Perhaps a goblet of wine."

He clapped his hands and commanded a slave that it should be brought to them in the garden; they sat in the shade drinking, and talking mainly of his poetry.

She enchanted him. She was ethereal, so different from the woman rumor had painted for him. She was so gentle, even more fragile than usual after her recent illness, and that she should be one of the notorious Borgias seemed incongruous while it added to her attractions.

"I cannot stay long," she told him. "We must get back to Ferrara before dark."

He said he would show her the herb gardens; he was interested in herbs and had made additions to Strozzi's collection. And as they walked through the gardens he made poetry for her, and this told her that her coming was something he would never forget as long as he lived.

"You will visit me again here?" he asked.

She smiled a little sadly. "I could not come often. It would be noticed. Then, I do not doubt that I should be forbidden to come. But why should you not come to Ferrara? You could meet your friend Strozzi, and there are often parties in my apartments. You would be very welcome."

He took her hand and kissed it fervently. Then he walked with her to the barge.

She stood looking back as they glided away; he stood watching. They were both aware of a tremendous attraction, different from that which either had ever felt for any other person.

Pietro Bembo came to Ferrara, and he was seen each night in the little rooms of the balcony.

As he was famous thoughout Italy his presence added luster to those gatherings. Bembo was accustomed to adulation and it affected him little as he was completely absorbed in his friendship with Lucrezia. For the first time in their lives each was indulging in an absorbing friendship which was as yet Platonic. It was a friendship of the mind, of spiritual love; and it was felt by both that should it descend to a physical level it would deteriorate and become another love affair such as each had known before.

Lucrezia, weak from that recent illness which had almost proved fatal, Pietro seeking a sensation which would lift his muse to even greater heights, found in each other all that, at this time in their lives, they longed for. Each of them felt exalted—together, apart from the rest of the world.

Strozzi looked on, content. This was as he wished. He had brought them together; he could watch them indulge in their unusual relationship and know that it was what he had intended. He could feel godlike; he could say to himself: I took these two prominent people and brought them together, I knew that they would behave thus, and it is what I wished. It would be interesting to see how long the friendship lasted on this level, how long before passion gained control and brought them tumbling from their lofty eminence down to earthly pleasures. Two beautiful sensual people, mused Strozzi; how long before they went the way of all flesh?

He believed he could keep them where they were or bring them down to Earth. It was a sensation of power which appealed to him mightily, which soothed the pain in his leg, which eased the fatigue which came so readily because of that pain, which made him say to himself: Ercole Strozzi, if you can rule the lives of two such people, why could you not rule the world?

Angela, so abandonedly in love with Giulio now that she made no secret of the fact that she spent half her nights in his company, was delighted by Lucrezia's friendship with Pietro.

"Why, cousin," she cried, "Giulio tells me that his sister Isabella is furious because Pietro comes here. She prides herself that all great poets are her property. How glad I am that *we* have secured him."

Lucrezia smiled gently at her exuberant cousin. Poor wayward Angela, thought Lucrezia, she would never understand the delights of spiritual love.

"Giulio tells me that Isabella is offering him bribes to go to her in Mantua," went on Angela. "She wants him there, not only because he is a great poet, but because he is so devoted to you. At last you have a chance to pay her back for all the insults she heaped on you at the time of the wedding. It must give you great pleasure to contemplate that."

But spiritual love was certainly beyond Angela's comprehension. It seemed a strange way for two lovers to behave . . . to meet only to quote poetry.

"It will not last," she said to Nicola. "You wait. Soon they will be lovers in the true sense."

Nicola was not sure. Angela was such a sensual little animal, a madcap who might one day find herself in a difficult position. Nicola, now that her love affair with Ferrante had faded, was quite ready to believe in the beauty of that new kind of love practiced by her mistress and the poet. Indeed the character of Lucrezia's little court had changed. There was less pandering to sensation. Instead of aromatic baths and leisure hours spent in Moorish shirts, there was continual reading of poetry and playing of music.

Only Angela went on in the old way.

One day Ercole Strozzi gave a grand ball in his palace in Ferrara to which the whole court was invited. Alfonso, back from his inspection of the fortifications, was present; so were all his brothers.

Pietro Bembo was naturally a guest, and it delighted Strozzi to watch his two Platonic lovers together. Lucrezia had changed. In this sedate ethereal young woman it was almost impossible to recognize the girl who, during her wedding celebrations, had taken her castanets and danced the erotic dances of Spain for the amusement of the court.

Strozzi guessed that Alfonso was thinking that it was time they attempted to get an heir for Ferrara, and decided it would be interesting to see how Lucrezia kept these two relationships apart—that entirely physical one which she would be forced to share with her husband, and the Platonic one with Bembo.

It seemed that Lucrezia had discovered the art of dividing her personality. She showed no revulsion for Alfonso, and at the same time she preserved that unworldly air of a woman spiritually in love with an ideal.

Duke Ercole's agreement to pay her 12,000 ducats a year was proving to be a small victory for Lucrezia since he paid the difference in kind, as he had said he would; and there was continual complaint about the quality and short weight of the goods he supplied.

Lucrezia however, immersed in her devotion to her poet, could not concern herself, as she had previously, with material matters; she accepted the stinginess of Duke Ercole without complaint; and while she continued to receive Bembo at her gatherings Duke Ercole left the court for a quiet sojourn in Belriguardo, taking with him the State ledgers so that in the peace of his retreat he could go over his accounts and try to discover a way of saving money.

In Rome Cardinal Ippolito was learning how dangerous life could be for those who incurred the dislike of the Borgias, and those days when

Lucrezia lay between life and death were very difficult for him, as the Pope made no secret of his suspicions regarding the Este family. He railed against Duke Ercole in the presence of Ippolito, and it was not easy to stand by and listen to complaints against one's own father.

The Pope had given Ippolito an income of 3,000 ducats a year that he might live in the style expected of him during his stay in Rome, but he did not allow Ippolito to forget that he was a hostage for the good behavior of the Este family toward Lucrezia.

"I begin to doubt," said the Pope ominously one day, "whether my daughter is being treated with due consideration in Ferrara."

Ippolito shivered at those words. He was not a coward, but the rumors concerning the Borgias' methods of disposing of their enemies were enough to make anyone who might be deemed an enemy shiver. The terrible Cantarella was not a myth. During his stay in Rome Ippolito had seen strange things happen to men who ate at the Borgia table. Others disappeared, to be discovered later in the Tiber. It was slyly said of Alexander in Rome that he was the true successor of St. Peter, for without doubt he was a fisher of men.

Sanchia, Ippolito's mistress, warned him.

"If Lucrezia dies you should not stay another hour in Rome," she told him.

"Of what use would my death be to them?" demanded Ippolito. "Could it bring Lucrezia back to health?"

Sanchia looked steadily at her lover. "If Lucrezia dies," she said, "the Borgia will no longer be the Grazing Bull. It will be the mad bull and the devil himself could not protect a man who stood in the way of that animal."

"The Pope is a man of good sense. He would see that my death could avail him nothing."

"Do you know nothing of the affection between members of this family? They are not normal, I tell you. They are a trinity . . . an unholy trinity if you like, but they are as one. If you have not seen them together, then you would not understand."

"It would seem," said Ippolito lightly, "that you are tired of your lover and would wish him gone, so that you might spend your time with others."

"Your presence here, my love, would not prevent me spending my time with others."

"And does not," said Ippolito lightly.

She laughed. "You would be unique if you could alone satisfy me. But I am fond of you, my little Cardinal. That is why I warn you. Be ready to fly."

There were times when he did not take her seriously; others when he did. When Alexander read letters from Ferrara and he saw the emotion in his face, he believed what Sanchia told him.

But the news was good. Lucrezia recovered. Bells rang throughout Rome, and the Pope went from church to church giving thanks that his treasure was spared him.

He was not going to wait any longer, he declared. He was going to Ferrara as soon as he had made his preparations to do so, and those preparations were to begin at once.

He went about Rome, a delighted smile on his face, a song on his lips. He was like a young man again; and watching, Ippolito was inclined to agree that there was something superhuman about these Borgias.

Cesare returned to Rome, and Ippolito prepared to welcome him, for there had been a time when friendship had blossomed between them; it was not long ago, at the time of Lucrezia's departure for Ferrara, when they had discovered a mutual dislike for Cardinal's robes.

Cesare came riding into Rome, and the faces of the people were averted and cautious while they hailed him as the conqueror. There were whispers of the cruelties he had inflicted on his victims, of the harsh rule of his new territories; and it was known throughout Rome that even Alexander now bowed to Cesare, and it was the son, not the father, who ruled the city.

Ippolito was with Sanchia when Cesare called on her. Tension was apparent, and Sanchia, chatting lightly with her two lovers, was aware of this.

Ippolito left her with Cesare. He was not a coward, but he could not escape that sense of threat which seemed now to emanate from Cesare wherever he went.

Cesare was clearly not pleased to find him with Sanchia, and it was obvious that any friendship which had ever existed between them was rapidly fading.

Sanchia sent for him a few hours later.

She put her arms about his neck, and her blue eyes were affectionate.

"Ippolito, my dear Cardinal," she said, "I shall miss you bitterly, but take my advice and leave Rome at once."

"Why so?" asked Ippolito.

"Because I have loved this handsome body of yours dearly, and I do not wish to think of it as a corpse. Go straight from here, take your friends and ride out of Rome. Ride for Ferrara as fast as you can. You may be in time to save your life."

"From whom?"

"You waste time in asking. You know. He strikes quickly. He is so practiced. No need now to make plans. He merely says, Method number one, or two, or three . . . and the person who has irritated him is no more."

"I have not irritated him."

"You have been my lover. Occasionally Cesare decides that he does not like my lovers."

Ippolito stood staring at her.

"Ippolito!" she cried. "You fool! Go . . . go while you have time. Give my love to Lucrezia. Tell her I miss her. But hesitate not a moment. I tell you, your life is in danger."

Ippolito left her and went down to where his groom was waiting for him with two squires. They were nervous. He saw that. The whole of Rome was nervous, and all those who caused annoyance—however slight—to Cesare Borgia should beware.

Within an hour Ippolito was riding away from Rome.

Pietro Bembo was now recognized as Lucrezia's court poet. They exchanged letters, cautiously written yet brimming over with love and devotion; they were both careful to keep their relationship on its Platonic footing, both fearing that to change it would in some measure degrade it.

Those were happy days for them both. They lived for each other; and Lucrezia felt that she had never been so peacefully happy as she was at this time.

She could not understand how she, who had taken such delight in physical love, could find this contentment in such a different relationship. Perhaps she missed her family very much; perhaps when she was with one who loved her carnally she remembered them too vividly. She was, after all, still seeking that escape, that opportunity to be herself—and herself alone—which had made her long to leave Rome for Ferrara.

Ippolito arrived and, although she had during the first weeks of their meetings been attracted by him, she was disturbed by his presence at court.

He was determined to be her devoted brother-in-law. All her brothers-in-law were her devoted friends, but Ferrante and Giulio were always busy with their love affairs, and Sigismondo with his religion, so that they had no time to pry into her affairs.

Ippolito however was ready to be very interested, and she feared his curiosity concerning her friendship with Pietro. There was scarcely a person at court who would believe in its Platonic nature, and Lucrezia was aware that there were many who would like to catch the lovers in a compromising situation so that they might explode this story of Platonic love between a poet and a Borgia.

Moreover the Ippolito who returned did not seem the same man as the Ippolito whom she had known in Rome. Nor was he. He had run away from Cesare Borgia and he was ashamed of himself. Always haughty and quick tempered, these qualities seemed to have been magnified by what had happened to him. He was charming to Lucrezia and bore her no grudge because it was her brother who had made him run from Rome, but his conduct in Ferrara was at times rather like that of Cesare himself. For instance when he imagined himself insulted by one of Alfonso's soldiers he flogged the man so unmercifully that he almost beat him to death. Alfonso was furious, but the harm was done before he could intervene, and Alfonso was not one to make much of what could not be mended.

It seemed to all in Ferrara that the Cardinal must be treated with the utmost respect lest his anger should be aroused and that happen to them which had happened to Alfonso's soldier; which was exactly the impression Ippolito had wished to create.

Ippolito was now at Lucrezia's side most of the day, which made it difficult for her to snatch those precious hours alone with Pietro, but Strozzi was doing his best to make communication easy between the lovers; one day he wrote a letter to Pietro in which he described conversations between himself—Strozzi—and Lucrezia, and told of the flattering things which had been said of Pietro. Lucrezia read the letter before it was sent and, because Strozzi had deliberately not signed it, she wrote her name at the bottom so that it should be known that she endorsed all that it contained.

That letter was an admission of the love, bordering on the passionate, which existed between the two.

But Ippolito, always at her side, was making meetings more and more difficult.

There was secret correspondence between them now, and because Lucrezia knew that she was surrounded by spies she signed herself as FF, by which she was to be known to Pietro in the future.

These difficulties and subterfuges were conducive to Platonic love, and Lucrezia's happiness seemed to flower during those months.

❧ 👑 ❧

Strozzi, seeing this love affair, which had been of his making, drifting into a backwater, could not resist trying to change its course.

It was during the heat of August when he came to Lucrezia and found her with Ippolito. He had heard that Pietro Bembo was sick of a fever and he wondered how deep this Platonic love of Lucrezia's went. Was it an idealistic dream of which Bembo merely happened to be material manifestation; or did she really care what became of him as a man?

It was too interesting a problem for Strozzi to ignore.

So he said in front of Ippolito: "I have bad news, Duchessa. Poor Pietro Bembo is sick, and it would seem that his life is in danger."

Lucrezia rose; she had turned slightly pale.

"Poor fellow," said Ippolito lightly, but he was alert.

"I must go to see that he has all he needs to help him recover," said Lucrezia.

"My dear sister, you should not risk infection. Let some other do what is necessary."

Strozzi was watching Lucrezia, watching the panic shown in her eyes.

She loves the man, thought Strozzi. Leave them together in his bedchamber and they will forget this elevated talk of spiritual love.

"He is my court poet," said Lucrezia, recovering her poise. "I owe it to him to see that he has comfort now that he is sick."

"Delegate someone to visit him," suggested Ippolito.

Lucrezia nodded.

❧ 👑 ❧

The streets were quiet and deserted, the heat intense, as Lucrezia's carriage made its way to Bembo's lodgings. Hurriedly she left the carriage and entered the house.

He was lying in his bed, and his heart leaped at the sight of her.

"My Duchessa," he cried. "But . . . you should not have come."

"How could I do otherwise?" She took his burning hands and kissed them.

His eyes, wide with fever and passion, looked into hers.

She sat by his bed. "Now," she said, "you must tell me exactly how you feel. I have brought herbs and ointments with me. I know how to make you well again."

"Your presence is enough," he told her.

"Pietro, Pietro, you must get well. How could I endure my life without you?"

"Take care, my beloved," whispered Pietro. "There is plague in the city. It may be that I suffer from it. Oh, it was folly . . . folly for you to come here."

"Folly," she said, "to be with you?"

They held hands and thought of the dread plague from which he might be suffering and might impart to her. To pass together from this life in which they had loved with all purity and an emotion of the spirit, seemed a perfect ending to their perfect love.

But Lucrezia did not want to die. She wanted both of them to live, so she refused to consider this ending and busied herself with the remedies she had brought.

His eyes followed her as she moved about his apartment. He was sick—he believed himself to be dying—and he knew that he loved her with a love which was both spiritual and physical. Had he been less weak there would have been an end to their talk of Platonic emotion. His sickness was like a flaming sword which separated them from passion. He could only rejoice in it because it had brought her to his side, while he deplored it; and as he looked into her face he knew that she shared his thoughts and emotions.

"It will be known that you have been here," he said.

"I care not."

"We are spied on night and day."

"What matters it? There is nothing to discover. We have never been what would be called lovers."

They looked at each other longingly; then Pietro went on: "I shall never know the great joy now. Oh, Duchessa, Lucrezia, my love, I feel our love will remain forever unfulfilled."

She was startled, and suddenly cried out in an access of passionate grief: "You must not die, Pietro. You *shall* not die."

It was a promise. Pietro knew it, and a calmness seemed to settle upon him then; it was as though he were determined to throw off his fever, determined to live that he might enjoy that which so far had been denied him.

❧♛❧

Pietro's recovery was rapid.

Within a few weeks he was ready to leave Ferrara, and Strozzi was at hand to offer his villa at Ostellato for the convalescence.

Before he left, Lucrezia had decided that she too would leave Ferrara for a short rest in the quiet of the country. Alfonso was once more visiting fortifications; Ippolito had his duties at court; and Giulio was the only member of the family who was free to accompany her. This he did with the utmost pleasure, since Angela was of the party.

So Lucrezia set out for the villa of Medelana, which was close to Strozzi's at Ostellato; thus during that convalescence the lovers could frequently enjoy each other's companionship.

There, in the scented gardens or under the cool shade of trees, they could be together undisturbed. Lucrezia would set out for the Strozzi villa with Angela and Giulio in attendance; but when they arrived and Pietro came out to meet them, Guilio and Angela would wander off and leave Pietro and Lucrezia together.

Thus in those golden days of August they mingled the spiritual with the physical, and Lucrezia believed that she had come at last to perfect happiness.

During those warm days in the gardens at Ostellato she lived solely in the present, taking each day as it came, refusing to look beyond it, because she dared not.

She would treasure, as long as she lived, the scents of the flowers, the softness of the grass at Ostellato; she would remember the words he had written for her, the words he spoke to her.

"If I died now," he told her, "if so great a desire, so great a love were ended, the world would be emptied of love."

She believed him; she assured him that the love he felt for her was no greater than that she felt for him. Each was conscious that there was so much to be lived through in a short time.

And so passed the happy days of Pietro's convalescence and Lucrezia's escape from Ferrara.

In Rome ALEXANDER was preparing for his visit to Ferrara. He felt younger than ever. He had numerous mistresses and he had proved that he was still capable of begetting children. Never had seventy-two years sat more lightly on a man than they did on Alexander. He was beginning to believe that he was immortal. The prospect of the long and tedious journey did not give him a twinge of uneasiness. He felt that he was at the very pinnacle of his powers.

Cesare came to Rome. He stayed with his father and there were many intimate encounters. Cesare declared that he would remain in Rome that he might join in the celebrations which were to be given in honor of Alexander's eleventh anniversary as Pope. This was not quite true. Cesare's relations with the French were not so cordial as they had been. Spain was beginning to play a bigger part in Italian politics. She had been content to look on while Southern Italy was in the hands of the Aragonese, but if they were unable to hold the territory, then the King of Spain must step in to prevent its falling under French domination.

If Spain was to be victorious over the French their King decided that it was imperative for the Borgias to cut their alliance with France—and what more natural than they should turn to the Spanish who were, in no small measure, their own people? In this uncertain state of affairs it might be that Cesare would have to rely on his own efforts to hold the kingdom of Romagna, and he was going to miss French support quite disastrously.

This meant that he was going to need a great deal of money to keep his armies intact, and accordingly Alexander fell back on the old method of creating Cardinals who were ready to pay dearly for their hats. In this way he made a profit of 150,000 ducats in a very short time.

There were other methods of raising money, and it was noticed that, at this time when the Borgias were hard-pressed, many rich people died mysteriously.

The very rich Venetian Cardinal, Michiel, was given a poisoned draught by a certain Asquinio Colloredo who had been paid to administer it by the Borgias. Michiel died, and his vast fortune went to the Pope and proved very useful.

But a great deal of money was required for the armies of the new Duke of Romagna, and Cantarella had a big part to play in obtaining it.

There was a feeling of perpetual insecurity among those who knew their deaths could bring profit to the Borgias. Cardinal Gian Battista Orsini was suddenly accused of plotting to poison the Pope and lodged in Castel Sant' Angelo. He denied this charge and was tortured in the hope that he would confess. It would have pleased Cesare and his father to be able at this time to pin the charge, of which they had so often been suspected, on someone else. But Cardinal Orsini refused, even under torture, to confess; and the powerful Orsini family were infuriated that one of them should be so treated. They realized however that the Papal State was now under the complete domination of Cesare, and that this brutal man led his father in all things.

They knew that the real reason for these persecutions was the fact that the Orsini family were rich, so they offered a great reward for the release of the Cardinal. The Cardinal's mistress loved him dearly and it happened that in the possession of this woman was a pearl of great price, so famous that it was known throughout Italy. The woman appeared before the Pope and offered him this pearl for the release of her lover.

The Pope, gallant always, smiled at the woman, for she was very beautiful: "I envy the Cardinal," he said, "in his possession of your love. This pearl you offer is unique. You know that."

"Give him back to me, and it is yours."

"I could refuse you nothing," answered the Pope.

Cesare was furious when he heard that the Pope had agreed to the release of the Cardinal.

He raged about his father's apartments. "He will disclose the fact that he has been tortured. There will be more evil rumors concerning us than ever. Moreover, we want the death of this man."

Alexander smiled serenely at his son. "There are times when I feel you do not understand your father," he murmured.

"I understand you well," stormed Cesare. "You have only to hear a request from the lips of a pretty woman and you must grant it."

"We have the pearl. Do not forget that."

"We could have had the pearl and his life."

The Pope was smiling pleasantly. "I see we think alike. This lovely woman must receive her lover, since I have promised her that. Already he has been given his goblet. She will receive her lover this day. I did not say whether he would be alive or dead. We have this priceless pearl and, in exchange, our little friend will have the Cardinal's corpse."

Other members of the Orsini family had been murdered recently. These were Paolo Orsini and the Duke of Gravina. The Orsinis were friends of the French, and Louis, furious when Alexander put Goffredo in charge of a company and sent him against the family, declared that his friends must be no more molested. Alexander ignored him.

It was during August when Cardinal Giovanni Borgia of Monreale died suddenly. The Cardinal was a very rich man; he had been a miser, and his death revealed that he was even richer than had been hoped. The Pope and Cesare could not fail to be delighted with his wealth which fell into their hands.

A few days after the death of this Cardinal there came to Cesare and his father an invitation to a supper party in the vineyard of Cardinal Adriano Castelli da Corneto outside the city.

Corneto was one of the richest of the Cardinals and was having a palace built for him in the Borgo Nuovo by the brilliant architect Bramante. He urged the Pope and Cesare to come, that they might first inspect the building which he was sure would be of great interest to them, and afterward retire to his vineyard for the party, which should not be large but nevertheless worthy of Their Eminences.

Cesare and his father were delighted with the invitation. They made their plans.

Cesare HAD HIS men in every important household in Rome. He issued orders that a dose of Cantarella should be slipped into the Cardinal's wine. Not a big dose. The Cardinal should not be immediately smitten. His death should not occur until a few days after the banquet.

They set out for the Borgo Nuovo where, at his unfinished house, Cardinal Corneto was waiting to receive them.

"It is a great honor," murmured the Cardinal. "I appreciate your coming on such a night. The heat is overpowering." The Pope laughed lightly, implying that the heat did not disturb him; he was as strong as a man half his age.

Cesare, admiring the work, declared that Bramante should build a house for him, and his smile was sardonic as he glanced at his father. Bramante was an artist; he should be allowed to finish his work, but it would not be for Corneto; it would be for the Borgias. It was a situation which appealed to Cesare. The poor fool was boasting of his treasures, little knowing that they would not long be his to boast about. But both the Pope and his son showed a deep and unfeigned interest in everything they saw. The wealth of Corneto would be a fine acquisition.

"Come," said the Cardinal at length, "let us ride to my vineyard. 'Tis thirsty work, on such a night, inspecting a palace in the process of being built."

"I confess to a thirst," said the Pope.

So they came to the vineyard where the alfresco supper was ready for them.

"We will first slake our thirst," cried Corneto; and Trebbia wine was served.

The Pope was very thirsty; he drank deeply of the wine; Cesare watered his a little, and Corneto watered his considerably, as did the few others present.

When the feasting began Cardinal Corneto gave no sign of the uneasiness he was feeling as he covertly watched his guests.

How heartily the Pope's laughter rang out! How smugly contented was Cesare! Did it never occur to them to count their enemies? Did they not realize that there might be people who were ready to risk their own lives for revenge? They had made life cheaper, yet they did not understand this. There might be a slave whose daughter or son had been taken by Cesare for half an hour's amusement, or perhaps had offended the Lord of Romagna in some way and had lost a hand or a tongue because of it. Were Cesare and his father so ignorant of human nature that they thought a slave had no feelings? Such a man, who had suffered through loved ones, would be ready to risk twenty lives, if he had them, for a glorious moment of revenge.

And the Cardinal himself? He had possessions which were envied, and his life was in danger. It did not seem to him an unworthy action to save the lives of others which were threatened while he saved his own.

He knew he could trust his servant who had good reasons to hate the Borgias. The powder which the Borgias had intended should be put into Cardinal Corneto's wine should be put into that of the Pope and his son. But the Cardinal had decided that all his guests must take a little of the poison so that every one at that supper table should suffer slightly. Then it might be believed that the malady which he intended should kill the Pope and his son would appear to have been caused by some poison in the air, for at this time of the year the condition of the Roman streets had a poisonous effect and many people suffered "summer sickness" on account of it. But even if it were suspected that the Borgias had died of poison, everyone would be ready to believe that there had been a mistake and the wine intended for the Cardinal had been given to the Borgias.

The Cardinal was waiting for the effect of that poisoned wine, but it seemed to have none whatever on the Pope who had drunk it without water. He continued to amuse the company with his brilliant conversation and when he left both he and Cesare seemed unaffected.

All through the next day—it was the 11th of August—the Cardinal waited in vain for news from the Vatican of the Pope's death. He called on the Pope to find that Alexander was his jovial self.

Is it true, wondered the Cardinal, that these Borgias have supernatural powers? Are they really in league with the devil?

THE POPE AWOKE early on the morning of the 13th August. For the moment he could not remember where he was. He tried to rise and as he did so was stricken with a terrible pain in his abdomen.

He called to his attendants, who came running to his bedside.

"Holiness," they began, and stopped, to stare at him.

The Pope tried to demand why they stared, but he found it difficult to form the words.

"Help me ... Help me ... to rise," he muttered.

But when they tried to obey him, he sank back swooning on the bed, and for some minutes he lay there, the sweat pouring from his body, the pain so overwhelming him that he could think of little else.

Then that dominant will asserted itself, as always in moments of crisis it had. He lay very still, fighting pain and sickness, forcing himself to remember who he was: Alexander the invincible. Alexander who had conquered the Sacred College and ruled the Papacy, Alexander whose son was one day going to rule Italy and the world.

And because of that great power within him which he had nourished until he really believed it was invincible, Alexander triumphed over his pains. He began to think clearly of what had happened during the last few days, and he said to himself: "I have been poisoned."

He thought of the supper party, of sly-eyed Corneto. Could it be possible that someone had blundered? Or was the blunder deliberate? He remembered the visit to the half-built palace, and how thirsty he had been. He remembered sitting at the table, and the slave who had handed him the wine.

Was it a mistake? If so . . . he was doomed. No, he was not. Other men might be. Not so Alexander. He could not die yet. He dared not die. Cesare, not yet secure in Romagna, needed him. Lucrezia needed him. How would she be treated in far-off Ferrara if her father was not waiting to avenge any insult directed against her? He must not die.

The pain was coming in waves, and he knew he was fighting with Cantarella, that old friend turned enemy.

He stammered: "Go to the Duke of Romagna, and bid him come to me. I must have speech with him at once."

He was trying to concentrate on the fight, but the enemy was a bitter one.

Cantarella seemed to be mocking him: Now you know, Holiness, how it has been with others. This torment was inflicted a hundred times on your enemies. Now, by some fluke of fortune, it is for you to suffer.

Never, thought the Pope. It shall not happen to me. Nothing can defeat me. I have risen above all my difficulties. Corneto shall suffer for this. When Cesare comes. . . .

Men were coming into the room but Cesare was not with them. Where was Cesare?

Someone was bending over the bed. His voice sounded like a whisper, then a roar.

"Most Holy lord, the Duke of Romagna is sick . . . even as is Your Holiness."

Cesare, twisting in agony on his bed, cried out: "Where is my father? Bring him to me. This instant, I tell you. If he is not here within five minutes someone shall suffer." But his voice had sunk to a whisper and those about his bedside looked on, feigning horror; they believed that Cesare Borgia was on his death-bed.

"My lord Duke, the Pope has sent for you. He cannot come to you. He too is sick."

The words danced in Cesare's brain like mocking devils. "He too is sick." So they had both drunk of the wrong wine. He remembered even as his father had. The thirst after the visit to the half-finished palace in the Borgo Nuovo, the pleasure of the shady vineyard, and the cool sweet wine.

He tried to rouse himself. A trick had been played, a foul trick, he thought. He wanted vengeance.

He cried: "Send for Cardinal Corneto. I would speak with him. Bring him to me at once. Tell him it would be wiser for him not to delay. . . . Holy Mother of God . . ." he whispered, "this agony . . . it is hell . . . surely hell."

The news was brought to him. "Cardinal Corneto cannot wait on your lordship. He is confined to his bed with a sickness similar to your own."

Cesare buried his face in his pillows. Someone had blundered.

There were whispers throughout Rome.
"The Pope is dying."

Outside the Vatican the citizens waited. When the moment came they would rush into the papal apartments and strip them of their treasures. There were usually riots in Rome when a Pope died, and this one was the richest of all Popes.

All through that day they waited, the question on every lip: "How fares His Holiness?"

He was fighting, they heard, fighting, with all his fierce energy, for his life. They were not normal, these Borgias; they had made a pact with the devil.

Clearly the Pope and his son had taken a dose of their own medicine; who could say whether that dose had been intended for them or whether they had taken it by mistake? That was of no moment now. The important matter was that Alexander was dying.

And in his apartments immediately above those of his father, the dreaded Cesare Borgia was fighting for his life.

Great days were about to begin in Rome.

Cesare could hear the murmur of prayers in the apartment below him. Down there men were praying for the Pope's life. He was ill, on the borders of death, and even his giant constitution was weakening.

Cesare lay weak with pain, refusing to think of death, wondering what he would do if his father died. He was no fool. He knew that he had been bolstered up by his father's power, his father's wealth; he knew that when towns opened their gates to him it was not entirely due to his own military skill or the fear he had contrived to instil; it was the knowledge of the power of the Papacy.

If that power ceased, what would happen to Cesare Borgia? Whom could he trust? He could not leave his bed, but he guessed that even now people were gathering outside the Vatican, that many a man and woman in the city was praying for his death.

Never had he felt so weak as he did at that time, never had he been so certain of all he owed to his father.

There were two men in his room now. He called to them and they came and stood beside his bed. One was his younger brother Goffredo, and it was gratifying to see the anguish in Goffredo's eyes. Goffredo, whose wife had been Cesare's mistress, had the Borgia devotion to the family; to him the most important person in the world was Cesare. There were tears now in Goffredo's eyes, and he was not wondering what would become of himself if Cesare and his father died; he was grieving for his brother.

"Brother," said Cesare, "come closer. You see me prostrate here when I should be on my feet. You see me sick when I have need of all my strength."

Goffredo cried: "I will be your strength, brother. But command me and I will obey."

"May the saints preserve you, Borgia brother."

Goffredo's eyes shone with pride, as they always did when he was called Borgia. The greatest insult that could be hurled at him was to suggest that he did not belong to that family.

"Who is that in the shadows, brother?" asked Cesare.

"Your good servant, Don Micheletto Corella."

"Ah," said Cesare, "bid him come forward."

Micheletto Corella knelt by the bed and took Cesare's hand. "My lord, I am yours to command."

"How fares my father?" said Cesare. "Come, I would have the truth. Do not seek to soothe me. This is no time to soothe."

"He is very sick."

"Sick unto death?" demanded Cesare.

"Were he an ordinary man, one would say so. But His Holiness is super-human. It is said there is a slight hope that he will throw off the effects of the poison."

"God grant he will. Oh my father, you must not die."

"He'll not die," cried Goffredo. "Borgias do not die."

"If it is humanly possible to survive, he will do it," said Cesare. "But we must be ready for whatever should happen. If my father dies, you must immediately get possession of the keys to the vaults, and my father's treasure must be carried to a safe place. Brother, my friend, if my father should die, you must get those keys before the people know. Once they have stormed the Vatican there will be no hope of saving my father's treasures."

"I will do that, my lord," answered Corella.

"And in the meantime my father and I must appear to be recovering. Do not tell any how sick we are. Say that we have had a slight attack of fever, probably due to the poisonous August air."

"Many who were at the Corneto party have taken to their beds. The Cardinal is saying that it is due to the poison in the air, and that the sooner Leonardo da Vinci, your fortress engineer, can do something about his drains, the better."

"Let them say that. So other guests are afflicted, eh? But not as my father is . . . not as I am. I find that very suspicious. But say nothing. Tell all that we are recovering. Listen! Who is that coming?"

"Some of the Cardinals from the Sacred College; they come to ask after you and the Pope."

"Prop me up," said Cesare. "They must not know how sick I am. Come . . . we will laugh and chat together. It must be as though in a few days I shall leave my bed."

The Cardinals came in. They had visited the Pope, and the disappointed expressions on their faces made Cesare feel exultant; it seemed that Alexander too had realized the importance of impressing them with the belief that he and his son were suffering from a slight malaise from which they would soon recover.

⁂

SUCH WAS ALEXANDER'S strength of mind and body that, only two days after he drank the poisoned wine, he was able to sit up in his bed and play cards with members of his household.

Cesare in the rooms above heard the laughter below and exulted.

Never before had he realized the greatness of this father of his; and the sweetest sound in the world, to Cesare that day, was the laughter which came from the Pope's bedchamber as the cards were played.

Corella and Goffredo came to him to tell him what was happening.

"You should see the faces of some of them," cried Goffredo. "They can't hide their disappointment."

"I trust you noted who they were," said Cesare. "When I rise from this bed they shall be remembered."

Cesare lay back and, ill as he was, he smiled.

None can overcome the Borgias, he was thinking. No matter who comes against us, we will always win.

It occurred to him that the poison had not affected the Pope as much as it had himself. Yet the Pope had drunk the wine undiluted, and he had weakened his with water. Perhaps this foul disease, which had dogged him since his early youth, was largely responsible for his condition.

When he was well enough to visit his father—although it seemed that his father would probably be the one to visit him—he would show him more tenderness than he had of late. He would insist that the Pope must take greater care of his health. Alexander was that strong stem from which the Borgia power had grown. That stem must not be broken yet.

He could have made merry with his brother and his trusted captain if he did not feel so ill.

ALEXANDER WOKE in the night.

He cried out: "Where am I?"

His attendants hurried to his bed.

"In your bed, Holiness."

"Ah," he said, "I wondered."

Then he murmured something which sounded like: "I have come to see the children, Vannozza. You too . . . and the children . . . and Giovanni . . . Giovanni. . . ."

The attendants looked at each other and whispered: "His mind has wandered to the past."

He was a little better when morning came. He heard Mass and received Communion.

He then muttered: "I feel tired. Leave me, I beg of you. I would rest."

Goffredo and Corella heard that the Pope was resting and did not seem so well as he had the day before. They did not tell Cesare, who had had a painful night, as they did not wish to worry him.

That day the atmosphere in the Vatican was oppressed by gloom which did not seem entirely real. It hid expectancy and perhaps hope and some jubilation.

The Pope was seen to be very weak and listless; the alertness seemed to have vanished from that vital face; he had changed a great deal in a few hours, and now that the veil of vitality was removed he looked like a very old man.

One of his attendants bent over him to ask if there was aught he wished for.

He put out a burning hand and murmured: "I am ill, my friend. I am very ill."

All the light had gone from those once-brilliant eyes and the man in the bed was like the ghost of Alexander.

Night came and the Cardinals were at his bedside.

"He should be given Extreme Unction," it was said; and this was done.

Alexander opened his eyes. "So I have come to the end of my road," he said. "There is no earthly path open to me now. Farewell, my friends. Farewell, my greatness. I am ready now to go to Heaven."

Those about his bedside looked at each other with astonishment. There was no fear in the face of this man who many had said was one of the wickedest who had ever lived. He was going, so he believed, to Heaven where he appeared to have no doubt a specially warm welcome would be waiting for him. Was he not Roderigo Borgia, Alexander VI, Christ's Vicar on Earth? He did not see the ghosts of the men whom he had murdered. He saw only the gates of Heaven open wide to receive him.

Thus died Roderigo Borgia.

THOSE ABOUT THE bed were startled when the doors were flung open and soldiers under the command of Don Micheletto Corella came in.

"We come to guard His Holiness," said Corella. And turning to the Cardinal Treasurer, who was at the bedside, he cried: "Give me the keys of the Papal vaults."

"On whose orders?" demanded the Cardinal.

"On those of the Lord of Romagna," was the answer.

There was silence in the chamber of death. The Pope could no longer command. In the room immediately above, that tyrant, his son Cesare, was lying near to death. There was one thought in the minds of those who had been disturbed by Corella: The Borgian reign of terror is over.

"I cannot give you the keys," answered the Cardinal Treasurer.

Corella drew his dagger and held it at the throat of the man whose eyes involuntarily turned to the ceiling. Corella laughed.

"My master grows nearer health each day," he said. "Give me the keys, Eminence, or you'll follow His Holiness to Heaven."

The keys dropped from the man's fingers. Corella picked them up and made his way down to the vaults to secure the treasure before the mob entered the Vatican.

Cesare LAY on his bed cursing his sickness.

He knew that the servants were already stripping his father's apartments of rich treasures. Corella had secured that which was in the vaults, but there was much that remained.

Throughout Rome the news was shouted.

"The Pope is dead! This is the end of the Borgias!"

All over Italy those lords and dukes who had had their dominions taken from them to form the kingdom of Romagna were alert.

Cesare was not dead, but sick in his bed, unable to be on his guard; and, if ever in his life he had needed his health and strength, he needed it now.

There would be change in Rome. They must be ready to escape from the thrall of the Grazing Bull.

Cesare groaned and cursed and waited.

"Oh my father," he murmured in his wretchedness, "you have left us alone and unprotected. What shall we do without you?"

If he felt well he would not be afraid. He would ride out into Rome. He would let them see that when one Borgia giant died there was another to take his place. But he could only groan and suffer in his sick bed, a man weak with illness, the greatest benefactor a man ever knew lost to him, his kingdom rocking in peril.

THe DeLiGHts of Medelana were suddenly shattered.

Lucrezia was being helped to dress by Angela and some of her women, when one of her dwarfs came running in excitedly to tell her that a distinguished visitor was arriving at the villa, none other than Cardinal Ippolito.

Lucrezia and Angela looked at each other in dismay. If Ippolito stayed at the villa it would put an end to that delightful intimacy between Medelana and Ostellato.

"We should send a message to Pietro immediately to warn him," whispered Angela.

"Wait awhile. It may be that my brother-in-law is paying a passing call."

"Let us hope he has not come to spy for Alfonso."

"Hasten," said Lucrezia. "Where is my net? I will go down to meet him." But Ippolito was already at the door. He stood very still, looking at

Lucrezia; he did not smile, but his lips twitched slightly; it was as though he was desperately seeking for the right words, and in that moment Lucrezia knew that some terrible catastrophe to herself had occurred.

"Ippolito," she began, and went swiftly to his side.

There was no ceremony; he laid his hands on her shoulders and looked into her face. "My sister," he began. "Oh my dearest sister, I bring bad news."

"Alfonso . . ." she began.

He shook his head. "The Pope, your father, is dead."

Her eyes were wide with horror. It was impossible to believe that he who had been more alive than any other could now be dead. He had seemed immortal. She could not accept this dire calamity.

Ippolito put his arm about her and drew her to a chair. "Sit down," he said. She obeyed mechanically, her expression blank. "He was after all," went on Ippolito soothingly, "by no means a young man. Lucrezia, my dearest sister, it is a terrible shock, but you will understand that it had to happen some time."

Still she did not speak. She looked like a person in a trance. It was as though her mind was refusing to accept what he said because to do so would bring such grief as it would be impossible to bear.

Ippolito felt that he had to go on talking. Her silence was unnerving, more poignant than words would have been.

"He was well," said Ippolito, "until a few days before his death. He went to a supper party with your brother on the 10th August. It was in the vineyards of Cardinal Corneto. Two days later he was taken ill. It was thought at first that he would rally, and he did for a while. But there was a relapse, and he died on the 18th. As soon as the news came I rode over to tell you. Oh Lucrezia, I know of the love between you. What can I say to comfort you?"

Then she spoke. "You can do nothing to comfort me because there is no comfort now that life has to offer me."

She sat idly staring ahead of her.

Ippolito knelt beside her, took her hand, kissed it, told her that he and his brothers would care for her, that though she had lost a father she had others who loved her.

She shook her head and turning to him said: "If you would comfort me, I pray you leave me. I can best bear my grief alone."

So Ippolito went, signing to her women to leave her also. She sat alone staring ahead, her blank expression slowly changing to one of utter despair.

SHE CROUCHED ON the floor. She had wept a little. "Dead," she whispered to herself. "Dead, Holiness. So we are alone. But how can we endure life without you?"

There had never been a time when he had not been there. She had sheltered beneath his wing; he had always been benign, always tender for her. He was an old man, they said, but she had never thought of his death; she had subconsciously thought of him as immortal. The great Cardinal of her childhood whose coming had brought such joy to the nursery, the great Pope of her adolescence and early womanhood, feared by others, loved so devotedly by herself, and who had loved her as it seemed only a Borgia could love a Borgia! "Dead!" she murmured to herself in a bewildered voice. "Dead?" she demanded. It could not be. There could not be such wretchedness in the world.

"I should have been there," she whispered. "I would have nursed him. I would have saved him. And while he was dying I was here, making merry with a lover. He was dying, dying, and I did not know it."

Pietro Bembo seemed remote. This Platonic love, which had blossomed into passion during the summer weeks of his convalescence, what was it compared with a lifelong devotion, a deep abiding love of Borgia daughter for Borgia father?

I should have been at his side, she told herself again and again.

Now she must think of the last time he had held her in his arms. That room in the Vatican when he had held her as though he would never let her go; outside, the snowy street, the impatient horses champing their bits and pawing the ground. The last farewell!

How could life ever be the same again?

THEY WERE AFRAID for her. They did not know how to comfort her. She would not eat; she would not sleep. She remained in her apartments, crouching on the floor, looking back into the past, remembering; her golden hair falling loose about her, just as it had been when Ippolito had brought her the news.

When Pietro Bembo came riding to the villa her women were relieved. Here was one who might comfort her.

He went to her and found her crouching on the floor.

"Lucrezia!" he cried. "My love, my love!"

She burst into wild sobbing then, and buried her face in her hands.

He knelt and put an arm about her shoulders. "I have heard," he whispered. "I have come to share this grief with you."

But she shook her head. "It is mine," she said. "Mine alone. None can share it or understand its depth."

"My dearest, to see you thus, so steeped in wretchedness, breaks my heart. Do you not see that it is I who am in need of comfort?"

She shook her head.

"Leave me," she said. "I pray you leave me. There is nothing you can do to help me but leave me with my grief."

He tried again to comfort her, but there was no comfort for Lucrezia. There was none who could understand the depth of her grief. There was none who could realize the height, the depth and breadth of that love of Borgia for Borgia.

VIII

DUCHESS OF FERRARA

Those weeks which followed her father's death were like an evil dream to Lucrezia. She could not escape from the memory of her loss; she grew pale and thin, for she still could eat little and her nights remained sleepless. Often she would sit crying quietly, and sometimes she would talk of her father, recalling every incident which proclaimed his devotion to her.

"Something within me has died," she said. "I shall never be the same again."

There was no sympathy for her from Ferrara. Duke Ercole openly rejoiced. The court, he declared, should not mourn one who had never been a true friend to Ferrara; and he added that for the honor of the Lord God and benefit of Christendom he had often prayed that the scandalous Pope should be removed from the Church. Now God had seen fit to answer his prayers, so there was little for him to mourn about.

It was Pietro who provided the comfort she needed. It was natural that he should. To whom else could she turn?

He would present himself at the villa each day, waiting for her to ask for him; and at length she did ask, and there he was waiting to offer comfort.

He was the one person to whom she could talk of her grief. He listened tenderly; he wept with her; he told of his undying love, and he wrote verses to commemorate it.

"Oh Pietro, Pietro," she cried. "What should I do without you?"

Ercole Strozzi arrived at Ostellato one day.

He came to Medelana with Pietro. He had not seen Lucrezia since he had heard the news of her father's death, and he kissed her hands tenderly and commiserated with her.

"But I come," he said, "to give warning. Alfonso intends to visit you here. It may be that he has heard of Pietro's visits and the friendship between you two. It would be wise if Pietro left Ostellato before Alfonso arrives."

"He does not care who my friends are," said Lucrezia.

"My lady Duchessa, I beg of you take care. The death of your father weakens your position and it will be necessary to act with the utmost caution."

"I will visit Venice for a while," said Pietro. "You have suffered enough and I would never forgive myself if I added to those sufferings."

"You must not stay too long away from me," Lucrezia implored. "You know how I rely on you now."

Strozzi watched them with interest. This love affair, which he had planned, was ripening, he fancied. It had outgrown the Platonic stage, he was sure; and he would be interested to see what effect it had on Pietro's work.

He must certainly make sure that Alfonso was not so irritated that he forbad the two to be together. Therefore it was wise for Pietro to disappear.

Alfonso arrived almost immediately after Pietro had left.

He was shocked by his wife's appearance. Even her hair had lost its luster.

He remonstrated with her. "Why, it was many months since you had seen your father. Why should you make all this fuss now?"

"Can you not understand that I shall never . . . never see him again?"

"I understand it perfectly well. But you might not have done so in any case."

She began to weep silently, because his reference to her father had brought back more tender memories.

"I did not come here to listen to your lamentations," said Alfonso, who could not bear the company of weeping women.

"Then you should have left me to mourn alone," she told him.

"Were you mourning . . . alone?" he asked.

"There is no one . . . no one . . . who can really share such grief with me."

Alfonso, who was practical in the extreme, could not begin to understand the nature of the love which had existed between Alexander and Lucrezia. He knew that that mighty influence had been withdrawn and he imagined her grief to be partly due to fear for her own future. He could understand such alarm. The King of France had already hinted that if Alfonso wished to repudiate the marriage he would put no obstacle in the way. Ferrara had been forced to accept the Borgia as a bride but Ferrara should not be forced to keep her.

Did she know that the friendship of France for her family was a fickle thing? Was she weeping for the loss of that Apostolic mantle which had protected her so firmly all her life? To practical Alfonso it seemed that this must be so.

He sought to comfort her. "You need have no fear," he said, "that we shall repudiate the marriage. We shall not take seriously the hints of the King of France."

"What hints are these?" she asked.

"Is it possible that you do not know? Are you so shut away here at Medelana?"

"I have heard no news since I heard that which so overwhelmed me with grief that I could think of nothing else."

He told her then of French animosity toward her family. "But have no fear," said Alfonso; "we shall not repudiate the marriage for we should have to pay back the dowry if we did, and that is something my father would never do."

He laughed aloud at the thought of his father's parting with all those ducats which he loved so well. He placed an arm about Lucrezia and tried to jolly her toward an amorous mood, but she was unresponsive. She repeated: "The King of France would not dare.... Though my father is dead I still have my brother."

"Your brother!" cried Alfonso.

She turned to him suddenly; she was vital again, her eyes suddenly brilliant, not with joy, but with a terrible fear. "Cesare!" she cried. "What of Cesare?"

"It was a sad thing for him that he fell sick at such a time. He needed his strength. But he was lying sick almost to death while your father's enemies rioted in the streets, ransacked the Papal apartments and made off with jewels of great value—which, it seems, your brother's servants had failed to put into safe keeping."

"Where is he now?" asked Lucrezia in anguish.

"He went to Castel Sant' Angelo for safety."

"And the children?"

"They went with him. Your son Roderigo and the *Infante Romano*." Alfonso burst out laughing. "Do not look so downcast. He had his ladies with him. Sanchia of Aragon was there and Dorotea, the girl he abducted. I wonder how they liked each other."

"My brother ... a prisoner!"

"Your brother a prisoner. How else could it be? He conquered many towns, and the whole of Italy feared him. He strutted about like a conqueror, did he not? But he took his power from the Papal standards, and suddenly ... he finds himself a sick man and the Papal influence withdrawn from him."

Lucrezia had taken her husband's arm and was shaking it in her distress.

"Oh, tell me everything ... everything!" she begged. "Can you not see that it is agony for me to remain in suspense?"

"The French King has withdrawn his support from your brother. All the small states are rising against him. Why should they not at such a time regain what was theirs? Even that first husband of yours, even Giovanni Sforza, is back in Pesaro."

Lucrezia dropped his arm. She turned away from him that he might not see her face.

"Holy Mother of God," she murmured. "I have been immersed in my own selfish grief while Cesare is in trouble, Cesare is in danger."

Thus in the brutal frankness of a few minutes Alfonso had done more to make her forget her grief in her father's death than Pietro had, with all the gentle comfort he had to offer, because in her fear for her brother she could best forget her sorrow for her father.

Fortunately for his peace of mind Cesare was too ill to realize the full extent of his defeat. The shock to his system, which drinking the diluted but poisoned wine had given it, although it was not fatal had deeply aggravated that other disease of which he had been a victim for so many years. During the sojourn in Castel Sant' Angelo he was not only sick in body but in mind, and therefore only half aware of what was happening in the world outside.

A new Pope had been elected. At such a time of unrest it had seemed advisable to the Cardinals to elect a very old man until the situation became more stable. The old man, Pius III, was almost on his death-bed when elected and therefore not inclined to meddle in Cesare's affairs. It was thus that the latter was able to earn that respite in Castel Sant' Angelo. But Pius died after a reign of twenty-six days, and there was all the furore which attended a Papal election to begin again.

Cardinal Giuliano della Rovere, that old enemy of the Borgias, now had his eyes on the Papacy; he had hoped for it at the time of Alexander's election and he was determined to secure it now, for if he did not he would most certainly never do so.

He was shrewd; he was clever; he was, indeed, a man of immense vitality. He was of the same type as Alexander himself, and this may have been due to the fact that they had both been born poor, although each had possessed a powerful Pope for an uncle. Sixtus IV had advanced his nephew della Rovere even as Calixtus III had given his nephew Roderigo Borgia his start in life; and both of these nephews had decided that they would one day wear their uncles' robes.

The time of Conclave was one of great tension for every Cardinal, as even to those who did not expect themselves to be elected Pope it was of the utmost importance which Pope was elected, since a friend or an enemy in the Vatican could make all the difference to their future.

Cesare, a sick man, with much of his conquered kingdom restored to those from whom he had taken it, was still a power in the Vatican, for Alexander had practiced nepotism as blatantly as any of his forbears, which meant that there were several Borgia Cardinals whose fates were so bound up with their family that they would vote for the man Cesare chose. Therefore Cesare still retained a certain influence, and della Rovere needed every vote he could lay his hands on.

He came to Rome and went to see Cesare.

He feigned shock at the sight of Cesare's emaciated body and the ravages of sickness on his face; inwardly he was filled with exultation. He had always hated the Borgias. Alexander had been his great rival, and now he turned the full force of that hatred on Alexander's son.

"My lord," said the wily Cardinal, "you are very sick. You should not be in Rome. You need the sweet air of the country."

"This is a time," said Cesare, "when men such as we are must be in Rome."

"Ah, the election. Poor Pius! But he served his purpose. He gave us that breathing space which was so necessary."

"It is to talk of the election that you have come to see me?" asked Cesare. Della Rovere replied: "I will not deny it."

"It surprises me that you should come to me for help."

Cesare was looking back over the years. He knew that his father had never trusted this man, had looked upon him as one of his greatest enemies, had known how desperately he desired the papal chair; he remembered he had said that della Rovere was an enemy to be watched with care because he was one of the cleverest and therefore most dangerous men in Italy as far as the Borgias were concerned.

Della Rovere smiled with an air of candor. "Let us be frank. A few months have changed our positions. You were a short while ago Duke of a large territory and there was not a state in Italy which did not tremble at the mention of your name. My lord, your kingdom has shrunk since the death of your father."

Cesare clenched his hands firmly. He retorted coldly: "Everything I have lost shall be regained."

"It may be so," answered della Rovere, "but you will need a friend in the Vatican to replace the one whom you have lost."

"Could there ever be one to replace my father?"

"There could be one who would give help for help."

"You mean . . . yourself?"

Della Rovere nodded. "My lord Duke, look clearly at the position before us. You have been sick. You have been near to death, and your enemies have taken advantage of that. But already you recover. Much power still lies in your hands. It is for you to strengthen that power. You could not make a Pope, but you could prevent any Cardinal's election by withholding the votes you command through the Borgia Cardinals. You need help now. You need it desperately. I need your votes. Make me Pope and I will make you Gonfalonier and Captain-General of the Church."

Cesare pondered in silence. Della Rovere had risen; he stood by Cesare's couch, his arms folded, and Cesare saw in him that glowing vitality, that power which had been so much a characteristic of Alexander.

Cesare tried to see into the future. Gonfalonier and Captain-General of the Church? It would be a blow to his enemies. He saw himself marching to conquest; he was visualizing the recapture of all that he had lost; he could see his enemies cringing before him.

Della Rovere bent over him swiftly and murmured: "Think of it."

Then he was gone.

Cesare lay thinking, and a letter was brought to him from Lucrezia. He read it and smiled; it was an expression of devotion. She had heard of his plight; she had forgotten her terrible grief over her father in her anxiety for him. She could find little support for his cause in Ferrara, but she herself would raise men; she had valuable jewels which she could sell.

He kissed the letter. It seemed to him symbolic that it should arrive close on the visit of della Rovere. It was a good omen. He had but to recover his health and the world was waiting, waiting for him to conquer.

When della Rovere was elected Pope and was reigning as Julius II, Cesare waited for him to fulfill his promises.

There were many men living—among them the great Machiavelli himself—who marveled at Cesare's simplicity in trusting Julius. It seemed to these men that Cesare's illness had indeed weakened his mind.

Cesare set out from Rome for that part of Romagna which his troops had been able to maintain. He was full of hope. He knew that the King of France had immediately on the death of Alexander withdrawn his support. The King of Spain had not forgiven the Borgias for their alliance with the French; and now Spain was in possession of a great part of Southern Italy. Cesare, his forces considerably depleted, stood alone, and his enemies watched him, wondering what he would do next. They were astonished that he did not seem to realize the desperate position in which he found himself. Rarely had a man been stripped of his power so quickly as had Cesare Borgia. Alexander had died, taking the Borgia glory with him; but Cesare, it seemed, had yet to learn this.

Della Rovere had no intention of bestowing on Cesare the titles he had promised. He was secure in the Vatican and he wanted no more of Cesare Borgia. He was prepared however to let him escape from Rome, though for this concession he was going to demand the surrender of all that part of Romagna which was still in Cesare's hands.

So when Cesare was ordered to surrender Romagna, and refused, he was taken prisoner by the Papal forces and imprisoned in a fortress at Ostia.

Here he was treated well, and did not believe he was in truth a prisoner. He would not believe it. He dared not. The new weakness within him frightened him so much that he would not contemplate it. From the battlements of the fortress he fired salvoes into the sea and shouted with mad ferocity as he did so. Those who were aware of what he did marveled at his conduct, yet they knew that he was in some way deceiving himself, deluding himself into believing that he was firing at an enemy.

Since Cesare refused to give up Romagna, della Rovere decided that he must be brought back to Rome. He must understand that the days of Borgia greatness were over, and that he was no longer a mighty conqueror.

So back to Rome he was brought while della Rovere considered what to do with him.

It was impossible to believe that this man was the brilliant Cesare Borgia. He seemed to have lost his sense of judgment completely. It was as though something of him had died with Alexander—his fire, his cunning; was there something superhuman about these Borgias? Were they different from all others? Was there some family unity which was not understood by ordinary men, so that when one died part of the others died also?

"His mind has been affected by his misfortunes," said della Rovere. "We will have him put in those apartments where the young Duke of Bisceglie was lodged at the time of his murder. How will this weakened Cesare feel when he is forced to live with the ghost of a man he has murdered?"

It would suit della Rovere very well if Cesare Borgia went mad.

⚜️👑⚜️

Lucrezia was back in Ferrara for the state visit of Francesco Gonzaga, Marquis of Mantua.

Lucrezia, still in mourning for her father, had taken to wearing flowing robes in thin material which clung to her figure and made her look more slender than ever; she was once more washing her hair frequently, and against the dark draperies it seemed more golden than ever.

She was conscious of the lack of sympathy in the court; she longed for her solitary meetings with Bembo. But when they met, others were usually present and he had recently been called to Venice on the death of his young brother.

Both her husband and her father-in-law were irritated by her sadness; Ercole took no pains to hide his jubilation at the death of one whom he considered his old enemy, and it was obvious that but for the rich dowry he would have availed himself of the French King's suggestion to annul the marriage. Alfonso was indifferent to his father's rancor and his wife's suffering. Both seemed to him a waste of time. His military duties and the work of his foundry occupied him fully; and he had his mistresses for his night time, as well as Lucrezia to get with child.

Both the Duke and his son were not very pleased by the coming visit of Gonzaga. They did not like him, and it was very rarely that he came to Ferrara although the distance between the Este territory and that of Mantua was not great.

The Este family thought that their Isabella was far too good for the Marquis of Mantua, and they made this plain. Clearly they thought he should have handed over the entire government of Mantua to the capable Isabella, and since—easy-going as he might be—Gonzaga had not done this, they were inclined to be resentful.

Thus the visit was to be a very formal one.

Francesco, as he rode with his cavalcade toward Ferrara, was thinking of Lucrezia Borgia. He smiled wryly recalling his wife's animosity at the time of the wedding. Not that it had decreased since. Isabella was furious because of the way in which Lucrezia kept the poet, Pietro Bembo, in Ferrara. Isabella believed that all poets and artists belonged to her. Often she had tempted Pietro to come to Mantua, and always he had refused.

Isabella had ranted and raged. "He is her lover, doubt it not! The sly-faced creature. So demure! So gentle! A Borgia! My brother should be warned lest she decide to introduce him to Cantarella. You must warn Alfonso when you are in Ferrara."

He smiled. Did she think that because she had behaved badly to Alfonso's bride he was going to be ordered to do the same?

He was chivalrous by nature, and, as he remembered her, there had been something fragile and feminine in that young Lucrezia whom he had met—it must be nearly ten years ago—which had appealed to his gallantry even then. It must have appealed a great deal because he could recall it vividly now.

And so he rode into Ferrara.

The old Duke, he thought, was ailing, and could not last much longer; Alfonso was as bucolic as ever; Ippolito even more haughty; Ferrante more thoughtless; Sigismondo more pious; and Giulio more vain. He was going to be somewhat bored in Ferrara.

Then he met Lucrezia. He caught his breath at the sight of her; she was more fair and fragile than he had been thinking her. Her grief was so recent that it seemed to hang about her in an aura of melancholy. Slender as a young girl in her flowing draperies, her jewels restricted to a few brilliant diamonds, she was almost unearthly in her beauty; and he was deeply moved by the sight of her.

He kissed her hands and managed to infuse a tender sympathy into the kiss. He felt that he wanted to make up for all the insults and humiliations which his wife had administered.

"It was with the utmost sorrow," he said in a low and tender voice, "that I heard of your loss."

Tears came to her eyes, and he hurried on: "Forgive me. I should not have recalled it."

She smiled gently. "You did not recall it. It is always with me. It will be with me until I die."

She enchanted him, this girl with one of the most evil reputations in Italy, who yet could look so innocent. He longed then to discover the true Lucrezia, and he was determined to do so before he returned to Mantua.

The visit was to be a brief one, so there was not much time for him to do this; moreover he sensed an aloofness in Lucrezia. She was genuinely concerned, he knew, with her father's death; and if it were true, as Isabella insisted, that Pietro Bembo was her lover, that would account for her polite indifference to his offer of friendship. She was charming of course, but he sensed she would always be that. He wanted to bring a sparkle to her eyes; to see them light up when he approached as he felt sure they would for a good friend. After all, the poor girl had not many friends whom she could trust—friends of some power, that is to say. Ercole was a hard, mean man; and Alfonso's indifference to the sort of wife he had was obvious. Her father dead, herself childless—as far as Ferrara was concerned—the French King suggesting there might be a divorce, her brother a prisoner of the new Pope . . . poor girl, did she not realize the difficult position in which she stood? She should do everything in her power to win the support of a man such as the Marquis of Mantua. But she did not seem to think of her own position. She did not seem to care.

He turned his charm on her ladies. With them he was most successful.

Later they chattered about him to Lucrezia. Oh, but he was charming! Not handsome—they would admit that. His eyes were slanting, yet that gave them a look of humor. His nose was flattened as though his mother had sat on him when he was a baby; but did that not call attention to the tender mouth? He was fond of women; that was understandable. What a life he must have with that harridan, Isabella! They could love him out of very pity because he was married to such a woman.

What a remarkable horseman he was! Why, when he rode out with a party he sat his horse in a manner that set him apart from all others. Did Lucrezia notice how his horse welcomed his approach and became lively and spirited as soon as he mounted?

"He has devoted much of his time to horses," said Lucrezia.

"It is to be understood," cried Angela. "Such a wife would drive anyone to something else. It is to his credit that it is only horses."

"Women," added Lucrezia lightly, "have also come in for a good deal of his attention, so I have heard."

"It does not surprise me," retorted Angela. "I can well believe that he would be . . . irresistible."

"I beg of you do not make Giulio jealous of the man," cried Lucrezia in mock seriousness. "Is it not enough that you give him anxious moments on account of Ippolito?"

"Ippolito!" Angela snapped her fingers. "Let him go back to Sanchia of Aragon."

Lucrezia laughed at her fiery young cousin, but she was still thinking of Francesco.

Francesco walked in the gardens of the palace and thought of Lucrezia. Never before had he wanted to linger in Ferrara; now he was going to be loath to leave. She excited him. She, with her gentle appearance, her evil reputation. She looked virginal, yet he knew Alfonso was her third husband, and there must have been lovers. Heaven knew there were scandals enough. What was it that excited him? That essential femininity? Or was it that gentleness? He grimaced. She was the complete antithesis of his wife. Was that the reason?

He felt a little sad, contemplating his overbearing Isabella. If she had only been a little less clever or a little less capable, how much easier she would have been to live with! But perhaps if she had been a little more clever she would have understood that she could have ruled him completely. He might have been ruled by gentleness; he never would be by arrogance.

There were times when he hated Isabella. Surely the gentlest of men must rebel against such a wife. Isabella was determined that everyone in Mantua should be her subject, including her husband. There had been times when he had been amused; but there had been others when even his natural placidity had been ruffled.

She no longer appealed to him as a wife or a woman. It seemed sad that this should have happened, for when they had first married he had marveled at his good fortune in having a wife who was possessed of all the virtues.

He was a sensual man, a man of action, yet a man of peace. He had often given way to Isabella, shrugged aside his own preferences, devoted himself to the horses he loved so that now his stables were famous throughout Italy, and the Gonzaga horses renowned for their excellence. He had also loved many women. That was his life, his escape from Isabella.

His courtly manners were the key to his success; that gentle charm, that tender care he was always ready to display, were irresistible. He used them diplomatically although they were not feigned, and it was their very sincerity to which they owed their success.

But toward Lucrezia he felt differently from the way in which he had felt toward any other woman, for Lucrezia was different. So depraved, said public opinion. One of the notorious Borgias. So gentle, said the evidence of his eyes, innocent no matter what has happened to her.

He must solve the riddle of Lucrezia although he was half aware that in solving it he might come to love her differently from the way in which he had ever loved a woman before.

This was clear, because had she been any other he would have planned a quick seduction, an ecstatic, but necessarily brief love affair, and would have returned satisfied to Mantua, fortified against the nagging of Isabella.

But this was different. He must seek to please Lucrezia, to win her confidence, to discover what really lay beyond that serene expression, to understand her true feelings for the poet Bembo.

This he set out to do.

At the balls and banquets he would not with obvious intention seek her out, but it was surprising how often she found herself partnered by him. Often when she walked in the gardens with her women, he—also accompanied by his attendants—would meet her. He would bow most graciously and pause for a few words, calling her attention to the flowers and discussing those which bloomed in the gardens of his palace on the Mincio. The others would fall in behind them.

As the time came nearer when he would be forced to leave for Mantua he began to grow desperate, and one day when they walked in the gardens, their attendants following, he told her, with that fervent sincerity which was so attractive, of his desire to be friends with her.

She turned to him and the candor of her expression moved him deeply. "You are truly kind, my lord," she said. "I know that you are sincere."

"I would I could help you. I know of your sadness. You feel alone here in this court. You long for sympathy. Duchessa . . . Lucrezia, allow me to give that sympathy."

Again she thanked him.

"The Este!" he snapped his fingers and grimaced. "My own family by marriage. But how cold they are! How unsympathetic! And you . . . so young and tender, left alone to bear your grief!"

"They do not understand," said Lucrezia. "It seems none can understand. Until I came to Ferrara I lived close to my father. We were rarely separated. We loved each other . . . dearly."

"I know it." He looked at her quickly, thinking of all the rumors he had heard concerning that love; and again he was deeply moved by her look of innocence.

"I feel," she said, "that nothing can ever be the same for me again."

"You feel thus because the loss is so recent. Your sorrow will moderate as time passes."

Her eyes filled with tears. "My brother said that once. . . . when I was unhappy about another death."

"It is true," he answered.

When she had mentioned her brother's name there had been a tremor in her voice, and Francesco knew then that her fears for her brother exceeded the misery she felt on account of the death of her father. What was the truth concerning this strange family relationship which had provoked more scandal than any other in Roman history?

Francesco longed to know; he wanted to understand every detail of her life. He wanted to take her in his arms and comfort her, make her gay, as he felt she was intended to be.

Then he realized that through this family relationship he might win her confidence.

He said softly: "You are anxious on account of your brother?"

She turned to him appealingly. "The news I have heard of him frightens me."

"I readily understand that. He trusted the new Pope too well, I fear. He seems to forget that Julius has always been an enemy of himself and your father."

"Cesare has been sick . . . sick almost unto death. I have heard disquieting rumors that his sickness has such a hold upon him that it has deadened his judgment."

Francesco nodded. "He is a man deserted by his friends. I understand full well your fears, now that he is a prisoner in the Vatican."

"I picture him there . . . in the Borgia Tower. . . . I remember every detail of those rooms."

Haunted by ghosts! she thought, seeing Alfonso—dear and most loved of husbands—lying dead across his bed, Cesare's victim. And now Cesare, weakened by sickness, humiliated by defeat, was a prisoner in those very rooms.

Francesco laid his hand on her arm, and whispered in that tender voice which had so delighted her women attendants: "If there were aught I could do to ease your anxieties, gladly would I do it."

An expression of joy flitted temporarily across her face, so that he was immediately aware of that latent gaiety within her. He wanted to arouse it; he wanted to make her joyous. Was it at that moment that he began to be in love with her?

"There might be something I could do for your brother," he went on.

"My lord . . ."

"Say 'Francesco.' Need we stand on ceremony, you and I?"

He took her hand and kissed it. "I mean to earn your gratitude. There is nothing I crave more than to bring back the laughter to your lips."

She smiled. "You are so kind to me, Francesco."

"And there has been little kindness. Listen, I beg of you. Pope Julius and I are the best of friends, and I will tell you a secret. He is asking me to take command of the Papal army. You see, these are not idle promises I make. I shall devote my energies to making you smile again. And if you saw your brother restored to health, and once again Lord of Romagna, would you be happy?"

"I should still think of my father, but I believe that if I could know all was well with Cesare I should know such relief and pleasure that I *must* be happy again."

"Then it shall be so."

There were more delightful walks, more tender conversations, more promises, but eventually Francesco found it necessary to depart for Mantua, and this he did with the utmost reluctance.

Lucrezia missed him when he went; she told herself that she longed for the sight of Pietro Bembo; but she did enjoy hearing her ladies discuss the charms of Francesco Gonzaga.

As for Francesco, he rode into Mantua marveling at himself. What were these promises he had made? Was it possible for him to advise Julius to pardon the son of his oldest and most bitter enemy? Should not the heads of states such as Mantua be greatly relieved to have Cesare under lock and key?

But he had told the truth when he had said that above all things he wished to please Lucrezia.

Cesare lay on his bed, his drawn sword by his side.

In this room little Alfonso of Bisceglie had waited for his death. They had put him here, Cesare knew, hoping to unnerve him, to remind him of that long-ago crime. They were wrong if they thought they could do that. There had been many murders in his life and he did not look back through a mist of remorse. He did not *feel* remorse; he felt only frustration. He, Cesare, who felt the spirit of emperors within him, who knew that he had had a genius for military conquest, believed that ill-luck had dogged him throughout his life.

He thumped his pillow in sudden rage against fate, which had made him first fight to free himself from the Church and then had taken that great prop, his father's power, from beside him before he was strong enough to stand alone. Worst of all was that ill-fate which had struck him with a sickness at the time when he most needed his strength.

But he would come back to greatness. He swore it.

He felt the power within him. That was why he lay in the darkness of this room, which for weaker men would have been haunted by the ghost of a murdered young man, and laughed at the darkness, laughed at Alfonso's ghost, for he was truly unafraid.

He must get well again. He must eat heartily and sleep for long periods, that he might cast off the lassitude of the last weeks.

He began to carry out his plans. Special meals were prepared at his command, and he spent much time—he had plenty to spare—discussing the menus; he retired to his bed early and rose late. He engaged in card games with his guards; and he exulted because he felt his strength returning to him.

His guards grew friendly; they looked forward to the games; this Cesare

Borgia, whom they had expected to dread, seemed but a mild man after all. They told him they marveled at his calm.

He shrugged his shoulders. "I put many people in positions similar to that in which I find myself," he said. "I remember this now, and mayhap that is why I am so calm. Some of them were freed. I do not believe that this will be my home forever."

The jailers exchanged glances; they watched him regaining his strength.

"My lord Duke," they would ask, "is there aught we can do for you?"

He would give them small commissions and he noticed their increasing respect. It filled him with exultation. It meant that men still feared Cesare Borgia. It meant that they too believed a prison in the Borgia Tower would not always be his home.

🙠👑🙢

With Francesco gone and Bembo far away, Lucrezia brooded continually on the plight of Cesare.

Something must be done, she was convinced. Cesare could not remain indefinitely a prisoner in the Borgia Tower. The subtle cruelty of choosing such a place for him was not lost on Lucrezia; for although she knew him well enough to realize that he would suffer little remorse for the murder of her husband which had taken place in those rooms, it was in those very apartments that he had sat with their father and discussed great plans. She believed that Cesare must be near to madness, and that he must be released at all cost.

Therefore she went to see Duke Ercole and, throwing herself on her knees before the old man, she cried: "My dear father, I have come to ask you to grant me one request. I have asked for little since I have been here and I trust you will bear this in mind."

The old Duke looked at her sourly. He was feeling ill and was displeased with life. Often he wondered what would happen to Ferrara when it was ruled by his son Alfonso; he remembered too that he hated the marriage which had allied his house with that of the Borgias—a family which was now of no consequence in Italy; moreover there was no son yet. If this marriage was going to prove unfruitful he would do all in his power to undo it—ducats or no ducats.

"Well," he said, "what is this you would ask?"

"I would ask you to allow me to invite my brother to Ferrara."

"Are you mad?"

"Is it mad to wish to see a member of my family?"

"It would be madness to invite your brother here."

"My brother is sick. Remember how he brought me back to life. He needs nursing. Who should do that but his sister?"

Ercole smiled unpleasantly. "We want no scandals brought into Ferrara," he said.

"I promise you there would be none."

"There always will be scandal where two Borgias are together," retorted the Duke cruelly.

"You are a man with a family," persisted Lucrezia, "you must know something of the ties which bind families together."

"I understand nothing of the ties which bind the Borgias. Nor do I wish to."

"But you must hear me. Allow me to invite my brother and the children of the Vatican to Ferrara. Let it be a short visit. I promise you it shall be so. But I beg of you, give me your permission to ask my brother here. He would not wish to stay. Maybe he would go into France. He has estates there."

"The King of France has written to me that on no account will he be allowed into France in spite of your supplications. He advises me to have nothing to do with the priest's bastard."

Lucrezia was unpleasantly startled. She had had high hopes of Cesare's being able to go to France. The French King had always been his friend, she had believed; and he had a family there.

She looked pleadingly into the tight-lipped gray old face, but the Duke was adamant.

He closed his eyes. "I am very tired," he said. "Go now and be thankful that you made a good match before it was too late to do so."

"A good match?" she said with an air of defiance. "Do you think I am so happy here?"

"You're a fool if you prefer a prison in Rome to your apartments in the palace here."

"I see," said Lucrezia, "that I was foolish to hope . . . for kindness . . . for sympathy."

"You were foolish if you thought I would have more than one Borgia at my court."

He watched her sardonically as she left him.

Cesare took a last look round the apartments. No more would he lie on that bed, his drawn sword at his side, no more order those elaborate meals, nor play cards with his jailers. He had done that which, such a short while ago, he had sworn he would never do. He had surrendered Romagna as the price of freedom. Now he could walk out of his prison; but he must leave Rome.

He was filled with hope. His sojourn in the Borgia Tower had given him back his strength. In some safe place he would make his plans, and within a few months he would win back all he had lost.

He wished that he could go to Ferrara. He needed Lucrezia at such a time. By the saints, he thought, I'll remember old Ercole for this insult. He shall wish that he had never been born before I have done with him.

But at the moment Ferrara was no place for him.

There was one other: Naples. At Naples he could make his plans.

Naples. It was now in the hands of the Spanish, which was perhaps better than being in the hands of the French. The Spanish King had been annoyed at Cesare's one-time friendship with the King of France, but that was over now, and the Borgias were after all Spanish. Oh yes, it was at Naples that he could expect to find that temporary refuge which he sought.

So he set out for Naples and during the ride south great plans were forming in his head. He must find new allies. Sanchia was in Naples; he flattered himself that he had always been able to subdue Sanchia; his brother Goffredo was there, and Goffredo was still eager to tell the world that he was a Borgia, so Cesare could count on Goffredo's loyal support. The children of the Vatican had also been taken there, so there would be an element of Rome at the Naples court.

Perhaps there would be others less pleased to see him; for instance there would be the relations of Lucrezia's second husband, the Duke of Bisceglie. They might still harbor resentment, but he had no fear of them. In Naples he would make new plans.

The first of these would be to strengthen his friendship with the man who had been set up in charge of Naples by orders of the King of Spain. This was a pleasure-loving handsome young man, Consalvo de Cordoba, who was known as the Great Captain. He had been a friend of the Borgia family, and Cesare saw no reason why, with this man's help, he should not find sanctuary while he gathered together an army and prepared to go into battle.

How different was this journey into Naples from others in which he had taken part! He remembered riding in triumph, the people running from their houses to look at him, calling a welcome to him, while the fear of him showed in their faces.

Now he rode in unheralded.

WHEN HE WAS installed in the lodgings allotted to him he was told that a visitor had called and was asking to be brought into his presence.

"Is it the Captain?" he asked.

"My lord," he was told, "it is a lady."

That made him smile. He guessed who it was, and he had expected her.

She came into his presence and, when they were alone, she threw off the cape and flung aside the mask she was wearing.

Her adventures had not impaired her beauty. There was Sanchia, voluptuous as ever, her dark hair falling about her shoulders, her blue eyes flashing.

"Sanchia," he cried and would have embraced her, but she held up an imperious hand.

"Times have changed, Cesare," she said.

"Yet you come hot-foot to see me, the moment I arrive in Naples."

"For the sake of old friendship," she said.

He took her hand and kissed it. "For what else?" he asked.

She tore her hand away and he caught her by the shoulders. Her eyes flashed. She cried: "Have a care, Cesare. The Captain is my very good friend, and you do not come this time as a conqueror."

He dropped his hands and throwing back his head burst into loud laughter.

"The Captain is your friend!" he sneered. "Well, it is what we must expect.

He is in command here, and Sanchia must command him. Is it due to you that I owe the hospitality I now receive?"

"It might be so," she said. "At least it is friendship which brings me here. I have come to warn you."

He looked disappointed. "I thought you had come to recall—and relive—old times."

"Nothing of that sort!" she flashed. "Everything of that nature is over between us. I see that though you have lost Romagna you have lost little of your arrogance, Cesare. Times change and we must change with them."

"That which I have lost, I will regain."

"You will need to go very carefully if you are to do so, and it is for that reason that I have come to warn you."

"Well, what are these dire warnings you have to offer?"

"Firstly do not arouse the Captain's jealousy."

"That will be difficult to avoid, dear Sanchia. You are as desirable as ever, and I am but human."

"Your life is in his hands. He is a good man who does not forget his friends in adversity; but you need to be careful. Your only friend in this court is your brother Goffredo."

"Where is he now?"

"I know not. He and I rarely meet."

"I see the Captain is a jealous man who will not tolerate husbands!"

She lifted her shoulders. "The court abounds with your enemies, Cesare. Naples did not love you after the murder of my brother."

"Yet you continued to love me."

"If I ever loved you Cesare, I ceased to do so then. There was passion between us afterward, but it was the passion of hate rather than love. Do you remember Jeronimo Mancioni?"

Cesare shook his head.

"You would not of course remember such a trivial incident. There have been so many like it in your life. He wrote an essay on what took place during the capture of Faenza. Doubtless it was a true account, but it did not please you. No, of course you would not remember Jeronimo. He remembers you though. His family remember also. Payment was demanded of him for writing that essay—his right hand was cut off and his tongue cut out. Such things are remembered, Cesare, when a man is in decline. I warn you, that is all. Have a care. You will need to walk more warily here in Naples than you ever did in your Roman prison."

Cesare shrugged aside her warnings.

He would have taken her into his arms, but she would have none of that. He laughed at her playing the game of loyalty to her Spanish Captain. How long would that last? he asked himself. He visualized that before he was ready to set out on the re-conquest of Romagna, Sanchia would be his mistress and all his enemies in Naples would be fawning on him.

⚜ ♔ ⚜

Hope HAD returneD. Goffredo was there, with the old admiration shining in his eyes. Goffredo was ready to serve his brother, heart and soul. It was wonderful at such times to recall the devotion of his family. Lucrezia was raising men, selling her valuable jewels, writing letters to influential men begging their help for her brother; and now here was Goffredo. Alexander the great central figure was gone but they were still the Borgias.

Cesare was himself again. His arrogance had returned in full force. Sanchia was not yet his mistress, but that would come. Soon all in Italy should learn that the Borgia star had suffered but a temporary eclipse.

Consalvo de Cordoba was uneasy. He fervently wished that Cesare Borgia had chosen a different refuge. Consalvo was a man who prided himself on his honor, and from the moment he had heard Cesare was on his way to Naples his anxiety had began. He had received honors from Alexander, and he was not the man to turn from his friends when they were no longer of material value. He wished to help Cesare; yet at the same time he must not forget that he was in the service of his King.

In the days which followed Cesare's arrival in Naples, Consalvo received no orders from Spain; therefore he welcomed Cesare and made it clear that his ill-fortune had not altered his friendship for the Borgia.

But he was wondering what orders he would receive when the knowledge that Cesare was in Naples reached Spain.

Sanchia was aware of his anxieties and sought to comfort him, for Sanchia was enchanted by her Great Captain. Handsome, powerful, he had won

her admiration, and she had quickly surrendered herself to the new ruler of
Naples. She was with him when orders came from Spain.

He read them and was lost in thought. Sanchia wound her arms about
him and whispered: "What ails you, my Captain?"

He looked at her and smiled sadly. He knew that she had once been
Cesare's mistress for their love affair had been one of the scandals of Rome.
He wondered about her, this strange tempestuous woman who had continued
her relationship with Cesare after the murder of her brother whom she had
dearly loved.

His own relationship with her had taught him something of her character.
He wondered whether Cesare still attracted her; he wanted to find out, and at
the same time he wanted to ease his own conscience; he therefore decided to
confide in her.

"Orders from my King," he said.

"Concerning Cesare?"

He nodded.

Sanchia went on: "Cesare has made himself hated by the world. The King
of Spain, I can believe, does not wish him to regain his Kingdom."

"You are right. I am to arrest him and send him to Spain. My King does
not trust the Italians to keep him prisoner."

"If he goes to Spain it will be the end of his hopes."

Consalvo agreed.

"Why should this make you sad, my Captain? What is Cesare Borgia to
you?"

"His father was my friend."

"The Borgias were friends only to those who could be useful to them."

"I have given him my word that he shall find sanctuary here."

"And you *have* given him that. It is only when the matter is taken out of
your hands that you must cancel it."

"The Duchess of Gandia has pleaded with Ferdinand, my King, that justice be demanded for the murder of her husband Giovanni Borgia."

"So Cesare is now to be made to pay for that long-ago crime, the murder
of his own brother!"

"Crimes have long shadows."

Sanchia was suddenly afraid. "If you go to his lodgings, he will fight. He is surrounded by men whom he has made his own, either through bribes or fear. My Captain, I am afraid. I am always afraid of Cesare."

"I must lure him from his lodgings. I do not wish for bloodshed. I must get him to the Castel del Ovo."

Sanchia nodded.

※ ♔ ※

Consalvo waited awhile.

Would Sanchia warn her old lover? He wondered. There was an uncanny power in these Borgias; Consalvo had been conscious of it since Cesare had come to Naples. He was a man who had suffered terrible sickness and heartbreaking defeat; yet his resilience was becoming more and more apparent every day. With a little help Cesare *would* regain his kingdom.

Oddly enough Consalvo had wanted to give that help. He was not a man who wished to stamp on the lame. He would have wished to plead Cesare's cause with King Ferdinand, to have passed on Cesare's explanation of the need to make the French alliance when he had done so.

Consalvo believed that he could have done that successfully; but Cesare's old crimes were creeping up on him. The pleading of his murdered brother's widow had decided Ferdinand that Cesare should be brought to Spain where he could answer that charge and make no more trouble in the Italian States.

Consalvo must do his duty. He was first of all a soldier. But he wondered—and in some measure he hoped she would—whether Sanchia would warn her old lover of the danger in which he found himself.

Now in the Castel del Ovo troops were waiting, and Consalvo must lure Cesare to the castle with some false tale of danger. He, Consalvo, must invite the son of his old friend to sanctuary which would in reality be a trap.

Such conduct deeply perturbed a man of the Great Captain's conscience. He hoped that when his messenger arrived at Cesare's lodgings, the Borgia would be gone.

※ ♔ ※

Sanchia had shut herself into her apartments and would allow none of her women to come near her.

Her eyes were as brilliant as sapphires and as hard as diamonds.

Very soon Cesare might leave Naples—for a Spanish prison; and it was in her power to save him.

She thought of their stormy relationship, of all the pleasure it had brought her. She was recalling those tempestuous scenes which had delighted and exhilarated her. She remembered the hate she had felt for Cesare, the deep satisfaction which she, a strong sensual woman, had derived from their encounters.

Often she dreamed of Cesare . . . Cesare bending over her, quarrelling with her, Cesare making love.

She was remembering also her little brother, Alfonso, so beautiful, so like herself. Insignificant little incidents from childhood would occur to her—the way he smiled, the way he lisped her name, the way he trotted after her with so much admiration in his bright blue eyes for his clever sister Sanchia. Then she thought of his coming into the Vatican with the hideous wounds inflicted on Cesare's orders; she remembered his casting himself at the feet of herself and Lucrezia, clutching their skirts, begging them to defend him from Cesare.

Then she remembered his limp body lying across the bed with bruises, made by Cesare's murderers, on his throat.

And remembering she covered her face with her hands and wept, wept for the little brother whose life had been cut short by Cesare Borgia.

Cesare was in his lodgings when the messenger came.

"I come from the Great Captain," he told Cesare.

"What news?"

"My lord, you must leave this lodging at once. My master has heard that enemies of yours are gathering in large numbers and preparing to attack you here and do to you what you have done to one of them."

"Who are these?"

"It is the family of Jeronimo Mancioni, my lord. He who lost his tongue and right hand. This night they will strike. The Great Captain offers you refuge in the Castel del Ovo. He says that it is imperative that you leave at once."

Cesare was angry. He was not a coward, and he disliked the thought of running away, but he must guard against his enemies. That was one thing he had learned. When his father was alive he had been able to ignore them; now they massed about him, determined to strike while they found him defenseless.

He pictured those maddened relatives of Mancioni. They would humiliate him, mutilate him, if they had a chance. He would fight them and kill a few; but how many of them would there be? A large band, the messenger told him; not only members of the Mancioni family, but others who had suffered at his hands.

Cesare turned to his servant. "Make ready," he said. "We will leave at once for Castel del Ovo."

Oh the humiliation of this! He, the great Cesare, to skulk from his lodgings into refuge! When he recovered his kingdom all those who had dared humiliate him should pay a thousandfold for every slight they had inflicted. He would come back to Naples; he would inflict such torture on the Mancionis as they had never dreamed of.

But there was no time to think of that now. Through the silent streets he hurried, all the time alert for sounds which might indicate that his enemies had discovered his flight and were in hot pursuit. When he reached the castle—sweating with exertion and relieved that he had been spared the humiliation of meeting his enemies—he was surrounded by soldiers.

"Cesare Borgia," said one of these, "you are a prisoner of His Majesty, the King of Spain."

Cesare looked about him, but he could see nothing for the mists of anger which swam before his eyes.

It was a trap, a trap conceived by the Great Captain, that honorable man!

For a few seconds it seemed as though he would venomously attack all those who surrounded him; but he was too late. He was firmly held and bound.

Very soon afterward he was put on the ship which was waiting to take him to his Spanish prison.

Lucrezia was overwhelmed with sorrow when she heard that Cesare had been taken prisoner and incarcerated in the fortress of Cincilla.

She wept to recall how often he had talked of going to Spain—the country of their family's origin—in the utmost splendor, even as his brother the

Duke of Gandia had done. No, it would have to be greater splendor. Cesare must outdo Giovanni at all costs. And now he had gone ignobly, taken there by force, a captive.

She heard that the King of Spain was wondering whether he should be brought to trial for the murder of his brother, found guilty—which he undoubtedly would be—and executed. But it might be that Cesare Borgia was more important to the King of Spain alive and a menace to Pope Julius. On such did the life of one who had hoped to rule all Italy depend.

The Court of Ferrara was growing more and more antagonistic toward Lucrezia as her family's fortunes further declined. There was only Goffredo left, and Goffredo had never been of great account. Never before had Lucrezia been so lonely; never before so completely shorn of that power in which her family had so tenderly wrapped her.

Alfonso had gone away on a foreign visit and, without even his casual protection, life at the castle was unsupportable. Therefore Lucrezia retired to the country retreat of Comacchio.

Pietro Bembo arrived and stayed nearby at one of Strozzi's villas which the architect of this affair had put at the disposal of his pair of lovers.

There was comfort in Bembo's presence. There were walks in the beautiful gardens of the villas; there was music and the reading of poetry. But the love which she had once enjoyed with Bembo had lost its ecstasy. How could she indulge in ecstatic love when Cesare was in misery? Moreover into Lucrezia's thoughts there intruded a man quite different from Bembo—a man of action, the breeder of horses, flat-nosed, completely sensual Francesco Gonzaga.

Pietro would gently recall her attention to the poem he was reading.

"You are sad, beloved," he would murmur.

"How can I be otherwise," she asked, "when I think of my brother? He less than any can endure prison. What is his life like, I wonder."

Pietro shook his head. He did not remind her that what was done to Cesare was not so cruel as that which Cesare had done to others.

"He would have been a good ruler, a good and wise ruler, once his king-dom was in his hands," she insisted. "He had great plans which he discussed with his fortress engineer, a man who, I think, is called Leonardo da Vinci. There were to be sanitary systems which would have drained away the refuse in the cities, and that, Cesare used to say, was one of the first steps toward ridding the country of periodic plague. He planned to do all this, and he would have done it."

Bembo tried to lure her back to talk of poetry, but the magic which the early days of their association had brought with them was lost to her.

There came a day when messengers arrived from Ferrara. They had come to warn Lucrezia that old Duke Ercole was very ill and there seemed little hope that he would recover. Her brothers-in-law, Ippolito, Ferrante, Sigismondo and Giulio, thought that she should return at once to Ferrara.

She was preparing to leave when she saw Bembo coming across the garden to her, and the sight of him, his poems in his hands, walking quietly across the gardens, seemed to her so utterly peaceful that she was filled with a longing to spend the rest of her life at Comacchio or some other quiet retreat.

"I love Pietro," she murmured. "Oh, that I were free to marry him." And her mind went back to Pedro Caldes whom she had once loved so dearly, the father of little Giovanni, and she thought, had I been allowed to marry him when I wanted to, had I been allowed to live peacefully with him, our lives would surely have been lived in surroundings such as this. And Pietro and Pedro seemed in that moment like one and the same person; and she loved that person dearly.

She ran out to meet him, for she was overcome by a longing to stroll once more round the gardens, to snare the happy moments she had enjoyed in this place that she might preserve them in her mind forever; she knew that the death of Duke Ercole was going to make a great deal of difference to her life, and that when she was truly Duchess of Ferrara—if Alfonso decided to keep her as his wife, and if he did not she could not begin to imagine what would become of her—she would not be allowed to leave Ferrara to indulge in an idyllic love affair with a poet.

In the shelter of the trees Pietro embraced her fervently. "We cannot guess," he said, "what his death will mean to us. But know this, my beloved, always I shall love you, always cherish these hours we have spent together."

She dared not delay now. In the absence of her husband her brothers-in-law had summoned her, and she guessed that Ippolito was already aware of her love affair with Pietro.

So she rode out to Ferrara, but before she came into the town a letter was delivered to her. As she read it a faint flush rose to her cheeks and she felt a tremor of excitement within her as she recalled the ugly charming face of the man who had lately intruded on her thoughts and refused to be dismissed.

He had written that news of what was happening in Ferrara had reached him. If she should be in need of a friend, he, Francesco Gonzaga, Marquis of Mantua, would be ready to come at once to her aid.

She rode on, her spirits lightened; such was the power of that man to comfort her.

THere was an atmosphere of tension in the castle of Ferrara when Lucrezia arrived. Alfonso was, unfortunately, traveling in England, and Ippolito was watchful of Ferrante, Ferrante of Ippolito. Giulio, hot-headed and haughty, was already putting himself at the disposal of Ferrante with whom he had always been on terms of friendship, which had grown deeper out of his hatred for Ippolito. Sigismondo spent his time praying that no discord befall Ferrara on the death of the Duke.

Lucrezia was received with pleasure and relief by her brothers-in-law. As Alfonso's wife she was, in his absence, acknowledged as the most important person at court; for it pleased the brothers, in this time of uncertainty, to have a figurehead whom they could regard as temporary head of the state.

Lucrezia remembered those days when the Pope had left Rome and had placed her at the head of secular affairs. That experience stood her in good stead now, and she slipped naturally and calmly into the new position which was awaiting her.

She was conscious though of the tension which existed between the brothers, and she prayed that soon Alfonso would return.

In the meantime with her natural serenity and dignity she was able to keep the bubbling passions of the brothers at bay, while they waited for the return of Alfonso and the end of Ercole.

She was glad at that time of the company of her lively and beautiful though somewhat empty-headed cousin Angela Borgia, who could not conceal her delight in being back in Ferrara, since during the stay at Comacchio she had been deprived of the company of her lover, Giulio.

Angela, completely immersed in her own affairs, was unaware of the dangerous discord which prevailed in the castle at this time. She had never forgiven Ippolito for turning from her to Sanchia when they had first met, and as her mind was completely occupied with her own attractiveness she could not forget the slight.

It was a different matter now. Ippolito was regretting his earlier conduct. Ippolito was a lover of women, and there was quite a scandal in Ferrara because of the way in which he caressed young girls as a lover might, while he feigned to be blessing them as a Cardinal.

Angela seemed far more desirable to him now than she had at the beginning of their acquaintance, and this was no doubt due in some measure to his knowledge that she had for some time been indulging in a passionate love affair with his half-brother Giulio.

Ippolito had long been irritated by Guilio; the young man's vanity was maddening, particularly as, through Angela, he could flaunt it before the Cardinal.

He never lost an opportunity of talking of Angela before Ippolito, and the Cardinal felt his desire for Angela grow with his murderous feelings against Giulio.

Now Guilio had ostentatiously put himself on the side of Ferrante.

Ippolito longed to discountenance the conceited Giulio and, even at this time of anxiety, when Angela returned from Comacchio he made another attempt to take her from Giulio. He followed her into the gardens one day and asked for a few words with her.

"I am growing weary of your continual refusals," he told her.

"There is one alternative, Eminence. If you cease to ask there would be no more refusals."

"There will continue to be demands," he declared angrily, "until what I ask is given." She looked pensive, as though she were considering him, and he cried passionately: "Angela, you know that I love you. I have loved you earnestly since our first meeting."

"I remember the occasion well," she said. "No doubt Sanchia of Aragon remembers it also."

"You were such a child," he pleaded. "I respected your innocence."

"That respect began," she retorted, "when you set eyes on Sanchia. Do not imagine that I may be dropped for the sake of others and picked up when they are no longer available."

"You are mistaken. You turn to that young fool Giulio . . ."

"Giulio is no fool. He loved me from the first and has done so ever since. Think of him—my lord Cardinal. Think of Giulio and think of yourself. Why, I love his beautiful eyes more than the whole of you and your wealth and all your fine promises. Understand that."

Laughing she ran lightly across the grass to the castle.

As soon as Alfonso heard that his father was dying, he made plans to return to Ferrara immediately; and no sooner had he set foot in the castle than the tension lessened. There was a quality of strength about Alfonso; he was practical in the extreme; he might lack the dignity of Ippolito but he was also without that blind arrogance; he might lack the vitality of Ferrante and the charm of Giulio, but he was possessed of a strength which inspired the confidence of all.

"How fares my father?" demanded Alfonso on his arrival.

"He lives, my lord," he was told, "but he is very weak."

Alfonso was relieved. He had reached home in time. He greeted his brothers and Lucrezia and immediately went to the sick-room.

Old Ercole's expression lightened when he saw his eldest son, and Alfonso hurried to the bed and knelt to receive his blessing.

"My son Alfonso," whispered the Duke. "I rejoice to see you here. Very soon Ferrara will pass into your hands. Never forget the Este traditions, Alfonso, and keep peace within the family."

Ercole's eyes went to those standing about his bed—his sons and the wife of Alfonso. He wanted to warn Alfonso against the ambitions of his brothers and the extravagance of his wife, but he was too tired. Alfonso sensed this, and remembered that one thing which he and his father had in common. "Father," he said, "would you like a little music in your bedchamber?"

The Duke smiled. Music, which he had always loved; music to soothe him in his passing, to delight his mind so that it was lost in that pleasure which would prevent his worrying about the future of Ferrara.

Alfonso gave orders that musicians should come to the bedchamber. Surprised, they came, and Alfonso then commanded that they play those pieces of music which his father had best loved. And thus, to the music of the harpsichord, Duke Ercole left Ferrara forever.

ALfonso's vital personality filled the castle.

Custom demanded that the new Duke should be crowned before the court went into mourning for the death of the old one, so the first task which lay before them was the coronation with all its attendant ceremony.

Now that he was among them none feared that the rivalry between his brothers would ever become serious. The new Duke of Ferrara was a man who would make all pause and consider very carefully before they crossed his will.

It was winter and the streets of Ferrara were icily cold as Alfonso rode out from the castle to the Cathedral to be crowned Duke of Ferrara; but in spite of the snowy weather the people turned out to cheer their new Duke.

And when he returned to the castle Lucrezia was waiting to greet him. She stood on the balcony, that the people might see her, wearing a great cloak of white watered silk lined with ermine about her shoulders, and, as the people cheered her and she bowed and waved her acknowledgments, the crimson and gold jewel-spattered gown beneath the cloak became visible.

The people did not seem to hate her, for their cheers were spontaneous; but she was wise enough now to know that they could cheer one day and call for her banishment the next.

Everything depended on Alfonso, and she realized suddenly that she knew very little about this husband of hers. How could it be otherwise when their acquaintance had seemed to begin and end in the bedchamber? And even there he had never confided to her his hopes and ambitions, his likes and dislikes. All she had known was that he wished for sons, and during the time they had been married she had disappointed him in that respect.

He was entering the castle now, and she came down from the balcony to greet him. She was at the entrance of the castle as he reached it and before the eyes of many eager spectators who, she knew, were as curious concerning her future as she was apprehensive, she knelt and kissed her husband's hand.

Alfonso laid his hands under her armpits and raised her as easily as though she were a child. He kissed her cheeks and everyone applauded. But his kiss, Lucrezia noted, was as cold as the snowflakes which fluttered down upon them.

Then he took her hand and led her in to the banquet; and those festivities began which would go on until the next day when they must put off all signs of rejoicing, change white and red and gold for black, and conduct the old Duke to his last resting place.

✦ 🙟👑🙝

THe ceLeBration BOTH of the coronation of the new Duke and the funeral of the old were over, and for the first time, it seemed to Lucrezia, she and her husband were alone together.

Here was the well-known routine. Alfonso, saying nothing, treating her merely as the means of getting children.

After the idyllic relationship with Pietro she was in revolt against this man, and yet when she thought of those sunny hours with Pietro at Medelana and Comacchio there seemed about them an air of unreality; they were light and transient; they could never be repeated.

She realized now that she was afraid of the future, and the knowledge that it lay within the power of this prosaic and cold man was alarming.

Never until this moment had she felt so alone. She thought of those who had stood between her and the ruthless cruelty of the world and, by their own ruthless cruelty which exceeded that of all others, had protected her from evil.

"Oh my father," she wanted to cry. "You have left me undefended. Cesare is a prisoner and I am alone . . . at the mercy of Ferrara."

Alfonso had taken her into his rough embrace.

"It is important now," he said, "that we should have sons."

His words seemed to beat on her brain. Did they convey a warning? Sons . . . sons . . . and you are safe.

It was like a reprieve.

🙟👑🙝

In a few weeks Lucrezia was pregnant. The Duke expressed his pleasure. Not that he had had any doubt that this would soon be so. He had had numerous children, and Lucrezia had already shown herself capable of bearing them.

He was waiting now for the birth of the heir of Ferrara.

Once my son is born, thought Lucrezia, my place here will be firm.

She knew that Isabella was receiving reports on her conduct; she had made several attempts to lure Pietro Bembo to Mantua and, now that she knew she could not, she was writing to her brother urging him to put an end to the love affair between his wife and the poet.

If you do not, she implied, when your child is born you will have all Ferrara looking for the features of a poet rather than those of a soldier.

Alfonso grunted as he read Isabella's warning. He knew that the child Lucrezia now carried was his because she had not seen Bembo since long before its conception. He had known of his wife's fanciful friendship with the poet and had cared not a jot for it. But Isabella was right when she said that the world might suspect his Duchess of foisting on to Ferrara a child not his.

Poets were not the sort of men he felt much sympathy with. As for Lucrezia he had little interest in her apart from the nightly encounters in the bedchamber. She was worthy of his attention then; he did not deny her beauty; she was responsive enough; but he would always prefer the tavern women; Lucrezia's perpetual washing of her hair and bathing of her body vaguely irritated him. A little grime, a little sweat would have been a fillip to his lust.

Now that she was pregnant he was less frequently in her bedchamber; but he did like to visit her now and then for a change.

Pietro came back to Ferrara, and Lucrezia was delighted to see him, for it was wonderful to be with one who shared her love of poetry, whose manners were gracious and charming and who treated her as though she were a goddess, only part human, which was very different from the way in which Alfonso treated her.

Alfonso was alert. Never before, it seemed, had he shown so much interest in his wife. He gave her new attendants and they were all Farrarese.

"I have my women," she told him. "I am satisfied with them."

"I am not," he retorted. "These women shall be in attendance on you in future."

They were not her friends; they were his spies.

She wondered why Alfonso thought it necessary to spy on her. And one day she heard the sound of workmen near her apartments and, when she went to discover what was happening, she found that they were making a new passage.

"But why are you doing this?" she wanted to know.

"We have orders from the Duke, Duchessa."

"Are you merely making this one passage?" she asked.

"That is so, Duchessa."

"And how long is it to be?"

"Oh . . . it merely runs from the Duke's apartments to your own."

A passage . . . so that he could reach her quickly and silently.

What had happened to Alfonso that he was preparing to spy on her?

It was impossible that such mundane matters should touch the love she had shared with Pietro, which had no place in this castle with its secret passages through which an angry husband could hurry to confront an erring wife.

Lucrezia shuddered at the possibility of Alfonso's discovering her and Pietro Bembo together. No matter how innocently they were behaving Alfonso would suspect the worst. What could he—that great bull of a man—understand of love such as she and Pietro shared?

She was careful never to be seen alone with Pietro; and it was only when they met, surrounded by others in the great hall of the castle, and he implored her to tell him what had changed their relationship that she could trust herself to explain, and tell him about the passage which Alfonso was having made.

"Soon," she said, "it will be completed. Then he will be able to come swiftly and silently to my bedchamber unheralded, unannounced. He has had this made so that he may try to catch me in some misdemeanor."

"Where can we meet and be safe?"

"Nowhere in Ferrara . . . that is certain."

"Then come again to Medelana, to Comacchio. . . ."

"It is different now," she answered sadly. "I am in truth the Duchess of Ferrara. Alfonso needs an heir. Do you not understand that I must produce that heir, and he must come into a world which is satisfied that he can be no other than the son of Alfonso?"

"But if we cannot meet in Ferrara, and if you cannot leave Ferrara, where shall we meet?"

"My dearest Pietro," she whispered, "do you not see—this is the end."

"The end? How could there be an end for us?"

"The end of meetings. The end of our talks . . . the end of physical love. I shall love you always. I shall think of you always. But we must not meet, for if we did and we were discovered I know not what would happen to either of us. Our love remains, Pietro. It is as beautiful as it ever was. But it is too beautiful to be subjected to the harshness of everyday life."

He was staring at her with dumb anguish in his eyes.

Too beautiful, she thought. And too fragile.

IX

THE BROTHERS

OF FERRARA

Pietro was lost to her. The tender relationship was over, as were the flowers which had bloomed so beautifully in the gardens which had provided its background.

Lucrezia was trying to give all her thoughts to the child who was due to be born in September. Her pregnancy was a difficult one and she often felt very ill. Alfonso, who could not endure sickness in women, left her very much alone, and now that Pietro had gone from Ferrara the suspicious husband no longer made his unheralded visits through the corridor.

Alfonso had many difficulties to contend with in those months and little time to spare even for his foundry. The plague had been more devastating than usual during the hot summer days; and the results of famine in Ferrara had been alarming; moreover the death of old Ercole seemed to have brought certain festering sores to a head. These were the petty jealousies and rivalries between the brothers.

The most disturbing of these brothers was the bastard Giulio. The very fact of being a bastard made Giulio constantly anxious to prove that he was every bit as important as his brothers. It was unfortunate that Giulio happened to be the most handsome member of the family; he was also the wittiest, and he had the gift of ingratiating himself with the people. He was more popular than any of his brothers, although the solid worth and practical ability of Alfonso were appreciated.

Ferrante was like a pale shadow of Giulio, almost as madly reckless, but lacking that quick wit of the bastard. And it now seemed that Ferrante and Giulio were ranging themselves against Ippolito. Sigismondo however could be ignored; his ideas were becoming more and more mystic, and he would never be a menace to the dukedom.

In his new position Alfonso was quick to realize that harmony within his dukedom was essential, and he tried to placate Giulio by presenting him with a palace and a good income such as he could never have possessed under the rule of mean Duke Ercole.

This however, while it made Giulio more arrogant than ever, also aroused the jealousy of Ippolito, who showed his rancour by arresting a chaplain who belonged to Giulio's household. The man may have slighted Ippolito; no one but Ippolito was sure of this, but what did seem obvious was that Ippolito was trying to show Giulio, and Ferrara, that his upstart bastard brother must remember his place in the dukedom and that therein he must behave with due respect to his legitimate brothers.

This was the state of affairs during that hot summer when the city, with a hundred noisome smells, was the breeding place of plague.

It would be folly, Lucrezia decided, to remain there for the birth of her precious heir; and she called her women to her and told them that she planned to leave for Modena where, in more suitable conditions, her child should be born.

She noticed that her cousin Angela seemed to have lost her usual high spirits, and she wondered whether this was due to the fact that she would be leaving Giulio.

She decided to speak to her, and eventually sent all her women away with the exception of Angela; and when they were alone she said: "Now, cousin, you had better tell me about it."

Angela began to protest vigorously—too vigorously—that nothing was wrong; then she broke down and sobbing blurted out: "I'm going to have a baby."

"Giulio?" said Lucrezia at length.

"Who else?" demanded Angela fiercely.

"Giulio knows?"

Angela nodded.

"And what says he, my dear?"

"He says that we must marry."

"Well, then you should be happy."

"We are afraid that there will be obstacles. Alfonso's permission must be obtained."

"I doubt not that he will give it."

"Ippolito will do all in his power to frustrate us. He hates Giulio."

"And you, my pretty cousin, are in part responsible for that."

Angela, always the coquette, smiled through her tears. "Was it my fault?"

Lucrezia smiled gently. "Well, do not be distressed. I doubt not that all will be well for you. But in the meantime I would advise caution. It would not be wise for you to marry without Alfonso's consent, as Giulio would then arouse the enmity of his eldest brother as well as that of Ippolito. Heaven knows, enough trouble is caused by the quarrels between himself and Ippolito. Now listen to me. Keep this matter secret for the present and ask Giulio to do the same. Believe me, this is the best way if you would marry in the end. Your pregnancy can be kept secret for a while. We will make a new fashion for skirts. Leave it to me."

"Dearest and beloved cousin, how I adore you!" cried Angela. "What should we do without you?"

"You will need more than my help," said Lucrezia. "You have urgent need of more discretion on your own part."

And looking at Angela she wondered how she was suddenly to acquire that valuable asset in which so far she had shown herself to be entirely lacking.

LUCREZIA AND HER party set out for Modena. When Lucrezia traveled a large retinue went with her. There were her dressmakers and many personal servants, her jesters, dwarfs, musicians.

Angela had regained her spirits and seemed to have reconciled herself to parting with Giulio, in a manner which surprised Lucrezia. But when a few miles from Ferrara they were overtaken by a small party of horsemen at the head of whom rode Giulio, she understood the reason for Angela's contentment. He looked very handsome, very sure of himself, his dark eyes flashing as he scanned the company for a glimpse of Angela.

"Guilio!" cried Lucrezia. "What are you doing here? Why have you followed us?"

He brought his horse alongside hers and taking her hand kissed it tenderly.

"Sweet Duchessa," he said, "how could I bear to be separated from you!"

"Your soft words do not deceive me," Lucrezia told him with a smile. "You have other reasons."

"Allow me to ride with you, dear Duchessa, and I will tell you why I have found it necessary to fly from Ferrara, although, my dear, dear Duchessa, I insist on your understanding this: Whether it had been necessary for me to fly or not, I should have followed you, for how could I bear to cut myself off from the light of your bright eyes?"

"And Angela's?" she added softly.

"Ah, and my sweet Angela's," he answered.

"You and I must have a talk about that matter soon," said Lucrezia quietly. "But not here."

"The saints preserve you for your sweet goodness, Duchessa."

Angela had taken her place beside Lucrezia, and she and Giulio exchanged passionate glances.

They were reckless, thought Lucrezia, but how could she blame them for that? As they rode, Giulio told them why he had found it necessary to ride full speed out of Ferrara.

"You will remember that my accursed brother, Ippolito, had the insolence to imprison one of my chaplains. I could not allow that so I have stormed the man's prison and freed him. What my brother Ippolito will say when he discovers I can well imagine."

"He would like to have *you* imprisoned for what he would call violating the sanctity of his castle," said Angela shortly.

"One day," said Giulio, "I shall have followers to equal those of proud Ippolito. Then I shall stand and face him, and if it be necessary to fight to the death I will do this. It would seem to me that there is not room for the two of us in Ferrara."

Angela's eyes shone with admiration for her lover, but Lucrezia was sad.

"I wish for an end to these troubles," she said. "I should like to see you friends."

Angela and Giulio smiled at each other. Dear Lucrezia! they thought. What did she know of passionate love and passionate hate?

PLAGUE AND FAMINE were sweeping across Italy and, as Lucrezia came into the town of Reggio where she was to rest for the birth of her child, no banners were hung out, no shouting crowds waited to welcome her. The hot streets were deserted and the people hid themselves behind their shutters.

It was depressing for Lucrezia who was always conscious of the miseries of others, and she remained melancholy as she awaited the birth of her child.

She longed for an encouraging message from Alfonso. None came. It was as though Alfonso implied: Produce the heir of Ferrara, and then I shall congratulate you. Before you have done that, what is there to congratulate you about?

There were tender letters from two men, and she knew that she was continually in their thoughts. One of these penned her exquisite lines of poetry— that was Pietro Bembo; the other wrote as a soldier whose arms were always at her disposal. This was Francesco Gonzaga.

These letters brought great comfort. She was delighted that Pietro should continue to think of her. She could not help laughing, when she remembered the cold welcome which had been accorded her by Isabella at the time of her marriage, to consider how solicitous and tender toward her was Isabella's husband. This seemed Fate's revenge for all the slights which she had received at Isabella's hands. Lucrezia was convinced that the proud and domineering woman, while she accepted her husband's infidelities with other women, would be very put out if she knew that he had some tender feeling for the woman whom she hated and whose position she had resolved to undermine.

But of what importance were these matters? All that mattered now was that she should come through this difficult pregnancy, escape the plague and give Ferrara a healthy heir.

Messengers brought her a letter from Alfonso.

She seized it eagerly. At last he seemed to have remembered her existence. But as she read the letter her eyes clouded with disappointment, for there was scarcely a reference in it to herself.

She threw it aside and asked Angela to bring Giulio to her; and when he came she said, "I have bad news for you both. I am very sorry."

They waited breathlessly and she went on: "It is from Alfonso. Ippolito has complained about your storming of his castle and freeing your chaplain who, Ippolito claims, insulted him. Alfonso is weary of the strife within the family, and he says that Giulio must immediately leave us. You are to go far away from trouble, Giulio, far away from us all."

Angela let out a wail, and Giulio's eyes flashed. "I'll not go," he declared.

"Giulio, Angela, you must think of your future. You must obey Alfonso. Only if you do, shall I be able to persuade him to agree to your marriage."

And after a passionate leave-taking of Angela, Giulio left.

❧ 👑 ❧

During the heat of September Lucrezia's baby was born. She called him Alexander, for as she held him in her arms she believed that he might bring her a joy which would help her to forget the loss of that other Alexander.

But the baby was very small. He did not cry; he lay very still; he did not want to be fed. There was surely something wrong with a child who did not cry and did not want his food.

She longed for a word from Alfonso but there were only the letters from Pietro and Francesco to bring comfort.

And one morning when Alexander was scarcely four weeks old Lucrezia awoke with a terrible sense of foreboding. She knew that her baby was dead.

❧ 👑 ❧

A letter from Francesco Gonzaga brought her out of her melancholy.

His condolences, his most tender thoughts, he sent to her. He knew how she must be suffering. He thought of her constantly in that gloomy town of Reggio. If she would forgive the presumption, he would say that she was unwise to stay there. Let her leave Reggio and all its memories; she should not remain, brooding on her tragedy. She should return to Ferrara, and she should do this by barge, which would be so much more comfortable in her present circumstances. He would suggest that she break her journey at Borgoforte, a small fortress in his possession, on the banks of the Po. It would give him the utmost pleasure there to wait upon her, and entertain her. He was a rough soldier and was no poet to charm her with words, but he could offer something of equal value, he believed. For instance he knew how she suffered on account of her brother's imprisonment. If they met they could discuss this sad matter. Who knew, he—as a soldier—might be able to suggest some means of alleviating her brother's suffering. And this he would be at great pains to do, because he knew that the suffering of her brother was hers also.

That letter roused her out of her apathy.

She read it through and read it again, and she found that a smile was curving her lips because she was comparing his blunt phrases with those flowery ones of the poet, Pietro Bembo.

But Francesco was right. What she needed now was a soldier's help for Cesare. Only in helping her brother could she forget her own misery.

Alfonso's neglect—he was clearly annoyed by the death of the boy and seemed to blame her, first for bringing a sickly child into the world and then losing it—had hurt her deeply, and this gallant soldier's tender interest soothed her, wiped away her humiliation.

She called her servants together and cried: "Make ready to leave. I am weary of this place. We shall travel back to Ferrara by barge. But first we shall stop at Borgoforte."

There was bustle throughout the apartment. The atmosphere had lightened.

Everybody knew that they would now begin to move away from the tragedy which had been wrought by the death of little Alexander.

❧♛❧

Francesco was hastily trying to transform the meagre fortress—which was all he possessed at Borgoforte—into a palace worthy to receive the woman he was hoping to make his mistress.

He had not been so excited since the days of his early youth. Lucrezia was different from all other women. That mingling of latent passion, that serenity— they were such an odd combination.

The enchantment of Lucrezia lay partly in the fact that there could not be a woman less like Isabella in the whole of Italy.

The gentle Lucrezia...the domineering Isabella. How different! He believed he was on the verge of the greatest love affair he had ever experienced.

Recently she had been said to be the mistress of a poet. Was she in truth his mistress? Had there been physical love between those two? No one had proved that. They had wandered in gardens together and he had written verses to her; they had set the verses to music and sung them together. It seemed to this rough soldier a poor way of conducting a love affair.

Still he did not dismiss Pietro. He wanted to say to Lucrezia: I can give you all your poet gave you, and more also.

He had even written sonnets to her. He blushed to recall them. Yet all poetry seemed to him equally foolish, so why should his be more so than any other?

If only he had a palace to offer her instead of a miserable fortress! But he could not invite her to his palace of Mantua for Isabella would be there and her alert eyes would be upon them; and although she allowed him a mistress or two, she would never tolerate a love affair between himself and Lucrezia.

But love affair there should be, even though it must flower in a fortress.

His servants were now draping magnificent tapestry about the pillars; the musicians were arriving; and a messenger had come with a letter. He frowned as he took it, for he saw that it was from Isabella.

News had been brought to her, wrote his wife, that he was making an effort to transform the fortress of Borgoforte into a palace in order to entertain some friends. She was surprised that she had had to hear of her husband's activities from others than himself. Would it not have been more seemly, more gracious, if he himself had told her of his plans? Should she not have been invited to welcome his friends?

Francesco was melancholy. He pictured Isabella's arrival, her determination to humiliate Lucrezia as she had at every opportunity during the wedding celebrations in Ferrara. This visit he had planned as a preliminary to seduction. Isabella could have no part in such a plan.

Then suddenly Francesco threw off his melancholy. In that moment the great campaigner was in command and the servile husband of Isabella subdued. A curse on Isabella! She had put herself in command in Mantua, and like a fool he had a hundred times given way to her. But this was not Mantua.

Deliberately he wrote a note to his wife telling her that he had not asked her to make the journey to Borgoforte, and had no intention of doing so. She had recently recovered from an attack of fever, and was not in a position to travel. Not only would he refuse to invite her . . . he would forbid her to come.

He sent off the note and turned his thoughts to the decorating of the fortress.

But Isabella could not be dismissed from his thoughts as easily as that.

Francesco searched his soul and had to admit that he was afraid of his masterful wife.

Therefore he wrote to her once more, telling her that one of his guests was her sister-in-law, Lucrezia, Duchess of Ferrara, who would call at Borgoforte on her way back from Reggio to Ferrara. Perhaps it would be a pleasant gesture if he invited her to visit Mantua on her journey. He was sure Alfonso would be delighted if his sister entertained his wife.

Having dispatched the message, Francesco asked himself whether he was a fool or not. If, during Lucrezia's stay at Borgoforte, he advanced his relationship with her as he intended to, would it not be visible to the alert eyes of Isabella?

SLOWLY THE BARGE drifted down the Po toward Borgoforte. Surrounded by his muscians whom he had commanded to play sweet music, Francesco saw it take shape through the mist as it glided past the banks thick with birch trees.

As the barge came nearer he saw the brilliant colors of the women's dresses, and there in their midst Lucrezia herself, her freshly washed hair golden about her shoulders, and a smile of pleasure on her face. As she stepped ashore, he took her hands in his and his heavy-lidded eyes shone with emotion as he studied her slender figure. She seemed more frail than ever, and sorrow had seemed to give her an appearance of even greater childishness.

Francesco had never before felt such pity mingle with desire. Poor child! he thought. Poor, poor child, how she has suffered!

He realized that her stay at Borgoforte was not going to be the merry one he had anticipated; he doubted whether she would become his mistress while there. Quite suddenly that seemed unimportant; the only thing that mattered was to make this young girl gay again.

The gay music seemed out of place in the misty meadow.

He said: "I knew you loved music. I but wished you to know that, while you stay at my poor fortress, I mean to do everything I can to make you happy."

She had placed her hand in his and had given him that childlike smile.

"I have felt happier since I received your invitation," she said. "I feel happier still now that I have seen you again."

He led her into the fortress. She was astonished at its magnificence.

"But you have gone to much trouble," she said.

"It was of small account," he told her.

"But no, it is of great account. It was done to cheer me. I know it."

"Then if it has cheered you one little bit, the effort was well worth while. I have arranged a banquet for this night. You and I will dance a measure."

She shook her head and the tears filled her eyes. "It seems such a short while since I held my baby in my arms."

"It is over," he answered her. "No grieving can change it. You must try to be happy again. If I could make you so, I should be the happiest man on Earth."

"It is in no man's power to make me happy, I fear."

"You speak with your grief fresh upon you. There shall be no dancing if you do not wish it."

They went into the hall which, with its cleverly painted murals, gave an impression of vistas opening out beyond the walls of the room. She was effusive in her praise, and that pleased him for it showed her awareness of all he had done to attempt to charm her. But still she was sad, and her mind dwelt on the child she had lost.

He could not make love to her. He could not even speak of love. He could only show by actions that he cared for her, that her fragility appealed to him, that her insecurity made him long to protect her.

It was not easy to be alone with her at the fortress. They could only talk during the banquet or while the guests danced together.

"You know," he said earnestly, "that if you should need my help I would come to you at once."

"Why should I need your help?" she asked.

"My dearest Lucrezia, you, who were a short time ago protected by the most powerful relations, are now alone." She was immediately melancholy, thinking of her father's death, of Cesare's captivity; and the last thing he had wanted to do was increase her sadness. But he persisted: "Alfonso wants an heir . . . needs an heir."

"And I have failed him once more."

"Do not brood on that. Understand now, that should you need my help at any time and send word to me, no matter where I should be, I would hasten to your side."

"You are good to me," she told him.

He did not touch her, but she saw the smoldering light in those heavy-lidded eyes that seemed suddenly robbed of their sleepiness. "It shall always be my greatest joy in life . . . being good to you."

"Why are you so good?" she asked. And when he was silent for a few seconds she laughed a little uncertainly. "During my first days in Ferrara I came to know your wife as my most bitter enemy."

His eyes smoldered. "She was cruel to you. I could hate her for it."

"You . . . hate Isabella, your wife!"

"Do you not understand why?" Lucrezia's heart had begun to beat a little faster; this man was succeeding in making her feel alive again. She waited for the answer. "It is because I am falling in love with you."

"Oh no! It cannot be so."

"I was a fool not to know it before. Do you remember our first meeting? Do you remember how you made me talk of my battles? I thought you a child then . . . an enchanting one, but only a child."

"I remember it well."

"And you stood on the balcony and watched me ride away."

"Giovanni Sforza was there . . . my first husband."

Francesco nodded. "He spoke slander against you even then, and I hated him. Yet I did not know why I hated him."

"I thought what a great soldier you were, and if Giovanni Sforza had been like you I might have felt differently toward him."

"Lucrezia . . ."

"You must not misunderstand me. There can be no love between us two."

"But there *is* love between us two."

She shook her head.

"Have I not told you that I love you?"

"They are the words of a courtier."

"They are spoken from my heart."

"But of what use is love if only one feels it? Love must be shared to be beautiful."

"It shall be. It shall be," he cried passionately.

But she only shook her head once more.

"I will show you the extent of my love," he told her.

"I pray you do not. Did you not know that the men who love me are unlucky?"

"Alfonso . . ."

"Alfonso never loved me." She turned to him smiling. "But it is good of you to show me such kindness. You know how heavy my heart is. You know of the sorrow which has befallen me during this most tragic year. You seek to make me light-hearted. That is so kind of you. I do not forget how kind."

"You do not believe that I love you truly, and that my love is greater than any you have ever known before. Do not think that poets, who have a gift for flowery speech, can love with the same passion as a soldier. My verses make you smile—or would, had you not the kindest heart in the world; but love does not consist of writing verses. I will show by my deeds that I love you. You have a brother on whose behalf you suffer much pain."

She had clasped her hands together in an agony of expectation, and he smiled believing he had found the way to her heart.

"I have some influence in this land and in that of Spain. If I sent an envoy to the court of Spain begging for your brother's release, my request might not go unheeded. What would you say to me then, Lucrezia?"

"I should say you were the kindest man in Italy."

"Is that all?"

"I could, I believe, begin to love one who could bring so much good to me."

"How you love this brother of yours!"

"We were brought up together. There are family ties. We have always been of great importance to each other."

"I have heard that said. I believe, Lucrezia," he went on seriously, "that there will never be happiness for you while your brother is in captivity."

"It is as though we are one person," she said. "While he is a prisoner, so am I."

"The prisoner of your own emotions, Lucrezia," he said. "There shall be one in your life who means so much to you that even your love for your brother will seem of small significance. I intend to be that one."

"You forget Isabella," she said. "Isabella and Alfonso."

"I forgot nothing," he answered. "You will see in time Tomorrow I send that envoy to Spain."

"How can I thank you?"

"Between us," he said, "there shall be no formal gratitude. You will see that I shall put my life at your service and in exchange . . ."

"Yes?" she asked. "In exchange you will require?"

"Only that you love me."

Isabella was waiting to receive her sister-in-law at Mantua. She was suspicious. Why had Francesco suddenly become so bold as to forbid her to attend the two days' festivities at Borgoforte? And who were the guests? Lucrezia and her miserable attendants! All that fuss, all that preparation for the Borgia woman!

Yes, Isabella was very suspicious indeed.

She had been almost unbearable to her servants that day. She had been dressed three times before her appearance satisfied her.

She was assured that no dress in Italy could compare with the one she was wearing. The Borgia woman in her morello and gold would look coarse beside her; she was so slender, so dainty. Isabella cuffed the woman who said that. "Am I a fool?" she demanded. "Can I deny the evidence of my eyes? I am neither slender nor dainty. These are the Borgia's qualities. But I fancy I have as good a shape as any woman in Italy."

The more apprehensive she grew, the more she wished to flaunt her superiority. She practiced her singing and dancing steps, as she had before the wedding; she went through her galleries admiring her works of art. The woman would never have seen such treasures, not even in the Vatican. That rogue, her father, had collected women rather than art treasures.

But what annoyed her more than anything was the thought of her husband Francesco's daring to dance attendance on a woman who she had decided to hate.

She sent for two of her women who she knew had been his mistresses. They were quite handsome still and she bore them no grudge. She had, though he had not known this, chosen them for him. She complimented herself that she knew him so well that she was aware of those occasions when he was ready to go, as she called it, a-roving. That did not worry her. All she asked was to rule Mantua, and if he was deep in a love affair he was more likely to leave her in command than if he were concerned with matters of state. She liked him to have his mistresses in the household so that she could watch the progress of his affairs. What she would not tolerate was that he should choose his own women.

"We must show the Duchess of Ferrara that we can give as good a banquet here as ever she enjoyed in the Vatican," said Isabella. "And you two shall have new dresses. There is not time for me to design them for you, so I shall select from my own store what most becomes you."

The women were delighted. They understood, and she knew she could rely on them to use all their wiles to lure the Marquis of Mantua from any fresh love.

ISABELLA TOOK LUCREZIA in her arms and gave her the kiss of Judas.

"How it delights me to see you here!" she exclaimed.

Lucrezia's smile betrayed nothing. She stood before Isabella, child-like yet self-contained; not in a dress of morello striped with gold but in dark draperies which clung to her figure and which were even more becoming than the bright colors had been. In spite of her troubles she was still a slender and lovely girl.

"Come," said Isabella, leading the way into the castle, "I long to show you my treasures. I trust my husband entertained you in a manner suited to you?"

Isabella's eyes were mocking and cruel, full of suggestions, hinting that she suspected Lucrezia of being her husband's mistress.

Lucrezia replied: "The Marquis and his friends gave me a hearty welcome at Borgoforte. I fear my low spirits disappointed them."

"Then I trust they were able to raise them a little."

"It is always comforting to have good friends."

"Alfonso was not pleased by your sojourn there as my husband's guest, I gather. He is a jealous husband."

"He has no need to be."

Isabella's laughter rang out.

"The Duchessa has had a long journey," said Francesco, "and she has not yet fully recovered her health."

"Forgive me," said Isabella. "I am forgetful. We will refresh ourselves, and later I will show you my paintings and statues. I'll swear you have rarely seen a better collection. I pride myself on it."

Isabella would not leave Lucrezia's side; she watched her husband's two ex-mistresses waiting upon him, and Isabella had to admit that they seemed gross beside the newcomer.

It was clear to Isabella that Francesco either had made or determined to make the woman his mistress. Lucrezia with her air of innocence might suggest that she was unaware of this, but she did not deceive Isabella. She is a Borgia, thought Isabella, and therefore a monster.

The light of battle was in Isabella's eyes. There shall be no love affair between those two, she told herself. I'd see Francesco dead first. He may have all the women in the world if he wishes to—but not that one.

It was a situation which was quite intolerable to Isabella. What was going on behind those sly meek eyes? Was the girl laughing at her? Was she thinking to take her revenge for what had happened at the wedding?

She took Lucrezia's arm and with a party they toured the castle, for Isabella had a great longing to show Lucrezia the treasures she possessed. She wanted to accentuate the fact that she, Lucrezia Borgia, was no longer a power in Italy, and that even the possessions still left to her were held insecurely.

Francesco was in the party, so were the two women whom she had dressed in two of her most becoming gowns. They were chattering as coquettishly as they knew how, but Francesco was scarcely aware of them.

Lucrezia must gasp in admiration at the beautiful works of art which Isabella had to show her, and even Isabella gloating over them briefly forgot her enmity toward Lucrezia.

Isabella was a born collector with a sincere love of what was beautiful, and as she stood before the glorious Mantegna painting of the Triumphs of Julius Caesar her eyes filled with tears.

Lucrezia was similarly affected, and for a moment they were drawn together.

"It must be one of the finest paintings in Italy," said Lucrezia.

Isabella nodded. "Painted for me by Andrea Mantegna when Francesco became Marquis of Mantua."

Isabella had broken the spell; immediately she was herself once more. Painted for *me*. Arrogant and possessive, implying everything within this castle belongs to me—including Francesco.

There were the beautiful paintings by other artists of note; Isabella had made sure that all the greatest works of art should be housed in her palace. Here were works by Costa and Perugino; the rarest books were in her possession; ornaments finely wrought in gold and silver and decorated with precious stones. She had her grotto to which she took Lucrezia, and there, among the most exquisite sculpture in the world, Lucrezia discovered that which was perhaps the most beautiful of all.

Her eyes dwelt on Michelangelo's Sleeping Cupid which had once been in the possession of the Duke of Urbino. To Lucrezia it represented more than a beautiful piece of work by one of the world's most brilliant artists; it was a symbol of Isabella's ruthless cupidity. Lucrezia remembered that, when those whom Isabella had called her great friends were in distress, her first thought had not been for their safety but for the Sleeping Cupid; and at Cesare's request she had banished the Duke and Duchess of Urbino in exchange for the Sleeping Cupid.

Did Isabella think of this every time she looked at that exquisite statue? What was she thinking now? Isabella's mocking eyes held those of Lucrezia briefly, as though to imply: Understand the sort of woman I am. Ruthless to my friends, how much more so should I be to my enemies!

But there was one treasure Isabella had kept to show her visitor, which she guessed rightly would cause her more pain than anything else she could show. This was the handsome young heir of Mantua, one of the most beautiful boys in Italy: Federigo, son of Francesco and Isabella; and Isabella made sure that Lucrezia, who had so recently lost the heir of Ferrara, should have plenty of opportunities to envy her the heir of Mantua.

She sent the younger of the ex-mistresses to her husband's bedchamber that night, but the woman returned to Isabella and told her she had been dismissed. Isabella then sent the second of the women, and she too failed and returned to her mistress.

Lucrezia's bedchamber was well guarded. She should not have the comfort of Francesco during her Mantuan nights, decided Isabella; and after a two-day visit of great strain and tension, Lucrezia re-entered her barge and sailed away from Mantua, leaving behind a regretful, unsatisfied lover and his bitter and revengeful wife.

THe barge glideD on its leisurely journey along the Po, turning from the main stream on the way to Ferrara, and so it came to rest at Belriguardo.

Here a pleasant surprise awaited them. Giulio was standing on the bank to welcome them.

Eagerly he kissed Lucrezia's hand and even more eagerly his eyes sought those of Angela.

"But . . . Giulio!" cried Lucrezia. "Should you not be far away?"

"Have no fear," Giulio reassured her. "I have not broken parole. Alfonso was in a benign mood when the baby was born. He gave me leave to return to court."

"I am glad, and so will Angela be."

Angela certainly was. She was a little anxious also; her pregnancy was drawing toward its end, and it was becoming increasingly difficult to hide her condition which by now several of the women had guessed. Therefore for Angela's sake, Lucrezia was delighted to see Giulio and still more delighted that Alfonso had decided to forgive him.

Giulio explained that he had called at Belriguardo to welcome them, and was going to ride on ahead of them the very next day to warn the court of their imminent return.

Lucrezia arranged that he and Angela should be alone together, and when the lovers had embraced they began to discuss their plans.

"We must marry soon," Giulio declared.

"If we do not," grimaced Angela, "our baby will be born before we do."

Giulio hesitated. He told her that he longed to marry her immediately, but at the same time he did not wish to offend Alfonso.

"You see, my beloved Angela," he explained, "after this affair of the chaplain he warned me that there must be no more rash escapades. If there were, he said, he might not forgive me so readily next time."

"We want no more banishments," said Angela.

"No. But I will speak to Alfonso. He is not unreasonable, and I feel sure that had I not been banished I could have arranged our marriage before this. The menace is of course Ippolito. He hates me, largely because he knows you love me."

"A curse on Ippolito!" murmured Angela. "He will do everything within his power to prevent our marriage. I know. But we'll outwit him. The first thing is to get Alfonso's consent."

"Then I will ride to Ferrara tomorrow and consult him on this matter at once."

True to his word Giulio left Belriguardo the next morning. He rode alone not wishing to be encumbered with attendants. He had not ridden many miles when he saw horsemen approaching, and he laughed to himself when he recognized his half-brother Ippolito at their head.

"Good day to you, Cardinal," he called in insolent tones.

Ippolito pulled up sharply and gave his brother a look of hatred. He had never seen Giulio look so handsome, so sure of himself.

"You looked pleased with yourself," cried Ippolito.

"As you would be, were you in my shoes."

"You have just left the Duchessa?"

Giulio nodded. "And . . . Angela," he added softly.

"I have heard news of that girl."

"That she is to have my child?" said Giulio.

"You speak with pride of that which should fill you with shame."

"Shame, brother? When you would give so much to be in my place?"

Ippolito was filled with a sudden rage. He thought of Angela, and how his desire for her had become important to him, because it contained more than a physical need; her rejection of him was the symbol of his brother's superior attractiveness and powers with women. She had said that she cared more for Giulio's beautiful eyes than all the Cardinal's power and wealth. For the moment Ippolito's fury was beyond control; and as Giulio was about to whip up his horse Ippolito shouted: "Seize that man. Put out his eyes!"

His grooms hesitated a second, but Ippolito snarled: "Obey, you knaves, lest that which I command you to do to him be done to you."

That was enough. They fell upon Giulio; they had him spread-eagled on the ground while they jabbed at his eyes with their daggers and wild agonized screams came from Giulio.

"It is enough," said Ippolito; and he and his men galloped away, leaving Giulio frantic with pain, lying half dead on the blood-stained grass.

It was some hours later when a rider came panting into the castle of Belriguardo to tell of the terrible sight he had seen in the meadow close by.

Angela, in floods of helpless tears, fell fainting to the floor while Lucrezia gave orders that a litter be hastily made, and Giulio brought back to the castle. There was a doctor present but she sent messengers to Ferrara, demanding that all the best doctors should leave at once for Belriguardo.

And Giulio, more dead than alive, was brought to the castle.

When Alfonso heard the news he was both angry with Ippolito and filled with pity for Giulio; then he was apprehensive. That which he had always feared had broken out: enmity within the family circle.

His first impulse was to send for Ippolito and punish him severely for the terrible thing he had done; but Alfonso was quick to remember that he was first of all Duke of Ferrara and that he could not allow personal feelings to stand between him and the good of his dukedom. Giulio was of little importance to Ferrara; whereas Ippolito was a Cardinal and as such would wield some influence for Ferrara at the Vatican. Therefore Alfonso could not afford to mete out justice at the expense of that man who, next to himself, was the most powerful in Ferrara. Moreover Ippolito, in spite of his haughty and ungovernable temper, in his calmer moments was a sound statesman and there had been many occasions when his advice had been invaluable to Alfonso.

Alfonso was a plain man, and a man who took his duty seriously. He wanted to do what was right and honorable; he had only shortly taken over the reins of government, and fervently he wished that his father were alive to deal with the terrible quandary in which he found himself.

Ippolito in the meanwhile had ridden out of the state of Ferrara, fearing the severe punishment which he had earned; and Alfonso was aware that very soon the terrible story would be spread throughout Italy, and the weakness of a House, in which brothers warred with one another, exposed for all to see.

He wrote at once to his sister Isabella and her husband Francesco, telling them what had happened; and his letter was a plea for advice. When Isabella heard she was maddened with fury, for one of the few people whom she loved was her dashing young half-brother Giulio.

Francesco had rarely seen her so moved. "To think of him," she cried. "My dear little brother. . . . To have left him there lying on the grass . . . in agony! I could murder Ippolito. And Alfonso asks what he should do. He should summon my lord murderer back to Ferrara and he should slash out his eyes. 'Twould be a just punishment."

Francesco watched her quietly. It is strange, he thought, but I believe I have come to hate Isabella.

He had thought continually of Lucrezia since she had sailed away, and he remembered vividly every little hurt Isabella had given her.

Yet Isabella truly loved Giulio. She did not understand why Alfonso hesitated. She did not realize that to punish Ippolito would be to wound his great pride and make him an enemy of Alfonso and therefore of Ferrara for the rest of their lives. No greater harm could come to Ferrara than strife between these two brothers, and Isabella, in urging the punishment of Ippolito, was urging also the weakening of that structure which was the Este family; yet in her grief she could not see this.

And Francesco? He hated the Este family even as he hated Isabella. He hated their pride, their arrogant feelings that they and they alone were worthy to rule. What did he care for the downfall of Ferrara! But he did care. The matter was of great importance to him. He would be secretly pleased to see his wife's family in decline. Ferrara and Mantua had never been true friends. And how he hated Isabella!

"Why do you stand there saying nothing?" demanded Isabella. "Is it of no importance to you that Giulio should be mutilated in this way?"

"I am thinking," he said. His eyes smoldered beneath their heavy lids. "Certainly Ippolito should be brought to justice."

She put out her hand and he took it.

In this way and this way only, he thought, can I indulge my hatred of Isabella.

She had risen. "I will send doctors to Giulio at once. At least he has a sister who will do all in her power to save his life."

So the reply was sent to Ferrara. But by that time Alfonso had considered the matter with the utmost calm, and Alfonso Duke of Ferrara was in command over the sentimental brother of the wronged Giulio.

He had already sent word to Ippolito. He must return at once to Ferrara. His absence weakened the Duchy. They must stand together, no matter what happened, against all those who were ready to be the enemies of the state.

GIULIO LAY IN the dark room. There was pain . . . pain all the time. He could not escape from pain, and even in sleep he would be haunted by dreams of those cruel men standing over him, their daggers in their hands; he would feel again the stabbing pain in his eyes; and he would awaken to more pain.

He would lie still, hating . . . hating the world which had been so cruel to him, which had first made him strong, handsome, gay—and in one short hour had taken from him all that had made his life good. Hate dominated his thoughts and there was one man to whom all that hatred was concentrated, one man whom he longed to destroy even as he had been destroyed. The only thought which comforted him during those days and nights of pain was of revenge on Ippolito.

He had lain in the darkened room; the slightest shaft of light could make him scream in agony. But even as he cursed his fate he remembered that he had good friends. They—Isabella, Lucrezia, Alfonso—had sent the best physicians in Italy to his bedside. They had not only saved his life, they had prevented him from being completely blind. He knew now that the sight of one eye was left to him, for he could see the outline of objects in the darkened room. Yet as he twisted and turned on his bed he wished that those kind friends had been his enemies, that they had left him to die as Ippolito had.

Lucrezia came into the room. She was a slender graceful shape, a perfumed presence which bent over his bed. She took his hand and kissed it.

"Dearest sister," he murmured. "My dearest Lucrezia. I should have been dead but for you."

She touched his forehead lightly and he strained to see her face. There was no mirror in the room and he did not know how much he had changed. They had removed the bandages from his face and at first the air on those scars had been excruciatingly painful.

"You can see me, Giulio?" she asked.

"Yes, sister. Your face becomes clearer to me as I look."

"Then we must rejoice, for you are not to lose your sight."

"Angela?" he asked.

"The child has been born," she told him. "We have kept it a secret. Do not worry. Foster parents have been found. They will be well paid, and perhaps in a short time you will be able to claim the child."

"I see that you have looked after us both, Lucrezia," he said emotionally.

"It was my pleasure to do so."

"Has Alfonso been here?"

"No."

"He will see justice done," cried Giulio. "I know Alfonso to be a just man."

Lucrezia was silent, and Giulio went on: "All Ferrara shall know that Alfonso will not allow any—even the great Cardinal Ippolito d'Este—to deal thus with me."

"Angela is waiting to see you," said Lucrezia. "And Giulio, there is another. Ferrante is here."

He smiled: Lucrezia forced herself to hide the repulsion which the smile aroused in her, for it made the poor mutilated face grotesque.

"Ferrante!" he said. "He was always my friend."

"Poor Ferrante!" said Lucrezia. "You will have to comfort *him*. He is both furious and heartbroken."

"On my account," whispered Giulio. "It would be thus with Ferrante."

"I will send Angela to you," Lucrezia told him, and she left him.

He felt the sweat on his face. He was terrified. Why was there no mirror in his room? Why was he not allowed to see himself? He had cared so much for his looks; he had swaggered before his servants in his fine garments; he had extorted flattery from them. And now?

Angela was in the room. She stood by the door and although he could not see her clearly he sensed her hesitation.

"Angela!" He tried to speak calmly but his voice faltered.

It seemed to him that she took a long time to reach his bedside.

"Why . . . Giulio!" she whispered.

"Angela . . . come near to me. . . ."

She fell on her knees by the bed, and he put his face close to hers; he had to read the expression in her eyes, but she had lowered them. She was steeling herself to look. Lucrezia had prepared her. She could still hear Lucrezia's unhappy urgent whisper: "Angela, do not let him know . . . wait until he is stronger. Look straight at him. Smile . . . do not flinch."

But frivolous Angela had never learned to hide her feelings. She could not look; she dared not.

She felt his hands on her face; he had grasped her chin and was forcing her to look.

She stared; she flinched; she could not hide the horror in her eyes, for instead of handsome Giulio a hideous mask was staring at her, a travesty of a face, cruelly battered, the left eye enormously swollen, the right lidless, and in vain did she try to suppress the shudder which ran through her.

He released her as through she were some poisonous animal. He lay back on his pillows, his head turned away from her.

"You . . . you will get better, Giulio," she stammered.

He answered her: "All the money in the world, all the justice in the world, will not buy me a new face, Angela."

She tried to laugh, and he hated her laughter. He hated her weakness and the hurt she had given him. Ippolito had not only robbed him of his beauty but of Angela. He had removed handsome and charming Giulio from the world, and put a hideous misanthrope in his place.

She seemed to shrink from the bed. She talked about the child, but he had no interest in the child, for what would the child do when confronted with the creature he had become? Turn away in horror. Everyone would do that in future.

"Holy Mother of God," he cried out suddenly in his anguish, "you too were cruel to me. You should have let me die."

Angela had one desire; it was for escape.

"I will come again, Giulio," she said.

But he shook his head and would not look at her. She went and he knew she would never come again—not the Angela who had loved him.

He could have wept, but how could a man, mutilated as he was, shed tears? Tears would have eased his pain, but there was no comfort.

The door had opened and someone else had come into the room.

"Go away," he cried. "Go away from me. You cannot deceive me. I am hideous . . . hideous . . . and it is embarrassing you all to look at me. Do not come with your lies. Do not tell me I shall be myself once more. I am fit for nothing but to be put into a cage and wheeled through the streets, that people may come from their houses to laugh at me . . . to stone me. . . ."

"Giulio . . . Giulio . . . this is unworthy of you."

He was held in a pair of strong arms; he was embraced; someone was kissing his scars.

"Ferrante!" he said. "So you came, brother."

"I came, you old villain. I have been here several days. They would not let me see you. 'Not see my old friend Giulio!' I cried. 'Know you not that he is my brother and that he and I have been together in adventures, so mad that we would not dare speak of them to any other?'"

"Those days are over."

"Never."

"Look at my face, Ferrante. Now don't tell me that I am as handsome as ever or that I will be, that everything will be just as it was if I am a good boy and take my medicine."

Ferrante took his brother's face in his hands. There was no shrinking in those strong hands, no faltering in the gaze which met his.

"Giulio," he said, "I am your handsome brother now. There are scars on your face which will never be healed."

"I have the truth from you, brother."

"Did you doubt you'd get it? Listen, Giulio, the women are not going to lose their virtue to you so readily in the future. But perhaps they will. There is Strozzi, the cripple. The ladies seem very fond of him. Who can account for women?"

"Ferrante, you seek to cheer me. I am hideous, a monstrosity. You admit it."

"It's true, brother. But you'll grow used to it. You must accept what is."

"Ferrante, tell me, do you hate to look at me?"

"Fool of a brother, I never loved you for your beautiful eyes. I never loved the long lashes, the red lips. No, it was brother Giulio whom I loved. He is the same."

"Ferrante!"

"Come, come . . . no dramatic scenes, I beg of you. I was always bad at them. I shall stay here, Giulio, until you are fully recovered. You and I have much to talk of. Alfonso is our good brother. By God, Ippolito is going to pay for this."

"Ferrante, brother . . . stay with me. Life seems suddenly bearable."

Then Ferrante embraced his half-brother once more and Giulio releasing himself said: "There are tears in your eyes, brother. There would be in mine were that possible. But what is there to weep about? I thought I had lost all that made my life worth while. I was a fool, Ferrante, to have forgotten that my life still held you."

Lucrezia, a close witness of Giulio's tragedy, forgot her own sorrows in contemplating it. She believed that more trouble was brewing. Alfonso would never bring Ippolito to justice, and in the dark room of pain where Ferrante was a frequent visitor plans for vengeance were discussed. Lucrezia knew that it was only these plans which gave poor tortured Giulio a reason for living.

As for Angela, who was terrified of having to look at her once handsome lover because his distorted face filled her with horror, Lucrezia believed that the kindest thing she could do was to get the girl married and away from Ferrara.

She had arranged for the care of the child of that tragic love affair even as her father had arranged for her own child, the *Infante Romano*, the fruit of another such tragic love affair.

Alfonso was helpful in this matter and eventually a bridegroom was found for Angela in Alessandro Pio, Lord of Sassuolo, who held a small territory.

Angela was excited at the prospect of marriage and escape from Giulio, and became absorbed in accumulating her trousseau. Lucrezia bought a dress of cloth of gold for the girl to wear at her wedding and was glad when the ceremony was over and Angela had gone away, though she missed her for, frivolous as she was the girl had been amusing and absolutely loyal to Lucrezia.

It was a long time before she could bring herself to tell Giulio that Angela had married and gone away.

✦✦✦

Lucrezia intercepted Alfonso on his way to Giulio's apartment. "Alfonso," she cried, "I must speak to you . . . about Giulio."

Alfonso studied his wife. He supposed she was very beautiful; he had heard it said that she was; it was a pity she was not his type. He liked fleshy women. Not that he was averse to doing his duty by her; but it did seem as though she was going to prove disappointingly infertile.

"Something must be done for Giulio," she said.

Alfonso raised his eyebrows questioningly.

"All these weeks have passed and there is no attempt to administer justice. This harbors dangerous thoughts in Giulio . . . in Ferrante."

"So they are plotting together!"

"They do not plot. They fret for justice."

"You are a fool," he said, "if you think I can afford to estrange Ippolito."

"You mean you will shrug your shoulders at what he has done?"

"You speak of Cardinal Ippolito d'Este. I could not show favor to a bastard at his expense."

"Favor! I did not suggest favor. Only justice."

Alfonso looked exasperated and Lucrezia for once abandoned her serenity. "Oh, I know I am only a woman," she cried. "I am here to bear children . . . nothing more. But I tell you this, Alfonso; if you do not administer justice in some form you will have trouble between your brothers."

"Trouble in the family must be avoided at all cost," said Alfonso. "I plan to bring my brothers together; there shall be a reconciliation."

"You think Giulio will ever be reconciled to Ippolito!"

"He must be . . . for the sake of Ferrara."

✦✦✦

Eventually Alfonso prevailed upon them to meet each other. He stood between them—the mighty brother to whom they both owed allegiance.

"Ippolito, Giulio, my brothers," he said. "This has been the saddest thing I ever witnessed. I would have given ten years of my life that it should not have happened."

"Do not look at me," said Giulio bitterly. "I was but the victim."

"Giulio, I am asking you to forget your wrongs. I am asking you to forgive your brother."

"Why does he not speak for himself?"

"I am very displeased that this has happened," said Ippolito, inclining his haughty head.

"Displeased!" cried Giulio. "I would describe my own feelings in stronger terms." He snatched up a torch and held it to his face. "Look at me, Alfonso; and you, Cardinal, look at your work. This hideous thing you see before you is your once handsome brother, Giulio."

Alfonso's voice was broken with emotion as he cried: "Stop, I beg of you. Giulio, my dear brother, stop." He went to him and embraced him. "Giulio, I grieve for you, brother. But think now of Ferrara. Think of our family and, for the sake of our ancestors, who made Ferrara great, and of all those who will follow us, make no trouble now. Forgive your brother."

And Giulio, weeping in Alfonso's arms, murmured: "I forgive him. It is over and done with. Long live Ferrara!"

It was easy to say one forgave; it was difficult to continue in that noble attitude. He must lie, poor Giulio, in his darkened room, for even after some time passed he could not bear to face the light. He listened to the sound of distant music from other parts of the castle and brooded on the old days.

Ippolito would be flashing his brilliant robes, making assignations with beautiful women. Ippolito who had ruined his brother's life and thought he had made amends by lowering his haughty head and saying he was sorry.

There was only one comfort in his life: Ferrante.

Ferrante spent most of his time in Giulio's room, where they talked of past adventures. Ferrante could often make his brother laugh, but such laughter was always followed by melancholy. What could memories of the joyous past do but lead to the melancholy present? Why should they not talk of the future? What was the future for him? Giulio demanded. He would spend long hours in a dark room, and if he ventured abroad he would have to be masked to hide his hideous face; even then people would turn from him, shuddering.

There was only one way to bring Giulio out of his melancholy, and that was to talk of revenge. Revenge on Ippolito the author of his miseries; revenge on Alfonso who had taken Ippolito's side against his brother.

It amused them to make plots—wild plots which they knew they could never carry out.

Ferrante, always reckless, sought means of enlivening his brother's fancies, and one day Giulio in a fit of depression cried: "What fools we are with our pretences! Our plots were never meant to be carried out. They are idle games which we play."

From that moment Ferrante decided that they should have a real plot, and he set about finding conspirators who would join them. It was not difficult to find men who believed they had been ill-treated by Alfonso; it was even easier to find those who resented Ippolito's high-handed ways. There was a certain Albertino Boschetti who had lost some of his lands to Alfonso; and his son-in-law Gherardo de Roberti, who was a captain in Alfonso's army, was ready to join in the plot. They would meet with a few others and discuss the Borgia methods of poisoning and wonder whether they could lure Lucrezia into becoming one of them. This they abandoned as impossible; but a priest, Gian Cantore di Guascogna, who was possessed of a beautiful voice and for this reason had been favored by Duke Ercole, joined the plotters for his own reasons. It might have been that he realized the plots were not serious but merely a simple means of bringing a little excitement into Giulio's life. The priest had received nothing but friendship from Alfonso, and indeed had accompanied him on many of his amorous jaunts.

Giulio lived for the meetings which were held in his dark room; often the sounds of laughter would be heard coming from his apartment. One day Lucrezia, hearing them, smiled with relief. She did not know what was causing the laughter.

Giulio was saying: "As for Alfonso, it should not be so difficult. You, my dear Gian, often accompany him to his low brothels. So what could be easier? Take some of the girls into your confidence. Pay them well. They will do anything for ducats. And when he has drunk deep, tie him to his bed, and then . . .

it should not be difficult to find those who, with their daggers, would be ready to do to him what has been done to me."

THE woman was to Alfonso's taste. She was voluptuous and silent. He preferred silent women. They had drunk deeply and he was drowsy; he lay stretched on the bed waiting for the woman, while she hovered about the room.

"Come, hurry, woman," he growled.

But she laughed at him, and he half regretted that he had drunk so deeply that he felt disinclined to rise. She was kneeling at the foot of the bed.

He cried: "What do you there?"

And still she laughed.

She did not know that he was the ruler of Ferrara. Part of the pleasure in these nightly jaunts was that he ventured forth incognito.

He jerked his foot. It did not move. But he felt too listless to care, and the woman was now flitting to the head of the bed.

He reached out an arm to catch her; she took it at the wrist and held it. She had moved behind him and, keeping his arm outstretched, she kissed it at intervals.

He grew impatient; he was never a man to fancy the preliminaries of lovemaking. He implied that he was a practical man; he made no secret of the purpose which had brought him here. Therefore delay irritated him. But tonight he was strangely listless.

Then he found that his feet and hands were securely tied to the bedposts, and he was at the mercy of this woman.

Now he was alert. For what purpose had she tied him thus? How could he have been so foolish as to have lain supine while this was done to him? Suddenly he understood. Something had been slipped into his wine to produce this lassitude.

He was in danger, and the thought of danger, and the need for prompt action, cut through the fumes in his head.

Then the door burst open and there was Gian Cantore di Guascogna, the rascally priest with the divine voice who, like his master, enjoyed a tour of the brothels.

"Free me, you rogue," shouted Alfonso.

The priest came and stood by the bed. He had taken his dagger from his belt. He lifted his hand as though he were about to plunge the knife into the Duke's heart.

"Enough!" cried Alfonso. "Come, you old rogue. Cut these ropes at once. 'Twas a good enough joke, and I its victim, but 'tis over."

Alfonso had been accustomed to command all his life, and there was authority in his voice. His laughter rumbled in his throat, and the priest, under the spell of that strong personality, leaned over the bed and cut the ropes.

Alfonso jumped up; he was laughing heartily, slapping Gian on the back, calling him Scoundrel.

Then he pushed Gian from the room. Gian stood outside the door trembling.

WITH THE COMING of the spring Alfonso left Ferrara for one of his missions abroad and, as was the custom, appointed Lucrezia as Regent. Ippolito being so powerful in Ferrara—the most important man next to Alfonso—could not be ignored, so that it was necessary that he should be co-Regent.

Lucrezia was glad of her brother-in-law's help, for Ippolito, when he was not suffering from imagined slights to his dignity, was a statesman of no small ability.

But Lucrezia was aware that Ippolito's hatred of his half-brother had been increased through the terrible injury he had done him. Ippolito could not dismiss Giulio from his thoughts; he knew that many people deplored what he had done, and he sought to put himself right in the eyes of Ferrara. To do this he must prove Giulio worthless, and as Ippolito had always had numerous spies in the castle, he was fully aware of the meetings which took place in Giulio's apartments.

He listened gravely to Alfonso's account of how he had been tied to a prostitute's bed, and Alfonso had accused him of lacking a sense of fun. Ippolito had said nothing. He intended to teach all his brothers a lesson.

That the plotting had begun as a game, and had never been anything else, mattered not to Ippolito. He was determined to set himself right in the eyes of the world while he brought some balm to his own conscience.

He did not tell Lucrezia what was in his mind, as he believed Lucrezia might warn Giulio and Ferrante. She was forever searching for some means of making Giulio happy, and Ippolito did not trust her.

Ippolito discovered that an ambush had been laid for Alfonso at some place on his journey. That this was done half-heartedly was of no account; and that the plotters had waited at a spot which Alfonso did not pass was quite unimportant. Ippolito arrested Boschetti and his son-in-law who, when put to torture, confessed that there had been plots against the life of Alfonso and Ippolito, and these had been concocted in Giulio's room.

Lucrezia came to the dark room.

"Giulio," she cried in alarm.

He sat up to stare at her.

"Alfonso is back," she went on, "and something is wrong. Boschetti and his son-in-law have not been here for three days. They are in prison."

Giulio leaped off his bed; the sight of his poor stricken face made Lucrezia want to weep.

"They are Ippolito's prisoners," she said. "There is talk of treason."

"So . . . he has done this! He has made a monster of me and now he wants my life."

"I believe it to be so," said Lucrezia. "There is little time to spare. You should leave at once, Giulio. Do not let yourself fall into Ippolito's hands again."

"Do you think I care what becomes of me?"

"Giulio, you must live. You must live to prove to Alfonso that you had no intention of taking his life. There is only one way you can do this. It is through immediate escape."

"And where should I go?"

"Isabella, your sister, loves you dearly. She hates Ippolito for what he has done to you. Go to Isabella. She will help you. And her husband is a good man."

Giulio kissed Lucrezia's hands; and soon she had the satisfaction of hearing him gallop away from the castle.

But Giulio came back to Ferrara. He came back because Ferrante was in the hands of his enemies, and Giulio could not rest in Mantua while Ferrante was their prisoner. He had to return to explain that their plots had no roots in reality. They had had a hundred opportunities to kill their brothers, but they had not taken advantage of these.

Isabella and Francesco had listened to the demands of Alfonso for his return, and they had allowed him to leave only when Alfonso had given them his word that Giulio's life should be spared.

Thus Giulio came back to Ferrara where in the company of Ferrante he was forced to witness the barbarous execution of some of his friends.

Ippolito had won. He had assured Alfonso and the people of Ferrara that his prompt action had saved Ferrara from terrible civil war and bloodshed. Ippolito's conscience was salved. He had attacked his brother in a fit of rage; but see what a villain this brother was—he was a traitor to Ferrara!

Giulio and Ferrante were sentenced to death, but the sentences were reduced to those of life imprisonment, and from that time they were placed in one of the towers of the Castle of Ferrara, there to live out their long lives, there to listen to the music of the balls which took place in the castle, to hear the sounds of the people who passed the castle's walls. So near to the life they had known, and yet shut away from it, they were two young men before whom the long years stretched out, yet whose lives were over.

X

THE BULL IN THE DUST

In the highest tower of the fortress of Medina del Campo Cesare paced up and down, clenching his hands, biting his fists, uncontrollable fury within him.

"How can I endure this life?" he shouted at his attendants. "Why should this happen to me . . . to Cesare Borgia! What have I done to deserve such a fate?"

His servants cowered before him. They might have answered that he had imprisoned many men, had condemned them to a worse fate than that which he now suffered; but none dared speak to him, even though their silence could irritate him as much as words.

He had not been ill-treated. In Spain he was recognized as a prisoner of rank. He had his chaplain and attendants, and he was not entirely denied visitors from the outside world.

But to a man such as Cesare Borgia, who had dreamed of ruling all Italy, this fate was the most tragic that could have befallen him.

There were moments of fury when none knew what he would do next. He had during one of these, which had come to him while he was in the prison of

Cincilla, lifted the governor in his arms and attempted to throw him over the battlements. Cesare was emaciated by sickness and frustration, but anger gave him strength and the governor's life had been saved just in time.

As a result Cesare had been removed to this high tower in the fortress of Medina del Campo.

When he looked from his narrow window he could see the valley far below. He would sit brooding for hours over the view from that slit of a window. He longed for freedom and each day he cursed his evil fate, until those about him believed he would do himself an injury.

Then he would call for writing materials that he might write to his sister. "Lucrezia," he would cry aloud. "You are the only friend I have in the world. And what can you do for me? You are almost as much a prisoner as I am. To think that this evil fate could befall us . . . the Borgias!"

He would sink into melancholy, and none dared go near him.

But there were moments of hope. He had heard that King Ferdinand was not pleased with the work of the Great Captain, Consalvo de Cordoba, in Naples, and that he considered he was a traitor to his country. Ferdinand had a plan. He would release Cesare Borgia, set him at the head of an army and send him to make war, in the name of Spain, on Cordoba. Cordoba was the man who had delivered Cesare into the hands of Spain; but for Cordoba he would not be a prisoner now. Ferdinand decided that Cesare was indeed the man to subdue the Great Captain.

So hope was born. There was laughter in the tower of Medina del Campo. Cesare cried: "Soon I shall be marching at the head of my army. Soon I shall be in Naples. I was dying, my friends, for a breath of Italian air. The thought of breathing it revives me now."

He discussed his plans with his visitors; he would spend hours stretched out on the floor, studying maps. There was an atmosphere of excitement in the tower—until news came that Ferdinand had changed his plans and had set out in person for Naples.

Then it seemed that madness possessed Cesare. He threw himself about the tower so that his servants were sure he would do himself an injury. He stood at the window looking down, and all believed that he planned to throw himself out.

The Count of Benavente, a nobleman who lived close by, had visited Cesare out of curiosity, and become fascinated by him. This Count, seeing thoughts of suicide in Cesare's eyes, said to him: "Are you thinking of throwing yourself out of the window, my friend?"

Cesare answered: "It would be an escape from what is rapidly becoming intolerable."

"By the window certainly," said Benavente. "But why jump out? Why not lower yourself down by means of a rope?"

"I have my visitors," said Cesare. "I am treated as a prisoner of some state. But my jailers would never allow a rope to be brought to me."

"It might be arranged," said Benavente.

Cesare now had an object in life. His spirits revived and the old vitality was with him. His chaplain and his servant Garcia were in the plot, and eventually, a little at a time, the rope was smuggled into the tower.

There came a day when, afraid that the guards were becoming suspicious, Cesare decided that there must be no more delay. The pieces of rope were securely joined together, and the escape planned for a certain dark night.

Garcia descended first and to his horror he discovered, when he reached the end of the rope, that he was too far from the ground to jump with safety. But jump he must; and he lay groaning in the ditch about the castle, his legs broken. Cesare had by this time descended and seen what had happened; there was no alternative but to jump; he did so and, as with Garcia, both legs were broken as were his wrists and several bones in his fingers.

Writhing with pain, cursing his ill-luck, he lay on the ground. But it was not long before Benavente came hurrying to him and, seeing his condition, picked him up with the aid of his groom and set him on a horse.

Cesare was in agony, but at least he had escaped. As for Garcia, there was not time to save him as the castle was already alert.

Garcia was left to be captured and executed, but Cesare was taken by Benavente to Villalon, there to have his bones reset and recover sufficiently to undertake the journey he had planned into the Kingdom of Navarre, which was ruled over by his brother-in-law.

At last he was well enough and, thanking his friend Benavente, he left him and with two attendants rode with all speed toward Navarre.

Lucrezia never ceased to think of her brother.

The times were anxious. Julius was proving a warlike Pope and, although during Alexander's lifetime he had been his bitter enemy, decrying the ambitious desire to subdue the neighboring states of Italy, now that he was sure of his own power he was determined to restore the Papal states to the Church; and it seemed that his policy ran along lines similar to those pursued by Alexander.

He had made an alliance with the old Orsini, marrying his daughter, Felice della Rovere, to Gian Giordano Orsini; his nephew Niccolo della Rovere was married to Laura, the daughter of the beautiful Giulia, wife of Orsino Orsini. Laura was said by some to be the daughter of Alexander, but Julius chose to ignore this and accept her as an Orsini.

Having made peace with the Orsinis and the Colonnas, Julius felt that he was safe at home; he was therefore ready for conquest farther afield, and went forth to attack the Baglioni of Perugia and the Bentivoglio of Bologna.

The Bentivoglios had always been firm friends of the Este family, but Ferrara had been forced into alliance with the Church. Julius however had never had a great opinion of Ippolito and had reproved him often for his vain dress and manners, suggesting that he behaved more like a woman than a man and did not conduct himself in a manner befitting a member of the Sacred College. Moreover Julius had been shocked by recent happenings in Ferrara, and considered that Alfonso had been wrong not to have punished Ippolito for his terrible outrage on Giulio.

Therefore there were rumors in Ferrara that this friendship between them and the Pope was an uneasy one, and that the latter might, when he had completed his conquest of Perugia and Bologna, turn his attention to Ferrara.

Lucrezia felt apprehensive and ready for any terror that might come; never did a day pass without her thinking of those two young men who had been her frequent companions and who were now shut away in the tower of the castle. Disaster could descend, swift and unexpected. Who could know what would happen next?

Her old friend, Giulia Farnese, wrote to her now and then. Giulia was once more installed at the Papal Court now that her daughter Laura was married to the Pope's nephew. Giulia recalled the old days when they had been constant companions and had washed their hair together and competed for Alexander's attention. She wrote without nostalgia, which meant that life to her now was as good as it had been in Alexander's time; and Lucrezia had heard that Giulia, even now only a little more than thirty, was reckoned to be the most beautiful and attractive woman in Rome. She was surrounded by admirers and even her young daughter, herself a beauty, could not compete with her.

Giulia had known great triumphs. Not so Sanchia, that other friend. Sanchia had died recently in Naples in the prime of her youth and beauty, deeply mourned by her last lover Consalvo de Cordoba, the Great Captain who had lured Cesare to the Castel del Ovo that he might be made prisoner of Spain.

It was into this uneasy atmosphere that the great news broke.

Lucrezia was with her women when she heard that a messenger was below and had news of such importance that he refused to impart it to any but the Duchessa herself.

The page knelt at her feet and poured out the great news: Cesare was free. He had reached Navarre. He was preparing now to regain all he had lost. He needed the help of the one he trusted more than any other in the world.

Lucrezia listening felt young again. She laughed as she had not laughed for a very long time.

Then she took the page into her arms, and kissed his forehead.

"You shall never want while you live," she told him, "for bringing me this news."

Lucrezia was light-hearted. She had another reason for rejoicing besides the escape of Cesare. A guest had arrived in Ferrara and a ball was to be given in his honor.

She had not realized how much pleasure this event would give her and she was astonished that she could feel so happy. Often she would look up at the tower in which those two young men were incarcerated and, thinking of the melancholy turn to Giulio's life, had come near to weeping. She had pleaded with Alfonso, and the two brothers had been allowed to be together. She knew what comfort this would be to them, and it must have been indeed a happy day when Giulio and Ferrante were told that their confinement was no longer to be solitary.

But Lucrezia was not allowed to see them for Alfonso had forbidden any to visit them. Their names, he warned Lucrezia, were to be no more mentioned. He had shown mercy to his brothers who, he declared, had plotted against his life; they were together in captivity, and they were allowed a window from which to look out on the world. They would be fed and clothed until they died; he had commissioned men to look after that side of their lives. As for the rest, they were dead as far as all others were concerned.

"Why do you treat them thus?" Lucrezia had demanded. "Is it because you, like Ippolito, dare not look at Giulio's face and know your own injustice?"

Alfonso's eyes were cold. "If you would concern yourself with your business and leave mine alone, I should be better pleased with you," he said.

"Is this not in some way my business?" Lucrezia asked with unwonted passion. "Am I not your wife?"

"I would pray you remember it," Alfonso had answered. "A wife's task is to provide children for her husband, and you have not been successful in that respect."

That subdued her. She was always subdued by her inability to produce an heir.

But within the next few weeks she was again pregnant and Alfonso's manner warmed a little toward her.

And now she must put aside thoughts of those two sad prisoners. She was with child, and she prayed that this time she would not disappoint Alfonso. But what made her so happy was that there would be a guest at the ball who, she did not doubt, had made the journey to Ferrara for the purpose of seeing her; that guest was Francesco Gonzaga.

She was dressed in cloth of gold with velvet and brocade; she wore her hair loose and a great diamond on her forehead.

Her old friend, Ercole Strozzi, whispered to her that he had never seen her look so beautiful as she did tonight. She smiled at him well pleased. Since her love affair with Pietro Bembo, Ercole Strozzi had been one of her most trusted friends. It was pleasant to sit with the crippled poet discussing poetry and music; and talking of those days at Ostellato seemed to bring them back endowed with a fresh beauty.

But this night, if she thought of Pietro Bembo, it was as a figure of unreality; their love now seemed like something they had read in a poem, too fragile for truth, too rarefied for reality. And here was a man who was virile—a man who could arouse her senses, and make her feel young as she had in those days when she had loved Pedro Caldes and Alfonso of Bisceglie.

Francesco, as the guest of honor, took her hand and led her in the dance, and his eyes were ardent beneath the hooded lids.

"It seems many years since I said good-bye to you in Mantua," he said. "Did Isabella hurt you badly, Lucrezia?"

Lucrezia smiled. "No," she answered. "At that time nothing could hurt me. You had made me so welcome."

"I mean to put a shell about you . . . a protective shell to guard you from her malice. She hates you because I love you."

"She hated me when you were scarcely aware of my existence."

"I have been aware of your existence since the day we first met. Nothing shall come between us now. Not Alfonso nor all of Ferrara. Not Isabella with all her malice."

"We could not be lovers, Francesco," she told him. "How could we? It is impossible."

"Love such as I bear you can conquer what may seem impossible to conquer!"

"Come, we must dance," she told him. "We are watched, you know. All will be wondering of what we talk so earnestly."

"They must know that I love you. How could any man do otherwise?"

"I have my enemies," she said. "But dance, I pray you. Alfonso watches."

"A plague on Alfonso," murmured Francesco.

Lucrezia's dancing had always been of the utmost grace and charm. It had delighted her father and her brothers, and Alexander had been wont to have the floor cleared when Lucrezia danced. Here in Ferrara it attracted attention, and many watched as she circled the floor.

She seemed inspired on this night. She radiated happiness. She was full of such spirits as had been hers before the death of her father, and those watching her marveled.

"Madonna Lucrezia is happy this night," people said to one another, and they laughed behind their fans. Had it anything to do with her attractive partner? Francesco Gonzaga could not be called a handsome man, but he was known to appeal to women.

"How can we meet . . . alone?" demanded Francesco passionately.

"We cannot," she told him. "It would never be allowed. We are watched closely. My husband watches me, and I wonder too how many in your suite are Isabella's spies."

"Lucrezia, in spite of all, we must meet."

"We must plan with care," she told him.

There was another matter which she did not forget even as she danced with Francesco and allowed her senses to be exhilarated by his desire for her: the need to help Cesare. Who could be more useful to Cesare than the powerful Marquis of Mantua, the great soldier whom the Pope had made Captain-General of his armies?

"You know of my brother's escape?" she asked.

He nodded. "It was one of the greatest sorrows in my life that my efforts on his behalf should have failed with the King of Spain."

"You did your best to help. Do not think I shall ever forget that."

"I would give my life to serve you."

There was nothing they could do but dance together; only thus could they touch hands and whisper together. So they danced and danced until the early morning, and Lucrezia seemed like a child again.

She did not realize how exhausted she was until her women helped her to her bed. Then she lay as in a dream, her eyes shining, recalling everything he had said, the manner in which he had looked at her.

I am alive again, she told herself. Cesare is free, Francesco Gonzaga loves me, and I love him.

SHE AWOKE. It was not yet light. Something was wrong, and as she tasted the salty sweat on her lips, she was suddenly aware of acute agony.

She called to her women and they came running to her bedside.

"I am ill," she said. "I feel as though I am near to death."

The women looked at each other in alarm. They knew.

The doctors were brought; they nodded gravely. There was whispering throughout the apartment.

"She was mad to dance as she did. It is certain that by so doing she has lost the heir of Ferrara."

ALfONSO STORMED INTO her apartment. He was too furious to contain his anger.

"So," he cried, "you have lost my son. What good are you as a wife, eh? You dance through the night to the danger of our heirs. What use are you to me?"

Weak and ill she looked pleadingly at him. "Alfonso . . ." she began, "I beg of you . . ."

"Beg . . . beg . . . ! You will indeed be a beggar if you do not do your duty, woman. This is the third child we have lost. I tell you, you have no notion of your duty here. You bring frivolous Roman customs to Ferrara. We'll not endure it, I am warning you."

Lucrezia wilted, and the sight of her fragility infuriated Alfonso the more. He wanted a big strong woman, lusty, sensual and capable of bearing children.

He knew the dangers which threatened those states without heirs. Ippolito had already made trouble; there were the two prisoners in the castle tower. There must be an heir. Lucrezia must either cease disappointing him or he must get him a new wife.

He could no longer bear to look at her lying there among her pillows, elegant even in her present state. The ordeal through which she had passed had made her thinner than ever.

"Are you incapable of bearing children for me?" he cried.

He strode out of the room, and Lucrezia lay back exhausted and trembling.

Melancholy had seized her. There was no news from Cesare; Francesco had gone on his way; and there was a threat in Alfonso's last words.

ALfONSO STRODE fURIOUSLY through the town. He was dressed as an ordinary merchant because he was eager not to be recognized; he did not wish his subjects to see him in this angry mood.

He was regretting that he had ever made the Borgia marriage. Of what use were the Borgia now? Their influence had died with Alexander. He did not believe that Cesare would ever regain his kingdom. Lucrezia was still rich, and that was to the good, but she was not rich in children.

She should certainly not have with her in Ferrara her son by the Duke of Bisceglie. She must be made to realize that her position was a very precarious one and would continue to be so until she gave Ferrara an heir.

He was passing a humble dwelling, and as he did so, a beautiful girl stepped into the street. She was carrying a box—the sort which was used for bonnets—and she walked with grace.

Alfonso immediately felt interested, and so great was that interest that he forgot his resentment against his wife.

He followed the girl. She went into one of the big houses, but he knew she would soon come out since he guessed that she was delivering a bonnet to the lady of that house.

He was right. She soon emerged. Alfonso had rarely seen a face and figure which appealed to him more strongly. She walked with a feline grace although she was large of hip and bosom. Her long hair fell to her waist; it was unkempt, perhaps a little greasy; and her skin was brown. She might have appealed because she was so very different from the elegant wife whom he had just left.

He caught up with her.

"You are in a hurry," he said, laying his hand on her bare arm.

She turned a startled gaze on him. Her large eyes were soft and without anger.

"I am in no hurry," she said.

"It is well, because I would talk with you."

"I must return to my mother's house," she said.

"The bonnet-maker?" he asked. "I saw you leave with the box on your arm."

She recognized him suddenly; she turned to him and dropped a curtsey.

"You know me?"

"I have seen you riding in the streets, my lord Duke."

"Do not be frightened," he said softly. "I would know your name."

"It is Laura Dianti."

"Laura Dianti, the bonnet-maker's daughter," he repeated. "I think we shall be friends."

They had reached the little house. She pushed open the door. It was dark inside.

"There is no one at home," she said. "My mother is at the house of a lady, making a bonnet...."

"So much the better," laughed Alfonso.

He laid hold of her. She was unresisting, earthy, the woman he needed to make him forget his frustrated anger against Lucrezia.

He was well content; and so it seemed was Laura Dianti, the bonnet-maker's daughter.

Lucrezia soon recovered from her miscarriage. There was so much now to make her gay. Cesare was a free man; she had constantly believed so firmly in his destiny, so godlike had he always seemed to her, that she was inwardly convinced that he would now achieve all his desires.

When a few of the younger Cardinals rode into Ferrara from the suite of Julius which was now installed in neighboring Bologna, Lucrezia was as lively as she had been since she came to Ferrara. She forgot Alfonso's threats because, surrounded by Cardinals, she was reminded of the old days in Rome; and the homage these men paid her made her feel young and important again.

Francesco was passing through Ferrara once more, and this time she was determined that there should be some means of meeting privately. She began feverishly designing new dresses and spent so much time on these frivolities that Friar Raffaela da Varese, a strict priest of the Court, began preaching sermons against the wickedness of feminine vanity, and even condemned the use of cosmetics.

Lucrezia and her ladies pretended to listen to him gravely, but they ignored his warnings of hell-fire. There was gaiety in the little apartments of the balcony; and always at the side of Lucrezia was the lame poet, Ercole Strozzi.

Alfonso disliked him; he had no use for poets and, since he had ruled in his father's place, life had gone less smoothly for Strozzi. Certain lands which had been bestowed on him by Duke Ercole had been reclaimed by Alfonso. Strozzi could have forgiven him that, but what angered him was Alfonso's attitude toward his literary work.

Alfonso would laugh slyly when poetry was read, and there were many in the court who were ready to follow the example of the Duke.

Moreover Strozzi was a great friend of Francesco Gonzaga, and Francesco and Alfonso had never been fond of each other; now that Francesco desired Alfonso's wife they were less likely to be so.

The proprietary attitude which Strozzi had assumed over Lucrezia, during the affair with Pietro Bembo, persisted. There was a strong bond between Strozzi and Lucrezia which neither of them understood. There was deep affection, although there had never been any suggestion of their being lovers.

Strozzi was now entirely devoted to the beautiful Barbara Torelli whom Lucrezia, when she had heard her sad story, had taken under her protection.

Strozzi was an artist; he longed to create, and because he felt a certain inadequacy in his poetry he wished to use his creative ability to mold the lives of the people he loved.

Barbara Torelli had appealed to his pity, for hers had been a very tragic story. She had been married to Ercole, one of the Bentivoglios of Bologna, the lowest sort of sensualist, in whom Barbara's cultured manners inspired a great desire to humiliate her. He had therefore set about making her life as miserable as he possibly could and his greatest pleasure was in devising means of insulting her. There came a time when he invited a Bishop to his home and offered to rent Barbara to him for a period, for the sum of 1,000 ducats. Barbara refused to agree to the transaction; whereupon her husband told her that if she did not he would publicly accuse her of attempting to poison him. Barbara's reply to that was to leave him. She found refuge in Mantua and stayed in a convent under the protection of Francesco Gonzaga.

It was Francesco who had made her story known, and although he could not induce Ercole Bentivoglio to return her dowry, a great deal of sympathy was aroused for Barbara.

The poetic Strozzi was deeply moved by her story; he sought her acquaintance, and her charm and dignity in adversity so moved him that he fell deeply in love with and married her. As for Barbara, she found this second Ercole such a contrast to the first that she began to return his affection, and the passionate and tender love between Ercole Strozzi and Barbara Torelli became an inspiration for many of the poets of the day.

Lucrezia had been equally moved by Barbara's story and Strozzi's devotion to her, and it seemed the most natural thing in the world that she should offer her protection to Barbara. So Barbara was a frequent member of Lucrezia's circle, and Strozzi yearned to repay her and Francesco for all they had done for Barbara while at the same time he sought vengeance on Alfonso, who had not only deprived him of his property but was so uncouth that he could not appreciate his poetry.

Thus, when Francesco came to Ferrara once more, Strozzi determined to use all his ingenuity so that the lovers might meet in the intimacy they desired.

Lucrezia's love affair with the attractive soldier blossomed under Strozzi's care, and there were meetings between the lovers while Strozzi, Barbara and those few intimate and trusted friends made the necessary cover.

During those weeks Lucrezia began to love Francesco with the strength which came with maturity. Francesco declared his one desire was to make her happy; she believed him; and so those idyllic weeks passed.

It was night, and Cesare with his army was encamped about the Castle of Viana.

A terrible melancholy came to him as he went to the door of his tent and looked out at the starry sky. There was a knowledge within him that his dreams would never be anything but dreams, that he had lived his life recklessly and had failed to see the truth, which was that all his greatness had come from his father.

Now in this little camp, the little commander in this little war was a disappointed man, a man of no account.

He, Cesare Borgia, must this tragic night see himself as he really was.

He had offered his services to his brother-in-law, the King of Navarre, and this was the task assigned to him: he must break the siege of the Castle of Viana and defeat the traitor Louis de Beaumont. It might be, if he could prove that he was still the same Cesare Borgia who had struck terror into the hearts of so many during the lifetime of his father, that he would yet get the help he needed to win back his kingdom.

But what was the use? He must face the truth. What had become of the Borgias now? Who cared for the emblem of the Grazing Bull? Alexander, that most fortunate of men, had died in power; but he had taken the might of the Borgias with him.

Cesare's wife, Charlotte d'Albret, had made no effort to help him. Why should she? He had forgotten her when he did not need that help. He had escaped from the King of Spain, and the King of France had become his enemy. What was his standing with his brother-in-law? He had no illusions. Should the King of France demand him to be delivered up, the King of Navarre would not refuse.

He was alone and friendless. There was only one in the world whom he could trust; she would give everything to help him, his beloved Lucrezia.

But what of Lucrezia? Her power had waned with his, for they were bound together as Borgias, and his danger was hers. Lucrezia would give her life for him, he knew; but that was all she could give.

"Little Lucrezia," he murmured, looking up at the stars. "What big dreams we had in our nursery, did we not? And bigger dreams when our father ruled the Vatican. Dreams, my dearest, only dreams. I would not accept this fact before tonight. It is significant that I do so now. Cesare Borgia believed himself capable of ruling the world, but I see these idle fancies of mine as dreams."

There was sudden tumult within the camp. One of his men shouted that the enemy were taking stores into the castle under cover of darkness.

"To horse!" cried Cesare, and he leaped into the saddle.

He could see the party riding with great speed toward the castle; he shouted to his men to follow him, and he was off.

He rode with such mad fury that he outstripped all his followers. He reached the raiding force which was now joined by men from the castle who, realizing what had happened, had come out to do battle.

Cesare rode into their midst, slaying right and left, shouting triumphantly as he did so. But he knew that the others were far behind, and that he was alone . . . alone and surrounded by the enemy.

He laughed within himself. In that mad moment, when the need for action had intruded on his reverie, he had determined on this.

They were all about him; he heard their blood-thirsty laughter. He heard his own, loud, demoniacal. He raised his sword and slashed furiously.

He was brave, they said; but what was one among so many?

He went down, the mad and bitter laughter on his lips; and as he lay bleeding from his many wounds Louis de Beaumont rode up to see who this man was who had so eagerly sought death.

There were many to bend over him, to strip him of his shining armor and his fine raiment.

When they had done this they left him naked for the buzzards; and the thirty-one-year-old Duke of Romagna and Valentinois, the dreaded Cesare Borgia, was no more.

Lucrezia was dreaming of Francesco in her apartments, asking herself if he would come again, when into the courtyard there came a dusty rider.

Lucrezia did not know that he had come, and it was Friar Raffaela who brought her the news.

He came to her, and there were tears in his stern eyes as he laid his hands on her shoulders and blessed her.

"You are so solemn," said Lucrezia; "you are so tender that I am afraid."

"I would ask you to prepare yourself for tragic news."

Lucrezia waited tense.

"Il Valentino has been killed in battle."

She did not speak; she stood staring at him, her expression blank as though she refused to believe him.

"It is true, my daughter," said the friar.

She shook her head. "It is false . . . false!" she cried.

"Nay. It is true. He died bravely and in battle."

"Not my brother, not Cesare. He would not die in battle. He could not. He was a match for all."

"Would you like me to pray with you? We will ask for courage that you may bear this grief."

"Prayer! I want no prayers. There has been a mistake. Good friar, you must go to Navarre. You must bring me the truth. There has been a mistake. I know it."

He looked at her sadly and shook his head.

Then he led her to her bed and signed to her women to help her. She seemed limp until they laid hands on her. Then she threw them off.

She looked pleadingly at the friar once more before she covered her face with her hands. They heard her whispering to herself: "Cesare . . . my brother! My brother . . . Cesare! It is not possible. Not Cesare . . . anyone but Cesare. . . ."

She signed to them to leave her alone. They did so and she threw herself on to the floor still murmuring his name.

"My father . . . Giovanni . . . my first Alfonso . . . all those . . . yes . . . but not Cesare. . . ."

Her women were afraid when she remained thus for more than an hour. They came to her and tried to rouse her, but she would not be roused. She would neither eat nor drink; but eventually she allowed them to help her to her bed.

She lay there woebegone and during the night they heard her sobbing.

Many times she called his name; it was uncanny, they said, as though she were imploring him to come back from the dead.

In the morning they tried again to rouse her.

It was a terrible blow, they said; but she would grow away from it. It was the sudden shock which had stunned her.

"Grow away from it!" she cried. "You do not understand, for Cesare was Lucrezia, and Lucrezia Cesare; and one without the other is but half alive."

It was Strozzi who sought to rouse her.

She must not give way to her sorrow, he implored her; she was young yet and there were many years before her. He understood her grief for her brother, but there were many who loved her and grieved to see her grief. For their sakes she must not become so sad that she would surely die of melancholy.

To him and to Barbara she tried to explain this bond between herself and her brother which had begun in their nursery days and had continued through their lives. They assured her that they understood, but that she must throw herself into some activities or lose her reason.

What of Francesco who loved her so tenderly? Was it fair to him that he must in anguish hear these reports of her misery?

Strozzi had devised an intricate plan whereby Lucrezia and Francesco might correspond with each other. They must not forget that they were surrounded by spies here in Ferrara, and it was certain that Isabella had heard by now of her husband's infatuation for Lucrezia.

Strozzi's plan was that he should write letters to Francesco on Lucrezia's behalf, and that he would send these to his brother—Guido residing in Mantua—who would then take them to the Mantuan court and present them to Francesco. The answers would come by the same route. But they dared not use their own names for this correspondence in case it should fall into hands not intended to receive it; Francesco, for instance, should be called Guido since the letters were to be addressed to Guido, and Lucrezia should be known as Barbara. They must also have faked names for others such as Alfonso, Ippolito, Isabella, who might be referred to.

Lucrezia must admit that it would be a means of corresponding with her lover, and what she needed now in this time of terrible melancholy was an interest which would make her forget for a time the death of Cesare.

Lucrezia, at first half-heartedly, allowed herself to be drawn into this scheme; and after some weeks she realized what Strozzi had done for her, since this correspondence which brought her assurances of Francesco's devotion was, she believed afterward, the means of saving her from a breakdown at this time.

Then she discovered that she was pregnant.

ALfonso refused to take any great interest in this pregnancy. He had been disappointed so many times. He was finding the bonnet-maker's daughter absorbing; she appealed to him as no woman had before, and what he had thought would be a passing fancy had developed into a love affair already of some duration.

He spent a great deal of time in the woman's company; and Lucrezia was glad of this. She was determined this time, though, that she would do nothing rash, and she lived quietly during the months of waiting, longing for the arrival of the baby.

She never danced and was very careful of what she ate, spending her time in writing letters with Strozzi and designing the baby's garments. She instructed the court engraver, Bernardino Veneziano, to make her a cradle which should transcend all other cradles, and when this was completed members of the court came to marvel at it. It was made of gilded wood with four pillars at its corners. The roof was a pergola of gold branches and leaves; the curtains were of satin and the miniature pillows embroidered with gold.

It was in April when her pains started, and there was excitement throughout the castle. Alfonso however reacted by leaving at once. He could not endure another failure, and he did not trust Lucrezia to give him the heir he so much needed.

It was some hours after he had left when the baby was born—a healthy little boy who cried lustily and who, all declared, would most certainly not go the way of his predecessors.

When the little boy was laid in Lucrezia's arms she felt a great load of sadness lifted from her. She had her son and she would try to live her life in him; she would try to forget all the sorrow which had made up the preceding years and she would endeavor with all her might to stop grieving for Cesare.

Alfonso came riding back to Ferrara when he heard the baby was born and was male and healthy.

He stormed into the bedchamber and demanded to see the child. He held it in his arms and laughed aloud with pleasure. This was a true heir of Ferrara.

"We will call him Ercole, after my father," he said. "Come, Ercole, my son, come and meet the ambassadors who are all waiting to welcome Ercole who will one day be their Duke."

And in the audience chamber, where many waited to see the new heir, Alfonso held up the child; then he removed the robe, crying: "See. He is healthy, this one, and provided with all things."

There was great rejoicing in Ferrara.

THere were rumors concerning the baby, for many remembered the last visit of Francesco Gonzaga and, although the lovers had believed at the time that their meetings had been secret, there could have been some servant whom they had believed erroneously that they could trust.

There were covert remarks concerning little Ercole's appearance.

Was that the Este nose? Perhaps it was a little too wide? A little too flattened? Did it resemble the very distinctive nose of a certain neighboring Marquis?

Lucrezia heard the rumors through Strozzi, a born intriguer who had his spies everywhere; she shrugged them aside. They were quite ridiculous, she said, and everyone must know them to be so.

Strozzi however warned her to be careful. Ippolito was watching her closely and she should remember the havoc he had wrought in the lives of his brothers. She must never forget those two young men, still captive in their tower. No one spoke of them nowadays; they seemed to have been quite forgotten; but she should never forget and, remembering them, be reminded of the might and malice of Ippolito.

Her first indication that Alfonso was aware of Francesco's love for her and hers for him was when he sent the announcement of little Ercole's birth to Mantua. She read his message and expressed astonishment that it should be addressed to Isabella.

"I see," she said, "that you do not mention Francesco Gonzaga."

Ippolito, who was with his brother, said: "Isabella is our sister."

"But Francesco Gonzaga is ruler of Mantua."

"We do not think it necessary to tell him of the child's birth," retorted Ippolito.

Lucrezia did not answer. Alfonso was looking at her directly. She knew then of their suspicions.

Alfonso said: "I shall shortly be going to France. You will be Regent with my brother while I am gone. Doubtless"—he waved his hands—"after recent happenings you may be feeling incapable of governing. I would have you know that Ippolito is always here to help you . . . and to help me."

It was a warning. She went back to her apartments and sent a message by her chaplain, to Strozzi. She trusted the chaplain completely. He had been with Cesare and had helped him escape from Medina; he had come to her asking for refuge, and most willingly she had given it; she was very fond of his company, for they would sit together and talk of Cesare for hours, so that Lucrezia was able to hear details of his captivity; and it was almost as though Cesare were not dead, when she talked with his chaplain. Moreover this man and the page who had brought her the news, were, she knew, her very trusty servants, and she had need of all those whom she could trust.

When the chaplain brought Strozzi to her, she told them what Alfonso and Ippolito had said.

All Strozzi's love of scheming was aroused. He was determined that the love affair should prosper. He then wrote a letter to Francesco, through his brother Guido, in which the perfidy of Camillio (their name for Alfonso) and Tigrino (Ippolito) was deplored. Camillio was leaving for France, very shortly, so why should not Guido (Francesco) pay a visit to Ferrara in his absence?

Isabella was angry. All her malice against Lucrezia had its roots in jealousy; and now Lucrezia had inflicted the greatest humiliation upon her; Isabella's husband was in love with her rival.

A light, passing affair with humble women, Isabella accepted; a light passing flirtation with Lucrezia she might have endured. But Francesco had changed; he was melancholy, brooding; and he had given up all other women.

What power was there in that quiet slender girl to arouse such devotion? Isabella demanded of herself.

She was determined however to ruin Lucrezia, and Francesco too if need be.

When she thought of Francesco, cunning came into her eyes. As his love for Lucrezia grew, so did his hatred of Isabella. He was asserting himself against her and was reminding her twenty times a day that he was the ruler of Mantua, and the power which she had once seized as her right, was now being taken from her.

If Francesco were involved in disaster at Ferrara, she would not be heart-broken. Her son, Federigo, was young yet. If his father died there would be a regent, and who should that be other than the mother of the young Marquis Federigo?

She wrote to her brother Ippolito, that lover of intrigue. It was no use writing to Alfonso; he was too prosaic; and Ippolito had taken a dislike to Lucrezia since the affair of Giulio and Ferrante, because he knew that Lucrezia's sympathy had been with his brothers.

It might not be a bad idea, suggested Isabella, to lure Francesco to Ferrara and there expose the lovers. Ippolito should burn her letter when he received it, as she would burn the letters he wrote to her. She believed that there might be considerable correspondence between them over this matter.

✿ ♛ ✿

SHORTLY afterward Lucrezia was visited by a gentleman named Masino del Forno, who was known as the Modenese; he was a much favored man at the court of the Este family and Lucrezia knew him to be a great friend not only of Alfonso but Ippolito.

Conversation was general for the first minutes of the visit. Masino del Forno asked to see the heir and young Ercole was brought in. He was a very healthy baby, and Lucrezia was delighted with him.

When Ercole had been taken away, Masino said quietly: "What a pity it is that relations between Ferrara and Mantua are not more cordial."

"The Marchesa is devoted to her brothers," said Lucrezia cautiously.

"I was not thinking of the Marchesa. After all it is the Marquis himself who is the ruler of Mantua. We must not forget that."

"I do not forget," said Lucrezia lightly.

"It is a grievous thing in these times that there should be misunderstandings. I firmly believe that a visit from Francesco Gonzaga would do a great deal to improve relations between the two states."

Lucrezia felt her heart leap. She longed to see Francesco again, but something within her warned her. She knew Masino del Forno to be an intimate of Ippolito and since the terrible fate of Giulio and Ferrante she had been afraid of Ippolito.

Del Forno went on: "I believe that if an emissary went from Ferrara to Mantua to persuade the Marquis to come here, he would do so. I myself would travel to Mantua with the greatest delight. Should I go with your blessing?"

Lucrezia was tempted, but it was as though the grotesque face of Giulio rose before her to warn her of the perfidy of Ippolito.

She said coolly: "In my husband's absence my brother Ippolito is co-regent with me. I pray you discuss this matter with him; and if he agrees that you should travel to Mantua with an invitation for the Marquis, then I should put no obstacle in the way."

The Modenese went away; Lucrezia sensed that he felt disappointed.

In Mantua Francesco, waiting impatiently for the letters which brought him news of Lucrezia, was suddenly aware of a change in Isabella. She was less haughty, less arrogant, less fiery-tempered. When he asserted his rights she would press her lips firmly together as though she were holding back words which she longed to utter; and all the time there was a look of expectancy on her face as though she were urging herself to have patience . . . for a while.

Isabella was plotting. Against whom? wondered Francesco. Against Lucrezia? Then that would be against him.

What was the meaning of that air of looking forward? She was like a cat at a mousehole. Why? There was her attitude to their son, Federico. It was indulgent yet firm. It was as though she was determined to win the boy's respect and affection while she kept a restraining hand on him.

A visitor arrived at Mantua. He came quietly—almost in secret—and he came from Ferrara. He sought an early opportunity to be alone with the Marquis.

This man Masino del Forno, the Modenese, was not entirely unknown to Francesco. He knew him to be an intimate of Ippolito, and he believed that on more than one occasion he had performed a shady deed for his master.

Francesco had been walking in the gardens when del Forno sidled up to him; del Forno looked over his shoulder and back at the castle windows apprehensively.

"I come, my lord," he whispered, "on a secret mission, a mission from the Duchessa."

Francesco was immediately alert. This was strange. Why should Lucrezia send a message by this man, when already there was the excellent means of corresponding which Strozzi had arranged for them.

"A secret mission? You surprise me."

"The Duchessa longs to see your lordship. She would have you know that the Duke will be away for many months. It would give her great delight if you could slip into Ferrara . . . unheralded . . . a secret mission, you understand."

Francesco turned to the man, who could not know that he had received a letter which must have been written at the very time del Forno had set out from Ferrara. This was a very suspicious method of procedure, and Francesco did not trust it. He thought of Isabella's demeanor of the last weeks and his suspicions increased.

"I doubt not," he said, "that if my brother of Ferrara feels I should visit his dominion he will ask me to do so. As for going in secret, I see no virtue in that."

"I have been entrusted," pursued del Forno, "to give you this."

He held out a miniature, tiny but exquisite. There was no mistaking the face portrayed there. It was Lucrezia's. Francesco looked at it and longed to take it, but by now he was sure that his enemies were aware of his love affair with Lucrezia, and he believed he understood the meaning of his wife's expression of late.

She wished him to be lured to Ferrara. The man who stood before him, he believed to be a hired assassin of Ippolito's and possibly Alfonso's.

"Thank you," he said, "but I have no wish for this trinket, and I cannot understand why it should have been sent to me."

With that he turned away from the man. He immediately went to his private apartments and wrote a letter to Zilio (Strozzi) which was meant for Lucrezia, explaining all that had happened and giving a strong warning that he believed them all to be in acute danger.

❧♔❧

Isabella faced the Modenese and listened to his account of what had happened. She was angry. Francesco was not such a fool then. He might be in love with Lucrezia but he was not going to risk his life.

"You have been clumsy," she snapped.

"Marchesa, I was tact itself. Depend upon it, they suspect us."

"They would never suspect us, those two. They are besottedly in love like a shepherd and his lass. It is that man Strozzi who is managing their affairs. It seems to me that he is cleverer than my brothers. Go now. There is nothing else you can do. I think it would be well for you if you set out at once for Ferrara. If the Marquis suspects you, you yourself may be in danger. Go at once."

Del Forno was only too glad to obey; and when he had gone, Isabella angrily asked herself why Lucrezia should be able to inspire such devotion, not only in Francesco, but in a purely Platonic way as it seemed she had with Strozzi.

She was more jealous of the girl than ever. One would have thought that, with her father and her brother dead and the name of Borgia no more of importance to the world, she would have been defeated. But no! For always there were some to rally round her.

Francesco was far away, but she still had Strozzi—Strozzi, the power in Ferrara, the lame poet who had taken Barbara Torelli and made a public heroine of her with his verses about her, who was no doubt after the dowry which the Bentivoglio were determined they would not relinquish.

Strozzi must have many enemies in Ferrara. There were not only Alfonso, who disliked him because he was a poet, and Ippolito, who objected to his influence over Lucrezia; there were the Bentivoglio who were violent people and very loath to part with money.

Isabella was thoughtful. Then she wrote to Ippolito.

"I pray that this letter may be burned, as I burn yours," she finished. "This I ask for the sake of my honor and benefit."

On a **HOT** June night that chaplain who had been Cesare's faithful servant, and therefore especially cherished by Lucrezia, left her apartments for his own quarters in the Convent of San Paolo.

It was a dark night and, as he came along the narrow streets, two men leaped upon him and one silently seized him while the other, equally silent, lifted his dagger and cut the innocent priest's throat. Lightly they dropped the body on to the stones and crept away.

Next morning Lucrezia was heartbroken to discover that she had lost a trusted friend.

Strozzi came to see her that day.

His happiness in the baby girl Barbara Torelli had just given him was clouded by this tragic happening.

"What means it?" asked Lucrezia.

He looked at her obliquely. "Of course it may have been robbery."

"Who would murder a poor priest for his money?"

"There are some who would murder any for the sake of one ducat."

"I am afraid," said Lucrezia. "I believe he has died because my enemies know that he is my friend. How I wish Francesco would come, that I might tell him of my fears."

Lucrezia began to weep quietly. She had loved the priest, she said; and what harm had he ever done in his life? He had done only good.

Seeing her in this mood of despair Strozzi said they would write to Francesco and beg him to come to comfort her for, reasoned Strozzi to himself,

Francesco would know how to take care of himself, and none would dare harm him. Moreover he feared that if her lover did not come, Lucrezia would lapse into melancholy.

"Come to see your Barbara (Lucrezia)," wrote Strozzi. "Show her that you love her, for she wants nothing else in the world."

The letter was dispatched, and he left Lucrezia to visit Barbara who, in bed with her baby, had not heard the news of the priest's death. He gave instructions to her woman that she should not be told. Barbara's clear mind might read something in that death which would make her very uneasy, and a woman after child-birth needed the serene happiness which he had always sought to give her.

He left Barbara happy, after they had discussed the future of their child; he then shut himself in with his work and wrote a little of the elegy he was composing. Reading it through afterward he thought it sounded melancholy. He had written of death—although he had not intended to—for the memory of the priest's murder would not be dismissed from his mind.

Later that day he went again to see Barbara and when he left her apartment he limped back to his own house, the sound of his stick echoing through the quiet streets. It was at the corner of via Praisolo and via Savonarola that the ambush caught him.

He had half expected it. He had arranged other people's lives to such an extent that he knew that this was the inevitable end of the drama.

He was unarmed. Their daggers were raised against him. He faced them almost scornfully. He knew who his enemies were; it was the house of Este who wished him removed. It was Alfonso who saw him as the man who had arranged his wife's love affairs with Pietro Bembo and Francesco Gonzaga; it was Ippolito who was determined to isolate Lucrezia from all those who might seek to make a political figure of her; it was the Bentivoglio family who feared he would discover some means of wresting Barbara's dowry from them.

Then suddenly he did know fear. It was for Barbara. He thought of all the miseries she had endured; he thought of her at this moment, weak from child-birth. Barbara would be alone once more, alone in a cruel world.

But there was no time for thought. Strozzi sank fainting against the wall of casa Romei, while his enemies, determined that this should be the end, bent over him and thrust their daggers again and again into his dying body.

Lucrezia was bewildered. Cesare, her chaplain and now Strozzi—all lost to her. She was frightened; never before had she felt such a stranger in a strange land.

There was only one person in the world now to whom she could turn: Francesco.

Francesco must come to her. No matter what obstacles lay between them, he must come.

But who would now write those letters for her? Who would make sure that they reached their destination? By striking at Strozzi her enemies had cut her off from Francesco, the only man in the world who would help her.

She summoned Strozzi's brothers, Lorenzo and Guido, to her; she wept with them over their brother's death and she implored them to send a message for her to Francesco. "There is no one else whom I can trust," she said. "You are his brothers, and you will do this for me."

They did so and Francesco's response was to offer a reward of five hundred ducats to any man or woman who could name the murderer of Ercole Strozzi.

The reward brought no murderer to light and, since little effort was made in Ferrara (where the police were famous for their successful work) to bring the murderer to justice, it became clear to Lucrezia that, whoever had committed the murder, it had been done with the connivance of Alfonso and his brother.

The desolate weeks passed. She would sit by the baby's cradle, brooding. Only in him could she find comfort, yet she longed for a strong arm to lean on, and she realized that never before had she lacked that support. She saw herself clearly, saw that she lacked the self-reliance of a woman such as Isabella, that she had been dominated by her father and her brothers to such an extent that she felt limp and bewildered when forced to stand alone. She needed Francesco, yet he did not come.

Again she wrote to him, pleading, begging him not to forsake her. She would go to Reggio, and the journey from Borgoforte to Reggio was not a long one. She must see him, if it were only a brief meeting. She needed him as she never had before.

She set out for Reggio, and there she waited in feverish impatience.

Isaʙella watcheᴅ Francesco with malicious lights in her eyes.

"Why do you not take a little holiday?" she asked. "You are looking strained, husband."

He tried to read the thoughts behind her eyes. Was it true that she wished him to go to Lucrezia, that he might be murdered as Strozzi and the chaplain had been?

Isabella . . . Regent of Mantua. It was what she wanted, and if the life of her husband stood between her and that goal, she was ready to sacrifice him.

Francesco was torn between his desire to see Lucrezia and his need to preserve his life, between his wish to comfort his mistress and the triumph of outwitting his wife.

Just a short visit, he promised himself. A little trip to Reggio. It could be a walk into a death-trap. They have killed Strozzi so that we can no longer arrange our communications; they have stripped her of her friends, left her desolate so that I shall go needlessly into the trap they have prepared for me. They know she will implore me to go to her, because without Strozzi to warn her, how can she understand that this is a gigantic plot either to kill or to ruin us both?

He replied to her, that he longed to be with her but he was unwell and was in fact too ill to travel at this time.

Wʜen at Reɢɢio Lucrezia received his letter she was filled with anxiety. Francesco ill; then she must go to him. She would not lose a moment. She called to her attendants and told them that they were leaving next day for Mantua.

She could scarcely sleep that night, so eager was she for the journey. She lay restlessly waiting for the dawn.

Daylight brought visitors to the castle—important visitors, she knew, for there was a great commotion below and, as Lucrezia started up from her bed, Alfonso himself strode into the room.

He stood, legs wide apart, laughing at her.

"What's this I hear?" he said. "You plan to travel to Mantua?"

"Our brother is sick," she answered him, although her voice shook with fear. "As I am not far distant I thought it but courteous . . ."

Alfonso's laugh was louder. "You thought it courteous! The reason for your intended courtesy is well known. You are not going to Mantua to visit your lover."

"I have made my arrangements."

"Then we will unmake them."

"Alfonso, what can it matter to you?"

"It matters this," he said. He came to the bed and taking her by the shoulders shook her angrily. "You are my wife and Duchess of Ferrara. We have an heir, but we should have many children. Ercole needs brothers."

"That . . . that he may . . . bury them alive?" she cried with a show of spirit.

He swung his heavy hand across her face. "That is for your insolence," he said. And he repeated the action. "And that is for thinking to cuckold me and bring flat-nosed bastards into my house."

She cowered back in the bed. Alfonso's sudden burst of anger had passed. "No nonsense," he said. "Daylight is here. You will dress, and we shall return to Ferrara without delay."

"I have sent word that I am visiting our brother's sick-bed."

"Sick-bed! He's in no sick-bed. He tells you so, hoping to excuse himself for not coming to you now. There is nothing wrong with Francesco Gonzaga. He is a man of good sense. He knows when it is unwise to continue a flirtation." He put his face close to hers. "And that time has now come," he added.

She leaped out of her bed. "Alfonso," she cried, "I will not be treated thus. I am not one of your tavern women. I am not the bonnet-maker's daughter."

"Nay," he said, "you lack their freedom. You are the Duchess of Ferrara, and in future you shall never forget it. Prepare yourself. I am in a hurry and impatient to return."

"You forget that I am Lucrezia Borgia, and when I married you . . ."

"I forget nothing. Yours was a name which carried some weight in Italy. It was no credit to you. Your glory came from your father. Now he is dead, and your brother is dead, and the power of the Borgias is broken forever. So subdue that pride which cries 'I am a Borgia!' Be wise, woman. Cultivate modesty. Bear me children and I shall then have nothing of which to complain."

So **she came** to Ferrara; and as she rode beside her husband she seemed to hear his words echoing in her ears. Alexander is dead, and with him died the power of the Borgias; Cesare is dead, and with him died all hope.

As they came near to the castle she looked up at the highest tower and she thought of the two young men who were prisoners and would remain there for the rest of their lives.

She rode with Alfonso into the castle, and she felt as the walls closed about her that she too was a prisoner, sharing their fate.

There was a pain in her heart and a longing to see a loved face again; and the cry which rose up within her was not Francesco, but Cesare.

EPILOGUE

Lucrezia was pregnant. How many times in the last ten years had she been pregnant! And each one left her a little weaker and a little less able to endure the next. Yet never had she felt so ill as she did now. She was growing old, although at times she still looked like a girl, for she had remained slender and her face had never lost its look of innocence. She had remained serene, accepting her fate since the day Alfonso had brought her back to Ferrara and had told her so clearly that her future depended on her ability to do her duty.

Little Ippolito had been born after that, and Alfonso was not displeased. Two sons now for Ferrara. Young Ercole had continued healthy.

What pleasure there had been in the children! They had provided all the happiness of the last years. Alfonso's pre-occupation with the wars which had at one time threatened Ferrara had kept him away from her for so long that after Ippolito there was no other child until little Alexander was born. Poor Alexander, that ill-fated name! The first of her children by Alfonso had been Alexander who had lived less than two months; her second Alexander had died at the age of two years, which was even more heartbreaking. But by that time she had her little Eleonora, and Francesco, the baby, had come the following year.

She had recaptured her youth playing games with them in the castle. Games of battles and hide-and-seek, and in those games never, never going near the great tower in which two men—young no longer—remained shut away from the world.

When they were tired of games they would call to the quaintest of the dwarfs, Santino, whom they would stand on the table that he might tell his wonderful fairy stories. And as he talked others would creep in from all parts of the palace, lured by the spell of the teller of tales.

Those were happy times.

She had now ceased to grieve for Francesco Gonzaga. He had remained her very good friend, and had wanted to tell her of the plots against them, of the reasons why he had thought it necessary to make illness his excuse for not visiting her. Yet they had discovered a means of continuing to correspond, and through this she had at one time found her greatest happiness.

There had been a time when he had been captured in battle by the Venetians, and kept in prison where he had suffered deeply. It was then that the whole world came to know Isabella as she really was, for she had refused to allow her son to become a hostage for his father, even though there could have been no danger to the boy; and it had become clear then that Isabella wanted her husband to die, and that she hoped the melancholy dankness of his prison would kill him.

Francesco had never been the same man after that, but there had been a return of hope, a sudden outburst of passion when the Papal forces rose against Ferrara, and Gonzaga planned to carry her away as his prisoner. He had prepared the Palazzo de Té to receive her, and the letters which passed between them at that time were like those of young lovers.

It was a dream which was never to materialize. Alfonso was too good a soldier, and his beloved cannon served him well.

Francesco was now dead; he had died at the beginning of this year and Isabella was at last triumphant. But how short-lived was that triumph as her son Federico soon showed his determination to rule alone, and the death of her husband for which she had longed brought no power to Isabella.

Lying back in her bed Lucrezia thought of all the unhappiness which need never have been. She thought of the malice of Isabella and the murder of Strozzi and the chaplain. She thought of her love for her young husband, Alfonso of Bisceglie, and of his wanton murder by one whom she had never ceased to love, more she believed than any she had ever known.

It might have been so different. She had wished to live happily and serenely, away from violence, but the milestones of her life were stained with blood.

She was in pain again and with pain came flashes of a memory which seemed to impose itself on the present; she saw the handsome face of Pedro Caldes and remembered the anguish of the love they had shared in San Sisto. There had been many reminders of that love when she had had Giovanni Borgia, the *Infante Romano* and son of Pedro, brought to her in Ferrara. Alfonso had at last relented and allowed her that, although Roderigo, the son of Alfonso of Bisceglie, had never been allowed to come to her. Poor Giovanni, he had been a wayward boy and she feared he would never make his way in the world. As for Roderigo she would never see him again; he had died some years before.

"Why should you grieve for him?" Alfonso had demanded. "Have you not healthy sons in Ferrara?"

But she did grieve. She grieved for the past, which had been so sad and might have been so different.

Pain had seized her although the child was not due until August. She called to her women, and they came hurrying to her bedside.

That night a seven-months child, a daughter, was born; the child sickly, refusing to take nourishment, was hurriedly baptized.

Lucrezia lay in a fever.

Her long rippling hair hung heavily about her shoulders. She lifted her patient eyes to those who watched her, and implored them to alleviate her pain.

"Your hair, Madonna," they murmured, "it is so heavy. Shall we cut it off? It would mean great comfort to you."

She hesitated. She could not clearly remember where she was. She thought of long afternoons, lying on a couch in a Moorish shirt, her hair damp about her; she remembered washing it with Giulia Farnese whose hair had been similarly golden.

Cut off her hair, of which she had been so proud? She would not have believed that she could ever consent to such an action.

But the heat was unendurable, the pain intense and she was so tired.

She nodded slowly, and lay quietly listening to the click of the scissors.

Alfonso came to look at her, and she saw the alarm in his face.

I am dying, she thought.

Alfonso had moved away from the bed, and was beckoning to the doctors. "What hope?" he asked.

"None, my lord. She cannot survive. She is dying now."

Alfonso nodded slowly. He stared at that once beautiful head now shorn of its golden glory. Lucrezia . . . she was thirty-nine; it was young to die. She had given him the future Duke of Ferrara, and in time had become a good and docile wife, but he had never understood her, he had never wanted an elegant lady. He thought of his Laura, grown rich and plump under his protection, Laura the bonnet-maker's daughter who was the mother of two children. Laura whom he had called Eustochia, the good conceiver. Laura, earthy and passionate, a woman whom he could understand and who could understand him.

He wanted a steadier life now; he wanted a wife who could be both mistress and mother of his children.

Watching the life slowly leave Lucrezia's body he thought: I'll marry Laura.

He went back to the bed. Lucrezia's eyes were glazed and, although she appeared to look at him, she did not see him.

She was thinking of all those she had loved and who had gone before her; her mother, Vannozza who had died last year, her brother Giovanni, her father, Cesare, Pedro, Alfonso of Bisceglie—those people whom she had loved as perhaps she had never loved any others. Three of those six people had been murdered, and by one hand. Yet she had forgotten that as she slowly slipped away from this life.

I am going to them, she told herself, I am going to my loved ones.

Her lips moved, and it seemed to some of those watching at her bedside that she murmured: "Cesare."

A hushed silence had fallen on the apartment.

Lucrezia Borgia was dead.

TURN THE PAGE TO SEE ALL OF

JEAN PLAIDY'S

HISTORICAL NOVELS

AVAILABLE FROM

BROADWAY PAPERBACKS

Read all of Jean Plaidy's
Novels of the Tudors
in historical order:

To Hold the Crown
The Story of King Henry VII
and Elizabeth of York
$14.95 PAPERBACK
978-0-307-34619-3

Katharine of Aragon
The Story of a Spanish Princess
and an English Queen
$16.00 PAPERBACK
978-0-609-81025-5

Murder Most Royal
The Story of Anne Boleyn
and Catherine Howard
$14.95 PAPERBACK
978-1-4000-8249-0

The King's Confidante
The Story of the Daughter
of Sir Thomas More
$13.95 PAPERBACK
978-0-307-34620-9

previously published as
St. Thomas's Eve

The Sixth Wife
The Story of Katherine Parr
$13.95 PAPERBACK
978-0-609-81026-2

The Thistle and the Rose
The Story of Margaret, Princess
of England, Queen of Scotland
$13.95 PAPERBACK
978-0-609-81022-4

Mary, Queen of France
The Story of the Youngest Sister
of Henry VIII
$12.95 PAPERBACK
978-0-609-81021-7

7

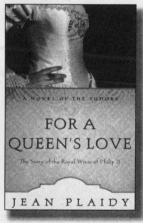

For a Queen's Love
The Story of the Royal Wives
of Philip II
$14.00 PAPERBACK
978-0-307-34622-3

previously published as
The Spanish Bridegroom

8

A Favorite of the Queen
The Story of Lord Robert Dudley
and Elizabeth I
$14.00 PAPERBACK
978-0-307-34623-0

previously published as
Gay Lord Robert

9

Available wherever books are sold

Read all of Jean Plaidy's
Novels of the Stuarts
in historical order:

The Royal Road to Fotheringhay
The Story of Mary Queen of Scots
$15.00 PAPERBACK
978-0-609-81023-1

1

The Captive Queen of Scots
The Story of Queen Mary
$14.95 PAPERBACK
978-1-4000-8251-3

2

3

The Murder in the Tower
The Story of Frances,
Countess of Essex
$14.00 PAPERBACK
978-0-307-34621-6

4

The Loves of Charles II
The Stuart Saga
$16.00 PAPERBACK
978-1-4000-8248-3

previously published as
three separate volumes:
The Wandering Prince
Health Unto His Majesty
Here Lies Our Sovereign Lord

5

The Three Crowns
The Story of William and Mary
$14.00 PAPERBACK
978-0-307-34624-7

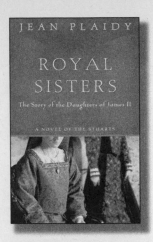

6

Royal Sisters
The Story of the
Daughters of James II
$15.00 PAPERBACK
978-0-307-71952-2

previously published
as *The Haunted Sisters*

7

Courting Her Highness
The Story of Queen Anne
$16.00 PAPERBACK
978-0-307-71951-5

previously published as
The Queen's Favourites

Available wherever books are sold

Read Jean Plaidy's
Queens of England series
in historical order:

1

The Courts of Love
The Story of Eleanor of Aquitaine
$15.00 PAPERBACK
978-1-4000-8250-6

2

The Queen's Secret
The Story of Queen Katherine
$14.95 PAPERBACK
978-1-4000-8252-0

The Reluctant Queen
The Story of Anne of York
$14.95 PAPERBACK
978-0-307-34615-5

The Lady in the Tower
The Story of Anne Boleyn
$13.95 PAPERBACK
978-1-4000-4785-1

The Rose Without a Thorn
The Story of Katherine Howard
$13.95 PAPERBACK
978-0-609-81017-0

In the Shadow of the Crown
The Story of Queen Mary I
$14.95 PAPERBACK
978-0-609-81019-4

6

Queen of This Realm
The Memoir of Elizabeth I
$14.95 PAPERBACK
978-0-609-81020-0

7

Loyal in Love
The Story of Henrietta Maria,
Wife of Charles I
$14.95 PAPERBACK
978-0-307-34616-2
previously published as
Myself My Enemy

8

9

The Merry Monarch's Wife
The Story of Catherine
of Braganza
$14.95 PAPERBACK
978-0-307-34617-9
previously published as
The Pleasures of Love

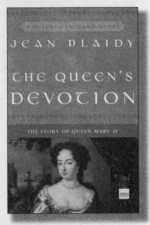

10

The Queen's Devotion
The Story of Queen Mary II
$14.95 PAPERBACK
978-0-307-34618-6
previously published as
William's Wife

11

Victoria Victorious
The Story of Queen Victoria
$16.00 PAPERBACK
978-0-609-81024-8